THE COLLECTED SHORT FICTION OF

Published in Canada by Engen Books, Chapel Arm, NL.

Library and Archives Canada Cataloguing in Publication information is available upon request.

Print: 978-1-77478-177-7
eBook: 978-1-77478-178-4

Distributed by:
Engen Books
www.engenbooks.com
submissions@engenbooks.com

First mass market paperback printing: March 2025

THE COLLECTED SHORT FICTION OF

ENGEN
BOOKS

CONTENTS

The Crustman..007

The Theogony..012

Invasion..039

Reptilia...041

Revving Engen..073

Jacobi Street...088

The Hunters..149

The Shoe...157

The Lakehouse..159

Rituals of the Celestial Ram...166

Touch Your Nose...169

The Spy...218

Remembering...220

Young Republicans..245

Interlude..248

The Game..259

The Views..286

The Sacking of Outpost Toth...289

Flickers in the Night..347

The Chair...356

GENRES

HORROR

The Crustman..007
Reptilia..041
Jacobi Street..088
The Hunters...149
The Lakehouse...159
Flickers in the Night...347
The Chair...356

FANTASY

The Theogony...012
Rituals of the Celestial Ram..166

SCIENCE-FICTION

Invasion..039
The Shoe...157
Young Republicans...245
The Views..286
The Sacking of Outpost Toth...289

CRIME & ESPIONAGE

Revving Engen..073
Touch Your Nose...169
The Spy...218
Remembering..220
Interlude..248
The Game...259

THE CRUSTMAN

The memories of my childhood are viewed through a deep fog not easily penetrated.

I grew up in a place that isn't there anymore.

We all do, to some respect. Disused schools get torn down. New construction changes the landscape. Well-worn paths grow over. But the town where I grew up was literally removed from the map. You can only see it on old versions.

There's a known psychological phenomenon that occurs when a man lives longer than his father ever did. A fatalism that creeps in. You start to feel like death is around every corner. Like your time is up. The clock wound down for your father right about now, so time to set your affairs in order.

I wonder if there's a recognized effect on men whose home is no longer on the map.

The sample size likely isn't large enough to get results.

***

I putter into Paris Cove and tie my boat up to a government dock that has had all the signs of government torn away, leaving discoloured rectangles and oblongs where the touch of the sun has tanned it unevenly.

There's slick moss over the dock cleat that makes it harder to get a rope around than it should have been. But I do it and I get up the ladder near it. Have to jump a little to do it, the tide is low. The ladder is slick as well with algae and seaweed. I slip twice.

I remember a time when the government wharf was the crown jewel of Paris Cove, always fresh and clean and proper. Always teeming. Other docks could fall into disarray as the men who worked them grew old or died or became disinterested, but the government paid people to keep its wharf pristine and up to code. They had to. They had to be vigilant. Negligence would mean that an accident on the government wharf would be the government's responsibility, so they took every step to avoid negligence. Ripping the signs that indicated government function was as good as putting up a warning sign: You can't sue now. Play at your own risk.

The boards of the wharf are decaying with edge-rot that has all but taken some of the boards. They're coated with bird shit and guano. Discarded nets where the wharf met the shore are littered with dead gulls that were caught in them while trying to peck leftovers out, only to become the thing leftover to provide temptation for the next bird hungry enough to try.

Did the gulls ever leave once they came? Gulls came because humans came, congregated and bred because humans congregated and bred. Took their meals from the bits of carcass we left behind as we fed our own. But there were still gulls here, stragglier than they'd been when there were people. Meaner looking. Thin. Aggressive. Did the leftover gulls ever leave once they had nested? It seemed like the answer was no.

Gulls might be more hearty than people.

People will not abide by the level of starvation these gulls have, generation after generation. People will revolt, speak out. Leave and encourage others to leave. The government kept their signs up until the last people left, but they had pulled up their anchor long before; when the cod fishery closed and there was no reason for Paris Cove to exist anymore, save habit; when the people asked for money the way the gull asks for scrap, to keep themselves fed until the fish come back.

Until the fish come back.

***

There's grime on the houses, tears of salt from sea spray left to evaporate over time. Buildings decay. I saw a show on Discovery Channel about it. How fast the fruits of man's labour fall into disrepair without men there to hold nature back. Streets are islands of concrete beneath my feet with crushed stone between platforms. Years of moisture getting into cracks and then freezing and then coming apart and then filling anew, pushing itself further and further apart.

Siding has been scraped off many of the houses, and the bark from the electrical poles that now house no charge. I look across the harbour and see an elk grinding its antlers against the corner of a house. If it knows I'm here, it knows I'm far enough away to not pose a danger. Were I to come closer to it, it would scamper and maybe not come back. Something in its mind would tell it that the humans were not gone, that they could always come back. I stay clear of it.

This place isn't mine now despite my attempt to reclaim it.

Across the way I see time has not been as kind to all the homes as to just leave salt spray. Some houses are gone with only parts of their frames remaining. Gavin Fudge's house--gone. Mary Moore. Trevor and Tina Heartridge. All gone. Every last bit of it save for a few support beams. I turn my gaze to Paddy Marsten's demolished house and I see the culprit, a large boulder sitting in its middle.

Just as the water got in around the cracks in the sidewalks and forced them apart, so too did snow pack in among the hanging rocks that surrounded the basin of Paris Cove. It froze and pushed them up, only to have them fall back down once the melt arrived. Slowly, over time, nature dislodged boulders from their perch. Slowly it encouraged them to fall, and with no one around to stem that fall, they rolled like thunder from the gods and crashed through anything in their wake. Homes. Stages. Boats.

Nature was taking back Paris Cove, piece by piece. It had been erased from the Newfoundland map but not from the landscape, and that was being seen to. The results had made a topography that loomed over the town that was reminiscent but not familiar. Caves that had once been the warrens of imagination had ceased to be with the changing of the landscape.

But one cave, right in the center, was still there. It still looked over my grandmother's house. A maw in the cliff-side, deep and black. A birth canal from with only darkness came.

***

My grandmother's house was still standing. It had avoided the assault from both land and sea that its neighbours had not. The furniture was rotted but still there, patterns still familiar. Plastic over the couch that had never been removed to keep it fresh had sealed in air, making it mildewy. The old tube television was there, rabbit ears jutting up to the low ceiling. It looked like it would have still worked had there been electricity to run it. If we even broadcast television over signals anymore.

It had been made at a time when things were built to last. It outlasted the world it had been made for.

Like all of us.

From my grandmother's old kitchen table, I remember the summers spent there, eating oatmeal. Eating cream of wheat. Eating toast with butter and sugar on it. I can see her there next to the old wood stove, watching me eat with a smile on her face. Happy that she could provide, having lived in a time when that wasn't a certainty. I see her there, and I see her smile fade as she looks at my plate. See her motion to the window, to that darkened cave in the middle of the cliff's side.

"Eat your crusts," she said, eying the way I'd nibbled around them to only get the soft warm parts of the homemade bread. "Eat your crusts, or the Crustman will get you."

***

The Crustman was a nightmare figure in my childhood. A Boogey Man with purpose.

My grandmother told me that he was a man. She told me he was a man who lived in that cave, in the very centre of the cliff's side. She didn't say what he looked like, but my imagination told me. He was gangly and long and wore a thin black suit and hat. He walked with big, exaggerated steps on spidery legs. He smiled. He was a crooked man, and he would walk a crooked mile.

He lived up there with a sack, my grandmother said. A big black garbage bag. And it was filled with all the left-behinds. He came down from his perch at night, she said, and filled his bag with all of the crusts that had been left behind in the trash, and they'd gone mouldy and blue and rotten. It was full of them, she said, filled to the breaking with mouldy stale crusts. I pictured it like the inverse of Santa's sack.

He would come down, grandmother said, when he heard of little boys and girls not eating their crusts. He would come down for them in the night and take them away to his cave and tie them up. He would tie them to a chair and he would make them eat, she told me. He would make you eat all of those crusts. Mouldy crusts and blue crusts and mildewy crusts. He would pinch your nose and make you open your mouth, and he would stuff them in, one after the other, until the bag was empty and you were full of them.

He spoke with a rattle deep in his throat, a croak.

My grandmother would tell me that the story would end with me fat from the crusts that had made his bag fat. That it would be limp now, and that he would roll me down the hill back to my home, I'd be so fat. This never stuck with me, this whimsical fairy-tale end to the story. She would tell me this and my mind would continue to play the horror, play to truth with her false narration over it. I knew that he would keep you there with his needle and thread.

I knew that he needed a new bag.

***

A shiver ran down my spine as I remembered it, but, at the same time, I chuckled at the absurdity of it. The lack of logic behind it. If the Crustman filled his pouch with all of the crusts children left behind, and if he made each of his victims eat every crust in the sack... then there would never be any crusts in the sack. Each child would throw out a crust, to be discovered by the Crustman and placed into his sack. He would then take the child hostage and make them eat all the crusts in the bag... of which there would be only one. And then the sack would be empty because the child would have eaten all it contained. And so the next child would have to eat exactly one crust, their own.

There were other reasons it was ridiculous of course. Fairies did not exist. Haunted caves did not exist. Demons did not exist. But of all those lies, half-truths, and legends my grandmother told me to get me to do her bidding, the Crustman was the one that seemed the silliest. It was the one that had fallen apart under its own logic, the one that didn't make sense even within its own narrative.

***

I went to sleep that night in my childhood bed, surrounded by memories of my grandfather that my grandmother decorated the house with like talismans. Rabbits' feet from hunts he'd been on. Pictures of him that had been left behind in her passing. Jewelry he'd brought back from other ports when he'd been away from her for months at a time.

***

I woke up unable to move, pinned to my bed by unseen binds. I struggled against them, but my arms were anchored tight. They were pressed to the bed, unable to move or be moved. I didn't scream, for there was no one in the town to hear me.

I thought that then.

But as my eyes adjusted to the dark I saw that I saw wrong.

There was a man hunched over himself in the corner of my room. His back was all of him at that moment. He was wearing a black suit so old that it had gone translucent, and I could see the individual rungs of his back. I could see his ribs protruding out of his flesh like knives. I could see his breath, hear the rattle in his throat that came with each one.

I froze.

He turned to me, glaring with the glint of one eye. Dry gray hair crackled like hay with the sudden motion. His flesh was ashen. He turned to me and stood, grew, and I was paralyzed. I had been paralyzed before but had wanted to move, but now that desire was sapped from me. I didn't want to move, didn't want to breathe, didn't want to do anything that would bring him to me any faster.

He opened his mouth, a black maw filled with corn kernel teeth, and croaked out one single, horrifying word.

"Leftovers."

I said nothing. I did nothing. But deep in my mind, that same part of me that had questioned the logic of my grandmother's legend niggled at me. I had not had bread. I had not had anything. I had eaten in the boat, and my food was in the boat's cooler, and I would eat again tomorrow after I left. Beyond the horror of everything, there had been some mistake. This was not just a horror movie, this was an injustice. I had eaten my crusts since that day as a child living under my grandmother's rule.

I had been good.

He reached down and picked up the sack at its feet. It was heavy. Despite my logic, it had been heavy. He lifted it with great effort and brought it down near my bed, and it landed with a weighty wet slop. It rustled as he plied it open, over the edge where I could not see.

"Leftovers."

He reached out with cold fingers I could feel the bones through and pinched my nose, tilted my head back. When I could not wait for air any more I opened my mouth. He reached into his sack and withdrew a fish head and placed it on my tongue, grimy and salty and rotten. He shut my mouth and held it with his thumbs, those cold fingers splaying out over either of my cheeks as I reluctantly chewed and swallowed.

"Leftovers."

When I was done he pinched my nose again and tilted my head back. This time he withdrew a gull. A dead gull, left to rot in the sun. He snapped its neck and twisted its head until it came clean. He pushed it into a shape that would fit in my mouth, and when I was desperate again for air he put it in. It tasted of bile and gangrene.

He twisted off more of the bird, snapping it into bite-sized chunks and bringing them to me one at a time, and before each would say the same, the only word he would speak: "Leftovers."

"Leftovers." "Leftovers." "Leftovers."

The thing that made the logic of my grandmother's tales work was that he didn't punish the little boys and girls who hadn't eaten their crusts by making them eat all the crusts. He punished them by making them eat their *leftovers*.

And in Newfoundland, there was never any shortage of leftovers.

Fish parts left to rot on the docks when we thought they would never end. Gulls left to cannibalize and scavenge when the humans they had nested for had left. Remnants the government had left behind when it had packed up and moved on.

He reached into his bag when the gull was gone and took out a foot. A human foot, up to the knee. He began wrenching the meat from it, as though it were nothing more than a steak at the butcher. But it was more than just a leg. It had scars I remembered, gathered during summers running the torn streets of Paris Cove. It had grime on the bottom that I had meant to clean in the sea before getting into my childhood bed.

It was not a leg. It was my leg.

It was then that I realized the harsh truth of Newfoundland.

We were the leftovers.

THE THEOGONY

He lay alone on his cot with his legs curled up near his waist like he was cold, but he'd kicked all the covers off. They laid on the floor in a crumpled mess that looked like a used tissue: pure white except for the dark pits of shadow that the folds created and the subtle remains of yellow piss stains that were somewhere on every sheet.

It was a single room and the walls were cushioned. All the hearers got cushioned rooms, whether or not they'd ever been violent or shown themselves to be violent. There was nothing in the room except his cot, pressed up against the wall, and the empty space alongside it where Dr. Brakman's chair went.

He'd been lying there for days, it felt like. Sometimes they would leave him there for longer. Once he would have sworn he'd been left there for weeks: the light from the window hadn't changed, and it was too high up for him to look out through. The light could have been coming from anywhere. It could have been a spotlight that they'd pushed up to the window to try and fool him. Or they could have moved the Clinic to the Arctic Circle. It could be daylight for months there.

Sometimes these thoughts occurred to him and it was almost impossible to get them out. Most of the time he knew that they weren't right, but other times they latched in deep. Sometimes, lying there in bed, he thought he could almost feel the concrete base of the Clinic as it slid along the snowy field of the Northwest Territories and up toward the North Pole. Sometimes he could hear the little Inuit boys that the Orderlies paid three bucks an hour to pull it along, each with their own chain strapped to their arms and hauling with all their might. Of course, the Orderlies did this for nothing more than their own amusement. There was a switch in the fuse box that turned on treads that ran below the Clinic like a tank. The Orderlies would grin out the windows and flip the switch, then watch as the Clinic lurched to life and started down across the snow, the little Inuit boys running and jumping to get out of the way.

"Theo?" Dr. Brakman said, leaning in with a smile full of teeth and getting his attention.

Theo blinked twice. His eyes hadn't been closed, yet somehow Brakman had just appeared in front of him. He was sitting on the chair that was usually left just outside his room. It was only brought in for Brakman. Anyone else who came in to talk to him had to stand or lean against the far wall.

Brakman was a short man with a large nose that came out of his face and tried to stab you when he spoke to you. He would always inch closer and closer when he talked, until there was nothing of your personal space left and your chest felt itchy and claustrophobic from it. He said his name like brac-MAN out loud and when people asked him how it was pronounced, but in his head, it was BREAK-man. It was on the billboard he rolled in with him now, standing up behind him with spotlights shining up at it from every conceivable direction, blue letters on a bright green background:

BREAK MAN.

Theo fidgeted, then squinted his eyes and turned away from the lights. His pillow had been pushed up against the wall next to him and he grabbed it, pulling it close until his face was buried in it.

Brakman frowned, then nodded and got up. He took the chair with him as he left. No sooner was he gone than one of the Nurses came in. She was holding a syringe up in the air, its tip long and dripping as she flicked it twice and pushed on the plunger. The liquid came out in sporadic little spurts that reminded him of squeezing juice boxes too hard as a child. She bent over and shoved the metal end into the meat of his buttocks and the world went fuzzy around the edges again, slowly working its way in until all he could see was the glowing white gauze that was his world.

They may have left him like that for days, he wasn't sure. The light outside was always on.

***

The Group Meeting room, like most every other room in Black Springs Clinic, was painted the same greyish white on all four walls. The far wall was almost completely made up of tall windows that stretched from just a foot off from the floor to the top of the ceiling, the glass covered by a thick wire mesh on either side. Outside, it was bright. The sun glistened off the sand that they were always told was at a beach, but you could never see any water past it, no matter what window you looked out of how hard you craned your neck. Many suspected that it wasn't actually there, that it was a cruel joke they'd made up to try and get some of the Closers to escape. They'd get it into their head to escape, and make it out in a laundry trolley and get out only to discover that there was nothing but sand and a few patches of crabgrass for as far as the eye could see. Some would just go back inside. Others would be caught within hours by the Orderlies. A few would actually die out there in the hot desert sun.

The room was one of two common areas in the Clinic, which were attached to one another by two doors on the Eastern wall. The Public Room (as it was often called by both the Residents and the Orderlies) was large and bright and always clean, with tables and games and a TV that could be turned, it seemed, to any channel in existence, though Brakman seemed to only tune it to the news stations. The Group Room was dark and grey and always seemed cold. While the Public Room only had one purpose, the Group Room served as a multi-function room. There were easels stacked against the far wall that were used for what the Pretty Nurse called Art Therapy. There was clay beneath a sink in the corner, too. But mostly it was used for the meetings, when the Pretty Nurse and Dr. Brakman would sit at one end of a circle with all the Closers and Hearers around them, and they'd talk. Everyone would talk. Sometimes they would talk about themselves, sometimes they'd talk about each other, sometimes Brakman would give a person or topic for them to talk about, but they always talked and nobody ever told the truth.

Theo sat on the far left, his chair pushed back just slightly so that he could see past Johnny's head and out the window. There was sand out there all right, mounds of it. It seemed to go on forever. He wondered how long they'd left him in his room. Long enough to make it from the North Pole all the way down to the desert. He squinted at what he saw through the windows, watching the way the light reflected off the fine grains and made it look white. It could have been snow, he thought. It might still be. They could have done something to the window to make it look like sand when really it was snow. Or it might not be real at all. They could have ordered one of the pull-down backdrops that they used to use all the time in movies before they started using computers for everything. It could have been the sand from Ben-Hur he was looking at. The more he stared at it, the more it was.

"Theo?" Dr. Brakman said, scribbling something down on the clipboard he held against his knee.

Theo's head snapped forward and he rolled onto his knees without a word, looking from patient to patient to see who was talking and then pretending to make eye contact with them to make it seem like he was listening. He'd discovered some time ago that if you stared at the spot in between a person's eyebrows, you could fool everyone that you were looking right at them, even the person doing the talking.

It was Jerry talking right now, one of the older Closers. He'd been here almost as long as anyone had; at least that was what he said. He was a thin old man with white hair that straggled down behind each ear, and a pointy nose and mouth that made him look like he had a beak that was always open. His eyes were sunken and dark under his forehead, only lighting up from time to time.

Paul Pike was next to him, a stutterer who couldn't even say his own name. The rest of the Closers were on him about it constantly, especially when they went around introducing new patients on the Ward. "That's Davey, and that's Fred, and this over here is Pill Poke."

"P-P-P-P-Paul P-P-P-P-Pike."

"T-T-T-T-Tall T-T-T-T-Tyke?"

"P-P-P-P-Paul P-P-P-P-Pike."

"M-M-M-M-Mall M-M-M-M-Mike?"

This would continue until Paul finally got sick of the game and found a spot on the floor and stared at it until they went away. Most times he'd stay that way until the Pretty Nurse came back to him and took him off to bed.

Carl was fidgeting with the sleeves of his shirt, trying to fix it so that people couldn't see his scars. Nobody ever could, but he always thought they could. He'd tried to kill himself twice the year before he'd come to Black Springs, and now all he wanted was to be out. He'd tried only once since he'd been inside, and Theo couldn't completely say that he blamed him. He never spoke except in the group meeting, and even then only when he was asked to.

Lindsey complained about his wife, always. He'd been in the Clinic for ten years and his wife had died after five waiting for him to get out, but he could still do nothing except bitch about The Wife.

Danny Cliff sat backward in his chair toward the group and thought he looked cool. He'd been convicted of six counts of sexual assault (four on women and two on a man) and had been sent to Black Springs as a sex addict. He'd been here three years and was no better than the day they'd brought him in. He was always smiling, always happy, and loved playing Monopoly and Gin. He also loved masturbating in the corner when he thought nobody was looking, or had until Brakman had found the right combination of drugs. Now he could rarely get it up, but sometimes he still grabbed hold of himself in the corner, even when it was nothing more than a limp noodle.

There was a guy named Pedro that everyone called Ruffles. He talked all the time, but didn't make any sense. He'd go on about Russia and The Bomb for hours, no matter how many times you tried to tell him that the war was over and that it was all good. Once Danny Cliff had told him that the Russians had finally got The Bomb into Cuba and Ruffles lost his mind so badly that the orderlies had to give him two helpings of Haldol to calm him down.

Rob was a Bruins fan that could not stop shitting himself in public. He never once did it on the Ward, but they'd let him out five times now, and every time he'd be back in a week later to tell them all the places he'd shit.

There were others that didn't talk, usually twenty (give or take) on the Ward at any given time. Some never shared, some only shared. Some never talked, some never stopped talking. The only thing that was true of all of them was that they all brought their own signs.

Each of them had billboards that sat behind them like giant TV sets all tuned to different channels. There was a different volume control for each one, but someone had set all of them to blast at all times. Sometimes if he tried, Theo could make a particularly annoying one (like a song playing on repeat) fade into the background, but it always seemed like the others would get louder to compensate. It almost wasn't worth it.

Rob was thinking about the last Bruins game he was at. The game was in 3D and almost came off the billboard at them every time someone shot or passed the puck down the ice. The crowd cheering droned into a white noise that was almost blissful, except that every time the Bruins scored (which they did often in Rob's memory, more often then Theo suspected was likely), a loud buzzer went off that cut through the cheers and made him want to cover his ears.

Ruffles' billboard looked like something out of science-fiction theatre, with a bunch of men wearing white coats all standing around a device that Theo could not recognize, but he assumed was Ruffles' twisted nightmare vision of what a nuke looked like. There were wires that looked like claws coming out of it everywhere. All the men were looking down at it and writing onto their clipboards. It wasn't a video; Ruffles' billboard never was. It looked like one of those slide shows that the General used to brief his men in the old spy movies, all shaky and sepia-toned. There was a flag with a sickle and hammer on it in the background.

"The Bomb," Ruffles said, looking intently at a line in the palm of his hand as though he were reading from some secret document in it. "They've got the Bomb."

Danny Cliff's billboard was replaying an old episode of Gilligan's Island. It stopped and strayed to a different thought whenever Mary-Anne came onto the screen, though. He'd somehow managed to rescue her from the island and she was back in his bed and he was towering over her. She still had her hair in her pigtails and her eyes were closed, her face drawn out in an expression of simultaneous disdain and ecstasy. These only lasted a second before jumping back to the main plot of the Professor making a radio out of a coconut shell. It was as if someone had inserted single frames of pornography into an otherwise wholesome movie reel.

Lindsey seemed to be actually listening to Jerry. His billboard was of his mother. He was looking up at her as she cut potatoes at the kitchen table. Judging from his height, he was no more than four. Her lips were red, and her dress was blue with a white apron in front, and there was just a little grey catching along her hair at the temples. She looked absolutely beautiful.

Theo hung on that one for a moment, watching out of the corner of his eye (so that Brakman wouldn't notice) as Lindsey's mother picked him up and hoisted him into the air, laughing. He could smell her perfume. It smelled like lilies.

Carl's billboard was a still picture of the album *Dude Ranch*, the bull on its cover looking back at Theo from over its bulbous backside. *Dammit* was playing loudly from speakers on either side of the sign, and Carl was bobbing his head along with the beat. If the music hadn't been there, he would have just looked twitchy, but while it was playing he looked like he was ready to start singing along at any point.

Paul's was filled with static. Every so often there would be a flash of something, like a clown or a star-filled sky, but it would be gone again before Theo could really see what it was. It was like his sign was a television that some inept child was trying to adjust the rabbit ears on and failing miserably.

Everyone had a sign it seemed, except Theo. He wondered sometimes if they'd forgotten to give him one upon admission, but then he remembered that it wasn't just people in Black Springs that had the signs. If he tried hard, he could dimly recall that people out in the World had them too. It was harder to see them out there though. The lighting was better in here.

He shifted uncomfortably.

Even Dr. Brakman and the Pretty Nurse had billboards. Right now Dr. Brakman's was just the Group Room from his point of view, as though his eyes were cameras that projected the image out a lens in the back of his head and onto the screen. There was music though, a rendition of Beethoven's Fifth with pianos and oboes that seemed to keep his blood pressure down. The Pretty Nurse was thinking of her son, a young man named Christopher. He was two, and the image of him made Theo smile.

She saw Theo smiling at her, and it made her shift uncomfortably.

Jerry's billboard was dark, like a house at night after the lights have been turned off and your eyes haven't gotten a chance to adjust yet. Even now, there were bits of blue coming in from the moonlight, touching the edges of a dresser and a nightstand, as though someone were painting in the scene as they went.

"It was always my mother, you know," Jerry said, fumbling with his hands. He was looking down, but there was a sparkle in his eyes hidden deep within the shadow of those bushy eyebrows. "She could be so nice sometimes, but she didn't understand how being so horrid made all that go away. She could erase the nice by being horrid, but she couldn't erase the horrid by being nice."

The scene moved back and forth, as though the camera were on some kind of rocker that never seemed to stop. The wall was visible now, the moonlight reflecting off it and giving light to the other items in the room.

"She would always punish me. Most of it I didn't even know what for. Made me take a bath in ice water once, I thought my nuts were going to come off. I think it was because I had a wet dream."

The camera shifted focus rapidly, skewing down to look away from the wall. It was on a bed, not a rocking chair, and now there was enough light bouncing off of the wall that a girl could be seen wedged uncomfortably between the camera and the bed, the blue moonlight making her features soft. She was saying something, but the sound had been muted on her. Not everything had been muted though; Theo could still hear the squeaking. Could hear it even above the blare of the Bruins's latest goal.

"One time when I cut my hands chopping wood, she made me put them in bleach," he said, running his fingers over a deep scar on the back of his hand. "Another time she locked me in the cellar for a whole week, only fed me twice. It was dark and cold, and I hardly got any sleep on account of the rats. I don't even know why she did that."

"It was because you took your little sister to bed with you," Theo said, his voice monotonous and far away. He was meeting Jerry's gaze for real now, and Jerry returned it with a stare that could have frozen fire. He was snarling, but there was still that twinkle in his eye. The movie on the screen continued, but it was flickering now, as though about to change reels into a different picture.

Brakman looked up from his pad at Theo, his eyebrows stretching to reach where his hairline should have been. "Theo?"

"I never did no such thing," Jerry said, staring across the circle at Theo. "I loved my sister. She was an angel."

"Yes, you did," Theo nodded, motioning to the billboard behind him as though everyone could and should be able to see it. He tilted his head to one side. The incestuous film was playing again now, but this time with more light. It was still flickering though. "You went into her room sometimes after your parents went to sleep. You told yourself not to and that you'd never do it again and that she wouldn't remember, but you always kept doing it. It was like someone else took over you, like you couldn't control what you were doing when you did it."

"Shut up. That never happened."

"Theo --" Brakman started to object, but did it low enough that he knew Theo would not stop.

Danny Cliff's billboard had changed now, Theo could see out of the corner of his eye. It was a twisted imaginary version of the scene on Jerry's board, with Jerry the same age as he was now and the girl slightly older than she had been in Jerry's memory. The girl was blonde in Danny's version and brunette in the real one, but otherwise they were about the same. The cameras moved back and forth at different speeds and made Theo so motion sick that he thought he might get nauseous.

"You never even found out how your mother found out," Theo continued, "You came home one day and she started screaming at you and hitting you with her shoe and telling you all the things you'd done. You hadn't thought about it in weeks... it was always a few weeks between times, and for a while after each one you didn't think about it at all. Didn't even remember doing it. She hit you with her shoe and pushed you down over the stairs and left you there for weeks."

"Shut up!" Jerry yelled, and Theo snapped out of his trace and blushed.

Jerry's billboard had finally fully changed. It was like Brakman's now, his eyes turned into cameras that showed Theo himself from Jerry's point of view. After a second, the camera rose and came across the circle at him, arms reaching out from behind the fourth wall and gripping Theo around the neck, forcing him off the chair.

Theo almost had to look around and assure himself that it wasn't really happening.

Jerry was still burrowing holes into Theo's head with his eyes, with the sparkle back there again now, as (on the billboard behind him) Theo gasped for air through purple lips.

"I think we should move on," Brakman said, and the Pretty Nurse nodded in agreement and flipped to the next page in her chart and showed it to him. "Paul, we were talking last day about an incident between you and another boy when you were eleven."

***

Everyone showered at once. All twenty-something residents on the Ward, at least the ones who could stand, crowded into a shower room that looked like a gas chamber out of a World War II biopic. It got Ruffles going every time, kicking and screaming and saying that they were going to gas him. Every day they tried to get him in, and every day they wound up giving him a shot and scrubbing him down themselves with the Vegetables while he was out.

There was one door and there was one Orderly at it at all times to make sure nobody got out and snuck off into the desert nude. They didn't like tanned Closers. He was supposed to be watching them to make sure that Danny Cliff or someone like him didn't try to sodomize the others, but most of the Orderlies were too liberal to spend fifteen minutes every day looking at twenty-something dicks flapping in and out of the stream in the room.

Theo loved the shower. The water was always hot (the entire building was heated by hot water), and it was the only time he felt clean and sane while he was here.

He leaned forward and pushed his head under the spray, letting it wet down his hair. He closed his eyes and felt it run down over him. There were dozens of songs in his head, and the few times he'd tried to sing, he'd ended up stuttering worse than Paul.

Jerry punched him in the face while he had his eyes closed, sending him crashing to the floor.

The fist had connected with both his left cheek and eye, and he could already feel the skin bruising as blood rushed to the surface. Redness streamed down his nose into his mouth and dripped from his chin, cleaned away almost instantly by the hot water and making deep pink swirls as they travelled down the tile and into the drain in the center of the room.

Jerry looked down at him, rage twinkling in those horrible sunken eyes of his. His fists were clenched tight at his sides as he waited to see if Theo would get up, prepared to smack him down again if he did.

Theo didn't say anything, just stared up into Jerry as blood seeped down from his face.

Jerry just breathed harder and harder until he finally turned and stepped away without a word.

Theo stayed on the floor until the Orderly turned off the faucets.

***

The Public Room was called so because it was the only room that anyone from the outside could regularly see. Once a week (although it seemed like much longer sometimes; in fact Theo was sure there had been a year between visits once), friends and relatives would come in and sit at long tables to chat, visit, and play board games.

It was easily the largest room in Black Springs, fitting ten long tables from the front of the room to the back. There were windows looking out at the beach again, although they didn't go as far down the wall here, leaving room for shelves that held books, magazines, videos and games. There was a ping-pong table in the back with no net next to some armchairs and a television (which was too high up for anyone to reach, even Danny Cliff, who was well over six and a half feet when he wasn't slouched over).

The time when the visitors came was the only time when all twenty of the patients at Black Springs were there at the same time. Of the twenty patients, there were three groups, though they were not equally divided.

There were two Vegetables who lay in their beds by the windows with tubes coming out of them everywhere. These fed in IVs and heart monitors that were carted around with them everywhere. They couldn't move or eat or talk, but the Orderlies carted them around to all the group meetings and public visits anyway as though they were a part of it somehow. Theo didn't know their names, but one had been named Carrot because his Mexican heritage gave his skin an orange complexion. The other had been named Turnip, just for virtue of consistency.

There were fifteen Closers, named for being 'closer' to getting released than any of the other groups. They comprised the majority of most mental institutions. They were self-committed or committed on behalf of family or, in rare cases such as Danny Cliff, here by some mercy of the state in lieu of a prison sentence.

Theo was a member of an elite class of clinic patient called Hearer (or Listener, alternatively, though they'd stopped using this moniker as it implied that the patients were hearing something that was actually there). They were the true schizophrenics, according to Brakman. They heard the voices that told them to do things. Caught somewhere between the lucid Closers and the catatonic Vegetables, they were unfortunate enough to likely be permanent occupants of Black Springs and unlucky enough to be aware of that fact. There were two others at the Ward at the moment, Ruffles and Rob, although there had been a fourth named Terry when Theo had arrived. He'd tried to kill Paul with a fork during Theo's first week. The next week he'd pushed the same fork so far into his own eye that he'd bled out before the Orderlies could do anything about it.

Jerry's wife came every week to visit him. Most days they'd talk at 'their' table closest to the door, but sometimes they'd play Gin or Bridge. A few times they'd laugh, and if they managed that, then Jerry was pleasant for days afterward. His billboard would be turned to her smile until something would be said in Group to make it flicker out, and he'd be back to mean Jerry again.

The Vegetables had what seemed to be a nearly endless supply of family that took turns coming in and taking care of them. The two clans seemed to know each other, and know each other very well, and would talk for hours over tea while Carrot and Turnip lay there staring out the window, oblivious to what was going on around them. It was as though the families had formed their own little club: Vegans of the Psychiatric Ward.

Paul's parents would sit with him and he didn't stutter nearly so much then, only on his M sounds, which he could try to avoid. Lindsey's son visited every second week, and Carl's wife seemed to be the first one in every time. Sometimes it seemed like she camped out in front the night before just to get in as early as she could.

There were three people visiting with Danny Cliff alone. Two were older and clearly his parents, while the third was a young blonde girl that looked about nineteen. She might have been his girlfriend, or possibly a much younger sister. There was a pink stripe in her hair and she wore metal hoop earrings so big they almost touched her bare shoulders. She wore a top with horizontal black and white stripes under a brown leather jacket with no zipper and jeans. Her navel was showing, and it was pierced as well. She was leaning against the wall a few feet from where Danny and his parents spoke, eyes moving freely around the room from one patient to another. She looked like she should have been smoking.

Everyone had somebody.

Theo sat alone at a long table in the middle to the room, caught between the Vegetables and the Closers. There was a bag of potato chips in front of him that was opened and pointing at him, though he did not remember how they had gotten there, and he hadn't eaten a single one. They smelled disgusting, like old cheese.

He sat alone until the Orderlies told him it was time to go.

***

It was dark in Theo's room when he went back to it. He could not remember the last time it had been dark. Had they turned off the light? Or was it time for the six months of darkness now? He hoped not.

His pillows and sheets smelled fresh and new, so he curled up in them instead of tossing them away as he usually did, even though he knew that by midway through the night, he would hate the stench of them and they would be a gaggled mess on his floor.

His head hit the pillow and he closed his eyes, and for one blissful moment there was silence and darkness, and he felt sleep take the first tentative tugs at his eyelids. His mouth was still numb from the pill the Pretty Nurse had given him before closing the door, but it was fading fast. Soon he wouldn't even remember it.

There was a small sparkle in the darkness that made his eyelids flutter. It looked like the twinkle of Jerry's eyes, or maybe even the headlight of some far-off train. It glimmered in the distance for a moment, then came at him at warp speed. Suddenly the darkness was gone and his padded walls turned into flat-screens, all of them turned to their own channel and bawling at them at their highest volume. His bed was gone, even though he could still feel it beneath him, and the screens started to close in on him as they did every night, the sphere of his personal space becoming smaller and smaller. His heart beat faster and faster as the glowing, yelling images descended upon him until finally he was inside the screens. All of them. At once.

The Pretty Nurse was on his bed and was about to fold the sheets when Danny came up behind her. He bent her over the bed and she fought at first, but only at first, and after a minute she turned over and let him climb on. Her breasts were bigger here then they were in the Group Meets, enlarged to an almost comedic size as Danny settled himself down between them.

Jerry punched him in the cheek and he went down. There was so much water falling down on him that he thought he was going to drown.

There was a field then. The walls all collapsed away as though the Ward was actually a house of cards that just got a good easterly gust. Danny was still fucking the Nurse on Theo's bed and they hadn't even noticed that they were in a field even though the tall grass was tickling their bare skin. Jerry was still standing above him. Carl sat on a log near them and was laughing wildly, slapping his knee repeatedly as he did. His wrists were clean and there were tears coming down his face, he was laughing so hard. His kids were behind him, and for a moment, Theo thought he was laughing at him.

"Don't be silly now, boy," Carl said, motioning Theo to turn around. "You're missing the show."

Theo turned and saw that there was a Circus Tent behind Jerry, with clowns running in one side in all sorts of silly matters. Carl's kids ran out from behind him to go and play, all thirteen of them, and they ran right through Jerry and made him disappear.

Theo breathed a sigh of relief.

"That's better now, ain't it?" Carl smirked, offering Theo a hand up.

There was a monster hanging back in the shadows. It was large and purple and looked like it was made of slime. It wouldn't come into the tall grass, but it swiped at it with its long talons and cut it down with each pass. Theo hoped he wouldn't be smart enough to use this method to cut a path toward them.

Lindey's mother stood next to Theo's bed holding a plate of cookies in her hand and looking for all the world like Barbara Billingsley. She smiled that unflappable smile down at Danny as the Nurse again tried to push him off with that face like Mary-Anne had had, wanting but not wanting what was happening.

"Well, that's not very nice now, is it?" Barbara said, taking one of the cookies off the tray and having a bite.

Jerry punched him in the cheek and he went down. There was so much water falling down on him that he thought he was going to drown. Jerry bent over and grabbed him around the throat, squeezing the wet flesh until it was impossible for him to get air.

The Purple People Eater started mowing the lawn with huge swipes of his claws.

Paul's brother was yelling at him and he was running away from it. He went over to his girlfriend's house, but she was eating zebra and working a pedal with her foot. It looked like the pedal of a sewing machine, but it wasn't, it was a pump for poison gas that started to come in through the vents even now.

The poison did not affect the monster.

Carl laughed and laughed. The gas was Nitrous Oxide, at least partly. Paul's girlfriend was pumping the Nitrous Oxide that she'd stolen from the Russians who were trying to find a way to mix it with Mustard Gas and send it to every Dentist in Amerika, a fiendish plot if ever the Commie Bastards had ever had one. They would have stopped her too, but they were too busy dealing with Ruffles. He'd found their secret plans for The Bomb, and he wasn't going to give them back until they gave him thirty-six Twizzlers and a Cherry Coke.

"Oh, Danny. You feel so good," the Pretty Nurse moaned; and for a moment, Theo forgot where he was and when he turned around the Greased Lightning was there and Danny was screwing Sandra Dee in the back seat in some weird never-before-seen outtake. He blinked and the car was still there, but now it was Danny Cliff and the Pretty Nurse in the back seat, still dressed like their fifties counterparts, Danny with his hair greased back and his leather jacket on.

Carl laughed so hard that he pissed himself.

Paul's girlfriend kept pumping Nitro into the air, feeding her pet poodle a few scraps of zebra under the table.

Jerry punched him in the cheek and he went down. There was so much water falling down on him that he thought he was going to drown. Jerry bent over and grabbed him around the throat, squeezing the wet flesh until it was impossible for him to get air. Theo's lips turned blue as he fought for air, but Jerry seemed unaffected by anything he did.

"Stop it," he said weakly though bloated lips. The blood vessels in his cheeks were bursting. "Stop... stop it."

He closed his eyes as they rolled back into his head.

When he opened them again, there was light bathing in through the windows and getting caught in the stream of sweat he'd made. Had they only turned the lights off long enough to fool him? Had they ever been off at all?

The pads on the wall were ripped and torn in long, winding patches as though something had dug its claws in deep at the top and dragged them right down to the baseboards. At first he'd thought it had been the People-Eater, but then he'd noticed the scrapes of white fabric still underneath his nails.

There was a knocking sound from beyond the wall, and when he looked, he could see that the billboards were still there. Carl was still on his log and Danny was still fucking the Pretty Nurse to high heaven even though he'd came three times over already. He didn't seem to be losing his drive any. The billboards weren't on top of or inside of him now; they were floating away as if he were driving past them on the highway.

A new billboard that looked like Snow White singing about whistling while she worked was there too. It belonged to the Pretty Nurse, and Theo could hear her whistling along with the movie as it played in her head. She knocked on the next door in line and the billboard of Carl laughing fizzled out into nothing before becoming static for a half second, then turning into the Pretty Nurse. It was like his eyes were cameras again, looking out at her as she peeped in through the window in the door to make sure Carl was getting up.

There was a knock at the next door and the image of her on her back in the Greased Lightning vanished, replaced by her soft face peering in through Danny's bedroom window again. It wasn't long before it was replaced by the same movie-reel porno though.

She came to Theo's door and looked in, noticing the fabric that had been ripped from the walls immediately.

He sat on his knees in the middle of the room and looked like he was in prayer, hunched over so that his shoulders looked huge and glaring out at her through wisps of hair.

She shook her head.

***

The easels had been pulled out from the wall and arranged around the Group Room in symmetrical, evenly spaced little cubicles so that everyone could have their space.

They were all there. Jerry was one seat behind Theo and one to the left, enough that Theo kept seeing him move out of the corner of his eye.

The billboards were nice now, like watching psychedelic colours move to music, each stroke making something magnificent.

"That's good," the Pretty Nurse said. She walked between the easels with her hands clasped behind her, and looked more like a Nun in a Seminary than a Nurse in an Institution. She might as well have traded in that purity-white uniform for a Habit and Whipple.

She walked behind Paul and looked over his shoulder. He was painting a bust of a fox with the night sky behind it. The moon was bisected by the beast's ear and the stars behind it seemed to twinkle in the dark blue mat he'd made for them.

"That's very nice, Paul," she said.

He smiled, then went back to his painting.

Lindsey was painting something in light blue that looked like one of the Rorschach tests that Brakman used on them from time to time, but on his billboard it was clear that it was the dress he remembered his mother best in. He'd left the white from the apron unpainted, and it faded into the background and looked like something a real artist might have done.

"That's wonderful."

Ruffles had made a few marks on his canvas with his brush, but had quickly moved to using his hands. Despite the mess he'd made on himself and the floor around him, the resulting cacophony of blues and yellows and reds did look stunning, if random.

"That's good."

She walked behind Theo and threw a glance toward his canvas.

It was blank, the rivets in the white paper staring back at him. The paintbrush was in his hand with bright orange paint on the top that had dried on it had been there so long. It had dribbled down the wood of the brush and down across his knuckles.

She sighed and looked away.

"That's very good, Robert."

***

The Public Room seemed larger today.

Doctor Brakman said that there was something wrong with the Air Conditioner and that he'd already called the electrician, but when they piled all the Closers and Hearers and Vegetables into the room again to wait for their families to filter in, the heat and humidity ratcheted up with every warm body that came into the room until it was like an oven. The walls sweated with the immensity of it, and every inmate had beads rolling down into their eyes. The walls seemed to expand and contract with the heat, as though they were breathing.

Carl's wife was the first one in again, slinging her arms around him as though she hadn't seen him in months. It made Theo wonder if maybe it *had* been months. Maybe the lights had been out in his room for six whole months of darkness and he had been too far gone to realize it. He twitched out the corner of his mouth and brought his hand up to examine the level of scruff on his face. Was it more or less than the day before? Or the same?

Danny Cliff's father was back today, but not his mother. They were sitting over in their usual spot and playing chess while talking about her now that she wasn't there. When the Pretty Nurse walked by, the father looked her up and down and asked his son if he'd tapped her yet. Danny only smiled in response and moved his knight to king seven.

Theo sat alone at the long table between the Vegetables and the Closers with a Snickers bar unwrapped in front of him that he had yet to take a bite out of. The plastic wrap that still covered its lower half had started to curl from the heat and the humidity in the room.

"Well, don't you look happy," a blonde girl said, flopping down on the chair opposite Theo in such a way that she was laying down across several, her entire weight supported on the crook of her elbow and the meager swell of her lip. Her hair bounced on her shoulders with the impact and she smiled at him, a perfect row of white between two thin slivers of crimson.

She was the one who'd been visiting Danny the day before. That pink stripe was still in her hair and came down on either side of her earrings, getting caught in them and wrapped up in them. Her shoulders looked as white as milk as she brought one colourfully painted fingernail up onto the table and used it to spin the chocolate bar around to face her.

"Mind if I take a bite?"

He didn't say anything, just shrugged.

She laughed a little. "I said: Mind if I take a bite?"

"Nn," he said at first, as though it took great effort to speak. "No. No, go ahead."

She nodded politely and picked up the bar between her thumb and forefinger. It entered her mouth without touching her lips and she bit off the tip, bits of caramel running out of it and staining that picturesque smile of hers. "Heaven."

She held it back out to him as though it hadn't been his to begin with. "Want some?"

"No," he said again, and it came out much easier this time.

"Why not? You don't eat? Is that what they got you in here for; you anorexic?"

"No. It just all tastes bad. Like feet. Really bad, smelly feet."

She looked at him without a smile for a moment, a kind of understanding buzzing behind her eyes as she mulled that over. She wrapped her hand around the bar and grabbed it fully now, taking a tearing bite of it. A chunk of peanut fell to the floor.

He was silent again then, listening to the drone of voices all around him and the TV behind him until it all became white noise. He stared past her until his vision focused on the row of chairs behind her and she became soft and blurry until it was like she wasn't there at all.

"So what're you in here for if you ain't anorexic, anyway?" she said. She had a drawl as though she was from the street even though she didn't look like it. Her clothes, her accent, her hair... it was all fake, he thought. There was something wrong that he could't quite put his finger on.

He didn't answer her.

"And where're your folks? You can't be the only guy in here without visitors every day. Young stud like you, I would've thought you'd've had a different girl here every day of the week... tell the redhead that visiting day is Tuesday and tell the brunette that it's Wednesday."

He didn't answer her, but she was in focus now. Everything was in focus now.

"And what about your parents? One of them has got to still be kicking around. Why aren't they camping out and waiting to come in like poor old Carl's wife?"

An Orderly walked by and she sat up in her chair as though she were about to get scolded. She leaned in close to Theo as though they were having an in-depth conversation about the answer to life, the universe, and everything.

Their hands touched for a moment and she bit her lip, looking from their hands to his eyes and then back again quickly.

"I --" he started, his mouth drenched with saliva and yet somehow dry at the same time.

"No, wait. Don't tell me." She smiled, peeling back his fingers until his palm was open on the table in front of her. "I'm psychic."

He smiled a little at that.

"Hey, worked already," she said, smiling back wider and wagging her head from side to side. Her earrings bounced. "Let's see what else we can get."

She bent over and began to study his palm, the tips of her hair tickling it and making him jerk away reflexively. She held on as though she'd done this a million times and was used to this response. His hands were rough and dry with yellowed nails that had been broken and split by the previous night's escapade. There was a line of blood blisters along the base of his fingers that he'd never even noticed until now. Each knuckle was like a tiny, dry, swirling bit of dessert sand. Her fingers were smooth and quick, running over the rough hewn lines of his palm and studying each one, tracing them all from start to finish and then using her nails to measure the distance between each.

"Interesting..." she said, humming contemplatively.

"What?" Theo asked, leaning forward to try and see what she was talking about.

"This is very interesting."

"What is it?"

"Well, you've got a fate line. Not many people do."

"Fate line?"

"Mm. See this one here that runs straight down from the middle finger to your wrist?" she said, tracing it gently as she did so and sending shivers up and down his spine. "That's your fate line."

"What does it mean?"

"It would seem, Mr..."

"Theo."

"It would seem, Mr. Theo, that you are the unlikely wielder of a destiny. You have a deep fate line, and are strongly controlled by fate."

Her eyebrows jostled from side to side as she spoke with a fake Scandinavian accent like some mystical palm reader at a county fair.

"What else is there?" he asked, leaning in closer now.

"Well, your head line is curved, so you're creative."

"I'm not."

"Yes, you are," she corrected, poking her nail into the line as though she were pointing out a certainty in a signed contract. "But there's a cross in it here. You, my friend, are in some sort of emotional crisis."

He met her eye and said nothing, then looked back at his own palm as though it were some foreign object.

"Your life line tells me you're often tired, but you have more than one here so there's a chance to change that. You have extra vitality in you and... oh." She smiled.

"What?"

She gave him a coy look.

"What?"

"Your heart line, Mr. Theo... I never would have pegged you for the romantic type."

He stared at her with a puzzled expression on his face.

"It starts here at the middle finger and reaches down to touch the life line here and here. And there are little circles and smaller lines cutting into it... you fall in love easily, Mr. Theo, but I think you've had your heart broken."

He took his hand away, and this time she let him. "I haven't."

"Maybe you will," she shrugged, popping the last of the candy bar past her lips.

He shifted uncomfortably. His stomach rumbled, loud enough that he could hear it above everyone talking and the TV and the sound of the Air Conditioner trying to cut back in.

She squinted at him, feeling bad about the empty wrapper between them.

"That's a not a very nice thing to tell someone," he said finally, his hands darting under the table and away from her.

"Everyone gets their heart broke from time to time," she smirked. "There's no shame in it."

He shuffled uncomfortably.

"So why don't you eat anything anyway? You holding out for some good home-style cooking like your Mama used to make, or are you just picky?"

He did not respond to that.

"Or do you like your meals simpler? Maybe waiting for some good-old meat and potatoes like the one's your dad used to fire up on the grill on hot summer days."

The side of his mouth twitched again, and he found a small black stain on the table to stare at and avoid her eye.

She smiled, then nodded. "Well, if you ever get out of here, there's a little restaurant about a half mile off the highway that I think you'd like. The Olympic it's called, and it lives up to the name. Best steaks you ever had..." She paused. "Better even than the ones your daddy fried up."

He let out a short, frustrated sigh. "Why're you even here?" he asked the table, skulking. "Shouldn't you be over there with Danny?"

"Oh, I'm not here to see Danny, Mr. Theo," she smiled.

For the first time he realized she had no billboard behind her head. That he couldn't see any more to her than just her, all blonde hair and green eyes and white, smooth skin. He looked around for it for a moment, as though she might have somehow left it leaned against the wall on the far side of the room, then turned back to her. She was still smiling at him and hadn't moved a muscle.

"I'd like to be left alone, please."

She exhaled through her nose and let her hands fall down by her sides. "Of course you would," she said, as though they'd had this argument a thousand times or more. "I mean, why wouldn't you? A man learns he has a destiny and all... it'd take the fun out of anyone, I guess."

"Please," he said, finding his spot on the table again and letting everything become blurry. He might not have been able to see her thoughts, but there were still plenty around. They screamed at him now, like fifty television sets all turned to different channels blaring information at him at the same time. "I just want to be left alone."

"Yeah," she said, standing up and straightening her shirt. "Too bad they don't have a line on a palm for Daddy issues. I bet that one'd run real deep."

He blinked, then looked up at her. She towered above him now. He hadn't realized how tall she was. "What?"

"Old man Theo, whoever he is... I bet he must be a real piece of work to have messed you up this bad. Did he put you in here, is that it?"

"My last name's not Theo."

"I know. That's not the damn point I was making."

"It's Flaherty."

She stopped speaking with her finger in the air like a cartoon character, frozen for a moment. "Flaherty?"

He nodded.

"Flaherty? Eff El Ey Hurty?"

He nodded again.

She brought her nail to her mouth and started to chew it, finding her own spot on the table to stare at and sat back down.

"What is it?" he asked, wishing she had a billboard so that he could just see whatever she was thinking all on his own.

"Nothing, it's... Nothing," she mumbled, waving the question away and then putting her hand right back into her mouth. She was picking at her nail with the minuscule gap between her two front teeth that he wouldn't have said was there a moment ago. "*Flaherty.*"

They sat there in silence until there was a full strip of paint gone from her nail.

"Did you..." he frowned, then stopped. He sighed, then forced himself to look up again. It was the first time he'd made himself do something consciously in months. He'd spent most of his time moving from white room to white room on the Orderly's commands. "Do you know my father?"

Her eyes moved to meet his and she studied his face, *really* studied it, just as she had his hand. His eyelids were shadowy and dark from lack of sleep, and there were deep torrents slicing down his face coming from either nostril, as if they had to be there to keep his frown from stretching clean off his face. He was white and his hair fell down into his eyes constantly, like the boys on the covers of pop singer albums. The lobes of his ears connected to his head. His eyelashes were long.

"Maybe," she whispered finally, reaching out and pushing his hair out of his face and squinting. Her touch sent shivers through him again. "Do you have any uncles? Brothers?"

He shook his head for each.

"There's this guy named Flaherty that I've seen on the road once or twice. Sharp dresser, always looks like he's to the nines."

His face perked up.

"I'm on the road a lot. I've seen him in a few different places, always with that briefcase and looking at things on his phone... I get the impression he travels for work a lot. He's got hair like yours, but he wears it different. Slicked straight back."

"That's him," Theo said, his voice almost a gasp. "That's my dad."

"Wow, look at that," she said. His hands were back on the table now and she clasped them. "Will wonders never cease?"

"Did you talk to him? Did he say anything to you?"

She tilted her head at him, a slow smile growing out one side of her mouth. "No. I mean, do I look like the type of girl your daddy would talk to?"

He looked her up and down. "Actually... yes."

"Hey!" she laughed, slapping him playfully on the arm. "I caught that. Watch your mouth."

He laughed, and the sensation was strange to him. Like a spasm in his throat he couldn't control. It died down after a moment, and he got quiet again. "So you never spoke to him?"

"Naw," she sighed. "Sorry. Caught his name from the truckers."

He nodded. His stomach growled ravenously. "Well, if you see him... just... make sure he knows when visiting hours are, okay? Take a pamphlet. He forgets stuff like that easy."

She smiled again, a real smile that showed off her teeth. "Why don't you tell him yourself? It's Wednesday, I bet he'll be there tonight."

He looked around the Public Room, as if she'd forgotten where they were.

"Come on," she said, waving his objection away again. "It'll be fun. Just you and me. We'll slip out of port via cover of darkness." The Scandinavian accent had returned, and he thought maybe she thought it was Russian. She smiled playfully at him. "We have ways of making you talk," she laughed, then hit him again. "I can have you out and back before light. That is, if you even want to come back."

Theo thought for a moment. He debated for an instant telling her that it was no use waiting until dark. That dark here never came, there was always the same light coming in through his window and that they never turned it off and they'd use it to catch them.

He opened his mouth to speak, then shut it again.

"Come on," she pleaded, running her thumbs along the edges of his hands. "You're not going to let me go out there all alone, are you?"

He met her eye, then smiled.

***

It was still light when the Orderlies tucked him in that night, using the sheets to tie him down to the mattress so tight he couldn't move. The padding on the wall had been replaced, the new pads a slightly brighter shade of white than the rest and glowing in the light from the window as though they were radioactive. It looked like the secret passages you'd see in old eighties animation, when the animators always coloured the part of the wall that would move a different colour than the rest so that everyone would know which one was supposed to move.

He didn't close his eyes for quite some time, and wondered if he even still had the ability to blink. The light from the window started to come in a slightly deeper shade of orange, then deeper again, and again, until it was always red and he wondered if someone was playing with the dimmer switch out in the hall. Before he knew it, it was dark in the room for the first time that he could remember.

All around him, billboards began to switch on to different channels, each one glowing in the dark and broadcasting in 5.1 stereophonic surround sound certified by George Lucas and the whole THX crowd personally. Danny was ploughing the Nurse again, this time in an awkward manoeuver that Theo didn't even have a name for and wasn't sure he wanted.

He raised his arm until his shoulder bulged up out of the sheet like an erection, until it hurt against the strain of the tightly-woven sheets. It didn't take much. He wondered if he'd been sewn in like they used to do to men staying at their fiancées' houses back in the old days, but he didn't remember the Orderly having a needle. His fingers *may* have been needles, they were long and pointed.

"Stop talking crazy," he told himself, trying to ignore the billboards that were coming on.

He raised his other shoulder the same way, straining until he couldn't any more and gritting his teeth so hard that his bite slipped and sent a loud crack ringing throughout his skull. He relaxed back onto the bed, feeling that the sheet was a little looser from the effort. He started rocking back and forth, making the bed squeak in a way that seemed to fuel Danny's fantasies, pushing one arm up and then the other until they were loose enough that he could reach his arm out and into freedom.

He gave a satisfied sigh and smiled.

He pulled the covers off of him and sat on the edge of his bed to make sure he didn't fall asleep. They'd given him the pills before they'd tucked him into his bed, but they never worked. They never seemed to work. Still, it was better to be safe than sorry. He looked up at the window in his door and expected her face to be there already, floating there from the second he'd gotten out of bed and ready to open the door for him.

Of course it wasn't.

He sat with his arms propped up on his legs and waited, staring at the chicken-wire covered window. Time seemed to draw out like a blade, and eventually he turned and found a spot on the floor (a sister to the one on the table, identical in almost every way) and lost himself in it.

Lindsey was dreaming about painting.

Theo focused until his billboard came closer and closer, like he was approaching it on the highway at top speed, until it took up his whole wall. Colours would start out of nowhere and fade in from the blackness, soft and warm, and in tones and shades that Theo couldn't name. He didn't think there was a name for them, that these were colours that couldn't exist in real life. There was a red so soft and warm that it was like the sky, and a brown like the tint inside a tree when you first cut into it that only lasted a second. Less than a second. Each stroke happened on its own and then disappeared. The paint faded back into the canvas so that Theo couldn't see what Lindsey was painting, but he knew it was beautiful. There was a long, blue, quivering horizontal line across the entire canvas that he was sure was the top of a water's edge. Was it the ocean perhaps? Or maybe a cabin on the lake? That would certainly explain the brown. There was green now, making little lines up and then out, out, out... up and then out, out, out... they were trees, he thought. Evergreens, the type that you didn't see much in California, but may well have been frequent wherever Lindsey was from. He thought he knew where Lindsey was from, but couldn't remember.

-Knock Knock-

His head turned back to the window and she was there, the pink highlights in her hair just visible in the frame of the window.

"Come on!" she mouthed, as though she were scolding him for still being in bed.

He got up and brought his face to the window, his heart beating furiously in his chest. Was it really happening? He didn't think so. He thought maybe this was Danny's dream. He turned to eye Danny's billboard to see, but found him to still have the Pretty Nurse bent over the desk that used to be in his old high school library.

Their faces, Theo's and hers, were both pressed so close to the glass that it fogged. It was almost like they were kissing.

"I can't get the door open," she said, just loud enough to hear. Her voice was muffled through the glass. "You have to."

He ran a hand through his hair and then looked around. There were long staples holding in the new pieces of mattress. He pried one out (hooking it under his fingernail and making it bleed, leaving a small smear on the otherwise pristine white pad) and inserted it into the small hole under the knob. His tongue poked curiously out of the corner of his mouth and he wriggled it around until finally it clicked.

He pulled down on the lever and it swung itself forward, revealing her standing on the other side clapping silently.

"My hero," she said, taking her chin in his hand and giving him a kiss on the forehead while he was still down on one knee. "Come on."

He got up and stepped out into the hall after her.

The hallway was long and dark, the lights having been turned off hours ago to let some of the more fidgety Closers sleep. There was a light at the end off the hallway that was so bright and white that it shimmered and reflected off the metal walls, floors, and ceiling, and cast bending, monstrous shadows everywhere.

She trolled along the highway two doors up, just a black silhouette against the cold metal of the hospital. "Come on!"

Theo started after her.

***

When the doors opened, he saw that Black Springs didn't exist in the Arctic right now, if it ever had. It wasn't on a beach either, although Theo thought he could hear waves crashing somewhere far in the distance.

It was in the desert.

The moon was high and red overhead. The road that led from the front entrance of Black Springs out to the highway was the same compacted dirt and sand as the rest of the grounds, as hard as concrete and yet light enough that a good gust of air could send it spiraling in mini twisters toward a person's eyes. The only thing to distinguish the trail from the rest of the barren land was its colour. It was a sort of light orange. The rest of the ground was the hard brown of true grit.

The highway was a thin gray line on the horizon, marking the edge of a long line of hills that looked like they'd been drawn on. The brown of them was layered, getting darker as it went down, as though somebody had shaded it lazily in Photoshop.

She was a few paces in front of him and still jogging, when she stopped, the dirt she'd kicked up by running still continuing forward for a moment before fading into the night air. She leaned over onto her knees for a moment to catch her breath, then spun around to look at him over her shoulder. The night was hot, and her golden hair clung to her cheeks and her breasts with glimmering sweat as she took deep, gasping breath after breath.

Theo was standing in front of Black Springs, looking up at it. His back was turned to her.

It was smaller than he'd thought it would be. He'd pictured it as a massive prison with a stone-and-wire fence that went up the whole way around. He'd pictured towers on either corner that rose up story after story until they ended at points that pierced they sky and caught stray bolts of lightning on stormy nights. The truth was that it was small. All of it one story, a rectangular white building with very few windows and a black slit for a door in the middle. It looked like one of the bunkers people used to use in the forties, only bigger. Dirt clung stubbornly to one side and yellow, powdery roofing dust tumbled over one corner onto the ground. Beyond it there was pitch black that he couldn't see, but he could hear and smell. It was the salt of the sea. It was there, after all, but it hid from him even now.

"You're not having second thoughts, are you?" she asked, turning toward Theo and the Clinic.

"No," he said, still staring at it. "No, not at all."

***

She didn't have a car, and the ground was hard against his feet.

Black Springs was far behind them. Its narrow, thin frame had sunk into the distance quickly, becoming just a slit on the horizon. No cars had passed them in the hour they'd been walking, and sometimes it felt as though they were walking in place. The monotony of the sand seemed to never end, though sometimes he thought he saw the lights of the city far in the background.

Their shoes were covered in dust almost immediately. Within ten minutes, it had worked its way up to their knees where it stayed now, flirting with rising only to retreat again every few minutes.

He twitched and turned around, then back to her. The night was hot and she was sweating. The striped shirt she wore clung to her body tightly.

Taking a deep breath, he closed his eyes and listened.

There was only silence. Silence and darkness. No screaming voices, no videos, no loud annoying billboards assaulting him and entering him and raping him... just the peace of the windless night, the air hanging thick around him as he walked through it.

"You okay?" she asked, stepping in tune with him as they made their way around a long, curvy bend. She looked the way he pictured hippies looking, all blonde and young and beautiful and hitchhiking safely through warm summer nights.

"Yeah," he said, and smiled the first real smile he had in months. He turned around again to make sure Black Springs wasn't following him somehow, even though he knew it wasn't. Knew it. It seemed that it had been forever since he'd known something, even longer since he'd known something comforting. "Yes."

***

"So, what's your father like?" Theo asked, when he realized that neither of them had spoken in an hour. The backs of his legs hurt, a sharp ache travelling from his ankle up to the back of his knee with every step he took.

"My dad?" she laughed, throwing her head back and smiling wonderfully. Her teeth were bright even in the dark of the night. "I bet you think a girl like me must have a real piece of work for a father, huh?"

He smiled at her. "No."

Her head came back down, hair tumbling over each shoulder stringy and damp. It hid her face for her when she spoke next, her pace slowing just a little when she spoke. "My dad's a bit of a scoundrel. Has what Mom used to call The Sickness. Said it was in his genes, that his father was like it, too."

"Were they married?"

She snorted. "He put the ring on, but he never married. Not one day in his life was that man ever married. Made my mom frightfully jealous."

Theo nodded slowly, turning his eyes forward.

The moon was in front of them, and sometimes it seemed like they were walking toward it instead of some unseen spot along the highway.

"He used to run around with women half his age, sometimes younger. Always cheating, always whoring... he never stopped." She sneered a little. It looked odd on her pretty face. "I told myself I'd never be that uncivilized."

"You're not uncivilized."

She did not respond.

"What did your mother think of it?"

"Other than the jealous bouts, she never really used to mind. At least not until a few girls started showing up pregnant."

Theo winced.

She laughed. "You'd think the man was setting up franchises, the way he went at it. Sometimes I think he had a different girl in every town across America. The first time I hit out onto the road was for one of those kids."

"You been there ever since?"

"No," she smiled, finally making eye contact with him again. "This isn't one of those stories. I make it back whenever I can. Dad's still the way he is, but he's gotten old enough now that no lady but Mom'll have him, and I think it learned him a thing or two. Or maybe one of his conquests got a hold to his heart and showed him how it felt... maybe it was just time."

They were silent again then.

***

"Can I turn around yet?" Theo asked, calling out into the air around him from where he sat.

"You can't turn around, period," she called back from where she squat behind him, trying to pee. "When I'm done, I'll come around to you."

He sighed and smiled, looking at the open land around him. The desert was timeless. It stretched on forever as it had when the first settlers had come here and the way it had been when the first natives passed through before that. The only difference was the sand, the way the rocks were striped and coloured darker the further you went down them... The rings had been less tanned then, their depth the only thing to show the passage of time.

There was a cactus off to his left that had blossomed bright pink flowers from the top of each of its four spires. They looked bright even now, their yellow centres beaming with enough light to rival the moon above. The spikes of the plant caught the moonlight and sent it glimmering in all directions, turning the green of the cactus into a dull gray.

A coyote stepped out into Theo's field of vision, and he felt his breath catch in his throat.

It was big, easily as tall as the smooth rock that Theo had found to sit upon. Its coat was reddish brown and its eyes were solid black marbles in a soft pinkish bed. They got no rest there, darting about quickly through the desert night for other signs of life.

Its eyes fell upon Theo, and it let out a low hum of a growl from deep within its throat. Air puffed out from its long snout and kicked up dirt that had scattered across the desert's surface, and it seemed not to have to blink as it stared Theo down.

Theo stared back at it, paralyzed with fear and unable to move or blink or call out to her for help.

It snorted again, then licked its lips and turned away. It looked back after a moment, but made no sound, then turned and ran back to the highway. When it got to the road it began to trot tranquilly back down the road the way they'd come, its great paws kicking up grit as it went and its bushy tail swerving from side to side behind it.

Theo told her nothing about it.

***

The desert seemed to go forever, until, some hours after they had left, the two of them came across a light that glowed from around a turn in a highway creating a halo around a large striped rock formation. It made her face light up, her smile stretching until the pink of her lips pushed the rise of her cheeks up and her ears wiggled.

"Is that it?" Theo asked, the backs of his legs burning by now.

"That's it," she laughed, taking his wrist in her hand and breaking into a jog until they were around the corner.

It looked like something out of a Phillip K. Dick adaptation. It sat in the midst of a vast wasteland of sand and gravel and grit, and was the only thing bright enough to compete with the bright white light of the moon above it. While everything around it was earthy and muted (the gray pavement, the caffeinated-brown sand, the maroon hillsides), this was bright and pink and neon.

The Olympic was one story that stretched so far back into the sand that the lights of the entrance could not penetrate the darkness, making it seem like the area behind it simply ceased to be. In reality, it skewed down on a steep angle and met with the desert floor so that anyone who wished to could simply step from the ground behind it onto the ceiling and walk their way up without any effort at all. There was no roofing dust on it, just regular brown sand from the desert that had blown up over time and had never been dusted off. The front-facing wall was painted a bright blueish green that seemed out of place here, as though someone had taken the ocean and brought it in to the middle of the dessert. There was a hot pink oblong with one rounded corner sitting at the top of the building and the rest of it jutting out over like a blob, a flowing tube of pink neon light travelling all around its edge. It buzzed constantly, the tube flickering near the top just enough for Theo's eye to register that something was wrong.

Written across the oblong in a glowing cursive script was the name, *The Olympic*.

There was a series of connected windows that took up the entire middle front of the diner, and even though it was early in the morning, there were still people inside.

Theo slowed down until her hand was tugging against his arm, then stopped.

She turned around and squinted at him, smiling. "You don't need to be scared."

"I'm not scared, I'm just..." he paused, trying hard to find the right words and coming up with nothing. "I'm not scared."

"Okay," she nodded, as though she were now completely in agreement.

He looked past her to the diner. The parking lot was unpaved and crowded with vehicles. Most were semi-trucks. Beyond that there were some old beater cars with wooden panels along the sides, but there were one or two nicer cars that a businessman might have driven, especially if he were driving a secondary car... something he used to get from place to place.

There were large plastic crates tracing the light on either side of it, the type that looked like they'd need a forklift to move. He didn't see a forklift anywhere. It was like all of the gray and gloom and bad from the rest of the world was captured by the light of the sign and compressed itself into cubes at its edge, frozen there forever.

He closed his eyes and took a deep breath, in through his nose and out through his mouth.

There was still a glow in the darkness, one that had nothing to do with the buzzing neon he could still hear. Within the diner's walls were small billboards of the same type that he'd always found in Black Springs among the Closers, small television screens that belted out their insanity in non-stop commercial free continuous coverage of the mind behind it. There was a man in the corner reading *The Bluest Eye* to himself, turning the pages every few moments. His billboard was an odd form of black that did not quite fit in with the black around it, the words on the page echoing through the dry heat in a British accent not his own, like some never-before-seen audio book only available in his mind. Another screen showed the psychedelic greens and red of an Alanis Morissette cover, one face in the foreground staring up into the vampire moon and another looking to the right, seemingly interested in what Toni Morrison was writing about. The lyrics radiated through the confined space, and Theo was surprised that everyone else in the diner wasn't bobbing their heads. *And I'm here to remind you of the mess you left when you went away. It's not fair to deny me of the cross I bear that you gave to me.*

He winced and opened his eyes. She was standing in front of him, her face and bust taking up the entirety of his vision. He hadn't realized that her hands had been on his shoulders, but they were. He could still see the screens though, shining through the supple skin of her breast as though she were partially transparent. The notion sent a shiver down his spine.

"Is something wrong?" she asked, biting the corner of her lip.

"I think so," he said, furrowing his brow and shaking his head. "I think... I think I just got used to the dark."

She nodded, then backed off from him a pace. "I'm going in now... I'd really like it if you came with me."

He nodded again, walking just a step or two behind her as they crossed the street into the parking lot.

The light from the sign hit the toe of his shoe and sent jolts of Electric Mirror Sundance up his leg and out through the back of his head.

There was a rustling sound in the darkness just to the right of them and they stopped frozen in their tracks. Theo's face grew taut with worry as his eyes bulged and searched the shadows of the gray boxes.

She smiled, even as the disheveled man came into view.

He looked old even though he wasn't, his neck and forehead were loose and full of wrinkles, but his cheeks were still high and smooth. They glowed in the pink light when he smiled his large smile out from over a battered novelty sombrero. A gray mustache the shape of handlebars came down from either side of a large nose filled with blood blisters that perfectly framed his swollen lips. He wore layers of clothing despite the heat, and the stench of sweat that came off of him was wretched. There were patterns in the clothes, but no colour, any colour having been drawn out of it after hours spent in the desert sun. Now there was just the gray of the dust that clung to it.

At first, Theo thought he didn't have a screen either like her, but then he saw it. It wasn't a song or a movie or a memory, just a feeling of deep, deep need. It scared him, and he backed off a pace into the light as the man got closer. "Watch out," he said, holding a hand out to her and motioning for her to step closer to him.

She rolled her eyes and tisked him, stepping closer to the man and bending down a little to match his height. Theo hadn't even noticed now short he was or how tall she was until this happened.

"Do you have any change?" the man said, looking from her to Theo and then back again. His lips barely moved when he spoke, and it sounded like his throat were almost completely devoid of moisture. "I need a... a cup of coffee."

He motioned toward the diner as though there were some choice as to where he would buy it.

She smiled at him, her hair coming down around either side of her face and looking like the colour of spun gold. Her mouth remained tightly wound, but she smiled with her eyes. Their noses were less than a foot apart, but they weren't touching yet. "How much do you need?"

"Ffffffffffffffffffffffty is all," he replied, the word getting stuck against his lip. "Fifty cents."

She nodded knowingly. She laid one hand down on his shoulder and looked him straight in the eye. "You don't need it."

A tear escaped his eye. His mouth was slack slightly, and he did not seem to be able to tear his gaze from her.

She smiled, bringing her other hand up and stroking his youthful cheek lovingly. "Whatever it really is, you don't need it."

He nodded slowly.

She released him and took a step back, then reached into the pocket of her jeans and pulled out a bill. She handed it to him, her arm stretched out as far as it would go. "Here."

He reached up and took it, clutching it as tightly as he would a life preserver. He turned from her and made his way into the desert one shuffling step at a time.

"What was that?" Theo asked, stepping up beside her to watch that man as he walked away.

She smirked, her arms crossed in front of her midriff, then turned and walked into The Olympic. He watched for a moment longer, then followed her.

***

The diner looked as though it had been ripped straight from a movie about the 1950s. There was a real bell hanging above the door that chimed happily as the two of them entered, not one of those robotic sensors that beeped angrily whenever someone stepped near them.

The setup was simple enough, with pink and red booths lined against the front window and far wall to form an upper-case L and the bar taking up the majority of the rest with stools in front and the kitchen in back. There was a large man standing behind the counter wearing a big smile and a bright apron, his palms both leaning flat against the blue counter and his sleeves rolled up to his elbows.

"Hey, Girl!" he yelled happily as they entered, coming around the counter.

She twirled her arms through the air and he picked her up, spinning her around so that her shoes almost hit the walls and stools around them. They both laughed like madmen until he finally put her down. "How have you been, Darryl? Keeping that wife of yours happy?" she asked.

"You know it," he smiled, winking mischievously at her. His hands were still on her hips. Her hands were still on his shoulders. "What about you? What've you been up to?"

She shrugged. "Making my way along, like I always do."

"You two... know each other?" Theo asked, shifting from one foot to the other.

Darryl turned to him and smiled. His mouth was comically small for the size of his face, but still showed that he was missing at least two teeth. His cheeks were bulbous and full of stubble. "Hell yeah, this girl here is the reason I own this place!" He hugged her close to his side and shook her joyfully one final time, then let her go. She seemed to shrink when he released her, as though he'd been holding her up that whole time.

"Really?"

"Oh yeah! Never would've been able to make something of myself if Little Miss here hadn't come along and civilized me! Was just around here, too!"

Theo looked from Darryl to her and smiled. "You don't say?"

Behind Darryl's head was a picture that showed a slightly younger version of the girl he was standing next to. It radiated joy and sadness all at the same time.

"He's exaggerating," she beamed, stepping away from him politely.

"Sure I am," he snickered. "Whole cities of men like me got lot to owe you."

Again she smiled respectfully.

"So what'll it be?" he asked, moving slowly back around to his side of the bar. "The usual?"

"Oh --" Theo said, laughing. "We're not here to --"

"Two usuals will be fine. Mash his," she interrupted. She turned to him with one eyebrow raised. "While we're here."

He relented, and the both of them stepped over to the nearest open booth alongside the window.

There was a man in the back wearing all black, from his tee-shirt to his jeans. His hair was combed to one side, he had a pencil-thin mustache and chin-beard and he looked like an art student. He was reading a book that he was too engrossed in to look up, the coffee in front of him having gone cold while it waited for him. His hand covered the front cover, but Theo knew that it was *The Bluest Eye*.

There were three large men squat into the booth behind Theo's companion, each of them wearing baseball caps with plastic mesh on the backs. One wore black and red checkered button-up shirt, the buttons on it pulled as tightly as the strings behind them would allow and sections of his chest visible between them. One man was sitting alone at the counter, his head bobbing along to the music streaming into his brain through his headphones. The track had moved on from *Oughta Know* to *In Bloom*, and the album cover hovering above his head had changed suitably. Four men sat symmetrically in a booth a few rows behind Theo, each of them wearing straight black ties except one who wore a tie with a Tasmanian Devil on it. The desert behind the character looked much as Theo imagined the desert he'd just crossed would have looked in the light.

Theo craned his head around and examined them all. She watched him with her hands clasped together and her chin resting on them, her eyes following his head wherever it went until he turned back and met her gaze.

"He's not here, is he?" he sighed, running his hands through his hair.

She frowned. "Doesn't look like it. Give it a chance though. He might show up."

He shook his head, then pressed the heels of his hands against his eyes hard enough that he saw spots. "This was a stupid idea," he said between gritted teeth. "I knew it the second I stepped into the parking lot that this was a stupid idea."

"Hey," she soothed, leaning in and touching the palm of his hand with her index finger. Her touch was light and feathery and made him feel warm, even though he didn't want to feel that way right now. "It'll all work out. You'll see. I can tell the future, remember."

He smiled despite himself as Darryl walked over to them carrying a graceful golden pitcher of water. He placed a small silver-plated basin between the both of them. They watched in silence as tipped the water over the basin so that his guests might rinse their hands, then nodded and stepped away wiping the excess water from the jug with his apron.

Theo dipped one hand gently into the basin and watched as the water surrounded it and distorted its proportions. It ran into the cup of his palm and made a small lake there, so clear and perfect that he could see the rough hem of his heart line within it.

After a moment, she took his hand gently in both of hers, her touch little more than a sensation running across his skin. The water poured from his hand and she began to massage it without rhyme or reason, rubbing the muscles and tendons of his fingers.

A moment later Darryl emerged at the table again, this time carrying two steaming hot plates. The smell filled the air as he laid them down, one in front of Theo and the other in front of the girl, and Theo wondered how he hadn't smelled it long before he'd done so. The sweet hickory scent of meat cooked just right. It was a porterhouse steak cooked to a perfect medium-rare. There was a half-cob of corn resting beside it and mashed potatoes brimming with volcanic butter. Hers was much the same, except instead of the mashed potatoes there were fries.

She dug in immediately, picking up her fork and impaling several fries on it with a few short stabs, and then shoveling them into her mouth all at once. As she chewed, she picked up her knife and started to cut her steak into small, bite-sized sections.

Theo looked down at his plate. His mouth was salivating and his stomach was rumbling, turning over upon itself with excitement as it got the signals from the rest of his senses somehow about what was in front of him. The steam rose up from the plate and fogged his vision. Even the aroma of it was better than any food he'd had in him in months.

She looked at him for a moment, her cheeks filled with steak and french fries. "Well?"

He smiled at her meekly, then turned back toward the plate as though it were an enemy. He brought his hand to rest on his fork, but did not pick it up. He stared at it like that for what seemed like a long time while she chewed. When she swallowed, she opened her mouth to speak (something sarcastic, he was sure of it); he spoke first.

"You don't know what it's like not to know your name," he said, looking away from the pile of rapidly melting butter and into her eyes, then back again. "I mean, I know my name. But it's like I don't know who I am... because I don't know who *he* is. All my life I grew up never knowing who he was. I could read his mind backwards and forwards and still have no idea who he was. And it just... I mean, the son of a big snake is a big snake, right? And the son of a big bear is a big bear too. But if you don't know where you came from, how're you rightly supposed to know--"

He trailed off, his eyes becoming damp. He picked up his fork and used it to saw off the end of his steak and pushed it into his mouth. It was warm and juicy and good, and it filled his whole being with flavour. He smiled, then laughed as he chewed, scooping up a heap of potato and eating it all. The need to cry was gone again now, but the few tears he'd made dribbled down over his cheeks nonetheless. He sniffed back hard, laughed, and took another bite of his steak. It was even more delicious than the first. And before he knew it, it was half gone.

She watched him and smiled at him, eating her own dish more conservatively now. When he was almost done, she reached out and laid her hand across his the same way that paper covered rock, gently cupping it. His eyes rose to meet hers.

"You, are Theo Flaherty," she said, her voice hushed and serious. "Nobody ever needed to be anything else."

He smiled.

Behind her, the large man with the red-and-black shirt's ears perked. He turned around and kneeled his arm over their booth (much to the surprise of the men he was with) and poked his head over until his nose was almost in her hair. His baseball cap had a large jewel-encrusted cartoon crown on it with a small pickup truck in all four corners. "Excuse me," he said, in voice that was almost too eloquent. "Did you say Flaherty?"

She smiled happily, turned from the man to Theo and then back again. "Why yes we did, good sir. Do you know someone by that name?" When she spoke, she was trying not to laugh from happiness, milking every moment out of it that she could.

"Don't call me sir, I work for a living," he chuckled, inching his way out of his booth and coming around to stand next to their table. His eyes locked onto Theo's face, and he seemed to study every inch of it. The long slope of his nose, the prominence of his chin. "The name's Nathaniel. Nathaniel Esther. Folks around here call me the King." He motioned to his cap, as if to illustrate.

Theo was looking past him at the billboard there. There was an image of him on it, wearing clothes he'd never worn and doing things he'd never done. And he was older, though not by much. He extended his hand. "I'm --"

"Theo Flaherty," Nathaniel said, taking his hand and pumping it heartily. "I've heard a lot about you."

The girl moved over so he could sit down, and he did.

"You knew my father?" Theo whispered, ducking his head down low.

"I know your father," Nathaniel laughed, an action that shook the table and most of the row. "Helped me out of a jam once. Me and my wife, Donna, we'd got in a little deep with the debt collectors. Seemed like everyone was coming after us, her especially. Almost drove us apart. Your daddy hired me on at a ridiculous salary... hell, you can probably tell I'm not worth it. He didn't keep me longer than I needed... said he didn't like better men than him working for him. Made him nervous. Don't know what I would've done that Christmas without him."

Theo listened with awe and intensity to every word, as though he'd found some heretofore-lost book of the Bible that mentioned him by name.

"It all worked out, but I wouldn't be where I am without him," Nathaniel said, getting up again so that he could fish out his wallet. He took out a hundred dollars in twenties and laid it on the table between them. "Your meal's on me, it's the least I could do."

He turned to leave, and Theo reached out and grabbed his arm. He turned around just enough to meet Theo's eye.

"Wait..." Theo said, holding his sleeve for a moment and trying to gather his thoughts. "What was my father like?"

Nathaniel stopped for a moment and thought, his face taking on a comical expression with his lower lip jutting out moist pick flesh. "He'd rarely give a man ten dollars when he only needed five, but he would *never* give a man five dollars if they really needed ten."

Theo smiled. "What's that supposed to mean?"

"How'm I supposed to know?" Nathaniel winked at him. "He's your father."

He turned and left the diner then and Theo let him, watching until he disappeared out the front door into the desert night.

She smiled at him from ear to ear as he stared at the place where Nathaniel had been, her hands laced in front of her.

"Come on," she said, tapping his arm. "It's time to go."

***

"Thank you," Theo said, when they reached the edge of the light The Olympic provided just at the edge of the highway.

"You don't need to thank me. Ever," she replied, rubbing her arms. A breeze had started in from the west, and even though it was warm it made her flesh dance. "It was fun."

He turned and looked at her over his shoulder and smiled at her, then turned back toward the highway. It stretched off to the left and right from where he stood seemingly forever... the left road taking him back to Black Springs, the right taking him... somewhere else.

He held up his hand to the light behind him, examining the deep trench of what she had called his heart line. Slowly, he brought his opposite index finger over and traced its edge from his middle finger to the edge of his palm.

"Hey," he said. "Do you think-"

He turned around to smile at her.

But she was gone.

***

When dawn with the rose red fingers crept her way over the horizon in the morning, Theo was back in his bed in Black Springs.

***

The easels had been pulled out from the wall and arranged around the Group Room in symmetrical little cubicles so that everyone could have their space.

"That's good," the Pretty Nurse said. She walked between the easels with her hands clasped behind her and looked more like a Nun in a Seminary than a Nurse in an Institution. She walked behind Paul and looked over his shoulder. He was painting a basket of fruit with a bright red cloth behind it. "That's very nice, Paul," she said.

He smiled, then went back to his painting.

Lindsey was painting another of his Rorschach tests.

"That's wonderful."

Ruffles had made a few marks on his canvas with his brush, but had quickly moved to using his hands. Despite the mess he'd made on himself and the floor around him, the resulting cacophony of blues and yellows and reds did look stunning, if random.

"That's good."

She walked behind Theo and threw a glance toward his canvas.

There was a beach on it with a roaring sea made up of blues and greens and reds and browns and every colour imaginable. It crashed and swirled out in the harbor, yet was calm by the time it reached the land, cresting in small laps against the golden grains of sand. There were a few rocks, but they'd all been worn smooth by the waves. There were two sets of footprints leading from the foreground up along the beach until they disappeared over the horizon, one slightly bigger than the other.

"Theo!" the Pretty Nurse gasped, smiling as she came around behind him. She laid a hand on his shoulder proudly. "That's absolutely beautiful!"

She beamed to herself, then continued walking over toward Robert.

He stared at the picture he'd painted for a long moment, the oil on it still wet. On the easel tray below it were the colours he'd used, small pails of red and brown and a bright, vibrant blue. It stared at him for a moment, then he picked it up and walked over to the solid gray wall of the Group Room.

He drew back and splashed it against the wall with all the force he could muster, the thick blue paint arching up from the pail and looking solid for a moment as though it were suspended in midair and then crashing against the wall in a great splash.

All the Closers jumped in their seats and turned to him, startled. He began to spread the paint around with his fingers, covering as much of the wall as he could.

"Theo!" the Pretty Nurse shrieked even as the Orderlies entered the room.

He kept painting, running his fingers along the dry, rough surface in spastic swirls and jaunts.

An Orderly took him by either shoulder and pulled him off, his feet dragging along the floor as he was pulled laughing from the Group Room.

There, on the west wall of Black Springs Clinic, was his ocean.

INVASION

Maria stood by the window, the teacup in her hand making long wreaths of steam that curled around her slender form. She was wearing the navy slacks I'd bought her two birthdays ago and had never seen her in and a simple gray top. Her arms were bare and she looked cold.

Far in the distance, not far from where Marlborough Mall would be, there was a tiny sliver of silver hovering in the air amidst a sea of perfect blue. It caught the light, but did not reflect it. It almost looked as though it had been painted onto the outside of the window, like a dime-store decal meant to amuse the young and the stupid.

Maria stared at it intently, and I saw a shiver run through her.

I tried to say something to her, then stopped and looked down at my tea. I watched as the steam from it turned my glasses into a world of fog, and then slowly ebb back to normal until it just hung near the corners of my vision.

"What do you think happened with Carol and David's kid after?" she asked finally, her eyes still fixed on the dull line on the horizon.

I paused and looked at her. Her breasts were pressing against the cotton of her shirt. I cleared my throat, realizing that I had been unintentionally staring at them for some time.

"I'm not sure," I said finally, picking up my cup with both hands and holding it in front of my face. The heat from the tea cascaded against my chin and neck, making them so hot that I could feel tiny beads of sweat form on them immediately. "It was a pretty bad thing what he did, breaking into the school like that. He tore the hell out of that old grand piano."

"Yeah," she said, and for a moment I thought I'd lost her yet again to the world outside our window. "I don't think that was him though, I think it was that other boy -- Johnny. I can't imagine Tyson getting something like that into his head all on his own."

"On Good Friday no less," I huffed.

She turned away from the window and rolled her eyes at me. "I don't think anyone but you and Missus Engleman realized it was Good Friday."

She sat down across from me at the table and laid her tea down in front of her. After a moment, she picked up the milk tin and added a healthy splash to her already pale drink, then stirred it absently with the sugar spoon.

I watched her, the way she sunk into the dusky walls behind her and became two-dimensional. I felt tears well up behind my eyes and turn everything into a murky gray mush, and then forced them back with a long sniff.

I felt stupid.

"I finally found something for your Dad for his birthday," she said. "It's a book with all these different types of birds in it. The pictures are drawn by that painter he loves, Nathan Shaw?"

"*Nigel* Shaw."

"Nigel Shaw."

Her palms clasped around her mug for warmth. There was none to be found anymore, the steam was gone and the tea inside was cold and filmy. She bit her lip. "What do you think they want?"

I frowned deeply and sadly, then got up and wrapped my arms around her as tightly as I dared.

Outside the saucer still spun, hovering over Marlborough with its dull gray sheen.

REPTILIA

"Rata-tat-tat-tat-tat-tata!" Tyler yelled at the top of his lungs, his tiny form vibrating as the invisible weapon he clasped tightly with both hands riddled the hot desert air with a hail of bullets.

"No!" Jamie cried, clutching her chest with one hand as she fell to the ground, kicking up mounds of dust as she did. Her fingers went slack and her tongue protruded from the corner of her mouth, then she was still.

The gun disappeared all at once, Tyler's hands falling to his sides. "That's not how you do it," he said, whining his frustration.

Jamie did not speak at first, lying in the sand with her mouth hanging open.

"Give it up!" he cried, kicking up dirt.

She looked up, her mouth drawn up in a bow as she watched him scuffle about. "What'd I do wrong?"

"You're so stupid."

"Mom says you're not allowed to use words like that anymore," she said, brushing the dust from her leggings as she did so.

"Mom's not here," he teased, shoving her shoulder and sending her back into the sand.

"Quit it!" she huffed, her cheeks livid for a moment as she scrambled back to her feet. "Mom says - -"

He shot her a look, and she stopped the sentence dead in its tracks. He ran a hand though his shaggy blonde hair, smiling as he lost all interest in what he and his sister had been fighting about and instead turned toward the sea of chestnut sand that surrounded them. "Come on."

She paused, bringing the joint of her finger to her mouth thoughtfully as she turned back and looked the way they'd come.

The walls of Stapleton were already a quarter mile behind them, its grey stones reaching out of the dunes toward the bright orange sky. The buildings inside stretched out like concrete fingers, long and bony as they tried their best to grasp the sun but never could.

Jamie couldn't recall any point in her nine years on this planet ever seeing the town from this far away. She was sure she had, driving over the hills to Kingian for supplies or just going out over the dunes with her father, but right now all she could think was how small it looked from where she stood. "I think... I think maybe Momma might need us."

Tyler turned back toward her, frowning. "Why would Mom need us?"

"I... I don't know. I just think... I think maybe she does, that's all."

"You're just scared."

"I'm not scared."

"Little baby Jamie, gets scared on the daily!" he sang, wiggling his fingers at her mockingly.

"I'm *not scared!*" she insisted, turning away from Stapleton and marching forward with clenched fists, stomping her way past her brother.

He laughed, jogging until his stride matched her own.

They walked in silence for a moment, with only the sound of their footfalls and bouncing displaced pebbles between them.

"What're you scared of, anyway?" he asked after a moment, bending over to pick up a rock and then throwing it. It landed in a splash of dirt in a nearby mound of sand, soon disappearing as the grains flowed over it.

"I told you, I'm not scared."

"Puh," he snorted, rolling his eyes. He turned away for a moment, his eyes surveying the landscape, then looked back at her accusingly, a wry grin on his lips. "You're afraid of the Northies, aren't you?"

Her plump face turned white, all the colour draining from it as she stared vacantly forward for a second, then turned toward him. "Am not."

"You are so. You're afraid that a big, bad Norther is gonna come up from the sand and grab you and take you away to be his wife!" he laughed, poking her arm with his index finger to punctuate every word.

"Go away!" she whined, jolting her arm away from his jabs.

"No, Jamie! Be my bride!" he yelled in a fake Northern accent, holding out his hands toward her.

"Stop it!" she squealed, turning away from him. Her heel got caught in the sand and refused to move, though the rest of her body continued to. The joint twisted harshly before she fell face first into a sandbar, sending sharp bits of stone into her face. She started to sob, even as she brought her palms flat against the warm mineral on either side of her to brace herself as she got up. "I'm telling Momma!"

Tyler did not respond.

"Puh," she spat, trying desperately to get the dirt out of her mouth. Each tiny pebble was like a bit of glass bouncing around the inside her mouth, slicing away at every gum, tongue and soft surface it found while there.

When she was done spitting, she looked over her shoulder at him. Tyler was standing a few feet behind her, his face as white as first-morning's light as he stared off into the desert beyond where she lay. One of his arms lay dead with shock at his side, while the other had gone up to meet his face in the same fearful, thoughtful position she had been in a few minutes before, the joint of one finger clasped between his lips.

Jamie turned around, lifting her head to see over the dune she'd fallen into. She shivered, her lower lip quaking violently even though the heat was blistering.

Thirty feet beyond the dune, a man lay in the sand.

He was almost invisible in the tattered beige uniform he wore, hidden against the soft bronze hues of the sands. His face was red, its lower half splotched with blood that still oozed from his mouth in slow seeping, congealed glops.

He looked at her with eyes that barely acknowledged what they were seeing, the pupils having shrunk to mere pinpricks in the blazing sun long ago. The skin on the right side of his face had blistered and peeled, turned a deep brown by the suns rays. After what seemed like an eternity, his chest rose ever so slightly to take in a breath.

Jamie opened her mouth and screamed.

"Mom-*Ma!*"

***

"Clear the way!" EMT Mark Baxter cried, pushing along the gurney as fast as he dared.

The doors to the emergency operating room at Stapleton General burst open as the gurney was wheeled through feet first, slamming against the tile walls on either side.

"Private Terrence Baker, 1054th Regiment. Found out in the desert thirty minutes ago suffering from massive dehydration, asphyxia, as well as multiple contusions and burns along the face and upper torso!" Mark belted out, holding an oxygen mask to the soldier's face as he yelled. His short black hair stuck to him with sweat that poured off him in buckets, even now that they were out of the heat and inside in the air-conditioned and sterile hallways of the hospital.

He positioned the gurney such that it was right next to the operating table. Three nurses gathered around, each clasping their own side of the sheet that Private Baker had been laid upon, then hoisted him over onto the smooth stainless steel table.

Blood shot up like a fountain from Baker's mouth, splashing against the surgeon's apron and turning it a deep, wet red.

"Christ," the surgeon cursed, backing up a pace a watching the blood make its way between his gloved fingers.

"Heart rate is slow, but steady," Mark continued. "I think his lungs are filling with blood. There might be a bleed in his left--"

"Well, what was your first clue?" the doctor barked, motioning down at his apron. It was hard to gage the man's expression with his surgical mask and goggles on, but his tone was very clear.

"Dr. Sutton, I was merely suggesting that --"

"Get back to your car, Mark," Dr. Sutton interrupted again, already unbuttoning the patients shirt. "There are plenty of scraped knees and broken wrists out there that are in desperate need of your help."

Mark stared at him for a moment, then looked down at the man on the table. Blood spewed from his mouth again, almost hitting a nurse before splashing onto the floor in a great wave of crimson. He frowned, then shook his head and left the way he came in, closing the OR doors behind him as he went.

Dr. Sutton finished unbuttoning Baker's shirt, spreading the torn fabric wide to reveal the entire torso. The skin was loose and rubbery, as though it were two sizes too big for him. His chest was covered in patches of short, curly hair turned white by the sun's rays while lying out in the desert sand.

Just below his right nipple was a small round puncture wound, trickling blood slowly.

"You think that might be the source of the bleed?" Sutton called, winking at the nurse next to him.

She smiled back. He couldn't see her mouth below the mask, but the laugh lines under her eyes told him all he needed to know.

"I'm gonna need a number five blade and a clamp. Get ready for some sutures too, people. Lots and lots of sutures. This guy's lung seems to think it's his stomach, and last time I checked those two things weren't the same."

He glanced up into the observation deck.

There was an older man standing as straight as a pole looking back down at him. His gaze was unblinking and unmoving, his features withered by time and seeming to melt down into his collar. He wore a clean white suit with brass buttons polished to a starry gleam. Red epaulettes were the only spot of colour of the whole thing, standing out like gaping mouths. His hands were clasped firmly behind his back and the only sign of movement was the slight tap of his smooth, black shoes.

Dr. Sutton nodded once, then turned back down toward his patient.

The Officer nodded back as well, in a movement so slight it may not have happened at all.

***

Mark sat on the bench near the front entrance of the hospital, staring at the baseboards in front of him. The automatic doors were only a few feet to his left, and every time someone went in or out he was blasted with a wave of heat from outside, contrasting the almost biting cold of the hallway. The contrast played havoc with his body temperature, sweating when he was warm and then being drenched with it in the cold. His face was a low, deep purple around the cheeks as he let out a deep sigh, leaning forward onto his knees.

"He's like that with everybody."

He looked up to see Chauna Deeds standing a few feet to his left, her fists resting against her hips. One hand was clenching her surgical mask and cap tightly as she stood staring down at him, one leg cocked out in a relaxed, ready pose. Sweat lined the brim of her brow and soaked deep circles into the armpits and collar of her salmon coloured scrubs. "You look hot," he said.

She raised an eyebrow to him quizzically, then looked down at her sweat-drenched form and smiled, showing all of her teeth. "Oh, yeah," she laughed, taking down her ponytail and letting her curly brunette hair fall down onto her shoulders. "Air conditioner is broken in radiology. Been there all day taking scans."

"Hm."

She sat down next to him on the bench, looking up at the air conditioning vent on the ceiling above them and letting the cool breeze blow down onto her for a moment before turning toward Mark. "Like I was saying, don't be pissy about Sutton. He's like that with everybody. Man just doesn't have any people skills."

"You heard?"

She laughed. "It's a small hospital, Mark."

"It's a small settlement."

She nodded slowly. "True."

He brought both hands up to his face, stretching it downward and making a low, moaning sound in his throat. "Ugh. I gotta get outta here, Chauna."

She rolled her eyes. "Thought you liked it here. Allie does."

"Allie's an idiot."

The comment took her aback. Her mouth stayed open for a moment before she finally found the words with which to fill it, her brain catching up with the rest of her. "That's... okay, yeah. I thought you two were doing better?"

He snorted a laugh then turned to look at her. She was still warm from the hours spent in radiology, her breathing heavy and her chest heaving up and down with every breath she took. He mumbled something, then turned back to staring at the wall.

"What was that?"

"I said I wish you'd make up your damn mind," he spat, turning toward her again. The veins in his cheeks turned the deep purple they did whenever he got angry.

"Excuse me?"

"Excuse you. A month ago you didn't much care whether or not Allie and I worked it out, did you? Month ago you were sitting bare-breasted on my bed asking me to leave her. So which is it?"

"Neither... both," she huffed, shaking her head. "I thought we got past this. This snapping at each other."

He took a deep breath and closed his eyes.

Biting her lip, she reached out to lay her hand on his shoulder.

"What're you doing?" he barked the second contact was made, getting off the bench and glaring down at her.

"Whatever, Mark," she huffed, grabbing her mask from her lap and turning to walk away.

"Chauna," he called after her, his face softening.

She made a curt wave without even turning around, then went around the corner and disappeared from sight.

He sighed, placing the heel of his hand against his throbbing eye. He held it there for a minute, wishing for it to stop, before turning and punching the wall as hard as he could and turning toward the exit.

The automatic doors opened, surrounding him in the dry heat of the desert and sand blew by him, slicing at his skin.

Red streaks radiated out from the dent he'd left in the wall, seeping downward toward the floor.

***

"Jesus," Dr. Sutton cursed as another dollop of blood splashed onto his shoes. He stepped back, holding the scalpel in his steady grip as he looked toward Private Baker's mouth, still drooling blood. "Can somebody trach this guy before he chokes on his own blood, please?"

"I'm trying, sir," one of the nurses sighed, holding the tube in front of her in exasperation. "But he keeps--"

"You're useless," he shot, turning back to the large opening he'd sliced in the centre of the Private's abdomen. "Get Stein to do it. I think she actually went to medical school."

The nurse huffed, then passed the tube and laryngoscope to the person next to her.

"You can sponge," he said, nodding to her. He paused a moment, then added, "I do mean now."

She grabbed a cloth from the way station, brought it to his forehead and dabbed the moisture from it, careful not to interrupt his field of vision.

He took a deep breath, then moved Baker's gallbladder aside and continued to manoeuvre his blood-spattered, gloved hands further and further into the victim's chest.

Nurse Stein brought her own scalpel to Private Baker's trachea and made one clean slice. Redness gurgled out, spilling onto the table as though she'd turned on a faucet. "He's anemic!"

"Well, he can't be anemic," Sutton drawled, nodding his head toward his hands, both of which were submerged within Private Baker. "Because if he was, I'm fairly sure this would be a bit of a problem."

Nurse Stein cursed, washing the blood away and continuing with the tracheotomy.

***

Chauna flopped down into the soft suede chair that had stood against the wall of the surgeon's lounge ever since she'd been stationed there, smiling as its familiar grooves bent and flexed to the contours of her slender form.

Across the hall, Dr. Adrian Janes looked up from his paperwork at her and smiled. He was much older than her, in his mid-forties, but had managed to maintain a full head of dark, neatly styled hair. He even retained his boyish good looks, in Chauna's opinion, when he kept himself clean-shaven, which he was at the moment. He watched her reach into the mini-fridge next to the chair without even so much as glancing in its direction, pulling out a fruit cup and peeling off the vacuum sealed cover. She looked at it hungrily, then glared at the cutlery drawer all the way on the other side of the room. Weighing her options for a moment, she tilted her head back and drank the fruit from its container as if it had been juice. He laughed.

She brought her head back, wiping a dribble of pineapple juice from her chin. "What's so funny?"

"Nothing, just... nothing," he smirked, turning back toward the x-rays in his hand, holding one up to the light for a better look.

Her smile broadened, stretching from ear to ear. "What? Oh, you've got to tell me now."

He smiled, laying down the sheet. "Five years you've worked here. At least three times a week, I watch you get a fruit cup from that fridge; most of those times you end up eating it with your hands."

"And?" she chirped, picking a strawberry out of the cup with her thumb and forefinger and placing it gently between her lips.

"Does it never occur to you to get a spoon *before* you sit down?"

She paused as she chewed, reflecting on the question, then swallowed. "It has."

He looked at her, waiting for more.

"Priorities, Janes," she hummed, sinking even deeper into the chair. "Priorities."

He chuckled, shaking his head at her as he noticed a speck on the x-ray. He tried to wipe it away, discovered that it was indeed a part of the image, then scribbled something down in his file.

She ate the last piece of fruit from her cup, then tipped it back and drank the juice that remained in the bottom. The mix of all the different flavors made it taste like punch and reminded her of the boxes her mother used to pack in her lunch tin as a child.

"Did you see the guy they brought in from the desert?" he mumbled after a moment, still making notations.

"Yeah. Poor guy. Looked like a train wreck."

"You think it was the Northers?"

"What else could it have been?"

"Exposure. I've seen heat exposure do some weird things to the skin, things you wouldn't believe. If the guy was even a little allergic to sunlight or UV rays, the toxicity to his liver alone could account for the blood."

"Maybe," she sighed, laying her cup down on top of the fridge. "I dunno. I guess we'll find out if Sutton patches the guy up."

"Hmm," Janes hummed, tapping his chin as he examined another x-ray.

"What?"

"Nothing, just... you don't see many people like that pull through. I don't care who Sutton thinks he is."

Chauna watched him for a moment, then settled back down into her chair.

***

"Ow," Jamie whimpered, her lower lip sticking out as her mother dabbed a cotton swab soaked in peroxide against her face.

"Shh, sweaty," Karen Reynolds soothed, stroking her daughter's hair as she tried to be softer with the swab. "Its okay. It'll be over in a minute, don't cry."

"Yeah," Tyler spat from the corner, a handheld game covering the lower half of his face. "Stop being a baby."

Jamie's eyes began to tear up again as she waited for validation from her mother,

her face stinging intensely.

"Jamie, that's not what I said," she assured her, taking a moment to smile at her daughter warmly before examining her face for more scrapes and cuts. Finding none, she turned toward Tyler. "And you'd best be good, mister, unless you want your father to hear about it when he gets home."

Tyler closed his mouth, then turned back toward his game.

Karen continued to watch him for a moment before turning her attention back to Jamie. "I heard the Officer say that you were the bravest little girl he'd ever seen," she said, straightening the collar of her dress.

Jamie sniffed once, her finger once again stuck in her mouth. There was a glob of red on it, almost hidden between her index and middle fingers.

Karen tisked as she grabbed her wrist gently and pulled it from her mouth, wiping the blood away with the cotton swab.

***

"What the hell?"

Nurse Stein looked up from the ventilator she'd been preparing, her eyes traveling from Dr. Sutton to the patient and then back again in the span of a second. "What is it, Doctor?"

Sutton looked at her for a moment, then up toward the observation deck. The uniformed man was still there, in almost the same position he'd been in nearly two hours ago, leaning in only slightly to see what the doctor was talking about.

"It's the bullet," Sutton said finally, wiping the sweat off his own forehead into the shoulder of his pale blue scrubs. "I found the bullet, but it's nowhere near the lung. It's lodged in some fatty tissue a few inches shy of the liver. It's not really hurting anything."

"Then what's causing all that blood?" she asked, motioning toward Baker's mouth, which was still seeping blood around the corners.

"I don't know," Sutton sighed, reaching for his forceps. "But there's nothing wrong with this guy's lungs. Whatever's causing the blood is happening from someplace else."

Above them in the observation room, General Freemantle let out a long sigh as he watched Dr. Sutton remove the bullet.

***

Mark closed the door to his apartment, letting out a long sigh as he took off his shoes and laid them down next to the doormat.

"Honey?" came a voice from down the hall, followed closely by the sound of a faucet squeaking shut. "Honey, is that you?"

"Yeah, Allie," he called back, his voice strained and low. His face was still sweating from the heat outside as he peeled out of his burgundy EMT jacket. He held it out in front of him, staring at the closet just to his left, then dropped it onto the floor and left it there.

She came out from around the corner at the end of the hall, wiping her hands in a dishtowel before laying it on the kitchen counter and walking toward him. Her smile was big and bright, her thin lips pulling back and showing all her teeth. "You're home early," she chimed, wrapping her arms around his shoulders and squeezing him. "I can't remember the last time you came home early."

Mark grunted. Her hands smelled like cigarettes, and now that smell was all around him. He felt like it was choking him, killing every last strand of oxygen just as it reached his mouth. He reached up and placed both hands against her chest, calmly moving her away. "What's for dinner?"

She paused a moment, fixing her bun and straightening her left sleeve. "It's a roast. Your favorite."

He nodded, then made his way toward the kitchen.

She followed after only a moment's pause, walking past him as he sat down at the table. She stepped over to the counter and started to peel an onion, the skin coming off it large crackling husks.

The kitchen was small but serviceable. It had a stove with three burners, all of which were in use at the moment, as well as a fridge and a neat little table. The counter came out too far and there was an oddly vacant area at one end, but it did them just fine.

He grabbed the glass of water off the table in front of him and took a large gulp, watching her intently as she peeled the vegetable.

Her foot tapped aimlessly to whatever beat had been caught in her head, the sandals she wore to combat the heat flopping this way and that every couple of taps, trying to work their way off her feet but always failing to do so. Her legs were smooth and dark where they met her feet, her tan deeply ingrained into her flesh from many hours spent sunning on the back patio. She was wearing the jeans he'd bought her last year. They clung to her frame as if they were a part of her, moving with and spreading along her curves.

He got up from the table.

She felt his breath on her back before he touched her, hot against the nape of her neck. She tisked, letting both her hands fall to the counter, laying down the onion and knife. "What do you think you're doing?" she scolded playfully.

He did not respond. His tongue moved softly over the roof of his mouth, making a slow, barely audible clucking sound as he placed his hand on her hip, slowly moving inward.

"Not now," she cooed, squirming just a little. "I have to get these done, hun. The roast's already in. If I don't add these soon, it'll be too late."

He reached up with his other hand, placing it firmly on her chin and tilting it to one side, exposing the tender, moist flesh on her neck before he brought his lips to it.

She rolled her eyes, a smile beaming over her face. "Mark, seriously, not now," she shrugged.

He pushed her head forward, slamming it against the kitchen cabinet.

"Guh!" she shouted as she rocked back, hitting her shoulder off the table as she fell. Blood gushed from her nose and into her mouth, mixing with mucus and spit and becoming a mess on her blouse that was the same texture of tapioca pudding. "What the fuck is the matter with you?" she screamed, bringing one hand to her face as she looked up at him.

She squirmed back a pace when their eyes met, the burning and stinging sensations shooting from her nose ignored now.

The skin from his shoulders up had gone a deep shade of maroon, the blood rushing to it like she'd never seen. His cheeks were now royal purple, almost every vein in them clearly visible as they pumped even more blood into his face. He was sweating more than she had ever seen him, droplets the size of ball bearings falling off of him like rain. His teeth were barred, his upper lip quivering and shaking in a snarl. His skin split before her eyes along the creases of his forehead and cheeks, so dry and tight that it broke under the weight of its own movement. Blood ran down into his eyes even as the blood vessels there burst, making the whites a shallow pink but becoming a deep crimson with the blood from his face.

He was literally seeing red.

His tongue clacked against the roof of his mouth again for a second, his whole body rising and falling with each deep breath he took.

"Mark..."

"Raaagh!" he yelled, bringing both fists into the air and then crashing them down toward her.

She scrambled out of the way, knocking her head against the kitchen counter once more. She grabbed the handle of the cutlery drawer and pulled herself up even as he swung around again, drawing his fist back behind his head and plowing it forward toward her.

She grabbed the knife and spun it around, the cold steel meeting his hot flesh and jabbing into his palm.

"Argh!" he huffed, lurching forward as blood gushed from the open wound.

She grabbed the saucepan off the stove and flicked it at him, spraying hot gravy into his face. He howled in agony again, opening his eyes despite how they burned and staring at her with more rage and frustration than he'd ever felt toward anything. He charged at her again.

She ducked, swooping just barely under his arm and turning just in time to see him smash his face head-on into the fridge door.

He fell backward, slamming the back of his head against the table. He shook a little, at first looking as though he were going to get up and then like he was having a small seizure... and then he was still.

Her lower lip shaking, she reached for the phone.

***

"Sponge."

Sutton brought his hand up quickly, the needle that carried the wire he was threading throughout the Private's innards flitting about like a baton. In that moment he looked more like the conductor of a symphony orchestra than a surgeon, commanding the sutures of the patient's right lung to close shut. Instead of the soft radiance of harps and flutes, the only sound to react to his motion was the soft, moist sound flesh made as it was moved by some external force.

He paused with his hand in mid-air, the twine stopping its dance at once and hanging lifelessly at the end of the pin. "*Sponge*," he said again, casting a glance sideways.

Above them, General Freemantle leaned in and placed a hand against the glass.

One of the nurses stopped to stared at him, letting the oxygen mask fall from the patient's face. She was sweating too now, putrid liquid squeezing from her pores in bullets.

"For Christ sake!" Sutton yelled, letting go of both the needle and thread as he reached for the sponge that lay in a saucepan of water near him. They both fell into the patient's body cavity, the muscle twitching in reaction to their presence as they glistened and sparkled in the overhead lights. Sutton doused the sponge twice, slathering his face with it before squeezing it over his head and letting the water trickle down over him. "When I say I need a sponge, that means I need a sponge *now*, you idiots!"

He huffed and turned back to the patient. For a moment all he could see were millions of tiny black dots, dancing about his vision like a swarm of flies. When they went away, he saw the needle he'd dropped, resting comfortably against the patient's still-open lung. "Jesus," he cursed at himself, wiping brow again, this time simply using his sleeve. "Uh..."

The nurse still stared, even as the patient's oxygen saturation levels began to make the machines beside her howl.

Freemantle huffed, his hand reaching to the wall and pressing a large red button he found there with his thumb.

There was a soft, almost inaudible clucking sound in the air that sounded like the air conditioners cutting either in or out.

Sutton looked up from the open cavity, finally noticing the nurse. His forehead had split open, the blood on it watery and diluted from the sponge, and when he saw the dumbfounded expression on her face his own contorted with rage. "What the fuck are you looking at, you little twit?" he barked, reaching up and ripping off his surgical mask. He took several deep breaths though clenched teeth. "What is it?" he barked again, turning toward the sink to get another mask.

Nurse Stein lashed out, raking her nails across his face. Her surgical mask had been peeled away, revealing the same house-of-mirrors snarl that Dr. Sutton wore, her breathing heavy and labored as she hunched over him, her hands hanging poised and ready to strike at her sides. Her bun had been let down at some point, her previously permed hair sticking off in wild directions and making her appear ever more feral. Sweat drenched her face, dribbling off her chin and onto the floor like water from a leaky faucet. The whites of her eyes were gone; her blood pressure raging with such unrestricted animalism that reddish liquid seeped from her tear ducts and ear canals.

Sutton hit the floor as the other two nurses screamed, finally stopping their work altogether. There was a hunk of nail embedded in his cheek that spewed blood freely, smearing the left side of his face like war paint. Propping himself up against the table, he glared at her from under his massive brow, a series of clucks coming from somewhere deep in his throat and running together like a low growl.

They stared at each other, each of them swaying back and forth even though there was no breeze in the room, like cobras awaiting the opportunity to lash out.

The heat wafting off them made the air palatable, raging against the air conditioners and winning.

The nurses clamored against the far wall, as far away from the patient, Stein, and Sutton as they could be. "D-doctor?" one of them stammered finally, reaching out her hand gingerly.

Sutton spun, foam and saliva spewing from his mouth and splattering against the wall as he did, letting out a long roar. His pupils were small and beady, engulfed in a sea of red as he pushed his way past the table, knocking Private Terrence Baker onto the floor. He lunged at the nurse, grabbing her by the neck as she opened her mouth to scream. The sound was quelled by his strong, clubbed fingers, coming out as nothing but a quick gasp of air.

The other nurse had no such problem screaming, a sound that erupted from her in shrill waves, using up one breath before taking another and then continuing. She fell to the floor, grabbing at a tray for balance as she went and only bringing it down with her, sending an array of scalpels and the infamous sponge onto the tile.

His fingers clamped down like vices, pressing in on the smooth, dry flesh of her already slender neck until he began to feel it give way beneath his grasp. Grunting, he jutted his face forward quickly, his neck craning about above the blood-slathered scrubs he wore. Opening his mouth wide, he engulfed it around her upper lip.

Her eyes grew wide as she felt the hot, wet surface of his tongue at first... then bulged as his teeth dug in, ripping through the flesh, their enamel scratching against her own.

This time she did scream.

The sound was muffled and stilted as blood gushed down her throat, its coppery tang filling her to the brim. The blood engorged her, filling her mouth so much that it ran out through her nose in massive spurts. She pushed hard against his wiry shoulders, trying to force him off as his hands finally left her throat and went to either side of her head. Bracing her, he pulled his head back, taking with it the flesh from her upper lip right up to the bridge of her nose.

She screamed as she fought for air, each of his thumbs riding her eye sockets and making it impossible to see anything but great burgundy blotches of pressure. Tears forced their way out painfully, the ducts closing off to make extra room for her eyes as they bulged and contorted under his grip.

The flesh slithered and sputtered about like a fish in his mouth. He fought with it for a moment, shaking his head as though he thought it were still alive, then sucked it back like a spaghetti noodle until it was all inside. He chewed it vigorously, blood and bile seeping out from between his lips.

Nurse Stein was on him at once, pouncing at him from the side. Her nails dug into his scalp and pulled, taking great chunks of hair and flesh with it as they crashed into the medicine chest, sending hundreds of syringes cascading down on top of them.

He grabbed her by the side of the head, slamming it into the stainless steel chest so hard that it left a blood-smeared dent.

She twisted her neck so far that he could hear the calcium in her neck pop. She opened her mouth and dug her teeth into his palm, hard. He pulled back, his mouth open in a silent howl as he wrenched his hand away from her mouth, taking one of her canines with it. Both his fists slammed down on her face, crushing her lower jaw. Clicking his tongue against the roof of his mouth, he leaned in again, digging his teeth into the taut flesh surrounding her eye and clamping down hard.

Nurse Sloan kicked away from the scene, backing up until her back arched against the stomach of Private Baker. The Private had stopped breathing, something she didn't consciously register but filed away nonetheless, somewhere in the back of her mind. She saw movement just to the right of where Doctor Sutton was sucking juice out of the open wound in Stein's head, her legs still kicking at him fiercely, and turned toward it.

The other nurse lay propped against the far wall, her neck and chest drenched with the blood that spewed out of her mouth more and more with every breath she took.

But she was still breathing.

Sloan crawled over to her, keeping one eye trained intently on Sutton, until she was hauled up next to her against the wall. "Beca?" she whispered, as loudly as she dared. "Beca, are you conscious?"

She stared straight ahead. The only sound she made was the soft whistle coming from her forever-open nostrils every time she exhaled.

Sloan sighed. Grabbing some gauze, she started to wipe the blood from Beca's chin.

From deep inside her throat, Beca let out a low, broken growl.

Sloan stopped, her face expressionless as her mind clicked over and realized what had happened.

***

Freemantle stared down at the bloody mess below. Shaking his head, he reached for the phone on the wall without turning away. He pressed the number one on its base and then brought it to his ear. He watched blood squirt up so high that it splashed against the glass, but did not flinch. "Get a team together in Observation One," he said calmly, in a voice that spoke of black lung from either cigarettes or the mines. He leaned over slightly to see the source of the blood, watching as Nurse Sloan's throat was opened up for the world to see. "We've got something of a situation."

***

"Jesus!" Allie hissed, jerking her head away as Chauna dabbed the gash on her upper lip with iodine.

Chauna frowned, giving her a look that was half concerned and half annoyed before she continued dabbing, albeit a little softer. "Sorry. Hard to gauge this with the gloves on."

"It's okay," she replied, moving back to the position on the couch she'd been in before. The doctor's lounge was empty now, Adrian having left long ago to tend to a patient. His papers were still scattered along the desk, next to a half-eaten tuna sandwich that caught her eye. Tuna, along with any other seafood, was a rarity here. Depleting fish stocks had led to a cut down in its production in the last twenty years and besides that, supplies were usually at a bare minimum by the time they reached the border colonies like Stapleton. She guessed that it had been sent to the good doctor in a care package from home, most likely accompanied by a homemade sweater that didn't fit right and a greeting card bought for two dollars at a local drug store. Still, she'd forgotten how much she missed tuna until she saw it.

Chauna turned, following her gaze for a moment. She smiled. "You can have it when we're done, if you want."

"I couldn't."

"No, really, it's fine. He gets them every few months. Doesn't have the heart to tell his mother he grew out of tuna around the same time he grew out of acne cream." Chauna laughed, reaching back onto the coffee table without looking and grabbing an adhesive strip. "This might sting."

"Thanks," she said, bracing herself. "And you can tell Dr. Janes that if he can't stomach the tuna anymore, there's a buyer right here in town."

"I'll pass that along," she smiled, pushing her hair back behind her ear as she hovered the strip just above Allie's lip, trying to make sure she got its placement right the first time. Applying pressure to a facial wound was torture enough, she didn't want to have to rip it off and then reapply it again. Her tongue sticking out of the corner of her mouth slightly, she pressed the strip down gently.

"Ow," Allie said without force, almost as a psychological reaction to the notion of pain rather than to pain itself.

"Sorry," Chauna said again, tisking to herself. She stood up and looked down at the top of her patient's head. She parted the hair there quickly, trying to get a good look at as much scalp as possible. "Doesn't look like there's any bruising... are you experiencing any blurred vision?"

"No."

"Sensitivity to light?"

"No."

"Vomiting?"

"Christ, no."

Chauna paused.

"A little, but it was the blood. I could taste that mentally taste all the way here."

She paused for a moment, waiting to see if there was more. "You should be fine. I don't think you have a concussion, thankfully." She stopped again, bending over to pick up some alcohol wipes from the table. "How about Mark?"

Allie shot her a look. "Are you asking because you care for him, or because you're a doctor?"

"Both," she replied honestly, unwrapping the swab and starting to clean the blood off Allie's forehead to make sure there was no bruising underneath. "But after today, I think I care for him a lot less than I thought I did."

Allie did not respond, barely even noticing the cool pad against her face.

"Hem," she huffed, clearing her throat. "I'm actually surprised you called me. Glad you still think of me in a time of crisis, even though --"

"I called you because you're the only one I can trust to keep this off the books," Allie snapped, looking up slightly to meet Chauna's eye.

Chauna stopped wiping and stepped back a pace so she could look at her patient properly. She sighed, dropped the pad to the table in a bundled up glob and then sat on it, bringing them both level. "You might have a concussion. You're definitely going to need x-rays, and I'd like to ultrasound to make sure you're not bleeding into your brain. Tests mean paperwork. Paperwork needs a place to be filed, and that place is your file."

"And putting it in my file means that it'll be seen by Freemantle. He'll take Mark off of active duty and you know it. You're keeping this off the books."

Chauna looked at her side on, shaking her head slightly. "Why're you protecting him? You can't seriously be staying with him after this."

Allie looked away, fixing her collar. After a moment, she grabbed the alcohol wipe from the table and started to apply it herself, meeting Chauna's gaze again. "He's done worse."

"Listen, I --"

The door to the lounge opened, Adrian's white coat flapping against it as he stuck one foot in. His eyes were wide, but they narrowed a bit in confusion as he looked from Chauna to Allie and then back again.

There was a moment of silence.

"Just cleaning up," Chauna said finally. "What is it?"

"Uh, emergency," he said finally, forcing his brain to snap to attention. "We're needed down in Observation One."

"I'll be there in a minute."

Adrian nodded, casting another glance toward Allie and then back to Chauna.

Chauna nodded, and he left.

She turned her back on Allie, grabbing her scrubs and surgical mask off the table. "Eat the sandwich and do whatever you need to," she said without looking at the other woman as she walking toward the door. "Call the police or don't, either way it's on your head at this point."

Allie curled her upper lip as she closed the door, turning toward the mirror to see if she'd gotten all the blood. There was still a great glob of it there, just above her left eye.

Frowning, she brought the wipe up to it.

***

Sutton snapped the bone of Sloan's finger between his teeth, sucking hard at the stump that remained until the marrow was gone. He put the finger in his mouth then, biting down hard. His teeth gave way in some places, but the flesh and bone of the appendage finally broke and started to fall apart in his mouth, its sweet, salty taste filling him. He swallowed hungrily long before the pieces were small enough for him to do so safely, wanting to make room for more.

He was hunched over the table enjoying his meal. He was bleeding from his scalp and shoulder. His arm appeared to be dislocated, although that did not stop him from using it, and his foot had the remnants of a hypodermic needle tip sticking out of it.

Through the thick glass of the observation lounge, the scene looked staged and fake, the glass fading the colours and blocking their ability to hear and smell what was happening in the operating room.

Chauna brought her hand to her mouth but did not turn away, instead taking a step closer to the glass to try and see as much of the horror as she could.

"What the hell are we looking at?" Adrian asked in a hushed voice, standing firmly between Chauna and General Freemantle. Another doctor stood directly to Freemantle's right, a tall, portly man with a comb-over so poor that the slightest breeze rendered it useless.

"All due respect, Doctor, that's why I called you down here," Freemantle said, tapping the glass twice with his knuckle. "Diagnose this."

The other doctor, Drover, scoffed. "If you want a diagnosis for insanity, you're going to have to sedate him and get him over to the capital. We're physicians, not psychiatrists."

Freemantle and Adrian both turned to look at him.

"Oh, come on," he continued. "Sutton goes nuts and kills three nurses and you're looking for a medical excuse? The guy was an asshole. And a drunk. And Christ only knows what else. Trank him and let the police sort him out."

"He didn't kill three nurses," Freemantle corrected, motioning down toward the corner, which was mostly obscured from view. "That one killed Nurse Sloan while he was killing Stein. Then he killed her when she tried to eat a chunk of Stein's foot."

Drover's face went white as he turned back toward the scene, gulping back hard.

"I locked the door," he added, nodding to the button on the wall.

"Oxygen... depravation... has been known to cause hysteria," Adrian offered, taking his time to get the words out as he processed the information. "Have you checked the ventilation system?"

"Mmm," he nodded, taking off his cap and resting it under his arm, running his hand along the bristle-like hair on his head before putting it back on. "Once myself. Computer says it's okay. Got a couple of the boys from R&D doing a manual check, but I doubt they'll find anything. Told them to strap on the hazmat gear just in case, though."

Adrian nodded.

"What about toxins?" Drover offered, stepping forward as he started to get some colour back into his cheeks. "Some sort of adrenalin injection or steroid."

"Never heard of this sort of affect before," Adrian sighed, sitting down.

"That doesn't mean it's not the case now."

"I wasn't trying to dismiss it. Just saying: never heard of it before now." He paused and leaned his elbows against his knees. Freemantle turned away from the window for the first time in hours, looking down at the boyish doctor. "It could be rabies."

"Came on far too quickly to be --"

"It looks like rabies."

"Had a dog with rabies once," Freemantle said finally. "That doesn't look like rabies to me. I'm no doctor, but it's not just the way they're acting... it's their eyes. Their eyes go red. Blood red, Doctor."

"Trauma can cause that, sir," he offered, getting up again and looking through the window, trying to get a good look at Sutton's eyes. They were mostly closed, eating the muscle off a rib now. "It might not be a symptom of--"

"Happened before the fight started, Doctor," Freemantle corrected gently, then pointed toward what remained of Nurses Sloan and Stein. "To both of them."

One palm pressed against the glass, Chauna cursed to herself finally.

Freemantle turned to look at her. "Something to add, Nurse Deeds?"

"It's a contagion, sir," she said, turning away from the window. They all turned to look at her then, the sight of Dr. Sutton sucking on spinal fluid momentarily not interesting. She paused, organizing her words before she gulped back saliva and spoke again. "I don't know what kind. All I know is that it's blood born... and that it's already spread beyond the confines of the lab. We need to get a team out to the residences, sir."

Freemantle picked up the phone again without so much as turning to the two doctors for validation.

For their part they did not object. Drover stepped closer to the glass with a trembling right hand wavering in front of it as if afraid to make contact, while Adrian made his way to Chauna, touching her elbow softly.

"Freemantle," he said into the phone. "I need armed forces on the ground at Camp One ten minutes ago, you're looking for --" he paused, turning to Chauna.

"Mark Baxter," she said softly, wincing as if the words had physically harmed her.

"-- Mark Baxter. Restrain, use force if necessary. Do not make physical contact." He paused, then turned toward the glass one last time. "And cancel the R&D's examination of the vents. Have them torch the place instead. If there's anything but carbon left in that room by the time I get back, I'll have your head."

He hung up the phone and left the room through the south exit, followed quickly by Drover and Adrian.

Chauna moved to follow, then stopped. She turned quickly, pushing open the door to the north exit and running up the stairs.

Sutton gripped Sloan's liver between his fingers, squeezing it before taking half of it into his mouth and biting down hard.

***

Karen Reynolds picked up the dishes from the floor in front of the television, huffing audibly. She briefly considered scolding her children, who were now colouring at their table a few feet away, but decided to let it slide. They'd been through a lot for one day. She could stand to let the small things slide. She turned to look at them, watching as Jamie scribbled fiercely on her sheet with a red colouring pencil, going way outside the lines that the horse had presented her with.

She smiled.

Turning around to grab their glasses off the coffee table, she glanced out at the late afternoon light streaming in through the window.

There was a man outside staring intently at her mailbox.

He had a gash on his forehead about an inch long that looked a few hours old, the right half of his face covered with congealed blood so dark that it looked black. His fists were clenched tight at his sides and there was a sneer on his face that was filled with hate, as though the mailbox were the worst thing he'd ever seen in his life.

It was Mark Baxter.

All at once he swung a fist at it, his knuckles grating against the metal box. It wobbled on its base, moving backward for a moment before springing forward and connecting with his central plexus.

He looked to scream, though she couldn't hear it.

Then he lashed out again, this time with both fists, wailing on the offending object and ripping off the small red flag on its side.

Karen reached into the jeans pocket and pulled out her phone, holding down the number five and then bringing it to her ear. It rang three times before someone picked up.

"Rachel? It's Karen. Look out your window. You're not going to believe this."

***

Chauna opened the door to the lounge wide, her eyes doing a full sweep of the room as she tried in vain to catch her breath. Her scrubs were soaked with sweat by now, and it rolled down her face in barrels. She could barely hear anything above her heart and the sound of her gasped, labored breathing.

There was nobody in the room, just the same stack of papers Adrian had left out earlier.

Minus the tuna fish sandwich.

She cursed, took note of the blood-soaked gauze on the table, then turned and left the room again, running down the hall despite the objections her lungs were screaming at her.

***

Two floors down, Jim Keating was pushing his mop bucket along the main hallway on its wheels, humming softly to himself.

He stopped in front of the large automatic doors, grumbling when he noticed the amount of sand that had passed through them. Sometimes if the storms got bad enough the sand itself set off the motion detectors as it flew around, making the hallway a thousand times worse than it was now. In any event, mopping up sand was not his idea of a good time.

He stopped after one pass, grabbing a stick of gum from his front pocket and passing it through his cracked, dry lips. He let out a sigh as the minty cool filled his mouth, then smiled.

When he opened his eyes again, he saw the reddish dent on the wall.

He raised an eyebrow and dragged his finger along one of the red smears, the liquid coming off easily. He rubbed it between his thumb and forefinger, shrugged, took his rag out of his breast pocket and began to wipe it down.

***

The wind blew hard against the back entrance of the hospital, always did. It had started off the same eggshell white as the rest of the building, but the constant assault of sand had revealed the stainless steel underneath in less than three years.

Adrian pulled the collar of his lab coat up, trying to shield himself from the sand as it swirled around him like a million tiny razor blades. It only lasted for a few feet until he ducked into the backseat of the white limousine waiting for them right behind Drover and Freemantle. "What are we doing?" he asked, trying to catch his breath as he wiped dust from his lips.

"Getting the hell out of here," Freemantle said gruffly, taking off his dress uniform and tossing it to the other side of the cabin along with his cap. He looked infinitely more approachable in the sky blue shirt he had been wearing underneath, making the blue eyes that had seemed as cold as steel a moment ago appear warm and inviting. "There's a helicopter on the other side of the compound big enough for about twenty people. I've sent a message for police to meet us there with as many unaffected as we can."

Drover balked. "How can we be sure it's even spread beyond Baxter? Or that it's even contagious the way Deeds described? She's bright and all, but I'd rather a dumb doctor than a smart nurse any day."

Adrian shot him a look through the corner of his eye, then turned back to Freemantle.

In the two years they'd lived on the same compound, he had never once seen the General without his dress uniform on. It had been a private joke between he and Chauna that the man even wore it in the bedroom. To see him without was disconcerting, no matter how pleasant he appeared. "What about the rest?"

"I'm calling in a team," he assured the doctor, nodding. "It'll be fine. It'll be dealt with. I just want to make sure the only people in the town to be hurt are other people with this... this whatever this is."

Adrian nodded, turning back out the tinted windows toward the back entrance.

Freemantle tapped the intercom panel just to his right. "Drive."

"No!" Adrian objected, turning back toward him with a shocked expression on his face. "You have to wait for Chauna!"

Freemantle raised an eyebrow. "I think you'll find I don't have to do much of anything anymore, Doctor."

Adrian huffed. "So much for never leave a man behind."

"We're not leaving a *man* behind," Drover corrected, winking at the General.

Freemantle turned toward Drover, giving him a stern look. All three men were frozen there for a moment. He nodded, pressing his index finger to the intercom again. "Belay that, Reynolds."

There was only silence for a moment then, with the faint sound of static on the other end of the line and the wind howling outside.

Freemantle paused, touching the call button again. "Reynolds?"

The tinted window separating the driver from the rest of the cabin cracked, spider-webbing in all directions and letting them hear the low, clucking growl that it had blocked a moment before.

"Jesus!" Adrian yelped, pushing himself as far back against the seat as he could. Drover joined him, reaching for the door handle.

Freemantle dove for his uniform, fumbling with the pocket until he pulled out his service revolver. He turned it toward the window as a massive fist pounded on it again and let out three sharp blasts, shattering the window and sending shards of it cascading to the floor in all directions.

The driver hunched back against the wheel, struggling to draw breath as his eyes burned red with hatred. Duel bullet holes in his chest spewed blood, hissing slightly every time he inhaled. His hands were hauled up in distorted, bloody fists, the fingers curled back and spasming wildly.

"Hold on," Adrian gasped, reaching for the stethoscope in his pocket. "We might still be able to --"

"Do nothing," Freemantle finished, though it was not an order. He raised the barrel of the gun again, then fired one final shot into the forehead of Justin Reynolds. The body twitched twice more, let out a breath, then stopped moving altogether. He turned back to Adrian. "You'll get the blood on you."

Adrian nodded, grabbing the handle away from Drover and opened the door. "We can't drive this then, either. My car's out front, I'll drive."

Freemantle nodded, then followed him out.

Drover took one look back at the driver, shaking his head. "Monstrous," he breathed, stepping out into the sandstorm again.

He bumped into the chest of General Freemantle.

"I'm sorry, sir, I didn't--"

"That was not monstrous," Freemantle corrected, his glare making his look menacing even in the absence of his uniform. "That was a man. A good man who was never late for work, never sick and always made time for his children's softball games. And for mine, for that matter. You're going to be sending his family condolence cards every Christmas for the rest of your life." He paused, looked at Reynolds for a moment, then turned back. "And a check."

Drover tried to respond and even managed to sputter out a syllable or two before Freemantle turned on his heels as fluidly as though he were running drills.

Adrian nodded at him once, holding the door to the hospital open.

Chauna appeared in the doorway, her breathing labored as she bent over and rested on her knees. "I think we've got another patient," she huffed, bringing two fingers to her neck and feeling for her own pulse. She threw a glance toward the white limo and the blood spattered all over the inside of the windshield. "What the hell happened here?"

"Get back inside, Miss Deeds," Freemantle said by way of response, stepping past her. "Your friend Doctor Janes is going to be driving us today."

Drover followed Freemantle inside. Adrian and Chauna exchanged a look before he stepped inside to join her, closing the door behind him.

***

Sweat poured down Allie Meridian's face and neck as she leaned against the rack of chips, facing down toward the filthy tile floor as drool dripped from her open mouth. Her head was pounding, the beat rivaling that of the teenage pop-rock that played in the background.

"Guh," she grunted, reaching up a hand to wipe the moisture from her milky white face and knocking several bags to the floor as she did.

"Miss, are you okay?" called out the store clerk from behind the counter, craning his head to see what was going on. He was about sixteen with long blonde hair that looked like it had been straightened with an iron, the tips frayed and singed badly.

Allie turned to look at him, her eyes bulging. They were mostly white still, but the veins in them were bright red and looked ready to pop at any given moment. She opened her mouth to speak but found that no words would come, only a faint sound from the back of her throat that reminded her of a single popcorn kernel popping. Grunting in frustration, she turned her attention back to the shelf beside her.

Lined up in a row were hundreds of bottles of aspirin, each white bottle blurring together in her vision. She reached up to try and grab one, batting five to the floor instead. Groaning, she let go of the chip rack and let herself fall to her knees and grab one.

"You better not be making a mess back there!" the clerk called back, his voice annoyed and wavering either from fear or from hormones or both.

She crawled several steps before pulling herself to her feet, walking toward the counter with the pill bottle clenched awkwardly in one hand and the other contorted and misshapen so that it looked more like a paw than a hand. She started to fumble with the lid, her cheeks turning red with frustration as she bumped into the counter without even realizing it.

The boy looked at her a moment, her lips curling up as she stared at the pill bottle, her eyes open as wide as they could be and unblinking. After a moment the pupils moved, no longer aimed at the bottle but at the clerk's mouth.

She opened her mouth slightly, and several clucks came out even though her tongue did not move.

"Take it," he said finally, reaching into his back pocket and pulling out his wallet. "It's on me."

She stared at him a long moment, then shuffled herself sideways until her shoulder connected with the door and pushed it open. She stayed there for a moment with her hair caught in a gust of wind, still staring at him, as one of the blood vessels in her eye broke and starting leaking blood into the white cerca. She turned, running as quickly as she could.

"Junkies," the boy huffed, ringing in the bottle of pills and shaking his head.

***

Mark growled at the mailbox again as it rocked back and forth in the sand. It was hard to think, but he was sure of one thing: he knew he'd hurt it. It was covered in blood.

His knuckles were almost completely ripped down to the bone except for the slightest remnants of tissue and hair. His lower lip was a bloody maw that looked more like a used wad of chewing gum than a part of someone's face, and he sucked it in again and continued to chew on it.

He turned his head to one side and spit, the saliva light and foamy, making a tiny oasis in the sand a few feet from where he crouched.

He was missing hair. He had pulled it out of his own scalp in frustrated clumps when the enemy kept refusing to go down.

"Mark?" someone called from behind him.

His eyes grew wide with fear.

Rachel White took another step closer, her cordless phone still pressed tightly against her breast. She had shoulder-length dirty-blonde hair that caught the evening light fully, and lips such a dark red they might well have been already bleeding.

Back in the house, Karen held the phone to her ear. "Careful, Ray," she whispered, knowing full well her friend couldn't hear her.

"Mark?" she called again, reaching out a hand to touch his shoulder and then thinking better of it, noticing the state of the mailbox for the first time since exiting her home.

He turned his head slowly, almost further than he should have been able to. His eyes met with hers, the red of them such a dark crimson that they were almost indistinguishable from the pupils.

She stopped mid-step, her face dragging down in fear.

Before she could speak or move or even think he turned, thrusting himself at her and grabbing her by the hips.

She flopped down in the sand, the impact sending thousands of grains into her skin as she finally let out a scream.

He grabbed the right side of her head with one hand, pounding on the left with the other until he could feel his fist and his hand clapping together. When he opened his eyes, there was a red stain in the sand where her head had been a moment ago, dotted with chunks of enamel and white matter.

"Oh my God!" Karen yelled, dropping the phone and bringing both hands to her face as she watched in horror.

Mark turned toward the window, locking eyes with her.

Behind her, the children still coloured.

***

Adrian held the gas pedal of his jeep down as far as it would go, the treads of the large rubber tires kicking up dirt and dust in all directions as the hospital became smaller and smaller in the distance.

Freemantle sat next to him, loading his gun and taking the occasional glance up to make sure they were still in the clear and that they were headed in the right direction.

"You have enough ammo?" Adrian asked, never once taking his eyes off the road nor his hands away from the ten-and-two position.

"Should be."

"There's more in the trunk if you need."

He shot the doctor a glance, squinting as the sun glared off the red-tinted sand. "Whatever happened to do no harm? Thought they made you folks take an oath."

Adrian did not respond, gripping the steering wheel even harder.

Behind him, Drover rubbed the bridge of his nose. His eyes were closed and every few minutes he would let out a silent but horrendous fart that made the already humid cabin even more unbearable. He was mumbling something softly to himself that could only be recognized passingly as the Our Father. And he was crying.

Chauna sat behind Freemantle, staring out the porthole window of the jeep. "What are you doing with ammunition in your trunk?" she asked, not turning away from the window.

"Used to go out to the range when I lived in the city," he sighed. "Thought there might be time for it out here, but haven't found any yet."

"With any luck we won't need it," Freemantle said, sliding the last round into his gun and flicking it shut.

"Because luck is something we've been blessed with this far," Adrian said, making a sharp turn toward the township. The jeep's tire bounced quietly against a large boulder to just one side of the road, rocking its inhabitants for a moment before righting itself again.

Chauna gasped, placing her hand against the porthole. "I think I see Mr. Keating out there!"

"Is he --"

"I think he's carrying a boy under his arm," she finished, erasing Adrian's need to ask the question. She forced herself to turn away from the window. After a moment she ducked her head down between her knees and threw up.

"Alright, that's at least three confirmed infected and six or more dead," Freemantle said, clutching his gun. "That's one fifth of Stapleton's population. One third if you don't count the men down in the ore mines away from it all right now. We are officially calling this one. The four of us are getting to the copter and getting the hell out of Dodge."

"What?" Chauna exclaimed, looking up at the back of the General's chair in shock. There were still chunks of half-digested fruit stuck to her lips, but she unbuckled her safety belt and leaned forward into the front seat. "You can't do that! There are people here. Children! We have to get them out!"

"For all we know they could already be infected," he said, adjusting the side-view mirror so that he could see the hospital. There was a cloud of dark smoke rising from the wing that the operating room had been located in, and now, he assumed, no longer was. "We are getting out of here and getting a team together to stop this. Nearest base is two hours out."

"That could be enough time for this thing to kill everyone in town!"

"And what, prey tell, do you think our remaining here will do to dissuade that?" Freemantle barked, his cheeks growing livid for less than a second as he raised his voice.

Adrian took his eyes off the road for a moment and cocked an eyebrow at the General. This was another first, the raising of the voice. He glanced at the older man's eyes and discovered nothing but the pale blue that had been there a few minutes ago, then turned back toward the road.

The General calmed himself. "If we don't get out of here, then no help will come. This will continue until the entire town is overcome by this... this plague and then one of two things will happen: those infected will just kill one another like Sutton and the others... or they'll get out, and things will spread. One of those I can deal with. The other, I can't."

Chauna remained silent for a long moment, then leaned back into her seat. She nodded once.

Adrian's jeep sped toward the town's outer ring.

***

Karen slid the metal door of her hall closet closed, holding one of her children firmly to each breast. It was dark inside, except for the narrow bands of light that filtered in from the turrets of the metal. She could smell both the freshly cleaned coats that hung overhead and the old, damp sneakers that now rested in the arch between her buttocks and her feet, the mixture of both the pleasant and the pungent agitating her olfactory senses.

She remembered, briefly, a conversation she'd had with her husband when they'd moved in here. In choosing a location to live, he had mainly been concerned with square footage and yard space. She, on the other hand, had only two decided factors: neighbors and closet space. The latter was not important in Stapleton, however, as the houses here were of the cookie-cutter variety, with each one nearly identical in layout. Her decision to live here, then, had been made when she had met Rachel White.

At once, her mind shifted gears and she could almost see the scarlet stain in the sand outside her home where Rachel's head had been a few minutes before.

-Parr!-

The sudden sound of soft flesh against solid, sturdy wood reverberated through the boards and beams of her home. She felt the vibrations through the floorboards, making her yelp and jump a little.

"Mom?" Tyler called, turning to look up at her.

"Shh," she soothed, holding him closer and bending down to kiss his head. His hair got caught on the hot, sticky tears that had started to roll down her face. Her chin had become wrinkled and shook as her eyelids continued to fill again and again.

-Parr!-

Came the sound again, louder this time.

"Ah!" she said, despite her own efforts to bite her tongue.

Jamie did not speak, her index finger held in the cusp of her lips and her eyes wide.

-Parr!-

-Tuh!-

-tin, tin, tink.-

She'd never heard that sound before, and yet knew exactly what it was. It was the solid wooden door of her home hitting the scratched hardwood floor, the tiny bolts that used to make it swing so gracefully bouncing along behind it.

And then there was nothing.

She sat in the closet, her knees bent up into the fetal position and her children held to each breast as though she were feeding them.

Her neck itched wildly as beads of nervous, fearful sweat rolled down it in odd, winding paths. She tried so hard not to make a sound but her body simply would not comply, her breathing quickening into short, loud gasps and her blood pumping so loud that she was convinced anyone could have heard it, let alone Mark Baxter.

Tyler shifted at her side, squirming to get comfortable in the confined space. His heel knocked against the baseboard, creating a dull thump and an accompanying vibration that she felt but wasn't sure if it was enough to filter through to the rest of the house. She dared not shush him, squeezing his shoulder firmly but gently to try and make him be still. She debating using her nails for a moment, though she never had before, but decided that the risk of his hissing or crying out in pain or surprise was too great.

He moved once more without a sound, then settled back in.

Still, there were no more sounds from beyond the closet.

She strained her ears, trying hard to hear any sign of the intruder. She could hear the wind outside through the now open doorway, howling like a dingo baying at the moon. She could hear the sound of sand and dirt as it got kicked up into small cyclones, spinning about and scratching against the wall of the house as well as the children's play-sets with a series of light, metallic clinks. There was even the hum of the electronics that made life easier in the desert: the fridge cutting in and the steady, surreal clambering of the air conditioner.

For seven agonizing minutes there was nothing.

Karen leaned forward, peering out through the divides in the metal door that was all that separated her and her children from the rest of the house.

The cappuccino-coloured couch sat in the center of her field of vision, catching the light that streamed in from the bay windows in front of it. The coffee tables, freshly dusted, glimmered and gleaned. There were crayons scattered all over the floor, and she couldn't help but take note of a yellow one that was under her husband's recliner and would have been obscured from view at any other time. The floors were dusty but clean and, most importantly, devoid of any shadows. They didn't bend, creek or volley in response to a person walking on them.

Biting her lip and taking one last glance around the room, she slowly reached up and laid her hand on the door handle.

Mark Baxter stepped into view.

She jumped back, clutching her children's heads so tightly that for a moment they could not breathe. She bit her lip so hard that it bled, closing her eyes the way Jamie did when she was convinced that there was something under her bed and just willing it to go away.

When she opened her eyes again, she could see the backs of two long legs through the openings in the door. He was seven feet away from her, just to the left of the couch.

A drop of blood fell to the floor next to him, splashing up and crowning into several smaller droplets that cascaded down around it.

He stood straight, his entire body moving with each of his wet, heavy breaths. Even the back of his legs seemed to be a part of the motion, tightening and relaxing with every hackneyed sound.

Karen's teeth started to chatter despite her every attempt to grind them down and gooseflesh waved over her body. She brought her hand to her mouth and squeezed, so tightly that her nails left for small half-moon indentations in her cheek.

He stopped moving, standing rod straight for a moment. Then he turned, slowly bending over until he was sitting on the couch, hunched over and craning his neck backward like an animal watching out for fellow predators. She could see him through the spaces in the closet door now, his typically full-bodies hair whetted down against his skull with blood and sweat and bile. His face was the hued pink of boiled lobster and he took his breaths through clenched, grinding teeth. His eyes were what she noticed most, though. The white had ruptured and ripped, leaving only great swells of red, gelatinous goop behind. Rosy tears streamed down his face, so hot that they might have evaporated instead of falling from his cheeks and onto the floor.

There was a can clasped between both his hands, held so tight that his knuckles turned white. He cradled it against his chest for a moment, his eyes still glued to the hallway he had come from, before turning toward the coffee table and raising his hand high.

-BARM!-

"Mf," Karen mewed, stifling the yelp that had wanted to erupt from her lips as the edge of the can bashed off the corner of her coffee table.

He stared down at it, squeezing it as though it were a neck he was ringing and let out a long, vengeful grunt before raising his hand and bringing it down again.

-BARM!-

This time the top cracked, sending juice and pulp gushing onto the table in a bright orange wave.

He laughed, though it sounded strange and forced, as he poked the tip of his finger through the gouge in the metal. It sliced at his finger though he didn't seem to notice or care, worming it about until he got a good grip and pulled. The tin peeled back slowly, opening enough that he could see the sweet treasure inside. It also ripped at the calloused flesh of his forefinger, turning those contents vermilion in the process.

When he reached in again, he produced a juicy, if slightly discoloured, peach and placed it between his lips, slurping it back and sending it down his throat without so much as biting it. The instant it was gone he went searching for another one, his lips smacking together wildly as that constant low cluck in the back of his throat continued.

Karen sighed.

He stopped. His finger stopped rooting around the can and he even appeared to stop breathing for a moment.

She stopped, clamping her fingers down across her lips again as she felt Tyler squirm beside her.

Mark's head spun around like an owl's, his eyelids braced open so far that she could see the curvature of his eyes as they locked onto the closet door. His cheeks turned a dark, vein-drenched red again as that angry bird sound started to sound from his throat, his adam's apple bobbing up and down with every hark.

His eyes seemed to be staring directly at hers, though she knew that wasn't possible. Couldn't be possible. There was no way he could see in through the tiny spaces between the metal into the darkness of the closet, let alone lock eyes with her. Her eyes would be nothing but slivers of shadow to him. Yet he did lock onto her, his nearly invisible pupils focuses intently on her.

Slowly, he laid the can of peaches down onto the coffee table, his blood dribbling from the gouge he'd made in it as though it had gotten stabbed. The muscles in his legs tensed considerably as he rose to full standing position and she could hear his stomach growling from where she and her children sat huddled in a mangy closet, not wanting to think about what it that might mean. Hot blood was raging through him again now, if it had ever truly stopped. When he finished rising, the grate she had been looking out through held an almost perfect frame of his pelvis, demonstrating that indeed the blood was running rampant through his entire body. His pants throbbed and pulsed as though there were something inside that wanted desperately to get out and she watched his fists clench to either side of it, the veins on their backs popping out nearly a quarter centimeter and looking ready to burst. His abdomen mounted and relented so quickly that it almost resembled a seizure, the muscles around his portly stomach dancing and moving about with a mind of their own.

He took one lumbering step forward, his body slanting comically to one side before he righted himself and looked almost normal, but only because she couldn't see his face. She was infinitely thankful that she couldn't see his face in fact, yet still wanted to know if he was still staring at her.

His steps became lighter now, almost soundless. Every one seemed planned and well-thought out, something that seemed to be very much the antitheses of the way he'd acted only moments ago in opening the can of peaches. His left foot stepped out in front of the right in a smooth, graceful arch, not ruffling a single article of clothing or making any sound. When he brought it down to the tile floor, he laid the outside arch of his foot down first, then slowly rolled it down until it was flat. Again, there was not a sound, even as the metal toe of the boot touched down. The right foot came around from behind and repeated the moment almost identically, and before she could even remind herself to breathe, Mark Baxter's feet were less than and inch in front of her closet door.

Tyler stared at it wide-eyed as Jamie just turned away into her mother's breast again.

For her part, Karen laid her head back against the wall as quietly as she could and closed her eyes despite her body screaming at her not to and whispered a prayer to herself, one she used to recite as a child and hadn't even thought of in twenty years until that moment. She opened them again when she heard a dog bark outside.

Mark's right heel turned, pivoting slightly at its base in the direction of the door, which she could only imagine was irreparably off its hinges. The clucking from his throat got louder and quicker and before she knew it, he was running toward the door. Allowing herself a rueful, desperate laugh as tears flew down her cheeks, she listened as his heavy footfalls got further and further away, then heard the familiar -Pff!- sound as they made first contact with the sand outside and kept going.

Laughing and sobbing as mucus drooped down into her mouth and onto her chin, she turned toward Tyler and kissed him softly on the head, then to Jamie and did the same, squeezing her tightly. She hadn't realized how much pain her position had been causing her until she tried to move, bracing herself on either wall and letting out a heartfelt "Umph" as she pushed off them and started to rise to her feet, twisting her neck quickly to throw her hair back out of her face.

"Come on, Jamie," she tisked, hoisting her child under the arm. She forced a smile to let her know it was okay, turning back to the door and grasping the handle.

Mark Baxter glared at her through the metal grate with eyes that burned like hellfire.

She opened her mouth and let out the longest, loudest scream she ever had as he grabbed each side of the closet door violently and began to shake, the metal frame clanging against itself until it's own squeal rivaled hers. The children began to cry as well as Mark opened his mouth hungrily, letting that same click spew out like venom from deep below his uvula.

He reached one hand high, clenching his fist tight before bringing it down onto the door.

-BAM!-

She jumped, her back slamming against the wall as her feet pushed off against the floor, instinctively getting her as far away from the brutal, snarling thing in front of her. But never once did she lose eye contact with it, much less take her eyes off of it.

Nostrils flaring, he reached back his fist again, knuckles ripped to pieces and staring at her like four infected eye sockets.

-BAM!-

The shamrock-green door buckled inward. He stared at her exclusively, barely even taking note of the children on either side of her. His teeth ground together so fiercely that she thought she saw flakes of enamel falling away from them like dandruff just beyond her peripheral vision. Eyelids twitching for moisture yet refusing to blink, he lifted him fist again.

-BAM!-

Blood spurted from the left side of his head as several large chunks of his skull separated themselves from the rest, falling to the floor a brief instant before the rest of him did.

For a moment that seemed like forever, she could not process what had just happened. She kept staring into the space where Mark Baxter's eyes had been a second before, waiting for them to return but seeing only the final sputtering spasms of his left leg.

As if by will, eyes did appear, though they were not red or monstrous or even unkind. The soft, cobalt blue spheres were turned upward in pity, accented only by the worry-lines that had formed beneath them many years beforehand.

"Karen," Freemantle said, his voice possessing a quality of calm she'd never heard from him before. "You can come out."

She hesitated for a moment, clutching her children before lunging forward and thrusting the door open as quickly as she could, tossing herself into Freemantle's arms. Slowly he laid his hands on her back and for a moment she wasn't in Stapleton. She was at home and it was twenty years prior and she was as safe. Tears that she'd tried so well to hold back for what had seemed like hours came gushing out now, and for a brief time she even forgot about her children, skill clutching on either side of her blouse.

"It's okay," he said, some of the gruffness returning to his voice. He patted her back twice with the hand not holding his service revolver. "It's all right."

When she opened her eyes again, she saw the other three, standing in her hallway and partially obscured by Freemantle's shoulder.

Adrian stood close to the kitchen cabinets, playing with something absently and trying to avoid looking at her as she was caught in Freemantle's arms. He didn't appear uncomfortable by the display so much as respectful, his eyes darting over every now and again out of simple, human curiosity.

Chauna stood near him, her hands at her sides and sweat still pouring off her and onto her scrubs; she was breathing hard and wasn't turning away, though wasn't staring at her either. She was staring at the children, watching them as they grabbed at their mother with needing hands. Her eyes darted toward the body of Mark Baxter then, welling up slightly before forcing themselves away again.

Drover stood the furthest away from her, staring down at his feet and shuffling about uncomfortably.

"Come," Freemantle said finally, tapping her on the back again as he began to rise to his feet. "We haven't a lot of time, I'm afraid."

She nodded to herself, rising to her feet and bringing the children with her as she made the first, tenuous steps toward the door. Her legs almost buckled beneath her, the adrenalin rushing through her turning them to butter.

"Here," Chauna said, forcing a smile and she stepped to Karen's side. "Let me help."

Karen smiled, taking Chauna's hand as the both of them walked out the back entrance to the Reynolds home, the children and Adrian close behind them. Adrian picked up Jamie, letting her head rest on his shoulder.

Freemantle straightened his shirt with one swift tug on the bottom with both hands, then started for the door himself. When he reached the hallway, Drover lay a hand on his arm.

"Who is she?" the shorter man whispered, leaning in close to the General. "Who is this woman that you'd risk all our lives to save her?"

Freemantle stared at him for a long moment, the muscles in his face retaining their stanched and stern form. He looked down at Drover's hand on the crook of his arm, then back again.

Drover released it quickly, then slowly let his arm fall back into place.

"She is Karen Reynolds," Freemantle answered crisply. "Daughter of Katherine and Michael Peachtree, mother to Tyler and Jamie Reynolds. Spouse to Justin Reynolds, my driver of many years."

Drover opened his mouth, saying nothing as he nodded.

Freemantle leaned in until his dry lips were almost touching Drover's ear. "Remember their names. You'll be addressing sympathy cards to them for many, many years."

Drover stiffened as Freemantle walked past him. He waited until he heard the General's feet hit the sand outside before he turned to follow, taking one last look at the body of Mark Baxter before he did, still bubbling hot blood onto the floor. "And checks," he added, exiting the home.

***

Allie sat on the sidewalk and fumbled with the bottle in her hands, the beveled edge of its stopper grating on her nails as she tried desperately to open it.

Blood ran down her cheeks in several waving streams now, fed every few moments at its source, as her vision became more and more alizarin.

Her mouth scrunched and twisted uncomfortably as she fought with the pills, writhing in all manner of shapes. Her nostrils even contorted as she let out several small, monosyllabic grunts that until today she had reserved only for when she was mid coitus.

Andrea Mercer poked her head around the corner at the sound, one of her carefully drawn-on eyebrows perched skyward quizzically.

Allie did not notice her, continuing to fight a losing battle against the plastic capsule as her hair swung about her head in a wild, sweaty mess.

She turned, biting her lip as she looked back toward the car, then took a step closer to Allie. "Is there something I can help you with?"

Allie looked up from behind her ragged bangs, her eyes so deeply red they approached purple. The pupils had long since disappeared, yet somehow Andrea knew that the girl was staring right at her. Her breath became short and heavy as she dropped the bottle, letting it roll along the ground between her feet in small concentric circles, finally coming to a stop against the curb.

Andrea took a step back, bringing her hands to her face.

Allie arose slowly, her back hunched and her arms hanging low. She opened her mouth, revealing chipped and missing teeth that ripped at her own gums every time she clamped down. She let out a low, menacing growl made up of a long series of short clicking sounds.

***

Karen lay her head down in her hands as she willed herself to stop crying, staring down at the checked teal carpet and rubber mats that made up the floor of Adrian's jeep. Her face and hands had taken on the complexion of sour milk, that chalky white mixed with the slightest hint of green. There was a layer of sweat on her forehead that had nothing to do with the heat of the desert, though they kept the air conditioner blasting air at her regardless.

"Water?" Freemantle offered, holding a clear plastic bottle just in front of her. Its contents looked almost crystalline in the sharp light off the sand.

"No," she said dryly, her lips making an audible sound as they parted. "Yes."

She took the bottle from him and brought it to her lips, letting the first few gulps wash their way down naturally before stopping. She took another sip and swished it around her mouth, making every cranny and vein feel human again before swallowing that too. She handed him back the bottle, which he took back into the front seat gently.

To her left, Drover reached out and placed a hand on her back. "How are you?" he managed to ask, every word feeling forced and unnatural.

Not responding, she looked out the window between Adrian and Freemantle. From this angle all she could see were electrical poles whizzing by and the dark blue cloudless sky beyond them. She turned toward her children, both of them coiled up in tight little balls on either side of Freemantle. Neither spoke, but they were both skill awake. Her thoughts swimming and dazed, she lolled her head to her right and met Chauna's gaze, who promptly turned away and looked out the small circular window of the jeep's backseat.

"What am I going to do?" she said to no one in particular, her head swinging back down and looking at the floor. "What am I going to- - Justin, he was - -"

"Karen," Freemantle said, laying a hand on Tyler's head.

She stopped, looking from the General to her child and then back again, then nodded. Licking her lips, she held her hand out for the water again and got it.

Chauna sighed, watching as the houses that zipped by got fewer and further between as they approached the outskirts of town. They looked peaceful enough. Happy even. But just beyond them to the next street over and the street after that she could see the signs of something more sinister. Billows of smoke too big to come from smoke stacks. The frames of people walking not quite right, their shoulders lurched or their legs limping. The sound of sirens both getting louder and further away simultaneously as the last few squad cars were dispatched to whatever residents still had the sense to call in.

Adrian spun the wheel quickly, making a wide turn that kicked up a cloud of gravel.

She steadied herself, turning to frown at him although he wasn't looking anywhere near her. When she turned back toward the window it was on the last arc of their spin and one house had come perfectly into focus.

Its siding was a deep full red that made it stand out amongst the greens and the whites that had dominated the majority of the street if not the settlement. The door was metal but had been painted a soft, woody colour and stood perfectly in the middle of two great bay windows, giving the house a 'face' of sorts. The tiles on its roof were the same auburn as her hair, the white trim acting as the perfect highlight for each colour.

There was artificial grass covering most of the front lawn. Real grass was nearly impossible to maintain here and most families chose to adorn their yards with cheap stone or, cheaper still, leave the natural sand. The thin plastic blades of green made the house look like a vibrant oasis amidst the dunes, a symbol of life and unity tapered in by a white-picket fence that looked like it had been taken out of a movie.

Just beyond the furthest post of the fence, a German Shepard and a Labrador Retriever fought over the tattered, mauled remains of a human arm.

Both dogs growled viciously, their throats incapable of making that click but trying nonetheless as blood seeped out of each dog's ears and eyes, matting their mangey fur into wet, slimy clumps. Their eyes were completely red, without even the slightest hint of anything else. Foam dripped from their jowls in massive froths. As the jeep sped by, the Retriever raised its paw and batted the Lab across the snout, getting a better grip on the supple pink flesh in its teeth.

Chauna gasped, turning away from the window as her eyes darted back and forth inside her skull.

Adrian took his eyes off the road for a second, gazing up into the rearview mirror at her. "Everything okay?"

She did not respond at first, bringing one hand up to her temple and using her nails like a comb to rake the hair away from her face.

"Chauna?"

"Hate," she said finally, looking up into the mirror. His eyes appeared to just float there in the middle of the sky as he squinted at her from the front seat.

"Excuse me?"

Freemantle turned slightly to hear.

"It's a hate plague. A contagion that somehow it, it --"

"Makes us angry," Drover finished, nodding. "Yes. Raise the blood pressure, increased cranial pain: rage."

Freemantle nodded, turning back toward the road ahead.

"But it's preposterous," Drover continued, almost to himself. "There aren't any natural factors that would account for a blood born, communicable contagion that affects hormone levels this way and can be spread from man to animal this quickly."

Freemantle frowned, turning his head slightly to give him a look.

"It wasn't natural," Chauna said, speaking for him.

"Up ahead," Adrian said finally, bringing the jeep to an abrupt halt and making them all lurch forward.

The airstrip station lay before them, its flat grey surface stretching out over the desert to seemingly no end.

It was empty.

The helicopter was gone, and had been long enough that the telltale stench of diesel and clouds of black smog that it left behind weren't even present.

Freemantle got out of the jeep without a word, leaning one arm against the door as he surveyed the situation, moving his eyes slowly from one end of the horizon to the other.

Adrian got out a moment later, running his fingers through his hair as the wind gusted about and displaced it once again. "I don't understand. It should be here."

"Could they have left?" Drover offered, leaning forward between the seats. "I mean, I know they could have left, but would they?"

Freemantle leaned down until his eyes were just a smidgen lower then the frame of the door. He did not answer, nor was there any expression on his face one way or the other.

Drover nodded, then sat back.

Standing again and straightening his shirt, he turned back toward the station. Adrian was a few feet in front of the jeep now, and he moved to join him.

"Is this seeming a little too coincidental to anyone else?" Adrian asked under his breath, turning back to watch as Chauna got out of the jeep.

Freemantle nodded. "Are you familiar with history, Doctor?"

"Moderately, sir. Took a few courses as electives while I was at University."

"War and science have always seemed to go hand in hand throughout our history. If necessity is the mother of invention, than violence is its father. Or grandmother. Or what have you. Either way, wars have always proven great boons for scientific breakthroughs... and breakthroughs, as I'm sure you're aware, require experiments."

Chauna raised an eyebrow, walking a few feet toward the right of the jeep. The mines were in sight now, the small cavernous entrance to its eastern tunnel just a few hundred yards away. Her head was tilted downward, the rest of her body following suit, as she examined something on the desert floor.

"And experiments require control groups," Adrian finished, turning back toward the empty fueling station. "Must make sure the rats don't leave the cage."

"We need to get out of here," Freemantle said. There was a gravitas in his voice that Adrian had never heard before, and if he hadn't known the man as well as he did, he might have described it as fear. "We need to get the tanks in here and blow this entire place back to Shangri-La, and I mean right now."

"Reptiles."

Freemantle and Adrian both turned toward the sound, as did the passengers still in the jeep. Chauna was still bent over, examining two small creatures in the sand.

They were two small salamanders, each no longer than a human hand, sitting calmly in the sun. One was inanimate except for the occasional blinking of its eyes, the other moved forward awkwardly on its webbed purple legs.

Both were covered in deep crimson, congealed blood.

Drover leaned forward. "Incredible."

"This plague, whatever it is, it's activating our reptile genes. The R Chromosome that we haven't used since Lord knows when, but it's in all of us. Each and every one of us. And this thing activates it somehow... but for them it's already active. That's why they don't --" she stood, turning back to Freemantle and Adrian.

They were staring in her direction, but at the same time were not looking at her. They were looking through her and past her, to the area beyond the jeep. She turned, following their line of sight even though she was certain she didn't want to.

Less than four hundred yards away, a large group of the infected stared at them with massive, unblinking red eyes as they lumbered forward on unsteady and broken legs.

"Get back in the jeep," Adrian said, stepping toward the vehicle and then running after his first footfall. "*Get back in the jeep!*"

Chauna turned and dove back into the door as Freemantle and Adrian clambered inside. Adrian shifted the stick to drive and pulled forward immediately and with no real direction in mind except away, spinning the tires and then tearing away from the station in a wide arc.

"Where are we going to go?" Drover yelled to nobody, his head pivoting between the front window and the back. "Where do you think we can go that they can't follow? There's too much desert out there and too many of them in here! We're dead! Dead!"

"Shut up!" Chauna said finally, giving him a look before turning back to Karen. "We're not dead. We are not dead until we're dead, and we're not dead."

Adrian glanced up into the rearview mirror at her, meeting her gaze all but briefly.

"We're not dead," she said again, in response to some phrase her colleague hadn't spoken.

They were almost to the mines and the infected were disappearing behind them again, though they were still coming. Even if they couldn't see them, they could *feel* them, the way you feel panic as it ebbs its way up from the lining of your stomach and becomes something ravenous.

"Here!" Freemantle yelled, grabbing the wheel and jolting it to the left. "Hold on!"

The jeep lurched to the side and spun until it was facing the entrance to the caves and then plunged forward, slamming into the solid rock mouth and sending all seven of them into the dashboard and seats in front of them.

For a moment, nobody moved or spoke.

"Everyone okay?" Freemantle asked, breaking the silence as the jeep's engine wound to a final halt.

"Fuck is wrong with you?" Drover asked, rubbing the back of his neck gingerly.

"No, look," Adrian smiled, craning his head too see as much of the windshield as he could. "We're plugging the hole. The entrance to the cave is sealed. They can't get in."

"But we can't get out."

"That doesn't matter," Freemantle interrupted harshly, clearly in pain as he checked to make sure the children had not been harmed. "There are twenty miners in these tunnels with enough supplies and rations to last eighteen months, should anything happen. We'll be fine in here until we find a way out or a way to contact the outside world." He leaned forward and slammed his elbow against the plate glass windshield. It popped out on the second strike, sailing three feet into the cavern before landing on the solid stone floor and shattering. "Come on."

***

The walls of the cave were magnificent simply in their continued existence. What at first appeared to be solid rock was actually compressed sand, pressed together to the point that any weight put upon it by the surface was evenly distributed amongst the grains. Navigating them by flashlight was like being shrunk down to the size of a doll and exploring a sand castle built as a child, its construction weaving and intricate.

The swirls and twists of multicolored flecks of sand left patterns and shapes in the walls. They formed long flowing faces stretched out in agony and horror, red-sanded eyes watching them wherever they went.

Two miles into the cave the tunnel became narrow with sharp stalactites jutting up from either side, and it became necessary to walk single file. Freemantle led the way with the flashlight, careful to test every rock and crevice that looked suspicious to make sure it was safe for those following. Karen walked behind him, holding Tyler in her arms. Then came Adrian holding Jamie, Chauna, and finally Drover.

Chauna mumbled to herself, some of her words audible and some not, as the counted off digits on her fingers.

Adrian glanced back once or twice and noticed her get to four or five, stop, then start again. "What's wrong?" he asked after a moment of trying to figure it out on his own.

"Trying to figure out the route the pathogen took."

He raised an eyebrow at her.

She frowned, stepping carefully to avoid a large boulder. "Infectious diseases are transmitted from one source to another. Respiratory, gastrointestinal, sexual... they all have to be transmitted from person to person."

"Of course."

"Well typically it's hard to tell what sequence it happened in... but a blood born disease, and a new one at that... it shouldn't be that hard to track its progress."

"And?"

"And I can't. No matter what I do or how I do it, I can't figure out how the disease moved. Somewhere, somehow, it jumped the tracks."

He frowned, turning to Jamie to make sure she wasn't paying attention. She appeared to be asleep despite everything that was happening, nuzzled into the nape of his neck. "Talk it out."

"It started with that Private, we're all clear on that."

"Baker, yes. That was definitely patient zero."

"Then Mark and Sutton, in that order."

"I'm following you so far."

"And after that the disease takes a fairly clear path through town, albeit unbelievably quickly. It spreads from person to person in a predictable fashion for a blood born infection."

"What's the problem then?"

She leaned in, whispering. "I can't for the life of me figure out how the General's driver got it. Karen's husband. No matter what way I think about it, I can't figure out how someone with the infection managed to infect --"

Adrian screamed, turned quickly, and fell to his knees. Sharp rocks dug into his kneecaps and out the other side in a glorious spurt of blood and he thrashed forward, slamming his head against the pact sand in the narrow cavern. He dropped Jamie to the ground as her mother and Freemantle turned around, the girl landing on her feet next to him, her head still buried in his neck.

She pulled back, taking a chunk of his neck the size of his fist with him as a fountain of blood splashed out onto her face and hair, almost obscuring the opaquely red eyes that turned toward the light just as Freemantle shone it upon her. She opened her mouth and screamed, the sound coming out a long squeal and clicks and clacks that echoed off the walls and came back in all directions.

She darted at Freemantle, too fast for him to see, and pushed him into the rock wall. He fell, letting go of the flashlight and letting it tumble to the ground to catch himself. She bellowed at him, opening her blood-drenched mouth wide and yelling so loud it shook the molars of the tiny round teeth.

Freemantle started to get up and reach for his gun as Jamie turned, leaping at Chauna and clawing at the older woman's chest.

"Fuck!" Chauna yelled , trying her best to hold the child at bay.

Jamie roared back, turning and biting at Chauna's wrist and coming back with a vein caught in the gap of her two front teeth, pulling back hard until it came clear like a boiled noodle.

Freemantle stood and aimed his weapon, taking one step forward to steady himself before firing.

His steel-toed boot came to ground on the base of Adrian's flashlight, and the steady beam went out, bathing them in darkness.

***

The jeep that pulled up to the cave was eerily quiet, its treads packing the sand beneath it into jagged rectangular patterns. It came to a stop in silence, the well cared for breaks never once squealing in defiance as it came to a halt. There was a moment when all was still, and for once there wasn't even a breeze to carry grains over the dunes. The main turret of the tank stared out upon the entrance to the cave, an unblinking eye watching mournfully over the tomb.

The door at the top opened, and an officer wearing a black uniform with duel rows of black buttons stepped out and jumped down onto the sand, sending waves of it cascading in all directions around him. He took off his cap and wiped the sweat from his brow with a small red handkerchief, then placed it carefully back into his pocket.

A younger officer poked his head out from the jeep after a moment, then finally allowed himself to fall to the ground as well. He made a grunt when he did, as though the feeling of dirt beneath his boots were foreign to him.

"Any sign, sir?" he asked, his voice wavering in a way it hadn't since puberty as his eyes darted across the horizon. The town lay in ruins, the only sign left that there had ever been anything there a smoldering building a mile to their west that reports claimed had once been a hospital, the embers burning so hot that the ground around it had turned to glass.

The senior officer chewed slowly, moving the toothpick in his mouth from side to side as his eyes passed over the cave. The sand at the entrance was tinted a crimson he knew had nothing to do with their planets tone. He let out a long sigh. "There's nothing here," he said finally, turning back to his second-in-command. "Get the old man on the line, direct contact. Let him know Reptillia is good for mass produ--"

There was a sound behind him, not unlike the rattle of a child's toy, slow and rhythmic. A soft, almost soothing cluck that under any other circumstances might have been hypnotically pleasing.

His withered eyes went wide for the first time in years as he turned around on his heels so fast he almost ripped a ligament in his hip.

They say screams can't echo off the dunes. That they absorb the sound and prevent it from continuing on.

If they're loud enough, they do.

REVVING ENGEN

Coral Beach, Maine

Tash leaned back on the wire-mesh chair she'd found at the supermarket, her cell phone pressed tightly to her ear and her coffee slowly getting cooler in front of her, bleeding steam into the cool September air.

There was a table with an umbrella sticking up from its centre that was almost exactly like the other ten that surrounded it, differenced only by the placement of the freckles of rust that decorated them. The balcony that surrounded the top floor of the supermarket on all sides was rarely used to the point that most people had forgotten it was there. They stopped and stared at her now as though she were some alien being as they shuffled past, their plastic bags of groceries cutting deep gouges into their fingers on their way to their cars. She smiled and nodded at each one that looked at her. Some smiled back, most looked away quickly.

"Small towns," she mumbled softly to herself, then sat up. Her voice became louder and clearer as she spoke into the phone. "No, sorry. Yeah. Yeah, I have it here in front of me."

She reached for the paper she'd bought while in line for her coffee (which tasted for the world like motor oil). It was a *Star* weekly, the type of tabloid that could be found in any checkout across the country. It had bold headlines like MY BABY'S DADDY IS FROM DIMENSION X and ELVIS IS LIVING IN MY BASEMENT accompanied by horribly photoshopped photographs.

"You know, that might be worth checking out. If Elvis is still alive after all this time..." she stopped, turning to the second page. There was a one-column piece there about the LUCKIEST MAN ALIVE, without the benefit of pictures. "I'm just saying, it would be great. I'd switch it up so that you get the kids and I get the adults, and I'd reenact King Creole every Saturday. You're sure? Damn shame. I'm reading it."

She grabbed her paper cup around its cardboard sleeve and brought it to her scant lips. They were a small bow in the middle of her pointed chin, amidst the faded freckles that dotted her otherwise smooth complexion. She took a long sip as her eyes scanned their way down the article, their brows climbing a notch with every paragraph.

"Wow. This seems like it could be legit." She stopped, listening to the person on the other end of the line for a moment as she finished the article and laid it back down on the table. A second later her coffee was laid down too, and she pried her phone out from between her head and shoulder, rubbing the spot where it had been tenderly. "That's a lot of cash. He could just be good, you know. Despite what he used to say, sometimes a cigar is just a cigar. Be careful. Kid's twenty-one and sitting on that much cash, he's going to be jumpy. Maybe."

Her brow furrowed, and she took another sip of her drink now that both hands were free.

"Back to the Future?" she asked quizzically, her mouth curling up in a smile. After a moment, the smile went away and she rolled her eyes, her voice taking on a frustrated tone. "Back to the Future *Part Two*, then? Yeah. Uh-Huh. Do you think it's anything like that? ...Alright, well, be careful. I'm here, but I don't know how I'm going to find anything in this place. I really hate Maine. Read too many Stephen King novels and now I'm scared of every shadow in every small town it's got. And this one's weird. It's small enough that it barely shows up on the map and doesn't show up online at all, but here it is. It's actually bigger than most towns; it's almost a city. And the people here are cagey... I think it's going to be hard getting anything out of them without looking suspicious."

She stopped talking long enough for the person on the other end to respond, a concerned look flashing over her dark eyes. "Okay, well be careful. I miss you... Out."

She pulled the phone back from her ear and watched as the connection went dead, then laughed and shook her head as she placed it back into her pocket. "Who the hell says out to end a conversation?"

She pushed the weekly Star to the far side of the table and picked up another paper from the seat next to her, the *Beach News Daily*.

***

Sara Johnson forced her locker door closed, putting all her weight behind her shoulder as she forced the metal door flush with all the others that lined the hallway. Her tongue was sticking out of the corner of her mouth a little as she did so, the pink of it just different enough from the pink of her lips to be noticed.

She heard the mechanism inside it click, then smiled and stepped back from it.

It groaned for a moment, then snapped back open, spilling books and papers out across the hall in a V-shape spreading out from the door.

"Fuck!" she huffed, stamping one foot before dropping to her knees and shoving all the loose sheets of paper into a pile. She had a brief memory of her father teaching her how to play fifty-two pickup as a child, but it left as quickly as it had arrived.

"You know, that wouldn't happen so much if you didn't have your whole life in there." Nick said, leaning against the locker next to her.

She looked up at him even as she continued to gather her books together, having to crane her head back to the point of pain to do so.

He was tall, several inches above any other male in his grade. His brown hair was spiked and gelled up and make him look even taller, monstrous even. It was something he'd been teased about in elementary school but in recent years had become one of his defining attributes, along with his pale blue eyes. Sometimes in the sun, his eyes almost looked white. His height, along with his speed while dribbling and passing, had made him a force to be reckoned with on the school basketball team.

She didn't know how long he'd been standing there, but she assumed that it was long enough that she had made a fool of herself at least once. She gave him a little smile, the right corner of her lip curling just enough to make her irresistible as she fixed her top to make sure he couldn't see down it. There were fishnet stockings wrapped around her hands that had rips along the wrists from where they'd become caught in her large hoop earrings. There were at least two rings on each of her fingers, silver rings on the left hand and gold rings on the right. The gold ones had been polished recently and sparkled in the fluorescent lights of the hallway, while the silver ones were dull and faded.

"I wouldn't know what to do with myself if everything wasn't at arm's length," she said, shoving a hardcover geology text into the locker with such force that the spine creased.

"Come on, take a lesson from Tom Petty."

She raised an eyebrow at him.

"You don't have to live like a refugee."

She rolled her eyes as she continued to shove books and papers into the locker without any concern for their state or the creases created.

He sighed, then bent down and started to help her. He recognized a math book from seventh grade, a hardcover text with a bear juggling beach balls. The bear was smiling stupidly at the fourth wall and reminded him of the bears from the Coca Cola commercials every time he thought of long division. Most people had sold theirs to the next crop of grade seven students during the first week of grade eight, but here was Sara's copy, still occupying the bottom of her locker just in case she ever forgot how to use cosign and needed a quick reminder.

"It's like you're a damn nomad," he sighed, flipping through an array of used notebooks with coiled metal spines.

"A what?"

"Nomad." He smiled. "A person who moves from place to place."

"Always got to be ready for the next big thing," she said, shoving the last of her belongings into the locker and slamming the door shut again. "Can you get this?"

He nodded, then braced his feet against the tile floor and shoved against the door as hard as he could with both palms. There were odd scuttling sounds as the items inside shifted under the weight of the door before finally finding a comfortable position as the lock clicked into place with a solid, metallic tone.

"Thanks," she chirped.

"No problem."

She motioned toward the hall as she started to walk toward the front entrance. He nodded and stepped up beside her, hoisting his book-bag onto his shoulder and jogging the first few steps to catch up.

He stopped after a moment and looked around, a confused look coming over him. "Where's Xander?"

"Out with Grendel. Apparently there was some special kind of speaker he needed for his party on Friday, but he didn't know what kind... so he called on the Nerd Patrol to come help him pick it out."

"Frightening."

"What is?"

"Grendel doesn't have the time of day for him most days, but he needs him for something and: bam. Let's hang out after school."

She stopped and turned to face him, squinting her eyes and tilting her head slightly to one side. "You're not coming to Grendel's party this Friday, are you?"

Nick rolled his eyes. "What was your first clue?"

She frowned, and they continued walking. After a few paces, her tongue clicked against the roof of her mouth (as it always did when she was about to try and convince someone of something) and she continued, "You really should come, you know. It's going to be the social event of the season."

"Why're you talking like that?"

"It's fun."

"It bugs me."

"That's what makes it fun." She smiled. "Anyway, everyone's going to be there... maybe even Teresa Conway..."

He turned and looked at her, her voice having gained a musical tone as she said the girl's name. "Isn't she with Jamie Dawkins?"

"I have it on good authority that she'll be in need of some male companionship before too long."

He sighed. "I'm not coming to the party. I don't like Julian Grendel even under the best of circumstances, I'm certainly not going to pretend to just so I can sit next to Teresa Conway while she downs Cuba Libres until she pukes."

She shot him a look. "You're testy today, aren't you?"

He paused. "Sorry. Rough class."

"That's okay. What're you doing now?"

"Right now I am walking down the hall with you."

She shot him a look.

"Oh, you mean later? Later, I'm doing nothing."

"You want to come to the Factory? ...could be fun. I think Jamie's going to be there if you wanted to play pool."

He smiled. "I'll think about it."

***

A crack filled the air of the Factory as Nick sent the cue ball crashing into the assembled balls at the other side of the table, the sharp sound echoing off the walls until it seemed to be coming from everywhere.

The Factory was a local arcade, club and dance hall where almost every teen in Coral Beach went when there was nothing else to do, which was almost all of the time. It jutted up from the otherwise calm landscape that had been named 'downtown' even though it was only a small distance from the city centre or even from the outskirts of town, and was always loud and exciting and neon.

Nick leaned back from the table and watched as the billiards began to dance about, ricocheting off each other and the torn green fabric that lined the sides until finally coming to a stop. They were scattered nicely, with the one ball teetering very close to the corner pocket at his right and a small cluster of balls still remaining at the far end of the table. Nothing had been sunk.

"Your decision," he said to Jamie Dawkins, motioning to him with his stick.

Jamie frowned, observing the table. "It's not much of a decision." He leaned over the table, raising an eyebrow as he tried to figure out his shot. His leather sports jacket crumpled and scrunched noisily every time he moved, forcing him to push up the sleeves over and over again. His brother had worn that jacket when he was captain of the Coral Beach Cougars, and his father before that. Now that he was finally captain, it barely ever left his back. Some even said he showered with it on. He squat down to make his eye line level with the path between the cue and the one, finding that it was blocked by the eight. He sighed.

"You could always bank it," Nick offered.

Jamie shot him a look.

Nick shrugged. "Just saying." He turned toward the bar just as Sara was shaking her head at him. She had a tall glass of soda in her hand that was so cold there was fog coming off of it, bathing her neck and chin in chilly, cool condensation that was like fresh morning dew on the leaves outside his house. Julie Peterson was next to her, finishing off the last few bites of a local burger called the Slaughterhouse that dripped sauce and grease onto the paper plate she had strategically placed on her lap. Randy Owchar was there too, his eyes shifting back and forth between the pool table and Julie's exposed tailbone.

"Good break," Sara said, taking a long gulp of her drink and then using it to salute him in a 'cheers' motion, even though he didn't have a drink himself. "But you shouldn't make fun of him like that."

"Like what?"

"The 'your decision' thing?"

He smiled. "Come on... it's that old basketball-football competition."

"Be nice, Lardo," Julie smiled, nudging Sara in what both girls would often refer to as 'her fat'. "It's fun watching them play like this. It's like watching the apes on Animal Planet."

"You have never in your life watched Animal Planet," Sara replied, moving away from her.

"Have so."

"Oh, yeah? When?"

Julie was silent for a long moment, then eventually let her shoulders slump. "Sometimes you can be a real bitch."

Sara smiled, then turned back to Nick. He wasn't watching them and he wasn't watching the game, even though Jamie had made his shot on the one and missed, leaving the choice of balls in Nick's hands again. He was staring past the both of them into the null space at the other end of the bar. It was a place where nobody typically sat, and was usually occupied by stacks of cola bottles and unopened milk cartons. She turned to follow his line of sight, her hair getting caught on her lip balm as she did.

There was a woman sitting on the furthest seat of the bar.

She was wearing a dark blue hooded sweatshirt that disguised most of her features and even hid her eyes in shadow, but there was a femininity to that slant, triangular nature of the lower half of her face that made her gender impossible to hide. Her lips were small and bright red, and Sara guessed that they had been what had first drawn Nick's attention... they looked too red to be real, standing out bright and vibrant against the comparatively sepia-toned color of the Factory wall. It was as if someone photoshopped crimson lips into an old black and white photo.

She was sipping tea in long mouthfuls from a cup that was so hot that steam poured out of it without the slightest pause, yet she seemed to have no trouble taking it in. Her hands were soft and delicate, the nails on the end of each painted to match her lips.

Sara caught herself staring much in the way that Nick had, finally forcing herself to turn around. She scrunched up her face in an exaggerated scowl and rolled her eyes. "Skank alert."

Nick shook his head, then met her eye again and smiled. "What?"

"Skank alert," she repeated, motioning toward the end on the bar with her head. "As in, be alerted to the presence of skanks. I really didn't think it needed any more explanation."

Nick wrung the edge of his pool stick, turned to look at the table and then back to the stranger. "What makes you think she's a skank?"

"What would you call a thirty-something year old man that came into here, sat in the shadows and watched us while sipping on tea?"

"A pedophile."

"And what would you call a female pedophile?"

"...A skank."

"Hence the skank alert."

He watched the woman for a moment longer. The steam from her drink seemed to dance up from her mug and caress her chin, hugging against the flesh without even touching it and continuing up over her head and out into the atmosphere.

He turned away from her and bent over the table, making his own shot at the one and sinking it effortlessly. It slammed against the back of the pocket with a loud crack before finding its home in the soft leather net below it.

"I'm low," he said, moving to the side of the table without taking his eyes off the balls. They moved for him in his mind like atoms, each one coming into clear focus for a moment while the rest faded into his peripheral vision until each had been examined and reexamined into the equation that was this pool table.

He bent over and made a shot at the five, sending it into the far side pocket with another loud smack that made Julie and Sara both jump, even though they'd been watching as the action unfolded. The cue rolled back until it was almost touching the two, and Nick quickly made his way around to the other side of the table and gave it the final tap needed to send it into the side pocket.

Jamie huffed, wringing his stick but leaning against the pillar closest to the table and getting comfortable.

Nick continued around the table again, finally coming across a clear line between the cue and the six. He pulled his stick back hard and nailed it, leaving a dent of blue chalk in the side of the cue as it rocketed across the table and collided with the six, bouncing off it and sending it into the corner pocket.

He glanced up at Sara and smiled, winking at her. She smiled back, but he couldn't help but notice the woman behind her was still watching them... had even stood up a little to see over the edge of the bar. Although that small, rosy mouth of hers was still held in the exact same expression, he couldn't help but think that there was a smile building across the edge of it somehow.

He turned back to the table and moved around it again, with each step his eyes continuing to flutter back and forth over the balls so fast that the blues of them almost looked white, zipping about in their sockets so quickly that even the irises took on a grayish tone. He found a clear shot at the three and took it, making another shot at the seven before either ball had even stopped moving and sinking both.

Sara smiled and took another sip of her drink. She had the same calculating expression on her face that he did, although she wasn't measuring distance and force. Julie noticed her and smiled, poking her in the side again.

"What?" Sara laughed.

"Leave something for the rest of us, why don't you?"

"The big lion gets the most food," she smirked. "Deal with it."

Nick waited for the cue to stop rolling and finally lined up his shot with the four, cracking the cue into it so hard that it would have been bruised if it hadn't already been purple. He stood up and surveyed the table again. There were seven high balls still scattered around it with three still in a small cluster where they had been since they'd been racked, and the black eight ball sitting alone along one side.

He smirked at Jamie, then bent over and made his shot at the eight. He did not slam it as he had almost every other shot, instead tapping it as gently as he could and letting the two balls collide before sending the second one rolling smoothly toward the top corner pocket. It was like watching it in slow motion compared to the rest of the game, and as all the other eyes in the room (including the stranger's) watched the ball roll its way across the felt, Nick made his way around the table until he was in front of Jamie, his hand out in front of him.

"Pay up," he said, just as the eight sunk into the pocket and clicked against the balls already waiting there.

Jamie peeked up over his shoulder to make sure the ball had actually sunk, frowned, then shoved his hand deep into his pocket and produced a wrinkled and crumpled five dollar bill. He held it up between them for a moment, then slammed it down into Nick's waiting palm. "Next time," he said, meeting his eye with mock contempt.

"I've heard that before," Nick smiled, laying his stick down and making his way over to the bar. He sat down on a stool away from the others and waited for Roxanne to come over and take his order, seeing her shadow move in the back of the house as she tried in vain to clean the grease off the deep fryer.

Sara came over and leaned over the bar next to him, her hair falling down around her. Her arms were crossed across her chest and it pushed her breasts up until they were almost escaping her shirt. He hated himself for noticing, it was one of the things he despised most about Julian Grendel - the obviousness with which he ogled most of the girls in their school - but he simply couldn't help it. The more he tried not to notice them, the more conspicuous they became.

"That was pretty impressive," she said, looking from him to the five he'd won and then back again.

"Thanks," he smiled. It *had* been impressive, he knew, but it was something he'd become accustomed to and almost had to remind himself that it wasn't normal from time to time.

"Any chance I can play the winner?"

He smiled at her. "I get the feeling you've been playing the winner since grade eight."

Her smile spread and she laughed, not outright but the strange, subdued little hum that was her typical way of expressing herself.

There was an arcade game playing against the far wall behind her, flashing lights and strobe effects every few seconds to try and entice patrons into shoveling quarters into it. The lights were caught in her straight blonde hair and made it glow around her like a halo, first red then green and blue and then back to red again. Her eyes remained the same though, that same sparkle of light that had always been there present even now. She was beautiful, and he found his throat getting dryer and dryer the closer he got to her until the five dollar bill in his hand felt like a pitcher of water at the end of a long walk across a desert highway.

Her lips were pink with lip balm, shimmering in whatever light source had made her eyes sparkle.

He felt himself inching his head closer to hers, and it was as though his body were maneuvering on autopilot without his control. Her eyes fluttered from his to his lips again and again, watching as events seemed to happen in that same slow motion that had made the sinking of the eight ball so dramatic.

"Is this okay?" he heard himself whisper, though he wasn't entirely sure why. He'd seen men try to make unwanted moves on Sara Johnson before, and it typically ended with them getting kneed somewhere very unpleasant.

"Mmm," she said, with that same sort of hum she'd used to respond to him a moment before. Her mouth opened, and he could again see the pink of her tongue against the pink of her lips. Could feel the heat of her breath on his. "I've been waiting for you to kiss me since I noticed those eyes in eighth grade."

He stopped, suddenly in control of his body again. Their lips were almost touching, to the point that a bead of condensation on either's lip would have been felt by the other. They hung like that for a moment before he took a step back.

"What?" she asked, hurt filling her eyes almost immediately.

He swallowed back hard, then cleared his throat.

"What is it?" she repeated, taking him by the arm and forcing him to face her.

"It's nothing," he said, his voice almost breaking as he did so. "Really. Just, ah... just feel like sitting this one out is all."

"Oh."

"Yeah. Maybe I'll play next game. I think Jamie's ready to play now, if you still wanted too."

"Yeah." She nodded, then pushed away from the bar and took a step backward towards the others. "Are you sure you're okay?"

Nick nodded, swallowing back hard again.

Her brow furrowed in worry, but she did not ask again. She turned away and walked back to the pool table, picking up a short pool stick off the wall rack along the way.

He stared at the cash register against the wall from him, the rest of his vision becoming hazy and mossy as he focused in on it. There were thirty-two buttons on it, five of which had cracks in their plastic casings. Two had their labels peeled off, and one number (the seven) was upside-down. It had a thick layer of dust on it despite the fact that Roxanne cleaned it weekly and used it often, and was the same colour of faded pears that seemed to have adorned all mid-nineties technology.

He let out a long sigh and dropped his head, bringing the wood grain of the bar into focus instead. His hands found his way into his hair despite the fact that he knew Julie and Randy might well have been watching him right now and he fought the urge to simply curl into a ball and start to cry.

"That was quite a show," came a smooth, silky voice. For a moment he thought it was Sara. The voice had that same smooth, summery feel to it... as though warmth was a sound that could be heard rather than merely felt.

He turned and saw that it was the stranger, just gliding into the seat beside him. She wasn't looking at him, was instead examining the cash register in much the same way he had been. It was only now that he could see how taut her skin was... it clung to the bone around it for dear life, the muscle of her profiled face pulled tight and ready at all times. Her lips looked like a sideways heart from this angle, but were still that same deep red that he'd noticed before.

Skank alert, he caught himself thinking, but dared not say it aloud.

"Not really," he said finally, standing on his toes to try and see if Roxanne was coming yet. "I didn't even get to do any bank shots. Usually they're the hard ones. The balls just went in the right places."

"Not the pool," she smiled, laying her cup down on the counter in front of her. "The *girl*."

He turned and looked at her, narrowing his eyes until they were just tiny white slits in his head. "What do you want?"

She smiled. "I think the more appropriate question would be: what do you want?"

He looked at her for a long moment, his tongue massaging the top of his mouth.

"I want to show you something," she said finally, moving just a little bit closer to him. The arm of her sweater grazed against his leg and he felt shivers run up and down his spine like gooseflesh.

"I don't - -"

"*Please*," she said, leaning forward until the light off the counter caught her face. Her skin was smooth and milky white, with just the slightest tint of yellow around each cheek. Her nose was petit and straight, and made her already impressive eyes look large. She reached into her pocket and returned clasping a small metal gadget. It had holes for each of her slender fingers and seemed to make been made specifically to fit her hand. There was a small red dial at the top where her thumb could get at it that was switched to off at the moment, but she lingered near it, ready to turn it on at a moment's hesitation.

He stared at it, taking in every groove and pivot of it. "What is that?"

"I can't show you in here," she whispered, in that voice like the sun. "Please, just step outside with me for a moment... you'll see."

He frowned. Roxanne finally came out from the back and noticed the two of them, eyeing the pair suspiciously. He turned back to his friends and saw that Julie and Randy had stepped aside to play a pinball game, Randy standing close behind Julie and helping her work the buttons on either side of the machine. Sara was leaning on the pool table with her stick in one hand while the other gripped Jamie Dawkins's back, her nails digging into the smooth leather of his captain's jacket. His hands were cupping her hips in the same place Julie had been poking, and their lips were moving back and forth against each other. Her hair, previously straight, was now one big curl across the top of her head.

Nick stopped, his mouth again going dry. He became aware again of the bill in his hand and clasped it until it became hot as he watched the both of them. She finally dropped the pool stick, letting it fall to the floor with a loud clang.

"Thought he was with Teresa," Roxanne said, scrubbing the grease off her thumb with an old rag.

"Past tense," he replied, then turned back toward the stranger.

She was gone. All that remained of her was the cup of tea she'd been holding, which was still billowing out steam at such an alarming rate that even now, almost empty, he dared not touch it. Out of the corner of his eye, he caught the motion of the door closing, and turned just in time to see the blue arm of her sweatshirt disappear behind it.

He turned back to the pool table where Sara and Jamie still stood with their lips locked together as he hoisted her up until she was sitting on the table, then sighed and turned to follow the stranger out the door.

Sara opened her eyes as Jamie began to kiss the side of her fragile neck and watched as Nick left the Factory. She bit her lip, a look of concern coming over her as she closed her eyes again.

***

The Factory opened up into a large gravel parking lot that eventually tapered off into grass before becoming the street again. There were no lines or guides in the front lot to let you know where to park, only the occasional divot where the weight of multiple cars had dug ditches into the ground and made guidelines for the next parker to follow. When Nick came out of the Factory, there were no cars parked in the entire lot, nor were there any cars on the road. The closest light he could see was Derek Smith's house across the way, both of its upstairs lights and one of its downstairs lights on and shining brightly at him.

He turned around, finding himself panting even though he wasn't exhausted at all. His tongue felt dry and desolate inside his mouth, and he thought that if he tried to talk it might spread to his teeth and turn them into sand they way they always did on cartoons when the characters went to the dentist. The Factory door had already shut tight behind him, locking all the neon flashing strobe lights of the place inside. It couldn't even be heard from out here, years of complaining neighbors resulting in some of the best soundproofing a very small amount of money could buy.

There was a small sliver of an alley alongside the east wall of the building that led to nowhere. It had once been null space between it and the storage building next door but had since been bricked over on one side to create an area devoid of wind and drifting snow that could be used for a smoking section or garbage disposal, even though neither building did anymore.

He paused and watched the small, dark space for a moment as if expecting it to do something. He could see every inch of it even though there was very little light... every crack or crevice in the brick, every dent on the plaster, every bit of garbage pilled up alongside it.

Slowly, tentatively, he stepped toward it. With each step, his view of it became more and more fixed and narrow, until almost all he could see was the black absence of light that it made. Even he had a hard time seeing into it, the moon above providing little to no aid.

Finally he entered the mouth of the alley and stood there, staring into the darkness and waiting for his eyes to adjust.

She was standing halfway down the alley, almost exactly in its centre. Her hood was still up and the light caught off the fabric on her head and shoulders, draping her face in the same darkness that surrounded her. It made her look like the Grim Reaper, a thought that made Nick turn back toward the Factory's door. He took a step back out into the open, an act that made him feel safer without actually making him safer.

She reached into her pocket without a word, again producing the same small device. She wasn't wearing it now, only cupping it in the palm of her hand. She bobbed it twice, then tossed it into the air and let it come down on the alley floor between the two of them, kicking up clouds of dust and dirt as it landed.

He stared at it again, looking from it to her and then back.

She nodded at him, then took a step back from the device.

Licking his lips, he threw one last glance toward the door of the Factory, then stepped into the dark of the alley. He took one step at a time, always careful to hold his eye on the stranger with every movement he made. Just like with the pool table, his every move altered his perception of her and the way he evaluated her threat... each movement bringing him more and more information.

When he got close enough, he bent down and reached out, caressing one of the slots on the device with his index finger and pulling it toward him until it was close enough that he could clasp it. He stood up immediately and held it in the palm of his hand, examining one side and then flipping it over to examine the other before starting again.

She reached inside her hood, past her head to the area between her shoulder blades.

He looked from the device to her, and was about to ask her what it was again, when she pulled a small blade from the darkness of her hood. It was like it came right out of her face, a reverse of the sword-eaters he'd seen as a child. He dropped the device to the floor again, splashing more dirt onto his jeans as he took a step backward.

She raised the blade high, moving it between her fingers until it came to a comfortable position and then stopped, the tip of the blade in line with his neck.

"Hey," came a harsh voice. It was stern and hard like he would have expected hers to be. He turned to the end of the alley and saw Tash standing there, her fists clenched at either side. Her face was slender and shadowed by the moon behind it, her eyes blazing white and her face curled up in a snarl. "How about you just fuck off?" she finished, thrusting a finger out toward the stranger.

The stranger tilted her head as Nick began to pant again, turning from one to the other. Slowly, the stranger reached up with her free hand and clasped the nub of fabric at the cusp of her hood and pulled it down, revealing her full face. She was Asian; that thin face finally seen fully with almond-shaped eyes. The skin just over each of them was the same yellowed tint he'd noticed on her cheeks a few moments ago, and bled up into a long mane of jet black hair that went far down her back a disappeared somewhere behind her. When the rest of the sweatshirt hit the ground, he saw that she was athletic, dressed in a red jumpsuit with black edges all the way down it. The handles of twin katana blades protruding from sheaths on her back, the straps crossing her chest in a giant X. She put her knife away and drew one of the blades, again moving it around her fingers until it became comfortable and then readying it to strike. It had four gold spikes coming off the handle, making the legs of a spider, with two red rubies making up the body and the head.

Tash stared at her for a moment, her head tilting slightly to one side. "Swords," she said finally, clicking her tongue against the roof of her mouth. "Sure, why wouldn't it be swords?"

The stranger crouched, moving from side to side like a spider swaying on its web in a spring breeze, her hair remaining perfectly still as her eyes shifted from Nick to Tash and then back to Nick again. A wry smile spread over her lips as she took a step forward, bringing her sword up high.

"No!" Tash shouted, taking her first step forward even as the stranger brought down her blade toward Nick.

Nick wanted to close his eyes but couldn't, could only watch as the blade moved up to the highest point of its arc and caught the moonlight in its path, sparkled briefly, then started its descent back down toward his head. It seemed to be moving slow even though he knew it couldn't be, and he swallowed back hard as it became almost invisible, its sharp thin edge lined perfectly with the area between his eyes. It occurred to him that if he followed it the entire way down, he would be cross-eyed when it struck and that that would likely be how his parents found him: a boy with two heads cross-eyed. As the blade came closer and closer to him, he turned his head and rolled out of the way, diving with such force that his head rammed into the brick wall and split open.

The sword clanged against the concrete and the stranger sneered at Nick, surprised that he wasn't where he had been when she'd struck. The entire passage had taken less than a second to happen, even though it had seemed like an eternity.

"Hey!" Tash yelled, grabbing the stranger by the collar and slamming her against the wall opposite Nick. The stranger tried to raise her sword, but Tash brought up her knee and slammed it into her wrist, pinning it between her bone and the wall. The sword fell from her fingers onto the ground.

"Jesus," Nick gasped, trying hard to catch his breath. "Jesus."

"I think the next time I tell you to back off, you're going to," Tash continued, their foreheads almost touching as she locked eyes with the strange woman.

The stranger pushed her back, making Tash stumble and almost trip over Nick. She pulled back and punched Tash in the side of her neck with such force that she felt her molars rattle. She coughed once, tasting blood as it erupted up from her mouth, then spun back to face the stranger.

"I didn't care for that," she said, hauling back and hitting the woman in the face. The stranger fell back and slammed the back of her head against the brick wall, then fell forward against the ground and spit up a heaping mouthful of blood herself.

"Come on!" Tash yelled, hoisting Nick up under one arm and running with him toward the mouth of the alley.

"Will that stop her?" Nick asked as he turned briefly to stare at the woman from over his shoulder.

"It might slow her down," Tash replied, turning around the corner and breaking into an all-out run.

***

Sara stared at herself in the bathroom mirror of the Factory. It was cracked and dirty despite Roxanne's best efforts to keep it clean. Coupled with the gray walls around it, it looked depressing when she saw her reflection in it even on the best of days. Tonight it seemed especially dismal.

She tilted her head to one side and pulled her hair away from her neck to reveal a large red spot that Jamie had put there while she had sat on the pool table. She tisked, then reached into her purse and took out a small pad of makeup and started the task of covering it up. When her finger touched it, the memory of watching Nick leave the Factory came back to her, and she let out a deep sigh.

There had been a look on his face that she'd seen before... a loneliness and a heartbreak that she knew she'd caused in some of the other men in her life - one in particular. She'd wrestled long and hard with the responsibility of that, and had held firm to the belief that some people just were that way... that if they hadn't been pining over her they would have been pining over somebody else. But now she'd brought it out in Nick... someone who up until this point had always been strong and kind and happy.

She sniffed as her hand trembled against her neck, and she forced herself to steady it.

"You okay in there?" Julie called, knocking on the door twice.

"I'm fine," she lied, then turned back to the mirror and slathered on some more foundation.

***

Nick gasped for air as his lungs threatened to burst, each one a hot ball of fire within his chest. Tash ducked the both of them into the shadow of a house and tried to catch her breath, still clutching onto the loose flesh between his neck and shoulder.

"What the hell was that?" he asked, squirming out of her grip and standing a few feet from her. He tried to stand up straight but couldn't, bending over and resting his hands on his knees.

"If we live, I'll be sure to tell you," she replied, pressing her head flush against the wall of the house and looking around its corner. There was nobody coming up the street from where they'd come from, nor was there any sign of movement in the street at all... it was more disturbing to her than if there had been three of that woman bearing down on them with swords drawn. She'd spent most of her adult life in America's cities, and for any street to be this vacant was like looking into the soul of a ghost town. "Is it usually this quiet here?"

"Ah," he started, standing up and squinting at a nearby street sign. "We're close to Laird Street, more the residential area. So yes, people don't tend to stay out late here unless they have a curfew."

"Right," she nodded, glancing over the street once more.

-click-.

He stared at her for a long moment, then shook his head. Sweat dripped off it when he did. "Who the hell are you?" he said finally.

"My name's Natasha. You can call me Tash, most do. And, don't take this the wrong way... but I think I'm here for you."

-click-.

"Me? Me? I'm sorry, how am I not supposed to take that the wrong way?"

"It's a long, crappy story, kid," she frowned, touching her face where she'd been hit gingerly. She winced once, then pressed harder. "The point of it right now is, I'm here to help. If you don't want my help, that's fine too... it's your call."

Nick stared at her even though she hadn't so much as glanced at him since they'd stopped.

-click-.

"I'm still not sure what you're -"

"Shh," Tash hushed, raising a hand to silence him.

"What?"

"Shh!"

They both paused, each standing as still and as quietly as they could as the cool September air blew around them.

-click-.

"There," she said, raising one finger into the wind. "Right there."

"What is it?" Nick asked, his voice hushed.

"Metal scraping... probably against the concrete."

"Is it her?"

She paused again, her eyes fluttering over the horizon line. "No," she said finally, standing up straight again. "No, it's coming from the wrong direction."

-click-.

"What should we do?"

She frowned, scanning the area from one side to the other. "Let's get the hell out of here."

***

There was a deli on fifth street that was famous around town for two major accomplishments: they had the worst meat products of any place that served meat products in Coral Beach, and the best coffee of any place that served coffee in Coral Beach. They even topped Dunkin' Donuts, as hard as it was for anyone from out of town to believe - until they actually tried a cup.

There was one booth in the entire deli that still seemed like it was new, and it attracted the most patrons. Every other cushion had holes and rips in it and springs that struck out in uncomfortable places, but these two adjacent seats had somehow managed to escape the fracas and were comfortable at the same time. Nick sat in one and stared down at his coffee as Tash sipped on hers regularly, pain shooting up the bruise alongside her skull with every sip she took. The gash on his head had stopped bleeding, but it hadn't been hard for the cashier to tell that they'd both seen trouble recently. To his credit, he hadn't asked about it.

"So that's it, huh?" Nick asked, still staring down into his untouched coffee.

"Pretty much," she smiled. It was a warm smile that hurt her lips, but she couldn't help it. He looked sad and cute all at the same time, and her heart went out to him... like a little lost puppy. "Point of it all is, the world's going to hell. In more ways than one... it's been on a tipping scale for quite some time, and now some bastard has come along and decided to give it a little nudge, like someone always does every few decades."

"What does any of that have to do with me?" he asked, almost pleading.

She frowned. "Absolutely nothing," she said honestly, reaching out and taking his hand. "In truth, I don't think much of this does... not really. But I've got a friend who's trying to make it better. And I really think he could... but we figured out a while back that we can't do it alone. We're going to need help."

Nick twitched. "You're talking about me?"

She paused. "... No. No, not you. Maybe someday, but for now, you're too young. It's just not fair. But there are people out there that don't care how fair it is or how young you are. You met one of them here tonight. I think if we'd stuck around, you would've met a second."

Nick turned around and looked out the big windows that lined the deli into the darkness beyond. "They're still out there, aren't they?"

Tash nodded.

"And when you leave... they're going to kill me."

She let out a long sigh. "Probably."

He stared out into the dark for a long moment. "Why me?"

She smiled. "Don't tell me you haven't figured that one out yet."

He turned to her and scrunched up his face.

"I've met a few people with your kind of talent in my time, kid... hell, my friend's tracking one down right now that might have passed his whole life if it hadn't been for a lucky tabloid reporter... but you're not one of them. It's a good mask, I'll give you that, but not to my eye."

His face changed, as though it wasn't sure whether to be hurt of scared or angry or all three.

"Why don't you take out the contacts?"

He swallowed hard, then reached up carefully and touched his eyes lightly with his thumb and index finger. When he withdrew them a coloured contact lens was sticking to each, and when he looked at her again, his eyes were pure, irisless eggshell white. He felt them fill up with tears but forced them back.

Tash got up and moved over to his side of the table, and he immediately broke down and buried his head into her shoulder and started to cry.

"I didn't ask for this," he said after a moment staring out into the darkness beyond the window. He wasn't sure, but he thought he saw something moving in the shadows... like two figures dancing against the night sky.

Tash's face became sallow as the stroked his hair around his ears. "Nobody ever does," she said softly.

***

Sara forced her locker door closed, pinning her History textbook beneath her arm as she put all of her weight into her shoulder. She forced the metal door flush with all the others that lined the hallway, her tongue sticking out the corner of her mouth a little as she did so, the pink of it just different enough from the pink of her lips to be noticed.

"Christ," she sighed, snarling at the sticky feeling under her arms and knowing that she'd have to feel that uncomfortable, muggy feeling the entire walk home now. She turned to see that Nick had been standing beside her locker, and almost jumped. There was a vacant look in his eyes that she'd never seen there before, and it took her a moment to remember the events of the previous night. She resisted the urge to cover her hickey with her hand. "Hey," she said, as soothingly as possible.

"Hey," he replied solemnly. He looked as though he was about to cry, but didn't. There was unshaven scruff on his cheeks; that was news to her, as she hadn't been aware until now that Nick had even needed to shave. There were bags under his eyes and he was wearing his good coat even though it was still far too warm outside for it. The book bag slung over his shoulder looked full.

She shot his a wry look, then smiled. "What's with the hobo look? Is there a new trend I'm not aware of?"

He did not respond, his lips pursed until they were white.

Her smile faded. "Look, if this is about last night..."

"It isn't," he assured her, waving his hand to one side. He locked eyes with her again. He took a deep breath, then reached up and took her chin in his hand. Her skin was soft and warm. He leaned in and their lips met, hers warm and wet and pink against his. She seemed surprised at first, then pushed up on her toes to get closer to him. He put his arms around her waist and held her like that for a long moment before finally breaking it off and letting her back down.

Her eyes were wide and she didn't seem to be looking at him, blinking several times. "Wow."

He smiled, but somehow he still looked sad. He touched her face again, stroked her cheek with his thumb, and almost leaned in for another kiss... but he didn't. He knew that if he did, he wouldn't be able to do what he needed to next.

"I'm going to be gone for a while," he said finally, almost having to force the words out. "My parents are sending me to school down south."

"What?" Sara asked, shaking her head and coming back to reality. "Then don't go."

"Kind of have to," he said, sighing. "I just... can't be a nomad anymore, I guess."

She stared at him for a long moment, then nodded.

"But you stay here, okay? You stay... you. As long as you're here, there'll be a home in Coral Beach for me to come back to."

Her stroked her cheek one last time, then pushed himself off from the locker and walked down the hall and out of the school without looking back once.

She watched him go until he was long out of sight, still feeling his kiss on her lips and the jolt it had given her... there had been something in his eyes that had been different than any other time she'd seen him, and she felt like she never had gotten the kiss from the boy Nick Carry that she'd been wanting ever since eighth grade, but that maybe she'd been the first person to ever lay eyes on Nick Carry the man.

She smiled a little at that, although she wasn't sure why, then turned to the boy standing at the locker next to her.

"So, you going to Julian Grendel's party on Friday?" she asked him, paying little attention to his response or even if he gave one.

JACOBI STREET

1

Chelsea walked into the gift shop a full half hour later than usual, carrying a big gray paper bag with rope handles that stuck up of their own accord. She was wearing a deep-red blazer with two large black buttons just below her central plexus that stared out at him like the bulging pupils of a heavily stoned person.

Bob closed his eyes and tried to make the image go away, turning toward the candy dish alongside the cash. There were a dozen or so chocolates in the shape of the Mona Lisa there. They were wrapped in tinfoil that was supposed to color her curves and contours correctly, but usually just made her look as though she were wearing someone else's skin, like Leather-Face. Once Bob had tried to fix them and had ended up buying twenty or so when the foil had become ripped irreparably.

"Good morning!" Chelsea chimed, laying her bag down against the floor so she could shake the cold out of her hair.

Bob turned and smiled at her, but kept fiddling with the order of the chocolates. "What kept you this morning?"

"Woke up with a hangover," she grinned, rolling her eyes a little. "Stopped by the market to get me a little Vitamin C from Booster Juice and ended up stopping in this quaint little boutique that's opened up there. You know the one?"

"I don't know *all* the boutiques."

"Of course. Well, they had this marvellous little shawl there that I had to try on, and when I was paying for it I saw they had these adorable little handmade necklaces for sale."

"I don't know *any* of the boutiques."

"I told them they should bring a dozen or so by for us to sell. Put them out when they get here, twenty per cent markup. They'll sell."

Bob forced himself to stop fiddling with the chocolates and wiped his palms on his jeans.

"Make it twenty-five. They'll sell. I bought five."

"I'm sure they will. Speaking of, it is the tenth so—"

"Right, the new shipment comes in today. Fuck me, I'm gonna need more coffee in me before I deal with that!" She laughed, shrilly and honestly, slapping the glass counter top. Her hand made her way to the Mona Lisa chocolates then, and when she took one out, she displaced the large semi-circle around it.

"Yes," Bob nodded, letting out a deep sigh. "Yes, definitely. But in addition to that, the tenth is when you said you'd—"

"Actually, can you handle it when the shipment comes in?" she asked, not meaning to interrupt. Not even acknowledging that he had spoken, really. "Don't tell them where to put them, I'll handle that, just make sure everything that's on the list are in the boxes.

Remember the Monet shipment? I swear, if I ever have to deal with that much red tape again, I'll puke like a freshman."

"Charming. Now, I was wondering if we could discuss—"

"I'd love to sweetie, but I've got to go." She smiled and picked up her bag again. The handles bent into odd shapes. "I can't just stand around here talking all day. Some of us have work to do!" She laughed again, then reached over and clasped another chocolate.

Bob reached out and plucked it from her fingers, pressing it back down into its plastic nest. "We're running low."

Chelsea paused and looked at him a moment, their hands touching over the small milk chocolate. After a tense moment, she smiled. "Yes," she said finally, smiling wide. "Duh, Earth to Chelsea, right? Lol."

She actually said 'lol' in speech, making it rhyme with 'doll.' It made Bob cringe every time.

Her fingers parted with his and fluttered deftly away. "Ta," she said, scanning the rest of the candy before leaving the way she'd come in.

Bob watched her go, cursed under his breath, and started arranging the chocolates properly again.

2

Bob leaned against the rotting guardrail that surrounded the unused back stoop of The Menagerie, looking out at the windowless red brick buildings and right angles that made up the back-alley of Jacobi Street. Overhead the sun beat down, reflecting off the stone and asphalt all around him and bathing him in the last of the summer heat. His vision was wavy near street-level, making the lower bricks of the buildings sway to and fro while the rest of them stayed ridged and upright, like old folks dancing the tango. He smiled thinking of that, and made a mental note to paint that at a later date.

Bob had lived on Jacobi Street for the last ten years, his entire life. He was older than ten, was in fact secretly thirty-five, but did not consider those first twenty-five years to have been living. They were more of an extended incubation period, as though he'd walked through his early childhood and teenage years and early adulthood in a fragile shell. Then Jacobi Street had just shattered it, with Bob emerging newly born: naked to the wonder and culture and the extreme heat.

Jacobi Street was famous for exactly one thing: not being famous. It was less than half a mile in length and existed as a side street just to the south of 14th Street. It was a one-way with both the exit and entrance to Jacobi being off 14th, giving it the impression of an appendix or small tumor. It was so small that it was often left off of maps entirely, and Google Maps refused to acknowledge its very existence. When it *was* acknowledged as existing, which was a rarity, it often was in the context of having the most street vendors, markets, theatres, and art galleries per square foot of any street in North America. They'd all been pubs during prohibition, when the small entrance and exit to the street had been false front houses to hide from the local constabulary. The streets were made with beautiful cobblestones, and five years ago the city had passed ordinance to lower the speed limit on Jacobi Street to 10 mph to preserve its natural beauty. That, and its narrowness, contributed to why the only vehicles ever seen on Jacobi Street were delivery trucks. It was the only area in the city where children could still play in the street without fear. There was no need for cars anyway: everyone who lived on Jacobi Street worked on Jacobi Street, though the only apartments were above businesses.

There was a hiss from down below him, a static sound that was nothing like a snake or a cat. He took a puff of his cigarette—the first he'd had in five months—and bent over the precarious wooden railing to see to the bottom of the alley, squinting his almond eyes against the strain of the sun.

Sloan Barkhurst was standing in front of the red brick wall scratching one of her pale cheeks. She had a can of spray-paint in each hand and was absorbed in the paper stencil on the red brick before her, already partially covered in pink and purple and baby blue. Her long brown hair was matted and tied off in random places and was clumped with spots of paint that had gone in wet, stuck together, and since dried.

She wiped her cheek with the back of her hand, smearing pink just under her right eye. She was wearing a white tank-top and camouflage pants filled with pockets that sagged because they were used to carrying cans of spray-paint. She held the a can of purple in her left hand and a can of pink in her right, both at her hips like a gunslinger ready to draw at any moment.

"Jeffrey Dahmer?" Bob called out, taking a puff of his cigarette.

Sloan scratched at her scalp and made a pensive face, though she did not turn for him to see it. "No, Dahmer was last month. Ran out of the yellow I needed for the M for the last few stencils and they just looked weird. Only had five left at the end so I scrapped them."

Bob nodded, leaning to try and get a better look at what she was doing until he felt the rail shift slightly beneath his weight.

Sloan was a self-proclaimed Street Artist. Officially, the state deemed her a 'Graffiti' artist, but she rejected that term as easily as she had rejected most of the terms the state had chosen to bestow upon her, including (but never limited to) terms relating to outmoded codes of gender identity, sexuality, and (briefly) humanity as a whole.

At any given time there were up to twenty street-artists calling Jacobi Street their home base, from which they spread their art throughout the city, each in their own unique style.

There was a Native American man who called himself Emilio, who lived above Cooper's General Market. He made wooden shoes and tied them together and hung them from lamp-poles. Because they were out of the way and took up a space unused by most other artists, they had an extended longevity. Bob had gone for a walk with him once and he'd pointed out a pair of shoes in a colour he hadn't used in seven years. When he put them west of 59th Street the locals had gotten uppity until they realized who had made them, as they had become 'in' in some markets. Now they were still taken down in well-off areas, but instead of ending up in trash bins they ended up on eBay with price tags of two grand and up.

Another street-artist, who was also a self-imposed street-urchin, was Obi. He could usually be found outside The Oz Theatre. He refused to tell anyone his full or real name. When pressed too much for it by those he called 'the authority' he would chuckle "Obi-Wan Kenobi, Motherfucker," typically with a marijuana cigarette clasped between his dried lips. He looked as though he'd time-travelled straight from the 90s punk scene, with three barbell-piercings in each eyebrow and bright jade hair. He made art out of trash, typically fast-food cartons. At one point he and Sloan had broken into The Menagerie late at night and added his plastic cup men to the Memorial Day display, and it was a week before anyone noticed.

Sloan did stencils, a complex form of art that involved paper, paint, knives, and lots of agility. The process began with the purchase each month of a ream of 200 sheets of thin canvas joined at the north end, which Sloan got a special discount on because she had once dated the manufacturer. When the mood struck, but usually once a month, she took her knife to the ream and carved an image into it, employing negative space, carving out the silhouettes or shadows in a face or the space around a letter, much in the way one would carve a pumpkin. The cuts would go all the way through the sheets, and she would have her stencils for the month. She would spend the next thirty days sticking them in strategic places around the city, painting them quickly, then ripping down the stencil and leaving only the color filling in the formally-negative space. The result was 200 hundred identical, yet unique, works of art. There were three websites dedicated to tracking her art, though none were affiliated with her or knew who she was. Last month's stencil had been of Jeffery Dahmer eating a Happy Meal, his cheeks plump and fat. She'd called it *You are what you eat.*

Bob had met her three years ago when she had borrowed a ladder from Eddie and he'd ended up going with her to the freeway at three o' clock in the morning to paint over all the ads and billboards with whitewash, giving commuters an advertisement-free drive to work for the first time in most of their lives. The billboards were back up by ten of course, but anyone driving into work that morning had driven free of what Sloan had called "the capitalist nightmare." Bob had come home to them both covered in white paint and drunk on cheap wine and laughing all over one another. When he'd come in, he'd raised a thick eyebrow at them and that had made them laugh even harder. After several minutes, Eddie had managed to get out the words: "This is Sloan," and that was how he met Sloan Barkhurst.

Sloan made two final sprays with each of the paint cans, repeating the same hissing sound that had gotten his attention in the first place. Her final statements made, she peeled off the paper stencil to reveal her newest masterpiece: a stern-faced Barack Obama giving the viewer the finger. The exaggerated and protruding middle digit had a plump top to it, giving it the impression of a phallus. The pink, purple, and baby blues came down in three stripes all around him and highlighted in various other points.

"Nice," Bob said, taking a quick puff of his cigarette. It was down to the butt now and he was burning the filter, the sick taste of roasting fibreglass filling his mouth. "Does it have a name?"

"*No, We Can't,*" she smirked, stepping back from her work as she shoved one of her cans into her pocket. She turned and looked up at him for the first time since he'd noticed her, just as he was flicking his cigarette out towards the mouth of the alley. "You smoking again?"

"Nope."

"Eddie's gonna kill you."

"Eddie can suck my dick."

"No he won't. He says cigarettes make your cum taste like death," Sloan smiled.

Bob fought the urge to laugh at that and failed. After a moment of chuckling he coughed twice, and the pleasant bubble of his laughter transformed into the sound of his throat rending.

A dull vibration filled the alley. Bob reached into his pocket and pulled out his phone. "Speak of the devil," he said, unlocking it with a swipe of his thumb. There was no need to lock it. He'd lost it twice since living on Jacobi Street, and both times it had been in his mailbox by morning, untouched save for accessing his address. It was a good neighbourhood.

"What's he saying?" Sloan asked, back to examining her work.

"'Bring Twizzlers,'" Bob read aloud, even as he punched in his response.

"Movie night?"

"Movie night." He waited for his answer to send, then put his phone back into his pocket. When he withdrew it it was holding another cigarette.

"Jesus Christ Billy-Bob, what's the deal?"

He took several quick, halted puffs to get the cherry started. The smoke billowed upward and joined the cloud cover that was finally starting to come in. It would rain later, the type of hot rain that could only happen at the end of a hot summer in the city. He could smell it in the air even now.

Sloan watched him and waited for an answer. When she didn't get one, she picked up the baby-blue can of spray paint and added a quick line to the bottom right-hand corner of her piece, giving the hint that Obama was standing in front of something. A podium? Who knew, that was up to the interpreter. If it was a podium, who was he giving the finger to? The American People watching at home? The Conservative Media? She didn't say and didn't want the piece to say: so much of the meaning of art was on the viewer, and she'd said too much already.

"Today the tenth?" she asked finally, willing the newest mark she'd made to dry before the rain came.

"Yeah," Bob said curtly, tapping the ash from the end of his smoke to punctuate it.

She nodded. "Talk with Chelsea didn't go well, huh?"

Bob snorted. "The talk didn't happen. We talked about the new shipment coming in that I have to inventory, because apparently I'm Receiving now, and we talked about some kitschy little necklace that I'm gonna have to find a place for in the gift shop, but that was all we talked about." He took another puff of his cigarette, and then threw it away in disgust, only half gone.

Sloan pursed her lips and nodded, but said nothing.

Bob was a painter. Not a street-art painter like Sloan, Bob worked on traditional canvas. He did landscapes and portraits and the occasional commentary or mood piece. He used a wet-on-wet style with oil paint in a similar fashion to another famous Bob who was also a painter. His work couldn't go on walls as quickly or easily as Sloan's: it had to be bought and mounted and framed and placed purposely on the wall in someone's home or office. So far in his career he had painted at least two-hundred paintings and sold ten. Most of them now occupied a storage unit on 59th Street that he shared with Sloan and Eddie. Sloan kept her name off the lease, and the most incriminating of her art supplies in the unit.

Eight years ago Bob had taken a job at The Menagerie, an art gallery dead in the center of Jacobi Street, as a way of getting his foot in the door and get his art on the walls. As of yet The Menagerie had yet to feature any of his work. It had had a tree with Emilio's wooden shoes hanging from it for a month in the main lobby and, for one glorious month last year, had had Obi's plastic-cup men on display (even though nobody had known), but never his. Chelsea, the gallery curator, had always managed to avoid the topic, although she had bought one of his pieces herself.

His phone buzzed again. He took it out, smiled, then typed something back.

"What'd he say?" Sloan asked, happy for the topic change.

Bob smiled. "He said, 'Shawshank,' with five exclamation points."

"That's a lot of exclamation."

Bob sighed, then chuckled despite himself. He had a throaty chuckle, with a cadence of a machine gun heard while underwater. When he tucked his phone away and looked down again, Sloan had finished putting her paint into her pockets. "Where you headed?"

"UES. Got a score to settle there at one of the Liberal Political Offices."

Bob saluted her, said "Stay safe," then opened the rusted back door to The Menagerie and stepped back into the darkness of the back hall.

3

The shipment was larger than most that came through the doors and took hours to sort out. When he was only a third of the way through the inventory, Bob began to hear the telltale pitter-patter of raindrops against the roof of The Menagerie. By the time he was halfway done, the pitter and patter had morphed into an all-out downpour.

There were three works by Pardy and four by Boone, the last of the latter of which was a ten-foot by eight-foot canvas that took three deliverymen to unload. The frame on it seemed thick, and he doubted that the studs in the wall where it was planned to go would hold it. They'd have to find somewhere else. Not only that, but Chelsea had earmarked it for the third floor, and he didn't envy the person who had to scale the narrow staircase with that particular piece.

There was a print by a young kid named Flaherty from the west coast that was quite good. Bob had taken the front off the crate, not recognizing the name. It showed a girl bathed in fire and the brushwork on the flames reminded him of that one William Blake: pale but lively. The bio card said he was a student, but Bob didn't recognize the name of the Institute as any art school he knew of.

There was a Pollock on loan from MoMa, as part of a series they were doing to commemorate some anniversary. It would replace their current piece, which had its own special room, and was kept locked except for tours. There were three Lairds and five works by Marsh. He didn't look, but assumed they were from her cat period. There was too much, he realized soon, to fit where Chelsea had allocated the space for the collection. They'd have to rearrange the Corben pieces to be all on the same wall to get some of these in.

As the deliverymen became frustrated, he began checking down the inventory list in front of him, making small ticks alongside each entry in pencil. When he was done, there was only one that had no tick next to it, an untitled work credited to O.K. Mal.

He paused and looked around to see if he'd missed something. Three Pardys, four Boones, a Flaherty, a Pollock, three Lairds, five Marshs, but nothing by anyone by the name of O.K. Mal.

"Hey, we're missing one," Bob said, raising his pencil into the air and stabbing at the humidity.

The deliverymen continued wheeling their carts back toward the front entrance.

"Hey," Bob said, looking up from his clipboard and annunciating. A small amount of colour had risen to his cheeks. "I said we're missing one."

A sleepy-eyed deliveryman with the name Nelson embroidered onto the breast of his uniform stepped over and took the clipboard from Bob, scanning his eyes down it. "It's all... here," he said, pausing before the last word for no discernible reason.

Bob tapped the line that the missing painting was on. "This one. I'm looking and not finding it, if I'm not finding it, you can't leave."

Nelson frowned with his big lips, his lower lip sticking out and revealing a thick purple vein running across it. He stuck it in and out contemplatively as he scanned over the assembled crates, then finally made a sudden *pop!* sound with it that made Bob jump. He walked over to where the four Boones all stood in a row, leaned against one another. There was a gap between the first and the second, and he carefully separated them and reached between them, returning with a small thin rectangular crate. He held it up triumphantly, and then handed it to Bob.

The inventory sticker on the lower right side indeed said the piece inside had been done by O.K. Mal, and that the title was unknown.

Bob looked from the sticker to the man, then back to the sticker. The colour left his cheeks and they returned to their normal shade. "You can go," he said flatly, signing the inventory and passing it to the deliveryman.

They left without another word, at least none that Bob heard, as he slowly stepped into Receiving. He walked by memory as he kept looking at the small rectangular crate. The crate was indeed much smaller than any that he had ever taken in at The Menagerie before. It couldn't possibly have held anything larger than an eight by twelve, once the frame was accounted for. It was heavy in his hands though, somehow having weight that belied its small stature: it must have had a very ornate frame or a very thick canvas, or both.

He reached the Receiving office and took out the original copy of the order. On it were the orders for Three Pardys, four Boones, a Flaherty, a Pollock, three Lairds, and five Marshs. He paused, squinted, then read the order again. Three Pardys, four Boones, a Flaherty, a Pollock, three Lairds, and five Marshs. There was nothing on the order form about an untitled piece by anyone named O.K. Mal.

This would not have been the first time this had happened. Shipments came from all over, and sometimes the entries for one order were mistakenly put with another: human error was a problem no amount of technological interference could truly ever account for. Usually Chelsea would report the error and track down the museum it was supposed to have been shipped to, but typically they'd just make room for it, and when the next shipment came in thirty days, it would leave with the deliverymen. Only once had a mistakenly-delivered order not gone on The Menagerie wall, a Georgia O'Keefe that had been desperately needed elsewhere and whose owners had been beside themselves by the time Chelsea had called.

Bob picked up the small crowbar with yellow stripes that usually sat on the desk of Receiving and worked it carefully into the groove of the small crate, steadying it on the desk and rocking the bar back and forth until the nails came loose. With one steady, practised pull, the front of the crate came free and packing tumbled to the floor, revealing the small painting that had caused him so much anxiety just a few minutes before.

It looked to be wet on wet from what he could tell, and quite old. He recognized the brush strokes, the hurried movements, from his own work. Wet on wet was a delicate art, requiring speed and precision and many, many spare canvases for all the versions you ruin. The image was of what looked to be an old style opera house, from the point of view of the singer looking out onto the audience. There were hints of thick red curtains along the sides and across the top, each with gold trimmed rope. The clarity of them was amazing for something so small, though still limited; there was only so small a brush could get.

The dominant features of the piece were the lifelike theatre seats, the perspective of which sloped in for a three-dimensional affect, which was done perfectly. The tone of crimson on each seat was marvellously crafted, slowly getting darker as it went further and further back into the cheap seats and finally faded into a patterned, murky back row, made not completely dark only by the golden pillars that held up the upper balcony, just out of frame.

The audience was not full. It held only nine patrons. In the front there was a portly man with tiny spectacles and a white wig sitting in the left of the second row whose face was blurred, as all faces are on a canvas of this size. Even though it was blurred it had a subtle, whimsical hint of expression on it, one that reminded him of someone who had just had their rear-end pinched on a crowded subway.

Bob smiled, taking out his phone and unlocking it with a swipe of his thumb. He quickly snapped a picture then sent it to Eddie with the caption: 'Check this out.'

The text went through with a small *wooloop* sound. A moment later he got back the reply: 'Thats cool! :) Twizzlers / Shawshank.' He snorted.

He laid the painting upright against the desk, then took out a post-it notepad and pen. He scribbled "find out who—" and stopped, unable to recall the artist's name.

He turned and looked over his shoulder at the painting's reflection in the mirror opposite it, the proportions of at least one patron looking not-quite-right when reversed. Still unable to make out the signature in the reflection, he leaned forward so he could see the painting again, and noticed that the artist had signed his last name first, followed by initials.

He finished his note: "find out who Mal O.K. belongs to" and stuck it on the ornate silver frame before heading back out into the lobby to deal with the rest of the inventory. Outside the rain came down hard.

4

Bob walked into the living room and stopped right in front of the couch. He was dripping wet with the rain outside and carried two gray grocery bags that were as well. There was water pooling in the bottom of them and they reminded Eddie of the way water balloons looked when they were half-full, their contents sloshing around unevenly.

Eddie looked from the bags to Bob, and then back again. A slow, wide grin spread across the lower half of his face as the soft blue light from the television caressed it magnificently. "Did you get them?"

Bob glared at him, his almond-shaped eyes fuming and the pupils within them becoming tiny little needlepoints. His nostrils flared and his lip curled, and Eddie had to keep himself from cracking up with laughter as he pictured little rivets of steam shooting out from each of Bob's ears.

"If you didn't get it, I'd understand."

Bob let out a breath through is nose, rainwater still dribbling down it, fuelled by the wet mop of thinning black hair that lay atop his egg-shaped head like a rug.

"It's hellish out there. Sixty-mile-an-hour winds, at least that's what it said during a commercial." Eddie's grin got larger. He stifled a laugh by tossing a handful of popcorn into his mouth. When most of it had been swallowed, he took a single fluffy piece, clasped it between his thumb and forefinger, and flicked it into the air. He caught it in his mouth, chewed for a moment, then motioned back toward the tv. "You missed your favourite part, by the way. When Andy asks Boggs if he can read."

Bob held out one of the bags before him, his arm meeting his torso at a ninety degree angle. Little spots of water dribbled off the plastic for a moment until he let it go, the bag crashing down onto the couch with a splash.

Water flickered onto Eddie, coating his lap and making him look as though he'd just had a rather embarrassing accident. The bowl of popcorn got it too, soaking into the fluffy kernels and turning them into soggy dead tarantulas.

Eddie looked at him for a moment, not even really noticing the water that was even now penetrating the fabric of his boxers. He turned and craned his head over the top of the bag, peeling away one of the handles to carefully look inside. He smiled, snatched up the bag and brought it to his lap. Humming happily, he reached inside and pulled out a bag of Twizzlers. "They did have them!"

Bob narrowed his eyes at him, then slowly sat down next to him on the couch. The cushion he sat on squished audibly as his bottom found the apex of the puddle he himself had just made, though aside from the sound he barely noticed it. He was already soaked.

He sat there for a moment and then let out a long sigh. The colour on his cheeks almost changed as he did this, going from the pale red it had become back to its typical jaundiced yellow hue. When the breath was complete, he bent over and reached into the remaining bag, his fingers getting wet again as he did so, and withdrew a bag of Lays chips. He opened it and shoved one into his mouth, crunching down hard.

Eddie looked at his unopened bag of Twizzlers, then at Bob's chips, then back again.

Bob turned, noticing this motion as it repeated once again, and rolled his eyes. He tilted the opening of his bag toward Eddie.

Eddie smiled happily, reaching in and grabbing a healthy handful of chips and piling them onto the top of his popcorn. He leaned in and gave Bob a quick kiss on his cold, wet lips. "Thanks Bob."

Bob had met Eddie halfway through his first year on Jacobi Street. He had lived on the Street alone just long enough to realize that he loved it, and not just his life with Eddie. He loved them both equally, with each taking up the same room in his heart. He felt as though he'd learned a lot about himself through his contrast with Eddie. From Eddie's messiness, he'd learned that he was neat. Through Eddie's humor, he'd learned that he could sometimes be uptight. Both things he'd managed to let go of a little, and found himself less stressed as a result. Eddie hadn't just been the ideal partner for him; he had made him better as a person, simply through the virtue of having been there.

It was also through his relationship with Eddie that he had learned that his parents were bigots.

His parents were first generation Asian-Americans, though their parents had not been from Asia. His ascendants had been Asian-Canadians, having been brought from China to help work on the great Canadian Railway in 1892. His grandfather used to tell him there was "one dead Chinaman for every mile of that track." Asians were used to doing dangerous jobs, like bringing nitro into mines to be exploded, or climb caverns with cables slung over their shoulders to set up a pulley system. He looked it up once out of curiosity. The track was 14,000 miles long. He thought of this whenever Canadian friends attempted to postulate their moral superiority over Americans, stating that race relations were so much better in Canada for never having had a slave trade: "Just because your slaves were yellow and not black, doesn't make them any less slaves."

Bob's parents had not had a problem with he and Eddie's relationship purely out of homophobia. Although he'd dated women while he was young and had lost his virginity to his first (and only) girlfriend, he'd realized his true lifestyle preference before leaving home. His father had caught him in bed with David Woodworth mid-way through senior year and they hadn't spoken for a week. At first Bob thought it was out of shame... only to realize it was the natural awkwardness that came from any parent catching their child in bed with any-one when, after a week of silence, his father had poked him proudly in the ribs with his elbow and had said: "Captain of the Football team, huh?" with pride in his voice. For the rest of the year there had been many Football-related sex puns; trying out for the team, going over manoeuvres. They'd even continued into Bob's next relationship, Tim Fowler, until Tim had found out what they were in reference to and had put a stop to it.

Bob had dated several men in college, none of whom his parents had taken issue with. One had even been a house-painter, someone with a 'low' job like Eddie had now. Had it not been for that, he might have given his parents the benefit of the doubt and assumed their disapproval for his relationship was based on class or concern for the well-being of their only son's future: if Bob was going to be a painter, he needed a partner that could bring in the money, a breadwinner. But it wasn't that. In truth he had dated men long enough and prolifically enough in his more promiscuous youthful days that there was only one mitigating factor left as the reason behind his parent's prejudice.

Eddie was Mexican.

Eduardo Alvarez, a third generation Mexican who had begun work at the Quaint Little Theatre. That was the actual name of the theatre, and also quite apt. His job had consisted of constructing and painting sets during a short run of a play called *Marks*, a musical about a detective who was tracking a killer based on the marks he left on the body, and who was also a Marxist. It hadn't lasted three shows, but the sets had been fantastic: so much so that the theatre director had hired Eddie on full-time. He'd commuted back and forth from the East End for the first year he'd had the job before meeting and moving in with Bob, in the big studio-esque apartment above the Hemp Emporium. He'd joked to Bob that he'd "left Mexico to get *away* from the drug-trade" while they were moving his couch up the narrow flight of stairs that led from street-level to the apartment, to which Bob had stone-face humourlessly replied to him: "You've never even *been* to Mexico."

Despite Eddie having never been to Mexico, Bob's parents had had a strong dislike of Eddie from the start and had never let go of it. And it wasn't because of disapproval of his sexuality or that he was with someone not considered economically stable, the reason came down to one thing and one thing only: every other boy Bob had brought home had been white and Eddie wasn't. First-generation Asian-Americans, whose ascendants had been brought to North America to work as slaves in all-but-name on the Central Pacific Railway, who had endured the internment and persecution of Asians by Canadians all through the 40s and who had raised their son with the old canard that all races were equal: racists themselves. One of the last things he'd ever said to his father had been on that very subject: after accusing him of his bigotry, his father had whipped out that old chestnut that all races were equal. "You say that," Bob had said, standing in the back yard of their retirement home in Western Maine, "But what you mean is, *your* race is equal." They'd never spoken again.

Bob squeezed Eddie tight to his shoulder as the rain came down outside.

5

The Corben Popart pieces on the second floor had indeed needed to be moved, just as Bob had thought they would. Previous to the arrival of the large shipment, all ten pieces had been in a horizontal line along the south wall of the second floor corridor. Now they occupied a space less than half that length in the western corridor. They were hung vertically, one on top of the other, their index cards stuck together on the wall just down from them. Bob had hated it: the pieces on top couldn't be appreciated, you couldn't really get up close, but Chelsea had overruled him.

Corben had been a popular part of their Popart series for well over a year and had steadily become the public face of it. Popart was an upper-class way of saying comic book art, although none of the art presented in any of the Popart showings had been remotely to do with comics and had merely been drawn by some of the betters in the medium: your Alex Rosses, your Richard Isanoves. Richard Corben was a mostly underground comic book artist known for heavy inks and tones. He'd worked on comics like *Grim Wit, Slow Death, Fever Dreams*, and had done some fill-in work for the original *Teenage Mutant Ninja Turtles* volume. He was best known, however, for his work on *Heavy Metal* magazine where his realistic portrayals of human anatomy and shading brought the larger-than-life fantasy images on the covers to life, making them leap off the page. He'd won the Spectrum Grand Master Award and had been indicted into the Will Eisner Award Hall of Fame, but no matter how many times Chelsea had to tell that memorized line to patrons visiting The Menagerie, when no one else was around Corben was still 'that comic-book guy.'

Bob had fallen in love with the line work from the moment he'd seen it, and couldn't have been happier when Corben had been one of the artists that had been brought into regular rotation... save of course, if Bob's own art had been. His favorite piece of Corben's was a large landscape that featured a unique Executioner's block. Four women stood around the block bare-breasted, wearing ceremonial headdresses, and stern, dower expressions while another hung back in the shadows. One was reminiscent of Cleopatra, another of Aphrodite. In the center was a tall, proud woman wearing only an executioner's hood and gloves, gripping an axe with both hands at crotch-level. She stood next to a stump and basket used for decapitations, and opposite her was a muscular man in the style of the perfectly-proportioned Greek statues. The nameless figure stared up at her as though in question, but she never returned his gaze. Though it was clear he was meant to place his head upon the stump, from his current position his manhood hovered precariously just above it and to the right of the axe's sharp blade.

The tones of the piece were what had captured Bob's attention at first: that was the key to lifelike human images, it was all in shading and tone. A man could be fully anatomically proportionate, but without a light-source and tone it laid flat.

Bob walked past the piece now, taking a bite of the hummus sandwich that was his lunch. There was a break room but it wasn't necessary: the gallery was all but vacant from noon to one on most days, and any patrons who were wandering about wouldn't mind. Patrons of the arts who found their way to Jacobi Street and to The Menagerie were typically not the type to turn up their noses because someone ate a sandwich in front of them.

Adjacent to the Corben art were the Marsh pieces he'd taken in only a week before during the big shipment. He'd been right without even having to have opened the crates: the pieces had been from her cat period. All five pieces were portraits of cats on vibrant coloured backgrounds: primary colours like yellow and blue and red that made the images they sat behind pop out at the viewer. Her brush strokes were clean and precise, with thick black lines accenting the figures of each fantastical feline. His favorite was a white cat with a Mona-Lisa-smile and a pink eyepatch covering its right eye. Bob smirked as he stepped past it and checked the card, noting the title of the piece: "Butterscotch." He snorted, and the sound echoed throughout the tiled hallway.

He turned at the end of the hall and stepped down the southern corridor, where the Corbens had been until last week. It was a long straight hall that terminated in a dead-end, unless one counted the fire escape hidden on its right. The terminating wall had been the best place to hang something eye-catching. It was where the Corben landscape of the Execution had been, with a small spot-light above it illuminating the piece. It served to create anticipation: when Chelsea did her tours the eyes of the patrons would always go to where she directed them at first, then slowly drift back to the piece highlighted at the end of the hall: "I wonder what that is?"

Now one side of the hall was home to the three new Pardys and the other to the four Boones that had come in. Pardy was a painter that used quick, expressive strokes to tell her stories. She was often called an expressionist, but dabbled in pop from time to time, and had become famous for constantly tweaking her works until they were out of her possession, sometimes even when they had been already paid for by a buyer. The most famous example of this had been a mood piece she'd titled 'fall' in the style of Pollock with oranges and reds and yellows splashed about the canvas with reckless abandon. It had been seen at a show and a young starlet had fallen in love with it and had paid the twenty-thousand dollar price for it on the spot, ordering it to be delivered to her flat the next week. When it arrived, Pardy had added a large triangular 'rip' painted into the center of the canvas, from which a man in a 60s era spacesuit poked his helmeted head out, his stubbly fingers holding onto the canvas to escape the star-field behind him. When the starlet had called, angry about the addition, Pardy had cooly answered: "The astronaut had always been there, she just hadn't painted him yet."

At the end of the hall now, in that coveted, spotlighted place, was the unnamed and unclaimed wet-on-wet of the theatre by O.K. Mal.

The formerly dull silver frame had been polished to a mirror shine since the last time Bob had seen it, and it glinted in the ambiance of the spotlight. The light reflecting off it moved and morphed as he got closer to it, bending and taking on new shapes as it travelled along the warped bends and creases on the weathered frame.

Bob put the last of his sandwich into his mouth and sucked the bit of excess hummus from his finger as he closed the gap between himself and the subtle white line on the floor that indicated how close one should get.

The man wearing the wig in the front row still appeared as comical to Bob as he had the first time he had seen it. Though his eyes were normal, they were overshadowed by the spectacles he wore and the glint from the light-source of the stage on them. The artist had made it seem as though these were his eyes, which made the already miniscule pug of a nose seem shorter still. His flabby cheeks seemed to vibrate, his mouth curled open in a bow as he just slightly turned around, adding to the overall expression that he was reacting to someone laying hands on his backside. The only person behind him was a large black man in overalls and a faded yellow shirt patted with dust and debris.

Bob smiled and furrowed his brow. Could this be a comment on race relations? When had this painting been produced? He had at first assumed it to have been at least a hundred years old from the style, but if that sort of message was in play that early on and it was intentional, then that would be quite impressive. So much so that he wasn't sure how he'd missed it before.

He checked his watch. He still had fifteen minutes of his break left. He smiled, wiped his finger on his pant leg, then brought his hand to his mouth contemplatively and looked back at the black man.

He was sitting alone in the third row, despite the fact that there were eight other patrons in the theatre. His shoulders were hunched over and his jowls saggy and depressed. There were red rings under his eyes and he stared out at the viewer forlornly, looking impossibly tired. He did not address the man in the front or seem to acknowledge him in any way, though now it seemed clear that the man in the wig was looking back in his general direction with concern.

Bob locked eyes with the large, bald black man, and for a moment the painting was almost so real he could step inside it. The man looked angry and sad all at the same time, yet resigned somehow. That racial tension, that anger... was that what this was about? He'd always tried to take what bothered him most about a piece and use that as a way of considering what the piece was actually *about*. With effort, he tore his gaze away from the steely eyes of the African and moved them up to the next row.

Just over the black man's left shoulder was a slender, gaunt woman with short cropped hair. She looked like a flapper girl, but couldn't have been. She was wearing a loose top that hid her breasts almost completely, and there were shimmering sequins down either side of the neck. She was dirty-blonde like Sloan, and had a hint of a smile somewhere behind her cheeks. It teased and played: a reference to the Mona Lisa, or a coincidence of the brush? It was hard to say.

Behind the flapper girl was a rough looking, scruffy man with sunken eyes. He had a long length of dark brown hair and wore a proper suit for the time period: that sort of puffy shirt that poofed out from the neckline. The hint of his belt, visible over the woman's shoulder and the seat in front of him, gave the impression that it was large and gold. His face was curled up in a sneer and his eyes were black. His cheek had been bloodied with a series of scratches.

Several seats to his right were a mother and child. The child was at its mother's exposed teet, the neckline of her dress hiked down to accommodate it. Its gender was ambiguous. It was nude and facing away from the stage. The woman however looked out at the viewer pleadingly. There were brush strokes down the face that were not present on any of the other patrons... the hint of tears? Her mouth was open in a wail to add credence to this. She wore a bonnet, pulled back to show the auburn hair on her sweat-strewn face.

Bob shivered, unnerved. The woman stared right into him, pleading with him, as her child drank from her. His eyes turned, involuntarily, back to the black man in the third row. He was angry about something, and this woman was scared. She seemed scared for her life, although the only reference Bob had for such things was in fiction.

On the next row up, seated almost an equal distance from the woman and the grim man, was a knight. He wore mail and had his helmet at his side and the sort of long blonde hair and unshaven gruffness one would expect of a classic portrayal of a knight. He wore a long white sash with a red cross on it and stood upright and straight, his eyes dead ahead but looking at nothing, as though he were standing guard over the five sitting below him. His chin was tight in a magnificent representation of a 'stiff-upper-lip.'

Finally, there were two women on either side of the knight in the row behind him: a nurse and a prostitute. The prostitute looked salaciously toward the stage with a wry smile, sitting in her seat lengthwise with one foot in the air. Her squared blouse showed her bosom to excess, almost as much as the mother who was feeding. The nurse sat quietly forward with her hands in her lap, the way people used to sit for portraits before cameras were invented. She wore a small paper hat and looked forward, but her eyes betrayed her: they darted to the right, towards the whore. Were these the angel and the devil on the Knight's shoulders? Bob looked back at the it, suddenly reminded of the Knight from the Wife of Bath's Tale from *The Canterbury Tales*. Did the women represent the Knight's choice between a hag and a maiden? Were they his warring morality, his desires as a man which had gotten him into trouble versus his virtue as a knight?

Behind the two women was only the darkness and shadow of the back of the theatre, framed by gold, inlayed pillars that matched the picture's frame itself.

The dark had seemed so fully dark when he'd seen it in the Receiving room, but now he saw that there were hints of purple in it as well. One winding S-shaped brush stroke, almost a semi-circle but not quite, was particularly noticeable. He squinted and leaned in, raising his hand to block the light from the spotlight to make sure it wasn't some trick of the light or reflection.

"The distributer doesn't know where it came from," Chelsea said.

Bob jumped slightly, pressed his hand to his chest, then smiled. "You startled me."

She smirked, then nodded toward the painting. "I decided to hang it until they sorted it out."

Bob turned back to the piece and nodded. Absently, he asked: "What do you tell people on tours?"

She shrugged. "That we don't know. Adds to the mystery."

Bob nodded. His eyes had gone back to the black man, who still stared out at him with an anger that would have been better described as vengeful fury. Bob noticed, for the first time, that there were three small gashes on the man's barrel of a chest.

He stepped back from the piece, realizing he'd inadvertently stepped over the white line while examining it, although Chelsea hadn't seemed to mind. The picture as a whole told a story, like the Hogarth etchings and portraits. These paintings of multiple figures always told a story and interacted with one another and said something about the society they came from: like ethnographic time capsules, perfectly capturing the culture and mood of that moment and place in human history.

"Remember to leave the key with Mr. Cooper tonight on the way home; he's going to deliver some refills to the gift shop once he closes up the General Market, okay?" Chelsea asked, checking something on her clip board. Bob kept looking at the picture, finally drawing her attention. "Hey? Your break's over."

He looked at his watch, nodded, and apologized.

6

Bob and Eddie stood on either side of the stage painting, with Sloan dead in the center. She was sitting cross-legged with her hair tied into a quick-and-messy bun that protruded from one side of her head, munching on dried mango with a sheet curled around her. She was wearing a black tank top that may well have covered no more than a sports bra on more-endowed women, showcasing just how miniscule she really was. She ate her mango and almonds mostly in silence, turning her head from one side to the other depending on who was speaking to her but otherwise remaining relatively still.

Had anyone been in the theatre to see, it might have looked like a scene from an indie comedy play. "Three's A Crowd" or "Odd Woman Out" would be the title, the story of a free-spirited young manic-pixie dream-girl who bridges the gap between two dissolved lovers. But the theatre was void of presence except for the three of them, and the distance between the two men was practical, not emotional: they were both painting.

To stage left, Eddie stood with a large, broad paintbrush making wide, firm strokes on the wooden figure he'd cut out not twenty minutes before from wood. He was applying a cream base before adding details to what would, eventually, be an image of Buckingham Palace for a small play titled *Et Tu Berlusconi*, which told of an alternate history in which Silvio Berlusconi had married the aging Queen Elizabeth in 1982. It starred an all-female cast, and the image of the twenty-something star bound and dressed as Berlusconi in the rehearsals made Eddie crack up every time he saw it. Twice last week he'd woken from sleep laughing about it, rousing Bob at the same time.

To stage right, Bob had sprayed the spatter from his oil paint all over the mat they'd laid down over the entire stage. There was a metal spiral at his feet between the legs of the easel that he used to beat the excess paint off of his brush when he was done with a colour for the moment. His palate was held out in front of him with a steady left hand, always at his side. It was a large circular piece of Plexiglas, its translucence worn away from years of use and scrapes with his knife. The knife sat on the tray of the easel now, one side of it caked in the adobe red he'd created.

He was painting the red brick walls of the ally he'd seen the other day with Sloan while having a cigarette. The buildings arose out of nothing, over the fog and ether of the smog and continued up past where the eye could wander. With great effort, he had used the edge of his knife to shift the paint on the lower halves of the tenement buildings back and forth until it had the same wavy, hot appearance it had had that day. Now he painted frantically, adding 'street art' to the red bricks of the buildings to give the impression of an elderly couple dancing, their legs blurred by the same waves of heat.

Sloan leaned back as far as she could, until she could see over Bob's shoulder. "Nice," she said, crunching on an almond. "Alley outside The Menagerie?"

Bob nodded, a motion barely perceptible from Sloan's point-of-view.

"The window on the right building looks amazing. It's like a photograph of the real thing."

Bob smirked. "Thanks," he said, turning toward her slightly, but not enough to even see her. He was working quickly, trying to get enough of the paint down before it started to dry. This was the hectic nature of wet-on-wet, and it was what made him not understand how others found it so relaxing. For him it was stressful, but a good kind of stressful: the type that amazing art was born from. He entered the first stroke tentatively, and by the third he had worked himself into a fury. Each painting was like a baptism through fire, and the image that came out the other side was better having survived the warzone of its creation.

Eddie turned to watch Bob for a moment. Bob had paint in his thinning hair, Eddie had paint on his cheek. Bob's energy of activity made him smile: there was something about him in the zone of creation, although it appeared so stressful, that brought a kind of serene calm to him. He took a deep breath, and then turned back to the leisurely pace with which he painted on the white base of Buckingham Palace. "You know Allie went home with that girl from the Fall Festival, right?" he said, absently.

Sloan's head whipped around so fast that her ponytail shifted its precarious placement. "Pardon?"

Eddie smiled. "Yea she went back with her and they spent the weekend together upstate."

"Poor Martin."

"Oh, Martin knows."

Sloan started to raise her eyebrow, then caught herself and laughed, shaking her head with bemusement. "Only Martin could justify staying with a girl that so clearly has no interest in him."

"You know they haven't been together in a year?" He bent down and got his drink cup and slurped through the straw.

"For real?"

"What I heard."

"Man."

"What I heard."

Bob pushed the canvas gently with one finger and let it crash to the floor, making the other two jump.

"What the heck?" Eddie asked without accusation.

Bob looked down at the piece which had landed upright and looked up from the dirty sheet at him. "It won't come out right. The couple... they look like marionettes."

"I thought that was intentional," Sloan smirked, playing with her own hair. "It's what I like about it."

"It wasn't."

"I swear I can see the strings, and their little joints where the pins get stuck like in the Robaxacet commercials."

"It wasn't though."

"Sloan," Eddie coughed, stepping away from his work. He passed the distance between stage left and stage right until he was just a foot from Bob, where he stopped suddenly as if Bob had a shield around him. He waited there as Bob took several deep breaths, his back and shoulders rising and falling, then stepped forward and put a firm, gentle hand on his neck.

Bob stirred briefly, twitching. Eddie kept his hand where it was, and eventually Bob brought his own hand to it and clasped it, giving it a tight squeeze.

Sloan arose; distressing the cloth at her feet until it inadvertently looked like an eggshell had risen in the center of the stage. She stepped lightly on her toes like a ballet dancer, her hair falling against her shoulder wildly until she'd found her way around Bob and Eddie, to where the picture lay. She picked it up gently by the dry canvas on one side and turned it until it was right-side-up, regarding it with a clenched brow and strumming her finger against her upper lip.

"It's a good painting," Eddie said finally, tapping the heel of his hand against the nape of Bob's neck.

Bob huffed through his nostrils, then calmed, massaging Eddie's hand with his own and leaning his head back. "It's not good enough. It looks like an assembly-line painting."

Eddie smirked. "Maybe that's why I like it. They're all the rage back home."

Bob rolled his eyes, but laid his head on Eddie's hand.

Sloan continued pressing her lips between her index and middle fingers. Her eyes moved from one part of the painting to another, finding each new element organically and lingering there. "It really is good," she said, mostly to herself. Her voice was far more critical than it typically was: there was no padding to her comments but no barbs either. The free-spirit had gone for a moment, to be replaced by the traditionalist buried deep within. "The brushwork is immaculate. The bricks are porous and catch the light correctly... it looks like you could step into it."

Bob turned and smiled at her. "Thanks, really. But it's not good enough." He reached for it and Sloan pulled it back. She withdrew a spray-paint can from her cargo pants and held it outstretched towards him like a weapon.

"Back!" she yelled, laughing. "Thou hast assaulted this maiden before! Not again!"

Eddie laughed as Sloan started to back up, spidery legs walking back towards the center of the stage while pinning the painting to her chest and keeping the spray-can aimed in Bob's general direction. When she was back to the eggshell rose she'd created, she stopped and pulled back the painting, checking it quickly to make sure she hadn't damaged it.

Bob looked at her, sighed, then started to laugh despite himself.

"You can have it back when you're in your right mind, and not before!" she said, thrusting her fist into the air when she said *and not before*, and yelling as though she were at a pro-choice rally. She tucked the painting under her arm guardedly. She looked like a cartoon character, her hair moving as though independent of the rest of her, her motions translating to it until long after she stopped.

Bob smirked, and then shook his head. He set up a new canvas on his easel, but after several minutes of staring at it, he moved to stage left to help Eddie, and did not start a new piece.

7

Frederick Cooper put the last of the tiny artisan chocolate Mona Lisas into their cardboard cradle, fastening the plastic crate that held them closed. The cooler had already been filled with carbonated drinks—there had been more Mountain Dew than he'd expected to be gone this week for some reason—and the gelatin-based candy packets had been topped up. Maps and pamphlets had been placed correctly and a bin of assorted brand-name chocolate bars had been topped up to its fill-line. The postcard rack had been filled and rotated. The ice-cream cooler had had its old stock rotated out and the new rotated in. He straightened the last of the stubborn Mona Lisa chocolates and then stood with his hands on his hips, surveying the gift shop in the glow of twilight until satisfied that he was done. He nodded once to himself, twitched his bushy white mustache, then picked up the remainder of his supplies and left the gift shop for Bob to contend with in the morning.

Frederick had lived on Jacobi Street for almost forty years, and for most of that time he had run Cooper's General Market. It hadn't always been *called* Cooper's General Market, but it had always been there in one form or another. For the first ten years he'd owned it it had been Davidson's General Store, a testament to his father-in-law from whom he'd inherited the business. After enough people had told him he'd honoured the man for long enough it had become Cooper's General Store for twenty years, until he saw the changes in the buying habits of those that lived on the street (and indeed, even in himself) and decided to make the change to Cooper's General Market. There was something about saying "I'm going to the market" that his clientele found cathartic when contrasted with "going to the store," and he found that he liked the way it rolled off the tongue as well. He sold seeds and artisan goods and unpasteurized pickles. He sold blankets made from wool from cruelty-free farms upstate that were hand-woven by local working mothers, bought and sold at living wages. He had embraced the sustainable market wholly and found that while he'd never felt bad about himself before, he felt good about himself now. His wife however had loved the change, embracing it fully and doing much of the product research herself. It was she that had struck the deal with The Menagerie, making sure to keep the highest-selling candy items available in The Menagerie and out of the Market's shelves to make sure they maximized profit without compromising what they held in their space.

The hallways of The Menagerie were long and dark in the evening. Sunlight was damaging to most paintings so there was very little natural light allowed in. When the running-lights were brought down and only the sleepy blue emergency lights were left, the halls had an impression of being permanently shadowed.

Frederick stepped down the dark second-floor hall now, unwrapping one of the chocolates absently as he did. He brought its milk chocolate head to his mouth and took a bite. The echo of his footfalls bounced and reverberated off the walls before finding their way back to his ears, the sound foreign to him by the time they did. Each footstep sounded like three in the cool light. The lights placement was such that the shadows cast on the paintings by the frames made each painting seem like a pitch black canvas. They weren't though. As Frederick passed each one, he saw details come into view, muddied through the fog of his poor vision in the evening, but there all the same. The harsh whites of the Corben illustrations came out even clearer now, the pale nude women in it shining like beacons in a sea of shadows. The black hood of the executioner sunk into the blackness surrounding it, giving the eye and mouth holes a skeletal appearance.

This had been the true perk of doing business with The Menagerie, Frederick had long thought. Not getting the carbonated beverages and gelatin off his shelves while still making money off them, not expanding his shelf space without having to pay for more real estate, this: for a brief period of time once a week, once he was done filling the stock, he had The Menagerie all to himself: his own private art gallery. What was more, he had it as nobody else in the world could have it; for the paintings were one thing in the day and quite another when under the veil of shadow. If anyone needed any proof of that, he referred them to play with the brightness and contrast on any photo they owned digitally and note the results.

He'd learned that Jackson Pollock was haunting in shadow, those bright oranges and yellows becoming eerily still. If colours could lie in wait for you to look away, that was what these colours did. The yellow hung back between the red and the orange, thinking it was camouflaged, like a predator convinced you cannot see it. Either action: proving you know it's there, or turning away, could prove fatal. He'd learned that Boone sometimes used fluorescent paints to change her images, making them mirrors of themselves when viewed in the dark. He'd never seen that in any of the literature he'd tried to find on her, and had decided to keep it his secret, something intimate that only he and the artist knew.

That was the truest word for this feeling: *intimacy*. He knew the paintings the way no-one else did, for he knew them as they looked at night when no-one else was around. To see someone in the dark, bathed in the blue light that was all-too like that of the moon was to know them in their flesh alone, to see them vulnerable, their secrets laid bare. When he had these paintings alone for a few minutes each week, they were his. He had never once contemplated cheating on his wife, seeing The Menagerie at night was as close as he'd ever gotten.

At the end of the hall there was one light still on, spotlighting the portrait oil of the theatre and casting black shadows on all the paintings around it. Frederick stopped and tilted his head at the piece, brushed the last of the chocolate from his nose, then stepped closer to examine it.

Nine figures sat in the seats of an old theatre. They were arranged in a way that was seemingly random at first, and Fredrick was sure it was meant to seem as though they were random, but thought they must have been arranged to say something by the artist.

Seated the furthest back were a Knight and two women, each of the females sitting behind and to either side of the Knight.

The Knight was wearing chainmail and clasped a sword, the hilt of which was gripped at his central plexus, the blade disappearing into the chair below him. He was square-jawed with pronounced cheekbones, and long blonde hair that came down in front of his eyes as far as his nose. His head was tilted upward and his mouth was not quite straight, giving the appearance of a sneer or a half-opened yell.

His eyes were almost invisible under that mop of sweaty blonde. They each appeared as large white splotches, almost too big for the rest of the features of the face.

Fredrick stared at the man made of oil and lead for a moment, then pulled his eyes away with some effort, swallowing hard.

The woman on the left wore a low-cut blouse and looked like the prototypical barmaid, of the type one was likely to see during Oktoberfest. Her body was leaning against the seat in front of her, showing off her ample bosom, leaning both toward the viewer and the Knight. Her face was turned away though, back towards the black in the back of the theatre, exposing the nape of her slender, supple neck.

The woman on the right side of the Knight appeared to be a nurse. She wore a small paper hat with a cross indicated on it in a shade just off from the rest of the hat. Her hands were in her lap and her body positioned forward, but she was turning back as if caught in mid-motion looking at the shadows behind her.

Fredrick bent closer, his nose almost touching the canvas.

In the dark blues and blacks that made up the vanishing point of the back of the theatre were a series of several small, purple swivels and one large S-shaped line. The swivels looked like something out of a Van Gogh: several small brushstrokes making something whole when viewed together. The small strokes were grouped below the large, slanted S-shape, contained by it.

Fredrick squinted.

Above the swivels were two deep red dots, almost so faint they weren't visible.

8

The static hiss of Sloan's paint-can filled the alley behind the theatre, along with the antiseptic stench of aerosol paint. She moved her hand back and forth in precise motions, pasting the stencilled outline of Barak Obama to the granite accent with bright blue paint until it was impossible to tell one from the other. She missed a large triangular section jutting in from the left side into Obama's suit.

"You missed a spot," Bob said from his vantage point over Sloan's shoulder. He was pinching his nose to dissuade any fumes from the spray can. It made his voice higher and more nasal than usual. In his opposite hand he held two more of Sloan's stencils, rolled up and tucked under his arm.

Sloan shrugged, not bothering to move the millimeter it would take to aim her spray-can at the void dagger currently stabbing into the heart of the forty-fourth President.

Bob twitched, shifting from foot to foot.

Sloan wiped some of the sweat from her brow, leaving a small trace of paint between her eyebrows. Her hair was wild. She had taken it down before dragging Bob outside the theatre with three of her stencils in tow. It had stayed mostly in place on the left side of her head for a few minutes, held together by some magic or (more likely) clumped together with paint, but it fell apart when a gust of wind had touched it and was now all around her like a lion's mane. She kept forcing it out of her line of sight, pushing it this way and that, never forcing it into the same position twice.

She caught him twitching out of the corner of her eye, moved her can to far east, and pressed the trigger. A line of blue paint not congruous with the rest of the picture appeared, jutting out from where Obama's raised middle finger would eventually be.

Bob huffed under his breath.

Sloan smiled. "What was up with the painting in there anyway?" she asked. She shoved the blue can into her cargo pants, still oozing paint, and withdrew the hot pink.

"What do you mean?"

She smirked and hunched her shoulders. When she spoke her voice was artificially deep and had an accent like a cave-man. She was doing an impression of Bob that was actually just an impression of all men in general: "Not good enough. Not good enough."

Bob lowered his eyebrows. "Droll."

"Thanks," Sloan smiled, making several calculated lines with the pink paint that would, when done, be the shadows on Obama's face and tie.

Bob watched her, knowing that right now it looked like a blue rectangle (with too little paint in a triangle on one end, and too much in a phallus on the other) with a few lines of hot pink spattered on, but that soon when she peeled away her original stencil it would transform into a recognizable representation of Barack Obama, giving the finger with a stern, paternally disapproving face.

"Well?" she asked, making one last mark with the pink before shoving it away and bringing out a can of deep black, almost the colour of India Ink. The pocket she took it from had a large sticky blotch of it along the bottom.

Bob twitched, then frowned, his ears moving along with his lower lip. "The painting was fine I guess. It was just too cartoony. It wasn't good enough for the gallery... for Chelsea."

Sloan looked at him for a long moment, then shook her head and turned back to her art, making several small, precise lines deftly to accent the President's features. "Bad reason to do art," she said finally, and not without a modicum of judgement.

She grasped the stencil by a corner she'd deliberately left loose and peeled it away in one quick motion, the excess paint falling away to reveal Barack Obama giving the finger to any who passed by. She'd drawn sunglasses on him with the black can at the last moment, leaving gaps in the frame to show through the pink paint, giving the impression that they were actually reflecting something pink in front of him.

Bob smiled.

"You like?" Sloan asked, wadding up the stencil for disposal. "I call this variation, *Cool Obama Don't Give a Shit*."

"You've been watching too much Randall."

She laughed. She turned and looked at it for a moment, watching as some of the paint from the sunglasses ran and dripped down Obama's face, a periodic consequence of doing spray-paint wet-on-wet. She ran her fingers back through her hair, not out of frustration, but because she loved the feeling of her nails on her scalp. "You know there's the Print Shop over on Anderson that has this great wall... great wall, adobe and shale base, all the street artists that know about it use it. It drives the owner nuts, he goes out every morning with a can of pressurized water to beat it all off. But the wall faces the morning traffic and catches the light just right, so it's almost worth it: you've gotta be quick. You've gotta get your thing up there in the night and know that by eleven AM the owner is gonna have it down, but you'll definitely get seen by that seven-to-eleven traffic so it's almost worth it. Anyway, I put *Where Are the Ponies* there and I liked the way it looked even though it ended up in a puddle at the guy's feet a few hours later, so when I did *Revenge of the Nerds* with that Sheldon guy as the nerd standing on Bush's head I put it up there too. Eleven AM, down it comes. I spray it on, he sprays it off, circle of life."

Bob nodded. "There a point to this?"

"Sure is. So I do three more pieces there: I do *Fuck Jonas* and *Why Stop Dreaming Just Because You Wake* and *Print is Dead*. I skipped the *Fuck for Chastity* pastiche because I think I remember someone telling me the guy's brother lost a leg overseas and I didn't want to be a dick."

"Big of you."

"Yeah. So I stuck around at the coffee shop across the road after I do *Print is Dead* and get a scone and a red eye, and as the sun comes up and people start to walk back and forth I see people start to notice the piece. I don't usually stick around to see people see it. It was the one with Rupert Murdock with the little black Charlie Chaplin 'stache."

Bob lowered his eyebrows. "Chaplin. Right."

Sloan laughed. "So these people start to look and they point and they start to talk. Some of them take pictures of it: I guess they know it'll be gone before too long, so if they want one they'd better take it now. I see a lot of people taking pictures, and I noticed a few of them show up on those 'Street Art' apps, with the location tags? Well, the owner must have noticed too, because when I came back to do *You Are What You Eat* last month, it wasn't gone. The guy had framed it, with glass and everything so that nobody else could go over it. There was this little engraving on the bottom edge of the frame: art by Sloan. They'd even tried to do my name like my signature, they screwed the N though."

Bob nodded, his brow furrowed. When she held out her hand for the stencils he handed them to her. "I suppose I'm supposed to get some kind of message from this? Do the art you want and the recognition will come?"

Sloan smirked. "I broke the glass and spray painted over *Print is Dead* in deep black. I don't think I'll go back there again, fucker can keep his nice wall. I kept the engraving though: pried it off and stuck it to my headboard. It trips the shit out of guys I have over when they notice it."

Bob paused in mid-step, shaking his head. "Why?"

"Because they're about to cum and I'm sucking on their neck, and all of a sudden they look up and see 'Art by Sloan' there with my signature on it. It's funny as shit."

"No, I mean—"

"I know what you meant," she smiled. "Because the moral of the story is: fuck recognition. The art is the art, and if I'd wanted it in a frame I would have painted it on a canvas."

They walked to the apartment tenement across the street and Sloan started pasting up her next stencil.

9

Fredrick Cooper hadn't been home in three days. His wife had tried to call the police for the first time on the first evening, when he'd been too late coming home from The Menagerie, but they'd told her that he'd have to be missing for at least twenty-four hours before they'd open a case file. At the end of the second day they had, in fact, opened a case file and found that Chelsea had already prepared the relevant security camera footage into a DVD for them: most of the cameras inside The Menagerie were dummies, with only a few protecting the entrance and some of the more expensive pieces. The footage showed Mr. Cooper finishing up for the evening in the gift shop and then turning to go through the halls, which Chelsea told the officers was common and not a problem, and his wife confirmed. Several shots taken from cameras targeting prominent pieces showed Mr. Cooper, either in shadow or in partial, passing by them. There was no footage of his leaving The Menagerie, but Chelsea assured the officers that she'd looked high and low for him, and that he must have left through the back exit.

The entire next day there had been no sign of him, nor had there been today. It was past the forty-eight hour mark when things were the most likely to turn up, and some people had already begun to assume that poor, sweet Fredrick Cooper had been the victim of a mugging gone wrong and were just waiting for someone to discover the body in some obvious-yet-overlooked corner of Jacobi Street.

Bob stared at the MISSING poster that Chelsea had put up on the sliding glass door of the Gift Shop, right at eye-level where people could see it. Usually there were several posters there, advertising upcoming exhibits or local shows on The Street or future events, but Chelsea had removed them all so that nothing could detract from the photo of Fredrick Cooper, cropped from a family photo taken while on vacation in Hawaii last summer. She'd printed it on high-quality paper in bright true-life colour, the pinks and blues of the festive tee he'd been wearing showing against the bright blue of the day. There was another version pasted to the front of the cash register, that one in black and white. She'd printed hundreds of those herself and had given them to Mrs Cooper, who had attempted to pay her for the printing cost and had been shooed away.

He picked up one of the small chocolate Mona Lisa dolls that Fredrick delivered every week, feeling the supple milk-chocolate body become pliable under the heat of his fingertips almost instantaneously. He reached into his pocket, produced two dollars, and then put it in the till without taking his change. He unwrapped the chocolate, cutting through the famous smile inadvertently, and ate the candy while staring out into the void space of the hallway.

"It's your break," Chelsea said as she stepped past his field of vision on her way to the drink cooler.

Bob straightened, startled. He should have heard her heels approaching all the way from her office, but he hadn't taken notice of her until he couldn't avoid her anymore.

She took a Mountain Dew from the cooler and pressed it against her brow, bosom, then back to her brow again before opening it. She took a long swig and motioned to him.

He took out a small booklet from under the cash, opened to a page with a green tab, and put a tick under 'Mountain Dew.' The page was headed 'Chelsea' and currently there were nine ticks under the heading Mountain Dew.

Once a quarter of the bottle was gone she gasped and released it from her lips. "Sorry," she said, wiping her lips. "I was out for a run this morning, took some of the posters with me. Did you put up any?"

"All around my building. I gave some to Sloan, she's going to take them when she goes out into the city and put them wherever she puts her art."

Chelsea nodded, then eyed the chocolate wrapper and the book.

Bob made the 'money' motion by rubbing his fingers together, nodding toward the register.

She nodded and took another gulp of her drink. "Go. It's your break."

He stepped out from behind the register and was about to walk past her, when he stopped himself. "Actually I was hoping we could talk again about maybe getting some of my stuff into the gallery."

She stopped on her way behind the cash to cover for him, turning back to him and looking him up and down.

"We said we'd talk about it on the tenth, but with the shipment and everything and getting in the new stock, we got distracted." *She* got distracted, he'd wanted to say, but restrained himself.

She took another, smaller, more contemplative sip of her drink, and then laid the bottle down on the glass postcard display. She paused to swallow, so long that she could have shot-gunned the entire bottle. "What do you have?"

He forced himself not to look hurt. She knew well and good what he had, had seen it multiple times. Had she forgotten or was this just a tactic to delay the conversation? The latter he suspected, but he couldn't back out now. "The cityscape landscape is still my best I think. There are a few good Natures and Still-Lifes I did while I was vacationing upstate. I've done a few quick portraits of the old men playing chess down at the park... I painted them but only in greys and blacks, so it's a painting that *looks* like those charcoal sketches, kind of experimenting with mixed-medium, but not really."

Chelsea nodded. "The cityscape has potential, and the men playing chess. I can see that all in a line, you know?"

Bob nodded, smiling.

She took a sip of her drink again, swishing it back and forth between her cheeks as she thought. "What's on the wall now is staying there for at least thirty days, or at least until we find out what's up with that mystery piece. I think I've still got some of your stuff on my phone. Tell you what, go to your break and I'll think it over, but it'd be best to wait until the tenth to talk to me, when we can actually do something about it."

His smile faded. He nodded again, then turned and made his way out into the hall.

'The Tenth' was the death knell of anything happening with any acquisition at any time, whether Chelsea knew it or not and he suspected she did. The tenth of every month was the arbitrary date which the previous curator had decided that any changes to the lineup would happen: old works came down and new works went up. It was chosen to coincide with the end of the business month, and although Chelsea had changed *that* when she started, the tenth had become recognized as the day when The Menagerie changed its displays by the community and she had kept that the same.

No new works could be decided upon until the old works were taken down... the problem was that by the time the new works had been taken down, Chelsea had already toured the city and seen the new pieces she wanted and hand-picked and ordered them: the wall-space a new artist was to enquire about was already spoken for and as such was unavailable.

She'd taken in the Boones and the Pardys after an extended stay at a bed and break-fast where a few of the pieces had hung. She'd seen a poster with Corben's art on it advertising his appearance at a local comic-book convention and had decided he would be perfect for her pop-art exhibit without knowing much more about his work with *Heavy Metal* or anything else about him: she saw something she liked out in the world and decided she had to have it.

That was how Richard Corben, a wonderful artist to be sure but a glorified funny-book painter to most who knew him, and a relative unknown to the rest of the world at large, had gotten an all-but-in-name permanent exhibit in the only art gallery on Jacobi Street while he still had yet to get a single piece on the wall. Bob had considered running off some cheap prints at Kinko's and pasting them around town in places he knew she frequented, perhaps advertising a fake convention, but had decided against it. For one thing, the money spent on prints was better off spent on rent.

Even someone literally unknown, like O.K. Mal, had managed to get a piece in the gallery, simply by virtue of a shipping error.

Without being totally conscious of it, Bob had auto-piloted his way to the hall with the majority of the Corben's exhibited, including the one with the feminist executioner he enjoyed so much. He had already passed that piece though, and was almost bin-ocularly presented with the piece by O.K. Mal that had been the subject of his ire just moments before. He stared at it, in its ornate but worn silver frame, the simple picture of an audience of nine and their interactions as some unseen play went on beyond the artist's point-of-view.

Ten.

There were ten people in the audience, he now realized. To the far right side of the third row, his shoulder partially obscured by the frame, was a gaunt man in a green apron. He was wearing a powder blue long-sleeve shirt underneath with one arm rolled up to reveal a thin, hairy arm. The brush-strokes on the arm-hairs were perfectly in sync with one another, and Bob wondered if Mal had used a single brush with most of the bristles taken out to achieve the affect. He'd done something similar when he'd done a portrait of Obi, to make sure all his hair was tossed to the side in unison.

The man's cheeks were gaunt and sallow, his skin so pale that one would be for-given for thinking the artist had used the same colour for the man's hair as he had for his flesh, though Bob noted a slight tonal difference. His eyes were sunken and dark, turning back and to his right, the small bushy white mustache underneath looking as though the artist had caught it in mid-twitch.

Bob squinted, raising an eyebrow. There was something familiar about the mus-tache, though it was just a single white line under the hint of a nose the artist had given the figure. Had he seen a similar technique used before? Perhaps in one of the Hogarth's he suspected that Mal was, in some way, aping?

He leaned back out, adjusting his neck and frowning. He let his gaze follow that of the man in the green apron to see what had him so worried, finding that he, like the man in the wig, was throwing a concerned look at the African man several seats away.

Bob stopped, startled. He looked at the piece again, letting his eyes move from the pale man to the black man and back again. Eventually he held up his finger at eye-height to use as a makeshift level, making sure that both figures were in the same row, the third row back from the stage. The African man still looked out through the painting and into the reader with exhausted, bloodshot eyes, returning the gaze of neither man.

Hadn't the black man been alone in his row? Hadn't that been a part of his entire thesis as to why the work as a whole was some commentary on racial tension specifically and tension in society in general: that the rest of the theatre had been so troubled by the presence of this black man that they all turned and stared at him in horror and disgust, *without* anyone sitting in the same row as him, effectively segregating him?

He leaned back further, frowning, taking in the picture as a whole after having focussed in too close.

"Hey," Chelsea called from behind him. He had once again somehow ignored her heels. Although it hadn't startled him this time, he decided that it meant he needed more coffee. "Your break's over."

He nodded, but did not turn away from the piece. Eventually she made her way up alongside him, her heels clacking on the tile floor and echoing with every step along the way.

"Earth to Bob," she said, with some mix of humour and seriousness only possible by a boss who considered themselves 'the fun boss' in their own mind. "You're needed back at base, Bob."

"It's different," Bob said quietly, almost to himself. He motioned to the third row and cleared his throat, repeating himself. "The painting. It's different."

She snorted, glanced at the painting, then back at him. "Take a moment to get some coffee from Receiving before you go back, would you?"

"I'm serious."

She laughed again.

"Look," he huffed, digging into his pocket and producing his phone. He unlocked it and opened up his photo album, which brought up the latest picture taken: the shot of the art of O.K. Mal he'd taken to show Eddie the night he received it. He brought it to full screen and pinch-zoomed in to the third row, revealing the large dead-eyed black man... and the skinny, pale white man in the green apron several seats down from him.

He stared at the pixilated, poorly-lit image on his phone screen for a moment, then turned back to the painting, then back to the phone again.

"Get some coffee, Bob," Chelsea smiled, placing a hand on his shoulder. She stepped away from him and started walking down the stairs.

Bob continued to stare at the painting for a moment, his jaw slackened. Now that he looked at it as a whole he saw details in the shadows in the back of the theatre that he'd missed as well: the purple S-shaped brush-stroke he'd seen before, but also several purple semi-circles of the same colour and two red splotches, where it looked as though Mal may have dripped some of the paint for the velvet curtains, and attempted to cover it up hastily with black.

10

Bob sat on the couch with his legs and feet spread out over it, almost lying down except for the haunch of his back and shoulders. He rested a large hardcover book against his stomach and read, his eyes darting back and forth in quick succession. The book was the deep maroon that it seemed like all hardcover texts from the 80s had to be by some unknown bylaw, the gold of the spine's text long since chipped away and the dust jacket misplaced. Wedged between the couch cushion and his side was his tablet, opened to a web browser and radiating heat. Next to the couch and within arm's reach were three more hardcover texts, which had been stacked haphazardly and were currently functioning as a coaster for Eddie's drink cup.

All four books were on art history, one of the few courses Bob had taken towards his major before realizing—thankfully before spending too much money—that one did not study art history to become an artist: one studied art history to become someone who looked at art and said 'Hmm.' The one currently resting on his stomach was titled *Hogarth and his Influence* by M.E. Way, who he had learned since was a female academic who'd shortened her name to initials as some women did to be taken seriously, but he still could not hear the voice in his head as anything other than a British man. He supposed that was a part of the same prejudicial system that had led to Way making the name change choice to begin with, but he considered it a benign sexism on his part. It was less, he thought, to do with systemic sexism and more to do with his long standing crush on Ian McKellen.

The other three books were *Art of the Seventeenth Century and Beyond, Sociology on Canvas*, and *Opera Houses of the World* by Thierry Beauvert, which he'd borrowed from the public library two streets up before coming home. It was the book that was now at the top of the pile, bearing the weight of Eddie's drink.

Eddie took a long, loud sip through the straw, laughed heartily at something on the television, then placed the cup back down on top of Beauvert's work.

Bob's gaze shifted from the page to the cup, then to the back of Eddie's head where he sat next to the couch. "If there's a stain on that book when I bring it back, I'm not going to be paying the fine," he said dryly.

Eddie nodded without turning away from his show. "Nor should you, fines are bullshit."

"What I mean is, you'll be the one paying the fine."

"Oh. I don't see that happening."

"Don't get anything on the book."

"I won't."

"It can come from more than a spill you know. Condensation can make a ring on the hardcover that you can't get out."

"I know."

Bob sighed, finally tearing his eyes back away from Eddie and continuing to read. Finding nothing on the page he was looking at he turned it, then two more, coming upon more text to scan through. Eddie reached up behind him and squeezed Bob's leg just above the knee, giving it two quick, gentle, affectionate tweaks before letting his arm fall back into place. As soon as he did he laughed at something on the screen again. Bob glanced up to see that it was a young man's head being bisected by a cleaver. He grimaced and turned back to his book.

Eddie loved horror movies. It was one of the few places where their interests divided and had never waxed or waned in the last eight years; Eddie's love never diminishing and Bob's revulsion never sating. There were a few other examples, such as Bob's love of brussels sprouts, his need to watch any movie starring Nicolas Cage, and his rubber band collection. Their shared bookshelf then was a study in contradictions, with the top shelf being regulated to books on art and the study of art, which was currently flopping to one side as it missed three volumes, and the bottom shelf being filled with classic monster movie DVD box sets like the Universal Horror set, classic novels, several hardback Stephen Kings, and many coffee-table books on the art and images of those early films. Once, as a gag gift for an anniversary, Chelsea had gotten them a book on the historical art of horror clichés. Eddie had loved it, Bob had ordered it wedged between two larger volumes as the cover itself had been enough to make his skin break out in gooseflesh.

Eddie had seen his first real horror movie when he had been just seven years old. He'd snuck in with his sister, Marlene, after they'd both paid the price of admission for a dime-a-dozen children's movie about sharing and working together, which had been nonsense kid's stuff to their jaded minds. Neither of them remembered what the movie was called or even much of the plot, but one scene stuck out in both their minds: a man entered an empty room and the camera panned around slowly, showing the entirety of the room before coming back to his face. Slowly and without him seeing, the door closed shut behind him to reveal an oozing old hag brandishing an axe. He'd never forgotten that tension and terror as the old woman slowly raised her implement without the protagonist's knowledge and without so much as a sound to warn him... Adding to the height of the terror in retrospect, was that the memory cut off before he could find out if the man made it out alive or not, probably because he'd ducked his head into his jacket at the last moment.

He wasn't even sure if Marlene truly even remembered that much of the film so much as she remembered him talking about it so many times over the years, as their memories started and stopped at the exact same frame. Whatever the case, the unnamed film had started them on a life-long journey towards cheap thrills and a love of horror. They saw every movie they could, renting and sneaking into theatres and staying up late to catch dirty horror B-movies on cable. Eventually the terror gave way to calm as the plots and jump-scares became more and more predictable and repetitive, and the props became more and more recognizable. Calm had given way to humour, the over-the-top kills being transformed into the punch-line of a twisted joke that the suspense was the set-up for. Every so often he and his sister, either in person or via Skype, would still sit and watch a horror movie together, seeking thrills but finding catharsis in the laughter instead.

Eddie wiped tears from his eyes as he laughed, the machete on the screen dripping corn-syrup blood in the center of the frame.

"What are you even watching?" Bob sneered, trying to keep his attention on the text but unable to completely.

"One of the Wrong Turn movies, I'm not sure which one," Eddie smiled, his laugh fading into a hum as he took another sip from his cola. He turned back to Bob, his grin so large it seemed to threaten to escape his broad face. "You?"

Bob turned his gaze on Eddie. The spine of the book he was reading, clearly imprinted with the name 'Hogarth' and the name of the author, stood between them. He waited a long moment to see if Eddie would pick up on this fact on his own. When either thorough ignorance or spite he did not, Bob replied: "It's a book on Hogarth."

Eddie smiled. It had been spite then, the sort of humour only he could get in asking something he already knew the answer to, just for the joy of having Bob answer it. Bob wasn't sure where the humour in that was, and in all these years Eddie had yet to adequately explain it to him. "He's the engraver right?"

"Among other things," Bob nodded. "I'm not looking for him though, I'm looking through the people that came after him. Someone he influenced."

"Who?"

"Not sure," Bob muttered, turning the page. "Remember that painting I sent you a pic of?"

"Oh, yeah," Eddie nodded. He paused a moment, the memory catching up to him. He turned and nodded more enthusiastically. "Oh yeah. Yeah, it was a little like his stuff. Kind of *Gin Lane* meets *The Analysis of Beauty*."

Bob shot him a wry look.

"I can know stuff."

Bob smiled. "So yeah, I'm thinking it was a contemporary of his, or someone aping him: your John Colliers, your Andrew Dykes. But for the life of me I can't find anything like the painting by this O.K. Mal guy in here anywhere, or any reference to him." He stopped himself, realizing that he had once again assumed that the abbreviated name was masculine instead of feminine, but then decided that for the purposes of his search it didn't matter.

"You try the web?"

Bob nodded toward the tablet, still wedged between his side and the couch cushion. He turned the page absently, no longer reading. After a moment longer he gave up, marked his place, then turned toward the screen. "What's the movie about?" he asked, his head on the heel of his hand.

Eddie raised an eyebrow but did not turn around. "A wrong turn."

"Yeah, but what's it about?"

"This isn't art history. It's a movie called Wrong Turn about yuppies who take a wrong turn and get killed. That's all."

Bob smiled. He reached down and picked up Eddie's cola, pretended to take a sip, then placed it down on the floor away from his books.

11

Bob and Sloan sat cross-legged at the end of the second floor hallway, with several boxes of home-fries and burgers in front of them from LiLi's, a small take-out restaurant on the corner that did American food in Asian styles. The food had been served in the sort of square folding boxes one expected of Chinese food. They sat, mirrors of one another, and stared up at the painting of the theatre in front of them, sipping their colas in reverent silence.

The gallery had been closed for an hour. Chelsea was still in her office making calls about donations. They could hear her over the hum of the cooling fluorescent lights, the sound of her high-pitched voice refracting off the walls and making its way through the entire building. Sloan had come by just as Bob had been settling up his cash for the evening, with a hot turkey sandwich burger and a tofu express burger in each if their own individual boxes, with fries. The fries were the main attraction of any meal from LiLi's, as anyone on Jacobi Street knew. Sometimes if the wind was right you could smell them from one end of the street to the other, a fact which nobody ever complained about.

"The brush work is incredible," Sloan said, munching on her fries without taking her eyes off the painting. They both had to crane their heads up to see it, like people sitting in the very front row of a movie theatre. "Immaculate even."

Bob nodded. "You see what I mean though?"

"Mmm. Yes, definitely inspired by Hogarth. The way all the characters are interacting... it tells a story through caricature, and the story is different depending on which figure you start with and which you end with. But it's telling a story, like Hogarth. I'm surprised there's not a little yappy dog in there somewhere."

They both stared at it, spotlighted against the dark by its own light fixture.

"So if Hogarth died in 1764, this painting had to have come after, we're saying?" Bob asked, consulting the notes he'd taken on his phone.

"Oh, way after."

"Oh?"

"The theatre they're all in... it's based on the Salle des Capucines, or some derivation from it."

"You're sure?"

"Absolutely. I've been there, it's like it was plucked from my memory. And The Salle wasn't completed until 1875."

"So it's a turn-of-the-century artist aping Hogarth."

She ate another fry, this one dipped in mustard. "There were more than one."

Bob nodded curtly, returning to his notes.

Sloan stared at the piece, taking her hand out of her fries and resting them on her lap, as though without life. "What's that in the back?"

"Oy?"

"There's something in the shadows in the back of the theatre."

"Nn," Bob dismissed, waving his hand. "It's a trick of the brush. When you do wet-on-wet you mix many colours together to get black. Sometimes when it dries you'll see swirls of the colours in with it."

"He mixed purple to get the black then?"

"Stands to reason."

"There's no other purple in the piece."

Bob looked up at that. The curtains were red, the seats were red, the stage was lined with gold. The patrons wore pinks and blues and whites and blacks, but none of them wore a stitch of purple. He opened his mouth, searching the canvas, working his jaw open and shut several times before speaking. "It's the blue and the red. The dark red of the curtains mixed in with a dark blue, made the black more purple than black."

Sloan shook her head and pursed her lips, scanning the piece from side to side. "The Salle is in Paris. Are we thinking this was a French painter?"

Bob rubbed his chin. "How exact is the image?"

"Like I said, plucked from memory," she said, her voice haunted.

"If we're saying this was done prior to photography then he would have had to have been there. He would have had to have sat on the stage with his easel and looked out and sketched it and drawn it."

Sloan leaned in, holding her hand up above her eyes to block the glare off the frame.

"What?"

She frowned, hesitated, then pointed: "You've got this guy down in the lower left, he looks like he should be a member of the Whig Party. Then you got this woman in the fourth row," she moved her pointer finger to indicate, "Who dresses like it's the Roaring Twenties."

Bob raised an eyebrow. "How's that?"

Sloan smirked, cupping her own breasts and bouncing them for effect. "She doesn't have any of this. She looks like she's doing the breast-binding thing that was all the rage back then. Flat chests were in." They laughed. She moved her finger. "Just up from her you have the Knight, who looks—"

"Medieval."

"Appropriately, yah. And the woman in the top right looks like she stepped right off the battlefield during World War One. *Maybe* 1812, but the little square hat has me thinking World War One."

Bob checked something on his phone quickly. "There were some like that in 1812, but mostly it was bonnets."

Sloan tapped her head. "Not just a hat rack."

"I'd assumed the aerosol fumes had killed any functioning brain cells long ago."

She shot him a dry look, then motioned back to the painting. "Finally there's this guy in the front, wearing a green apron. He looks like your stereotypical grocer... the type that didn't really show up on the scene until the 40s or 50s, in *America*."

Bob had begun to jot some of this down into his notes app.

Sloan looked from one end of the painting to the other, then motioned with both hands to encapsulate it all. "It doesn't make any sense."

Bob counted off points on his fingers. "It's a wet-on-wet oil painting by a French painter in the style of an English engraver and using subjects from European and American iconography." He paused. "And it had to be painted in the 50s at the earliest, because it includes reference to the 50s. It's one thing to have a piece of art look back, quite another to have it look forward."

Sloan winced. "Could have fooled me. I thought it was older."

"Yeah..." Bob whispered, "Me too."

Sloan shrugged, popped the last of her fries in her mouth and started to get up. "Well, if it wasn't until the 50s than it wasn't painted at The Salle." Bob looked at her quizzically. "In name I mean. By that time it had been changed to The Palais Garnier."

12

There was one cheap pub on Jacobi Street, which also happened to be its only eat-in restaurant. *The Belle Verde* was a name that didn't make much sense to anyone on The Street, and that in itself had become a part of the joke and its charm. The rapid shift from English to French, and from French to Spanish, left most people blaming Gordon Bowker for the state of American language, and roughly translated to *The Lady Green* or *The Green Lady*. While most patrons observed that *The Green Lady* was the more likely of the two intended meanings, there were a scant few who insisted on calling it *The Lady Green*, often to results that they themselves found humorous.

Eddie Alvarez was one of those people.

"How are y'all doin' tonight?" asked the waiter, a twenty-something named Gradey who seemed to be in a perpetual state of being in mid-grin. His lips had the sort of natural pinkish hue that most beauticians would kill to be able to reproduce, with a complexion always clear and radiant, his eyes always deep water blue. He only said colloquialisms like "y'all" when first greeting someone who walked into the restaurant: at all other times, he spoke in a perfect television-trained American accent.

"I'm feeling a bit peckish myself," Eddie said with a wry grin. Even as he said the set up, Bob's head fell into his hand and he rubbed the bridge of his nose. "I'm so hungry I could even go for a munch at the lady green!"

Sloan said a single 'ha' and Gradey laughed with that polite, bottled laughter that only those in the service industry can truly ever master.

Eddie had had two lagers at Sloan's before they'd decided to go out, and was feeling a bit loose. He walked between Bob and Sloan as Gradey showed them to their booth. He turned to Bob conspiratorially, speaking in a stage whisper: "First time for everything, hey?"

This time Bob did chuckle, more at the ludicrousness of his partner than the quality of the joke. "Stop it," he laughed, finding his seat. "Just stop. I can't handle you until I've had some carbs."

The restaurant, like most of the buildings on Jacobi Street, had been transformed from the conjoined tenements and low-income homes of years past through a gradual process of evolution, each likely starting as a home business and slowly becoming more a business than a home, until finally someone applied to have the lot re-zoned and the city tried to say "you can't put a business there" to which the owners and community likely said "you can't take that business away, it's been there for twenty years." It was the "easier to ask forgiveness than permission" style of business management, and in large cities it too often worked.

The building was one of the few on Jacobi Street which was *not* duel-zoned and did *not* have a living quarters on its second story. The second story was taken up by the kitchen and manager's office, and a small break room. Although the building seemed small from the front – barely fifteen feet across – it stretched far back past the property lines of its adjacent neighbours, interrupting the small alley that existed behind most of the buildings and stretching out until it met 14th Street. It had its own, rarely-used entrance on 14th Street, which was how most people discovered that Jacobi Street even existed: "Let's go out the back way... hey, did you know there's a whole different street back here?"

The majority of the restaurant's seating were booths that lined every wall. The bar was in the middle like an island and there were stools surrounding it and, while there were a few high tables scattered around, nobody wanted to be the unlucky soul who came late on a busy night and had to sit at them, with servers pushing back and forth and patrons heading to and from the bathroom or to get drinks. The booths were the way to go, with Bob and Sloan's favorite booth being dead center on the right wall. Eddie was ambivalent towards the choice in booth, and was more apt to weigh in on the choice of tequila on the rare night he felt the need to attend.

All the colours of the bar were maroon red and a woodsy brown, with the occasional mustard-yellow thrown in for flourish. There was something calming about those colours: not bright and exciting like primary tones, but subdued and earthy. A forest-green wouldn't have been out of place here, although it hadn't yet appeared. Bob had painted it once and had added in a small tree in the corner next to the men's room, and had decided that it looked good there. The owner had yet to take him up on his suggestion.

"What can I get you guys tonight?" Gradey asked, the 'y'all' conspicuously absent from his speech. He was Southern exclusively in greetings.

Neither of the three had to look at the menu. "Vegan Medley," said Sloan, taking off her coat and loosening her hair. "Fish," said Eddie, with a deep breath. "Like a lot of fish. Whatever the biggest fish you have is. You don't even need to put it on a plate, just throw it at me." The only fish they served was bass, and all parties already knew that.

"We'll manage to get it to you on a plate, I'm sure," Gradey smiled politely, writing down 'fish' in large block letters on his pad just as Eddie had said it.

"The Buddy Burger," Bob finished, handing Gradey the unused menus. "Hold the lettuce, regular onions instead of red onions, add chipotle mayo and extra mustard."

"Coming right up! Beers all around good?"

They all nodded, Eddie enthusiastically.

The Belle Verde was the sort of restaurant where beer, not water, was the assumed default drink of choice. The type of beer was never specified: it was assumed that the wait staff would bring whatever was local, artisan, and on-tap. If there came a time when for some reason that option was unavailable, though it never had, Hennessy was an acceptable substitute.

The menu was pages upon pages long, the sort of thing that would make any professional chef tear out his hair in frustration. Flipping through its pages was an archeological dig into food trends: there was an entire page of carb-free pub grub like burgers without their buns, which some cleaver person had repurposed as an impromptu gluten-free menu two years ago, checking two fads at once. There was a gelatin dish with pimento olives and cheese that would have been at home at a dinner party in the

50s but had no place on the menu of a restaurant that hadn't even existed during that time period. There were deep-fried pizzas and deep fried meatballs, which had started as an experiment but had become a house staple, with one small meatball accompanying everything but the vegetarian dishes. There were salads and shrimp and shareable fondues: a dish, it seemed, for every man woman and child living on Jacobi Street. And in practice, that was true. Nobody that lived on The Street had had to look at the menu in years, and it was easy to spot a tourist by looking for someone with theirs open. Everyone had their dish, and it was most likely the same dish ordered time and time again. When it came to The Belle Verde, everyone on Jacobi Street was an irregular regular.

"That was quite an order," Sloan teased at Bob, battling with her hair elastic. "I'm surprised you didn't specify how the cow was fed."

Eddie snorted.

The beers were delivered. Bob took a swig that drained the neck of his bottle all at once, said *ah* satisfyingly, and then put the bottle down on the table. "Nothing wrong with knowing what you want."

Sloan hadn't noticed. She looked as though she were doing a complex mathematical equation in her head, her fingers twitching as she counted items off. When it looked as though she was done she twitched, making sure, then turned to Bob and squinted. "A Buddy Burger with chipotle mayonnaise, extra mustard, regular onions, and no lettuce or red onions?"

Bob stared at her for a long moment. "Yeah?"

"That's a Southern Belle Burger, just with a little extra mustard. Why not just order that?"

"Because I didn't want a Southern Belle Burger," he replied in a matter-of-fact tone. "I wanted a Buddy Burger."

Eddie and Sloan both laughed, Sloan hiding her eyes behind her palm as she did so.

By the time the food arrived, Bob and Sloan were almost done their beers and Eddie had been long finished his, and so Gradey returned not long after with three more. It was good food, the type that could only be gotten at a local, non-chain, mom-and-pop style eatery close to where you lived. In many ways *The Belle Verde* was less a restaurant than it was a kitchen for the entire community; a place where the family could meet as a whole before heading out to their lives, with the assurance that they would meet back there again at the end of the day.

The patty on Bob's burger was almost three inches thick and the sort of juicy moist meat that was just the right shade of brown to be appetizing. The tomatoes they put on the Buddy Burger were fried before they were added, crunchy and crisp on the outside and warm and soft on the inside. It was the majority of the reason he got it sans lettuce: so that the greens would not detract from the crunch of the tomato's flesh. The chipotle sauce was spicy and succulent when mixed with the tangy dill mustard, the only kind that the cook employed. Both sauces soaked into the grilled poppy-seed bun they made special three blocks over, packed with so many seeds it would likely have registered on a drug test. Bob's eyes fluttered every time he took a bite of it, having to open his mouth so wide it aggravated his TMJ every time, but he didn't care.

Eddie's bass was served whole in a bed of strawberry-spinach salad. He'd only been at *The Belle Verde* once when it had not been served whole, the first time, and when he'd been asked how he had enjoyed his meal he had complemented them, but said: "It's just hard to get used to not eating it whole, like my mother cooked it." Since then Eddie had always gotten his bass whole without asking. He had inquired about this once, and was assured that 'the first time had been an aberration.' There were candied lemon slices in a line along the bass' plump body, the slit from gill to tail exposing the soft pink meat inside stuffed with a thin line of pico. He ate it slowly and reverently, taking a small bit of bass away with his fork and knife, pairing it with spinach or strawberry, and then repeating. He had two beers while he ate, taking the time to enjoy every morsel as the restaurant became more and more alive around him.

The Vegan Medley was a Vegetarian burger patty prepared and served as a part of a salad with cucumber, large tomato chunks, soy bacon, crisp lettuce, and black olives. The entire bowl was drizzled in sweet chili sauce and seasoned with lime, which Sloan gleefully added to her second beer when it was delivered. She ate each bite humming, her smile so infectious that everyone that passed her table said hello to her. Half way through the plate she became so relaxed that she had to loosen her hair even more.

A guitarist had started to play, sitting on a high chair below a lone spotlight in the far corner. He wore an auburn toque and large thick glasses that covered half his face, with stringy hair covering the other half. Only his large nose, bigger on him than his face or body would have implied, stuck out. He played soft jazzy guitar riffs with a Latin-American spin that made Eddie clap at one point. One song flowed seamlessly into the next, and the only way one could be totally sure they were actually different melodys was that some had lyrics and some did not. Those that had lyrics were kept simple, just one or two phrases repeated, often in French.

When the trio had finished their main meals and were eating the waffle fries that Gradey had placed in a large bowl between them, Emilio came in. Sloan called his name with a smile that was uncommonly wide even for her, and got up from her seat to give him a hug. He had hugged her back with equal enthusiasm, picking her off the floor slightly as he did. He'd talked for a minute about Fredrick Cooper and his wife. He'd asked Eddie how things were at the theatre and had taken the time to shake Bob's hand he hadn't seen him in so long. He'd come to play a hand drum for the last half of the guitarist's set, and when Eddie turned around to watch, he was shocked to see that the place had become full of life.

Obi had come in just after ten and Sloan borrowed another patron's hat and used it to collect small donations from the crowd to buy him a hearty meal. Gradey took the money even though it wasn't enough even with a major contribution from Eddie and Bob but served Obi anyway—they typically did. He was served a single beer and a Buddy Burger with two patties and a seemingly endless amount of waffle fries.

After her fourth beer Sloan had discovered that, underneath the removable glass top, the table for the booth was solid wood. Without asking, she had handed Bob and Eddie their drinks and had removed the glass covering with the rubber feet, and had begun using a small knife to etch a design into the table's surface. It was a collage of small images cascading and swirling out from a larger image in the center, a cartoonish representation of a French waiter, cross-hatching on his nose indicating an alcoholic's bulge. Eddie laughed when he saw it, and the faux Captain America shield just up from it, with a beer in its center replacing the star.

After his fifth beer and the third time Gradey had come around to fill their basket of waffle fries, Bob had begun to laugh. Not the practiced, polite laugh that he had honed for use on patrons who thought they were funny, but his real laugh: a loud, rattling, nasal snark that sounded like a machinegun blast. Eddie had just made some snide comment at his brother's expense and, unexpectedly, Bob had let out a long "Heh-he-hehehehehehehehehe" that in turn made the entire crowd laugh, although they hadn't heard the joke that had set it off.

That was the unspoken signal for when it was time to leave. They slowly made their way from the table (Sloan replacing the glass cover over her masterpiece) and settled their tabs.

They walked Sloan home despite her protestations and then Eddie and Bob walked home themselves. By the time they arrived, the last of the alcohol had set in, and Bob was thoroughly drunk. Eddie helped him out of his clothes and into bed, somehow miraculously still sober himself despite imbibing more, and the both of them settled in for a restful, peaceful, at ease slumber.

13

When Bob was in college, he'd written an essay about Munch's *The Scream*, which had included the phrase 'uncommonly deceptive.'

"The work," he had written, "Is uncommonly deceptive in its popular consensus in popular consciousness. The public at large believe they know what *The Scream* is about and what disturbs them about it: the balding, misshapen and incongruent head of the screamer, his skin the same pallid yellow as my own, staring out into the viewer is long thought to be the focus of the anxiety. This could not be further from the truth. We do not fear the screamer; we fear what we see in him, for we see ourselves.

"Of the twentieth century authors, only Phillip K. Dick seems to understand this, when he writes of the painting: 'The painting showed a hairless, oppressed creature with a head like an inverted pear, its hands clapped in horror to its ears, its mouth open in a vast soundless scream. Twisted ripples of the creature's torment, echoes of its cry, flooded out into the air surrounding it; the man or woman, whichever it was, had become contained by its own howl.' The word to note, here, is *oppressed*. With this single word, Dick illustrates that what we fear in Edvard Munch's masterpiece is not the screamer himself, but those that chase him."

Bob had had nightmares about *The Scream* after first having been exposed to it as a child. To have called them nightmares would have been to dismiss them though, they had been more like full-blown night terrors, the sort of recurring torture that plays on the mind and stays with it, like Hag Dreams or dreams of the Man in Black. His parents had told people, repeatedly, that he'd been scared by the screamer, but they'd been wrong.

He hadn't then been able to articulate what he had thought Dick was implying so well, that the terror in *The Scream* did not come from the screamer... it was in fact a terror you shared with the screamer, for the two shadowy men behind it.

The Scream featured the titular screamer on a long bridge overlooking a calm lake near sundown. Behind him, always at or near the edge of the frame, were two men draped in shadow against the light of the setting sun. Both men wore tall hats, either cowboy hats or fedoras, and were walking toward the screamer.

They were The Oppressors, as Dick had so cleverly coined. They walked at a brisk pace, somehow keeping time with The Screamer despite the way he ran. If it hadn't been drawn in the 1890s, Bob would have sworn that it was a piece of Vietnam art: the yellow man screaming in terror from the Americans as they bore down on him, the cowboy hat and fedoras long-standing symbols of American masculinity.

The Oppressors were what scared him, not simply in the way they looked or what he felt they represented... but in how they *moved*.

There were five known pieces by Edvard Munch known as The Scream. There was an 1893 pastel on cardboard, possibly the earliest version, in which Munch was still mapping out the composition. There was the most famous, the 1893: oil, tempera and pastel on cardboard. There was the 1895 lithograph, of which only 45 prints existed. There was an 1895 pastel on cardboard, and finally the 1910 tempera on cardboard.

In almost all five works, The Screamer remained the same... while The Oppressors stepped forward.

They did not move in order. The frames may not have come to Munch that way, or he may not have drawn them in order. Or he may have, and not released them in order. It was impossible to know.

When Bob arranged the paintings, he placed the 1910 piece first. Here The Screamer was looking out at the viewer, his pupils blank in abject terror. The Oppressors are stepping in time with each other down the long hall of the bridge: high above the water below, The Screamer cannot turn left or right, he has only the option of outrunning The Oppressors. He is trapped.

Next came the 1893 oil, tempera, and pastel. In this piece The Screamer has started to turn. His pupils are visible now, and it is only through this that we know he is turning his head back toward The Oppressors, who are closer.

The lithograph was third. The Screamer's face is more defined here, as though he knows his fate. The Oppressors are farther back than before: perhaps The Screamer has picked up his pace?

The 1895 pastel on cardboard was the most disturbing, and still sent gooseflesh down Bob's spine when he thought of it: The Screamer's head was fully turned back toward the man following him now, and one man was closer than the other, leaning against the rail of the bridge. His hand was up contemplatively, as if he were resting on it or hiding his face... that was what Bob saw when he looked at the piece, which had once sold for over one hundred and twenty million dollars: that the man on the right had recognized that The Screamer had spotted him and tried to shield himself, to turn and look casual, and appear as though he were not in pursuit. The body language was too ridged though, and the second Oppressor just stared forward ever-the-more menacingly. It did not appear casual, it appeared haunting.

Still, it was not so haunting as the final image, the first drawn, the 1893 pastel on cardboard. The man who had leaned on the rail was closer now, having sped up. They were closing in on The Screamer, but the man to the left stayed behind... but The Screamer's eyes did not latch onto them now. Though he seemed to scream louder than ever, his pupils stared to the right, off the part of the bridge and the page we could never see.

"What," Bob had written, "Could possibly be there that was more terrifying than the two dark, shadowy men looming down on him over the course of five frames?"

14

Sloan looked up at the blank ream of paper before her, which hung from a hook in her living room. She could see the image that would soon be cut away from it even now, before she had made her first slice: just as sculptors claimed that the sculpture had always been in the stone, they had just removed the excess so that everyone else could see it, so too did she see the stencils that would eventually emerge from each new ream.

She made her first cut not thirty minutes after Bob and Eddie had dropped her off over her protests that Jacobi Street, despite its proximity to streets where it was not safe for a young woman to walk alone, was not 'one of *those*' streets.

She cut the pulp away again and again, making tiny slits and then pausing before making another, constantly in motion. She pruned and preened like a gardener, adjusting every fragment down to the smallest detail until it was absolutely perfect. She worked long into the night, until her stomach panged with hunger and the sweat that beaded off her brow had rolled down and soaked into the neck of her shirt. Until she expended the last heat of the summer in one glorious cut of ecstasy that came from her wrist and up her arm, and flicked through the blade with beautiful terror, making one last ripple across the night sky she'd made.

She stepped back and looked at her work: it was a high tower with pillars on a hill. She had no idea why she had carved it.

15

The precarious and teetering fire escape of The Menagerie rocked even under the scant weight of Obi Caste. He paused on the third rung from the top of the ladder, feeling it give slightly under his foot, then skipped it and made it the rest of the way up the ladder without incident. Even the stoop itself rocked back and forth slightly, shifting to and fro beneath his Doc Martins.

When he felt as though he were steady, he brushed his mop of green hair back out of his face. Sweat licked from the tips out toward the brick beneath. He smiled and took a deep, satisfied breath of the late night air. He wished he had a cigarette.

The brick buildings of the next street that surrounded The Menagerie rose up in the dim moonlight, towering over him like stern gargoyles. They leaned in and looked down on him, erect and phallic and strong. He winced and looked away. Although the night was hot with the last sweat of summer, he felt a chill rise through him as he pried open the warped steel back door of The Menagerie and disappeared within.

***

The hall that the back door opened into was stubby and wide, like a tunnel facing the wrong way. In the day, light from around the disfigured borders of the door kept the room in silhouette, but at night there was nothing. The room was as black as pitch, as though someone had placed a veil of thick velvet over Obi's eyes without his knowing. There was a mop and a small shelf he couldn't see on the wall next to him. He reached out and touched them both to make sure they were there. Once they had not been where he'd expected, and he'd tripped on them and badly hurt his foot. Secure in their position, he peeled away his jacket and lowered himself to the floor, curled into a small ball, placed his jacket under his head, and shut his eyes.

There were three places on Jacobi Street where Obi felt it was safe to spend the night. The Menagerie was not his first choice of the three: that was the small storage closet above The Soper Boutique. They sold scarves and some hand-crafted jewelry, but he'd never take anything. The building had once been a small hostel, and the owners had since piled the old unused mattresses into a storage closet for a rainy day. Three perfectly good mattresses sat in the back storage closet, one atop the other, and on the rare instance that Obi could make it in to one, his back turned to gelatin upon touching that soft fabric, and he fell instantly to sleep.

A less favourable option, usually when it was raining and the ladder of The Menagerie fire escape was too treacherous to ascend, was the back porch of *The Belle Verde*, which was covered with a tarp on stormy nights and at least provided protection from the elements.

There was a homeless shelter on Eleventh Street, but he didn't feel safe there. It was run by evangelists, and he hadn't trusted evangelists since he had been twelve. There were transitional homes on D that had turned him away too often, and had made him feel like a louse. He wasn't a louse and he wasn't a thief. Nor was he a drug-addict or a pedophile, all of which their eyes had told Obi they thought he was.

The Menagerie was warm and quiet and nobody used the back hall due to the disrepair of the fire escape. He never took anything, nor would he ever, he simply needed a place to sleep. In the humid night air of the crowded room, sleep began to haze over Obadiah Caste's anxious mind.

Through that same foggy humidity, he heard the faint, watery sound of music beginning to play and opened his eyes.

It was a piano, of the type his father used to play when he'd gone on tour with a jazz troupe. They'd never gone outside The City, but there was a lot of money to be made circling the local bars and pubs and trendy spots at that time, if you knew how to play. And if there was one thing his father had known how to do; it was play.

The notes came in slow, haunting tones, one at a time and without trailing into the next, as though whoever was playing them was skillfully manning the instrument with one finger. They were high quarter notes that sounded as though they should have been played much faster. They should have been swift and playful, but had been slowed to the din of barely being heard.

Obi rose up onto his palms, his arms erect. "Hello?" There was no pause in the music, it neither increased nor decreased tempo. "Is someone there?"

He rose to his feet and listened, tilting his ear toward the unused hallways of the gallery. The sound rose for three notes and then fell one, then started again, over and over. A B C B, A B C B, timed with a low thromb travelling through it all that he hadn't heard while he had been lying down. It wasn't one-fingered playing after all, there were chords playing underneath it all. One two three, fall. One two three, fall. It played over and over again, then suddenly rose higher for a moment in a small flourish, before returning to its steady pace again.

It was in that moment that Obi knew he wasn't imagining things.

The sweat that had been on his forehead a moment ago rolled down his neck and into his shirt, tickling the soft flesh it found there. He'd had hair on his chest at one point, but it had fallen out. His green coif was pasted to the right side of his head, his left devoid of anything but natural brown stubble. His eyes bulged in the dark, unable to see anything. His pupils were large, soaking in all of the light they could and still he was alone in the pitch blackness of the closet. His world was void, all except that soft, light music, sneaking in from under and around the corners of the door to The Menagerie.

He swallowed hard, then reached out and turned the knob. He'd never spun it before, but it moved freely. When the door was open even a crack, the dull, shadowy light of the hallway cascaded into the closet and screamed at his pupils harshly, but the sound of the piano was no clearer.

When his eyes adjusted, the brightness became the dark blue haze that was The Menagerie hallway at night. Those dim lights looked so much like moonlight – artificial moonlight, in a city that rarely saw the genuine moon for the blazing sheen of neon and electricity. The turquoise light fell over the tops of the picture-frames and turned them into Morse Code: glowing dashes in the blackness of the night, interspersed with the small dots from where the lights originated.

The door to the storage room closed suddenly, making Obi jump. He turned back and tried the knob, making sure he wasn't trapped in the main section of the gallery. Finding that he was good, he allowed himself a thankful sigh before turning back to the long hallway before him. In the low light it seemed to go on forever, vanishing into the low-lit darkness just beyond his vision. He took one cautious step forward, then another. On the third, he noticed that the hard walls and floor of the gallery refracted the sound of his steps back toward him: but not the piano. The piano came to him whole, not distorted by bouncing off one wall and another before reaching his ears.

He could hear now that every second note was two notes, played is such quick succession that they had been almost indistinguishable from one another from behind the heavy door to the closet. He stepped forward slowly, straining his ears to hear, until he caught the far away caw of a baby crying.

"Hello?" he called, his voice hoarse from too many nights spent on the street. "Does someone need help?"

The music added the flourish that came every few notes on time, but did not respond. The baby either stopped crying, or couldn't be heard anymore.

"I was just trying to stay warm, but does someone need help?" he cried again. He could hear his own voice bouncing off the walls, echoing back at him, but the music still played as though it were coming from somewhere close by and devoid of distortion.

"Someone," came a voice from around the corner. It was gone as soon as Obi turned to it, the light just bright enough to convince him that whoever had spoken was not just beyond the power of his vision, hiding in the shadows. It had not been a voice like the voice of a child, it had been a man's voice: deep and guttural. It hadn't been the only word spoken either, just the only word that Obi had heard. The voice had faded in until those two syllables, and had then faded back out again, like a single line of a song heard while tuning a radio dial between stations.

Was there a radio on in Chelsea's office? Or a television? That might have been more reasonable at first, but the same melody—Russian, he thought, but couldn't be sure—had been playing for several minutes now without change.

Obi stepped with the sides of his feet, as he'd been taught while he had been in the service. Now his feet made less of a sound as he turned another corner, keeping his back as close to the wall as he could without disturbing the paintings. There was someone else here, likely more than one person. He wasn't one to judge, he shouldn't be here either, but what if they were doing something they shouldn't? A fire on Jacobi Street could take the whole street down to ash; the houses were so close together.

"Run," came another voice, this one had an odd accent. Not American, though not Russian either. It was something foreign to Obi's ear. The word hadn't been an imperative: the speaker wasn't telling his fellows to run, it was a part of a larger sentence that was unknown to him.

The music had reached a normal pace now. Its tempo seemed to shift the closer he got to it, rather than the volume. He could almost recognize it now, though he wasn't sure from where. It was haunting to recognize something so mysterious and yet not know from where: like recognizing a smell and not knowing if it meant there was danger.

He stepped down the east hall, silently stepping past two adjacent halls after looking down them to make sure there was nothing there.

"Help," came a woman's voice with a thick New England accent.

"Who's there?" Obi called out again, his voice returning to the resonate tenor it had once always employed.

All at once the baby started to cry again, louder now, deafeningly loud. It was a scream that came from everywhere all at once, and the music became so fast that one note bled into the next; ABCBABCBABCB over and over again without a break or flourish. The baby screamed so loud Obi thought that his ears would bleed, and no matter how hard he pressed his hands to them, it wouldn't even dull the sound. It was like it was coming from inside his own head, as though his brain was screaming at him while some tiny Russian sat on his cerebellum and practised his cords.

Obi screamed as he ploughed forward, but he couldn't even hear his own above the baby's. It was a scream beyond hunger or loneliness or fear: it was pain, the sort of torturous pain that only a child can experience, when they have no frame of reference or social context from which to frame it: when a child feels pain, the whole world is pain... and right now the whole world was its scream. There were no other sounds on the entire planet, Obi was sure: just the ear-shattering scream of that babe and the soft undercurrent of a Russian piano melody existed.

And then, suddenly, it stopped.

Obi stopped in his tracks, his breath heavy and hard. He thought at first that the blare of the scream had rendered him deaf, but he could hear the air whistling out through his nose and the drip of his sweat on the tile floor. It wasn't just quiet, it was deathly quiet. It had gone from so loud that he thought he would die to no sound at all in a fraction of a second, without even the echo as the sound travelled throughout the rest of the gallery.

Obi took one long breath in, shut his eyes, and then let it out again.

He turned, and down at the end of the hall was the one single painting in all The Menagerie which still had a light spotting it, even now in the wee hours of the night. It was a painting of a theatre from the point-of-view of the stage, he could see the red drapes falling on either side of the canvas.

With one green eyebrow raised, Obi stepped forward.

There were people in the aisles of the theatre. Not enough to call it filled, just a few in each row. Some were Caucasian, some were African. Some were men, some were women. Some were young, some were old.

All stared straight ahead.

They stared straight ahead in that way that still pictures sometimes did, looking directly at the focal point of the piece so that their eyes seemed to follow you everywhere. Indeed, as Obi stepped down the hall closer and closer to this, the first significant source of light he'd seen since entering The Menagerie, he swayed slightly and found that yes, the glossy globs of paint they had for eyes fixated on him.

At the far left of the fifth row was the only patron not staring at him: a babe at its mother's breast, crying so hard its face was flushed and red.

Obi stopped and stared at that a moment, the echoes of the screaming child still hanging in the back of his mind. A shiver went down his spine as he looked at the child's face, its cheeks a deep blood red.

Aside from the child there were ten sets of eyes staring back at him; four women, five men... and in the shadows in the back of the theatre, one pair of large, circular, deep red eyes.

When they blinked, Obi screamed long enough and loud enough to have put the sound of the infant to shame.

16

They were after him, the tall men in the dark hats, always ten or twelve feet behind. They walked with a tepid, casual gate and yet no matter how fast he ran, whenever he turned around, they were there.

Bob woke up with a gasp in a flop of sweat that had nothing to do with the diminishing heat of summer. His mouth was open and moist, and had a salty taste in it as he took several deep, panicked breaths in a row.

The morning light shone in through the window and reflected the faded red brick building that was their only view. Eddie wasn't next to him, but Bob could hear him in the kitchen. Still breathing hard, he reached for his phone without looking, patting for its place on his nightstand three times before finally laying his hand on it.

He opened his phone and his photo album app, and suddenly his breath stopped. The colour rushed from his cheeks and his eyes went wide with fear, and he felt his unused hand start to tremble and shake.

"Hey you want some—" Eddie started, coming into the room with a simmering pan in hand. He stopped when he saw Bob's face. "What's wrong? Is it your Mom?"

Bob did not speak, his lips pursed tight. Slowly, he turned the phone around to face Eddie.

Where there had been ten seats filled in the audience, there were now eleven. In the fourth row on the far left side was a gangly man with sunken cheeks, red blotches on either side of his neck, and green hair.

17

Eddie, Bob, and Sloan all stood before the painting, regarding it with their hands on their chins the way one would when appraising the brushwork of a new artist at a showing. Except here their hands frequently went to their mouths, registering their shock and horror as they stared at the newest addition to the portrait: a green haired man, slumped towards the frame and sullenly looking back behind his shoulder.

Sloan stepped forward with her hand out, as though to touch the new paint, then thought better of it. "It's...Obi."

"It wasn't there before," Bob said as a statement of fact. He knew this was the thing to get over, the hanger on which all their disbelief must be hung. It had to be addressed first, or there was no point in continuing. "We can agree on that, right?"

Sloan nodded. Eddie did as well, but he had taken a step back from the painting without even realizing it.

"We would have noticed it. We would have discussed it. When we were talking about the time period of the painting and all the people in it, we would have mentioned the guy with green hair. He's Grunge, it would have placed our estimate into the 80s and—"

"We get it Bob," Sloan swallowed, stepping back and touching him on the arm.

Bob closed his eyes and nodded, composing himself.

She moved back in to the picture of Obi. There was a red ring all the way around his throat, but it was not solid. It was thick on either side, but in the middle there was a single red line, between which one could see the pale hue of his flesh.

"What made you take out your phone and look?" Eddie asked, his voice small. He crossed himself. The others didn't see.

"I had the nightmare about *The Scream* again." They all knew of it. "I did a paper on it when I was in college, and I talked about how it wasn't just the people chasing The Screamer that changed position, his eyes do too. And I followed the line of sight of The Screamer to make my case."

Bob stepped forward so that he was level with Sloan. Pointing without actually touching the canvas, he started with the stuffy man in a wig in the bottom left. He motioned to indicate his line-of-sight, then followed it with a straight-line into the back of the theatre. He did the same with the grocery store clerk, then the woman with the baby, and the Knight, and both women in the back row. Finally, he did it with Obi. "The only one who doesn't do it is the black man, that's what threw me off at first. He's just staring straight ahead at the viewer... he's not scared, he's just resigned to his fate."

Sloan swallowed, finding it hard to breathe.

In the back of the theatre, at the junction where all the lines-of-sight had converged, were large, purple shoulders. It was just a hint, barely visible in the dim light, but they were there: large shoulders and a hunched back with a wild mop of black hair that hid it from the light and blended it with the shadows... and two large, perfectly round red eyes that stared bleakly out at the viewer.

On the seat just behind the Knight, almost directly between the whore and the nurse, rested its large purple hand. The knuckles on it were deeply defined and dry looking, and it had long, black nails that were tinted with the same red that had been on Obi's neck.

Eddie crossed himself again.

Sloan's eyes fluttered over the painting, taking in every tiny detail, looking for things she hadn't noticed before or that may not have been there before.

"Come on," Bob said, turning around and stepping down the hallway with great purpose. Eddie turned and followed immediately, while Sloan lingered for a moment on the red stain in the center of the black man's chest. When the two men were almost at the end of the hall she looked up and saw the fire-red eyes of the thing behind the seats again, then turned and quickly made her way down the hall to catch the others.

The three of them moved through the halls, turning this way and that past Boones and Pardys and Corbens until eventually arriving at Chelsea's Office, which he opened without knocking. She looked up from whatever she was doing on her computer and smiled. "Nice to see you in on a day off."

Bob nodded, his voice and purpose suddenly gone. He'd stepped down the hall knowing exactly what he needed to say... but now it was gone, sounding ridiculous in his mind.

"Sloan," Chelsea beamed, getting up and reaching out a hand to her. "A pleasure, as always. The new piece of Obama is yours?"

Sloan smiled despite herself, but didn't agree, merely tapped the side of her nose.

"Of course," Chelsea winked.

"The O.K. Mal," Bob blurted finally, so quickly it made Chelsea jump. She smiled from the start it had given her. "The picture, the one unaccounted for... of the theatre."

"Yes," Chelsea nodded. "I know the one. Yes?"

A long silence hung in the air that felt like an eternity.

"Have you found the owners yet?" he asked finally.

"No one's claiming it," Chelsea shrugged, looking back toward a pile of shipping invoices as if the stack itself could confirm her. "But it seems to be doing well. I like the way it—"

"You need to get rid of it," Eddie said, just as fast as Bob, his accent coming through in a way it only did when he was excited.

The smile slowly faded from Chelsea's lips. "Pardon?"

Bob sighed, rubbed his hands against his face, then stepped forward and sat at the seat across from Chelsea, hands forward. "I know how this is going to sound."

Chelsea raised an eyebrow.

"But there's something wrong with that picture. It changes. It changed last night, there's a man in it with green hair now." He took out his phone, unlocked it, and showed it to her.

She squinted, the shrugged. "It was always there."

"No, it wasn't."

"Well," she smirked, mockingly. "It kind of would have had to have been, wouldn't it?" She looked back at the photo. "This was taken in Receiving."

"The picture changed as well."

She smiled forcibly, composing herself and squaring her shoulders.

"It changed before, remember? Right after—" he stopped, more of his colour leaving him. He turned around and looked at Sloan and Eddie. "Right after Mr. Cooper went missing."

"Oh no," Sloan said, tearing up. Eddie took a moment longer, and Sloan turned to him. "The man in the apron." He cursed.

"Well, I do have a lot to do," Chelsea said in a high, too-polite tone. "Good seeing you all, as always."

"Please," Bob said. "You can dock my pay you can change my hours you can do anything you want but please, just take the painting down. Put it in storage, at least until we can find out who's supposed to have it and where it came from."

Chelsea folded her fingers together and smiled again, which did nothing to hide her unease and annoyance. "Well," she said finally, it that same too-chipper tone that revealed the opposite meaning of the words. "I do have a lot to do. Good seeing you, as always."

Bob closed his eyes, took a deep breath, then nodded.

18

The three sat in their booth at The Belle Verde, each with a cold cup of coffee in front of them. Despite the early hour, Gradey had given them an odd, side-long glance when they had deviated from the typical drink of beer. He had taken longer than usual to come back with the coffees, as though he had had to take both the grounds and the machine with which to percolate them out of some long-forgotten storage bin.

All three of them had taken it black, despite only Eddie taking it that way normally. They sipped the bitter, salty liquid sparingly until it had gotten quite cold, with Gradey coming over every thirty minutes or so and topping it back up but with the new hotness by no way having enough energy to warm the rest of the cup by a measurable margin. Still they thanked him absently, and each time he walked away with his pot mostly full and a grim sensation that there was something on his back.

Eddie looked as though he were ready to speak, stopped, then crossed himself again.

Bob's phone was on the table next to him. Every few minutes he would press a button or scroll or pick it up and type something, slowly becoming more and more irritable.

"I keep thinking of other things it could be," Sloan said quietly, finally breaking the silence. "Like maybe someone's kidnapping people and then painting them into the painting or... something. I don't know. Anything."

"Bad episode of CSI," Eddie said under his breath.

"I know right? But anything's more realistic than... well, what we're thinking." She paused, taking a deep breath. "But the pictures on Bob's phone. Every time I come back to that: the pictures on the phone changed too."

Eddie nodded, and the three of them again descended into silence.

"Damn it," Bob cursed, slapping his hand against the table and making the both of them jump. Sloan let out a small yelp, her cheeks flushing when she did from embarrassment. "I've searched for this painting everywhere. MoMa and Google and Engraved, everywhere I can think. I can't find it anywhere. There's no mention of the painting, and no mention of the painter." He put his phone aside and ran his fingers through his hair. "How does that happen? How does something just not exist online? There's scads of work by unknown artists everywhere that I can find with three clicks. Your stuff!" He gestured to Sloan. "You don't even sign your stuff but there's three websites where I can search your name and find it and find where and when it was with GPS!"

Sloan nodded knowingly.

"But this guy, we have his damn name! We have his name and I still get nothing, from anywhere, when I search O.K. Mal!"

He buried his face in his hands, and the three of them sat there in silence. Eddie reached out and touched Bob's shoulder, tenderly massaging the muscle.

Sloan's brow was furrowed.

"What?" Eddie asked, raising an eyebrow.

She opened her mouth, closed it, then opened it again. "Why do you keep calling it O.K. Mal?"

Bob looked up. "That's the name."

She shook her head and reached for his phone. "No it isn't." She turned it on and looked through his pictures. "You're turning it around, which some artists do, but there's no punctuation between the Oh and the Kay." She turned his phone back to him, having pinch-zoomed to the bottom right hand corner of the picture. Sure enough, in purple paint, were the letters: but there were not periods or dots between the letters. It was a trick of the light.

What there was, was an apostrophe before the Oh, so faint in the shadow of the dark red curtain that it was almost invisible.

The name, as presented, was Mal 'Ok.

"Mal 'Ok," Bob said aloud, zooming back out so that the picture was fully framed on his screen. He closed the image and brought up a browser again, and began to type. "I don't even think it's the artist... I think it's the name of the painting."

Sloan nodded, leaning forward in her seat to see what Bob was doing and tilting the glass surface when she did so.

Eddie's jaw had gone slack.

"There's nothing," Bob frowned. "Nothing relevant anyway. There's some gun and a weird Latin page, but nothing—"

"Malloch," Eddie said, his voice a ghost. "Type in: 'Painting' and 'Malloch.'"

Bob turned to him, looked as though he were about to question it, but then typed the words into the search window.

The page filled with hits, each one lighting up in blue. There were images of landscapes and cityscapes and a bright, lurid sunset that looked like something Munch himself might have done had he lived an extra century. Eddie leaned in, his face now so pale that he was almost unrecognizable, and touched the screen. "That one."

The page that opened wasn't an image, but a page of text.

Bob scanned down through, frowning. "How do you know that this is it?"

Eddie took a swing from his coffee. "Because it's on my shelf at home."

19

Horror in Historical Art had sat on Eddie and Bob's bookshelf for nearly five years, having been gifted to them as an anniversary present. It was a thick hardcover with glossy pages and had a wrap-around dust-jacket with the image of an 18th Century engraving of a shadowy goblin perched on a sleeping child's bed, an image so disturbing that Bob had ordered it to be wedged between two thick books so that it wouldn't be seen.

The pages were of the sort of thick, heavy paper that coffee-table books typically were: the sort that made the book seem to have more pages than it did. The edges were bevelled, every second period of ten pages alternatively a quarter inch short, then long, then short again. The images in it were glossy and tracked the light, especially along the black ink, giving the impression that the light was somehow coming from the shadows of the image as Eddie tilted the book.

"There," he said, planting his finger into the page with force. He was sitting cross-legged on the floor with the book in his lap, Bob and Sloan behind him on the couch. They both leaned in.

It was a full page on the right-hand side, page sixty-seven, across from an artist's rendering of Jack the Ripper. The heading, in scrawled Tosca Zero font like something from a B-horror movie, was *Malloch*. Unlike the page it was facing or every other page in the book, what followed the heading were two long columns of text.

"How do we know that's it?" Bob asked.

"Listen," Eddie replied, following his finger along the text as he spoke. "...Believed to be the common ancestral thread of many urban legends and suspicious beliefs, such as moving pictures and the idea that pictures or images steal souls."

Sloan sat up straight, a chill having found its way to her spine.

"Reports of The Malloch painting reputedly go back as far as 1475 in Wallachia."

Bob furrowed his brow. "That can't be right."

"What it says. It says that for a hundred years after tales of it popped up all over Western Europe. They have fragments of diaries and excerpts from manuscripts—" Bob took out his phone and started searching. Eddie continued. "Most are in Middle-English. A few are in German and Slovakian, and at least three are in Latin. Most of them are all but destroyed, but some accounts remain. Most surviving accounts reference silver, darkness, and no reflection prominently. 'No Reflection' has been found in many translations, although language historians debate this interpretation and authenticity. The Malloch painting then dropped from sight for over fifty years before resurfacing in France in 1898."

Bob grunted, clearing something on his phone with a swipe and then typing again.

Eddie stopped, looking over his shoulder. "There's more... about the different cultures that believe images steal your soul... should I...?"

"The dates don't match up," Bob frowned so deeply that it altered the line of his jaw.

"What do you mean?"

"Theatres like the ones in the painting didn't *exist* in 1475. They were... simpler. They weren't these grand, operatic things, just... stages in parks, essentially." He started typing again. "Sloan said she recognized the theatre in the painting as being an opera house in France, The Palais Garnier... that matches up with what you're saying about the picture turning up in 1898, but you can't type in 'Palais Garnier Picture' into Google because it'll just come back with pictures *of* The Palais Garnier."

Sloan leaned in over his shoulder to look at the screen. She pointed, accidentally touching it and stopping the scroll. "It wasn't called Palais Garnier in 1898," she corrected absently. "That wasn't until later. It was called Opéra Garnier at the time."

Bob stopped, then scrolled back up to the search bar and typed. "Same thing, just pictures."

"Try Mallock Opéra Garnier," she said.

"They list Chiapas here..." Eddie said softly, still reading from his book. "That's not far from where my parents were born."

"There," Sloan said, pointing and again inadvertently clicking. "Sorry."

"What is it?"

Bob squinted, skimming the article. "It's an account by a one Jean LaCrainte. Says he worked at the Opéra Garnier during the turn of the century."

20 - THE ACCOUNT OF JEAN LACRAINTE

June 10th

The walls have been repaired in the east wing, as well as the roof re-shingled. The signs of weathering are all but gone, and only a crack in the stonework remains to show where it once was. Julian has begun to decorate again and new textures and tapestries make it into the Opéra Garnier daily: fine red cloth and velvet and the finest oak this countryside has ever seen! We are rebuilding.

Eddie gestured with his hand outstretched. "Rebuilding from what?"

Bob shrugged.

Maria has given birth to a fine young boy, healthy and strong, the first son to bear the name LaCrainte since I was born no less than two and twenty years ago. He will be named Philippe, after my father before me and his grandfather before him, and will be a good, strong boy. He will grow in the shadow of The Opéra Garnier: his manger will be the soft tails of curtains, his nurse-maids will be the seamstresses, and his schoolyard chums those who come to watch him on the stage. I see him now, taking his first bow as the crowd cheers: Bravo, Bravo! And toss the same flowers they did as for the Romans and William before him.

The labour was hard on Maria—

"Vote to skip," Eddie said, raising a hand into the air. Sloan silently raised hers as well.

"Fine," Bob relented, scrolling down. "Here we go."

New paintings have been hung in the east wing to hide the faults in the reconstruction and the cracks in the walls. There is a large portrait of Shakespeare that is like nothing I have ever seen, Mama. He glares out at me with eyes lit with fire and a rueful, baneful sneer... and for once there is no doubt that this could be the man that did write those words, Will all great Neptune's ocean wash this blood clean from my hand? That man has contempt for the world in him, and shall see it down around his ankles as ash and soot.

There is yet another painting though that disturbs me yet more. This is small and sits across from the main stage, on the wall which divides the balcony of the east wing from the balcony of the west wing. From the stage it is center in one's view at all times if one knows to look for it, although I admit it is small enough that one would be forgiven for mistaking it for a part of the wall if not.

It is of a field of tall grass in the fall of the year, the grass turned dull and dead and yellow. The portrait faces west, the sun in the sky behind it low yet still visible. There are no mountains or trees or fiords to disrupt the ceaseless march of the grass blades across the canvas: nothing but dead leaves and sky, and the men who wait upon it.

Bob furrowed his brow. "Maybe he gets into it later. This isn't the painting."

"Keep reading," Sloan said in a hushed tone.

Four figures stand in a line across the field in perfect sections. Each stands before a long pole that stretches skyward behind them, and each stares down at their feet before them like a man awaiting his fate at the gallows.

The first is a Knight Templar if ever I have seen one, in such detail that I fight the urge to stand at attention each time I see him. He stands square-shouldered and clasps his sword before him, but its tip is to the ground and he will not raise it. Hair peeks from his helmet in grimy tuffs and there is blood mixed with the red cross of his sash: he is worn from battle, this Knight.

The second is a Knave. A Knight and a Knave? The Knave is filthy with soot and grime, his eyes darkened with it. He wears thick leather that has cracked in the sun and he, too, holds a sword: again, the sword is lowered to the ground. The battle has been fought and the judgement awaited, but in what battle did Knight stand with Knave and both reach their folly?

A broad dark man is third, and though he holds no weapon, nor should he, it is clear that he joined in the battle as well from the three cuts down his chest, soaking blood into the tufts of his shirt collar. There is water on his cheeks that has dried in the harsh sun only to be provided again.

The last man, I swear to you as clearly as I sit here today, is the image of that First Earl of Orford, Sir Robert Walpole! He stands, plump and saggy, with his bushy brows and white wig before his pole, awaiting punishment with all the rest, as though standing in condemnation of all the Whigs in the Church of England!

I must admit it fascinates me. Surely this could not be the end of any real battle, for in what battle did Knight fight along Knave? White fight along Black? Commoner fight along Politician?

None of which I am aware.

And the poles behind each man, dear sister, the poles that seem to mark the end for each man and raise high into the evening sky, as I look now I see that they are not poles at all. Each comes to a sharp point that I at first took for a trick of the brush, but they remain spikes or pikes or javelins: They are fierce weapons each for these men, who stand prostrate and await the punishment for the crimes of war.

And in the grass at their feet there is a fifth being, hidden among the blades. I see him only from the corner of my eye it seems, like some trick of the clever painter's stroke. Between the dark man and the Whig, nestled crouched like a tiger, a royal demon sits in wait for these four men to accept their fates.

I admit that of all this, nothing unnerves me more than the signature inscribed upon the canvas: Mal 'Ok.

"What does he mean 'royal demon'?" Eddie asked aloud.

Sloan looked pensive, her eyes flitting over the books still of their shared shelf until she came to one with a dark Tyrian Purple soft-bound cover. "It's the colour," she said, her head snapping back to the boys so fast her hair whipped around. "A demon coloured Royal Purple."

Bob thought back to the purple swirls he had first seen in the shadowy background of the painting.

June 25th

Philippe has been stricken with colic and Maria has been wrestling with Mother's Dread, the same that PaPa used to tell us took our poor grand-mère from us. I try to bring her 'round but she does nothing but sulk most mornings, leaving me to tend to Philippe. I apologize for my tardiness in returning your letter – yes, October will be fine for you and Robert to visit, of course. Will his sister Anna-Maria be joining you as well?

July 2nd
Dear sister,

The painting hung between the east and west wings has changed. The Manager and Producers believe I am mad, that I have come down with exhaustion from too many nights with Philippe without Maria's aid, but I swear it is true. Do you still have the letters I sent in June? Please keep them and bring them when you visit in October, they are the only record of my sanity.

What was once described to you as a wheat field has been replaced by a painting of the Opéra itself, as though the artist sat upon the stage and gazed out upon the empty seats and marked his brush in kind. When I try to tell anyone that it has changed, they mock me and say that it has always been this way: they only didn't look at it as I did.

I hear you in my mind even now, dear patient sister, how is it that it was not reported that the picture was merely moved or stolen and replaced with this forgery of the Opéra? Why would I say that the work itself must have been changed when such a more logical explanation presents itself? Discounting the ornate frame, which remains the same and shows no sign of tampering... the men, my dear sister. The four men I described to you in the wheat field are the sole occupants of this new theatre, and they no longer look down, but out at me.

The Knight sits near the back, still grasping his blade, the Knave just below him at his left. Seated near the front is the dark man, where he ought not to be, and he stares out at me with red-ringed eyes of warning. The Whig sits in the second row, and has grown a coat of flop-sweat since I 'ere seen him last.

I thought the Demon gone at first, until I caught a glimpse of it in the back of the theatre... where I then stood. Where the Demon appeared was where its painting hung, and when I realized this, chills ran through me. It was hidden by deep blacks and I admit to losing it more than once as a trick of the eye, having to follow the gazes of the patrons of the theatre to find it again, for all but the dark man glare back at it.

The Demon, however, glares at me.

The name has changed too sister. Still it says Mal'Ok, but now it is in the same royal hue as the monster itself, not the sheer black I first saw.

"Did he say the signature was black?" Eddie asked.

"Would you?" Bob shrugged.

It changed so as to still be visible against the shadow of the aisles I am sure.

Sister, this portrait has unnerved me in ways I cannot even put to pen. I have vowed not to approach that wall under any circumstance, to approach those wings through alternate means, but always I feel its red eyes on me when I am in its view: on the stage or between the seats. Late last night, I swear as I write this to you, I was alone in the theatre and heard a Prussian piano melody coming from that floor – where there is no piano. It was 'Standing Still,' a children's melody. The notes are in me now even as I write. The painting is with me at all times, sister. It haunts me as a phantom of the Opéra.

"Wait, what?" Sloan said, turning the screen toward her.

Eddie almost laughed, then didn't. Sloan took his phone from him without asking.

"It's a coincidence," Bob said, still staring at the phrase. "Has to be."

Sloan frowned. "It might be a coincidence, but there's more than one: "The Palais Garnier has been called the most famous opera in the world, a symbol of Paris like Notre Dame Cathedral, the Louvre, or the Sacré Coeur Basilica, at least partly due to its use as the setting for Gaston Leroux's 1910 novel *The Phantom of the Opera.*"

Bob turned to the word again. "Ten years later," then scrolled up.

Sloan shuddered.

July 12th

The Painting, I feel, has brought me to the edge of madness, and here it intends to leave me. It shifts and bends the few times I must see it: the patrons moving seats, the demon pacing to and fro in its shadowy den, as though pondering when to strike.

I attempted to sketch the beast, to provide some proof until October, but became quickly frustrated.

I inquired, with some distress, as to its origin. At my most recent request the director at last relented, and his logs revealed a long providence which ended in Wallachia, where it appears my original assessments of the demon have found credence. The picture came bathed in blood, I know that now, and more than the blood I have found on each o' the patrons.

"Blood?" Eddie asked.

"Shh," Sloan hushed, bringing a finger to her lips.

Four it has and thirteen it needs; that most unholy number that first came to the fall of the templar knights... like the Knight himself, the first. This I have found with the Director, but have mostly heard through the whispers in the night... at night the painting comes to life, and those four poor souls speak to me from their living hell.

Bob paused, then took a screen-shot of that section before moving on.

Dear sister, I may not be able to wait 'til the fall of the year. If I can implore you, send the letters now that I might prove myself and end my torment.

July 20th

Dearest Emilia; it is with great sadness that I write this passage. You may disregard my request for the letters if you have not already sent them. Keep them with you, or burn them if it suits your designs. It matters not.

Philippe and Maria had walked to the Opéra. I had been encouraging Maria to find herself outside more often, to lift her spirits. They were there for me... and there, they will remain. The Demon Mal'Ok has them, a part of the living hell which is his canvas.

"The mother and child," Sloan said, her voice quavering.

They cry out to me as though they can see me, their arms outstretched. I can see the tears on their faces and in their eyes as though they were moving and falling dear sister, the anguish and the pain on them is too much to bear, even before the blood. My Maria has her mark against her breast, a tally-marked herringbone calling her his fifth. And my poor sweet child – his sweet face is marred with three lines a cheek, salt water staining them.

It is with agony, my sister, that this will be my final letter and that I shall not be available to host you in the fall... not only for my deep sorrow... but for my fear. Seven more the demon needs, and though my last act may see me in hell, I take solace in that it will not be the hell that hangs on the wall of The Opéra Garnier.

21

The three sat in silence for a moment at the end of the passage, the air hanging still between them, thick with the dread of it.

Eddie crossed himself.

"Jesus," Sloan said under her breath. Then again, louder: "Jesus!"

"It's not true," Eddie said, kissing his cross nonetheless. "I won't believe it."

Bob's brow was furrowed, the flesh there clenched so tightly that his bushy eyebrows all but joined in the middle. He had closed the browser with the account of Jean LaCrainte in it and had opened his photo albums. He opened the screen shot he had taken first, repeating it out loud: "Four it has and thirteen it needs, that most unholy number that first came to the fall of the templar knights... like the Knight himself, the first."

"The mother was the fifth," Sloan said. "The man said she had a herringbone on her breast. That's what they used to call it when you made four marks and then crossed the fifth over it, a herringbone."

"Nana used to call it Making a Book," mumbled Eddie.

Bob opened the picture of the painting and zoomed in. The babe, Philippe, was still feeding in his version of the painting – but he could see the red smudges along her breast and his face where they met, as though hiding them from the viewer. "The marks are there," he said, his voice a low growl. "This is the one."

He scrolled over to the Knight, who had a single gash in the center of his chest. Next to him, the scruffy man who Jean had called The Knave, had two such marks on his neck, almost hidden from his collar. He realized that he'd seen the black man's when he'd first viewed the piece: the three red lines in the center of his chest, as if from a lynching, he'd thought at the time.

The man with the white wig had four slashes. The Prostitute had seven, the Nurse eight. The thin woman who sat in front of The Knave had nine, one herringbone and four scratches alongside, and he wondered how he hadn't seen them before.

His friend, Frederick Cooper, had two adjacent herringbones. And poor, lonely Obi had the same two bones and an eleventh strike besides.

"Ten," Eddie sighed.

"Eleven," Bob corrected. "We keep not counting the baby, from when we thought they were figures, Madonna and child."

Eddie nodded, his face pale and his eyes watering. After another long moment he said, hoarsely, "We don't go back there no more."

Bob turned to face him, then leaned in and kissed him, but did not respond.

Sloan took his phone and opened his search engine.

"What is it?" Bob asked, rubbing Eddie's shoulder rhythmically.

"He mentioned Wallachia... that was in Romania – yes, Romania," she said, clearly finding the evidence that she was correct. "A long providence that ended in Wallachia... and that his original assessments were true."

"What's providence?" Eddie asked.

"The history of who owned a thing," Bob said. "Like a record of owners."

Eddie worked his mouth and wiped his eyes. "Our record ended in 1490."

"1495."

"Whenever. It was maybe the same record?"

Sloan nodded, and typed 'Wallachia 1490' into the search bar. Articles regarding the History of Romania appeared. She frowned.

The three of them were silent for what felt like an age.

Bob picked up his phone and scrolled over the painting. The creature had moved from the last place he'd seen it, he noted. He scrolled to the bottom right, found the signature, and stared at its purple hue for a long time.

"Royal was the only thing he'd said about the creature," Bob said absently, turning the phone to face Sloan. "Royal Purple he'd been referencing – but unless we're missing letters, that's the only 'assessment' Jean made about it."

Sloan nodded, and amended her search to: 'Wallachia, 1940, Royal.'

A new article appeared, dedicated to Vlad the Third, the Prince of Wallachia from 1431–1476.

She went white even more than she already had as she scanned the selected article.

"What?" Bob asked, as Eddie sat up straight. "What is it?"

With a quavering voice that they'd never heard from her, she read aloud. "Vlad III served as the Prince of Wallachia from 1431 to 1475 or 76, as a member of the House of Basarab, also known as the House of Drăculeşti." She stopped and looked at them.

"I don't get it," Eddie said, tapping his hand on his knee.

"After his death, he was given another name; Vlad the Impaler."

Bob felt his throat run dry. At once the image of how Jean had first described the painting came to him: four men standing with their heads lowered as if they were at the gallows, each standing before a long, sharp stick, as the creature watched in the distance.

Eddie found his voice first. "Vlad the Impaler. *The* Vlad the Impaler? That was a real guy?"

Sloan nodded. "They made up stories about him. Said he was a cannibal, which is how some other stories about his family name got popular. You'd have recognized him by those anglicized names as well: when he was Vlad Dracula."

Bob felt his body start to curl and stopped it. He zoomed out of the photo and took a long look before closing it.

It was a portrait of a demon, whose first record came from Romania in the same year as Vlad Dracula's death. Since then it had travelled from region to region, feeding on the living, only moving at night. It needed thirteen souls, and it had eleven.

He stared at the image of The Knave, with the two gashes alongside his neck, with renewed horror, then turned off the screen.

22

Chelsea Whitmire stepped out of the receiving office into the dark halls of The Menagerie, the fierce brightness she was leaving making it hard for her eyes to adjust.

When it came to the evening lights at the gallery, she had always been of two minds: one voice in her head told her to leave them on, at least until everyone was gone. The thought of the liability alone—financial and personal—if Bob or one of the movers was in and tripped during the low light, was enough to birth that thought within her. The second voice, the voice she'd heard as her father's ever since she had been a child, responded with: "Just burn your money, it'll cast more light."

For as long as she could remember, Chelsea had been contending with those two voices. Was her father's voice the voice of her conscience? If he'd been alive and someone had asked him, he'd have likely said so. But too often the things his voice whispered in her ear were not truisms or nuggets of good advice or even good deeds: too often they were miserly, sensationalist, or downright wrong-headed. It was the voice that told her to round up the cost of admissions rather than down, to charge extra for the concessions, and to keep the most prized parts of their collection sheltered away for 'restoration' whenever a group of children came through the gallery on a field trip.

It wasn't that Hans Whitmire had been a radical or a racist—far from it, to her recollection. But he always erred on the side of caution, and often that overt caution too easily became xenophobia. She would receive warnings about her friends growing up: "You can hang out with that one, it's no problem, but keep your eye on him." There was never more said than that: just keep your eye on it. Despite the arguments and the distance it created between them in her teens and beyond, she found that voice, much to her dismay, at work in herself. When she met someone new, she heard that voice inside her: "She seems nice, but keep an eye on her to be sure." It had happened when she had met Bob, it had happened when she had met Eddie, it had happened when she had met Sloan. And as much as she tried to pin the blame on her father, in the end, the voice in her head was her own, just aping his tone.

She corrected the tilt of a Boone piece in front of her, which had somehow been knocked to the right. There had been children in earlier, and despite her father's warnings, she hadn't watched them. They had looked like children, but they had behaved more like wild cats and herding them had been roughly the same experience. They had all had sticky fingers no matter how many times she and their chaperone had tried to clean them. The fingers had been a mystery until they discovered one particularly gummy little boy had had a pocket full of gelatin worms and had been sharing them with the others.

She stepped back from the Boone and eyed it, tilting her head to one side, then the other, until she decided it was good. "Alarms, you should have these," the voice of her father said in his thick eastern-European accent. "If someone can bump, someone can take."

She smiled, shrugged the thought away, then reached back into the receiving room and got her coat and shut off the light. The darkness of the hallway was now near-total, with only the blue caress of the emergency lights to guide her way the short distance to the exit.

She was half way across the hallway when, far in the distance of the halls of The Menagerie, she heard the faint notes of a piano.

Chelsea turned and stared into the darkness of the hallway, then slowly laid her jacket down to rest on the tiled floor.

Deep in her mind, her father's voice told her to go; to not see where it was coming from; to leave.

As with most of the cautions he gave her, she pushed them aside.

been able to get it out. Her hands weren't in her hair though: one gripped the armrest as though trying to put her nails through its plush fabric, and the other was palm-outstretched toward the viewer. Tears and terror streamed down her face, her mouth open in a scream so wide that Sloan could see the pink of her uvula.

Her throat was slashed and gnashed where it met her collar, a herringbone on either side. Two further strokes travelled from the center of her throat to the areola of each breast, the blouse there ripped and soaked with red paint.

Sloan fought back tears. Despite the shivers that seemed to have made a permanent home on her spine, she couldn't turn off the analytical part of her psyche that still loved artistic composition. Chelsea sat in the back row, behind The Knight, yes, but directly between The Whore and The Nurse. Something about that lingered in the back of her mind, because wasn't that what Chelsea was: neither Madonna nor Whore, but rather somewhere in between? Wasn't that what all women were, all people; neither the good that was expected of them, nor the ill?

Her mind snapped back and she forced herself to look beyond Chelsea.

Behind her, the creature, Mal 'Ok as she now thought of it, stood in full view now. It no longer hid in the shadows. One of its heavy, misshapen hands lay on Chelsea's shoulder, and its glowing red eyes peeked out from over her other shoulder, pale with blood-drained flesh.

It was in the light now, no longer shy as it had been. The light source seemed to come not from anywhere in the painting, but from the spotlight on the ceiling of The Menagerie itself, as though the outer world were affecting the lighting of the piece. She was tempted to move it and see if the hue of the creature would change, but dared not.

Mal 'Ok stared out at her, not with malice of ill intent: it just watched, its hand resting heavily on Chelsea's tense shoulder.

It was mocking them, she realized slowly.

She backed away from it, not wanting to turn her back on it as she moved back up the hall to meet Bob.

23

Bob sat on the very edge of his stool, his feet resting on its metal braces and an untouched cup of cold coffee in his hand. His eyes had thick red bags beneath them and he hated himself for it. He wanted to be sterner, but every time he tried to summon a stiff-upper-lip he saw Chelsea's pale hand, her fingers splayed as she reached out to him for help from her world of oil and canvas.

Sloan sat on the floor next to him, her head just slightly touching his leg. The remnants of three juice boxes lay at her side and she moved her blade, the one she used to cut her stencils, back and forth from one hand to the other absently.

She hadn't cried. She wanted to, desperately. She felt as though the tears were just beyond the well of her ducts but refused to come forward; timid, tiny drops of salt-water. She didn't cry often and hadn't even as a child, but when she did it was followed by a deep catharsis. She craved that catharsis now, and it was denied her.

Eddie sat on the kitchen table, away from the two of them, his legs resting on the seat of a chair in front of him. He did this to face them rather than turning the chair around or sitting on it backwards. He'd cried. He had wept openly from The Menagerie to here, but by the time they had unlocked their door, the tears had gone. His jaw was set now, so set that it would have taken a crowbar to force it apart. He stared at Bob, the source of his rage, though not its focus. Every tear demanded blood, his grandfather had told him once, his accent thick and his breath smarmy with gin. When someone you love is hurt, for every tear there is blood that must be paid.

He sat, lip curled, unable to focus his rage on anything concrete for the first time in his life.

"She didn't deserve this," Bob said, breaking a silence neither of them had consciously built but that had hung around them for nearly an hour.

"Nobody deserves this," Sloan correctly reflexively, her voice a whisper.

Bob nodded, and another tear fell to his jeans. Unconsciously, Eddie marked and counted its passing.

They sat in silence into the night, finding sleep not far from where they sat.

24

Bob ran in the dimming hours of twilight, but no matter how fast he ran, they stayed behind him. He could hear the panting of his own breath and feel it in time with the heat in his cheeks, the lap of the waves far in the distance, and the steady plunk of old boards beneath his feet.

He'd been running for what seemed like forever, the splintered guardrails on either side of him going into the horizon. The wood creaked and moaned beneath his weight, threatening to bend and break with each footfall.

There were low men behind him, Low Men in tall hats. They were in shadow, silhouetted against the bright oranges and pinks and yellows of the setting sun, but each time he turned around he could see them. They were never moving when he turned, yet not matter how fast he pumped his legs, they were always behind him. Closer behind him each time as a point of fact, gaining. Not by much, not by enough that his heart would give and his legs might stop and he would turn to face them: just enough.

They moved as if playing a children's game of spotlight, only moving when he turned away from them and remaining as still as stone statues when he turned to look. Was he running in place? He couldn't see their faces and yet knew they bore no expression, as stern and emotionless as the face of his father the last time he'd seen him.

He made a sound, a dull N-sound, deep within his throat that was supposed to be a word but it wouldn't form. One of the Low Men was resting against the rail when he turned back next, looking out at the sailboats along the water. The sound of the waves thundered and roared in response to this, but the water itself seemed calm and placid.

The other one, the larger of the Low Men, had been caught in mid-stride with his left foot thrust forward. His fists were clenched and his jaw was set with determination. Eyes that weren't there stared into Bob, not at him but through him, daring him to attempt a false front of bravery because he could see through it all into the terror and the panic that lay just beneath the flesh.

Bob turned back around to the front reluctantly, and when he did he saw a lumbering, hunched purple mass in front of him, so large that it blocked the entire bridge. He screamed, long and loud, and then thrust himself up off of his pillow.

Sweat came from his brow in great round bullets, running down his cheeks and off his chin and down his back. He felt soaked in the sheets that barely covered him, the blankets having been kicked off. He'd been running in his sleep some part of him acknowledged, those sort of jerky bicycle kicks your legs managed during restless slumber.

He gasped for air he hadn't been able to get on the bridge as his heart raced. Somehow there didn't seem to be enough air in the world.

Next to him, by some miracle, Eddie remained asleep.

He didn't seem peaceful as he normally did. Typically Eddie managed to laugh off the troubles of the day by the time his head had hit the pillow, and managed to sleep with regular ease. Now his brow was tense, and Bob could see where lines might form in the years to come.

Bob watched him sleep for what felt like forever, allowing Eddie's presence to guide him back to reality. Eddie was never a part of *The Scream* Dream. He couldn't be. *The Scream* was about tension and fear and the unknown, and with Eddie everything was a known quantity. That, perhaps, was what calmed him the most about staring at the way the moonlight grazed the slope of Eddie's brow: his incompatibility with the world Munch had made. The two could not coexist, and if Eddie was real, then *The Scream* was the fiction. It was dubious logic, he knew, but the panic and anxiety of the dream world was not logical, it was visceral, like the world of art.

He got up slowly as he thought of this, bringing his jeans up over his bare buttocks. He took his eyes from Eddie only when necessary, as though his gaze kept him from stirring as it had the Low Men in the Big Hats. Eddie flitted and moved in his sleep though, the steady rise and fall of his broad chest teaching Bob's breathing how to return to normal, until slowly his anxiety had dissolved itself into a trembling tingle in his fingertips.

When he was dressed he stared at Eddie for a long moment, all of the blankets still curled around him, snug and sound despite the stress on his face. His black hair, thick and full and wild with the mess of the bed, shimmered in the ambient light filtering in from Jacobi Street.

Moments turned into minutes and he still stood in place at the foot of his bed, staring at Eddie and unable to move, until he began to wonder if the dream had really ended. Then finally, some part of him reached the decision he knew he would from the moment he'd jolted from his pillow, he stepped forward and kissed Eddie at his temple, then left the apartment they shared without waking him.

25

He'd had to walk to FDR to find a gas station; there were no gas stations on Jacobi Street. The bright red gas can had cost him $8.97 and the gas to put in it had rounded it up to an even ten. He'd paid with a twenty and not stopped to collect his change, walking back out onto the street without a word to the attendant, even as he called out, waving his lost ten-spot back and forth. In the end he'd decided that Bob couldn't understand him, and had made some vaguely ethnocentric remarks before he was out of earshot.

He didn't feel himself again until he'd crossed back onto Jacobi Street. The air was different here somehow, although he knew this was foolish. The air everywhere in the city was dank, the smog like the thick fog surrounding a haunted castle in a Hammer horror classic.

The gasoline sloshed back and forth in the gallon canister. He hadn't filled it even a quarter of its way, and hadn't needed to.

Bob entered The Street on the south end of 14th Street, legs moving like pistons the entire way up: past the home that he and Eddie shared, past Cooper's Market that wasn't really a market, past *The Belle Verde* and up the stone steps of The Menagerie.

He found his keys without difficulty this time. He stared blankly at the 'closed' sign that had hung, without comment, for days now in the front window of the gallery. He put the key into its lock without looking at it, staring instead into the dull blue darkness of the halls behind the sign. Dust had settled on the floor in a way it had never had a chance to do until the past few days, and when he pushed the door open it wafted up in a kinetic wave, the dust particles catching in the soft light and billowing into the darkness beyond his sight.

He closed and locked the door behind him. He stepped forward into the darkened hallway, then almost as an afterthought, turned back and faced Jacobi Street as he reached around the side of the entrance and hit all eight switches there. Lights blazed to life all over The Menagerie, the florescent hum noticeable only for its absence a moment before.

Somewhere in his vacant, almost entranced mind, it occurred to him that this could have been in defiance of Chelsea Whitmire. He could hear her voice behind him now, telling him to not to waste the electricity and the lifetime of the bulbs when there were not patrons in the gallery. He shrugged this thought away though. This wasn't about Chelsea, at least not wholly.

He turned to the left and set down his sloshing container, again producing his keys and unlocking the gate to the gift shop. The drink coolers buzzed with electricity. He didn't turn on the lights. He stood amidst it all in the darkness for a moment, surrounded by sugar and toffee and salt. Then he reached out with a hand that was almost a phantom, and picked up the chocolates shaped like the Mona Lisa. He placed one in the pouch of his hoodie and then went back for another, and another, until all five that had been left in the display were on his person. He left the gift shop without a sound or utterance, and without paying for the chocolate, stepped back into the hall and picked up the can he'd left sitting there, then stepped quietly into the halls of The Menagerie.

The halls were not as labyrinthine in the light, their white walls and colourful portraits seeming lively and bright. The colours complemented each other into a rainbow of thoughts and feelings and experience, and on any other night he wouldn't have been able to walk down those halls without stopping every few feet, his head swivelling, looking from side to side at the works of a community he had longed so desperately to be a part of a lifetime ago.

He reached the Corben hall. The spotlight at the end was no longer special now, the other lights stole its illumination from it. When all things were equal, it was just another painting in a building that saw them come and go with systematic regularity. The mauves were no different than the mauves used by Boone, the gold no different than the gold used by Pardy.

Bob made his way down the hall without turning to look at the fine pencil work of Richard Corben. The Mal 'Ok came slowly more and more into view, the glisten of the spotlight off its oil brushstrokes becoming less and less until the small piece seemed enormous in his vision.

He laid down his can.

Chelsea had settled back into her chair since he had last been to the gallery. Her hand was no longer outstretched, and he was glad for that. Even in his determined state, he wasn't sure his composure could have withstood that. She sat back with her head and neck rested on the back of her seat, as though exhausted and about to fall victim to sleep. Her eyes were wide though and she stared out past the fourth wall, to the painter or to Bob or to whatever it was they saw.

Mal 'Ok stood behind her, the light off his thick shoulders casting deep shadows on the rest of his frame. One shoulder was pushed forward, as though the artist had caught him in mid-stride, just as Munch had one of the Low Men in his 1893 pastel on cardboard. Could the creature move when it was watched, or did it just choose not to? It amounted to the same. Bob watched it, close enough to touch his nose to it, close enough for his breath to make the canvas flap in his wind, all but daring it to move.

Without taking his eyes from the canvas, he removed a long paintbrush from his pocket. It was a two-inch background bristle with a wooden handle, made of badger hair and stiff with its newness. He had chosen it over the other brushes, the ones he had used to create his tiny failures and masterpieces over the last few months: they had been used to create, and just as Eddie had been antithetical to the world of Munch's Scream, those brushes that had been used to make art seemed antithetical to the duty that lay before him.

He unscrewed the cap of the red plastic gas can and tipped it over the brush, splashing it onto the floor as the foul-smelling liquid soaked into the hair and was caught between the bristles. When it glistened with the moisture of it he stopped and stood upright, his dripping implement at his side like a gunslinger's revolver.

Had the creature's lidless red eyes gotten larger in the brief moment he had looked away, or was it his imagination?

He reached out and flopped the brush into the centre of the creature's face, spattering it with gasoline. Some of the paint smudged, but not much. He dragged the brush downward, soaking through Chelsea and The Knight and then through the African man, all of whom stared out with that same resigned, tight-lipped sternness that Eddie had had while sitting on the table some nights ago.

When his brush touched the frame, he brought it up and to the left, in the same motions he would when applying a base white to a fresh canvas, applying firm, steady pressure. It was like second nature to him now, muscle memory, the only thing breaking him from his trance the stench of the gas. He pushed the blade up through Fredrick Cooper, his green apron smearing into his face. He pushed it through the woman with the bound breasts and The Knave and The Nurse, who smiled sweetly out at him even as he doused her in gasoline.

He brought his brush back across Mal 'Ok then down over The Prostitute, the Mother and Child who were no longer screaming, Obi's green hair and the fake hair of the man of the Whig Party. He coated the canvas until it was all glistening with the flammable paint-thinner, the faces blurred and distorted in the glimmer of the spotlight.

Without a word, he reached into his pocket again and found a small lighter, of the sort bought for a dollar at any convenience store. Not breaking eye contact with the demon he reached out to the bottom right of the piece, the empty chair in front of Fredrick Cooper where he had first seen the words he'd mistaken for O.K. Mal, and sparked the flint.

The flame travelled up almost instantaneously, cascading up from lower left to upper right, defying gravity like a wave. There was a sound like skittering, chattering teeth, or the harsh buzz of voice heard through dense fabric.

Bob watched it and the paint began to curl and break, then stepped back and kicked the silver frame with the toe of his shoe. It came up from its mount easily, picture and frame crashing down to the floor as the flames overtook the Opéra de Paris, turning its seats to ash and its aisles to smoke and flame.

Bob stepped back a pace and then sat cross-legged on the floor. One by one he took all five Mona Lisa chocolates from his pouch, unwrapped, and ate each one as he watched the painting burn. He ate them all, the heat melting the milk chocolate before it had found its way past his lips and leaving its gooey residue on his fingertips.

He ate the chocolate and watched the fire burn until there was nothing left but the smouldering, charred silver frame.

He stared at the scarred pattern of the flame-kissed wall behind it, its stone unhurt by the flame but for the burn marks. The silver framed it and made it seem intentional, as framing something often did, just as Sloan had commented when the store owner had framed her street art.

The fire had been his brush, the flame his final statement.

After all his work, his art was finally on display in The Menagerie.

26

The Officer that had come to ask Bob about the fire had been named Stanley, and had been Latino. He had a thick goatee and bushy eyebrows so thick that they all but covered up his eyes. Bob had never seen him on The Street before, and he found himself looking at those bobbing brows as he answered the man's questions.

"Where were you?"

"Here."

"Have you seen her?"

"No."

"What was the painting?"

"Couldn't say."

"Nothing missing from inventory?"

"No."

They'd come to the conclusion that Chelsea had set the fire, due to her disappearance. Bob wanted too much to correct and contradict them, but he could not. He would not have been able to change their minds anyway. Officer Stanley left Eddie and Bob alone in their apartment as his partner questioned Sloan in the hall.

The Menagerie was closed until the owner could find a new manager.

27

Bob sat with his copy of *Opera Houses of the World* open on his lap, flipping the newsprint-thin pages one by one as he looked through the marked section. He was sitting cross-legged on a thick stone coffee table in the center of Sloan's living room studio, and not five feet away she was staring blankly at a long slice she had made in her newest canvas without knowing fully why she had made it.

She had heard his story of what had happened to the Mal 'Ok three times since he had burned it, each time at her request. There was something about how he viewed that last part of the story, the art that had come from the fire in patterns on the wall, that had changed how she viewed the way she worked with her blade. Was her art truly creative? She wasn't adding paint to the canvas to create the art, she was removing anything that was not the art from the canvas: her art, she was finding, was in its own way as destructive as the flame and the gasoline had been.

She had told the police what she had known: nothing. Bob had purposely not told her what had happened until after her interview was done, making it impossible for her to lie badly. She thanked him for this, though not aloud. There was a lie to it that she was glad to get away from, as though he had allowed her the take her blade to the parts of her life which were not art as well.

***

Eddie's brush went back and forth on the plywood board he'd leaned in front of him at an angle, painting the cedar-brown the dark gray of the walls of a medieval castle. The variety show that took over the theatre every second Thursday had requested it as a part of a sketch on Disney Princesses – each one being taken back to the castle to find the others there, the Prince Not-So-Charming having collected them all polygamously. From what he'd been told, or rather, from what he'd understood from the thick French accent of the Director, the skit was tentatively to be called 'Sister-Princess-Wives.'

He stepped back a pace from the castle to look at what he had done, his tongue sticking out the side of his mouth.

***

Sloan cut a third piece away from her canvas, completing a large semi-circle which she was beginning to believe was going to be the top-half of a rip-off Kirby's head, but wasn't quite sure yet. She looked up when she heard Bob make a loud huff, in time to see him lay aside his copy of *Opera Houses of the World* and pick up another, a thick text called only *Hauntings*.

Her face twitched. "What is it?" she asked, tentatively.

He frowned. "Net nikakogo otrazheniya," he said, touching a red-bound text behind him with a hammer and sickle on the spine.

"Pardon?" she asked, raising an eyebrow and lowering her knife.

"Pas de réflexion," he said in the same matter-of-fact tone, resting his hand on the copy of *Opera Houses of the World* he had taken from the public library. Finally he motioned to the book that was now on his lap. "No reflection. It's everywhere, it's the one commonality in any book that even hints at the painting. No matter how garbled or lost the rest of the text is, somewhere it will say the painting has no reflection, or something that seems like it was there, *something.*"

Sloan looked at him with pity. "Does it matter?"

He looked at her, then went back to his book. Several minutes later, after turning a few pages and becoming frustrated again, he finally replied, his voice low. "Yes," he said firmly. "It matters because it doesn't fit. Everything else... fits, this doesn't."

In the moments between she had made another cut, having decided that it would be Kirby, devouring all the money of the middle-class, and that she would use a separate stencil to give Kirby a Trump-style hairpiece. She put her knife down again, loosened her hair, then folded her fingers together and turned to listen to him.

"Look," he said, turning the *Hauntings* book toward her. It was an anthology book with no author listed. There was a small piece that seemed to be about the Mal 'Ok painting, or something like it, as an addendum to a piece detailing how early propaganda of Catholic cannibalism had contributed to the creation of popular myths regarding creatures who drink blood. "Everything else makes sense, and even this makes sense. The Romani reference, the blood, all of it. Even the no reflection makes sense, it's like that's where that part of the myth came from."

She glanced at the page, but mostly listened. "So then what's the problem?"

"It *did* have a reflection," he said with stress, remembering how it had looked that first day in Receiving. "And if it had a reflection then that can't be the basis for the myth and there's no reason for it to be in this book. But it *is* in this book, it's in *all* these books. It's the one part of the presentation that never changes."

She shrugged. "And lack thereof."

He turned back to his book, turned the page, then stopped and turned back. He looked up at her, brow furrowed. "Pardon?"

"You know, the presentation. The other thing they all have in common. There's no sketch or drawing or engraving of the picture; that was what took us so long to find it in the first place."

He nodded, and once again went back to his book.

***

Eddie finished painting a tree, having gotten far too into the intricacies of the leaves that nobody in the audience would ever be close enough to see. Painting trees had always brought him a certain amount of calm though: he could always hear the soothing voice of Bob Ross in his mind when he made them, expositing about "Happy Little

Trees."

His phone went off on the mat a few feet away, its screen lighting up. It was an alarm or a call, he wasn't sure which, but the tone was unfamiliar to him. He let it ring until it went to voicemail, not wanting to touch it with its paint-covered hands.

***

Bob closed the book slowly, and laid it aside. Sloan was working on the large round eyes of Kirby-Trump now, and was paying little attention to him.

She didn't see how pale he had gotten, as he stood up so that he could reach his phone.

He fished it out of his pocket and unlocked it, scrolling through his apps until he found his photo album and opened it. He went back several rows of images, found what he was looking for, and felt his legs turn to rubber.

He sat quickly, almost at free-fall, next to Sloan's canvas.

"What?" she said suddenly, seeing his cheeks with no colour. "What is it?"

"No reflection," he said, holding up his phone to her. "It wasn't a statement."

***

The ringtone blared through the theatre again and Eddie huffed loudly. It was a tinny piano melody that sounded European, not something he would have put on his phone. Bob must have done it, he decided. He stepped over to it and picked it up tentatively by the brushed band edges, turning the screen toward him.

There was no alarm or call notification, just the mp3 screen showing that a track called *Romanian Folk Dances - Standing Still* was playing. He frowned, and then unlocked the phone to stop it.

As soon as the screen was unlocked, it was filled with two glowing red eyes and the scant hints of the purple flesh which contained them.

Eddie screamed and dropped his phone.

***

Bob held the phone out toward Sloan, revealing that the Opera's patrons were still there, all twelve of them. The back of the house was empty though, Mal 'Ok was nowhere to be seen.

"No reflection was *instructional*," he said hoarsely.

28

The Quaint Little Theatre, as it had been ironically rechristened several years ago, was empty. The only light came from the stage lights, which shone down on wooden reconstructions of a knight, a castle, and an intricately designed tree.

Bob and Sloan made their way down through the aisles slowly, their brows thick with sweat and their breath strong but laboured as they stepped down the sloping aisle, row on row, until finally they were at the rickety staircase that led up to the stage.

There was a phone in the center of the stage.

Bob stepped over to it slowly. When he reached it, it lay between his feet and he stared down at it, daring it to move or make a noise of cease to be altogether. After a tense moment with Sloan standing back with her hands clasped to her lips, he bent down gingerly as if he were going to touch his toes and picked up the phone.

He unlocked it with Eddie's code, and as soon as he did the photo Bob had sent Eddie the first time he had taken the painting out of the box emerged, although it was so different now that it was almost a totally new piece.

Gone was the Paris Opera, replaced instead with the very seats that the stage now looked out upon: the audience of The Quaint Little Theatre on Jacobi Street. The house lights were on, not as they were now, and all the rows were in view. Chelsea, The Nurse and the Lady of the Night were in the farthest row back and seemed to be conversing about something privately. The Knight stood watch over everyone but them in the next row, followed by Maria and little Philippe and The Knave. Obi sat with the slender woman in the middle row, while Fredrick Cooper and the African American man both faced the audience (and away from each other) in row three.

To the far left of the first row was the man wearing a white wig. Two seats to his right, Eddie Alvarez sat with his fingers laced in front of him. He looked calm and ready to enjoy a show, were it not for the herringbones cut into each bicep and the three additional strikes on his forehead, marking him as thirteen.

There were no shadows for a demon to hide, and no demon presented itself.

Bob felt his eyes well up with tears even as he saw what he thought might be a playful smirk on Eddie's face. He handed the phone to Sloan who took it then fell to the mat, hysterical sobs escaping from her tear-stained lips. Bob did not hear them.

He stepped to the edge of the stage and hopped down, then stepped the short distance to the first row. He counted the second seat from the left and sat there, closed his eyes, and laid his hand on the arm rest.

For a moment he thought he could feel Eddie's warmth on the seat beside him. He leaned his head onto where the phantom shoulder would be and waited for time to catch up to him.

EPILOGUE

Sloan walked into the gift shop of The Menagerie, her hair pulled back in a makeshift – and unconvincing – ponytail, a full half hour later than usual. She was carrying a large sheet of canvas and was wearing a blue blazer that didn't suit her over a tattered Rolling Stones t-shirt, which did.

Bob looked up at her and smiled weakly, then finished arranging the chocolates on the cash. They were ears now: tiny chocolate ears with raspberry filling called "Van Gogh's Delight," which Sloan had found hilarious and Bob had found in poor taste, but delicious.

"Good morning!" Sloan chimed, laying her canvas down against the floor so she could shake out her hair.

Bob smiled at the patrons that walked by the gift shop entrance. The Menagerie was full, with more patrons on this Tuesday than it used to have on any given Friday. "What kept you this morning?" he asked, turning back to Sloan.

"Was out late putting up new pieces," she grinned, rolling her eyes a little. "Stopped by The Belle Verde to get me a little coffee." She handed him one.

He took it graciously, nodding in thanks.

She turned back to the large piece that was framed and hung in the center of the hallway, the first piece people saw when they entered The Menagerie, advertising one of its new exhibits. She watched as people walked past, each and every one stopping to stare up at it before moving on. "The piece is doing well," she said, almost smugly, or as close as Sloan could ever get to that.

Bob smiled, and nodded.

"Take your break," she smirked, slapping the desk to annunciate her point.

"Yes boss."

***

Bob stepped out into the hall with his coffee, still steaming heat. He walked up alongside a small elderly lady who was admiring it, gazing up with some difficulty but without complaint. He took a sip of the caffeine, grateful for it even though it burned his mouth. He stood alongside her and stared up at the painting, a slow smile spreading across his lips.

It was the last piece he had worked on while Eddie was alive, the wall of the alley with the old couple dancing the tango on the bricks.

In front of it was a small sign that read, 'Haung Exhibit - Third Floor.'

The old woman turned to him and smiled. "Lovely isn't it?" she beamed. He nodded, and blushed a bit, but did not respond. "It's almost like they're moving."

He forced his smile to remain, but broke away to enjoy the rest of his coffee outside in the early winter air.

***

"Lever ça là," came the thick French accent from the front row, waving his hands like a conductor.

"What?" a man with a bushy beard and a large belly said, turning back precariously on the ladder he stood on.

"Lever ça là," the man repeated, frustrated.

"English please, Jim."

The Frenchman frowned, so deep his wrinkles found their way off his face. "Raise that up, here," he said, biting each word.

The man on the ladder chuckled, then rolled his eyes and got up higher on the ladder.

Off from stage right, a thin man with a hooked nose and deep tan sunglasses chuckled to himself. He puffed on a cigarette that he knew he shouldn't have lit, as a large blonde woman beside him coughed and waved her hand in front of her face, glaring at him side-on. He pretended not to notice.

They watched as the man on the ladder raised the moon higher.

"You hear that?" the man in glasses asked after a moment of silence.

"Hear what?" the woman replied, not looking away from the ladder.

The man stepped back into the shadows behind the stage, the thick curtain blocking out all light, and reflecting sound as well to help with the acoustics. From here Jim's taunts and French curses sounded distant.

For a long moment there was nothing, and then, all at once, there was a sound again in the depths of The Quaint Little Theatre on Jacobi Street.

THE HUNTERS

Recording on. 7:54PM, June 11th, 2024.
Copyright *Cryptid Hunters NLPT,* 2024.
Interview #8661-967-001
Why don't you just start at the beginning.
Well, it's hard to know where the beginning even *is,* you know. You could say the beginning was a very long time ago. In my twenties, when I started the hunt. In my teens, when Fadder, he gave me my first gun. When he took me out to shoot for the first time… well, he thought it was my first time. I told him it was my first time, but I'd snuck his rifle out three or four times and practiced acing bottles off of ol' Brian Gumtree's fence years before. It was getting so that I was right good at it too, so when Fadder brought me out, thinking I'd never shot before, man, he was some impressed, b'y. He clapped me on the back and gave me attay'boys and later that night he let me try my first sip of rum he was so impressed, yessir.

But I imagine you don't need me to go back that far? No.

I'll just start. I know you can edit this down, I used to do some work in TV. I know how all this works.

They still call me *The Hunter,* you know. Even after the show went off the air, even after they stopped printing the trade books, there's still someone every day who calls me The Hunter. *The Newfoundland Sports Hunter* ran for twenty-one seasons! Can you believe that, sir? Twenty-one! Four-hundred and forty-one episodes of premium, Made-Right-Here content, and then all of a sudden? Bob's your Uncle, I guess. Gone. Pfft. Like nothing at all.

I was almost glad my dad didn't live to see it, I was. Shocking, b'y, the way they does you dirty. But there's some old timers, like I say, they still calls me The Hunter. I pass them on the street there off Smallwood or up at the Sobeys and they calls out to me, they says: "Hey, you're The Hunter!" and they says that they still turns on the TV to NLPT every Sunday at 2pm, just hoping I'll be back on. They never *really* cancelled us, you know. They're still calling it 'hiatus'.

But that's all well and good, right? That's the business, and twenty-one seasons is nothing to scoff at. When you two have been doing what you've been doing for twenty-one seasons, you'll know. How long have you had this on the air now, five? Six? Bah. Still wet behind the ears, sure.

I should have just retired, but I got *restless.* That's the thing that happens, right? That gets us old folk in trouble. You gets tired and you gets *restless.*

I tried to keep with the hunt. The government said we can't fish the cod no more, says they're almost gone. Well, they been almost gone for thirty years now, and they don't seem to be coming back. Maybe it'd be best to just let us have them. I tried the moose, but one year I didn't get selected in the license lotto, and the next when I did, I swear, there wasn't a buck to be found. In my basement there's a set of antlers for every season I was on the air, twenty-one of them, and there was spots there for those two years too, but I didn't see one dang animal. And you knows now that every time I heard a shot off in the distance, you knows that made me right mad. Murderous I was by the end of that season. Murderous.

That was when I started staying home. Watching too much TV, that kind of bad TV, you know. Daytime TV where everyone's talking but nothing gets said. You know what I mean? And I'm watching the TV and I sees you two. There was some interview with you two, and you were talking about Cryptids. You were talking about these beasts, these things, that people say they saw and that people think exist, but there's no proof of. And you guys, you goes out with your camera and you tries to find them. To film them. So the wife — my first wife, that is — she showed me how to look up one of your episodes on YouTube. And by jibber, it really looked like an old episode of *The New-foundland Sports Hunter*. Font was the same. Night-vision was the same, but there was more of it. Confessionals were the same. I said to myself, by jibbers, these young pups have gone and aped my whole style! You were even airing in my old timeslot!

But... no, calm down. That's not what I was trying to say here. That's not the point.

The episode, it was the one you did on the Bell Island Hag, you remember that one? Of course you do, what am I saying? You've only done a hundred and twenty-six episodes, you must remember them all. Talk to me when it's up over four-hundred and see how many you remember on a whim, eh? Anyway, you went out with the cameras, and it was at night and it was all night-vision mode, and you went looking for the Hag down in the caves of Bell Isle.

Only you didn't think it was a Hag. Mike, you had this wild hair that you thought it was a chupacabra. Goat Sucker, you called it, one of the beasts that's usually at home down South of the American border. But there had been reports, and by lord I looked them up, that there was one in Newfoundland, trapped on Bell Island. There were farms out on that island, and lo and behold, there were livestock killed. Neck injuries. Blood let. Enough to give you the creeps.

And maybe that was when the story started, when I saw your show. I saw your show and, I've got to say, I was excited again. Excited in a way I hadn't been since my first moose hunt. Since my first time reeling in a ten-pounder. Since I hit that first glass bottle off of Brian Gumtree's fence.

But I don't think so.

Because I watched that episode, and I remembered a time, years ago. Ages. Long enough that I'd almost forgotten it. I was out hunting moose with my father and Sam. That's how long ago this was now, that'll tell you, me fadder was still alive. We were hunting buck and we split up and I was creeping down this mucky, mossy old trike trail, trying to be as quiet as I could. Trying to be quiet, but you knows yourself it's impossible in terrain like that. Every step you takes sure, it's squelch, squelch, sssssquelch. Suction, as the mud tries to keep you.

I'm walking down this trail squelching my way along, and it's getting dark, but the moon is bright. Big and bright, lighting up the evening like it was midday. The kind of weather you pray for, hunting or filming. You know. Good visibility, able to shoot at night without tinting everything green.

The moon is bright and so I see it, clearly.

There's a footprint in front of me, in the mulch. Not just one footprint, many. Something had stepped out of the brush to the side of the trail here and stepped down into the mud, and goddamn if it hadn't sunk down four feet. The hole it made was *deep*. The heel was deep, real deep, the kind of thing that happens when you're rolling on it, when you're walking upright on two legs; but to have sunk down that deep? Damn thing must have been five-hundred pounds. I was only a stone's throw over twenty stone and even I was only sinking six or seven inches.

And there were more of them, footprints, leading towards me down the path at first and then back into the brush. Like something had been coming down the trail towards me and then stepped off.

And then I realized something that still makes the hair on the back of my neck stand on end, even now, years later, thinking about it. I bent down to look at the track, thinking if it was a beast that made that how good it would look on my wall, when I see that the swamp water, it's filling back into the print. I should get a picture soon, I think, because it'll be gone. I look up further on the trail and sure enough, the tracks that were farthest from me, they're filling in. The furthest one is all filled in, you couldn't even tell where it had been now!

I didn't get my camera out, because it occurred to me, then... it occurred to me that that meant the tracks were fresh, and that whatever made them? Whatever made them had stepped into the brush right alongside of me, and none too long ago. And when I realized that, I don't need to tell you, the blood ran from me a little. I could feel my face get cold from it, that feint feeling.

And right about the time I was putting two and two together, all the light from the moon at my back went dark. Like there was something between me and it, and there was a shadow over me on the trail. This massive shadow that I swear, must have been well over eight feet tall. I see that and I feel, on the back of my neck, I feel breath. Hot, humid breath. Stench of breath, that kind of rotted meat smell you only get from a carnivore's mouth.

I'm frozen. I don't know what to do, I don't know what I can do. And all of a sudden, the moonlight is back again, the shadow's gone. And then I hear that squelch... squelch... squelch as it's walking back away from me. Walking the same direction it had been before I'd interrupted it, made it step off into the brush. Before I'd bent down and looked at its prints and made it think that I knew it was there, before it had had to step out, beat its chest, show me what was what.

I think... I think that was the beginning. I've been on your site, seen some of your reference material. Some of the casts you've got, what people calls fake, from out in B.C.? The footprint casts? Yeah, they looks like what I saw that night. Sasquatch, you said you thinks it is. I don't know what it was. One name's as good as another.

Yeah. Yeah, I think that was the start.

***

So the old wife, me first wife, the ex-wife, you knows what I'm saying, she shows me more about the YouTube and shows me that you can upload to it yourself, too. No need for NLPT and their pocketbooks dictating everything. And she, the first wife, she shows me some of the channel numbers. Big viewership, more than we ever could have gotten on local cable, for some of it. And they're all getting brand deals and corporate sponsorships too... I'd been exited just from watching your show, just from the memory of having that thing come up behind me, but now the business brain was going. That's the thing about guys like us, it's one thing for an idea to turn us on *creatively*, but you also got to get the right-brain going, you know? You know.

The wife — the ex-wife now, you knows — she let me up with a channel *The Newfoundland Sports Hunter Hunts Cryptids*. Nice and simple. We had a few RED cameras in storage, a few lights. A few mics. No big setup, deal DIY kind of indie filmmaker style stuff. But where you and your lot was looking to catch one of these things on *film*, I was looking to take one down. I would have it on my wall, next to twenty-one sets of antlers, yes b'y I would.

We did a big press conference at The Rooms. I went up and stood in front of the giant squid they got pickled up there. I put my hand on the glass and reminded people — there was a time when they thought this thing wasn't real, either. Until they *caught one.* Until they had a corpse to cut open, test, prove that it was real and how exactly it fit into the ecological chain. And I was going to catch them all, I said. I was going to start on the island, but I was going to catch them all. And people laughed, of course, and the channel sent over lawyers because of the name, but I had lawyers too, and mine was better.

So we started filming, and the first episode, we went over to Bell Isle, the same place you did in your episode. And we talked to people, but you might have noticed if you seen it — it's a little easier for me to get people to talk to me, what? Yes, that's *The Hunter* charm. Being beamed into everyone's rabbit-ears every Sunday after church for twenty-one years has its advantages, you know. You could learn a thing or two, both of you.

We made a show of it. If this thing was real, based on what evidence we have and how we would track the things it's like, how would we track these things? We didn't catch it, of course, but we found evidence. We found blood. Blood all over pine needles, blood that had come off of it while it was resting. It probably got spooked, I'd said, probably couldn't run of a full stomach. It probably had crouched there, blood dripping from the proboscis it drank from, waiting until it was left by its lonesome.

That was where I met my wife, on that first day shooting, and her daughter. My second wife, not the first one. Not the ex, the current, and her daughter. My stepdaughter, though she's too grown for me to call her that. They'd owned the farm where that thing had hunted, and we interviewed them on camera. That was the first time I met my wife, my new wife, interviewing her about some goat-sucking chupacabra hag that had been after her pigs.

Between the new wife and the new show and the new animals, I got to tell you, I was feeling real good. Feeling young again, let me tell you. Not that there was anything wrong with my first, but at a certain age you start to think every new experience you'll ever have is in the rearview mirror, and it's nice to be proven wrong about that every now and again.

The wife? The first one? She's fine. She was fine at first, then she got a bit panicked when the show started to take off. Then she went on a trip, the wife said. She said they talked and she decided to go on a trip, and she hasn't come back yet. The new wife said that, I mean. About the old.

The new wife, and the new daughter, they came on and helped out behind the show, like the old wife did. They came with me out on the boat with me when we went hunting for giant squid. We didn't call it a giant squid though, we called it *The Newfoundland Sports Hunter Hunts the Kraken.* Because you've got to know how to sell this stuff.

You know what gets me mad? They tells us stuff like this doesn't exist, and we says it do, and we goes out looking for proof. And if we don't find it, they says we're nuts. But if we *do* find it, they just goes, "oh yeah, I guess that would exist" and they give it some boring old name. 'Giant Squid' my arse. That's a Kraken! The suckers on those things, you seen them? They can take down a Killer Whale! That thing is a Kraken, and you do the people who believed when everyone else said they were stupid a disservice by calling it anything but. That thing *is a Kraken.*

The Kraken episode, we got in some trouble for that one. See you can't hunt giant squid. But we went out to international waters, paid someone a lot of money to bring us there. When we got back people said it was illegal, but it wasn't illegal. We went out to where their laws didn't matter none. Got my lawyers involved again, the good ones. We never would have gotten away with it on NLPT, no sir. But I was running my own show now, and they couldn't tell me no. No sir. And all the controversy? It didn't hurt the view counts, I'll tell you that for nothing.

We found one, you must have seen that! Caused a stir. We found a Mongolian Death Worm, but not in Mongolia. *Here.* There were reports and I tracked one and I killed it, the scientists have it now, but I'm told I'll have it back when they've sequenced it. And just like with Kraken, they're already fixing to call it something else. The Death Worm, they're calling it a 'large intestinal worm' now, because that's what it does. It gets up inside you when you've stopped to squat. Eats you from the bottom up.

Blood red when it's full, and it's always full. It eats moose mostly, and wolves. I imagine it'd eat just about anything that squat to relieve itself. And that wasn't a problem, until we started to encroach on its territory. Then! Then you've got yourself a right big problem. Then it starts finding a home in outhouses, curling up for the night where it's safe from predators. And then some hiker comes along, squats over the hole to relieve his bowels, and suddenly it's chow-time.

It spits poison, this thing. Spits it. If it doesn't get you, if it doesn't latch on, it spits it automatically. Gets its victim in the rear and they're running away, and before you know it, they're falling over and rotting from the arse up. They fall down, hard to run when you're burning up down south, and the worm, it can just slither up onto you at its leisure.

Roy Chapman Andrews wrote about it once. Said he interviewed Mongolian Prime Minister Damdinbazar. That was how it got its name, although it's not specific to that region. Damdinbazar had seen one and lived to tell the tale. He said it was "shaped like a sausage, about two feet long. No head nor legs, and is so poisonous that merely to touch it means instant death." And man, he was right.

I tracked it from a populated park area, knew it couldn't stay there. Used my dogs, tracked it out far into the woods. It must have been so fast, in life. It must have been so fast to travel that far. It's hunting radius was massive. Tens of kilometers from its nest. I think what happened was, I think we moved into the nearby area and scared away its food source, so it had to slither father for it. It went out so far it went to us, where it usually wouldn't go, right?

I follow it back to its nest and the new wife and new stepdaughter, they follow me, cameras in tow. They follow me and we're up on it and it's curled around these eggs and it's hurking up whatever it ate before it got there and it's covering the eggs with them, like a mother feeding baby birds, except they'ms eggs. I think it scoffs up on them to keep them warm.

And it occurred to me, it couldn't shoot the poison all the time, or it would be poisoning its young right now. So I rushed it, and it spat at me, but sure enough what it spat was bile. It wasn't spitting using its venom sacks, it only did that when it was eating. It wrapped itself around my arm and, by lord, Damdinbazar was right. It burned. And then I... well, you saw the episode, I'm sure.

They came with me on all my adventures, the new wife and the new daughter did. But they didn't want me going back to that farm on Bell Island what they come from. They didn't want me looking for that chupacabra hag. No sir. Scared, they were. Brave when they were out in their field, braver than any sportsman I ever came across, but they'd been terrorized on that farm and didn't want to go back to it, and I could honour that. Ayuh, that was something I could do.

And they were right to be scared, I tell you, because we got tales of people who'd experience the hag everywhere we went. The Old Hag, the Goat Sucker, some combination of the two. We'd see them everywhere, everywhere we went there'd be a fresh story about them. People with slits in their necks that didn't bleed where the proboscis had latched on, like a leech. It wasn't just Mexico and Bell Island the thing was on, that was for darn sure. These things were everywhere.

The stories were the same. Cattle falling ill, getting drained of all blood. Goats running scared until they were out of breath, found days later with their blood gone, that one wound on their neck it was all sucked through. And sometimes... sometimes there were human victims. Sometimes the goat-sucker story would get mixed in with the hag story, and we'd end up in a place where there weren't any goats to be had. And in those places, you'd get the stories of people waking up paralyzed, unable to move. Waking up with a weight on their chests, opening their eyes, realizing there was someone sitting on it, leaned forward, taking from them.

Something in the way they suckled, it made you calm. Complacent. Paralyzed.

We started to hear these stories everywhere we travelled. We'd be interviewing about an Ogopogo, but one of the talking heads, they'd mention the chupacabra. The hag. The goat-sucker. We wouldn't use those clips of course, but I'd keep them. I have them.

It became so prevalent, it started to put me in mind of a *season arc*. That was what was selling nowadays, right? Season-long storytelling. I could make another Bell Island story. I could go back there at the end of the season, a kind of close-by-return, you know? People eat that stuff up. And then I would have all this footage, from every place I went to all season, but I would show *more*. I could show that the people I interviewed about the Kraken? They'd also seen the hag. And the people I'd interviewed about the Mongolian Death Worm? They'd seen it, too. I could use those clips like flashbacks, add some nice music to it, and show me on the Bell Island ferry: going back to finish what I started.

It would be amazing. Screw NLPT! They'd have me on Netflix if I could pull that off. Or CBC! Or, bless, maybe even FOX.

You know the problem, though. I already said it. It was the wife. The new wife and the new daughter, they wanted nothing to do with going back to Bell Island or doing anything with the chupacabra hag. When we found people who talked about it, which we did often as I said, they got nervous. They asked me not to roll on it. I told them we wouldn't use it in the episode, and we didn't, but they thought it was destroyed, and it weren't. It was all edited together on my cloud, waiting.

We got back from our crossover episode with the Haunted Hike people and I told them. I told them what I wanted to do and I told them how I wanted to do it. I told them that if we wanted to hit it big, this was how to do it.

And boys, they got *mad*. They got madder than I've ever seen them. I swear, their eyes turned red. I don't mean that figuratively. For a second, both of them, I swear their eyes. Turned. Red.

And then they were calm. It was like something just snapped, and they looked at each other, and they were calm. They just nodded and walked off, the both of them.

That was a month ago, and I've been working on the episode since. It has to be big. I've licensed some music, interviewed some celebrities what say they've seen the chupacabra hag. Alan Doyle. Ida Linehan Young. Vikki Barbour. You know, the ones you got to get quotes from if you want to make it big here. Linehan Young, she says she was attacked by it, even. Showed me a scar, right near her collar. Showed it on camera, too.

The new wife and daughter, they haven't been helping with these interviews. They want no part of it. It's been slower going without them... and if I'm honest, I've been slowing. At first I thought I was losing interest in the project, but no. If anything I'm more excited. I mean, come on. Netflix. You can have my 2PM timeslot if you want it, I'll be on streaming. On Demand, whenever people want me. But I was tired all the time, and it was slowing me right down.

And then last week, I was editing the footage from that interview with Linehan Young, and it was at the part where she was showing me her scar... and I felt myself scratching, and I was scratching at the same place. And I got that cold feeling in my face again, like the blood was gone out of me. Like there was something behind me, breathing down my neck with rotten meat on its tongue.

And I went into the bathroom and I looked in the mirror and sure enough, there it was. Just the same as what it had been on Linehan Young. A little sucker mark, a little bruise from the suction of it, and a little scar in the middle of it that looked like a starfish.

So that's... that's when I came to you. That's when I called you. Because even though I've been doing TV longer — and I *have* been doing it longer, and you'll be lucky to last half as long as I did — you've been doing *this* longer. The cryptids... thing. You've been doing it longer.

So I figure... I figure we do a crossover episode, or something, right? I give you the footage I have from all the people I interviewed about the chupacabra hag, you edit it together into a crossover episode of your show. "In this episode of *Cryptid Hunters NLPT, The Newfoundland Sports Hunter* becomes the hunted" and then you... help me find this thing. Stop it.

Save me.

You know, for the show. You save me.

Or just in general... please. Because I am in over my head and I don't rightly know how I got to be there, and I am really hoping you can help me see the other side of this.

End of transcript, Interview #8661-967-001

Copyright *Cryptid Hunters NLPT*, 2024.

9:01PM, June 11th, 2024.

***

He went home. The long way around.

When he got there the house was cold and empty. There was no food in the fridge. The clothes were gone from the closets. His guns were missing. It seemed like his new wife and stepdaughter had left, but he knew that was not the case. He knew because he could smell them, he didn't know how he hadn't before.

He ordered two moose burgers from the best place to eat them in the city, The Guv'nor, up at the top of Elizabeth Avenue. It cost an arm and leg to deliver it to him. They weren't even going to do it at first, but he'd told them who he was and they'd relented. The name of *The Newfoundland Sports Hunter* still had sway in this town. People used to tune their televisions to watch him every Sunday after church. You'd listen to God, you'd watch him while Momma cooked, and then you'd eat your Sunday supper. He was a part of that ritual for people, for a generation.

He ate them all, sopping with grease. When he was done, he took the soft bread they'd packed with the meal and soaked up the grease leftover in the paper plate with it, then ate that too.

It had been forever since he'd had a good moose burger. He remembered, suddenly, why hunters hunted. He remembered his dad, all those years ago, teaching him to shoot. And it hadn't been for fun or for ratings or for brand deals and sponsorships. It had been to put food on the table.

He patted his stomach full, took off his clothes, went to bed. Slept.

An hour later he woke up, but couldn't move. He struggled to open his eyes, but when he did, he saw that she was on him. His new wife sat on his chest, and his new stepdaughter sat on his legs, and he could not move. He couldn't move not because of their weight, but because he was paralyzed.

It was his wife, the new one, but he didn't know how he knew it was her. She was leaned over him, that stench he should have recognized that let him know she was still waiting in the walls with her brood. Her flesh was flaking, green skin that skittered, the texture of pine needles underneath. She had red eyes now, like when she was mad. The both of them did. Red multi-prismed eyes, like a fly's, and glowing red with retro-reflection. And there was a proboscis, hard and erect, come from her mouth and leading into the bruise on his neck that he had seen in the mirror.

And his new stepdaughter had one too, it lay flaccid against her chest, waiting for use.

And he tried to scream, but even his throat was paralyzed.

***

The Telegram
June 13th, 2024
Headline: Outdoor Enthusiast and Local Celebrity found dead in home.

The host of the popular NLPT series *The Newfoundland Sports Hunter* who entertained audiences all over the province with common-sense guides to hunting and fishing was found dead in his home late yesterday evening. Police suspect foul play. He is survived by his ex-wife, Mary, and their two children, Clara and Peter.

Mary Hunter could not be reached for comment. Children Clara and Peter have filed a missing person's report to ascertain her whereabouts.

He is also survived by his second wife and stepdaughter. They could not be reached for comment. The police were unable to find records of them with the city. If seen, do not approach.

***

Tonight on NLPT, a special *Cryptid Hunters* tribute to *The Newfoundland Sports Hunter*, where Mike and Maria try to finish his final hunt and track down the chupacabra hag in a special episode: *The Hunters of Bell Island.*

THE SHOE

To the untrained eye…

"Look here, sir!" Daniel shouted, his arms waving frantically. He dropped the small pick and brush that he had been using to dig in the delicate soil, turning to stare at his supervisor, Thomas Hopkins. Hopkins was busy flirting with one of the younger tour-guides, as usual, and looked very upset that Thomas had interrupted him. Maybe he wouldn't have been so mad if this hadn't been the fourth time that he had been interrupted. "Sir!" he shouted again as he clamoured around tremendous boulders and slipped on loose pebbles, finally stopping in front of his superior and bending over, his hands on his knees, trying to catch his breath as the sweat dripped from his forehead, moistening the desert-like sand that blew around them constantly, getting in their eyes and making the dig unbearable. "I really think I've found something this time, sir!"

Hopkins rolled his eyes and sighed heavily, not wanting to tear himself away from the sixteen-year-old blonde long enough to let Daniel discover move oddly shaped rocks and quartz. "Winters, I swear to Gawd. If this is another stupid dog bone, I will implant my foot so far into your- "

"No!" Daniel insisted, motioning over and again with his hands to come and see, the excitement emanating from each and every one of his pours, creating a stench that was not quite welcoming. "It's real this time! I swear! It's not even like a rock."

Hopkins frowned. "It's not solid? What the hell is it then?"

"I don't know… I think I've discovered some new artefact of the Now Yak Clan!"

A spark lit up in Thomas Hopkins' eyes, a sly smile spreading across his lips. He rubbed his chin, thinking of all the money that a brand new find would bring to the dig. *How many more slutty young tour girls could I get with an extra mill?* he thought whimsically, then discarded the thought and followed Daniel down the rickety old step ladder to where he'd unbrushed his little discovery.

Hopkins squinted against the harsh desert sun as Winters pulled out the centuries old artifact, holding it up for his eyes to see. His eyes went wide as they adjusted to the light, and he took in what had been displayed before him, his mouth watering as though it were one of his wife's four course meals. "My God," he whispered softly, his fingers trembling as he carefully took it from his trainee.

It was about a foot in length, but only a few inches wide. It was dingy and dirty with wear and dust, but still held some amount of sheen to its black surface. The bottom of it was hard, and oddly patterned with spirals and stars, and lines intersecting one another over and over again. However, that hard part gave way a half-inch up the item, giving way to a different material. While still black, there were spots of grey, and a weird checkmark of the side of it was the only color therein, bright and vibrant red. It still retained some smell, like the hide of a cow once it had been dried for several days in the warm summer sun. This part appeared hard like the first, but when Hopkins touched it, it gave way slightly beneath his finger. He pulled back suddenly, afraid of damaging it, then tried again with more care. It was smooth save for the tiny lines drawn in it, apparently for decoration. At the very peak was a hole that proved it was hollow, followed by a flimsy strap and several intertwining strands of felt, not terribly unlike string.

"Is that string?" Daniel asked, as if reading his mind.

"Don't be absurd!" Thomas chuckled, ruffling the boy's hair. "The Now Yak's were nowhere near pre-industrial. They couldn't have mass-produced string like we do!"

Daniel frowned, dismayed at his own stupidity. It faded after a moment, replaced again by the genuine wonder that was before him. The discovery of a lifetime. "What do you suppose it was used for?"

After a moment's thought, Hopkins smiled. He placed the hole over his right hand so that the star patterns faced upwards, tightening it with the straps and letting the flap rest against his palm for support. "Obviously, it is used in conjunction with a compass. You see, you would line this red marker up with true north, and then lift off in your space-craft and follow this map to the stars."

"You believe that the Now Yak's were capable of space travel?"

"No... Certainly not. More likely, it was left here as a learning tool for them by visitors of a long-extinct alien race."

Daniel hummed in acknowledgment, in awe of his teacher's seemingly infinite wisdom. "What is it called, Sir?"

Hopkins examined the item next to the red check mark, then smiled. "It is a shoe. Pronounced 'show'."

"A shoe. Amazing."

THE LAKEHOUSE

The memories of my childhood are viewed through a deep fog not easily penetrated.

I grew up in a small town near the easternmost tip of Newfoundland, in a place known for deep mists and heavy rain that hit with maniacal, unfettered fury.

The houses that were built near the sea were functional, though not made to last because they couldn't last -- not against the constant onslaught of the salt and the sea. They were saltbox houses, and were either kept in constant care or allowed to quickly deteriorate, like kidneys in the wake of rampant alcoholism.

It is a strange thing to watch a community crumble. The western mind is not adept at processing such things – we're used to buildings and monuments that last for generations, not ten years. We erect memorials to these lost homes in our minds, remembering every time we pass by a vacant lot or a skeleton of a foundation: "That's where Phanny Gilbert's son used to live."

The homes inland – the ones that lasted – held special reverence for me. They were like the cathedrals of my town, standing for generations even as the landscape changed around them, the Stonehenge of out-port life. Inland homes were where the upper class lived, and were the main source of envy for a young man who never had enough money for a cola from the school vending machine. The people who lived in the inland homes did not go to work in the fish plant at fourteen; they owned the fish plant at twenty-five. Inland homeowners existed in a special sort of limbo – nowhere near wealthy enough to matter anywhere outside the community, but so wealthy that their existence caused great shifts within the community.

From the time I was old enough to walk to school on my own, the crown jewel of those inland homes was The Lakehouse.

The Lakehouse was a building in the very centre of town, the sun around which everything else orbited. It was large and white with pale blue storm-shutters that were never replaced and always looked new. The Lakehouse was not just an inland home; it was protected on all sides by trees from the saltwater air that corroded everything it touched, remaining pristine and untouched in all the years I passed by it.

While the rest of the community crumbled and rotted, The Lakehouse remained strong and proud, towering above the sea-level shanties like a reaper as death came upon them, rotting the town from the inside out. I bought it in my thirtieth year, almost on a whim, for only five thousand dollars. Property values had plummeted in the years since my generation – the last generation to prosper there – had left for more urban developments.

In all the years I had walked past it and even all through the real estate process, it never once occurred to me to wonder why it was called The Lakehouse when it was nowhere near any lake, nor any other body of water in town.

***

I never met the realtor. The deal had been made online on lunch hours and after the nine-to-five grind of Town Life had ended each day. When I arrived at The Lakehouse, looking as tall and as sacred as it ever had, the key had been waiting for me under the front mat along with the deed, folded neatly into a zip-lock bag to keep out the moisture.

I had been in the market for a home for some time, but the market was not with me despite its sellers constantly claiming it was. The oil boom that had caused mortgage prices to skyrocket had ended, but realtors refused to lower the prices on their homes, not wanting to lose on their investment, so homes stayed on the market for years at a time with no-or-miniscule changes in price. It was a bubble that was soon to burst, but that didn't help me find a home now.

In my desperation I had expanded my search wider and wider, increasing the sphere surrounding St. John's for which I was willing to part with my hard-earned money, until finally the sphere had enveloped the town in which I'd grown up. I hadn't even realized it when it had happened... I had left in that time in youth when map reference was less important than relative space, and I hadn't noticed when the blue circle on the real estate website had devoured my tiny harbour.

The Lakehouse had appeared as available for purchase, the symbol for opulence and affluence from my youth, for only seven thousand dollars total, less than what I had saved for a down payment for a home in the city. As reckless as it may have been, my impulse led me to contact the realtor who wasted no time making me deals – he had had the home on the market for the better part of a decade with no offers.

The deal had been processed in less than a week. Any time my lawyer or I had an issue or concern, the realtor acquiesced by lowering the price immediately. By the time the deal closed, I had bought the building that in my youth had been the Tower of London and the Taj Mahal rolled up into one for a dollar less than five thousand dollars, cash. No mortgage, no down payment, no fuss, no muss. In seven days I had gone from immense frustration to a homeowner, and with the same amount of will as used to buy a pack of Skittles at the checkout counter at Sobeys.

***

My town had crumbled, a ghost of what it had been.

A black, tar-like moss had caked its way onto the side of every building that faced the sea. It looked the same consistency of thick black mold, toxic mold, and it stank like confervoid: the stench of rotten shellfish and salt that had a way of barrelling past all olfactory defenses and embedding itself between one's eyes for hours.

The houses closest to the sea looked like they were rotting from it, gaps in their structure giving way to the tattered remains of living rooms: couches and family photos and paintings still adorning the walls. The resettlement and destruction of my community had happened slowly over time, but people had left their belongings as though they had left on the run from some unforeseen natural disaster... or as if they thought they were coming back, and never did.

Despite that, The Lakehouse remained untouched.

The rest of the town seemed small, somehow, in the same way that returning to any place after a long absence did. Our minds distort the size of the things we see in our youth, but The Lakehouse was as large as ever, as though it had grown with me. It towered into the trees with twelve windows on the front end alone, and at least six on every other side.

There was no back door.

Inside the living room, like all the decaying living rooms I had seen on my drive, was fully decorated in the dated style that was old when I was young, plastic coverings over it to make sure no human ever enjoyed the feeling of its surface. It occurred to me when I ran my hand over the embroidered knit flowers of it that, to my knowledge, no one had lived in The Lakehouse in my lifetime.

The kitchen was completely new. The realtor had tried to update it several times over the years of trying to sell, investing more and more until he realized it was a sunk cost in a declining area and stopped, too late. I spent thirty minutes looking over the appliances – most with the stickers still on them – and realized that I could likely sell it all and make my five thousand dollars back immediately.

The bedrooms – nine of them – smelled of musk, and the bathrooms had been recently cleaned. The wallpaper was miraculously intact, and one of the bedrooms sported racially insensitive designs that were put on the walls of boy's rooms years before I was born, cartoon blackface caricatures and original peoples depicted with exaggerated features and stereotypical dress. Racism in Newfoundland was an odd thing, permeating a culture which had little-to-no contact with the cultures they maligned. The blackface caricatures were endemic of this, looking not-quite-right when compared with the figures that appeared in the Censored Eleven or *Gone with the Wind*.

I made the choice very early on that, historical significance or not, those papers would be taken down and the rooms repainted.

There was no hall on the first floor, each of the eight rooms led into the next and one had to step through them all to reach the last. This was strange to me – not just as an architectural curiosity, but because I had pictured the interior of The Lakehouse so many times in my mind's eye, and it was nothing like that. The main foyer led into the living room, which gave way to the reading room (currently packed with more hardcover books than I could read in a lifetime), then the kitchen, the dining room, the pantry, the laundry, and finally the back room.

The back room was an oddity, taller than the rest of the rooms on the floor. It was where the breakers were, and I deduced quickly that it had been built as an addendum to retrofit electricity onto the home, the ceiling built high to hide the wires travelling up to provide power to the upper floor. The room was tall but thin, with only enough space to open the door. There were two windows that looked out upon the back yard and a storm door that had been boarded up with several pieces of two-by-four and plank board. The boards had been poorly secured in place, the nails sticking out a half inch from the board like rusted hooks, waiting to slice unexpected flesh during a power outage.

I looked out that back window at the trees that bled into the forest that eventually became the wilderness that surrounded my hometown for the first time since I was a boy, and was filled with equal parts nostalgia and dread as the branches moved among their deep shadows conspiratorially.

***

The loudness of the quiet was unsettling that night. It settled over you like a sheet of plastic, slowly suffocating you by the time you realized it. One got accustomed to the city – the noise quickly became white noise, the sirens and horns and yelling facing into the background of existence. Without it the silence became deafening and distracting, the ears constantly reaching out to find purchase on something, searching to discover what was wrong – where had everyone gone?

I went to bed early that night, and with all the lights of The Lakehouse shut off, my ears finally picked up the soft, rhythmic sounds of the water, and they drifted me off to sleep.

I might have left well enough alone at that, if I'd known what would happen next.

***

It was on the third night, just as I was drifting off to sleep to the sound of the waves that had lulled me to sleep as a child, that it occurred to me suddenly and I sat up straight in bed: we were too far inland to hear the waves.

I told myself I was wrong, that reality was currently proving me wrong, as I continued to hear the soft crashing of calm water over and over again... that the sound would go further than it had in my youth because there were less people and devices to drown it out... But somehow I knew I was wrong; in that second of realization I knew.

I laid awake until three am and then went downstairs, through the reading room and the living room and the foyer, all the while hearing the crashing of the waves, until I stepped out onto my front stoop... where there was nothing. Nothing but the soft rustle of the evergreen trees, whose branches made shifting motions despite there being no wind, sending me back inside with gooseflesh on my arms.

The moment I was back inside I heard the waves again.

I spent almost an hour going from room to room, convinced there was some device making the sound: a Bluetooth speaker or some such thing, programmed to make soothing night time sounds that would lull the buyer into a false sense of calm, installed by the realtor in desperation. I found no such device, but the sound got louder when I went from the living room to the reading room, louder again when I went into the kitchen, the dining room, the pantry, the laundry, and was almost deafening when I entered the small back room.

The sound, I realized, was coming from beyond the boarded door.

***

When morning light came, the sound stopped.

I walked around my lakehouse to the backend, just as I had on my first day there, and confirmed there was no door on the backside. I went back in through the front door, through the foyer and living room, reading room, kitchen, dining room, pantry, laundry, and into the back room. I looked out the windows on either side of the barred door and saw my backyard, where I had been standing moments before.

I went to my car and got my crowbar.

I came back and pressed the hook of the bar into the wedge of space between the two-by-four and the door, sunk it in as far as it would go, and then pushed with all the leverage I could muster.

It came so easily I fell on my feet. It came as though it had *wanted* to come, as though I were not so much pulling it free as I was giving it permission to do what it had been anxiously waiting to do for eons. The board came loose not at the ends, but where the bar had been wedged, snapping in half with even my minimal force and falling to the floor.

The board cracked again when it hit the tiled floor, separating into two pieces. The back of it was covered in a thick, mossy blackness that looked very much like the black moss that had been around the decaying remains of the homes near the sea. It slithered and seemed to move in the uneven light of the back room, like snakeskin. The inside of the board had been corrupted as well and it oozed out of it with the consistency of Jell-O pudding, slowly spreading and forming a puddle at my feet.

The place where the board had been nailed to the wall hung limply now, each edge dribbling thick black ooze down the doorframe, tainting their white with streaks of black.

The second and third boards came just the same, and the fourth and final was so full of rot that it splashed into my eyes and mouth when I took my crowbar to it. I screamed and cursed when it happened and made my way to the washroom. For a moment when the tap was running, I would have sworn it was running the same blackness, but when I dried my eyes and looked again it was clear well-water, straight from my own pump.

By the time I made it back down to the back room, the liquid black rot covered the floor of back room fully three feet around the door. I avoided stepping in it as best I could, reached out, and against all sense, I opened the door.

***

The door opened onto a calm lake, roughly half a kilometer across and shaped like a kidney. There was a small stone beach all the way around it, and then thick, dense forest that the eye could not penetrate. The forest wasn't made of evergreen trees though; the trees had palm leaves. The sky was a bright clear blue even though I saw no sun in it, and the water on the lake matched it in kind: so calm that from the doorway I could see past the surface to the stone below in some areas around the shore.

There was a small island in the centre of the lake, no larger than what could allow a man to sit, made of nothing but stone.

I stared at this sight out my back door for quite some time, before I leaned back and looked through one window, then the other, seeing my backyard. I closed the door and walked around to the backyard of my lakehouse and found nothing but grass, *dry* grass at that. I got an orange pylon from my trunk and placed it in the center of the yard, directly in front of the area between the two windows, and walked back through the foyer and living room, reading room, kitchen, dining room, pantry, laundry, and into the back room. I craned my head through both windows and saw the pylon there, then opened the door and saw no sign on of it, only the lake.

There was a back stoop and stairs that led from my door to the beachside, in the exact style and color as my front deck. I swallowed, and despite all reasonable expectation of sanity, I stepped through the impossible door in my back room out into the lakeside.

The back of my house looked the same, although the trees grew tight to it. The palm leaf trees were not palm trees, but tall trees with wide trucks that sprouted a fresh crop of palm leaves every few feet of its shape. They grew so dense as to be a natural fence surrounding my home, a wall blocking me from venturing around to the front and seeing what was different there. Would my car be there if I could have circled around, or would something different have been in its place? If I had moved my car, would the thing have moved too? I have no way of knowing.

A thin layer of the black slime that covered my childhood home was spread over the back of this version of my lakehouse, still thin enough as to be translucent. It shifted and moved in the sunless sunlight, as though it were wriggling its way further up the architecture of the house over time.

The windows of my upper floor were boarded shut with plywood, a soft red light emanating from around their cracks. It was not the light of a fire; it was the light of neon, of the signs that buzzed at night in the city that would have lulled me to sleep and avoided this entire mess had they really been there.

I walked around the lake slowly, taking in the stillness of the air. There was a quiet and a calm that was familiar, but that I had trouble pinning down until I was about halfway across the circumference of it, crawling over a particularly large rock to avoid touching the water. I don't know why, but I knew I shouldn't touch the lake water... It was mostly clear, but there was a deep black cloud in its centre around the island that discouraged experimentation.

It was when sliding down the opposite side of that stone that the feeling was pinpointed in me: it was the calm of home. The calm that had been eroded away by years of neglect and decay and tumor was here, sitting placidly in the air of the lake, waiting to be breathed in. And I did breathe it in; I closed my eyes and took several deep, full breaths, filling my lungs in through my nose and out through my mouth and felt calmer than I had in years.

There was a rustle in the palm leaves behind me and I turned, too quickly on the rocks. My foot twisted and I fell onto my thirty-year-old back onto the uneven stone and felt bruises form that would cause me trouble for some time, my elbow penetrating the surface of the lake.

I removed myself from it quickly, ignoring the fierce pain of the movement. When I looked, the black cloud seemed to have moved, stretching from its place around the island for me. I backed up, kicking rocks as I went, until I was away from the water's edge and closer to the upper edge of the beach, where the line of palms started.

There was a slithering hiss over my shoulder, and when I looked behind me there were a pair of pallid yellow eyes staring back at me from between two palm fawns. I screamed and it came out of the wood after me, planting its – his – feet down on the stone. He was small – toddler sized – with bright yellow eyes and no mouth or ears. He was the shape of a toddler's shadow, but completely black, dripping the same swirling, living ooze that was trying to make its way over my lakehouse.

It was nude, that was the only way I knew its gender, and despite its humanoid shape and size I knew instinctively that it was full-grown.

It hissed at me through its eyes, the pupils shaking and shimmering with the sound like a rattlesnake's tail, and I turned and ran from it – I ran from a thing the size of a toddler, because I knew in my heart that if it touched me, it would morph its way over me and eat me like rot ate meat.

I ran over the stone I had slid down and along the uneven stone of the beach back toward my lakehouse, panting from fear and exhaustion. I looked over my shoulder three times to see if I was being followed: each time the swirling black mass boy was still there, waiting atop the stone... and each time there were more of him, coming out of the patchwork of trees as though they were the living shadows, standing at the water's edge and glaring at me with hissing eyes. Every time I looked, that black circle around the island was stretched toward me, an optical illusion that made it always aim at your eye.

My feet hit the stairs the led up to my back door and I looked up and froze in my tracks, and the color must have drained from my face.

There was a shadow of a man standing in the window of my back room, staring out at me and watching as I completed my frantic run towards my house. He stood mannequin-still for a moment, a paper silhouette on my window, before stepping forward into the light of the sunless sky.

It was me, my face ashen gray and my hair matted black from water, dark rings around my eyes... but it was me all the same. We stared at each other, the panting me and the darkened me, each on our own side of reality.

I turned away from the window and shut the door on the lake, locking it out once again, as the me on the stairs started to scream. I heard him banging for some time, and then I heard him sobbing, but these sounds grew more and more dull the more boards I nailed over the frame. Eventually they were far enough away that one could be forgiven for mistaking them for the white noise of waves on a distant shore.

I packed up my car and drove back into the city with my crowbar resting on my passenger seat, just in case. At three different stops along the highway I stopped and cleaned the blackness out from beneath my eyelids and from underneath my fingernails and gums. I kept seeing it build there in my rear-view mirror, catching my attention.

I showered when I got back to my apartment and the blackness went down the drain in congealed wet clumps. No matter how much of it came loose, there always seemed to be more of it.

I wondered, as the sirens and horns and sounds of the city lulled me to sleep that night, if it ever turned night on the lake. I wondered if those hissing toddlers ever made it beyond that stone border... and I wondered how thirsty I would have to get before I dipped my hand and face into that clear water with the shadow in its center, and risked taking a refreshing gulp from the lake itself.

***

House for sale. Spacious, nine bedrooms, three baths. Secluded location, within driving distance to St. John's. Perfect for cabin. All new kitchen appliances. $1000 OBO, as-is, with all faults.

RITUALS OF THE CELESTIAL RAM

During the period of my study of religious trends on the tiny island of Danloudfwenn (DAN – loud – FWIN) I discovered the emergence of a new and particularly addictive religious sect known as the Shrine of the Celestial Ram.

Since colonization by the colonials in 1495, Danloudfwenn has been chiefly thought of as a Christian-dominated region, with the majority of its population adhering to the divisions of Anglican or United denominations. However, at the turn of the 20th century a more scientific, modern knowledge belief structure took over, with science becoming the predominant answer to the native's questions of "why?" While this still exists today, the vast majority of the Danloudfwenns had converted to an unnamed new-age monotheistic religion where patrons worship and pay tribute to the drippings of a bean curd and its messiah, known mainly as Torton Him, but also referred to as simply Him, Himmy, He, It, or I Am in their holy scripts.

Unknown to the followers of Torton Him, a similar religious movement had begun in the south and had begun to work its way up into the mainland. While its followers seemed to have much in common with the Tribe of the Torton Him, (both of them worshipping the drippings of their bean curd) the new tribe, known as the Church of the Celestial Ram, practiced intense rituals of zoolatry, first worshipping a Mermaid with two tails and her breasts bared before evolving into a more modest version of the Mermaid, and finally settling on the Celestial Ram as its deity of choice.

The Church of the Celestial Ram seems to convert more and more followers from the Tribe of Torton Him every day. More and more of their temples pop up in populated areas all the time. In recent years a new trend has arisen: new Churches are being added to the few remaining Temples of Knowledge, creating a meld between the two and effectively converting the few remaining Knowledgers to the Celestial Ram faith. But how can two such opposing belief structures merge in harmony? I have made such a temple the subject of my field site and research.

This particular field site is located in the crux of an urban centre. Although it seems strange to find it here, it is nevertheless always teeming with devotees and those simply trying the bean curd drippings for the first time, hesitant to admit that simply by coming in they have converted.

Unlike the mechanical and routine atmosphere of Torton Him, the Church of the Celestial Ram is structured to be the centre of the community. There are chairs to sit in but also comfortable couches and a fireplace to warm oneself by. Followers are encouraged to come not just to pray, but also to work on secular accomplishments, socialize, converse, and even engage in pre-mating rituals. While the doors are open to all who come, there is one expectation made of anyone who walks through them: they must engage in the Divine Ritual of the Celestial Ram.

The Ritual, while never difficult, is highly adaptable and can be made to suit almost any worshipper. There is no specific time of mass, so followers can come and go as they please. If one has very little time, there is another Church of the Celestial Ram just up the street with a drive-by window where you can get your spirituality on the go. Despite the diversity of the Ritual, there are some elements that remain stagnant.

The Ritual begins with worshippers lining up to make a sacrifice at the Shrine of the Celestial Ram, either alone or in pairs. Often, one member of a group will wait in line while other members of their party wait in the designated resting area. This is seen by all as acceptable behaviour, and all will receive the coveted bean curd drippings despite only one of them having actively participated in the Ritual. Sometimes the line is long and other times it is nonexistent, though worshippers are still expected to wait a requisite amount of time before one of the four Priestesses on hand will see to their needs. While Priests are also welcome in the Church, it is generally frowned upon by the collective of the worshippers.

The Shrine itself differs from Church to Church, but many elements remain the same: there is a large table that divides the worshippers from the Priestesses. This is holy boundary that must never be crossed. Behind it are various tubes and pots where the holy bean curd drippings are first produced and then blessed, and for the un-ordained to enter there would sully their holiness forever. To one side of these pots is another table, often elevated higher, adorned with fruit and flower products as well and various spices and creams for those who wish to make further sacrifice to the Celestial Ram. Above it all is large tablet displaying the current selections of bean curd drippings, for this is another element of the Church that is customizable to the liking of the worshiper.

Once one has reached the first table of the Shrine, one must select from a wide variety of choices. There are bean-curd drippings that have been flavoured with various nuts and berries, as well as the fruits of many far-off lands. There are sub-categories of bean curd drippings that are pre-mixed with the whipped and beaten milkings of various bovid animals, some of which are even then further adorned with spices and herbs. While selections vary, at this stage there is no incorrect choice to be made from the menu: in the eyes of the Great Celestial Ram and its Mermaid ancestors, all bean curds are created equal.

There are several missteps that can lead to scorn at this juncture. While there is no slight so damnable that the worshipper will be denied service, repeated errors can result in patterns of gossip, ridicule and avoidance until the usurper is forced from the Church in shame. One such offence is to request "just plain" bean curd drippings. While variations of normal, unflavoured bean curd do exist, they are referred to by the holy titles of "Dark Roast" or "Columbian" (et al). To refer to the holy bean curd dripping as "Just" or "Plain" is seen as derogatory, and will be met with hateful stares and often the correction of the Priestesses. Another misstep is requesting the Priestess add sugarcane powder or bovid milkings to the sacred bean curd drippings on your behalf. While as stated above some of the drippings do come with such endowments, requesting changes to the potion's recipe is seen as a great offence and a sign of continued affiliation to the Torton Him, especially if the orders are barked with their specific vernacular of "double-double" or "triple-triple." But there is no slight as obscene as the disgracing of the sacred chalice. Bean curd drippings are provided in chalices of three varying volumes, each of them named with a different language to promote solidarity and community amongst the world's peoples. To refer to them as "small" or "medium" is seen as an affront to everything the Church stands for. Doing so will result in the Priestess pretending she does not understand you, as though you have begun to speak in the devil's tongue. This period of avoidance will continue until the worshipper either corrects himself or (in extreme cases) is corrected by the Priestess.

Once one has successfully navigated these social taboos and ordered the selected bean curd dripping, one is expected to pay tribute. The cost of the tribute is strictly monetary, a system left over from previous monotheistic religions. The amount of the tribute is not determined by what the worshipper can pay however, but rather is based on a static system in which each type and flavour of bean curd dripping is given its own symbolic value. In addition to this tribute, there is a second tribute to be left is a small circular cup located on the table. While participation in this part of the ritual is seen as voluntary, not participating will result in scorn from the Priestesses. One benefit is that there is no upper or lower limit to this monetary sacrifice. There are small things the Church attempts to give back however, such as tickets to the minstrels of the area, provided in conjunction with the Worshippers of the Pomaceous Occupation.

While Priestesses prepare and anoint the bean curd drippings, the worshipper then makes his way to the second table. After waiting patiently, if his heart is pure, he or she will be rewarded with the requested bean curd dripping. It is at this point that some measure of choice is allowed, and there are far less pitfalls for the uninitiated to fall into.

One can chose to perform further sacrifice, not to the Celestial Ram but to the bean curd dripping itself. Honey, sugar, and spices can be added alone or in combination to show your solidarity to the bean curd before consumption. Those who do not perform this sacrifice to unflavoured blends are not seen as sacrilegious however. Indeed, quite the opposite. These worshippers are seen as the True Believers of the faith, those who worship the bean curd dripping in its pure and undiluted state.

Once the bean curd dripping has been seasoned to taste, the worshipper is free to step away from the Shrine and rejoin his fellow worshippers or leave the Church completely, having fulfilled his part in the Ritual of the Celestial Ram for another day.

TOUCH YOUR NOSE

1

I was eighteen months deep cover when I finally got my first real in. Not deep cover as in fake mustache either, but real deep cover. No–friends–no–family–don't–forget–to–talk–with–your–American–accent deep cover. Eighteen months.

The first seven months were spent managing a failing restaurant in Virginia, a place so bad they did a two-episode stint of Kitchen Nightmares on it. After that started turning a major profit, there were three months as a management consultant – three months is not a long time to build a reputation though, so it was something of a smash-and-grab, a lot of dollars spent to get my reputation to where it needed to be. By my ninth month of deep cover, I was turning down interviews for Forbes. That got me the attention of head hunters, and then it was just a matter of waiting for the right offer. It took me a month to get a call from Tyler Carter, VP of the San Diego Valley division of Shane Enterprises. I'd been there eight months when I'd gotten my opening.

Eighteen months, and the accent was only just starting to feel natural in my mouth.

My name is Simon Monk, and this is what I do.

It was at an office Christmas party, which was being held in mid-November. December was a busy month for us; everything needed to be filed and catalogued and pressed and stamped and put into boxes, or so I was told – it was my first Christmas on the job. So Christmas got pushed ahead to November. Christmas in San Diego – in any month really – is an oxymoron. I spent any time I wasn't at the office going commando in shorts and standing in front of my AC for hours on end reading *Businessman Weekly*. At the party I was wearing a suit and tie – most were here for fun, but I was here to work. It was actually the first time I'd really been working in eighteen months.

Tyler had rented the penthouse suite of the convention center for the night. The room was huge and dark with Maplewood floors, three bars, and a glass ceiling that looked out over the whole city and up to a blanket of deep blue full of stars above. It was enough to make anyone feel romantic.

There was a patio that stretched all the way around the floor and looked out upon a view that dropped thirty stories to the street below. It was vertigo inducing. The patio was filled with smokers trying to escape the cool air-conditioned and clean-smelling interior of the penthouse for the stale swarmy smoke of their cigarettes. I wanted to be smoking. I'd quit eighteen months ago. Smokers are off-putting to non-smokers, but non-smokers appeal to everyone. This wasn't Mad Men and I wasn't Jon Hamm. Smoking and riffling through people's food doesn't mix well either, so Simon Monk had never been a smoker.

I was the only one not smoking on the patio, a bit of a slip. We all slip though; slipping isn't the problem. Trying too hard to correct the slip, that's where you're made.

I was drinking my third Scotch and Soda. Three was a good place to be at, enough that I could seem relaxed but not enough that I start pronouncing aluminum aluminium or anything else. The trick now would be to hold myself at this level of buzz for the rest of the night. Two virgin colas in the next forty-five minutes, one trip to the bathroom, then another Scotch. Rinse and repeat.

There was a large man named Craig Pollard on the other side of the patio auditioning for the role of the party drunk, uncontested, though still fighting the race with all his might. He was tall and heavy and battled to keep himself clean-shaven from the neck up to look as professional as possible throughout the day, but had an inordinate amount of multicolored body hair, with patches of fiery red and deep brown with a streak of white down his back. I knew this from my second night in San Diego, when he'd insisted on showing me the town and we'd ended up at three different full-nude bars. Each of these bars he'd snuck vodka into and insisted that I joined him in his libations. At the third one he'd insisted on buying me a lap dance, wherein a young girl with a badly concealed caesarean scar stared at me with dull uninterested eyes while trying (and failing) to make me erect. It was my first hint that life in San Diego was going to be frustrating, a portent proven true many times since.

Not long after that Craig had attempted to bring me to ComiCon, but that was where I had drawn the line. I give up a lot for this job, but I have not and will not go that deep into cover. If you stare into the abyss, and all that jive.

At the moment, Craig was surrounded by four interns who were marvelling both at his ability to hold his liquor and the fact that his beard seemed to have started to grow in in the brief time since the party had started. He had half a four-ounce steak in his left hand and would take a large bite absently when he felt like it, eating it as though it were a party favor.

One of the interns was a young woman named Cecilia, whom Craig had been covertly trying to get into bed for some time. Covertly for Craig, I mean, by which I mean that he hadn't openly approached her and asked her for intercourse.

I found myself staring at him. He was crass, and spoke using long words that he used properly but pronounced poorly. The three young men that looked at him did so with awe and respect as they asked him about his department's quarterly income figures. Cecilia was staring at him with doe eyes that seemed to take up her entire face. She was wearing a purple dress that sparkled and a perfume that danced on the night air. Craig turned and smiled at me and raised his glass; I smiled and nodded curtly back at him.

"I bet you could steal her away, if you went over," a woman said, siding up alongside me. There was a menthol cigarette clasped between her lips like a leg in a bear trap, the filter nearly crushed between those pursed red lines. Her hair was up and held together with pins and a net. She wore a blazer with the collar undone, and a skirt, and looked smart. She wore a broach the same color as her lips. Crimson.

I turned my head to face her. It was Lydia Carter, Tyler's wife. She was in the prime age to be a successful woman: too old to be a trophy wife, but not so old that she'd lose her husband to one. Not that Tyler has struck me as that sort anyway. They'd married at nineteen, when he was just an investment banker, or so he was fond of telling you when the subject of relationships came up.

She had been watching me for the better part of an hour. I caught her eye when I went back for my second Scotch and Soda, as I'd walked right past the group she was huddled into. A pack of lions, protecting their lionesses. As I said, everyone at the party had been dressed casually: pascal blues and pinks for the men, evening social wear for the women. In my black-and-whites I must have stood out like a sore thumb, or more appropriately, like a zebra. She'd pointed to me and asked Tyler who I was; he'd answered something I couldn't hear. I couldn't hear any of it actually, but body language is quite telegraphic at times.

She'd tried to approach me to say hello while I was on my way back from getting my third (and current) drink, but I'd managed to avoid her by placing a server between us. She'd stood there with her hand outstretched and light dancing in her eyes for a moment, like something motion-captured, and I'd known it was time to make my way out to the balcony and get some fresh, nicotine-saturated air.

Hence the slip, but not a slip.

And now here we were, the wind from the updraft catching a few stray wisps of her hair, and my tie. I turned away from Craig and looked at her, my drink caught halfway between my belly and my mouth. My mouth gaped a little at her beauty, quite deliberately. I turned from her to Craig and Cecilia the Intern again for a moment, as if not completely sure what she was talking about.

"Oh," I chuckled, taking another sip of my drink. "No, I wasn't looking at her."

Her eyes darted across me, up and down, finding their way to the empty ring finger that helped hold my glass. There were no tan lines from where one had been edged off, no green marks from cheap gold. Her eyes wandered a little beyond that, but not much, and even now I don't know if it had been an act to hide that she was looking for a wedding band or not. "She seems like a perfectly nice young woman," she said finally, turning away from me and sharing in my gaze across at them.

I paused. I'd known the words I'd use before she'd even walked over, before the party had even begun. Now all there was was the timing of them. "Young is the operative word."

She raised an eyebrow at me. I pretended not to notice.

"I'm not looking to get that kind of reputation around the office anyway," I continued with feigned levity, chuckling. "And I'm certainly not ready to settle down."

Her eyes locked onto mine and waited for me to turn. I took another swallow of my drink, counted to ten, and then did. All perfectly planned and rehearsed. Like a scene from a play.

All the best disasters start out that way.

"My name is Lydia Tyler," she said, extending a hand to me the way women in movies about the forties did. I took it and shook it once, firmly, the way I would have shaken a man's hand. I respected her, I respected what she did and how she did it – not that she knew that yet. Her hand was like spun silk or velvet, smooth with flighty fingers that even then tickled the inside of my wrist.

"Simon Monk," I said, smiling at her graciously. I took another sip from my drink and then placed it precariously on the banister of the balcony, so that there was nothing between us but the night. "Pleasure."

She beamed honestly, her cheeks red and healthy. She still kept eye contact with me, as though I were the only thing in the room. Not a lioness, it seemed, but a cougar. "The pleasure is all mine," she said, folding her hands before her.

I was eighteen months deep cover at Shane Industries when I finally got my first real in. Eighteen months.

2

There was a thick glass wall close to the main floor bar that was covered in evenly spaced rectangular notches. Each notch held a spoon with a taste of a different dessert on it, the epitaph of the trend towards smaller portions in fine dining. At least it was free.

Behind it was a ledge that ran all the way along the windowed wall and was cool and refreshing and looked out onto the sparkling city below.

It was possibly the most romantic spot on the west coast.

My shirt had become undone at some point, the knot of my tie loose and clinging to life near my nipple. My sixth Scotch and Soda was in my hand, and I was using it to mark time.

Lydia was still poised and perfect. She had champagne in her hand that the waiter refilled whenever it was low, moving in and out like a shadow. Even I wouldn't have been able to tell you what he looked like.

We'd been laughing for what seemed like forever and an instant at the same time. Lydia laughed truly and honestly, her chest heaving and her mouth taking up most of her face. She laughed the way children laugh, teenagers caught up in a whirlwind of flirtation they don't yet know is flirtation, playing games without subtext and without manipulation. Patty-Cake behind the pitcher's mound.

One story had parlayed seamlessly into the next so that there was no chance to catch our breath or realize how much time was passing.

Her champagne glass dangled precariously near her lips as her laughter faded again, and she looked at me side-on with those soulful eyes from beneath those perfectly preened lashes. "You must have been such a cad," she said slyly before taking another sip. "I'll bet the waitresses were all over you."

I laughed and tweaked my nose with my thumb and tuned away. It was a practised move, one of thirty fake-tells that had been repeated and endorsed until they became second nature. Nothing is as it seems, nothing fits where it's supposed to go. I stared out the window at the blinking red light of a control tower off in the distance and counted to ten. She must have thought I was looking at the stars and didn't move to follow my gaze. Her eyes have been locked intently – hungrily – on mine every since she approached me on the balcony.

I smirked. She leaned her head in every so slightly, tilting it to one side. I turned, made eye contact, and let the smirk grow into a smile. "Okay, there was one."

"Ha ha, I knew it!" she bellowed, uncaring of anyone who might hear. She slapped my knee playfully – an electric feeling that shattered the touch barrier. Outside the moon was big and full and bright orange, a hunter's moon. Focus. "Cad."

"Now," I objected, holding up one finger of the hand that was cradling the scotch by the brim. "It wasn't like that."

"Sure it wasn't."

I snorted. It's a hard thing to fake and takes a lot of practice. The act is like self-inflicted water boarding. "It wasn't. Honestly. And it wasn't a waitress, it was a hostess."

"What's a hostess?"

"The girl that greets you at the door and take you to your table."

"That's not a waitress?"

"Not if she doesn't take orders," I mumbled and finished my drink. A waiter eyed me and I waved him off with two fingers, quickly and discreetly.

She hummed. She was getting buzzed. She was also getting brave, leaning against the ledge now and casting her eye out over the crowd. She was looking for someone, but didn't find whoever it was. Her husband more than likely. Was she looking to make sure he wasn't watching, or was she looking *hoping* that he was watching? I did not know. All people, and all women especially, desire attention. The only mitigating factor was the type of attention they enjoyed most, consciously or unconsciously. Was Lydia Carter seeking the attention of a new lover or the attention of a jealous husband? In any event, the result is the same and the answer requires a deeper knowledge of psychology and sexual dynamics than I wish to have or employ.

"So this... Hostess," she said the word begrudgingly, as though it were distasteful to her. "Let me guess: tall, blonde, legs that go all the way up to Canada?"

"Now..."

"Sordid affairs in back rooms and dark freezers with strawberries and cream and cheesecake?"

I laughed, this time for real. I clipped it off though; real laughter can be a problem. Real laughter, once heard enough times, can make it far, far too obvious when fake laughter is being employed.

"Her name was Chanelle," I began, swallowing.

"Chanelle? Oh, I like her already. I see a good home-spun girl whose Daddy warned her about men like you."

A controlled laugh. "She was blonde, she wasn't tall though. That was actually how we met."

"You met because she was short?" Lydia finished her champagne and immediately motioned for another. The waiter produced it immediately, as if from air, and provided me with another Scotch and Soda as well, although one had not been requested. I'd have to nurse it now, but try not to make it obvious that I was nursing it.

"There was a jug on a high shelf she was trying to reach. She was jumping for it and trying to knock it down." I paused, taking a moment to try and be as delicate as possible. "She had... copious secondary sexual characteristics," I said, cupping my hands before me to mime what I meant.

Lydia laughed.

"So the kitchen staff wasn't helping her, they were just watching her jump for this jug. When I saw this, I, being a gentleman, retrieved the jug for her."

"And that was when she confessed to you about being good home-spun girl whose Daddy warned her about men like you and you started a sordid affair in back rooms and dark freezers with strawberries and cream and cheesecake."

"No, we rarely spoke until my last night at the restaurant."

"Ooooh, the last night. Those are always good stories. 'Come here, sir, I need to give you something to remember me by.' Ha."

She was being purposefully crass now, and was enjoying herself. Without even trying I realized that she'd been that girl, some years ago now, having affairs in closets and empty bathroom stalls. There was an age limit of such behavior to get the result that women wanted, to make a man feel as though this was his luckiest night on earth. You couldn't enjoy that level of attention as an attractive older woman, no matter how hard you tried to play the game. You could get a man lucky, but you could never be a man's lotto-win again. And there was a fierceness in a man when he'd just won the lotto, a manic energy that surges and is spontaneous and deadly and contagious. It's in his eyes and his hands and his heart, blood pumping, sweat dripping, everything exactly as it should.

Her eyes danced over the crowd for her husband again, and it suddenly struck me how unfair it all was. If a man wanted to "win the lottery" again, he could just play another ticket, to continue the metaphor. But Lydia had *been* the ticket, and now could not be anymore, and was thus shut out of the experience. What a horribly cruel twist of fate that the ones who are best at the game – in fact, the ones for whom the game even exists at all – are the first ones disqualified.

"There was this tradition in the back of house. I knew about it, but I never thought they'd do it to me. Anyone leaving, they nab and drag out into the alley out back and they pour freezing water over them, and then they pour flour over them."

Lydia's hands went to her mouth and she started laughing again. There was lipstick on her palms now. "Oh my god!"

"Ruined a perfectly good suit."

"Oh my god!!"

"So then, later in the night, Chanelle comes by to say goodbye to me when I'm in the freezer... and one thing did lead to another."

"Ha. I told you. Freezer," she chimed triumphantly.

I nodded. "Yes, well, nothing happened. Nothing to write home about anyway. But she didn't realize until she got home that night that she spent the rest of her shift with my handprints on the back of her pants in flour." I laughed at that. Lydia did too.

There actually had been a Chanelle. She'd been cute and sweet and had always had highlights in her hair at obvious and unprofessional places. She'd been exceptionally uncomfortable about those secondary sexual characteristics I mentioned, and often walked with a tray in front of her even though she never once took an order or delivered a drink. Camouflage was the art of making something that didn't belong look as though it did.

"Oh that poor girl," Lydia said, her laughter trailing off as she wiped her eyes. "Was she young?"

Truth comes quickly and without thought, but can get you in trouble. Tailored responses and selective honesty is better, but requires a level of insight I don't always possess. What was she looking for me to be here? Did she want me to be the caddish cradle-robber that could have any woman he wanted but chose to be with her? Or did she want me to be the mature man, interested chiefly in her type and ilk, for whom chasing a younger woman would be unappealing?

Immediately I realized it's the latter. She wanted to be the lotto ticket again, despite being the skilled hunter. But before I could answer, we were approached.

I almost mistook him for the waiter again, and held up my scotch to let him know I was still drinking the last one he provided me with uninvited.

It wasn't though; it was Tyler Carter.

He lumbered large above me from my position sitting on the floor, his shadow moving past me and falling over the city below. Interesting the way life plays out like metaphors sometimes, isn't it? So many things are only ironic in hindsight.

He regarded me for a moment, then smiled. "Simon."

I nodded and raised my glass to toast him. "Tyler."

Lydia smiled up at him, as though now that he was here, he was the only thing she had eyes for. It was impressive. Switching gears quickly was an art form in and of itself. There were no telltale stutters or stammers as she took Tyler by the arm, squeezed it, and kissed him on the cheek.

I realized with some trepidation that I liked her.

"Simon was just regaling me with stories of managing a restaurant in Idaho."

"Virginia," I corrected out of habit.

"Virginia," she smiled.

"Nothing too scandalous, I hope," Tyler said.

I got to my feet and brushed nonexistent dust off my knees.

"There was an affair with a young waitress."

She had assumed Chanelle was young.

Tyler grinned in that 'you old dog' sort of way that men did at one another and thought that women didn't notice.

"Your wife is a rare woman," I said, touching her gently on the arm. "You're a very lucky man, Tyler." I nodded to her and stepped away without another word, as though Lydia and I had not been deep in conversation, but merely passing ships in the night. Cecilia was by herself at the bar, the lummox she'd been swooning for likely passed out on the bathroom floor by now, and I slid along beside her and ordered a coke. Just a coke this time, nothing else. I left what remained of my alcohol on the bar for the waiter to dispose of.

I kept Lydia and her husband in the corner of my eye. They left soon after, and she threw me a glance over her bare, milky-white shoulder as she did. Her eyes were alive and forgiving and yearning and hungry, even hungrier than they had been when she'd approached me on the balcony.

"Nice tie," Cecilia said, smiling at me with wanton drunken delight. Her eyes were lazy and sleepy.

"It was," I replied. I drained my coke, then made for the exit.

3

People think they know what deep cover is and they don't. They think they know because they watched that one Val Kilmer movie where he goes home at the end of the day and tries on different mustaches and suddenly he's speaking in a Russian accent. People think deep cover is just another part of your suit you take off at the end of your workday.

With deep cover, the suit is never off. You go home and you are deep cover. You take a shower and you are deep cover. You take a shit, you are deep cover. You stay deep cover because if you stop once – even for a second – it's too easy to slip back into what you were before. Too easy to curse in your mother tongue if you stub your toe, or turn your head when somebody says the wrong name on a crowded subway.

I got home close to 4 AM from the party sober. My younger self hates me – he cannot imagine ever remembering how I got back from a party. But even that memory, that nostalgia, is a construction, because having been a wild child is a part of a wunderkind in the new millennium business world.

Have you ever told a lie so often you forget it is one? Maybe you told your friends you lost your virginity to Sally Plain-and-Tall when you were seventeen, when really it wasn't until you were twenty-one and wasn't to Sally, it was to Mary? But you've told the story and pictured it in your head for so many years that now you fool yourself. That is deep cover, but instead it's for your favorite food. For the way you speak. For the way you like to fuck.

I got home and I took off my tie and I laid it down against the green chair. It was a one-bedroom apartment with a small bedroom and a large living room with very little furniture in it. I liked being able to see all of it at once, like an infant being swaddled: I knew my boundaries. I showered and brushed my teeth and put clean pajamas in the dryer to heat them for when I put them on. The apartment was often cold at night.

You never practice deep cover. You are just it. There is never one moment, never one instant when you are not. Nobody can see you practicing reciting all your ex-girlfriends in front of a mirror so you can keep them in order. You have to know all of that – all of it – before you go. Hesitation is key, learning the right amount. Too much and it seems like you're making it up, too little and it seems like you're reciting regurgitated lines.

I took out my phone, a last-model Apple. Whatever was trendy at the time. I punched in my password – 0852 – and there was a message from Lydia. There would have been no indication of the message had I not put in the password. She had written:

"This is Lydia. I didn't get the chance to thank you, I had a great evening."

I had not given her my number, intentionally. This was a game of chess that was more like a game of dominoes, in which the moves you made at the start could inflict causations which you had no way of stopping. You had to be careful and deliberate. I thought that way then.

It was a gambit not giving her my number. I could not ask her for hers: far too typical an approach toward a married woman. Power is as much at play as flirtation -- in asking for her number, I would be asking for something of her. The power of the next move would be in my hands then. To ask a powerful woman for her number is to ask her to submit to your will. But I equally could not offer her mine: I could not surrender. If she wanted me to be the hunter, I could not act the prey. I didn't know what she wanted from me yet; there wasn't enough information. But doing nothing risked that first real lead in eighteen months. Eighteen months of going home smelling like grease and funneling money into failing businesses.

I looked at my watch. It had been two hours since I had left the party. Two hours in which she had gotten home – drunk and giddy – and found my number, on Facebook or on my resume site or on the company directory. I assumed the latter: she was business-minded and her head would go the business solutions.

"Me too ;)," I texted back, and waited for the animation to leave.

The result was instantaneous: ":)"

I waited, and said nothing. I made myself French toast.

The bread was beginning to crisp when she said: "You never did mention the waitress's age."

"What waitress?"

"Hostess*"

I paused. "She was in her thirties."

Chanelle had been twenty-two. She'd been finishing her GED and had had aspirations of one day being an advertiser, specifically for books. She thought that if *Fifty Shades* could have been marketed to more copies sold than anything else, than anything could be. She'd never actually read *Fifty Shades* though, only the cheap supermarket romance novellas that people said *Fifty Shades* was. She read them while sitting on a chair in the back hall of the restaurant and sometimes – just sometimes – would get so into the story that she would relax and let the book fall comfortably into her lap, exposing her cleavage to the ogling stares of the servers stepping by.

There was a several minutes pause. When she came back with the simple "okay" like I had suspected she would, I was almost done my toast. I ate it dry, without syrup. When I was completely done, I took two orange gel capsules I kept in the pantry by the fridge and swallowed them with a small glass of ice water.

I knew the conversation was over. I pressed the button on the top of my phone and turned it off, then pressed it on again and typed in my password – 2580. There were different apps now, none of them the same. There was no Candy Crush or Fruit Ninja or Bloons. I opened up the text app and punched in a number; there were no contacts. Remembering telephone numbers is a skill lost to the digital age one has to resurrect when one is deep cover.

I typed, "Contact," then shut off the phone and went to bed, and dreamed the dreams of a man I never was and would never really, truly be. That is what it means to be deep cover.

I had not dreamed my own dreams for eighteen months.

4

The next move happened fast. It had to. While emotions can linger for years or even decades, if one wants action and movement, you have to strike while the iron's hot.

Six days later, I was at the weekly staff meeting. Weekly staff meetings at major companies are exercises in masturbation: pictures and graphs and charts to illustrate how good each of us were at doing what we were paid to do that week. It is the grown-up equivalent of presenting your hastily drawn macaroni art to your mother for display on the door of the fridge.

I paid little attention to the numbers or the charts or the trends. Great leaps in success of companies that have already topped the one billion mark in pre-tax revenue rarely came from such minor factors. Once you grew so large that you were a part of the culture, it took great epistemic shifts within that culture to truly affect you.

I paid great attention, however, to the presenters. How much trouble did the peacocks go through to display their feathers in front of their master? Tyler sat at the back of the room and watched, making a note on the pad in front of him every once and a while. Were he and I the only ones really watching, actively listening? Were we watching for the same things, I wondered at the time. I suspected then that we were not, that he was hunting for some forbidden pattern in the numbers in front of him. I suspect now, perhaps, that he was looking the same as me.

The people that presented wore their hearts on their sleeves. I took notes on the numbers and discarded the paper immediately afterward. I took mental notes and filed them away forever. David was exhausted and fumbled his way through his presentation, but not because of alcohol or drugs. His eyes were never red, even deep in the corners where the Visine didn't help. He didn't stumble on every word, but always the same words: long syllables, usually with a 'b'. I decided at once it was a combination of nerves and the re-emergence of a long-dormant stammer. It would pass on its own. David worked for Shane, and you didn't get there by being weak or lacking confidence; therefore, his nerves were not caused by his work. Stress in the home life then – not kids; work provided an escape from kids. I narrowed in on issues with the wife or the soon-expected death of a parent. It went in the file without judgement. The file isn't for judgements; it's for information.

Craig had been drunk, but not recently. It was still in his pores. He was the one I'd been waiting for, the real act to follow. I wanted to impress – to leave an impression – and to do it, I needed to follow a weak performance. This was chess played with thin paper pieces, where even gripping them too hard would make them crumble and become useless. Seduction, no matter the method, is a delicate art.

I waited for Craig to finish talking about the boost his work caused in pre-tax revenue in the hardware division, a difference of cents on the millions, and said:

"Moon landing."

Eyes turned to me, as though I'd been invisible the entire time. I had been.

"Simon, something to say?" Tyler asked, punctuating his syllables with his pen.

I pretended to look surprised. I held my breath for a moment – heart rate increased, cheeks slightly flushed. "Oh, sorry. I've been doing research into this new company out of Virginia. Hometown boys, you know how it is. They've been working on this new hardware, much smaller than the stuff on the market today, but faster. They've been working on it in their basement and living off Kickstarters. They call it Moon Landing."

It was the most I'd spoken all at once in weeks. It was almost exhausting. Exposition always is.

"The things they're trying... well, it'd be great, if it worked. That's a big if though. The money you're saving, Craig," I turn to Craig. "I was just thinking we could invest there. Cents on the dollar don't mean much to us, but to start-ups... well, we remember."

None of them remembered.

"Anyway, sorry. Not the place. Sorry to interrupt."

Craig finished his presentation as Tyler scribbled a note onto the pad in front of him. As soon as I'm out of the meeting, I turned on my phone and texted, "Moon Landing."

It was time to trigger an epistemic shift.

5

See, all it takes is money, and knowing where the holes in the system are. That and people: you need a lot of people to act in just the right way for just the right amount of time.

Since the dawn of the Internet age, the stock exchange has changed so dramatically that nobody except the extremely wealthy can really trade stocks fairly anymore. It's an industry that relies heavily on speed: how fast can I act? Back in the day when all the traders were on one floor, that amounted to who could talk the fastest and the loudest to be heard. Now though, that speed isn't measured in minutes, but seconds. Not seconds, but microseconds. Not microseconds, but *nano*seconds. These distances are imperceptible to the human eye, but to a computer they matter immensely. Stock brokers pay big money to have their computer just a few feet closer to the server, trying to shave off as many tenths of a nano as they can. Private fibre-op lines are built to be as straight as they could so that packets of information aren't diverted.

All this is simple enough. It's hard to understand in such small terms, but if you squint your eyes and tilt your head sideways, you can kind of see what happened. But a few years ago, somebody really figured out how to exploit the system.

See when you buy a lot of stock on your computer, that order is broken up and sent to different exchanges all around the country – so it arrives at those exchanges at slightly different times. We're talking about thousandths of a second in the difference. Some of them go to New York and some of them go to Florida. Here's the trick: when New York gets a big order, it sends a message to Florida to let it know, and that message goes over their own high-speed connection. The warning arrives before your order does, and Florida knows to jack up the price of that stock. Now your money doesn't buy you as much. All that in the time it took you to click your mouse.

Essentially what this did was make it very hard for normal people – people who were not high-frequency traders – to make any money in the stock market. The system was usurped to work against you. What it did do, however, is make it extremely easy to *lose* a lot of money in the stock market.

Every time New York receives a large volume of purchases on a specific stock, and recognizes that action as just its portion of a much larger order, it sends that information off to Florida and they jack up the price. Click the buy button, then click the refresh button: uh-oh, you just paid more for your stock than you had intended to. Now the stock costs more, up to $1.08 a share from $1.06. Click 'buy' again, the same thing. It recognizes the trend, now it's at $1.13, a bigger jump than the last time. Each of these clicks represents huge transactions, thousands of dollars each. Tens of thousands more than likely.

I never ask how much money it takes. I don't want to know. I know it's enough that I can really only pull this trick once.

I watched the stock slowly rise, inch by inch, dollar by dollar. The transactions followed the Fibonacci numbers: the second purchase two minutes after the first, the second three minutes after that, the third five minutes after that, and so on. Two hours into our little pattern, there was a purchase out of order, a large one. The stock jumped. The new buyer, the one that wasn't a part of the pattern, went through at 3pm.

I dearly hoped it was Tyler, because immediately afterward the purchases came in rapid succession – as fast as they could be processed. At the time of the out-of-order purchase, the stock was at $5.08 a share. By the time the frenzy of buying was complete and the market closed, it was well over $10.

Eighteen months of unbelievably pedantic meetings and so many tens of thousands of dollars I didn't even want to think about it, all to potentially double the worth of Tyler Carter's personal stock portfolio. Tens of thousands of dollars just to impress a little man with a big hat enough that he'd mention me in passing to his wife.

6

The following Friday I was at a bar in downtown San Diego called Theories. It was dark and the carpet was poorly kept, and there were framed theoretical phrases every few feet along the wall with misaligned faded stock-photos of molecules in the backgrounds of each. These phrases ranged from the intellectual to the absurd:

Velocity equals the Hubble constant times distance.

$E = mc2$

If I fill my mouth with soda and ice cream, my brain will stop from brain freeze even if the soda was warm.

Things like that. There was a long bar and a dance floor that nobody danced at even though the music was impossibly loud, and roughly thirty pool tables. There were blue lights, but not nearly enough of them on, and children drinking far too much alcohol in the corner. One of them might have been old enough to get a learner's permit, and two were still clutching the book bags they'd brought to school with them, yet the bartender still hadn't carded them. They eyed everyone else in the bar suspiciously through secretive glances, as though constantly afraid that they would soon be caught and asked to leave.

I'd gone to Theories with Craig after work. Actually, that's a bit of an oversimplification: we had gone from work to Stompers, a restaurant that seemed to think it could get around various health-code violations by marketing itself instead as an 'eatery.' We had gone from Stompers to Liquid, Liquid to Flappers, Flappers to Wild Ones, and Wild Ones to Theories.

Liquid had been posh and upscale, and had it been twenty years earlier, I would have said that everyone there had been on cocaine. As it was, I wasn't quite sure what breed of drug they were on.

Flappers had been a VIP bar that we'd gotten into by virtue of our position and dress, but had received so many dirty looks thanks to Craig's boisterous humor that we'd been asked to leave after only three over-priced drinks. Cecilia had met us outside of Flappers and had followed us to Wild Ones and Theories. I could only assume that Craig had messaged her to tell her to come join us, though for the life of me I had no idea when. As far as I could tell, he hadn't even taken out his phone all night.

Wild Ones was an unnamed Irish bar next to a strip club, the name clearly applying to the strip club alone. Cecilia refused to go into the strip club half and I played the part of the gentleman by stubbornly agreeing with her, although there was nothing gentlemanly about it in truth. I was gravely concerned that Craig would try to order me a lap dance and that I would have to try and talk my way out of it. And so, outvoted, the three of us stayed on the Irish side of the bar with Craig craning his head to see the topless wonders that lay just beyond his reach until, finally, he gave up and suggested that we head to Theories.

I was having considerable difficulty maintaining the proper level of buzz through all of this, in large part due to Craig's destructive machinations. I had had my three Scotch and Sodas – that hadn't been an issue. I had even managed to have one virgin cola afterward, even though Craig tried to accompany me each and every time I went to the bar to order. But when my first virgin drink was running low, Craig took it upon himself to order tequila shots, followed by something with a name that sounded like a pornographic movie title, followed by the return of my Scotch and Soda, one for each of the three of us.

It quickly became impossible to control and moderate the level of drunk I was becoming, and I resolved to switch to virgin whenever I could sneak one past Craig – the issue was if he was not absent enough, I would get too drunk, and if he was absent too much, I would get too sober. The latter might not seem like an issue, but it could prove a dead giveaway if the situation turned. Despite what some actors will tell you, there is no perfect way to falsify an alcoholic stupor.

But there was very little hope of that happening; Craig rarely left my side and when he did it was to urinate, leaving Cecilia with me, always with instructions to "keep my hands off" followed by hearty claps on the back and strained chuckles from me. My vision was becoming unbalanced, and I resolved to try and avoid words that I might, in my inebriated state, pronounce incorrectly. Whenever possible, say 'home' instead of 'house,' 'leave' instead of 'out,' and under no circumstances talk about a certain malleable metal sheet that one can use to cover food or protect one's thoughts from alien invaders.

You might be wondering why I agreed to this if it's truly as much work as I'm making it out to be. And while it was true that barhopping with Craig was a lot like trying to care for a three hundred pound hungry toddler with Asperger's, it was something that a reasonable person would see as 'fun'. And 'fun' was a part of the personality that I desperately needed to protect and cling to, especially at this delicate stage of my plans.

You see, it wasn't just enough for me to be good at my job. Loads of people are good at their jobs, but very few of them are also likable. Many of them spend their days running TPS reports twelve hours a day, only get paid for eight, and then retire to the colourful world of an MMRPG for a few hours before knocking out for bed and starting the whole process all over again, only breaking the schedule when alcohol and desperate loneliness somehow produced overweight children. I couldn't be that: I had to be good at the job, and also be liked by those at the job, which translated into having to be *very* good at the job so that I would have enough time left over after having done the job in order to form the social connections needed to be liked at the job. Most Type-A personalities trying to accomplish this do so out of some self-gratifying need to be liked or need to be needed, and even then not without copious amounts of uppers.

I had to do this while remaining relatively drug-free, *and* doing the actual job of remaining in deep cover.

And the truth was I did like Craig – he was awkward in a way that he somehow owned. Was he obnoxious? Yes. Loud? Yes. Insistent? Naturally. But somehow still very likable. I think I envied him on some level, the way he careened from one moment to the next without so much as a thought or a plan; so different from the way I was forced to live. Craig was honest in a way I could never be and off-putting in a way I had never been. I'm not sure that I ever enjoyed being in his company, but it was certainly easier to feign enjoyment around him.

It was also easier to hide in his shadow. Craig was loud, and always over-spoke and under-thought, making it easy for anyone around him to simply blend in. In some strange way he became a part of my deep cover, one of the tools within my toolbox, like a jackhammer – yes, rarely used, but effective when it needed to be.

"Yeah!" he yelled, clapping his hands loudly at the end of 'Cotton-Eyed Joe,' as though the members of Rednex could hear his appreciation for them from wherever they were. When he lowered his hands, one of them clapped me on the back, and he arose. "I need to take a piss."

I nodded and held up my glass to him; he nodded back and stumbled towards the loo.

Cecilia stared at me from across the table. This had happened several times through-out the night, those awkward moments when two people who would have otherwise not associated were forced to make conversation with one another. I suppose we could have just ignored one another, but that could have proven problematic. The corners of her mouth twitched, her pupils floating in a gutter of alcohol that had permeated her body. "I slept with him," she said finally, matter-of-factly.

I raised my eyebrows and nodded.

This was actually the third time she had made the same admission to me, which gave a strong indication of just how drunk Cecilia really was. The first time had been after he had jumped the eight when playing pool to sink the six when caught in a tight corner, and had been said with pride and admiration. The second time had been after I had done something (I'm not sure what) that had presumably caused her to think that I was looking at a woman on the other side of the bar. That time it had been said as a gloat, in an "I'm getting something you're not" sort of fashion. This time it was with a twinge of regret, as though she was saying it to a priest during a confession. The depres-sant we were all drinking must have been getting to her, I decided.

"I haven't told my boyfriend," she said.

This information was new, but not unexpected. The way Cecilia had looked at Craig at the Christmas party, it had not been in the way one looked at someone when they saw something they want. It was the way they looked at someone when they saw something they wanted that they weren't currently getting. A subtle difference, but an important one. Still, she was young, and there would be plenty of mistakes ahead. We've made more than a few.

"I don't think I'm going to," she said, her brow furrowing into a tiny wrinkle be-tween her eyebrows. It vanished as she relaxed, and I saw that that would be a perma-nent fixture of her face as she aged. A wrinkle, perhaps even her first wrinkle.

"That's up to you," I nodded at her, listing my glass to my lips and then placing it back down again. It occurred to me suddenly that I might be able to find some excuse to dispose of the remainder of my drink now, while Craig was in the bathroom. Was Ceci-lia drinking the same thing I was? And if so, was she too drunk to notice if I poured the remainder of my beverage into her glass? When I looked, I saw that Cecilia's previously cola-saturated drink had been replaced with a deep blue one that could have only been an Aqua-Velva, and curled my lip in disgust before taking another sip of my drink.

"Have you ever cheated?"

She asked me this devoid of context, her voice trailing upward at the end of the word 'cheated' and making the query sound like something hopeful. Hopeful for what, I wondered. My brain was moving too sluggishly; it was discouraging. I had to stop this rapid consumption of alcohol in different types and quantities, and wondered all at once if I had it in me to feign some sort of alcohol poisoning event. Did she want me to be the saint who would never do such a thing, the scoundrel who had done it often and enjoyed it, or the mourner who did it once and always lived to regret it? Did it matter?

The fact that I asked myself the latter truly signifies how intoxicated I was becoming. Everything matters when you're in deep cover, you never know what might come back to bite you in the ass. You are always on, and every answer matters. I decided I would need to get out of there soon.

"No," I said finally, and did not elaborate. Was it true? It's difficult to say, so difficult that even I would have a hard time telling you with great certainty and great honesty. When one lies for a living, there become problems with matters of discerning the truth, and as this was not a steadfast fact like 'Where were you born,' there was some interpretation involved.

Craig returned then, with three deep brown drinks in small squat glasses and laid one of them in front of each of us. He clapped me on the back again; this was how I marked his comings and goings. His hand had still been wet, and I could feel the moisture from it against my suit. "Finish that quick, so we can all get started on these at once," he said, motioning to my Scotch and Cecilia's Aqua-Velva.

Cecilia downed hers in one gulp, and I reluctantly followed suit.

We played a game of billiards that I found incredibly hard to follow. There were three of us, so I swear we started by playing nine-ball, but at some point during the game, I remember looking down and realizing that the bright yellow sphere that was the nine-ball was no longer on the table, and yet we were continuing to play. There were also tens and elevens, so I deduced that we were actually playing eight ball.

What followed was a thirty-minute period during which I tried to discern exactly which brand of eight ball we were playing. At one point I had to shoot a scratch from behind the line, while at another I was afforded a ball-in-hand. At some point I resolved to simply bounce the balls around the table at varying speeds until Craig clapped me on the back and informed me that I'd lost. This, in turn, was followed by another round of shots named after a minor celebrity and another round of drinks supplied by Craig – Aqua-Velva's all around, this time.

My body's ability to abide alcohol can only go so far. As such, as you might have guessed, there are large portions of that evening which I do not currently have access to. I can only assume that at some point, later down the road, those memories will dislodge like a leaf caught on a rock in a stream and I will become privy to the fact that, yes – I did spend the better part of five-minutes discussing politics with Cecilia's chest, or some other such dubious action I would have otherwise abhorred.

We were sitting around a small round table, the seats of which were impossibly high and impossibly small and hard to balance on, when I came to the sudden realization that I had to get out of there.

Everything was blurring around me, all of the lights created lens flares on my retinas. Craig was talking about one of the theories on the wall – a hipster joke involving dating, which may or may not have been attributed to "The Bro Code." Cecilia was laughing honestly. There were people around – far, far more people than there had been when we'd entered. Was it still the same night? Was this bar ever going to bloody close?

Billiards. Loo. Bloody- fuck, I wasn't thinking in the right tongue, I realized, and forced myself to stand up from the table in the middle of Craig's sentence.

He looked at me, his eyes soft and concerned. "You okay, buddy?"

I must have made more of a scene than I'd intended to. "I'm fine," I said as I nodded, or perhaps I just nodded. "I just need to hit the... the... need to pee." I couldn't say bathroom. I was trying to, but all that wanted to come out was loo. How had I allowed myself to get so bloody fucked?

"Do you need me to come with you?" he asked, still concerned.

Oh God, I realized. *We're friends.* I shook my head, he nodded, and I turned and made my way to the washroom.

There was a theory framed above each of the urinals. Mine read that if there was a small defect or crack etched into the bowl of a urinal, men would attempt to aim for it and therefore spill less. I looked down and – sure enough – there was an image of a fly tattooed into the bowl I was currently urinating into, and the hot liquid that streamed out of me was cascading all around it. I wondered – likely for too long – if telling a man about that particular theory lessened its affect, like telling someone that you were prescribing them a placebo for their back pain: if you tell them, you've defeated the purpose.

I leaned my head against the clear plastic of the theory and waited until I was done. It seemed to take far longer than it should have. When I was finally done making water, I carefully tucked myself back into my trousers, washed my hands, and took out my phone. With great effort – and multiple attempts – I punched in 0852. There was a message from Lydia. I decided now would not be the best time to answer it, shook myself sober as much as I could, and headed back out into the bar proper.

I spied Craig and Cecilia across the room and realized I could just leave. I certainly had my facilities about me enough that I could sneak past the likes of Craig Pollard. I could leave, get back out into the night air, and find a cab to take me home. Certainly not the friendliest thing to do under the circumstances, but being slightly inconsiderate was a minor offense when one was blatantly, blisteringly drunk.

"Are you okay?" said the woman in front of me. I turned and made eye contact with her quickly, as my brain took a moment to play catch-up. I'd been staring at Craig and Cecilia, trying to make a choice as to whether to stay or go. This woman had been on her way past me, stopped and backed up into my peripheral vision, and asked if I was okay. She then stepped fully in front of me and asked if I was okay, which I clearly was not.

However, I said: "Yes, sorry, I'm fine."

"Are you sure?" she asked, brushing back dirty-blonde hair. "You don't look well. You're very pale."

I touched my forehead as though I would have been able to feel my paleness, and instead was treated to just how sweat-laden my brow had become. There was a seat not far behind me, and I found myself sitting. This woman's hand was on my arm. She had been guiding me into the chair and I had not even noticed.

"Sit for a moment," she said, and started to fumble with something in her purse. She took out her cell phone, let it bathe her face in pale light for a moment as she typed something, then put it away and returned her gaze to me.

My vision lolled past her head and I saw Craig, lumbering towards me with a drink in each hand. They were red and had fruit sticking out of them and there was some clear disconcerting liquid at the top that refused to mix with the rest. My stomach was already starting to protest this concoction, which I do not know the name of but have dubbed the "Kirstie Alley." It seems fitting, although I am not sure why.

Craig looked up from the drinks and saw me, sitting at the table with this blonde woman. His smile vanished, then reappeared in a different fashion. He backed up several paces without a word, nodding to himself, and sat back down with Cecilia and both drinks.

I looked at the woman with new light: she was a shield. A mystical, magical shield that repelled alcoholic beverages and lumbering idiots. A bartender came over to us and asked if we wanted anything, and she said: "Two virgin colas please."

Oh blessed Madonna! I was saved!

The woman turned back toward me, her hair tumbling in front of her eyes despite her best efforts. "Do you want me to stay with you a minute?" she asked, that same concern in her voice that Craig had voiced just a few moments ago.

Yes, I responded. "I would like that very much."

7

She told me her name was Maggie and that she worked in accounting, both of which were true. I say that not because anything she said or will say is a lie, but because there are so many lies and half-truths in my life that I have to distinguish when someone uses their *real* name and their *real* occupation. If that strikes you as sad, it's because it is.

Her favorite movie of all-time was *Ferris Beuler's Day-Off*, and she absolutely subscribed to the theory that Ferris was actually a figment of Cameron's imagination, a personification of his Id doing all the things he could never do, including (but not limited to) dating Sloan Peterson. She'd written a thesis paper on it in university during a film study course, which she'd minored in.

"Film Theory and Accounting?" I asked, smiling over the cuff of my suit. I had a tiny pink umbrella in my hand, and no idea how it had gotten there. Evidently I was still quite drunk.

"Mmm-hmm," she hummed. "I was going to be the first accountant to know the exact building cost of the Death Star."

I laughed again.

Unsurprisingly, the Cameron-Ferris Theory was not one of the theories displayed on the wall of the bar.

She told me she'd always liked acting when she was young, and had been in her high-school drama troupe. She'd tried again when she got to university, but had never been good enough to perform at that level. "At that level all I could do was minor in watching actors, not being one.

"Isn't it weird how jocks make fun of all the drama kids, but idolize all the actors?" she asked. She was drinking Virgin Cokes now too, either so that I wouldn't feel bad or so as to not get too inebriated around the complete stranger. Or both. "I mean, all those actors they fawn over are just the drama geeks they called faggot all grown up, right? It's so stupid."

I agreed that it was quite stupid. She said with word 'faggot' with distaste, her lip curling when the word was in her mouth. I adored her for it, and must have smiled. I told her that I had been in drama when I had been young too, as well as sports: the track team, to be precise.

Which was also true.

Not true of the deep cover, not a part of the carefully constructed identity I'd carved for myself since first putting on an apron and learning how to properly manage an allergy-order in a back-of-house kitchen: the real truth.

I wanted a smoke for the first time in years. I felt my shoulders relax, and then roll back. My posture changed, in a way I wasn't quite familiar with, and I was grinning out of the right side of my mouth as I stared across the table at those bright, seafoam-green eyes.

I paused for a moment, wiped my mouth, and said, "When I was fifteen, I got the lead in the school play. It–"

"Wait, let me guess," she grinned, holding the thumb and forefinger of each hand to make a screen and placing me in it. She had one eye closed and her tongue protruded as she 'focused.' "Thick cheeks, slender jaw, thin eyebrows... Hamlet."

I smiled and shook my head, "No."

"No?"

"No, it was an original play, something one the drama coaches cooked up, thinking they were being the smart auteurs that no high-school drama coach really is." I paused, not wanting to go on if I was boring her. She was watching and listening intently. "It was called "*How Good is It?*" It was about a young boy – moi – who was obsessed with finding out how good sex really was."

Maggie rolled her eyes. "Subtle. Ten bucks says it ends with a teen pregnancy."

I paused, for what must have been a little too long, because her gaze softened as it had when I was stumbling out of the washroom. "... It did," I said finally, smiling. I took another sip of my drink. "Actually, one night while I was rehearsing with the female lead, I confessed to being nervous about a scene where I would have to fake... oh, how shall I put this... Erotic Excitement."

She giggled.

"Of course I was nervous because I'd never had the experience first-hand – which she gratefully provided."

She rolled her eyes at me again, but was smiling. "A cad was born."

I snorted my drink.

It was the most I had spoken in eighteen months without thinking about the game of chess my words were playing. My shoulders relaxed some more, so much so that I felt calcium pop in the nape of my neck. Sometimes, you don't realize how tense life has made you until you finally relax.

We talked about the last election, a usual faux pas among strangers, but it came up organically and neither of us felt the need to artificially swerve the conversation away from it. We held differing political views but neither of us was far enough left or right that we couldn't respect and value what the other had had to say, and I think we both left the experience with more to think about on a few issues. I know I did.

I told her my favorite movie was *The Godfather*, a lie that she called me out on, claiming that "All men say their favorite film is *The Godfather* when their real favorite film would hurt their ego to admit." I admitted that it was a lie and that that was the reason, but would not tell her what the real choice was. She'd have to just take gratification in the fact that she'd done what few others could do, and caught me in a fib.

She told me that she didn't like chocolate, but ate a small piece of dark chocolate every night after dinner, for the antioxidants. She told me she'd had an acne problem as a teen but that it had faded, although she still had some scarring on her cheeks. I told her it wasn't noticeable (this too was a lie, but if she caught me in it she did not mention. What wasn't a lie was that it didn't detract from the overall aesthetic beauty of her face). She told me she listened to something called ASMR on YouTube to relax before bed sometimes, but couldn't remember what the acronym stood for.

Autonomous Sensory Meridian Response, by the way. I looked it up some time later.

I told her that the first time I had been drunk had been at my father's wake, and that I'd spent a great deal of it clutching the toilet off the parapet and vomiting into it while sobbing uncontrollably. This was a partial lie: I had actually been drunk the entire three days from the time of my father's death *until* his wake, on the coin of a good friend. It was not the first drink I had, but it had been the first time I had been drunk. And I hadn't sobbed or cried at all; I'm not sure why I said that.

She told me both her parents were alive, and all of her sisters. She only had one aunt, but they had never been close, and she didn't know now if she was alive or dead. All her grandparents had been dead before she'd been old enough to walk, a consequence of being born late in her parents' lives.

At some point I looked around the bar, and realized it was all-but empty. Craig and Cecilia had left, presumably together. I didn't think they'd come over to announce that they were leaving, but I might have missed it while in the deep troughs of my stupor. The house lights were still down, but the staff was cleaning up for the night.

"Oh," she said, looking around. Apparently she was as surprised as I was. "I guess we should leave."

There was a moment then, when she looked at me and expected me to suggest we leave together.

"I'll get you in a cab," I said, not making a show of it. I wasn't saying it to be gallant, but if it was a gallant thing to say, then all the better. She smiled and nodded.

We stepped outside and found a cab almost immediately, leaving little time for the awkward conversation that would usually accompany such a situation. Would I wait with her, would I just start on my way home? Would I try to split the cab in an effort to segue into sexual congress – all of that bypassed by an efficient cabby. I gave him some money without letting Maggie see how much and told him to make sure she got home. She would have had to live on the moon for it not to have covered tab and tip.

She stood in the door of the cab and looked at me for a long moment. I'm not sure if she was debating asking me to join her, or if she was just trying to find the right words to say goodnight... but I like to think it was the latter. The night had been smooth and easier, easier than any night I'd had in, well, much longer than eighteen months actually. It might have actually been years. I didn't like to think that that experience wasn't a shared one, at least on some level.

I decided to save her the trouble of whatever she was deciding either way. "Thank you for helping me tonight, Maggie."

She smiled and nodded. "I had a great time, Simon," she said, her voice almost lost on the early morning breeze. Then she leaned in and kissed me, ever so fleetingly, on the corner of my mouth. Her thumb had found its way to my cheek and stroked it once before falling away. She ducked into her cab before I could say anything, and was gone.

I stood there as it pulled away, basked in the crisp chill of the winter night. I turned and started my short walk home with a spring in my step and a smile on my face, stopping only once the entire way there to steady myself – as it turned out, despite all her help, I was still quite drunk.

So drunk in fact, that it never occurred to me then that I hadn't told her my name.

8

The text from Lydia had been precisely what I had hoped it would be.

You see, I couldn't chase her; there was something caddish about that. Going after a married woman includes equal parts of letting her come to you and knowing what to say when she does.

I didn't have that luxury.

Unrealized sexual attraction is something that can hang in the subconscious for years at a time, only to dislodge in the form of an awkward phone call years after the fact after watching a romantic comedy with a few too many poignant scenes. It can take the form of years of cat-and-mouse, with one person's situation becoming desperate enough that they call only to find the other person happy, or vice versa. Years can pass before the two sync up, if they ever do, and the result is almost always disappointing.

Very few sexual experiences can live up to ten years of foreplay.

And I'm sure it would have gone that way with Lydia, if I weren't who I am. I might not have heard from her again and been avoided by her at next year's Christmas bash, if she came at all. Tyler would realize the stir within his wife and do something uncharacteristically suave, a vacation more than likely. I would fade into the ether until he inevitably began to ignore her again, and nostalgia would take hold. Would things have been better with that cad, Simon Monk? I might have moved on by then to another job or another position; her desperation might have to reach a fever pitch before she got up the effort to contact me, and even then the dips and rises of marriage might have to make her contact me several times before we actually met. By the time she did, the young lady-killer she'd met at that one Christmas Party would be long dead, replaced by a silver-haired buffoon with too much weight on and sagging jowls.

While my timetable was by no means short, it was nowhere near that long. So a reminder had to be engineered, preferably coming from her husband himself. Necessarily, actually, since social media didn't reveal anyone that might have been better suited to deliver the message for me.

Hence the stock manipulation. By now the stock in the company that owned the rights to Moon Landing had fallen again (the market can't abide the type of inflation I'd facilitated). But the second it started to fall, Tyler Carter would have pulled out. Assuming the initial dip wasn't too severe (and it hadn't been), he would have doubled his already-large sum of money, all based on an off-hand tip that I gave him.

So Tyler Carter, sitting at home much as I was and watching this drama unfold with glee, turns to his wife and says something to the tune of: "That consultant I hired, Simon Monk? I just made a hundred grand off a tip he gave me on the stock market." Or something of the like.

Now that I think about it, it likely went nothing like that. I imagine he was celebrating on his own or calling a friend to tell him to buy while the buying was good as well, when his wife would have taken notice of his excitement and asked what had happened. *Being* excited, he would have had to frame the story from the beginning: he couldn't just tell her he'd made some money; that was boring. He'd have to tell about where it came from, where the idea struck him in that meeting, and whose off-handed comment had sparked it. Yes, my contribution to the story would be minimal from his point of view, but after mentioning my name (and in such a positive, impressive light) the rest of the tale would hold no context for Lydia Carter.

The text itself was more than I'd hoped for, and I suspect that she'd shared in a small bit of her husband's celebratory drink before making it: "Seems like I wasn't the only one impressed with you. ;)"

A text like that from a beautiful older woman would be enough to send any man's mind into a frenzy, especially when said woman happened to be your boss' wife: a prospect with simultaneous feelings of baleful vengeance and fear attached to it. I imagine some young men would analyze the text, possibly with the help of a friend or two, and decide the best course of action going forward. I am not speaking out of experience, unless one counts sitcoms that air on the television screens at the gym as 'experience.'

But in truth, the text still got a fair amount of analyzing from me, though in what I imagine is a far more intellectual fashion. It was hard to find a Lacanian Mirror Stage in a text of only ten words and an emoticon, sure, but I could certainly try.

It was obviously an overwhelmingly positive message, and had I not been in no fit state to do so at the time, I might have responded to it immediately and without much thought. But now that I looked at it, there were troubling elements. Notably, it was in the past tense. She had not written "Seems like I'm not the only one you impressed;" she had written "Seems like I wasn't the only one impressed with you." The difference was subtle but important, even if she wasn't totally aware of what she had said. People very rarely are aware of what they're saying, and it was one of the first traits I had to master when going into deep cover. Tense, tone, and emphasis: all this was vitally important to language.

The past tense was troubling; it indicated that the affair might have been over before it had truly begun. That she *had* been impressed with me, and in the days since moved on to something new or decided that the flirtation had been the drink and nothing else, a harmless bit of fun between strangers.

But if that were totally the case of course, she wouldn't have sent the text at all.

And then there was the wink, the herald of sexual promise of the emoticons. These messages were contradictory and troubling, but overall very positive. Lydia was still on the fence and I'd known that already – had she not been, my deep cover would have been over several days ago and I wouldn't have had the chance to get so drunk with Craig that many of my brain cells had collectively committed suicide rather than bathe in stinging hot alcohol.

I messaged back: "High praise from a rare woman is always appreciated."

Women as beautiful as Lydia have been told they're beautiful from the time they first bled and developed breasts, if not before. As such, the word has lost all meaning. Anyone hoping to actually make a legitimate impression should never use the word beautiful, unless the woman in question was well on her way to sixty and may not have heard it in some years, which Lydia Carter was not. There were several other euphemisms of beautiful, from the all-too-plain 'pretty' to the far-too-extravagant 'radiant,' but a smart man chooses a point of phrase that can hold many meanings for the mind to latch on to.

Beautiful can mean many things; it can even apply to more than aesthetic beauty (though usually not, and almost always in defense of its use). But of the things it can mean, they are solely complimentary and almost all of them are focused on the same attributes a woman has heard commented on since time immortal.

A true compliment, to stay in the mind and dig in its hooks the way one needs it to, should be much more opaque and obtuse than that. It should not be easy to discern its meaning through simple deduction, and perhaps even contain the possibility that it was not meant as a compliment at all. In times past, 'unique woman' might have been an acceptable choice, but unique has been co-opted by the loud, obnoxious manic-pixie dream-girls of the world since its hay-day of high praise and should not be used unless the woman in question embodies those qualities.

I have found 'rare' to be a much better choice. Such a small word, but it contains so much within it, like a small pouch packed to the brim with diamonds. What did it mean? Did it mean that I was beautiful, and in fact so beautiful that I was rare in my beauty? If so, then 'rare' would be better by definition than any of those words describing that beauty could have been. Did it mean that I was intelligent or engaging or witty or funny, and that the rareness of me was that those qualities were found in such a beautiful woman? If so, then 'rare' embodied many complimentary phrases at once and, even better, could embody those that the receiver felt was the most important. If the woman in question had always prided herself on her wit and you complimented her poise, that might fall flat. 'Rare' allowed for individual interpretation and meaning. There was also of course the possibility that it wasn't a compliment at all: was I rare because he's attracted to me despite my not being beautiful? Multiple interpretations, none of which I had any intention of ever expanding upon. Like the monster in a horror movie: the imagination could do more than the reality ever could.

"What are you doing?" she asked, without emotional punctuation.

In truth, I was doing very little: eating unsalted oatmeal and getting ready to swallow two capsules that were far too large for the human throat to withstand without pause. She pictured me watching TV or going over reports or reading a book as I chatted with her, the chat a bit of auxiliary entertainment to the main event of whatever I was doing to unwind after a long day. In truth, I was doing very little *but* scrutinize her texts and the tone of her texts, when compared to those previous. I was, after all, really working for the first time in several days.

"Reading," I lied, a partial lie. I am reading, though not a blog or a book or magazine or a report: I'm reading her texts, her social media posts, my notes on Tyler's behavior, and trying to construct a timeline of her mood and position.

"Reading what? :)"

The smile was a good upgrade. "Hemingway," I answer, upgrading what was first a misleading comment into the realm of total fabrication. I could have spouted any of Hemingway's titles, but nothing would hold the power of the synecdoche of invoking the author's name to stand in for his work as a whole. And of the authors I could have chosen – Hemingway, King, and Grant were all authors my deep cover was intimately familiar with – Earnest would hold the most meaning for a woman as... *rare* as Lydia.

I waited several beats, before adding: "And you?"

"Heading to bed." No emoticon attached. Dangerous invitation. A salacious invitation, or a polite way of ending the conversation?

After several tense moments, I texted back: ";)?"

As strange as it might sound, this was possibly the most daring move I had taken so far. More than my compliments, the disgusting amount of money I had unceremoniously flushed down the toilet to manipulate the stock exchange, or stepping away from Lydia at the party so that she would come out to the balcony to see me; this one, simple text was a very daring move.

I was not only expressing an emotion myself, I was asking her to impress one. Nay, I was actually placing the words into her mouth, and asking if I was correct in doing so. She had initially let the context of the comment hang, but I was forcing her to assign context to it, one way or the other. As much as you might hear everything I've done so far and judge me for it, this was the first truly forward move I had made yet.

A moment later, two texts came in quick succession: ";)" and "Goodnight :)."

If you had messaged me and asked me at this point, I would have thought that things were going very, very well.

8A

"Was that when you --" he asked, but was interrupted by the waitress. She was plump and had blonde hair with a pink streak in it, and was pretty when she smiled. He nodded at her and took his espresso, sipping it lightly. It was hot and stuck in the wisps of his facial hair. He did not finish the sentence once the waitress walked away.

Simon stared across the table at him. His own drink sat on the table in front of him, almost untouched, its dark liquid staining the pure white fabric of the cloth. The final remnants of the garlic bread he had been eating sat on the table next to it, bearing the marks of his teeth: one of the only things it was legitimately hard for him to fake for an extended period of time.

Slowly, he nodded.

9

Not long after that there was a late-night meeting at the office, with all senior staff and personnel in mandatory attendance. I was on that list and so was Craig -- and of course, so was Tyler Carter.

The reason for the meeting wasn't disclosed, even during its progress. Instead each team was given specific, even micro-managed tasks: correlating data from certain dates compared against other dates, finding productivity reports, seeing which accounts were outstanding and which were overdue, and – most importantly – seeing where fat could be trimmed. This resulted in catastrophic blitzkriegs of activity, followed by short lulls of refueling and coffee before another buzz of work.

Shane had military contracts -- and many of them -- in minor areas. Assembling nodes and complex circuits to be used in 'smart' weaponry. Programming. Simulations. All the work we were doing now rotated around these fields like planets around the sun, but did not touch them in any way. It drew my attention to them while trying to not draw my attention to them, like a murder suspect that goes too far out of his way to prove his innocence. We were filling this impromptu late-night with work that affected our military division without specifically addressing it, at such a micro-managed level that no one person had the chance to stop and look into that direction: there was no spare second when one could branch from their chosen task into the broader picture.

This meeting was announced in the morning, with no warning, and we were prepared for the very likely event that it would not be the last one of the week. As such, everyone looked tired, and I had to too. I pressed my thumbs into my eyelids to make them as bloodshot as everyone else's and reminded myself to get coffee every thirty minutes with begrudging movements. In truth, I needed very little sleep: humans are more productive in the morning, but since most people do not acknowledge this, networking is done late at night. Having to do both, I've gotten used to three-hours of sleep a night.

As a consultant my job – now – was largely to find places where business could be made better. This was ideal to my actual position, as I was afforded a greater glimpse of the big picture. This included things like which departments solely existed to generate revenue with which to fund certain other departments; which subsidiaries and auxiliary companies were generating the most business, and possibly why; and which patents paid off the greatest licensing dividends.

It was a complex web that this largely public company had created, and I passed many a tired, confused looking individual on my way to the kitchen for more coffee. Many complained, without compunction, about how their long hours at the office were affecting their home life.

That last complaint was the reason I was watching my phone.

Every time I went to get a coffee or to the washroom, I would discover an opportunity to check my public-facing profile and see if I had received any recent calls or texts.

It was roughly eleven when I checked and saw that the text had come in. Two in fact, sent in rapid succession: "How is the meeting?" and "I'm bored."

It is a myth constructed by a mostly-male power structure in our society that most women who cheat do so out of boredom. This diminishes the act while simultaneously shifting the blame for the indiscretion solely onto the female partner. In truth, anything that happens in a relationship is the cause of something systemic within the relationship itself: poor communication, lack of agency, lack of urgency to find time for one another... any number of things. But 'bored' was the shorthand men of the business world have adapted: they're worried about leaving their wife home alone, and that she'll get bored and cheat. Not that they're emotionally unavailable, not that they've spent less time together than strangers, not that he is, in fact, cheating -- she's just bored. It's insulting.

But in an odd turn, the phrase has been "taken back" by women in a fashion similar to other phrases used to diminish the disenfranchised which I will not repeat here. "She's bored" when said *of* a woman is an insult to her intelligence and her virtue. "I'm bored" when said *by* a woman was using the male coded language for her own gain, to stealthily initiate their own agendas.

In this new arena, where language norms change constantly, "I'm bored" was the equivalent of texting "I'm horny," without bringing to mind a Michael Myers persona.

I was leaning against the wall in the hallway between the door to the kitchen and a small-framed picture of the ocean with the sun hanging over it, a city skyline only just visible in the foreground. The Shane main headquarters was there. It was titled "Los Angeles Sunrise". It was the type of commissioned art that businesses hung on the walls to try and appear friendlier, having been told that drab expressionless walls lead to suicides at time of stock dips.

I know that I was standing right there. It's one of those moments I remember with complete clarity: the people walking back and forth in front of me, getting their coffees. The smell of the brewer, arid and hot. The constant white noise of the murmur of conversations through walls. The fact that I had just missed something, and had not realized it. The smell of multiple perfumes and colognes and deodorants.

I answered back two quick texts: "That's a shame" and "A beautiful woman should never be bored."

If we're following the logic of what I'm saying 'bored' was code for, remind yourself of what I'm saying to her.

Several tense moments passed, and I imagined that I had gone too far. 'Beautiful' was by no means a salacious comment, but it was certainly an upgrade in intent from 'rare.' I thought I could afford to be more direct now: the baser one's instincts got, the less one was expected to show class. Nobody jumps into bed with their bow tie still on, and all that rubbish.

I was about to put my phone away again, when two more texts came: "I enjoyed our talk" and "I want to see you."

I looked around. I was exposed, but not in a way that anyone would recognize. Still, I became acutely aware suddenly that this woman's husband was in the same building as me, on the same floor.

"We can meet for coffee," I returned. I debated leaving a question mark by it, and decided not to. Statements were more forceful. The question still lingered from that first night, that very first interaction with her: what did she want me to be? Did she want me to be the hunter, seducing the boss's wife for the sport? Or did she want me to be the prey, victim of a stealthy lioness?

"We can," she responded. "But that's not what I said. ;)"

I paused, scrolling back up over the messages she'd sent, and trying to understand where I'd slipped. I like to think I would have gotten there eventually, but she didn't feel the need to afford me the time.

"I want to see you," she texted again. A moment later, a picture of her was on my screen. The current term is 'selfie', I believe. Her hair was done but loose and tumbled over her shoulders, her eyes locked onto the camera. She wore a black robe and red underwear and little else, the downward angle of the photograph affording a slanted angle down her cleavage.

At once, I understood.

"Now," she texted again, before I could respond to the photo.

Any question of whether she wanted me to be the hunter or the prey had vanished. I very suddenly knew my place, like a gazelle grazing on some grass in an open field before hearing an overturned rock or the snap of a twig. I couldn't have planned for this, but it couldn't have gone any better than what I'd planned. Things were happening at such a fast pace now; I could all but see the finish line. Months of planning and small pieces of puzzles, all falling into place.

"I'm at work right now, can't come out...;)" I responded. I debated purposely misspelling the word come, and decided against it. Too crass for this stage of the game.

"I know," she said quickly. "But that's not what I said. ;)"

The same phrase again. She was leading me and enjoying that she was leading me, enjoying the hunt in a way any good predator would. This was good: when the people whom you are conning take agency of their own actions and set off in the direction you led them into, it can be a very good thing. That is... if you set them off in the right direction... if I did my job right. The pieces I'd set in motion were now moving on their own, and that inertia would be hard to stop – perhaps impossible.

"You saw me, I want to see you... now. ;)"

The realization of what she meant hit me all at once, and I imagine the color drained from my face. This had escalated far too quickly, and I've come to believe that she knew that. Lydia was headed in the right direction all right, but faster than I could have anticipated. For the first time in what was now nineteen months, I must have been sweating.

"I'm at work ;)" I messaged back quickly. It hadn't had the wink at first, and I had added hastily before pressing send. I was trying to slow down this inertia, not stop it completely, and I was not so far down this road with Lydia that I didn't have to tread carefully.

"I've been there," she responded coyly. "I know they have broom closets. ;)"

Fuck.

I may have cursed out loud. I'm not sure. If I did, I hadn't ascribed any attention to myself.

I turned off my phone and quickly turned it back on, switching profiles. The new screen came up, the one without Lydia's texts, and I opened up the messenger app and texted seven words that I had never thought, even in my wildest imaginations, I would ever string together: "I need a picture of a penis."

There was a long, tense moment. I imagine that no matter what circumstances a text like that was received under it would always be surprising. A moment later I received: "... What?"

"Lydia."

"There's this thing, it's called 'The Internet'..."

I huffed, perhaps outwardly frustrated for the first time. I couldn't text Lydia from this profile, and for all I knew that situation was spiraling out of control while I tried to contain it here. "I can't take an image from Google," I sent, followed by: "Anything I can find quickly, she could also stumble upon."

"For fucks sake..." I received. Several tense moments later, a picture of a penis appeared in my messages. The photo was sharp and in focus, so much so that individual beads of sweat were distinguishable on it. It was held erect by the taker's thumb, rising up from a curly tuft of black pubic hair, brightly lit in the glare from the flash. I paused to realize how lucky I had been that the hair had not been blond.

Most importantly the background was dark enough that it could have been anywhere, including the broom closet of Shane San Diego, and I suspected that Lydia would not be subjecting the photo to rigorous forensic analysis to see what lay hidden in the shadows of the background.

I pressed my thumb hard against the image, sending it to my other profile.

"Thanks," I texted.

"The things I do for you..." was the response I got, before shutting off the phone and starting it back up again, in the 'Lydia-Facing' profile. Sure enough, the photograph – which I believe has the moniker 'dick pic,' much in the same way the photo Lydia took has been labelled a 'selfie' – was waiting for me in her message box. I pressed send, and it sent.

There was another understandably tense moment that followed, as the three small dots that indicated she was typing something appeared, then disappeared. Appeared, then disappeared. Finally, I got two responses back to back. The first comprised of three letters and an emoticon, the second of four letters and an emoticon: "Yum ;)" and "Ttyl ;)."

I think if I had been a betting man, 'yum' would have been the least likely response I would have placed money on... remembering of course that it wasn't *my* penis she was referring to, but another man's.

In any event, the situation with Lydia was escalating quickly. At this rate, it was conceivable that my deep cover would last less than twenty-one months, a full three months shorter than I had originally projected. Not that projections meant much in my line of work: it took as long as it took, and that was all there was to it.

There are things that happen when you are deep cover that you have to respond to that you couldn't possibly have accounted for. When preparing myself for activity nineteen months ago, there was no way I could have predicted that I would need a cache of genital photographs for use at a moment's notice, but those were the realities of deep cover: you could not accurately predict the needs of human behavior, in that exact a detail, over that long a timeframe.

"Hello, Simon," Tyler said happily as he stepped past me on his way to the washroom. He clapped me heartily on the shoulder as he stepped past, clearly on the upswing of a caffeine-induced high. I watched him go, this man whose wife I had just sent a picture of a penis to.

At that moment, I probably thought that things couldn't get any more complicated. I was very, very wrong about that.

I stepped into the kitchen to get a coffee.

10

The sad truth about deep cover is that things are going to get complicated, and the longer it goes on for the more likely that will be. On a long enough timeline, any situation ends in failure. That's not pessimism; it's just the truth.

I was pouring the rich black sludge from the bottom of a coffee pot into my cup when I felt something sharp poke me in the back, timed almost perfectly with a deadpan delivery of: "Simon."

I turned. Maggie was standing behind me.

My mistake hit me at once, as it would have had I not been so colossally drunk when I'd bumped into her at the bar. She'd said that she was "in accounting," which I had taken to mean, "I am in the profession of accounting..." What she had instead meant was, "I am in the accounting department."

Maggie worked with me.

Maggie knew me.

I feel as though my brain didn't function for several moments there, but I know there wasn't any of that. At least while I'm sober, I can manage to sustain a baseline ruse even on autopilot. "Hey," I smiled back. Was the smile forced? I'm not certain. I put down the pot of coffee and turned to face her and leaned against the counter of the break-room. I needed to think but there wasn't any time to think.

"How were you after?" she asked, beaming in a funny sort of way. She reached past me and picked up the pot herself, draining the last of the coffee into her cup. "I mean, clearly you survived."

I don't remember what I said. Have you ever had the experience of having someone from one part of your life intrude into another unwelcomed? Like having an ex-girl-friend start working at the same place you're currently working at, or something along those same levels? This felt like that, but worse. I felt my shoulders fall a little, the way they had that night at the bar. My posture changed, in a way that I was just perceptually aware of, and I had to concentrate to bring it back to the way I'd stood and walked for the last eighteen months. This was why you had to keep the same thoughts, the same demeanor, the same everything at all times when you were deep cover: stepping out of that bubble once made it only too easy to do so again.

Tyler walked by the kitchen, but didn't step in. Tyler knew Maggie, Maggie knew Tyler, and Maggie had met me. The real me, not the deep cover me.

"I watched *Prometheus* the other night on Netflix. I don't know what people were bitching about," she said. She brushed past me again – making contact and making no effort not to, grazing my arm. This conversation wasn't about movies; this was about the kiss. She had kissed me, right in the corner of my mouth, little sparks of electric heat between the night and us. That same part of my brain that had pinned down Lydia's intentions so well sprang to life and, without meaning to, without *wanting* to, I was read-ing her: the cut of her blouse, the shape of her hair, the angle of her body, the color of her nails and lipstick. She had wanted to bump into me tonight, on this late night at Shane San Diego, when everyone had to stay late until god-only-knew what hour.

She wasn't drinking her coffee. She had poured it, but she wasn't drinking it, and now she was sitting at the table in the center of the break room, her head facing me. This angled her legs toward the empty chair next to her: an open invitation. She wasn't drinking the coffee, and the cup she was holding had been clean. Was there a full cup back in her office, amidst a sea of revenue reports and TKS slips? Almost certainly. She'd kept a weather eye on the break room and had waited patiently, knowing that at some point during a long night, everyone had to refuel. Even track-star drama-geeks.

I told her that I hadn't seen the movie, but that I didn't think anything could top Ridley Scott's first *Alien* movie. She replied that Scott had actually returned to direct *Prometheus*. I conceded that I would have to check it out.

She lingered, her posture wavering. She didn't understand why I was different than I had been the other night -- more than just workplace professionalism or being sober versus being drunk, I was different now. Which made a lot of sense: I was looking for a way out now, whereas before I had been content to allow things to progress however they progressed. Now I was avoiding questions and taking part in the conversation just enough to shut it down, but doing so without being rude -- being rude could get around as well, and the last thing I wanted was to jeopardise the personae I had cultivated for a year and a half.

She paused after talking about the report she was working on, and I could watch her decide which way to press the conversation. She could give up or plunge forward. She teetered on the edge between one or the other for several seconds, her pupils dilat-ing and pulse-rate quickening. "I think you should take me out to dinner," she said finally.

I raised an eyebrow at her. "Oh?" I asked quizzically. I knew why.

"To thank me for rescuing you the other night." Yes, that had been why. She got up then and stepped over to me, sliding her business card into my breast pocket. "I like Mexican," she said in a matter-of-fact tone, then turned and walked out of the room.

I had no idea whether Simon Monk liked Mexican or not, but it was looking more and more like I was going to have to find out.

11

I broke three wine glasses the next day when I got home. There's something deeply satisfying about the way wine glasses specifically fall and crash; awkwardly weighted, falling end over end like some bizarrely drunken trapeze artist until finally: *crash*. Glass heads in one direction and the stem shatters down the center almost perfectly every time. Whenever I gathered up the shards, I gathered those stems – those shattered, phallic halves -- first even though they weren't sharp. I was careful with them even though they were not even remotely sharp.

Have you ever lost a train of thought and been unable to get it back? Experienced those frustrating, headache-inducing moments afterward when you search the nooks and crannies of your mind and the broken fragments of your concentration until you find yourself just exhausted? That's what it's like when deep cover gets broken, except instead of a train of thought, it's more like an identity. I had chosen to play the prey for Lydia, but was now juggling two women attached to the same office, a decidedly Hunter thing to do (not to speak ill of the dead). So which was I? Who was Simon Monk that he was both being chased by this older woman and (apparently) chasing Maggie? And for that matter, who had spread glass all over his kitchen floor? Was it Simon Monk or someone else entirely?

This was why you had to stay in-character at all times during a deep cover operation: because life wasn't divided into segments like an orange, clearly divided parts that you can separate and arrange onto separate plates. The different parts of life are more like the different strands of a cobweb, unable to be pulled apart and impossible to untangle.

Simon Monk had absolutely no reason to be breaking three cheap wine glasses all over his kitchen floor, because Simon Monk had no reason or right to be this upset that Maggie had asked him out, because Simon Monk had never *met* Maggie. Simon Monk had gone into that bathroom at the bar and not re-emerged into the land of the living until late the next morning. Some spectre had taken over his body and done things with it he never would have and didn't remember doing, and now he was faced with the consequences. Now he was faced with two choices: turn Maggie down and hope that it didn't get around the office and back to Tyler and, by extension, back to Lydia that Simon Monk was a bit of a cad, or go out with Maggie and hope that that information didn't follow the same path, also back to Lydia.

There was, of course, an option somewhere in the middle that I didn't even fully consider. I had narrowed down my options to a simple, binary damned-if-I-do and damned-if-I don't – because the truth of the matter was, even if Simon Monk hadn't had fun that evening at the bar, I had.

12

When I was in college, I dated two women who were roommates. I juggled them both for about a week and a half until it all came crumbling down around my ears and they both left me at the same time, in a rather spectacular fashion. It was possibly my first experience with the pitfalls of living a double life, but more than that, it was one of my first experiences with compartmentalization. The fact was it never once occurred to me that I was doing something wrong until they confronted me. I legitimately felt horrible when I realized the truth. When I was with Betty, I really liked Betty and didn't think of Veronica much. When I was with Veronica, I didn't think of Betty much. I wasn't trying to be nefarious or anything.

No, those weren't their names; those are fictional characters and a part of Americana pop culture.

As much as I tried to tell myself differently, this wasn't that. Compartmentalization is an important part of deep cover, but Maggie was a part of both compartments. She knew Craig, or at least knew of him.

The only solution I could think of, then, was to move up the timeline of the Lydia situation. It was a risk certainly, but not as much as allowing these two systems to interact side-by-side was, as any chemist worth his salt will tell you.

I sat on my hands for seven agonizing days, afraid to make a move in either direction for fear of upsetting the delicate homeostasis that had been obtained.

When there was another late night at the office to go over the files and reports from the last quarter, I called in and let them know that I was going to be staying home sick. Tyler Carter called me back himself to make sure I was alright and to ask if there was anything he could do. I told him it was just a twenty-four hour bug and that I didn't want to give it to the rest of the staff, as busy as we were. He thanked me and told me to take the next day as well. I almost felt bad. If this level of trust hadn't been exactly what I had been working toward for almost nineteen months, I think I would have.

As soon as I hung up with Tyler, I opened up my text messaging and texted Lydia: "I'm not going in to the office tonight."

The message I got back did not contain any words, only a map reference to her home.

As though I hadn't known exactly where she'd lived for months.

13

Lydia and Tyler's home was beautiful, of the sort that people like you and I only dream about after seeing them on television. It was modelled after Victorian houses and had one of those massive spiralling staircases with every step ivory white and the size of my bed in college. There was a chandelier at the cusp of the staircase that hung down in a glistening crystal V-shape -- the shape of a womb. That's the difference between people pretending to be rich and people who are actually rich, you know: people who pretend to be rich cultivate things shaped like a phallus to overcompensate for their perceived inadequacy for not being truly rich. Those with real wealth didn't feel the need to prove anything, and as a result most things had the cupped, V-shape of a rudimentary womb.

I entered just after I knocked, not waiting for her to answer or acknowledge or even make sure I had the right house. I knew I had the right house, of course -- had discovered it before I'd even started my deep cover. That was where I had first seen Lydia Carter, sunning herself on her front yard when the Google van had come along to snap a picture of her property for Street-View. She'd been wearing a white two-piece and those big round sunglasses that only beautiful women can get away with wearing, her lips a small red smear beneath them. A bottle of lemonade sat on the grass next to her sun chair, a pink crazy straw sticking out of it lazily as condensation ran down the outside of the bottle. The entire picture looked hot. It looked like summer. She looked like an older woman -- not in the sense of what it means to me now, but what it had meant to me then: childhood summers spent mowing lawns for change under that watchful gaze of Megan Vance's mother, who in my teenage years was an 'older woman' at thirty-four. Those pictures, with the green of the grass and the white of her swimsuit and the red of her lipstick and the lens flare -- those pictures ignited the unrequited awe that comes only with early adolescence.

I entered just after I knocked, not waiting for her to answer, the ultimate display of ownership. I was entering the home of another man to bed his wife and I acted as though I belonged. I did not wait to be allowed in, to be led around and shown each room with passing interest ("Here is the living room." "Oh?" "Here is the kitchen."); I stepped in as though it, and she, were already mine to have.

She was standing halfway up those spiral stairs, white satin kissing her and hanging from her and dangling to just barely expose bare feet. She had not been in mid-motion, as though I had caught her coming down the stairs to meet me or do some chore. She had been standing there, her hair up and her eyes hungering for me, as though she had known I would enter of my own accord.

I maintained my eye contact with her as I shut the door behind me. For a long moment the air between us was tense, with neither of us knowing exactly what to say. Except that I did know what to say, and I knew exactly how long to wait before saying it. I knew how long to let the tension sit and let the heat between us build, separated by nothing but ten feet of open air for the first time since the Christmas party.

There's something about that moment that makes it the best moment in any relationship. That tense excitement when both parties feel as though there is no turning back from what will happen, but before it has actually begun to happen. That electricity is rare and only happens when it's new and so precious.

For a moment I envied her, because she alone was experiencing that jolt.

After I've waited what I knew was the appropriate amount of time, I smirked at her out of one side of my mouth and pushed my thumb back towards the door, and said, "It was open."

She smiled and laughed and came the rest of the way down the stairs, reaching out her hand to lead me into the sitting room.

Sexual encounters of this kind count among the most riveting games of chess on the planet. There's something about that sort of good strategy that just aches of pleasurable tension and makes it a universal human experience, as cathartic as the event itself. Both of us knew why we were there and both of us were there for that only reason, and yet the process of getting to that was better than the act itself. Curious, no?

We sat on a couch whose back leaned back in front of a roaring fire, the light from the dancing flames making her glow. She looked young, with the orange ambiance on her pale flesh and the white of her eyes, leaning against the back of the couch and facing me in a position reminiscent of the shape a woman takes when laying next to the welcome open area of a bed.

She handed me a drink and at first I was hesitant – not that I thought she would drug me or hamstring me, you understand, but because I did not want a repeat of the incident at Theories. I took it tentatively, holding it by the base so that I could smell the sweet scent of it. There were hints of plum and citrus and just this small, small hint of chocolate. I cannot emphasize enough how slight this hint of chocolate was, almost unidentifiable but just enough to tease at my frontal lobe and send a jolt through it. It was enough to take me by surprise, and I went back for another, longer smell, following up my "Hello there" with a longer "I'm fine thanks, and you?" to misquote Richard Paterson. I finally took a sip and let it rest on my tongue. "Walker?"

"Eighteen year," she smiled. She had been watching me enjoy the drink with rapt fascination. The care at which I took to fully enjoy it was metaphor for her expectations of my sexual prowess. All food and drink was metaphor for sex when sex was what one really wanted the taste of. I should have seen it back at the Christmas party in the way she watched me devour those tiny hors d'oeuvres: oral fixation, without a doubt.

I regarded the glass with some respect and took another drink. "It's been a while since I had something eighteen year," I said as I laid it down and turned back toward her. "I typically prefer something a little older on my tongue."

She laughed, and not the way I'd heard her laugh before. The laugh was honest, but at the same time held intent. She took her hand away from her cheek and pressed it to mine, touching it with the sort of deft feathery touch that I will never be able to accomplish. My hands are only capable of determined, punctuated motions. Hers moved on the breeze and caressed with the fleetingness of pure silk.

She reached for her own glass, and I took measure of it: scotch, the same amount and likely the same brand as mine. They had been laid down before I got here and hers may have been watered down. Discounting the first glass then, I would have to watch my intake carefully to remain in control above and beyond her.

She allowed her laugh to trail off into a hum; the way women on television do to let you know that they were laughing at the sexual joke you just made -- not to undercut it, but to affirm it. I say 'women on television' because I have never seen a woman I was in a real relationship with do that. It is a pattern of behavior exclusive to women of television shows, extramarital affairs, and one-night stands. Perhaps when we are not at our most comfortable we revert to the personality tropes society has taught us, and since the late 1950s, society has done its teaching through an idiot box filled with actors not good enough for film. She returned to the couch with a flop, the sort of fun and relaxed motion of those truly enjoying themselves. I think if I weren't me, I would look back on that moment with some guilt. She was beginning to relax, the firelight touching her like soft gauze and making her into a sepia-toned memory. With one pull of something that I hadn't noticed before and which disappeared immediately afterward, her hair was down and in luscious bobbing curls around her bare shoulders.

"What have you been keeping yourself occupied with?" she asked, taking a healthy drink from her glass.

I smiled. "Work, mostly. And school."

"School?"

"Yes," I said, a lie. "I teach a culinary class at the New School on Harvey Crescent." Another lie. "I'm also taking an intro course in fine art." Another lie. "The School lets instructors take classes for free." Possibly a lie, possibly the truth. I didn't fact check it. I know some better universities have such a program. "I try and take something new every term." Elaboration on a lie. "It broadens my horizons." Technically this would have been true if the classes were true, but they weren't so: lie. "Last semester I took anthropology." Such a lie. You know that one was a lie.

With every point I made, her head moved and twitched in that sweet, attentive way. She never broke eye contact, except to get more of her drink and to look at my mouth. I think she liked watching me talk in equal parts because of what I was saying and because she liked watching my mouth at work.

Oral fixation confirmed. I was almost insulted; I had spent the better part of a week researching her on social media and tailoring the perfect background for myself that would complement the gaps in my deep cover, and here she was more interested in the double-kiss my lips made when I said 'New School.' Whatever small part of me was insulted (likely none) was at the same time flattered by the attention though. I'm never arrogant enough to assume I'm attractive, but every so often when it's confirmed that I am (at least in the eyes of some), I wonder if all my pre-planning and memorization is necessary. Perhaps I could just walk in and bat my eyelashes and be done with it. The world will never know.

Her eyes were hungry and drank me in. I tried to lose myself in the moment almost entirely; some things cannot be faked. As I've said before, compartmentalization is a key part of deep cover. 99.9% of my brain was right here in the role of the salacious youth putting the moves on the boss's wife. Only that remaining 0.1% was monitoring the amount of alcohol I was sipping and making sure I pronounced words like 'mobile' correctly.

The firelight was on her skin and she looked too soft to be real. Her fingertips were grazing the edges of the straps on her shoulders, not moving them but teasing them, reminding me how little effort it would take to make them fall away. Her every gesture and look and smell was an invitation. She took another drink from her glass, finishing it. As she placed it back, I moved forward, completely in the moment, as one must be in times like this. There are some things that cannot be faked no matter how many months one has been in deep cover.

The air was thick between us. Closing the distance between our bodies was like swimming through warm, smooth gelatin. She closed her eyes just as they're lost in my peripheral vision, the first respite she'd given me from her hypnotic gaze since I entered. An instant later our lips met, our mouths open only slightly and then widening as we sank into the kiss, warm and smooth and just right. Her mouth was tiny, I realized, as I took her cheek into the cup of my hand.

Maggie.

The thought came to me from nowhere. The 99.9% didn't know Maggie -- it had been involved in a sordid affair with Lydia Carter for over a month. The 0.1% had been busy with my accent and alcohol and basic bodily functions. Now my eyes were open as the image of Maggie standing in front of me as she waited to get her cab, just before she leaned forward and kissed me, was in my head. All 100% of my brain was screaming red flashing cherry lights and clanging whooping alarms, convinced that this thought has come from some heretofore unknown portion of my mind: a secret percent that had until now been hidden, the grand total actually being 101%, the remaining one a vestige of evolution long thought deserted with Darwin's beaks.

I felt her hands on the back of my neck, lightly dancing fingernails, and hoped she didn't notice. Our bodies were pressed together, warmth meeting warmth. The only sound was the fire and our lips and she tasted and smelled of the same dark chocolate aroma that had been in the Scotch. At once, the 99.9% kicked back in and the kiss was almost all I'm doing again, my autonomous sensory meridian response sending goose-flesh all down my arms.

Maggie came to mind again, across from me at Theories and plopping complimentary peanuts on her upper lip before swallowing them.

I moved slightly, shaking her (and the alarms in my head) away. The motion was noticed by Lydia this time and the kiss ended, though gently and not abruptly.

"Mmm," she smiled as we parted, resting her head on her arm. In her youth, she would have said added wow to the end, but we're both far too old for such games. Neither of us would be the best the other has ever had, but we were both long past the notion that an act must top all others in order to be enjoyable. Our lips met again briefly as I leaned back and we both smiled; I hoped mine looked natural.

I wanted to ask the question, but we weren't there yet. Head-rush dulls the facilities quite a bit, but not enough that the wrong thought at the wrong time cannot snap one to attention. I glanced at her empty glass; mine was still three quarters full. I picked up mine with my right hand, obscuring its contents, and grabbed hers as well. "I'll refill."

She nodded, playing with her hair.

I walked to the bar and confirmed the bottle is Jonny Walker, aged eighteen years. I remember a time when I would have drank anything: pink sludge purloined from a parent's liquor cabinet with floating balls of gelatin in it, tasting of cranberries and shame. The memory came to me like something out of another life and almost set my pulse on fire, but I managed to stay calm. Where had it come from? And those thoughts of Maggie; why did they keep intruding? Where were they coming from, what forgotten corner of my misbehaving brain?

I mimed pouring myself some more Johnny Walker, and then did pour myself some more cola to water down what remained in my glass. It would taste like filth, but sacrifices had to be made. I poured Lydia two fingers and then a splash more for luck and topped it with just enough cola to change the color, not bringing it to the brim.

Advantage had to be gained somewhere, especially when it seemed part of my own mind was out to get me.

13A

Simon bit into his steak and moisture came out of it in succulent driblets. He chewed, looking down at the untouched salad on the side of his plate – a strawberry spinach concoction with dried almonds and red wine reduction – as he chewed. Once he swallowed, he looked up and realized that the man sitting across from him was shuffling uncomfortably. "What?"

"Getting a woman drunk?"

Simon rolled his eyes. "May I remind you I was doing it to avoid taking advantage of her?"

The man's eyelids bobbed, but he said nothing.

Simon took another bite of his steak.

14

There were several more drinks. I even had another non-virginal scotch and soda, poured myself to make sure it wasn't as full as the last. In many ways, it was the best sort of foreplay -- both parties knowing that the other wanted something from them, both wanting to come out on top and gain some edge on the other. I've always found that casual sex is at its best when adversarial... I'm not saying I like that truth or what it says about society or gender relations or sexual politics, it's just what I happen to have found to be the truth.

There were several more drinks and a lot more kissing, hot and sweet with the residue of the alcohol and cola on our lips. At one point, I was nuzzled in the nape of her neck for what felt like forever, suckling on the tender flesh I found there. It was one of the only times I lost myself in the action of the role, without thinking about what I was supposed to be doing or about Maggie or Tyler. There was something about the nape of a good woman's neck I've always found particularly appealing; I believe it has something to do with the fact that it's one of the key positions for depositing perfume. Whatever the reason, it was intoxicating.

There was conversation too. Those are the things they always leave out of the movies -- you know the ones. The spy and the girl go right to bed and the audience is left wondering how that even happens. While this type of encounter does happen, it often leads to the sort of awkward "putting on the clothes while avoiding eye contact" type of conversation after the fact that all parties hope to avoid. No, successful affairs can be some of the only times when adults have good, fulfilling conversations. You already know that the evening will end in sex, so you can be perfectly candid, and since there's a certain level of secrecy involved in the whole endeavor, you know that your words will be kept. It's like having a therapist you can go to bed with. Or in my case, *being* a therapist you can go to bed with, as I let her do most of the talking.

She told me about her childhood growing up in Algeria, her parents having been professionals working there with the UN at the time. She spoke of large stone cities built into the stone face of the earth until one was indistinguishable from the other, deserts that stretched so far that a child could become convinced that they encompassed the entire planet, lush greenery the likes that put the color in America to shame, and palaces that made one dream of being a princess as though it could be true. She told me about not wanting to leave when she was ten, but having to anyway, and of the culture shock of coming back to America and being surrounded on all sides by whites.

She told me about her first crush, a young boy named David Elgee who lived three houses down from her when she was twelve years old. He'd had blond hair and blue eyes and in her memory always wore horizontal-striped t-shirts as though he had stepped straight out of a sepia-toned photograph from the 1950s. He worked in Santa Cruz now, she said; she'd looked him up on social media.

The wonders of modern technology.

She told me about her first time, the sort of sordid hot affair in her parents' garage while they were still at home in the house: no time to be fancy, only the time to make it happen, the sort of quick, insane lovemaking that only children can do. She had been fifteen, which had at the time seemed impossibly old to be a virgin and now seemed impossibly young to not be.

As she told me this last story, I had become nuzzled in her neck and had perhaps faintly fondled her breasts, and may have missed some of the finer details. If she noticed, she did not seem particularly upset by this.

As I took my lips away from her neck, she caught them with her mouth and pulled me in with them; her lips grabbed me with sheer force that couldn't have been broken if I'd tried. Her legs were around me, the heels of her small feet pressing into the small of my back and pressing me close to her. She rocked me against her, grinding against me, her hands cupping the sides of my face and grazing the short hairs on the back of my head.

She was an intoxicating woman. When I tell people that I had to sleep with an older woman for the job, they picture some overweight behemoth with which I did the job for the sake of the job: this was not Lydia in any sense. This was not doing a woman I found distasteful for the purpose of a job I enjoyed; this was being unable to enjoy a woman because of a job I found distasteful.

The blood tried to rush from my head and I tried hard to keep it there, calculating my level of drunkenness: $3 - 1 - 1 + 1 = 2$. Two was not bad; at two I could still make logical choices and sense cues and meanings in subtext with enough virility to act on them accordingly in verbal chess.

Lydia was $3 + 2 + 2 + 1$ making her an eight, easily. Lydia was drunk, on the level that while she likely still wouldn't do things she wouldn't have wanted to, she was more apt to say things she wouldn't have meant to. She'd also had twelve fluid ounces of an eighteen-year-old depressant in her system in the last seventy minutes, which also worked well into my long-term goals. I estimated her weight at 120 pounds... she should have had a blood-alcohol level of 0.14, but was exhibiting signs of the 0.16 that I needed her to be at: the sort of sloppy drunk where social drinkers begin to feel incapacitated.

I do realize how this sounds, yes.

She must have had a drink before I'd arrived.

I felt her hand leave my face and slide its way down to my fulcrum. She gripped hungrily and urgently at the one thing I could not be disingenuous of. I took her hand away was a strong grip, lacing our fingers together and holding her hand above her head with force. She moved pleasingly beneath me despite this, her other hand still on the back of my neck. It took hold of my head by the ear and pulled to one side, bringing her lips to my neck and then breaking away as she gasped for air.

"Take me to the bedroom," she said, her mouth open and sensual.

I pause. For the act, this is for dramatic affect and to make sure she is sure. In reality, I am making last minute calculations, trying my best to decide whether or not she had had that crucial extra beverage. 0.16. 120 pounds. Twelve ounces.

It was time.

"What if Tyler comes home?" I asked, the first time I had dared to say his name.

She smiled sensually, her fingernails running up and down my neck. Her smile found me adorable, cute, like a boy anxious to get caught. "Tyler won't be coming home."

I smiled and took her into my arms, lifting her effortlessly. I realized at once I may have been slightly generous with the 120 estimate: we were at 0.16, I was sure of it. She made long, loud 'wooop' sound and then laughed as I hopped over the couch with her and back out into the parlor where we had begun and began ascending the stairs two at a time. She pulled my head to hers and we kissed, her teeth catching at my lip and pulling me in and forcing me out all at the same time.

I'm not sure how I made it to her bedroom with our faces locked in struggle that way, but I made it as though we'd done this hundreds of time before. I tossed her onto the bed and she bounced and laughed, and a moment later I was on her and my hands were everywhere at once: first in her hair and then on her face and then at her breasts and finally engrossed in the deep warmth where her legs met. We moved back and forth, rocking and kissing and locking eyes when we were not kissing. She grabbed my face with surprising strength, her fingers fanned like starfish on either side of my head as her body arched and angled against mine, her eyes never leaving mine even as the sounds of my bringing her to climax rang in my ears.

Without a pause, my hands slipped past her undergarments and slid them away, then turning to the warm, wet cleft framed by the wispy hints of pubic hair. She was like silk beneath me and I could see the surprise in her as I brought her immediately the downward direction of one orgasm into the upward climb toward another.

She reached for my trousers – pants, sorry – and began to unbutton them.

This was it. This was the real show. I didn't tell you about what I did with her to be vulgar -- deep cover necessitates you be well versed in a good many things and this was one of them. There was the setup, the promise of more, and then there was the 0.16 -- the thing that would make what came next possible and facilitate my getaway.

I brought my hand gently to hers as it unzipped me. I carefully made sure my voice had lost all machismo and that my eyebrows were upturned and innocent: "Are you *sure* Tyler won't come home?"

She laughed and kissed me. "My darling, Tyler won't be home all night... he practically sleeps at the office getting ready for the merger."

DING DING DING DING DING

We have a winner. There was going to be a merger. And now, knowing that, of *course* there was going to be a merger. A merger from which Shane would not emerge the controlling interest by a generous margin. A merger so secretive that only individual heads knew, no employees at any level, and investigations into finances had to be carried out under a vial of secrecy and lies.

I had brought Lydia Carter to climax after seventy minutes of anticipation and she had almost gone insane with it. My release came after almost twenty months of deep cover, and the sense of ease that followed was just as exponentially great.

I could take no time to celebrate. I brought my mouth down to her stomach and Lydia let her head fall back onto the soft down pillow behind her, her eyes rolling back into her head with anticipation renewed. I slid her dress up past her knees and thighs, exposing the milky flesh of her. Her hands touched the sides of my head, but after a moment fell to her side.

I kissed my way up to her breasts and then down to her stomach again, not striking her or paying any more attention to the fire in the joint of her legs. She moaned, softly, as I did this, avoided the areolas, remaining for a moment, then slowly and gently making my way back to her stomach.

Being bad in bed is as much a skill as being good in bed. Men brag about being good in bed, and I maintain I did not tell you about what happened above with the intent of bragging: exciting Lydia Carter then was as equally important as this was now. Men who brag about being good in bed neglect to realize that procreation hinges on our enjoyment of sex: we are made to enjoy it, our body tries hard to enjoy it, bringing blood to all the right places. One has to try quite methodically to not be arousing to a woman... to be downright boring. To be such that the weight of the pillows and the down sheets around you and the 0.16 blood-alcohol level in your blood suddenly has more urgency than the throb in your loins.

I kissed Lydia one last time and stood up, knowing full well by the steadiness of her breathing that she had fallen asleep.

I buttoned myself back up and made for the door, then stopped, went back, and placed an afghan around her up to her shoulders.

As I exited the Carter residence, Maggie was only on the peripherals of my mind. It had been the first time that night that my mind had not been screaming her name. The majority of my mind was alive with one thought and one thought only:

Merger.

15

Over the course of the next week, I sent a total of three texts comprised of that word and nothing else:

Merger.

Such a simple word, isn't it? Get one word in your train of thought long enough and it will start to lose all meaning, to the point that you have to start reminding yourself of that meaning. "Merger: a combination of two things, especially companies, into one." 'Especially companies': right there in the definition.

Do you have any interest in etymology? It's odd how many imperative words have single-syllables while two-syllable words are often much more... sinister. Single-syllable words include gun, food, drink. Double includes murder, merger, killer. When I was young I knew a ghostwriter who said he chose the names of his villains based on the two-syllable rule -- except that I didn't know him, Simon Monk knew him. And Simon Monk was a reality that was not only coming apart but was quickly proving itself unnecessary.

And yet, there was Maggie. That *other* two-syllable name.

Aside from the three single-word text messages I sent that week, I had had one awkward "post-coital" text conversation with Lydia; her 0.16 BAC appeared to have done the trick as intended. She neither had any memory of mentioning the merger, nor was she aware that we had *not* had intercourse. She assumed that we had continued and that she had lapsed in memory due to the drink. This wasn't ideal, but was better than the alternative. I had also had two brief textual interactions with Maggie: she asked me if I knew of any good Mexican restaurants; I told her The Pepper was good. She asked if I had had any plans that night; the answer was no.

By the time Friday rolled around again, I was sitting at my desk at Shane scrolling through these four messages, each set a day apart. I was thumbing the touch-screen on my phone to scroll them up and down even though all four lines of text were visible on one screen, the words bouncing uselessly against the top or bottom of the page with each flick of my digit.

Knowing that there would be a merger was not enough. It was something, but it wasn't enough. Knowing that there was going to be a merger would be enough to plummet Shane stock and certainly get Tyler Carter fired if either of those things had been my intention, and certainly if the information were to become public. A great deal of money could be made with the inside information during trading, again if that had been the intent. Neither was. For our intentions, it wasn't enough that there was to be a merger, it had to be known whom it was *with*.

For a week I had combed through any information I could without drawing suspicion: TPS reports, business trips (who, where, and for how long), meal receipts, and hotel bills. Were there adult movies ordered during the night at the hotel? Then he didn't actually stay at the hotel, it was a front. On Wednesday Tyler came to check on me, to make sure I wasn't working myself too hard to make up for the sick day I'd taken. I'd smiled and said I wasn't, that I felt fine, and shook his hand while some small hidden part of me chuckled with forced puritan awkwardness.

I received the documents from Accounting via courier.

As a general rule that was a bad idea. The more people involved in the actions of a deep cover, the harder it gets to maintain. Many hands do not make for light work in the realm of deep cover. It would have been far better for me to go down to Accounting myself to retrieve the records -- and yet I could not bring myself to do so.

What was happening? How I had I allowed everything to become so... un-compartmentalized? Despite all my efforts to the contrary, Maggie bled into all aspect of my cover. I would need to do the majority of my investigation in Accounting, which I was now avoiding like the plague. At the same time, any attempt to text her and honor our date for Mexican food (still necessary at this point for maintaining cover, above all else) was met with the brick wall of Lydia: I could see her face, held between my hands, and it left pangs in me. Was it guilt over betraying Lydia? No. I owed her nothing.

Maggie refused to stay in the box my mind had made from her, and nature abhors a vacuum, so the contents of the boxes she infested in to fill the gap. She was in everything and everything was in her, to my great frustration.

There had been a PDF detailing project headings for the last twelve months open on my desktop for fifteen minutes without my eyes glancing toward it. Craig had provided it without so much as a second thought, but instead of reading it, my thumb flicked the corner of my smartphone screen, making those four lines of dialog between Maggie and I bounce and twitter.

In one movement, in one of those moments when we act without fully aware of what we are doing, I turned off the computer screen and typed, "let's have dinner" and hit send.

16

We didn't go out to The Pepper. Apparently I didn't know anything about Mexican food, but that was okay, she was going to show me.

"As a rule of thumb," she said, wrinkling her button nose at me, "don't expect any good Mexican food from a Mexican restaurant with an Anglo name."

This was a good rule of thumb, and for the first time in years I did not file it away under compartment X or Y for later use, I just laughed and agreed that that was likely true.

We went to Capistrano, a small place downtown that had been made out of a converted home. The building still looked like a home in the front face, except for the neon sign that cycled the letters O – P – E – N in second-long intervals. Inside it was the heart of kitsch, the flaking paint the rust red of dried adobe and dollar-store framed pictures of quasi-Mexican art on the walls.

"That's the other thing," she said as she sat down opposite me in a small booth in the corner. She pointed to a print of an orange-skinned man with a wide face hefting a large knapsack filled with corn. "If there's good art, it's not a good Mexican restaurant. Real Mexican restaurants are too busy giving a shit about the food to give a shit about what's on the walls."

I laughed again. "There is no art on the wall at The Pepper. It's very chic, very modern. The walls are all this glossy white, I think they're paneled in plastic."

She raised an eyebrow at me. "Are you sure this wasn't an Apple store?"

We both laughed. As it trailed off, I cleared my throat, looking around absently. "How have the late nights in Accounting been treating you?"

"Mmm," she hummed, taking a sip of her water. "Uh-uh. No. No work please. That's what made our night out at the bar so great: there was no work talk."

She didn't know how true that was.

"What did you do this week that wasn't work?"

I stared at her for what felt like an eternity. Lying has to be second nature in deep cover; that is the *point* of deep cover. The answer has to just be on the tip of your tongue, as easily as the truth would be. Now ten different things that Simon Monk had done or would have done in his off time flashed through my mind, none of which I had actually done. Even if I had done them, they would have not been answers to her questions -- Simon Monk's leisure activities were still a part of my workweek. "... Nothing," I said finally, after far too long a pause.

She laughed, glancing my hand with her own. "I... had a bit of an RDJ marathon."

"RDJ?"

"Robert Downey Junior," she smiled. "It started out just watching *Bowfinger* because *Bowfinger* is one of those movies I watch every three years or so for no reason at all. It's like I have a little alarm clock inside me that somebody wound up and it goes off every so often and reminds me to watch *Bowfinger*. Weird, right?"

I nodded, and felt myself shifting and getting more comfortable. I was watching her talk. And not in some bored, un-fascinated way -- I was genuinely interested in not only what she was saying, but *how* she was saying it: the shape her lips made when she said the word *Bow*, curling like the word itself. The way her hair tickled the edges of her face when she laughed. Just how big her eyes were, and the way her cheeks pushed up into their territory when she smiled. I was watching it all, rapt.

"Then I had to watch *Kiss Kiss Bang Bang*, have you seen it? Amazing movie. It's almost a deconstruction of a movie; the way Harry – that's Robert Downey's character

– keeps addressing the audience in his narration and breaking the movie down. It's like it's aware it is a movie, or at the very least aware that it's a story that's being told. Really he plays two characters, Harry and the Narrator, because the Harry we see and the one the Narrator talks about aren't totally the same person. What's that called?"

"An unreliable narrator?"

"Unreliable narrator," she nodded, snapping her fingers. "So by this point I'm in full RDJ mode. Twice is a coincidence; three times is a pattern. So I break out *The Singing Detective* with a bottle of red wine and some cheese on cheap crackers."

"Naturally," I laugh.

"The next night I hit up *A Scanner Darkly*. I read every Phillip K Dick novel I could get my hands on in college after this one prof made us read *Do Androids Dream of Electric Sheep* and watch *Bladerunner*. Loved the book, movie was okay. Not the point. Next was *Good Night, and Good Luck.* -- and I know I'm not going in any way close to chronological order here, but who cares."

"Now I've seen *Good Night, and Good Luck.*," I said, raising my finger.

"Really? Not one of the better-known," she smiled. "What'd you think?"

"Loved the rhetoric. And just the whole examination of McCarthyism. Something about the news media back then, really taking on the estate... never happens today."

Maggie nodded enthusiastically.

I *had* watched *Good Night, and Good Luck.*, many times. Almost fifty times in the run of a week in fact. I had used it at one point to get a certain annunciation and affectation down pat... but I'd enjoyed it so much, I had put it on once or twice since when not in deep cover, even though I always inadvertently defaulted to examining how David Strathairn said the word 'can't' after a few minutes.

... was there anything left in my life I allowed myself to just enjoy?

"So I go from *Good Night, and Good Luck.* to *Zodiac,* and I think there's a certain logical leap there. Then I watched *The Judge* and then last night I watched *Chaplin.* I think I like him best when he's playing real people... or, roles based on real people... you get me."

It was a statement, not a question. I *did* get her. And on the tail end of this revelation, came another... why did this incredible woman even like me as it seemed she did? She said it herself, she preferred when the actor played roles based on real people, which I was not. Simon Monk was a fabrication, not some historically forgotten journalist. There had never been a man that had to waltz around town with a button that said, 'I am not Simon Monk' on his breast.

I shook the thought away. Where had this anxiety come from? I picked up the menu, but found that it was only a drink menu.

Her smile slowly grew as she watched the puzzled expression on my face, the straw of her drink lingering near her small mouth. "Real Mexican restaurants don't have menus either," she hummed when she finally thought I had suffered enough.

I raised an eyebrow at her just as the server walked over. She looked up at him, exposing her slender white neck, and in an instant any thought of question or anxiety was gone. All thought was gone, actually, except those of that thin line of flesh, the mouth they led to, and the scent of the perfume on it.

"Aguachile with bolillo to start," she said, her tongue rolling over the syllables as though it were her native one. "Then flauta, chicken and beef, with jicama. Fresh if you have it please." The waiter nodded once and stepped away without writing anything down, and she turned back to me and rested her chin on entwined fingers.

I paused a moment, then laughed. "You needed to know a good Mexican restaurant?"

She laughed as well, adjusting her straw again, then shook her head and smiled. "That's adorable."

I stopped, smiling. "What is?"

"After you laugh, sometimes you say words with an accent. It's too cute."

17

All of the food was sharable, all on one big plate between us. Our fingers touched often, sending sparks of electricity up my arm. Eventually we got used to it, and then we got comfortable with it, and then it became a sort of game with the food as tokens: I would reach for a piece of food and she would grab it, and vice versa. I took one succulent piece of flatbread with green salsa the consistency of silly putty from her and then offered it back to her. She opened her mouth and I put it in, the hand that was under it to stop any droppings catching the smooth skin of her chin. When she closed her mouth, it was millimeters from my thumb, and rarely had so small a distance seemed so important.

The appetiser was salty, succulent shrimp sautéed with chilli peppers and lime and coriander and thick slices of fresh red onion. There were fresh cucumbers on the side that were the only salve to my burning taste buds and I brought the mixture to my lips more and more readily, the spice only bearable in the moment the tasty seafood was first placed on the tongue. It was served with savory bread in the shape of an oval with a crunchy exterior and soft interior that felt good in the mouth. It was still warm, freshly baked.

The main course was rolled tortillas packed tight with chicken and beef and dipped in beans and sour cream and a yam blend that I learned from Maggie was the mysterious jicama that she had requested be as fresh as possible. She continued to eat this even after I considered it gone, collecting the last remnants on her small finger and then placing it in her mouth.

The food was good. The company was better.

Simon Monk did not eat like this. Simon Monk stuck to foods that kept him regular and out of gastric distress, because one did not know what the next day or even the next hour would bring. Simon Monk also did not shoot tequila for desert, but I did that too.

I walked her home. It was a long walk, but neither of us questioned it.

We talked about politics but about nothing particularly political. We laughed at a violinist still performing on the street and talked about music and got into a heated discussion about the films of Quinton Tarantino. We stopped at a small shop and got gelato in cones made in-house by a baker that knew her by name and spoke it with an elongated 'ie'. We sat on a park bench, not because we were tired but because it seemed like an unspoken thing to do -- neither of us suggested it, we both just did it. She sat close to me, my right side pressed tight to her left in the night air.

When we reached her front door, I did not ask to come in. I said goodnight and smiled at her. She jolted in as she had the night at Theories and kissed me, lightly on the lips.

As she was pulling back, I took her face in my hands and found her lips again, as well as her tongue.

It may have been the most perfect single kiss of my adult life, of the sort that we look back upon nostalgically and without regret.

We said goodnight and I stayed on her stoop until she was inside, then walked back to Capistrano to retrieve my car, feeling as though my feet did not touch the ground once the entire time.

18

There was this kid in IT Craig had introduced to me a month before, named Nelson. He was the young bookish type; you know the kind. One can't blame Hollywood for perpetuating the stereotype of the bespectacled social misfit in that role if reality keeps doing it for its own casting calls as well.

"Look harder," I said. My arms were folded across my chest and I stared at his screen over his shoulder. "There are files missing from R&D and Marketing. They were there when I did my audit and now they aren't; what happened to them?"

Nelson shrugged in that non-committal way fifteen year olds often do, though he was twenty-seven. "They're just gone."

I frowned deeply. "Nothing is ever gone on a Windows server. Not that quickly at any rate. That's why we destroy hard drives with a hammer before they go out the door to the dump. If you know what you're doing, just about anything can be recovered."

He turned slightly and looked at me over his shoulder. I straightened -- Simon Monk shouldn't have known that. At the very least, not on that level of condescension. I had slipped out of an uncomfortable shoe for an evening and now was trying to shove my swollen foot back into it and it wouldn't go.

He clicked from screen to screen, checking directories. "... It's gone," he said again, more to the screen than to me. "Not deleted. I can tell you that it wasn't deleted. It was moved somewhere, but I can't tell where."

I looked back at my files. The missing documents had been research into a synthetic pharmacological compound, ED – 01 – N, codenamed "Vitality." It sounded like a male enhancement drug. There had been several pages worth of animal trials and thirty identity-protected sheets of human trials, each with their own case number. There was a password-protected file that, once opened, would provide the name and social security number that corresponded to each case number. It had been a part of a long night of audits for me nearly a month ago, the files a red haze even to me. They'd had positive results in uterine cancer, it had been mentioned. Other test subjects had noted cognitive shifts, possibly a side effect? Who knew. The files itself didn't matter so much as the fact that they were gone. They had been in my hands, I had audited them personally, and now they were gone.

Nelson continued to click through screens of text, some of which made sense to me but most of it nonsense. It was the bios of the network, the programs running in the background on the Shane system. "There's something else gone too," he said, almost to himself.

I looked up.

"See here?" he pointed to a folder he had opened from deep in the directory. It was from the applied sciences subdirectory, and it was empty. "It's empty here, but click back," he did so, "and it says the folder has 368 files. The same was with your R&D files: gone but not gone. Not invisible, not hidden, and not deleted. There in all the ways the computer tracks and regulates but not there in practice."

"The files are in deep cover," I said under my breath.

"What?"

"Nothing." I straightened. "Can you tell me what the files were about?"

Several more clicks. "A specific sort of centrifuge? Maybe? If you trust the file directory."

I placed my hand on his shoulder. "Let me know if you find anything else. Only me, if you can."

He nodded.

19

Maggie and I attended a Charlie Chaplin double feature at the Bijou the next week. I'd gotten the idea after hearing her go on about seeing RDJ (I was calling him that myself now) in the Chaplin biopic. They played *The Great Dictator* and *Gold Rush*... I didn't think too much of *Gold Rush* either way, but I couldn't help but watch *The Great Dictator* with undue attention.

Did you know that the film was controversial at the time for being anti-Hitler? This was in the time while Hitler was in power, but before the second World War. There's so much of our history we've just... erased. Nobody would say now that there was pro-Nazi sentiment in the US prior to World War II, but it was there and prominent. But it has been whitewashed from history. America was in its own version of deep cover, inventing a new history for itself as it went along and insisting upon the fictional version as truth. History, Shane, Simon Monk: all of us under deep cover, hiding aspects of ourselves.

We went out for dinner afterward at a quaint little bistro that took cash only. The kitchen was in the middle of the dining room and the entire restaurant was filled with flavorful steam that permeated everything. They made this succulent lamb medallion that broke apart like butter the second you touched it with your fork... I tell you, there was nothing like it. It was the first time I had eaten something of my own choosing with my own tongue in twenty months, and it was like giving a dry man water: it filled me completely, made me whole and happy.

I walked her home again and again we kissed on her front stoop. It was neither her kissing me nor me kissing her this time, but rather something that happened naturally, like two halves coming together to make a whole. It was long and wet and slow and hungry, our lips still savory from the meal. Her perfume was on me and all around me; her hair was in my eyes and my mind and everywhere. After an eternity that felt too short, our lips parted, and a smile crept over hers.

I was smiling too, I realized. "Goodnight," I said, that dumb grin on my lips.

She took me by the hand, firmly and gently, and led me inside instead.

20

It was a familiar setting, and yet not. Old and yet wholly new: me on a couch, my lips pressed to a beautiful woman. Her hands were on me and in my hair and around me. She pulled me by the collar back onto the couch atop her, her lips soft and forceful in a way I am convinced no other thing in nature could be.

"Simon..." she said in hushed whisper, and I flinched. I must have flinched, for she flinched.

As I said: familiar, yet wholly new. Every touch was intensified, every caress, every graze. It had been too long since I had had an unexpected experience... even when I was the prey as I'd played for Lydia Carter, I was really the one behind it all. I had had no idea this was coming, and the spontaneity of it made my heart race and my blood pump in a way it hadn't in years.

I also couldn't remember the last time I had been in this position with someone I cared for.

The realization made me wince again.

"Simon—"

With the realization came anxiety. There's a reason American's hide the unfortunate political leanings of the past; through today's lens, it would make them think of themselves differently. It was the same with Shane when one came down to it: they hid what they did not want people to see, perceptions they did not want made public.

And what about Maggie? Would she have taken me by the hand and led me into her home and kissed me on the neck (and now the ear, oh my) if she knew some of the things I'd done? I'd love to be able to tell you that bringing a cougar to climax was the worst of my deeds, but we both know it is not. In my experience, one does not even enter the trade of giving up one's identity unless one is ashamed of something they've done to begin with. When Maggie learned the truth, would she want to erase me? Would I become another faded pencil line on the paper of her soul, forever rubbed out and forgotten along with college boyfriends and other past mistakes? Would she have been here with me if I had not been Simon Monk?

"Simon—"

Her hands grasped at the clasp of my trousers and opened them, each digit hungry and wanting more and more of me. Just as before, my hand reached up and touched hers gently, but forcing it to stop.

"Simon?" She stopped moving and kissing me, able to see me now for the first time. Her head jolted back and her voice took on a wet tonality. "Simon, why are you crying?"

My hand went to my cheek: I was. I hadn't realized it, but I had been crying. Not openly weeping, but there was a steady stream of tears down my face. "I'm sorry," I said. I buttoned my trousers reflexively. "Maggie, I'm so sorry."

I had never said those words before, to anyone.

Her touch was gentle on my shoulder. When she spoke, she said, "It's alright, Simon." She said it with certainty, with a level of conviction that I had never had toward anything... anything, perhaps, save her. It was not that she couldn't conceive of what it might be and was ignorant of the possibilities: she weighed the possibilities and decided that whatever they were, it was okay. Her faith was something I did not deserve, that Simon Monk could never deserve.

And so I told her.

20A

Simon took a long sip of his tea as the man across from him stared blankly.

"Well?" the man said finally, brushing his blond hair back from his eyes.

Simon looked up from his teacup, feigning ignorance. "Well, what?"

"What happened?"

Simon smiled. "A gentleman doesn't tell."

20X

"I'm a spy," Simon said, his hands clasped in a motion of prayer as they wiped the tears from his eyes. Moisture still dribbled from the cleft of his chin through the rough terrain of his five o'clock shadow.

A single syllable of a giggle erupted from Maggie Winter's lips. Had it not been for his tears, it would have been a full-fledged laugh. Even so the smile was in her eyes and she tried to fight it, tried to take it seriously... but it was so silly.

"I'm serious," he said again, his voice flat.

"Role play is a little much for the first time, don't you think?" She moved closer to him, but he shifted away. Her smile lessened slightly, and he hated to see it. He wanted to take it back, to laugh it off and take comfort in her lips and her touch and her body... But he couldn't. It had to be made clear. It had to be driven home.

"I manipulated myself into Shane as a means of industrial espionage, in order to get information for my employer."

Her smile was gone now, and she moved away from him. Not much, only a millimeter, but enough to send pangs through his heart. "Is this a joke? It's not funny if it's a joke."

He swallowed. "In order to get the information I needed on an upcoming merger --"

"Merger? What m--"

"I seduced Lydia Carter, Tyler's wife." He could not look at her when he said this last.

She looked at him, then away, and then back again. "Are you... What? How could... what? Who even does that, what could you..." She got up off the couch.

"Maggie, please."

"Don't you dare. Don't you dare. Is this why I'm here, is this why you're here, Mr. Monk? Did you need to get into the accounting books so you thought you'd go about it the fun way first? Is that how you get your rocks off?"

He swallowed. "Many years ago, I was in Niger. I was working for Turkey at the time... it's not important. Someone had gone missing, and when I found him there were two of them. Two men, the one I was looking for, and another." His accent slowly seeped in, adding a twang to the end of certain words. Salt water tears were getting in his mouth. "Those men... they changed me. It changed everything. Everything was different then... He and I went back to Turkey and took a message back to my employers, but these were not men easily trifled with --"

"*Why* are you telling me this?" she interjected, her cheeks livid and hot. "Why do you think I *care*? Why would you tell me any of this, Mr. Monk? What could possibly be in this for you?"

He sucked in his lower lip and took a deep, shuddering breath. "I couldn't be with you without you knowing who I was," he said finally. He reached out and took her cheek in his hand, and was surprised when she let him. "Not with you. Never, with you."

She looked at him, in the eyes, her cheeks still red with fury. After a moment she reached up and took his hand away from her cheek... but instead of forcing it away, she held it and kissed it, and knelt down in front of him finally. "That's a lot to take in."

"I know. I'm sorry... there's no easy way to say it."

She paused, for a very long time. "Is Lydia okay?"

He nodded. "We were not intimate. I... got the information I needed without taking it that far."

She nodded, bringing her hand up to wipe her face quickly, hoping he wouldn't see. After another long, tense silence... she laughed again, this time a full and complete laugh, not one stifled by poise or posturing. It took a minute, but he smiled. Her laugh made him smile, and he thought it was the loveliest sound he had ever heard. After a moment they kissed again, long but without hunger: it was a kiss of catharsis... another first for him in a long day of firsts, but for her as well.

"Well, Mr. Monk," she smirked at him. "Is that all now? Have you unburdened yourself?"

He looked at her pleadingly. "I'm sorry... my name is not Monk."

She made an exaggerated nod, as though she thought she should have expected that next. She put her hands against his biceps. "Well then, to whom do I have the pleasure?"

He smiled weakly. "Siaz."

She snorted again, releasing a long belly laugh that bubbled up from her and thrust her forward into his lap unintentionally. "I'm sorry, *now* you're kidding me. Simon Siaz? Your name is Simon Siaz?! As in, 'Simon Says touch your nose?'"

His eyes moistened again as she met his gaze through squinted, laughing eyes.

It took a moment to dawn on her, but when she did the laughter stopped. "Oh... oh, I see... Your name isn't Simon either, is it?"

"It is now," he said declaratively in his native accent for the first time in twenty months, and he brought his face to hers and kissed her.

21X

He kissed her with the sort of reckless abandon he hadn't allowed himself in years... perhaps ever. He held nothing back and kept nothing in, his hands cupping her face and then moving to her collarbone and then her shirt was gone, fluttering quickly through the air of her home until it landed softly against a chest. Her hair fell down over her shoulders like something out of a Sandro Botticelli, and for once in his adult life the only conflict he felt was whether he would rather gaze upon her forever or have her; if only he could have done both.

Once again she fumbled with the clasp of his pants, tugging the two halves apart... and once again, he faltered. "Maggie --"

She let out an exaggerated, exasperated, humored sigh, smiling at him. "What? Is there something else? Are you North Korean? Were you on the Manhattan Project?" She kissed him on the cheek.

"The men... there are cruel men in this world. Some of them I have worked for... some of them I no longer work for..."

She smiled. "I'm a big girl, and this isn't a comic book." She kissed him again, lightly, on the lips. "Nobody is going to come throw me off the Brooklyn Bridge."

"No, these men were not happy that I left, when I was in Niger... the man I was sent to stop, he helped me... but they were vicious men."

She took him by the ears. "Then I'll be gentle," she hummed laughingly.

"Maggie --"

At once, she understood. It all clicked into place, suddenly, and she nodded. Her face poised and sweet and serious, she leaned in and kissed him on the lips... the new best kiss of the newly christened Simon's life, and though he did not know it then, the best kiss he would ever have. The first kiss between a soul unburdened and another unfazed, each one seeing the other for what they truly were and accepting it, totally and without consequence or malice.

For a third time she reached for his middle, sliding her small hand between his skin and the fabric of his clothes. Her hand moved deftly and silently, up then down then up again, her lips pressed firmly to his the entire time. When her hand emerged again, she withdrew his penis.

It had been sliced vertically down the middle through four of its roughly eight inches, the two halves splaying in either direction like a dousing rod. The bulb was darkened and wrinkled. The foreskin had been wrapped around the half that stuck out to the right, giving the impression that the left half was a second, thinner member that splayed bare to the side due to bad plastic treatment. The foreskin, and indeed the skin of much of his groin, was noticeably lighter than the rest of him and did not move and twitch with the rest. The flesh that was colored 'correctly' was shrivelled and tight with scar tissue.

She broke off their kiss and pressed her cheek to his, regarding the part of him that lay limply in her hand. She moved it slowly, smoothly between her fingers, the right half between her thumb and forefinger as she led the foreskin over the bulb and back again, the left half cradled gently by her ring and forefinger.

Her cheek was hot and pleasant against his. They watched her actions together, each equally invested.

"How long has it been?" she asked quietly, without turning to look at him.

"It has been like this seven years."

"No, I mean, how long has it been since --"

"It has been seven years."

She nodded. "I'm sorry."

"No, I'm sorry." He winced. "I'm sorry after all this that I can't... I have pills, but they're at the house... and they're not much good. I hadn't expected."

She nodded, still manoeuvring his member slowly and carefully between her digits, then turned so that she could kiss him again as she did. When this kiss was done, she moved her mouth, moist and warm, to his chin and then his neck.

"What are..." he started, then caught himself somewhere between surprise and shame. "You can't."

She did not respond. Her mouth found her way to the right splay of his genitals and she cupped it gently along her tongue before taking it into her mouth almost to where the halves split, gently holding the left half all the while and keeping it safe. She moved it with her as she moved, down to exacting detail.

He winced once and tried faintly to object, then felt the muscles in his shoulders relax and refuse to stop her. She had taken him over. He was Pinocchio without his strings, lying prostrate before her power.

She cupped him gingerly as she moved, paying careful attention to every sound and motion he made, knowing then where to go and where not to go... and after what felt like forever, he felt something he had not felt in so long he had stopped believing it was a possibility, as he began to rise within the soft embrace of her lips. Blood filled him and expanded him, making him more a man than he had thought himself able in almost two Olympiads. She slowed as he grew, and as he thought she was finishing, she released him from her velvet tongue... then tenderly eased the left splay of his penis up so that it was in line with the right, lowering her head again until all of him was in her.

He tried again to object, but found he could not. Alarms and fireworks blared out the back of his skull and made it impossible to think. Pain mixed with ecstatic, revenant pleasure as she moved him within her and his vision went white around the corners, his every muscle going ridged and seizing with spasms of electric current.

He ejaculated, and the sound that came from him was ecstasy. His voice echoed off the walls and filled her home until it was bursting from the very floorboards, deep and full and in every cell of his being.

When he came back down to earth, she was at his side, her button nose stroking at the nape of his neck. He turned his head down and kissed her passionately. He was still cradled in the palm of her hand, glistening in the low light of her living room now. As he kissed her, she began to rock him again.

He smiled and chuckled. "Maggie... once was a miracle. I'm sorry --" But he stopped short, as his body made a liar of him.

She took his head in her hand and laid him back onto the couch until he was flat. She stood briefly, her breasts bare in the soft glow from her kitchen, and removed her underwear from under her dress. She lifted one leg and stepped over him, then again cupped him in her hands. She had become nimble at it now; there wasn't any hesitation. It was an instrument she picked up as though she had every night since time immortal.

He brought his hands to her thighs and slowly began to push her dress up. She stopped him in a mirror of the way he had her, her hands gentle on his.

"What?" he asked, his voice a whisper.

She smiled and laughed, a blush returning to her cheeks. "Promise you won't laugh?"

He nodded. "Never."

"... I don't like it when people look at me."

He did laugh, and she with him. He let her dress fall back around her and she gently brought him inside her, then leaned forward and kissed him as they rocked back and forth, her body clenching him as warmly and gently and lovingly as her hand had.

They arrived as one and she collapsed upon his chest with scant breath, where they remained for some time.

21

I awoke from a brief doze with her head on my chest, my legs spread along her couch, and I'd never felt more at ease with myself in my life. She was trailing her finger along the small nest of hair that existed between my nipples, not bored but aimless. It seemed like a reward in and of itself. I kissed her on the top of her head and felt her smile against me.

"So what are you investigating?" she asked, and I could tell by her tone it had been on her mind for some minutes. The question was casual though, with the air of someone who would accept any response even if that response was that I couldn't say.

"It's not like that."

"Then what's it like?"

"You're better not knowing."

She turned her head and gave me a look that told me exactly what she thought of any statement like that. "I'm an accountant. I could help."

"Too dangerous."

"And if I'm doing something wrong and not knowing it, I want to know."

I frowned, then shifted so that we were beside one another. I took several hard breaths, trying to find the right words. Lies were so much easier than the truth. "It's not a matter of doing something wrong, per se. Although there's certainly something going on. It's more..." I shifted again. She kissed me on the corner of my mouth, and it energized me, bringing my thoughts into clear focus. "There are epistemic shifts in the world, especially in the political world. Big events that change... everything. They upset the balance of power. The people paying me, they don't so much want to stop these shifts so much as be prepared for them."

"Who's paying you?"

Now it was my turn to give her a look.

"Sorry."

"It's okay. These shifts, sometimes they're unpredictable: like the stock market crash. But the more of them that happen, the better people get *at* predicting them. In the same way that we learned about the weather by first watching the weather, or how we developed profiles on serial killers by first looking at the profiles and patterns of existing serial killers. These patterns – these cultural shifts – have been mapped out for over a century now, and the people behind the people in charge of the world are finally getting good at predicting them."

She sat with that for a moment, then nodded slowly before lying back on me. Her eyes traced the patterns on her ceiling as though seeing it for the first time. "So... the people paying you, they think one of these big shifts in going to happen at Shane?"

I hemmed, bobbing my head back and forth. How to explain? "Something's coming. We're long past due, and the world seems to keep boiling over with no hint at stopping. Shane is one of three big players in a certain space that we think is going to make a big difference in the next few years. With that kind of growth comes money, and with that kind of money comes power: lobbyists, political partnering, campaign donations... Shane's interests become the world's interests... and if that's the case, it would be good to know what Shane's interests are ahead of time."

We were both silent then for a very, very long time. The two halves of me had returned, the man who now in some part belonged to Maggie Winter and the deep cover, returning from his evening of rest. I knew what to ask but didn't want to, even once I realized that she was all but waiting for the question. "Have you noticed anything strange, in your audits?"

I could feel her tongue moving about against the inside of her cheek as she contemplated. "No... well, yes. But not really."

I stopped and turned toward her. "What was it?"

She paused, pursing her lips. "I've been seeing a *lot* of money coming in from the Engineering department. A lot of money, easily a quarter of our income last year. I brought it up to Tyler twice and he said it was misrouted and that he would find out where the funds really came from – but for now I'm to just keep track of it so it can be properly allocated when he knows where it should have been coming from."

I mulled on that for a moment. "I don't get it."

"...We don't have an Engineering department, Simon."

22

Maggie loved watching Robert Downey Junior play real life journalists. So did I, honestly, but his were by no means my favorite portrayals. For me you had to go all the way back to 1976, when Dustin Hoffman and Robert Redford played Woodward and Bernstein... the simplicity of real investigation always struck me. It was never a mastermind stroking a cat felled by a dashing Scotsman – more often than not, it was something small and simple like it was in 1976: "Follow the money."

I got the keys to the hard files from Nelson, told him I was looking for my missing files. It was partially true, and that was what made him not question it. The files mattered, yes. There was something to the files, to ED – 01 – N, relating to that specific type of centrifuge and who knew what else, and lord only knew how important those things were... but they were symptoms. They were the fever that came with the virus that was going to kill you. I could spend the next twenty months digging through files and investigating targeting malware to try and find everything that Shane had been up to... but they were all of them symptoms.

The disease had been right in front of sweet Maggie Winter the entire time, and it made my lip curl to think of her soft hands organizing the files that helped clean the filth that came through.

Follow the money. Shane doesn't have an engineering department.

It took me less than five hours to find what I'd spent the last twenty months searching for as Simon Monk. Twenty months as Simon Monk bested by one word from the most amazing woman Simon Siaz had ever met.

Animal trials and clinical trials and human trials and synthetic drugs and new centrifuges and god-only-knew what else all had one thing in common: they cost money. Lots, and lots of money. The type of money that made the cash I had spent making myself looking like a good management consultant or a competent stock advisor seem like pennies.

Shane is one of three big players in the space that are going to make a big difference in the next few years.

Tyler won't be home all night... he practically sleeps at the office getting ready for the merger.

Money like that didn't come from just anywhere, and certainly not without a heavy caveat attached. Shane had been paid billions hidden through a department that didn't exist to do research and development on behalf of the payee. That much money doesn't just buy goods and services: it buys stock. Lots of stock, carefully changing hands outside of the public eye as the engineering department kept the money coming in... as the stock was slowly being filtered out. It was my stock shift I'd used to trick Tyler, on a massive scale. On an astronomical scale.

The money had come from different places, all filtered through engineering. OmegaGene and Crytech and Alpha Quadrant and Slipfire and private hands... all that money coming in and all that stock going out, no one the wiser that it was all filtering back to one place.

There are three big players in the space that are going to make a difference in the next few years.

It wasn't a merger... or if it was now, it hadn't started as one. It was the slowest takeover in history: thirty different small subsidiary companies contracting their work in exchange for money and stock options, the money staying with Shane, and the stock options all filtering back up to the parent company... until before Shane knows it, someone else holds that majority. Or close enough to a majority to render their management moot, and suddenly it's time to talk options. Does the current brass step down and let the void be filled with the people who took them over... or do they make a deal, becoming the largest of all the subsidiary companies in the process?

There are three big players in the space that are going to make a difference in the next few years.

23

I laid the folder down on the Joint Chief's desk. It was thick and meaty with pages, barely held together by the string that bound the manila-colored carrier together. I liked to make a show of it.

"That's all of it?" he said. His voice was high pitched and belied his sagging jowls. I wasn't sure how such a face could have even made such a voice.

I nodded.

He strummed his thumb down along the side. "I don't need to tell you that this stays between us."

"I've been paid, sir." It was the only acceptable answer to anything he said, ever.

"Thank you, Mr. Siaz. I have your next assignment." He held out a folder like the one I had handed him, but much thinner. I must have paused for a moment because he looked at me, but I snatched it an instant later. "Thank you, Mr. Siaz."

"Thank you, sir."

There is a part of me, a part that's still a spoiler, that would have loved to be a fly on the wall of that office when he opened the manila folder and realized that every one of those two hundred pages had been blank.

23A

Simon sat with his arm bent back over the mesh chair he'd been sitting in for over an hour, sipping his second cup of coffee. It had gotten cold twice he had been talking so much, and the waitress had been kind enough to heat it with fresh pots again and again. The Arizona sun was bright in the sky and warm on his face as cars and children passed him by.

The man across from him with long blond hair and a stubbly goatee wore a tight black shirt, his arms crossed in front of it. He looked grim and thoughtful, but not unpleasant. The muscles in his arms caught deep shadows in the sunlight. "That's it then?" he asked, nodding respectfully.

Simon nodded, smiling. "Yes, Victor, that's it."

Victor un-tucked his hands and laid one on the manila folder in front of him. "And these are all the files?"

"Eighty-Six fairly incriminating pages, along with two *very* incriminating ones. It wasn't hard once I knew what to look for... I'm sorry I couldn't get more, but once things start going missing... people start looking."

Victor nodded. "You told the Joint Chief there were two hundred."

"Like I said, I like to make a show."

He nodded again. "This is too big to hide."

"I know."

"You're not going to be able to play triple agent anymore."

"I know." He looked across the street at a trim woman in a dress blazer and the most perfect dirty-blonde hair he had ever seen looking at travel brochures from a spinning rack. "And I'm fine with that, honestly. I've got some money tucked away... and good friends." He smiled when he said the last, throwing Victor a wink.

Victor touched the folder again, gently, as though afraid to. "... And you're sure?"

Simon met his eye. "The hint is in the name. The money came through the engineering department. There is no engineering department at Shane. Of the two companies that would have the interest and the resources to buy out Shane... I'd bet anything that the money came from Engen."

Victor let out a long sigh, gazing out over the crowd himself and finally coming to rest on a young brunette girl that was eyeing the tag on an orange dress that suited the day well. He decided immediately that he would buy it for her; her smile had a way of making him smile, and that was something he needed desperately at the moment.

"All's well that ends well?"

"One of the most clandestine organizations on the globe has acquired its only major competition for use as a public face. I'm not sure what you call ending well."

"Nobody hurt."

"Yet."

"Nobody dead."

"Yet."

"You can be a real downer, you know that?"

The blonde made her way across the street during a gap in traffic, then finally came over to their table. Victor forced a smile. "You must be Maggie. I've heard... a lot about you."

She shot Simon a look.

Simon extended a hand to Victor. "We square?"

Victor raised an eyebrow. "When have we not been square?"

Pause. "For Turkey."

Victor took his hand and shook it stiffly. "We've always been square for Turkey."

"Never," Simon said, clasping Victor's hand with both of his for a moment before reluctantly letting him go. He placed a hand gently on Maggie's back, and both of them started to walk away. "Take care of yourself, Victor. Live well."

Victor smiled as he got up. "I will!"

Smirking, Simon turned around in the middle of the empty street and waved his finger chidingly. "I didn't say Simon Says."

THE SPY

"Where did you learn that?" He gasps, near the end.

I smile. Say nothing. State secrets.

The next day I'm on the other side of the iron curtain, listening to the gossip of everyday life. Ears open, trying to appear relaxed, although I'm not. You can't ever be totally relaxed, doing what I do, playing one side against the other. Double agent.

Behavior that comes natural to everyone else is rehearsed. Hide your natural accent, make sure you talk about the right things, laugh at the right jokes, order the right drink the right way. Culture that's a way of life for some is a performance.

I make the jokes that some part of me thinks are crude, engage in unanalyzed play that the analytical part of me knows is cruel. Tell a sly joke about the opposite team that you have to think on, and when they do, they jeer and congratulate. They're taken aback, they'd never heard that one before. They don't piece together that it's the type of humour – the type of insight – you can only get when you've spent time behind enemy lines.

The partners approach, and I'm made aware through whispered words and sly nudges that one of them is there for me. Later that evening she's on her back in her hotel room, asking that same question he did: where did you learn that?

I smile. Say nothing.

State secrets.

Properly plied, she starts to give information. Techniques only the forces on the other side are privy to. The best ways to loosen a tongue. She's trying to make me talk and I open my mouth and give her what she wants, but only enough. I'm never truly there, I'm taking notes on tactics, on style, on technique.

I've a catalogue of notes to bring back across the battlefield to make them talk, now. Secrets only someone who exists in the blank space between nations can know. They all think I belong to their camp, and they must continue to think that I belong to each of their camps.

If they found out A Spy was in their midst, I'd be excommunicated from both tribes. That is the nature of my unease. I can belong to both, or I can belong to neither. There is no in-between for a spy.

The one I got the information from has me out for coffee, her hand along my middle. Clenching, she thinks I'm hers. Her friends are there, their partners.

I see in one of them, that they're not there, too. Spies are often only visible to other spies. The way you count drinks, the way you hold your flowers, the way your accent slips on some words and not others. I see in one of them a fellow spy, and for a momentary glance, they see me, and I think they see me.

Thus begins a dangerous game: spy vs spy. They are hidden in plain sight as well, the person on their arm thinking they own all of them when they only own what they allow. Tentative smiles, nods. Furtive glances. We are a danger to each other here, the both of us double agents. We could unveil the other, or align forces. Trade state secrets like ships in the night, be on our way.

That night I'm on his couch, we're shooting pool at a local bar. Cover story.

My pants are around my ankles and I'm trying to keep notes. Tactic. Style. Technique.

Being a spy is hard work.

I think my head back and arch, open my mouth. I let out the words that, in our espionage, signal defeat.

"Where did you learn that?"

He smiles.

Says nothing.

State secrets.

REMEMBERING

I've been walking for a week and a half straight.

I push my body past the point of hunger, past the point of exhaustion... past the point where I have any right to keep breathing, let alone keep up the brisk pace I've set for myself. I run until my legs get rubbery and the bones in my knees threaten to snap under the strain... and then the womb's ability to heal kicks in and I get to start it all over again.

I've just passed Waterville on Route 65 when this dance starts again, black blood pumping up and surging through my joints and muscles, moistening them where need be, strengthening them in others. It gives me energy as if from nowhere, and suddenly the dull throb in the back of my head isn't pounding quite so hard, and the feeling of the highway against the soles of my feet doesn't make me want to die quite so much. A moment later those bad things are gone completely.

Deep down inside, I feel a rumbling that has nothing to do with my stomach. A kick and a squirm against my rib cage as the womb hammers at the walls of its prison, trying to get out. I swallow back hard to fight it, and that's when I realize my mouth is full of blood. But it's not the coppery, metallic taste one associates with red blood... it's a taste only I know. It's the putrid taste of the black blood that I have to thank for the sudden boost of vitality a moment ago. It tastes like rotten milk mixed with burning hair and silver.

My eyes shoot back open, and I realize for the first time that they'd been closed for almost half a mile. I pour on the speed as the night sky begins to cloud and threatens to rain on me. As my human heart and lungs begin to ache and strain, the womb finally stops slamming quite so hard.

Not altogether, just not quite so hard.

Its taken me over twice since I left home. Each time when I woke up, I found myself eight or ten miles back from where it overcame me. Trying to get back to Coral Beach. To the friends I left there. To finish the job it started.

The pack on my back feels like it weighs a ton easily, and the stench of sweat on my clothes makes me wish to God I didn't have enhanced senses, but I block it all out. I try to focus on something else... *anything* else but what's behind me. What I'm running from.

The forests to either side of me are dark and ominous. The evergreens make shadowy faces at me, waving about in the slight breeze that keeps me cool. I try not to stare at them too much, or the faces start to look familiar. The road in front of me seems to go on forever, and it's been hours since I've seen a car. Days since one has stopped to see if I needed help. The last one that did was a portly trucker, about forty-five. Overweight and clad in a flannel shirt and faded jeans, he looked like he'd stepped right out of Smokey and the Bandit. He'd pulled over about a quarter mile from where he'd passed me and waited for me to catch up, getting out of the cab when I got close. He had a grin on that was a little endearing, with a toothpick sticking out of the corner of his mouth and wearing a baseball cap with a faded picture of a bulldozer on it. He'd asked me if I needed help, and I'd looked him right in the eyes. I didn't need a mirror to know that when I did, he saw that they were as black as ebony... maybe even blacker. He'd stumbled backward and slipped on the slick, pebble-ridden pavement, slamming his back and skittering back toward the oversized wheels of his truck.

I'd flashed my teeth at him. Not the ones I was born with, the ones that stayed hidden until I needed them. The ones that were sharp and jagged like butcher's knives, and were yellow for no right reason other than they were. The ones that usually came out of my gums dripping with my blood, and went back in dripping with someone else's.

He'd slammed the cab door shut so fast that I thought the rusted hinges would crack, and then drove off with the roar of a powerful engine and the rankness of burning rubber. It made my nose itch and I coughed once as I watched him speed away, wondering briefly why I had frightened him off.

Then I remembered the reason I'd left home, and decided that the fat hick was better off having never known me. That a hell of a lot of people would have been better off if they had never known me.

My foot hits off a big rock on the side of the road, and suddenly I'm back to reality. I feel one or two droplets against the nape of my neck, and realize that all the stars are gone. I wonder what will come first, the rain or the dawn. Not that one would stop the other, even if it could.

The road ahead takes a sharp turn to the right and I stop to catch my bearings, kicking up a fair amount of dust as I do. It dissipates into the atmosphere around me slowly as I pop the calcium in my neck, releasing the tension in the cartilage and also giving me a kick jolt of pain that helps keep me awake. I lean down, resting the palms of my hands against my knees the way my father always used to after he'd spent a few hours chopping wood, and take several deep breaths before straightening. Squinting my eyes, I hear the faint squirting sound as blackness covers them anew. It's like the sound toothpaste makes when you squeeze it from the tube, that's the best I can describe it. Suddenly my vision is alive as if it were daylight. Better than daylight, there are no shadows to me.

The lights of Waterville are a dim memory on the horizon. Even if the womb escaped right here and now, it wouldn't get back in time to do any damage to the town or its people. Not that I'm about to let it out, it's just nice to know. The pavement has begun to sparkle and shine as raindrops slowly patter against it, like the stars I watched come out a few hours before.

There's a town not far west, I'll have reached it by morning. Might be able to reach it even sooner, but running in the rain is messy business, and I'd just as soon take it slow. I wrack my brain trying to think back to the maps of the state that Mr. Miles used to have hung up in homeroom, but for the life of me I can't remember any side road that will take me *away* from this small town, whatever it is. Every other place I've been able to avoid or bypass in some way, to stay out of sight of the people inside. I'd passed through Waterville, but it had been at night, and the only people who were around to notice me were a couple of teenagers, and they'd been too drunk to notice by the smell of them. High too, but that was besides the point.

I briefly consider cutting through the forests, but one look at them makes me reconsider. The contents of my pack might not survive the trees and branches, and that was the last thing I wanted right now. Those few items were all I had of home, and I carried them on my back as carefully as I could. I let out a heavy sigh and decide that I can easily get through town unnoticed, even in broad daylight.

I hoist the pack's shoulder straps with both hands, adjusting the weight a little. It wasn't until that point, when I felt the blood rush back into the pinched areas of my chest, that I realized exactly how long I'd been carrying it. I grunt and grit my teeth, grabbing the straps even tighter, until my knuckles turn white, and start toward town.

The rain made it before the dawn, and it poured.

***

A big, blue sign with white letters and a dent or two on it that looked to be made by bullets had welcomed me to the town of Kannibus, Maine about two miles back. Population one thousand and eight and dropping, although the sign had not advertised the 'and dropping' part. It had, however, advertised the best apple crumble in this county, which had started my mouth watering right then and there.

As I swallow back spit, I remind myself that I don't need food. Then again, I don't *need* cigarettes either, but since I'm going through town anyway, the temptation to pick up a pack is becoming too much to ignore. I also don't need the touch of a woman, but I never once turned it down from Julie Peterson... except for that one time. So, I decide that need is something very different from want, and that a smoke and some apple crumble might provide me with some natural fuel and the will to keep going on the road ahead, even when this town is far behind.

There's no snow on the ground here, and it takes a harsh wind to remind me that it's still winter. I can't see the buildings yet, I'm still about a quarter mile from that, but I can already smell them. The sun's about ten degrees into the sky, so I measure that it's a little after nine am, and my enhanced hearing picks up the groan of engines as people find their way to work. About five minutes later, three cars pass me in rapid succession heading back the way I came, probably going to work in Waterville. Something tells me that it's as close to rush hour as this town ever sees.

My head tilts from left to right like it's on a swivel, and I feel myself starting to lose my concentration on the road ahead, but decide that's a good thing. Someone looking too focused in a place like this might draw attention that I really don't need. Or want, for that matter. The trees that surround me are starting to get thinner, and the grass and marsh that surround them are scattered more and more with the sawed off stumps of where more had been. The type of tree is getting more diverse as well. Only a few hours ago there had only been those shadowy evergreen faces to keep me company, but now they're joined by maple, oak, and the occasional spruce.

The first sign of civilization I see (besides the sign two and a half miles back) is what remains of a park. Not the type of park with swings and see-saws, and those annoying metal horses on springs that I could never quite get to work right... it was a camping park, a nature park. It had rusted red gates across it now though, and looked as though it had for quite some time. An old wooden sign had a name on it that I'm sure is Native American and I am equally sure I am not going to attempt to pronounce, followed by a declaration of the park's hours of operation that had since been scratched out. The only thing within sight that looks less than ten years old was the chain and padlock that keeps the gates together, they sparkle like they're new. Somewhere not far beyond the gates, I hear the sound of a babbling brook, its steady stream caressing small, round rocks and probably making morning foam. I stop and eye the locked gate for a moment or two, and realize one thing the welcome sign hadn't read: Kannibus, Maine: Ghost Town.

Not abandoned, just dying, but a ghost town all the same. Probably built during the boom of the steel or coal industry and left to slowly bleed to death ever since. Seems like just as good a place as anywhere for someone like me, at least for a few hours.

I'm not even five minutes' walk past the gates to the park and I see the first buildings, a small convenience store and three houses.

The store's whitewash paint has been half chipped off its siding, revealing an odd dark blue color underneath in some spots, and nothing but rotted wood in others. It has gas pumps out front, two of those self-serve ones, but there's no sign saying the price and they look faded and unused... and I ain't smelled a lick of gas since those cars passed me.

The sign across the front reads : 'Hannah's Convenience and Garden Shop,' but there's no sign of vegetation anywhere, none of the tell-tale sights and smells that come with that sort of growth. No fertilizer, no bone-meal, and most of all: no plants. Not so much as a tulip or a turnip.

There are posters in the front window advertising movies for rent, and from what I can see through the open front door, that much appears to be true. But the posters are also advertising 'The Crow' and 'Seven Years in Tibet' as new releases, so it's obvious how much effort they're putting into it.

As I start to pass the battered old business, I catch a glimpse of snack food and bread on the shelves, and an old man wearing a green sweatshirt and Sunday pants sitting between the checkout and the cigarette display. The itch I've been feeling in my chest ever since I thought of smokes awhile back begins to get the better of me, and I feel my body turning toward the store without my knowledge. I stop myself, remembering how little money was actually in my bank account before I cleaned it out, and that there was nothing saying that this guy wouldn't be as forgiving about legal age as my home town was. But somehow, looking at the disinterested man struggling to stay awake behind the counter, I severely doubted that last part. Still, one had to admire him. He'd obviously tried every trick he could think of to keep his business alive, only to be met with defeat every time.

I know a thing or two about that.

As for the three houses, they're nothing much to write home about either. Bungalows, all three of them, each with a pretty equal stake of land. No fences, and some of the windows don't even have curtains on them, even though they're close enough together that John Smith A could probably see right into Jane Smith B's bedroom. Two of them have the same, plain off-white siding; while the other had chosen a ghastly shade of pink. That's right, *pink*. Either the person who was living there was color blind, or they had the worst taste I have ever seen in all my life. Or they'd lost a bet. But more than likely, the reason was because it was cheap. Aside from that obvious difference, the homes were pretty much the same. Roofs that peak just a little off center, chimney that hadn't been used in years, two windows on the front and three in the back and a rickety old porch that led up to the front door. One of the white houses has a barbeque accompanying its porch, and the pink house's lawn is scattered with children's toys. And they are all as quiet as a grave right now.

I think I see something move in white house number two, but choose to ignore it and keep on moving. Maybe it will do the same.

The trees are further back from the road now, but they're still there. The roads are kept up pretty good for a dying town, and I realize that's the reason it was built right on top of Route 65 instead of off of it: easy way to get the county to pick up the tab on the upkeep of your roads. These people might have been cheap, but they sure weren't dumb.

I step over a blind hill and there's another row of houses on the opposite side of the road, and trees on my side. I resist the urge to just back-flip into the cover of the brush and keep on walking, keeping a watchful eye on the windows and doors that seem to be staring at me like eyes now. Maybe I've just watched that episode of the Twilight Zone about the small town that doesn't like strangers one too many times, but I can feel the hairs on the back of my neck reach for the sky like they've been held at gunpoint, and can't for the life of me figure out why.

Maybe this place just reminds me a little too much of home.

The houses are getting more and more plentiful now. I'll be in the heart of town soon, and I try to distract myself by thinking of that sweet apple crumble in my mouth. Most of the homes seem about the same as the first two, just small dwellings for small families, some identical to the last and some with slight differences. There was one that was just a trailer, and there was a middle-aged woman gathering up children's toys out of the dirt and mud in front of its entrance. She turned and looked at me, first with surprise, and then with hallowed, sunken eyes. She glared for just a moment, then dropped the toys and went back into her house, shooing a young child back in as she went.

Then there was that house.

I'm so busy watching the woman picking up the toys that I almost don't notice. It's like it snuck right up on me, which, given its size, is no easy task. It is easily twice as long as the largest of the other homes, and the only two-story one I've seen since entering Kannibus. The bottom story is made of brick and opens to an extravagant porch which is the size of the trailer itself. Attached to its side is a three car garage with a convertible parked in the driveway. A quick glance around back and I can see a basketball court and a small workshop that's the size of the pink house down the street. It has four times the property of the other homes... and this one does have a fence around it. And not some dinky little picket fence either, one with wire and metal that was probably the most extreme thing the town council would allow. Several signs tacked to the fence warn to beware of the dogs, but I don't see any from where I stand. That doesn't mean I don't think they are there. It just means that I don't feel quite so uneasy about the other houses now.

And the very next house over is a one room with no siding that might as well be called a shack. It's easy to see which family has the money in this town.

I keep walking, and the road starts to wind and turn a little, up this hill and over that, swerving left and then veering right. I'd hate to see someone trying to drive over this drunk, which I'm sure happens more often than not.

I look up ahead and see a blind turn right next to an old bakery that looks to be still in business, next to an old gas station that clearly isn't. I smell the yeast cooking along with the distinct aroma of cinnamon rolls, and for a moment I've forgotten about the apple crumble and the cigarettes, no easy task. I lick my lips and realize how dry they really were as I pass the gas station, once again fumbling the change in my pocket, wondering exactly how much I have.

This station looks like it's been out of luck for the last five years or more, with all of the plate glass windows beaten in and scorch marks all along one side. I take the time to shake my head at the idiocy of someone setting fire to an abandoned gas station for fun, and then continue on my way, pushing the rolls out of my head and reminding myself that I'm not here to browse like some Yankee tourist, I'm here to get past this place, and get some apple crumble if it's on the way.

There's another house just past the bakery that I can only see the roof of. It's built on a plateau just a little way down from street level, with a set of hastily manufactured stairs leading down to it. There's no front yard, and the back yard is another steep drop off that seems to go on for some time, though it's hard to tell with all the trees. The house itself is little more than a shanty, with the dark green roof taking up its majority. The siding is again a plain white, the door a magenta red. The stairs (hastily built or not, on second glance appear sturdy) lead to a narrow porch which wraps around to the other side of the domicile, and I bet that the view from it is spectacular. There are toys scattered along this balcony. Nothing extravagant, just a cheap red and yellow plastic bike that looks like it could have belonged to a boy or a girl really, and a doll house which looked to be better maintained than the house itself. It was clearly a one bedroom house, and as I walk past I get a better view of it. The windows are cracked, one of them broken with panel board nailed over the front. The siding, while in good condition, did not extend over the entire house. Since winter (even the mild one this town seemed to be having) wasn't a siding season, I assume that whoever owns it had run out of money and couldn't scrounge up any more before the summer ended.

I soon have an image in my head of the occupants of the home, even though they were nowhere in sight. I picture the child, maybe three or four, wearing clothes that are ripped and much too small for her anyway, Mommy having long ago stopped trying to keep up with her growth spurts. She's still pudgy with baby fat and her first word will probably be a curse, but Mom will tell the neighbors it's something else, like 'duck' or 'shirt'. As for Mom herself, she wore tank tops and cut-off jeans, but she wasn't some 40 - something mom clinging to her youth, she was definitely young enough to pull it off. Daddy had worked on the mines and had to move to find work. First he sent checks every two weeks, then every month, then when he got around to it... then never at all and his phone was disconnected. For some reason in my mind she was a redhead, and she had a nice tan. Don't ask me why, I don't really know. Either way, I fully expect Tammy (that sounds about right, somehow, again I don't know why) to be a grandmother by the time she was thirty and a great grandmother by the time she was forty-five, and that both grandchildren and great grandchildren would end up referring to her as 'mom'.

I shake my head and just kept walking, noticing a corner store that looks far better off than the first one I'd seen just as I started to round that big blind turn, which turns out to also be a blind hill. I think for a second that this might be where my promised apple crumble lay in wait for me, but decide not, figuring that there would be some sign outside to advertise it further. Instead, there are signs promoting $3.48 Milk! And Hershey's Chocolate Bars: 2 / 99 cents. For some inexplicable reason there is a large blue cartoon cat next to the sign above the door, which proudly proclaimed: 'Neighbor's Convenience and Pharmacy' in bright red letters. I wonder how good business could possibly be. I've only seen ten houses since I've come into town, and so far two stores. This one, however, looks to be doing a little better. It's still quaint, but it's kept up well and if it had served the apple crumble I long for, I would have eaten it right off the table without a worry in the world.

I'm almost past the place, and the next house has caught my eye (again with the pink siding, it must have been a good sale) when I notice her.

She's small and fragile, having to use both hands and just about all of her body weight to push open the front door of Neighbor's Convenience, and one of those hands clutched a brown paper bag brimming with red licorice as if it were gold. She's about three, and is wearing a puffy little blue dress with white lace around the edges and up the middle, a matching white ribbon tied into the auburn hair that looks as though it might have been blonde just a while back in the summer months. I picture the girl's mother smiling as she put it in that morning, and the girl squirming impatiently as she did. Her eyes are big and hazel, and would no doubt give her some trouble with boys in about a decade's time, as they probably did her mother. Eyes like that never come from the father, I've come to discover. She's a healthy child by the looks of her, too. Plump, but by no means overweight the way most children are these days, and her cheeks jiggle just a little as she turns her head back toward the store clerk and says "Tank Hue."

I can't help but smile when she says that, my enhanced hearing carrying it over from across the road as if it were Dolby Digital. I stop walking altogether for the first time since I came into town, and watch as she trots along the parking lot toward the road and turns left once she was on it, her nose squarely planted into her bag of licorice, hair falling to either side of her face.

I get that sick feeling in the back of my throat again as the womb perks up, and I feel like punching myself in the side as hard as I can to shut it up, deciding to get out of town before I do something to this child that I pray I won't remember. My mouth has that burning hair taste I've come to dread over the last five months as I start to walk away... but then that black blood reaches my ears, and I hear something that doesn't make me smile. It's the sound of fast spinning wheels kicking up pebbles, followed by the scent of cheap motor oil and gasoline, and even a little marijuana (which shouldn't have shocked me in a town named Kannibus).

As I turn, everything's slow motion. I'm never quite sure if that's all in my head. Maybe that's just the way it happens, or maybe I'm moving that fast that everything seems to be in slow motion... but I try not to give myself that much credit. In any case, I can see the little girl in the blue dress walking along in red dress shoes about four feet too far from the edge of the road, and my eye just catches what appears to be a late eighties sport car coming up over the blind hill leading into the blind turn.

He'll hit her and not even realize it, the way these roads were made.

I take two steps and realize that I'm not going to make it, so I stretch out my arms and jump for all it's worth, my tired legs popping at the knees with the sudden elaborate use after days of monotonous walking. For a second, I'm convinced that the car is the only thing moving, getting steadily closer one inch at a time while I just hang there in the air and the child remains in mid step, still looking into her bag of candy (which wasn't that long, really. It had been about ten seconds since she had opened the store doors). The second my arms touch the girl time speeds up again, and I feel her tiny body topple under my weight, and allow myself a sigh of relief.

That's when the car's fender connects with my right hip.

As the lower half of body jolts to one side without the benefit of being followed by my upper half, the rational part of my brain tries to tell me that I'm fine. That I've felt worse than this. A lot worse, actually, and a lot more often. However, in moments such as these, the rational part of my brain is often minuscule in comparison to the portion screaming out in sheer agony as I feel what I've come to recognize as muscle pulling itself away from bones.

I hit the pavement about five feet away from where I made contact and just keep rolling, furthering the injuries even as they try and heal themselves.

In a lot of ways, the healing is worse than the original offense. Imagine the worst pain you ever felt, then imagine it happening again in reverse slow motion. Times that by ten and try to fight an unnatural organ or two from doing what comes naturally to them while keeping a lid on your emotions, and you're half way to figuring out what my day is usually like.

I finally come to a stop against a guardrail, at just the right angle to see the car speeding around the blind turn. I had been right, he wouldn't even know he'd hit something until he got home and saw the shape of my hip in his front bumper. Across the street, some old man is peering out his living room window at me, waiting to see what will happen. He probably got that house for this express reason, the same reason people go to stock car races or watch reality tv: as a people, we just love to see the wrecks.

I start to move just as the old guy reaches for the phone, no doubt to call 911... or maybe his friend in the next house over, who knows really. His eyes widen just a little. He's never seen road kill that moves before. If I could lift my arm, I'd give him the finger.

There's a whimper a few feet to my left just as my bones finish setting themselves with a wet snap that reminds me of the sound of ripping chicken off the bone after it's been in the fridge for a few hours, and I remember the reason I got myself into this mess in the first place. I look up and see her face down on the pavement, sobbing to break her tiny heart. One of those little red shoes has come off and rolled close to me, and my heart races as I pick it up.

The movement is sheer agony, always is. My body cries out in utter defiance as I force myself to my feet and take the two steps between the two of us, and that sour milk taste is threatening to burn away my tonsils. I can feel the blood pumping in my ears as I reach out to touch her shoulder. I stop, rethinking it. This isn't home, and this kid hasn't grown up two blocks down from me her whole life.

"Are you okay?" I croak out. My voice sounds odd even to me, either from disuse or misuse, take your pick as to which. I touch my throat just to make sure that didn't get damaged in the accident as well, and am pleased to find no blood on my hand when I withdraw it. That's good. Neck wounds tend to be hellish.

She turns toward me with a face filled with tears and eyes brimming with more, her lower lip looking to be set to constant vibrate, billowing up and down like a ruler snapped over a desk. Her hair is messed up now, strands of it going everywhere, and there's a small scrape across her forehead that's not even bleeding, but still was cause enough to raise warning bells within my psyche. There are now licorice scattered all over the parking lot and street, most of the sticky candy now covered with pebbles and smut, and I pray that is the only reason for her tears.

She doesn't answer me, not in any way I can understand anyway. She just shoves forward, wrapping her arms around me and shoving her salt water and mucus-strewn face into the only clean shirt I have, her pudgy little fingers grabbing the back of my shirt and holding it tightly. She starts to mumble what happened (as if I wasn't there), but I'm not really catching a word of it. Between her cute little girl way of mixing up words, the speed of her panicked speech, and the tears still caught in her throat, it comes out as one big wail with varying pitches where words begin and end.

Nobody can cry like kids can cry. They cry like whatever's going on is the worst thing that's happened in their entire lives... because really, it is. Kids have no reference for pain. They don't have that little voice in their head to says 'you've felt worse,' because they haven't. That scratch on her forehead is probably the worst thing she's ever experienced, judging by the relative lack of scars on the child.

There's no rationalizing a child's pain either, no explaining what's happened so they can just get over it. For all she knows, she's dying. No wonder she's scared. So, I do the only thing I can do: I stroke my hand against the back of her head as calmly and rhythmically as I can, and say the occasional "Shhh..." when her breathing tells me she might be getting upset all over again.

We stay there for about ten minutes before she starts to calm down, and I realize I have too. The womb isn't pounding at the gates anymore, and my adrenaline rush from a few minutes before is way down. My heart rate has slowed, and the blood in the back of my throat tastes like regular blood again.

I must be the only person in the world that gets happy when he tastes coppery blood in his mouth.

When her sobbing subsides enough that I think I can let her go without starting another fit, I take my hand off her head and back up a pace, kneeling down so that we're closer to eye level. "Are you okay now?" I ask, trying my best to make my gruff voice sound compassionate. I hope that it at least passes for human.

She nods, though her head is still turned downward, and the sobs (while few) still come, each one shaking her entire body.

"Okay," I say, forcing a smile onto my face. Those muscles haven't been used in so long it almost hurts. "My name's Alexander. What's yours?"

She sniffs once, wipes her nose in her arm, and then looks at me. "I'm Klarissa."

"Okay Klarissa. Do you want to tell me what you were doing out in the street like that?"

She huffs, rolling those big eyes of hers dramatically, her arms flapping down by her sides in exasperation. "Mummy was urking at the rest rant sos I had to go to Nannysmith's hose for little wile sos Mummy can rake enough money to boy mya pony someday and race it at nascar. She wasgonna tack me to par, but she had work and Nannysmith smells weir sos I went to par all by meself (cause eya bigurl) hen se watch stories. Not s'good as Dora tories but Nannysmith like sem. Sos I was goin two the par but I want sum candy and den I gots ome candy en den hue ushed me. And I'm spittin mad!" She stomps her foot once against the pavement, then spat milky saliva onto the ground, to show that she did indeed know what spitting mad meant.

"Okay..." I drawl, raising an eyebrow. "I'm not even gonna pretend I understood a word of that, but somewhere in there I think I heard 'Mommy'?"

She makes a very large nod of her head, and I begin to get the impression that she's patronizing me a little, which was more than a little amusing. The smile isn't fake now.

Another car passes us, and all the occupants turn their heads to look at the child and I as they drive by, even going so far as to slow down a little. The people are no doubt wondering what the stranger was doing crouched down next to one of their youth, with licorice scattered all around them. God only knows what their minds have already come up with. I turn toward the vehicle with the intention of flipping them off, but they've already disappeared behind that damned blind turn.

Almost growling, my hip still remarkably sore, I rise to my feet and extend my hand to the child. She takes it. I'm not sure if that's good thing or not, after all, I am a perfect stranger. But that's not any of my concern, really. Screw the apple crumble. I've been in this crappy little town for fifteen minutes and I've already broken three bones, been run over by a car, and looked like a pedophile. No pastry is worth this. I'm getting my cigarettes and getting back on the damn road. "Can you take me to your Mommy?" I ask, and she immediately turns, squeezes my hand a little, and starts walking down over the blind hill the way I was headed anyway.

***

I walk with her for about ten minutes when I notice her start to slow down considerably, and I realize that her little feet are getting tired, so I scoop her up onto my shoulder without a word. She laughs when I do, leaning forward to rest against my head and bouncing herself every few minutes, as if to say: 'giddy-up'.

We pass a few more houses and the park that my young friend must have been referring to (which I notice has not one but *several* of those horses on the metal springs that I can never figure out), and then another store. I'm beginning to wonder if the ratio of stores to houses in this community are 1:1, but Klarissa starts to fidget and I push the thought out of my mind. The houses themselves seem to be getting worse and worse with each step I take. Most of them don't have any siding now, or half-finishing siding. One was missing a north wall, which would have been fine for a house under construction, but the remainder of the home looks well lived in, as does the rusted out Ford parked haphazardly on the front lawn. The streets themselves are nearly deserted, with a car passing by every now and again. Only now they seem to slow more as they passed Klarissa and me... not much, but enough that I could see at least one head in each vehicle turn and look me up and down. The drivers were all young. Not as young as me, mind you, but young all the same.

One overweight man in his mid-forties peddles his bike up the road in the opposite direction as me on the other side of the road. His shirt is faded and full of mustard stains, and flip-flop sandals barely contain feet stained by tar and nails that were barely clinging to their anchors. He winked at me as he rode by, twitching his head to one side as he did, and I did my best not to make eye contact until he was gone.

The next house looks gawdy even by the standards that this town has set (pink is in season this year, after all). This one's color was normal enough, though (white with a dark blue trim), but everything else about it simply cried out for attention. On the lawn, three flamingos are perched in a semicircle facing one another, and they look somehow as if they're having a conversation about me. To the right of that is wooden cut out of the baby from 'Who framed Roger Rabbit?'. Three mannequins are sitting around a large fountain which spouts blue water, and there's an entire Smurf village which I can't help but think Mike would either love or be terrified of. There also appears to be a painting the size of a movie screen of a train on their back yard, actually sprayed onto the grass.

"That's Missusus Flarity's house," Klarissa states matter-of-factly, pointing a finger at the house. "She gives out candy apples for Hall oh wean."

We come upon a big hill on a very steep angle when we make the next turn. My young friend starts to squirm to get off as if she's used to having to hop down at this point, but I keep her up there, mainly because this is yet another of those blind hills, and I'm not keen on the idea of jumping in front of another moving vehicle. The march up isn't easy. It may not look like winter here at the moment, but it certainly is. You can tell by how slippery the roads are, and maintaining my footing on them hurts the backs of my heels like nobody's business... until the healing kicks in, that is. There's that odd slurping sound as a sore I hadn't realized was on the back of my left foot heals itself over, making a new layer of hardened, tough skin right there on the spot.

There's a little stream running by both sides of the road on the hill. The one on the other side of the road looks to be fed by the rudimentary sewer systems in the town, the water clear but still mossy and not something I would even stick my hand in, let alone drink out of. The water on my side, however, looks to be natural, and falls down over little rocks that stand in its way, making little splashing sounds as it did, this little babbling brook. I watch it intently, completely absorbed by its tranquility as I make my way up the dirt path on the side of the road.

Klarissa seems to notice me watching the water and starts to watch it herself, laying her head down on mine and sending a few strands of her auburn hair into my face, which I blow away without a care. As she watches the brook and listens to the rhythmic sound of the water pouring, I feel her little body relax, and it's only then that I realize just how shaken up she had been by the events of a few minutes before.

We reach the top of the hill and I continue straight, passing a post office with a battered and bruised American flag out front and graffiti all but covering one side. Klarissa taps me twice on the head with her full palm and I crane my head to look at her, stopping in mid stride. She points down a side road that I've passed, and I see a little take–out restaurant there, just a minute's walk into the road. I nod, then follow her instructions and turn around.

The establishment looks simple enough from the outside, a twenty-foot cube with wobbly wooden steps leading up to the front. The whole thing is painted a brick red and has two large windows on either side of its plate glass door. A large painted sign across the side facing the road proclaims: 'Marie's Restaurant and Take-Out, the best food in the county.' I'd begun to fear that that might not be as big a stretch as I would've initially thought, but my nose was picking up the scent of fried chicken and gravy (and fresh bread too, no doubt made at the bakery up the street), and suddenly my mouth is filled with more saliva than I can choke back in a simple gulp.

There are two signs hanging in the window to the right of the door, placed outside the white curtains patterned with roses. One gives the hours of operation (which, curiously, proclaims that it always closes for lunch), the other is hand-drawn and taped to the window itself: 'Home of Marie's Apple Crumble Special.' My eyes nearly bug out of my skull as I put Klarissa down next to me and open the door, its rusted hinges squeaking in defiance. I missed Christmas this year... but this little turn of fate will do just fine.

The inside of the diner looks a little better than the out, but not much. To be fair, they did wonders with what they had to work with. There are only four tables and eight chairs, all painted the same brick red as the outside. Someone tried to dress up the walls and make them look pretty, putting flower trim all around the center, but the tiled walls and the odd underlying odor that it wouldn't take my nose to smell tells me that this place was a butcher shop no more than five years ago. Just like the video store out on the edge of town, it had to change just to survive. Through an open door that reads 'employees only' I see the large sheering saw that used to be used for cow, and was now used chiefly for chicken. In all fairness, it was remarkably clean. A place this small with a cutting room, a kitchen and a bathroom should make a guy like me want to hurl from what I can smell, but all I get is the familiar scent of pine cleaner that makes my nose twitch just a little.

Behind the counter are racks of potato chips and soda, and another door into what can only be the kitchen, a phone attached to the wall next to it for taking orders. The door opens, and a tired looking woman comes out.

"Mommy!" Klarissa yells, holding out her arms wide as she runs under the counter and jumps up into the woman's arms. She hugs her mother tight, clutching at the apron patterned with the same roses as the curtains, but stained with grease and blood.

The woman smiles and laughs, running a hand through her daughter's hair and not realizing that she just left a gloop of some unknown black substance there, probably oil from one of the stoves in the back.

I feel ashamed for an instant as I look at them. Not thirty minutes before I had had her pegged as another neglectful teenage mother with more condoms in her pocket than common sense in her head, letting her child run free in the yard like an animal. Christ, I'd had her pegged as a great grandmother by the time she turned fifty, for crying out load. This girl was nothing like that. First off, she seemed older than I'd originally thought. There were lines around her eyes from either laughter or pain (or both). Her hair wasn't red at all, but a golden blonde that made her look positively angelic. I had been right about her daughter's eyes at least, those same hazel spheres glistened in her eyes too. Her smile was the best part, though. She had nice, freckled cheeks that moved at even the hint of happiness. Even a small smile for her reached from ear to ear, and made me realize what those lines around her eyes were really from. Her teeth weren't what you'd call straight but they were definitely properly cared for, never touched by nicotine and rarely by coffee. The only make-up on her face was on her lips, a pink gloss that made them shine and sparkle. Suddenly, the apple crumble didn't seem that appetizing anymore.

I'm about to estimate her age as actually being mid-thirties, when the rotary fan behind her finally turns and sends her scent in my direction. Behind the grease and sweat, she has a scent like marmalade. A natural sweetness that starts my mouth watering again, and I change my mind on her age. She's no more than twenty-five, probably a little younger, just aged a little too early by stress and a few too many disappointments.

"Klarissa," she tisks, getting down on her knees to face her daughter at eye-level. "What are you doing here? You're supposed to be at your Nanny Smith's house until after supper." Her voice has a hard edge to it, but it's natural and unintentional. Each word is doused in so much love, you'd have to ring them out by hand to make them mean. "Didn't she take you to the park?"

"See was gonna," Klarissa sighs, again slapping her arms against her legs dramatically, rolling those eyes of hers, "but see had to visit her friend Jack Daniels, but she never done that either... see just fell asleep watching stories, so I went to the park all by myself cause I'm a big gurl, but then on the way I wanted to go to the store sos I did an got some candy, but then the man pushed me."

Klarissa's mother turns toward me, as if noticing me for the first time. I'm leaned against the counter, trying my darndest to look casual, my hands clasped out before me. "You pushed her?" she says, her voice accusing as she gets up, dusting off her apron.

I back up a pace, stuttering a little as I do. "I - I mean - - there was a car! I pushed her out of the way of a car that was coming over the hill. It was a car, right Klarissa?"

Her mother looks down at her, and the child shakes her head slowly back and forth. "I din see no car."

My face goes white, and I realize that after everything, my chances of getting that apple crumble are fast fading away.

She looks up at me with dead seriousness, her eyes squinting in a way that doesn't look natural for them. I wait for a swift kick to a place where even my healing won't help me, but instead I see a smile begin to grow on her thin lips again, her cheeks rising until they nearly overtook her eyes. "Had her nose buried in a bag of candy, did she?" she asked, ruffling her daughter's hair.

I breathe a sigh of relief, feeling all my muscles relax, then nod. "Yeah. Some idiot in a car almost ran her over. Wasn't really her fault, but you might want to rethink your choice in sitters all the same."

She nodded knowingly. "Mm. She was a bit of a last resort. Usually Marie, the owner, looks after her when I'm working for her, but she had to go to a funeral upstate so Nanny Smith was really our only option." She looked me up and down, then extended a hand forward the way people do when they're not sure what else to do. "My name's Sandra. You can call me Sandi."

"Alex," I say simply, taking her hand and shaking it twice. Her hands aren't smooth like most girls her age. Lots of hard work and labor have turned their velvet touch into leather way before their time, but there's a softness to them that nothing on this earth can take away, I'd wager.

"What brings you to Kannibus, Alex?" she asked, trying not to sound as though she was prying even though she was. She might have been grateful, she might have been kind... but she wasn't stupid either. I was a stranger that had been alone with her daughter and I must have smelled like a pit bull by now. She had every right to have questions, so I decided to answer as best I could.

"Just passing through. Been keeping to the highways mostly, but this little place cuts right through it. If I keep going on the main road, will it take me back out again?"

She nods, even as she hands Klarissa a box of orange juice from the cooler and starts to wipe down the counter tops. "Yeah. Should only take you about an hour's walk to be completely out of town."

"Any place I can pick up smokes between here and there?" I ask, taking a quick glance around the place a realizing that not only are there none here, but I can't even smell that herb musk of nicotine anywhere close by.

"There's the gas station. It's the very last thing you'll pass when you're leaving the town limits. They're really expensive here, though. They know you can't get them anywhere else, none of the other stores sell them."

I nod in understanding, jingling the change in my pocket.

"So, what can I get you?" she asks as soon as she's done cleaning the counter, placing both hands on it and leaning forward, smiling. The top button of her checkered blouse is undone from the heat of the kitchen, and when she leans forward I can smell the sweat from her body.

"Nothing for me, thanks. I gotta get on the road and I haven't got much money." I say, turning back toward the door. It's time for me to get out of here, before something bad happens. Because with me, something bad *always* happens.

"Wouldn't dream of charging you. I think saving my little girl's life earns you a piece of chicken. Or at least some of Marie's apple crumble, there's a fresh one in the fridge, not even sliced yet."

I stop in mid-step. I remind myself, not for the first time, that I don't need to eat, strictly speaking. But my stomach starts to roar at me as it eats away at itself, and my dry tongue longs for the taste of something other than my own spit on it. I take my hand off the door and turn around, and before I know what I'm saying, I ask: "Ice cream?"

Sandi smiles again, as she gestures toward the cooler. "Your choice of three of the thirty-one flavors."

I walk back toward the chairs and sit down as she starts cutting up the promised apple crumble I've waited so long for. Every so often, Klarissa pokes her head up over the counter and grins at me as I wait, and I realize her eyes weren't the only thing she got from her mother.

She got her smile, too.

***

The apple crumble tastes like heaven.

I wolf it down like a savage, and it still takes me the better part of fifteen minutes to eat it. I think she gave me nearly half the whole pan, and she hadn't skimped on the ice cream either. It was vanilla and it was homemade by someone local or close to local, I guessed, and it's cool goodness in contrast to the steaming hot crumble makes the whole world disappear each and every time I shove another spoonful in my mouth.

She watches me eat the entire thing, head rested on her hand behind the counter. I apologize once or twice for my table manners, but she insists that she's enjoying watching me enjoy it. I smile at her (a feeling that if I'm not careful my mouth may get used to) and put another bite into my mouth, this one drenched in melted cream.

Klarissa's eating her own smaller version of my meal from a dish at the next table over, and I turn to her and wave my spoon in the air in a mini 'cheers.' She reciprocates the action, waving it a little bit too hard and sending droplets of melted ice cream spraying to the floor. The both of us laugh, followed in suit by her mother, who quickly wipes one of those droplets off the counter.

"So," she asks, smirking at me again. "What're you doing out on the highway in the middle of winter anyway?"

"Wandering," I say in a non-committal voice, motioning toward my pack in the corner. "Trying to keep warm and keep fed. Been on the road about a week and a half."

"Coming from the north or the south?"

"Neither," I answer, and don't elaborate.

She's polite enough to take the hint and get off the topic quickly. "Any idea when you're heading out?"

I put the last piece of apple crumble in my mouth and start to chew. I almost feel bad that as soon as I swallow I'm going to say: 'now,' then grab my stuff and leave, but it's not like I owe this girl anything. I don't know her from Adam, for god's sake. I can see both suspicion and curiosity in her eyes, and know that if I stay, one or both of us will end up hurt. Probably just her, and not in the way she would be worried about.

I swallow down and I'm about to make my exit, when I hear the roar of a suped-up engine pull into the driveway outside. Sandi hears it too, and the smile disappearing from her face just confirms what I already know : trouble.

I see dirt settling through the window, most of it being taken up and away by the breeze coming in from the north, probably bringing some snow with it, too. I can see just enough of the roof of the car to tell that it's red, shiny, and that the owner of the vehicle was definitely overcompensating for something. I hear shoes against the gravel outside as the scents start to make their way in through the doors before the men themselves. And they are men, I can smell the testosterone from here. I can also smell cheap motor oil and gasoline... and marijuana. More of it this time than the last time, I smelled it. My eyes narrow and my blood starts to pump, my fists clenching until the knuckles are white.

Sandi waves Klarissa over, ignoring me now as if I wasn't even there, the way any good mother would. Klarissa runs under the counter again and her mother shoves her into the kitchen, closing the door shut behind her, just as the door to the diner opens. Through it, I can see the red car, eighties model, suped up, with a dent in the front bumper where my right hip had hit.

I was expecting to see some stupid thug wearing army pants and a black tee-shirt with tattoos going down both arms like sleeves. I've really gotta stop assuming things like that, because for the second time since I marched into town, I'm dead wrong.

He's about a head and a half taller than me (which doesn't really take much), and he isn't the built up muscle man I was expecting, but he isn't weak either. It was hard to tell under that suit and tie he was wearing, the top button undone in a vain attempt to look casual. He looks like someone who works out, but not someone who thought working out was their life. He has short hair that's combed neatly to one side and gelled there so that it stays that way the entire day, and a perfectly groomed smile that looks like one a used car salesman gives you before he tells you the price. His hands were hairy and the veins were popping out of them at the knuckles, which were scarred in some places and scabbed in others. His eyes were that cobalt blue that made girls melt, made it so they couldn't see anything but those eyes until it was too late. People used to call eyes like that 'bedroom eyes.' I had another word for them, but not one I care to say.

Yeah, it's safe to say I don't like this guy right away.

Behind him is the big trouble, though. A walking mountain that looks to have the intelligence of half a mule and none of the charm. This one was wearing army pants, but he was wearing a white wife-beater instead of a black tee-shirt, and if the clothes ever made the man, they look to have with this guy. He looks like an ex-marine that beat his wife. He also looks like he would have no trouble taking me a round or two, and I'm glad when he hangs back outside.

"Get out of here, Kurt," Sandi says, pretending to be relaxed as she wipes down the Pepsi cooler frantically. "You know you're not allowed to come in here anymore."

"Sandra, baby," he smiles, his voice smooth and calm as he lifts up the door to the other side of the counter and walks in behind as if he owns the place. "I can do whatever I want, you know that."

They're both ignoring me, which is fine for now. I keep watching to see what I can learn, but with every second that passes I become more and more certain of what this is and where it's going, and I become painfully aware that my knife is in the pocket of my bag in the corner.

"You can't come in here, Kurt. I don't want you around Klarissa. She doesn't need to see you, not now." Sandi is backing up two paces for every one step he takes forward, and before she knows it her back is against the cooler. She jumps a little as the condensation hits her back, and suddenly she's sweating and looking downward as he closes the distance between them. The fan behind her moves again, and I can smell the fear coming off of her in waves.

"I'm just here to make sure she's okay. Old man Hickey says that he saw her almost get run over by a car today while she was alone. Is that any way to take care of our daughter?"

I remember the old man in the window and curse.

"She was supposed to be with Mrs. Smith!" Sandi yells, pleading now, tears ready to come at any moment. The only way she would have broken this fast is if this wasn't the first time, but more the latest of many.

This is where some people would make a discreet exit, and I hate to say that I'm tempted. This mess isn't any of my business after all, and in an hour I could be on the outskirts of town smoking a Marlboro with a full stomach for the first time in recent memory. Then again, it wasn't my business to jump in front of a speeding car to save that little girl either, but I'd done it. Far be it for anyone to say I don't see things through.

I get up out of my chair and it squeaks noisily, and suddenly both Kurt and Sandi realize that I'm here. I pick up my plate and fork in one hand and walk over to the counter, looking around it for a tray or something where I can put them. "Where do I lay these?" I ask stupidly, making eye contact with Kurt for the first time since he came in.

He glares me down, and suddenly I'm in a contest to see who'll blink first, and it's him. "Just put it anywhere and get out of here," he snarls, that salesman smile long gone as he pokes a thumb toward the door, then turns his back to me and pushes both of Sandi's shoulders against the cooler.

"Fine," I state, then toss the plate at his head. It hits just to the right and shatters against the cooler, sending sharp shards everywhere but where they intended to go. I realize I've gotten rusty, but try my best to make it seem like it happened just like I wanted it too.

"Fuck!" Kurt yells, brushing the bits of plate out of his perfectly groomed hair and messing it up in the process, making him look like a wild man. "What the fuck is the matter with you?"

"Throw a dart at a word that describes crazy, you'll probably hit one that fits me," I quip, smirking a little out of the corner of my mouth. "Now get the hell out of here."

"You've just made a really big mistake," he snarls, pointing a finger at me accusingly. There is no boasting in his voice, none of that wavering that usually comes with the empty promise of an evil man. "I own this town."

"Yeah, well I'm new," I say, feeling a little like Clint Eastwood. "So you'll have to pardon me."

He squints, making his blue eyes shoot fire if they could. "There are no pardons in my town," he says, then turns and walks toward the door, slamming his fist against the wall before he leaves and shaking one of the tiles down. The big guy outside looks as though he wants to come in after me, but he gets a slap upside the head and follows like any good lackey. It's almost comforting to know that no matter where I go, lackeys are still lackeys. Almost.

The engine roars back to life and he pulls away, the stench of dope staying in the air for a long while. When I'm sure he's gone I turn to Sandi, walking around the counter to where she's still got her back against the Pepsi cooler, as if he never left, shaking like a leaf.

"Hey, sorry if I was out of line..." I start, raising my hands in surrender, again ready for the possibility of a swift kick.

It doesn't come. "It's okay. I'm just sorry you had to see that," she says, voice quivering even as she reaches for the broom and starts sweeping up the plate I shattered. This time I help, bending down and picking up some of the bigger pieces. "Don't," she says, her voice full of concern, "You'll cut yourself."

I chuckle and meet her gaze. I don't know what my smile looks like, but whatever it is, it brings hers back. I don't bother explaining that it would take a whole lot more than a bit of plate to make me bleed. There's still no reason to get into that, much as part of me would like to.

"Thank you," she says finally, when all the little bits are in the pan. She opens up the door to the kitchen and dumps it in a hidden garbage, letting Klarissa out at the same time. "I don't know how I can repay you."

"That's fine," I say, and I feel my smile fading. I'm starting to get itchy to leave. I know where this conversation is headed, and I'm anxious to get out before it goes there.

"Do you have anywhere to spend the night?"

Too late.

***

Her shift ends a few hours later, and we go back to the little white house with the magenta red door next to the bakery. The walk doesn't seem so long this time, as she points out all the little houses that I noticed on my way up and tells me things about the owners. Nothing too scandalous, just cute little tidbits that one hears in a small town. The only house she doesn't even glance at is the one across from the store where Klarissa almost got run down, but I do. That same old man is in the window again, phone pressed to his large, swollen ears. You don't get ears like that by leading a peaceful life, you get them by taking as many hits as you dish out over the course of years.

She doesn't cook, and that's fine by me. She'd done enough of that over the last few hours I guess, and a microwave dinner was still the nicest full meal I've had in ages (but still didn't top the apple crumble).

Her home is small. The front door opens right up into the kitchen / dining room, which barely has enough room to walk around the table. Off of that is a living room with two doors in it, one for a bedroom and one for a bathroom. Only one bedroom, and that one had Klarissa's name on it in stick-on star letters. It was well cleaned, though, and warm despite the cool wind from the north that was only getting worse. All said, I was glad I wasn't on the road tonight.

After dinner, Sandi starts clearing away the table and Klarissa and I go play in the living room. We watch an episode of Dora the Explorer and then Sponge Bob Square Pants while playing a few rounds of shoots and ladders. She wins twice, I win once. I'd love to say I let her win, but when I suck at something, I really suck.

After a quick game of ker-plunk, I ask her if she'd like me to tell her a story. Her face lights up and she all but jumps into my arms, and out of the corner of my eye I see Sandi turning away from the sink and smirking at the two of us over her shoulder. I try not to smile back, but I can't help it.

I tell her the story of Klarissa and the Beanstalk, a classic. I change certain key things in the story and she eats it up. Klarissa doesn't sell a cow for magic beans, she sells licorice, and she buys it from a used car salesman that remains nameless. I get to the part where the giant (who I name Derek) says he smells the blood of a little girl, and I notice the fright in her eyes. I ask her if it's too scary, and she shakes her head no so quickly and furiously that her hair whips at my face. I turn to make sure that Sandi isn't watching, and then continue, pounding my fists against the floor to simulate the giant's footsteps.

I turn on the T.V. when Sandi goes into the room with Klarissa to put her to bed, much to the child's objection. There's nothing really good on, so I channel surf for about thirty minutes until a news station from the west coast catches my eye. There's a story on about the robbery of some high-tech industrial complex, followed by one about three homeless men found burned alive after they were caught scavenging for food. I turn the channel a few more times, landing on some sitcom and lean back on the coach, pretending to watch it. Over by the front door, my bag is calling to me again, telling me to take the opportunity and just leave. Now. But I don't, and a few minutes later, Sandi comes out of the bedroom wearing pajamas.

"Is she down?" I ask, smiling and poking my thumb out in the direction of the star-covered door.

"Yeah," Sandi smiles, taking her seat close to me even though there was plenty of room on the couch. "I had to listen to her retelling of Klarissa and the Beanstalk, but she fell asleep about half way through. I do hope she got out of it alive."

I blush a little, then smile. "I think that's a safe bet."

She reaches out and touches the short hairs behind my ear, and my entire body feels tingly.

"So, what was that guy's deal today?" I blurt out, trying desperately to change the topic and hoping it isn't obvious.

Her fingers stop, and she rests her arm across the back of the couch and sighs. "He's Klarissa's father, but I guess you figured out that much."

"I did, yes," I admit, that and more, but me telling her what I already know won't help her. She has to tell me before it eats her alive. Maybe someday I'll learn to take my own advice on that front. But I doubt it.

"I met him about four years back, right after he and his father had come into town. His Dad was some big shot Texas businessman with what seemed like all the money in the world to us. This community's been dying ever since the mine closed, and he promised he was going to make everything better."

"Did he?" I ask, raising an eyebrow skeptically.

"At first. He got everyone jobs at this factory in Waterville, everyone that didn't already have jobs, that is. And he started pouring money into the community. Like that playground down the street, or the baseball field up by the gas station. Everything seemed so great, he was like a father to the whole town... but he wasn't a kind man, by any means. He'd yell at kids if they made too much noise when he was trying to think. And the businesses, he started buying them up one by one, and those that didn't sell seemed to shut down pretty fast. There'd be some accident or they'd just run out of money. Or both."

I remember the abandoned gas station just up the road from here, the one with scorch marks all over one side, and understand what she's talking about.

"While all this was going on, I was dating Kurt. He seemed really nice at first. He'd take me on dates into the city and all over. He told me that when his father left for Texas in a few months, he was going to run this town, and he wanted me with him." A frown came over her face, and I knew what was coming. "But I wouldn't... you know. He said that didn't matter to him, that he loved me. One night I got mad with him when he wouldn't leave the video store on the other side of town alone, and he just... took it. Me, I mean. He just..."

Against my better judgment, I reach out and touch her shoulder. I don't say anything to coax her on, though. She'll tell all she wants to tell, and not one word more because of me.

"I went to the police. They took down every word I said and made it all really official. They said they'd get him. Then a week went by. Then two. Around the time I realized that I was pregnant, I noticed that all the county policemen for this area were driving new cars... and then I knew. It's been everything I can do to keep Klarissa away from him. He wanted nothing to do with her at first, but then a few months back he saw her at the county fair when she was eating cotton candy, and ever since then, he's been trying to take her away from me. And almost everyone in town helps, because if they don't..."

I nod, thinking back to the glares I got from the few people still in town when I walked through.

"I just know he's going to use this accident today to take her, I just know he will." That was it. As strong as she was (and she was, stronger than I'd be, or any of you, for that matter), the idea of losing her child was too much. It was too raw. The salt water finally came from her eyes in great rivets, and it was like a dam had burst inside the ducts. I wonder how long she'd been holding it in with nobody to talk to. I don't think a year would be a over-estimation.

I do the only thing I can think to do. I pull her close and lay her head against my heart, stroking her hair that still smells like grease over shampoo and let her cry a river onto my shirt. She's only there a moment before her arm is around me, clutching me as close as she probably did her pillow every other night. That marmalade smell fills my nostrils, and despite everything I've had to eat today, I find myself hungry again.

As if she's reading my mind, she takes her head off of my chest and looks at me with those hazel eyes. I hadn't even noticed that the sun had gone down until I noticed the way the moonlight sparkled against her lip gloss, making them so beautiful and succulent. I don't lean into her. I don't encourage her in any way. But I don't stop her, either. She leans in and kisses me, and suddenly that sweet nectar smell is everywhere, as is the taste as I feel her tongue, slow, then fast inside my mouth. Still embraced, I lean her onto her back and she wraps one leg around me, pulling me toward her. Her skin feels so smooth, her clothes so warm.

I break off the kiss and move my head back as she tries to continue it, her lips still moving as if it is. "I can't do this," I say, but she can feel my body rising, making a liar of me.

"Alex, I feel safe when you're here," she says, her voice equal parts seductive and innocent. It's almost more than I can bear.

"That's why I can't do this," I explain, getting up and helping her do the same. "It wouldn't be right. You have enough people taking advantage of you lately."

She smiles, then laughs as she starts to cry again. "You really are a nice guy," she beams, leaning in and giving me a peck on the lips and then a hug.

"No, I'm not," I say, but I'm smiling when I do, and I squeeze her tight.

"I feel so stupid," she laughs again, wiping away the moisture that the last hour brought to her face, and I'm happy to see that no more is coming.

"Don't," I say, rubbing both her shoulder as we part our embrace. "Believe me, it was my mistake."

She laughs again, and it's as if it didn't happen. We talk for a few more minutes and then she goes into Klarissa's room to sleep on the floor, giving me the couch. I try to say I won't sleep anyway, but that's another one of those things that would require too much explanation.

I turn the television volume down to zero, which is more than enough for my ears to pick up, and start flicking through the channels again. I watch an action movie until late, then get up to get myself a cup of coffee. A cigarette would make everything superb right about now, but what can I do? I sit back down and flick through the channels a little more, as the couch gets more and more comfortable and I feel myself starting to drift. I take another shot of coffee and continue to channel surf until I find a horror movie in black and white from the thirties and settle in, hoping that I can keep my attention occupied until morning. It crosses my mind that I can just leave whenever I want, but I don't want Sandi to think that there are hard feelings, so I stick it out.

It's about two a.m. and my eyelids are starting to get heavy. I hear a car go by, it's the fifth one this hour, and I wonder what these people are *doing* at this hour in the morning on a Tuesday.

My nostrils perk up as a familiar smell comes across them, and suddenly I'm more awake then I've been in weeks. Down at my right side, the womb perks up and starts to throb. This time my knuckles only turn white for a second before I let my fingers relax and the claws come out, one by one. My blood drips onto the floor from the wounds the talons make, and the pain makes me feel awake and alive. It's the same tingly sensation I got when Sandi kissed me, as grotesque as that sounds.

The smell of motor oil and marijuana is everywhere now, or at least it seems that way to me. I can feel the pressure in my veins building more and more with each and every breath I take it in with, both my hearts beating so fast I should be in pain, but I'm not. It's a strangely relaxing feeling, that little bit of calm before all hell breaks loose. In that moment, everything is clear. There's no right, there's no wrong. There's just me and the person in front of me, and the knowledge that in a few minutes only one of us is going to be left standing. There's a strange purity in that.

The knob to the front door clicks twice, and then the door comes open, almost off of its hinges. I hear the sudden gasps of air coming from the bedroom as Sandi and Klarissa awake with a start, and Sandi's knees scuttling against the floor. The door hits the kitchen counter, sending splinters of wood twirling to my feet as I take my first steps forward toward the barbarians at the gate. I feel the rumble of base in my throat that begins every growl, feel its vibrations against my chest and jaw. All of this happens in less than two and a half seconds after that second click of the door knob. At the three second mark, I'm facing off against a mountain with legs.

He's still wearing those damn army camouflage pants from earlier today, but he went shirtless rather than wear the wife-beater. Hard to dispose of blood-spattered shirts, way easier to just jump in the shower. His skin is the tan brown of someone that's been out in the sun just a little too long, but the lack of tan lines told me it was his natural color. I don't think this guy's a local, maybe a friend of Kurt's from around the south Texas border. His hands are clasped together tightly, combining to make one big fist that's the size of my head. His low, cave-man like brow (with a curious lack of eyebrows) rises as he lets out a long bellow and brings his hands across the side of my head, sending me flying across the room.

I hit the wall doing a forty, I think, and I somehow manage to leave a dent in it the size of my entire body.

As the room spins and the womb fights to give me back some semblance of control over my sight, I barely notice as Kurt walks in behind his thug, that used car salesman smile of his grinning smugly at me. I make a promise to myself that by the end of the day, he won't be smiling anymore.

We're six seconds in, and the world stops spinning just in time for me to see those two clasped hands connect with the bridge of my nose. It's one of those moments when I hate my enhanced senses. They make everything more real. I can hear the bone snap as well as feel it, and the sickening crunch as the healing factor rights it again. All said, a single, thin line of blood escapes my left nostril before it's completely healed.

The man-mountain looks at me, a perplexed expression on his dim-witted face.

"Get used to it," I bark, slamming my heels into both of his knees. He bellows loudly, but I don't hear anything break, and before I know it, he's struck a blow to my side. He hits even harder when he's angry, and that was my *right* side. My brain howls in agony as the impact makes the womb organ skip one beat, then another. It's not really hurt, but it's rhythm is just off enough that it's pumping air into my veins rather than that black tar that tastes like burnt hair.

The lucky fuck has gone and fucked me.

***

Sandi's eyes go wide as she stares at the silhouette of the man opening her bedroom door. Backlit the way he is, he looks as though he's all black... except that wide smile. That toothy grin of his is still pearly white. The combination of those two images is quite unsettling.

"Give me my daughter," he barks, and the smoothness is gone from his voice now. It's just demanding, like a child stomping his foot and demanding a new toy. It was the same tone he'd used the night he'd gotten her pregnant.

"No, Kurt!" she screams, holding her hands close to her heart. "You can't have her! She's the only thing you can't have. You can have anything else you want!"

He takes a step forward, reaching out and grabbing her around the neck and lifting her to her feet. "There is *nothing* that I can't have!" he yells, glancing into Klarissa's bed and seeing that she wasn't there. "Now where is she?"

Finally, Sandi understands, and smirks a little. "The only reason you want her is because you know you can't have her. Just like me," she smiles, looking him directly in the eye for the first time since she had dated him.

His upper lip curls as he grabs her by both shoulders and shakes her violently once, then twice, then lets her go, slamming her against the closet door.

***

I'm down but I'm not out. I've been without the power of the womb before, and I will be again. That does not mean I'm about to get my behind handed to me by some lummox with the intelligence of a gnat. I wait for him to rise for another strike (I think this is the third one since he made the womb-organ do the labamba, but I'm a little woozy on that point). He does with another of his massive grunts, and I slash out with my claws, raking them across his chest and stomach. He staggers back, confused and in shock. I didn't get very deep, but he definitely felt it. He looks down at the red coming from the four lines I've made across his torso as if this were the first time he'd ever seen his own blood, pressing his hand against them and hissing gingerly under the pressure, then looking at his blood on his hand in the moonlight.

He looks back at me and roars in anger, sending one fist forward. I swerve my head out of the way just in time, as he puts his hand through the wall as far in as his elbow. Turning toward me and bellowing again, he tries to remove his hand and gets about an inch. He's stuck, and I feel myself grinning. I slide under him and bring my knees up to my chin, then let loose with about thirty double-kicks to his chest and gut, around the same area where my talons tasted his flesh. He screams with every impact, and I pray to god it's not scaring Klarissa too much. But that thought's minor, I'm sad to say. Mostly, I'm just enjoying lacing into someone that actually deserves it for once. That's the one thing I love about thugs. No matter what I do to them, I never feel bad.

His eyes begin to water as my legs begin to ache, and I'm starting to have a massive headache because of all the air the womb pumped into my system, but it's well worth it. Out of the corner of my eye I see something coming out of Klarissa's room and stop, turning toward it just in time to see an expensive shoe coming toward my eye.

***

I regain consciousness no more than a minute and a half later, but they're already gone. The stench of their aftershave and that cheap dope still hangs in the air though, and it's better than smelling salts for waking me up. I get to my feet quickly, aching as the womb finally starts back at a normal beat, healing the bruises all over my body. I can't see out of one eye and my depth perception sucks, but I stumble my way over toward Klarissa's room.

My heart sinks.

Klarissa is still there, god bless her soul, curled up against her mother's breast and crying. There's a stream of blood going from the metal handle of the closet down to where Sandi's head is resting against the wall. Try as I might, I can't hear a heartbeat. It doesn't take a genius to figure out what happened, and that's good, because I might never have if it had. He'd pushed her way too hard. He probably hadn't even tried it the way it happened. Not that that mattered to me one little bit. Her hand is still wrapped around her little girl, just under the nape of her neck. Her last action had been trying to make the child feel better, to comfort her in some way. Her face is lifeless now, the muscles relaxed and fixated in that position. Still, I want to believe that I can still see that smile on her face. I know it's not really there, but I swear I can see it, just under the surface.

The cops arrive way too fast. Faster than anyone but me and Kurt could even know there's a crime. I kiss Klarissa on the forehead and bring my finger to her mouth. She nods in understanding as I slip back into the shadows of the room.

I'm there for an hour and forty five minutes. In that length of time, three cops and a coroner come through the place. None of them notice me. I could stay in this position for days if I had to, luckily that long isn't necessary. They talk about pressing charges and against who. There have been reports of a stranger in town they say. He attacked Klarissa, they say. I listen to it all, but more than that, I listen to the words behind the words. I listen to each of their heartbeats as they talk amongst themselves, to see which of them is lying. I'm surprised and gratified to find that none of them are, each of them deluded enough to believe what they were saying.

It's four thirty in the morning before the last of them leaves, and I finally step out of the shadows, stretching my stiff back muscles. I go immediately for the dresser and open it, rummaging around for something I smelled almost an hour before, but had no way of getting to. Something that smells like marmalade and skin moisturizer.

Something that smells like Sandra.

My hand hits something solid amidst the socks and shirts, and I haul it out immediately. It's a diary, brown with a coiled metal spine and a picture of a elk on the front cover, leaping over some tall grass. There's a pen sticking out of it to mark her page, and I open it with quivering hands.

'... *the only nice person I ever met. He's so kind and gentle, and he gets along with K. really well. He told her this hilarious story about Jack and the Beanstalk, but he changed all the names and things for her. I know he's going tomorrow, and that nothing I do can make him stay, but tonight he kissed me and made me feel special, because he cared enough to stop. He's the nicest, gentlest man I've ever met. And I just hope he remembers me after he's gone...*'

I feel the true womb start up again. Taste that burnt hair in the back of my throat as the black blood rises. Hear the soft squirting noise as that blood fills my eyes, rupturing the vessels there and turned them coal black.

"Black Womb lives."

***

"I'm telling you, it was that guy that attacked Klarissa yesterday," Kurt yells into the phone as he takes a puff of his cigarette, leaning forward in his chair and resting his elbow onto his knee. He reaches forward and doubts the smoke, joining a pile of ten within the last hour. "Who else could it be? Nobody else in our town could do such a thing. This is a good town, sir, with good people. Yes." He pauses, listening to the person on the other end of the line, then smiles. "Definitely. We'll start a full search in the morning. He won't get very far." He hangs up the phone and sighs, looking forward into the fireplace. It has started to snow outside, and he watches it fall for a moment before he sees something behind him in his reflection.

"Wasn't too hard to find the place," the Womb spits, grabbing Kurt by the collar and hoisting him up out of his chair. The room is filled with hunting trophies and expensive looking artwork that all looks positively ridiculous together, a mish-mash of culture from a thug trying to look better than he is. There's a picture of Sandi on the mantle, and it almost makes me throw up. "Just looked for the biggest, gaudiest house in town. Yours was the only one that fit the bill. It was also the only house whose owners could afford real siding."

I bar my teeth at him. I'm not quite sure what that looks like, really. I've never been able to sum up the courage to look myself in the mirror when I'm in Womb-mode... but judging from the expression on Kurt's face, it's the worst thing you've ever seen.

"Please, please don't kill - -" he doesn't even get the sentence out before I throw him against the mantle, his head bashing against its metal. It would be terribly ironic if I accidentally killed him like this, the same way he killed Sandi, but somehow I don't think I'm that lucky. It shuts him up though. He's not dead, but he's pretty out of it. I know that because his hand fell into the fire and he's not even twitching it to get it out.

I pour myself a drink of whiskey from a mini-fridge and sit in his chair while I drink it, watching his arm burn. When the skin starts to bubble I fish him out and sling him over one shoulder, and start toward the door.

***

I push his head under the water, and the son of a bitch finally wakes up. His eyes jut open like they're spring loaded, and bubbles start to come up from his every orifice. I know he can't really see me through the water. It's almost dawn, but with all the cloud cover, you wouldn't know it. There's a heavy weight of snow on the ground now, but that's not what's making me act so cold. It's the thought of two young lives ruined by one moron's temper. I've changed back into my human face. For some reason, that was important to me. It's not very stealthy, but at this moment, I don't care. I hear him curse beneath the current and pull him up by the collar, watching him as he gasps for air.

"What the fuck!?" he yells at me when he's got enough air in his lungs, although he's still coughing up water. He gets his bearings and looks around, seeing nothing but evergreen and elk. The only sounds are that of the river, the rustling of the trees, and the steady creak of the park gate as it swings back and forth on its rusty hinges. For some reason, I thought this would be as good a place as any to do this, though I don't know why. Maybe because it's the first thing I saw when I came into Kannibus, maybe because I didn't want people interfering... mostly I think it's because it's the one place I'm certain that Klarissa won't wander off to by herself. That girl's seen enough death for one lifetime. "Help!" he screams, and I smile a little.

"Yeah, like that's gonna happen," I snap back sarcastically. I'm sure there's something real meaningful I could say to him here. Make some kind of Biblical reference about the washing away of sins and re-baptism and all that jazz... but somehow, I'm just not in the mood. Grinning, I push him back down under. His eyes shoot open again, like one of those porcelain dolls whose eyes open and close depending on which angle you tilt them. His arms rise above the surface of the water and start grabbing at me, punching at my chest and pulling at my arms to try and get free. Once again I realize I was wrong in my earlier assessment: he's actually as weak as a kitten, and I almost feel bad about what I'm doing.

Almost.

He starts to kick as the bubbles get fewer and fewer, but his blows are getting less potent with each passing second. Finally, his eyes roll back into his head and the bubbles stop. I wait an extra moment and then haul him out of the freezing winter water quickly, laying him on his back. His lips are already blue and his digits are losing color fast, but that enhanced hearing of mine tells me I have plenty of time. His heart's slowed down and beginning to stop, but its beats are still strong.

I lace my fingers together tightly and press them against the center of his chest, timing it at five pumps every four seconds. I pause for a moment and look at him, realizing that there's no response. Again, I pump at his chest. One, two, three, four, five. Then I lean forward, pinch his nose and take in a long mouthful of air, then cover his mouth with mine and blow in until his lungs are full. He coughs, squirting water upwards as I move out of the way. He sits up, holding his chest tenderly. When he does I notice the pack of Marlboro's sticking out of his breast pocket, and reach out quickly to grab them. They're still dry, miraculously enough.

"What is the matter with you?" he coughs, turning toward me.

I grab him by the throat and push him back under the water again, using my free hand to push against his chest just like before, except instead of forcing the water out, this time it forces the air out. There's not as much of it left in him this time anyway. As soon as the bubbles stop, I pull him out again. That perfect hair of his is an absolute mess now, the moss from the stream freezing to it.

Again, I pump the water from his lungs and give him mouth to mouth, until all the water is gone.

Then back under he goes again. I marvel at how shocked he looks each and every time. I couldn't have hoped for as much.

Bubble... bubble... ... .

One, two, three, four.

Breathe in, breathe out.

Cough.

Bubble... bubble... ... .

I repeat the process eight more times before letting him go completely. That last time I held him under, he hadn't lasted more than a few seconds, and it was getting to be more work than it was worth to bring him back. I let him cough all of the water out of his lungs, and then he just sits there for a minute in the snow.

"If you're going to kill me," he says, and his voice is shaking from fear and the cold, "just do it."

I smile. I reach into the pack of smokes I just stole from him and light one up, taking a long steady drag. The smoke travels down and makes me feel relaxed, and for a brief instant, this moment is perfect. I know the way that sounds. "Kill you?" I chuckle, ruffling his hair as I crouch down next to him, blowing smoke in his face. "Who said anything about killing you?"

He looks at me with confusion, his eyes squinting with the effort of trying to understand what I've just said.

I decide to save him the effort. "See, if I kill you, then your pain's over. That doesn't sit too well with me, not after what you've done." I snarl, grabbing him by the collar and forcing him back into the water. I don't submerse him this time though, I just leave the back of his head in, in case he forgets his place. "I've got something much better in store for you. I'm going to *almost* kill you, again and again. And then I'm going to bring you back every time... just so you can feel what she must have felt all over again." I bring my face in so close to his that our noses touch, and that vibration of a growl happens in my throat again. "That's something you and me got in common, Kurt. See good people get to die just once... bad ones like you and me, we get to do it over and over again." I pull him out of the water, then turn my back to him and start walking back toward the street. "She said she wanted me to remember her... and I will, though I don't think this is what she meant. I want you to remember her too, Kurt. Remember what you did to her. Remember what it feels like. Remember that that's what you have to look forward to every day for the rest of your life."

As I walk out the trail toward the highway, I hear the seethe of a knife I hadn't even realized he had on him. I'm worried for a moment, until I hear that faint heartbeat of his.

A moment later, I hear his body hit the snow, and the soft squirt that only a jugular can make. The wind changes direction, and I catch the scent of blood, motor oil, cheap marijuana... and raw, primal fear.

It snowed pretty heavy that night. They didn't find his body until spring.

***

On my way out of town I stop by the take-out again. I don't go in, but I see Klarissa with a big plate of ice cream and apple crumble laid out in front of her. A middle-aged woman with a name tag that says Marie is talking to a woman dressed the way only a social worker can, and they're both calm, but sad. Klarissa looks up at me, and she smiles a little and waves. When I wave back, her smile gets bigger, almost hiding those perfect hazel eyes of hers. Sandi's eyes.

It occurs to me that maybe it's not just bad people that get to live over and over again, like I told Kurt. Maybe good people do too, just in a different way. A better way.

I carry the memory of their smile with me as I go, and somehow it lightens the load and keeps me warm through the snow and the cold. I remember them both fondly, and when I do, it doesn't seem like I'm walking alone anymore.

YOUNG REPUBLICANS

"Why does Mr. Collins eat outside?"

Everyone stopped eating, the silence of forks not clinking and teeth not scraping deafening. The Old Man sat with his mouth agape, an unhealthily large forkful of meatloaf hanging in the vacant space between his plate and his mouth. His teeth glistened in the dwindling twilight, the only thing that kept his from looking as lifeless as an oil painting.

Mom and Jesse had stopped eating, too. They stared at Brandy with the same astonishment: as though that simple question had unlocked some secret in them and now thoughts were flooding in at a pace that couldn't be dealt with. Brandy was staring out the bay window of the dining room, watching intently as Mr. Collins sat at the edge of the porch eating a sandwich. It was chicken slice, with mustard. He was sitting with his back to the house, unaware of the little eyes upon him or of the snowball their owner had nudged downhill.

Mom placed a gentle hand onto The Old Man's arm. He nodded briefly, then wiped his mouth with his kerchief and rose to full standing. He was a tall man, and with all of them sitting, he towered above them. It was only now that Brandy looked up, but was still unaware of what she'd done. She picked up her fork -- still too large for her small hands -- and continued to eat her greens.

The Old Man stepped around the table without a word, his heavy work boots thrumming against the oak floor. He made his way down to the cellar, and stayed there for some time before calling on Brandy.

***

It always starts with a question.

Questions are the cancer of the mind. Two synapses connect in a way that they weren't never meant to, just the same way a cell divides in a way it shouldn't, and then it's there: cancer. Cells and thoughts that misbehave until someone has to go in with a knife and take them out.

Questions were a cancer that could spread if left unchecked. It could come out the mouth and go in someone's ear and teach their brain to ask that question. It was worse than airborne, it was soundborne. Speechborne. It was the only disease you could infect people with by telling them about it, and it spread like wildfire in a dry season.

***

Jesse stood leaned on his rake, sweat showering his brow in the setting sun. The day had been as long as the grass. The latter was now piled in a tall pile behind him, the former was arranged in neat compartments in his mind. Suzie was the largest of the compartments, and his plans for Saturday.

He poured himself a glass of lemonade from a jug with mint leaves and ice in it, the condensation running from the sides of the glass jug like a waterfall. He poured until the tall glass overflowed, then wiped the sweat from himself and took a long drink. He poured it back until the ice hit off his teeth, then stopped and gasped for air and began to pour himself another glass.

He saw Mr. Collins staring at him from over his shoulder, his armpits stained and his brow drenched. He turned and started back on his hoe when Jesse saw him, working double time to make up for the seconds lost.

Jesse followed where the man's gaze had gone and realized he hadn't been looking at him at all. He frowned and drank the second glass of lemonade, then poured the remainder of the jug into the glass again. It only filled three quarters of the way, and most of that were yellowed cubes of ice. He brought it close to Mr. Collins and held it out to him, standing back a full arm's length.

It took Mr. Collins a moment to notice, and when he did, he startled. It took him a moment, then he took the glass from Jesse. He nodded but he didn't say a word. When he was done with the glass and had deposited some of the ice into his cheeks, he handed Jesse back the glass. Jesse threw it in the trash before bringing it back into the house.

The Old Man and Mom watched from the living room window. She touched his arm gently. He made his way down to the cellar, and stayed there for some time before calling on Jesse.

***

"Mr. Collins never has Sunday supper with his family," I said as I stared out the kitchen window. He was tending the goats and there was a light coming from the staff's house; we could see the shadows of his people around the table.

His people. I didn't think of them like that then, but I do now. I can't get that thought out of my head. Nouns are anchors, in every sense of the meaning.

The Old Man stopped chewing his greens, his mouth caught in an awkwardly aligned position jutting out to one side. He chewed vegetables the way a cow chewed cud, I'd realized long ago. I remember realizing it and knowing it and thinking it, but I don't now. Now it's gone.

Jesse and Brandy didn't stop eating. They shoveled full forks of beef into their mouths with the same zeal that they helped tend the fields: the motion perpetual in its repetition. They didn't look up into the window, where Mr. Collins was still tending the crops even in the low light of evening.

"Dina," The Old Man started. Mom put a gentle, guiding hand against the hairy tan of his arm. He stopped himself, then got up from the table. His heavy work boots thrummed against the oak floor. He made his way down to the cellar.

After some time he called to me, just as Mom was serving up cobbler to Jesse and Brandy. There was no plate for me.

I walked to the cellar door. I don't think I'd ever been there until then... maybe once, when I was much younger. It was hard to recall. The stairs weren't finished like the rest of the house. The rest of the house was that pristine white of polish and shine. The stairs to the cellar were unvarnished, the walls damp and glistening in the high-hanging dim light.

"Father?" I called, rounding a slight corner. The stairs went down like a corkscrew, burrowing into the very foundation of the home. I couldn't see what was next, only the continuation of the turn. Never the change, only the fact of change. There was a smell of gunpowder and musk, and that was the only hint that I was getting close to the bottom. The Old Man didn't answer me.

When I rounded that final corner, he was standing alongside an old wooden chair, the type that looked square-ish and uncomfortable, held together with L Brackets and strong bolts. It was the type seen in old films, back when they were only on physical media and the transfers were always rough.

There were leather straps against the arms of the chair, thick and meaty with bits of charred material around their edges. I must have been staring at them, because The Old Man said, "It's okay, Dina. We won't need to use those, will we?"

I shook my head and made my way toward the chair without being asked. I must have been there before, I thought, because it was like muscle memory. I got in the chair and shifted as I tried to make myself comfortable, even moving to avoid a stray bit of splintered sharpness I'd had no way of knowing was there, but did.

The Old Man turned from me and started moving things on his workbench. A blue glow started to rise from the table, as though he'd started a torch but no sound of a torch accompanied it. "You shouldn't talk about Mr. Collins like that," he said, almost under his breath. He reached for something, a small tank, and it disappeared behind him. There was a scraping sound, a hollow reverberation that got less and less each time it happened. "He does good work for us, and we don't want to have to lose him. You think you're doing him right, but you're just endangering him. If you get it in his head to step out, he will, and then where will he be?"

He turned around, and a face with glowing blue circles for eyes hung from his limp right hand. There was a bulging protuberance of leather where the nose would be, dual mouths jutting out from either nostril ended in sharp metal grates, each one the size of my small fists.

"Don't fight," he said, and instantly I felt myself tense. I'd been here before, I knew it now. I remembered, suddenly, that smell of chlorine and leather and something else bringing it all back. I pulled away in the chair but there was nowhere to go: he blocked the only way off, and I felt the rough of the straps beneath me and knew I didn't want them. The straps brought with them a whole host of bad memories.

I opened my mouth to scream but the mask was on me. I felt a pressure against the back of my skull and heard the clink-clink-clack of the straps being tightened. This was it now; there was no escape. I'd been here before and struggled, and all it had gotten me was a broken wrist. I remembered it now, that scar along my left arm, and where it had come from.

The Old Man stepped away from me and there was a mirror -- not a true mirror, just a hunk of polished steel -- and in it I saw myself, distorted and jumbled, a funhouse projection. I screamed but the mask muffled it; I raised my hands to get it off but I couldn't. The glow from the eyes was blinding, and the flickering as my hands passed over them made my brain hurt. There was steam and gas leaking from me, shrouding my reflection in a dim haze.

The Old Man returned with another canister. He pulled back my hair by the tail and forced it onto the rightmost of my dual mouths, that same hollow echo coming from my second face as he screwed it in. It's a gas mask, I realized, recognizing the distorted elements in my reflection, but not one that kept the gas out. This mask kept the gas in.

When it was finally screwed in and my Father's teeth were clenched so tight I could hear them grind even about my screams, a squeal of air sent a flush blue haze through the mask and into my mouth. It tasted like fluoride and coppery blood at first, but before too long the taste had morphed, and it tasted like Mom's meatloaf pie and apple cobbler.

***

The five of us sat at our table and ate our supper of fried chicken and greens, and outside Mr. Collins worked alongside his son, who was no older than me, showing him how to move the scythe through the hay with maximum efficiency.

No Questions were asked. They were in remission.

INTERLUDE

Sometimes it stank in Los Angeles. Stank like ashes.

She wasn't sure if it was the factories spewing out smoke or the millions of cars or the smog, but some parts of the town smelled like they were burning even when it was pouring rain outside.

More than that, it made her skin feel dirty. As though she'd been covered with dust or grime. She kept moving to brush at it but found nothing there each time. She did this even now, stroking her fingers over her left shoulder where she thought she felt the tickle of sand or some other debris. When she looked and saw that it was clean she rolled her eyes at her own lack of impulse control, then stared forward at the building in front of her.

It was a rather large teal townhouse, three stories high. Bay windows on the front showed that the first floor alone had ceilings of well over ten feet, with several fans placed around to combat the heat that dominated this city even in the depths of winter. There was a balcony circling all the way around the front, going wide on the west end to make a large gated porch used for barbecues and tanning. Stairs went up from it to a second entrance on the third floor, which looked dark and dusty from what she could see from across the street. She'd done some research on the place before coming. Hot-water heating with a propane back-up system, the three-acre property had a reported five underground tanks of water and contained enough stored food to last several months if need be. Apparently the owner had designed it personally to be completely self-sufficient after being taken in by the Y2K hysteria. She supposed that even though the world hadn't fallen into economic collapse, it still made for a hell of a conversation piece.

The woman's name was Leigh Blackheart, something that not many people got to know personally. She was slim and beautiful, but there was also something about her that was off-putting. The angle that her back bent at didn't seem quite right. Her limbs seemed to be able to move regardless of the limitations of her joints and her eyes quivered as though their hold to her face was tenuous at best. Like yolks shaking in the centers of fried eggs. She hadn't been on many dates in the last few years, but those she had been on had ended rather abruptly when the man (or woman) in question had gotten a real good look into those eyes. They were as black as tar yet somehow glowed in darkness, a glint in their corner even when there was no light around.

The skin on her face was a chalky white that looked more like a balloon shaped like a face, filled with too much water. Even though she wasn't chubby, her face still shook every time she moved as though she were. Her lips and eyelids were painted black and her raven hair was cut short, held down close to her scalp.

Other than her face, her shoulders were the only part of her body uncovered and were just as pale. The rest of her slender form was covered in a form-fitting sable jumpsuit that covered even her hands and feet. She looked as though she had been poured into it, like something out of a spy novel.

She spat out the gum she'd been chewing as she glanced in both directions (pausing to let one last car pass by), then stepped off of the sidewalk and onto the road, heading toward the house she'd been watching.

Her footsteps barely made a sound as she walked. When she was certain nobody could see her she broke into an run toward the far east side of the property, ducking behind a fur tree that had been planted there. The foliage looked out of place in the otherwise barren and rocky yard. There was still an orange ribbon with a price tag wrapped around the center of its trunk.

She peered through the house at the darkened windows, searching for any sign of movement or life. Another car sped by, illuminating her for a moment. She turned in its direction and the driver caught a glimpse of her pasty white face and starkly black eyes, but he was in such a rush to get home that what he had seen would not register until later that evening when he was home in bed next to his wife. The sight would give him nightmares for three weeks.

Once it passed she ran toward the house. She pressed her body against the concrete foundation and lowered herself until her eyes were flush with the basement window. Again, she saw nothing but darkness within. She frowned and squinted with concentration as beads of sweat formed on her forehead, her pupils widening to take in more light. After a moment, the basement den of T.J. Evans faded into existence.

It was quaint. In a different situation, it might have made her smile a little.

There was an old dusty-rose couch just a few feet off from the window she was looking in through, with a host of science fiction novels and popular mechanics magazines on a wire rack next to it. Just beyond that was a table that looked as though it might have been hand crafted, a few spots on it a little less varnished than others. It was either the least impressive professional job she'd ever seen, or the most impressive amateur work. She wasn't sure. On it was a stainless steel chess set with a few of the pieces moved about as if it had been left in mid-game, as well as a picture of what she could only assume were Evans' parents in a dark purple frame.

On the opposite side of the table was a chair that almost matched the couch, but not quite. This one was more of a pink, and had faded roses stenciled all over its cushions. They had definitely come from two separate sets, and had probably been picked up at a yard sale. Against the wall behind it was a powerful lamp with one of those energy-saving bulbs in it, aimed directly over the shoulder of the chair. The wall behind it was covered in pictures of family and friends, as well as some shots of random objects with black-and-white film. It was obvious that somebody in his family fancied themselves an artist of some sort.

Leigh turned her gaze away from the room once she was satisfied that it was empty, looking down at the hard white plastic that surrounded the glass pane. There was a crack running along the outer edge that terminated itself after a foot or two, as well as several growths of mold in each of the corners, but other than that it looked sturdy enough. She slapped her hand against both sides, then pushed on the hatch of the window just enough to make sure it wouldn't have come undone all on its own. Satisfying herself that there was no other way to enter the building, she closed her eyes and got ready.

Sitting down in the dirt and crossing her legs Indian-style, she rested her hands against her knees and tried to stay calm. She took a deep breath and then slowly let it exhale the way she had done many times before, feeling a tingly numb sensation work its way down through her body and then out through her fingertips. The way it felt always reminded her of electric energy, the way it surged right through her.

She pushed the thought away, inhaling again through her small black lips. To a casual observer she would have looked very odd sitting that way on the side of a stranger's house. With her eyes closed, she would have looked much more normal now as well. It was much easier to see just how long her eyelashes really were now as they lay pressed gently against her cheeks. She exhaled again. When she did she felt something move next to her ear. She had experienced this before but never the exact same way twice. She had found the hardest part to be not breaking her concentration to turn and look at what the movement had been. When she filled her lungs again a lock of her hair fell from its place against her scalp, bouncing gently next to her earlobe. It itched at the tender skin and sent more shivers through her, making her mouth twitch a little as she struggled to keep her concentration.

The hair began to move.

On its own, with no help from her or the wind, it started to curl upwards like a piece of plastic curling away from a fiery log. The tip narrowed to a point as it moved, swirling over and over with increasing speed as if being spun around some invisible finger.

She had to remind herself to continue breathing, suddenly letting go of a mouthful of air she'd almost hung onto for too long. When she did her mouth began to vibrate, as if it might fall right off her face if she wasn't careful.

Her hair had curled itself up almost to her head again as one last surge of electric energy shot its way underneath her skin. Suddenly the hair melted together and dripped, like two dewdrops meeting on a leaf and then tumbling off of it together. The greasy liquid fell to the ground where it landed with an audible -plop!-, seeming to hang in the air for a moment before finally splashing.

Leigh took one last breath and held it as her entire body erupted in one large splash, like a water balloon that was filled too tight finally bursting. Liquid shadows spread out in all directions, laying in one massive puddle in the mud next to the house. Another car passed by, its headlights shimmering off the trees in the distance. Other than that there was no movement and no sound.

A ripple made its way through the surface, its rings growing until they reached the edge and splashed up onto a nearby rock. The puddle started to flow toward the house slowly but surely, as though it were on a slope even though it wasn't. It pooled right under the windowsill, defying most of the laws of physics as it did, and started to flow up the concrete wall. Ripples began from some unknown place in its center and waved out, growing with every inch until it crashed forward like a tidal wave. Every time it did this it gained a hold on whatever it had landed on, pulling itself along the wall like that until it covered the entire window.

There was an odd sucking sound as it conformed to the shape of the glass, like when you open a jar of jam for the first time. At first there were air bubbles, but even they slowly deflated until it looked like someone had painted the glass black.

It stayed like that for several moments, with no movements or sounds except for the patter of rain all around the house.

The blackness covering the bottom right hand corner of the window seemed to twitch, no more than a heartbeat, and was followed closely by a loud slurping sound that seemed to drag on forever. It was like someone trying to suck the last bit of cola from a straw. A bubble popped where the twitch had been a moment ago, leaving behind a hole in the black sea.

The rest of the tar started to swirl around the hole like a whirlpool in a bathtub, that slurping sound getting louder and louder with every bit that got sucked up. The goop glistened as it slowly disappeared, pebbles and raindrops falling from it as it unstuck itself from its place on the window. One last sliver swirled around the edges of the hole for a moment before being sucked in, and then it was gone.

After several long moments, a car went by on the road, its headlights beaming into the trees again. Between the branches, they illuminated something the driver didn't see at all. Something whose eyes held onto the glow of the lights long after they were gone.

***

The last of the black ooze ran down the wall on the other side of the window, leaving a stream of moistness in its wake as it rejoined the rest of its mass on the floor. It had congealed together in a large lump rather than a puddle, like half-formed clay tossed onto a spindle. It didn't have any specific shape, just lumps on top of more lumps of darkness. Suddenly two eyes opened in the center and Leigh's head jutted out of the darkness. She struggled at first to get free as it clung to her cheeks and she gasped for hair. Her face almost blue at first, then slowly faded back to the pale white it had been a moment ago as she got more and more oxygen into herself.

Slowly her body began to take shape around her, the lumps and mounds folding inwards until she was back to her paper-thin figure. Her hair had once again taken on the close-cut style it had before she had melted. She gasped for air, afraid to close her mouth for fear of missing some even though she was drooling onto the homeowner's wooden floor. When she raised a hand to wipe off her chin it splashed against her face. She opened her eyes for the first time since the ordeal had begun and saw that it was still just a maw of dripping tar at the end of her wrist.

"Fuck," she cursed as she stared at the disobedient appendage, dark sweat dotting her forehead and cheeks. After a moment the liquid bubbled upon itself, boiling up until it had enough girth and then falling back, leaving a pale white hand with ebony fingernails behind in its wake. She smiled, nodding her head back and forth the way she did when she was proud of herself, but only when it was just her around. She stood and took a look around to make sure everything was the way it had looked from outside.

She picked up the top science fiction novel off the wire rack, the mostly red cover showing two starships passing by a small asteroid, each of them backlit by a star behind it. She rolled her eyes and tossed it back onto the pile, then turned her attention to the stairs that twirled up from the center of the room. At the top, almost obscured from view, was the outline of a doorway. From here it looked like a rectangle made of light painted onto the shadows.

Taking one last cautionary glance around the room, she moved up the stairs as though she were gliding off them, her legs not bending so much as arching. Each step stretched just a little too far, as if her body was ready to let go of her legs at any given moment.

She stopped dead in her tracks just as she reached the door, turning back down toward the floor. Her lips were drawn up small as she stared into the darkness at the bottom of the stairs, the faintest mist of light floating in from the window. Once again the rose-colored couch had been reduced to an outline to her, the metal pieces of the chess set claiming most of the light that had filtered in.

She squinted, waiting for her eyes to focus and holding her breath as long as she could. She couldn't see anything, but she was almost sure she had heard something upon reaching the top of the stairs. It had almost been like the pit-pat of the rain outside, but there had been more to it. It had been followed by a hissing sound like the one a cat made, only faster. She waited for it again, then turned and opened the door.

She barred her teeth as the door creaked, stepping through it as quickly as she could. She stared at it for a moment, debating whether or not she should risk making the sound to close it again, then decided to leave it open.

The house she had opened up to was as different from the one she'd peered into downstairs as murder was from suicide. The walls were a dark navy that usually showed dirt but in this case emphasized just how clean and pristine the home really was. There was a shelf with a narrow rectangular mirror behind it on the wall opposite her, her reflection fading into the dark blue within the white frame. On the shelf were tiny pictures of children in heart-shaped frames. They each seemed to have the same coffee-brown eyes and angular nose regardless of gender. She thought maybe they were siblings, but they were definitely all related in some way. The floor beneath her was hardwood and was freezing against the soles of her feet.

Using her thin frame to slide between the open door and the wall she passed into the main hall. It was wide and spacious, with plenty of scrapes and gouges in the floor that resulted from children's play. They had been touched up with varnish, the same type of almost-professional job that had been done on the table downstairs. Pictures hung on thick wires all around her. A set of french doors led into a room that looked like a sitting area, but was so immaculate she thought it likely that it had never been used.

She turned another corner and almost bumped into an end table, coming face to face with another long, winding staircase that led to the upstairs bedrooms. She smiled to herself gleefully, then started up them two at a time.

No matter how many times she did this, it still had the same effect on her. It was like the world's best drug and never lost its potency or dulled its edge the more she did it. Her heart doubled its pace by the time the arch of her foot touched the fourth step, adrenaline coursing its way through her bloodstream. She felt her calve muscles pump harder as more oxygen and glucose was fed into them, sending her up the stairs even faster.

She reached the top and stopped suddenly, steadying herself on a round oak banister when she slipped on the smooth floors. Her smile beamed wide. These were the only times she ever had on a real, genuine smile and she usually wished she had a picture of it to prove that it did happen from time to time.

The hallway up here was thinner than it had appeared from downstairs. Where the main floor had been open and lavish, this floor was far more utilitarian. The walls were still navy blue with white trim but boasted none of the elaborate hangers or pictures that the downstairs had. Instead there were a few scratches and scrapes on the walls, probably from children as well, that hadn't been tended to yet. The fact that these weren't a priority made her believe that very few people got to see this floor that weren't spending the night.

There were four doors, each one nearly identical to the next. They were all the same eggshell white, all with the same round gold knobs. Her eyes went over them one at a time from left to right, examining each one meticulously before moving on to the next. Her brain was still juiced from the surge she had felt a moment ago, moving a mile a minute to process the information before her. She stopped at the second-to-last door and smiled, her eyes focusing in on the knob. It was exactly like the others, with the exception of a thin vertical slit in its center.

It was the only bedroom with a lock on it.

She chuckled softly and shook her head as she walked toward the door. She reached out and grabbed the knob, twisting it sharply to the right. It turned ten degrees, then stopped with a hard -click!-, refusing to go any further without its key.

Leigh rolled her eyes and pointed at the lock with her right forefinger. It seemed to wobble on the edge of her knuckle, like a sword made out of silly putty. She pressed it forward into the lock and grimaced as it slid in, the jagged metal winces slicing at the liquid flesh. She felt something inside it snap and pushed the door with her free hand. It slid open gently, her finger sliding out of the lock. She watched it as it became solid again, sucking in air as bones and nerves re-knit themselves.

She stepped into the room slowly, her eyes darting everywhere. It had been months since anything had truly taken her off guard in either her professional or personal life, but she never stopped being careful.

-tak-

She spun around so fast that she felt her hips become liquid again for just a moment to accommodate the motion, almost leaving her legs facing the wrong direction. She stared back down the stairs into the hall. It was fed by a light in the adjoining room, casting odd shadows and reflections back at her. The light seemed to dance like a wild flame for a moment until her eyes got used to it, her pupils larger than a normal persons were capable of being to make sure she saw everything.

The tiny hairs on the back of her neck stood on end as she again felt that sudden rush when her adrenal gland pumped more and more epinephrine into her system. What had felt wonderful a moment ago now felt like too much of a good thing, her mind now working overtime to come up with different things that could be waiting in the dark for her. It didn't take much imagination. In her life she'd seen many amazing things... but many horrors as well. She'd seen a child that put her own darkness to shame sprout teeth and claws as if from nowhere and dive at her. She'd seen men that looked meek and gentle overcome her in one shutter-fast instant. She'd seen things large enough to flatten houses barrel down toward her at speeds they shouldn't have been capable of. At that moment in her mind, whatever was downstairs was all of those things and more.

After a moment of silence she smiled and laughed a little at herself. Still, she closed the bedroom door behind her as she turned around.

The room was small and windowless, its walls a pale cappuccino color. There were no scrapes on the walls here, or anything else out of place for that matter. The floor was hardwood with a single, multi-colored Vietnamese rug running up its center from the doorway. On either side of the rug were three large cases, each one perfectly shone to magnificent glory until one could barely tell where the air ended and the glass began. At the end of the felt walkway was a small table with three stainless steel boxes laid carefully upon it.

She took a deep breath and stepped forward. She almost expected alarms to ring out the second she stepped onto the rug, but they did not and she chided herself again for being so worrisome. If anyone had been watching her, they would have thought it was her first job.

It was, however, an important one.

Each of the six cases held items that on any other day would have given her (and any other thief in the country, she imagined) a wet dream. There was a curved blade accompanied by a jeweled holster that had been lifted from Saddam's fortress after the American occupation. An unfired bullet from the gun that had shot Adolf Hitler and Eva Braun. A suit of armor that had been worn by Genghis Khan.

She stopped by the last two display cases and turned to look at the one on the left. It was a small blade, only about ten inches long. The small card in the display window said that it was diamond-etched titanium, but that wasn't what had caught her eye. On the grip was an upper-case 'I' incased in a golden circle. On the card it was misread as the letter 'H', but she knew better. Had in fact seen one like it before, if not this exact one. When she leaned in a little closer, she thought she could actually still see a little blood spatter in one of the grooves.

She scoffed, curling her upper lip in disgust. She debated just reaching in and taking it, then thought better of it and turned back toward the table at the end of the hall, doing her best to ignore the display cases lest she get distracted again.

The desk was a deep black oakwood and looked to have been hand carved, although it was anything but ancient. Symbols representing Vlad the Impaler, Musolini Trepes and Judas Iscariot had been carefully engraved there along with too many others for her to count now, though she wanted to.

There was no doubt anymore. This was a War Room.

She had heard that T.J. Evans had descended from German war-criminals but hadn't believed it and still wasn't quite sure if she did. As bad as all of this looked in light of those rumors, it could still have been a healthy obsession with history and its battles. Either way, she tried not to think about it. Convincing herself that Evans was one of the bad guys would only serve to make her feel justified in what she was about to do and although she felt no guilt, she had no delusions of Robin Hood syndrome, either.

-sissssss-

She turned around, wondering if she'd tripped some alarm after all. There was nothing, not even a bug or shrew on the floor. The room was immaculate. She shrugged, then turned back to the desk.

There was a dark silk cloth laid elegantly over the table, upon which sat three identical tin boxes, each about the size of a cigarette case.

Pursing her lips together, she reached for the case furthest to the left and tapped it firmly with her index finger. A clasp inside came loose at the top and opened slowly without a sound, its inside lined with the same red silk as the cloth.

Laying there, staring up at her from a sea of red, was a floppy disc. Its metal slide-guard twinkled and winked at her even though it must have been ancient. She doubted it would even read in a computer anymore, but the words scrawled across it made her want it anyway. Even if it was worthless, just the idea of having it in her possession gave her the shivers.

It read: Srebrenica.

At the time the largest genocidal mass murder in Europe since World War II, killing over eight thousand Bosniak boys and men. It had been a specific and intended plot to obliterate Bosnian Muslims in the area of Srebrenica, a United Nations safeguarded area.

Some people had long suspected that there were other factors involved in the massacres, the answers to which were probably on the disk in front of her. That information could give tens of thousands of grief stricken families the peace they deserved... as well as fetch her at least eight mill on the international market.

Leigh reached out to touch the disk, but stopped short of it and moved on to the next case, tapping it once.

A smile spread across her black lips.

A slender piece of metal sat in the center of the box. It was almost devoid of anything with which to identify it with, except for the small USB connection sticking out of its head. A small piece of paper next to the flash-drive had the word Unstable printed on it in calligraphy.

She reached out and picked up the drive carefully between her thumb and forefinger. Smiling, she brought it to her lips and kissed the cold steel softly before tucking it into her blouse and turning to leave.

She stopped before she even made it a single pace, clenching her teeth as she tried to fight the thought that had just occurred to her. Letting out a hefty sigh she turned around, rolling her eyes at herself as she did. "One of these days you're going to run out of lives, Leigh," she scolded herself, even as she stepped back to the table. "And your curiosity will get the better of you."

Pausing only for an instant, she tapped on the cover of the last case and watched it slowly open to full view.

Her eyes widened.

"Oh, no shit," she whispered, leaning in to make sure she was actually seeing what she thought she was.

It was a mini- cassette tape of the kind that was popular in the mid-nineties for recording home movies on. They would be slid into larger, master tapes and played in any household VCR but were much more compact and easy to store than normal VHS tapes.

This one looked to be a security tape rather than a simple home movie awaiting Bob Sagat's approval and had been kept in remarkably good condition. She imagined it had already been exported to DVD at some point, but one never knew with things like this. There were no words on the label, just one hastily drawn symbol. It looked like a figure-eight with the bottom half of the lower circle missing and a line cutting diagonally through the top. Not a lot of people in this world would have recognized it and even fewer would have known what it meant, but she did.

It was the Zyphrius symbol.

Her mind racing, she reached out toward the tape. She stopped herself again, almost immediately. There were places in the world where you could be killed simply for having seen something like that, and this was one of them. How Evans had gotten away with having it out in plain sight like this for so long was beyond her, although she suspected that she would spend the next few nights laying awake thinking about it.

Biting her lip, she turned away and started back toward the door.

Thick, grey smoke barreled out from the crevice between the door and the floorboards, circling upwards in loops and spirals.

Leigh froze in her tracks, the drive almost popping out of her shirt as she did. "Oh, fuck," she cursed loudly, making no effort at stealth. Either she'd been caught or this was all some massive coincidence, either way she was still trapped in a burning room with no windows.

Wincing, she reached out toward the doorknob carefully, trying to see how close the fire was to the door. She felt nothing at fist, but then it was like her nerves woke up and realized what was happening. Searing pain scorched through her arm, traveling like a bullet through her system and exploding out the back of her brain. She screamed, yanking her hand away as quickly as she could.

Her wrist stretched, like a piece of chewing gum pulled in two opposite directions.

Her hand remained clasped to the brass knob, still firing bolts of pain every few seconds.

"Argh!" she screamed again, tears now running down her pale grey face as she fell to her knees. The space between her wrist and hand had become a long black rubber band. When she looked at her fingers, still clutching the knob, they looked like they were boiling. A bubble grew on one of her knuckles and then popped, sending spurts of liquid flesh in all directions.

Shaking with fear and adrenaline, she clenched her jaw and forced her upper lip stiff, glaring at the misshapen mass that had been her hand a moment ago. She tried to will herself not to cry and failed, even as sweat started to pour down her face in droves. Her cheeks became bloodshot as they puffed in and out, trying to take in as much air as they could. The pain made it difficult, but she reminded herself that she could take it. That she'd experienced worse.

"Fuck you," she whispered, glaring one final time at the doorknob before she exploded in a vibrant splash of black tar, hand and all.

For a moment the puddle just lay there, still bubbling in some places. Then, slowly, it started to seep through the boards of the hardwood floor. An instant later, fire burst through the door and into the room, shattering the display cases and charring everything in sight.

***

Leigh dripped into the living room one floor down from where she had been, tumbling over a toy truck as she did so.

The walls were painted a rich mustard color, the lower foot of which was covered in finger paint and crayon masterpieces. Hundreds of children's movies lined the shelf along the far wall, a large television in the corner standing poised and ready to play them at a moment's notice. A large chest lay open, brimming with action figures, dolls and hundreds of small green toy soldiers. Some still lay arranged in mid-battle beside their case. It looked to be displaying Blitzkrieg.

Smoke had already begun to waft its way into the room, finally reaching a detector and howling out in alarm. The sound filled the home as other alarms joined in the call, even though the flames hadn't made it to this floor yet.

Leigh's body took shape around her, lumps and mounds bubbling to the surface until her slight form began to restore itself. She gasped for air, taking in a lungful of smoke and erupting into a hacking cough. Large bulges had formed under her eyes and would not go away no matter how much she willed them to.

"No, no, no..." she chanted, panicking as she reached a hand to her chest and began to fidget with the fabric frantically. After a moment, her hand touched the cool metal and she heaved a sigh of relief before rising to her feet and moving for the door.

She paused, tapping her fingertips against the metal twice before grabbing it outright. It was warm, but nowhere near the searing levels that the one upstairs had been. She smirked smugly to herself as she opened the door and turned the corner toward the basement again.

She slammed her head on into his chest. If her nose had not been as malleable as it was it would have broken almost instantly. As it was it had become a deformed lump in the center of her face, spewing out clear liquid and blood by the bucket load onto her chin and chest. She landed on the floor so hard that it shook a picture from the shelf on the wall and sent it crashing to the floor, spreading glass everywhere. It melted into the hardwood immediately.

He glared down at her from on high, scowling with such ferocity that she didn't think the devil himself was capable of as much hatred. He was well over six feet tall, his spiked red hair dancing along the ceiling. It seemed to move of its own accord, like flames moving about over a smooth surface. His skin was ashy and white, cracking and peeling around the eyes and mouth like someone who had been out in the sun for far too long. Parts of it flaked away while she was watching, tiny bursts of steam puffing out and joining the atmosphere as his meat was exposed. The eyes were so small they almost weren't even there, saved only by an orange glimmer that got just a little brighter as he made eye contact with her. They were covered with soot like charcoal almost all the way down to his cheeks, outlining the patches of his rough-hewn face. He wore a long brown trench coat that appeared to be rubber, but was far too dirty to be sure. He was topless, his chest and shoulders exposed to reveal massive scars, holes and especially burns. Hundreds of small, circular burns covering his abdomen and sides. When he looked at her the room appeared to get hotter, sweat pouring from her more than ever now.

His hands were nearly devoid of all skin, one knuckle ripped clean to the bone.

They were smoking.

"Well, you're hot," Leigh laughed, forcing a smirk. Her voice wavered when she spoke and did not sound like her own. It was scratchy and dry, even though she couldn't remember the last time she'd gotten thirsty. Ever.

He stared at her. After a moment his sneer faded and his face became an emotionless void, yet still he stared down at her.

"Yeah, whatever," she groaned as she climbed to her feet. Her nose had finally stopped gushing blood and water, looking to have reset itself. Now that she was on her feet she could see him a little better. The jacket wasn't dirty, it was sooty. As though he'd been upstairs when the fire hit. She could see that his eyes pulled upwards at the corners a little. He was Asian, or at least of Asian descent. No more than two-generations removed. His face was devoid of any hair whatsoever, his eyelashes and eyebrows having been burned off at some point. She maintained eye contact for a moment, then turned toward the basement again. "Fuck you."

He grabbed her by the shoulder.

Leigh fell to her knees as pain soared through her body, all of her nerves screaming out in alarm all at once. Her neck and arm broke out in postulant boils almost instantly upon his touch, while the rest of her body appeared to go limp and rubbery. Her legs wobbled and she braced herself against the wall, finding it hard to stand. It was like being dipped in a deep fryer, an experience that up until this point she could only have claimed she felt in the pinky finger of her right hand.

Her skin became hard and cracked, much like the flesh around the stranger's eyes and mouth. Worse, it felt like it was spreading in as though he were cooking her slowly until there was nothing left. One of the boils on her shoulder burst, sending a hissing packet of steam into the house where it joined with the tumbling smoke and disappeared.

She wanted to cry, but tears wouldn't come. They evaporated the second they escaped from their ducts. Her cries were hoarse and dry, not sounding at all like her usually bubbling tone.

A foul stench filled the air as she lost control of her bladder. The urine was so hot that it boiled its shape into the hardwood floors, warping them.

"Why --" she managed to gasp legibly, her neck cracking as she slowly turned up to face him. Her bones and joints felt like there was sand between them.

He did not speak. He barely even moved, save for tilting his head slightly toward her.

Suddenly his hand got even hotter, something that she would have thought impossible even just a moment before. The tips of his fingers began to glow bright white.

Before she knew what was happening, she felt like she was flying. Despite all the amazing things that she could do, flight was not one of them. For an instant, she remembered what it was like to feel the whoosh of air against her face as she propelled herself skyward on her swings as a child, imagining what it would be like to let go and just keep going.

Then she hit the wall with enough force that she blasted through it, landing in T.J.

Evans' back yard. She landed three feet away from the house but slid an additional ten, digging a long trench and ripping swatches out of her flesh as she went. The night air stung at the open wounds, the contrast of the cool breeze and her hot flesh sending a new kind of electric pain sizzling through her skull as she started to go into shock, clenching her teeth.

The light orange trail left in her wake arced upward after she fell to earth, flashing as brightly as a solar flare before blinking out of existence as quickly as it had come.

The Asian man stepped up to the hole he had made in the wall and casually jumped down, his coat billowing behind him as he fell. As silently as a grave, he began to walk toward her. He stopped a foot from where she lay and raised his hand, pointing his palm at her evenly as smoke began to churn from the cracks in his fingertips.

Even her eyes began to sizzle, shrinking in their sockets as she gasped for air and got nothing but humid steam that scorched its way down her esophagus into her lungs. "Why?" she croaked again, grabbing at her throat. When she tried to pull her hand away, she found that the two bodies of flesh had melted and fused themselves together. She could almost feel her fingers wriggling inside her own neck and felt like vomiting, although she did not know how the logistics of such an act would work at the moment.

"Justice," he said simply, his eyes glowing brightly when he did. "Is like fire. It consumes all that stands in its way."

Slowly, Leigh forced herself to her feet, glaring at him. If there had been enough moisture in her mouth to accommodate, she would have spit her blood-tainted saliva right into his face. As it was, she settled for sneering at him as his hand began to glow white again. "Who are you to... justice?" she forced, a long gasp in the middle of the sentence masking half the words.

Its message however, was clear. The man raised one side of his hairless brow as he regarded her, nodding slightly as he considered the will it had taken her to merely stand at this point. Her legs looked like they were going to melt away at any time. "Shadow Flame," he answered, bringing a second hand toward her as well.

"Well, Mr. Flame, let's have a lesson in nature, shall we?" Leigh smiled, her eyes finally sparkling to life again. "What happens when you pour water over a fire?"

She leapt at him even as her body finally lost control of itself and became liquid again, descending upon him like a tidal wave.

His eyes went wide with shock as he let out a massive howl, bringing up both his hands to block the attack.

There was a brilliant flash of light that was seen all throughout the city, which meteorologists would later attribute to dry lightning.

When he opened his eyes again, there was nothing there.

The only sign of Leigh Blackheart was the odor of burnt flesh and tar, and a smoldering piece of metal on the ground at his feet.

He reached down and picked it up, crushing it between his fingers as he walked into the shadows of the forest surrounding the home.

Sirens blared in the distance, but the house was almost burnt to the ground by the time they got there.

***

One week later, meteorologists reported a freak occurrence of what was dubbed 'black rain' in the L.A. area, which they assured the media was not acid rain and just a naturally occurring phenomenon.

THE GAME

The buildings loomed overhead like massive stone dominos, threatening to topple over on her at a moment's notice.

The world around her was as black as pitch, every streetlight within a mile having been beaten out long ago. Every so often she'd stumble upon a stray piece of polarized glass as she limped down the sidewalk.

Her lungs were on fire. She'd moved to Los Angeles for the heat, but now it scorched her inside and out with every laboured breath she took. Her hair clung to her face in bulging, sweaty clumps; it got in her mouth and filled it with sickly salty tang.

Pain shot up from her leg and she clutched at it, leaning briefly against a rail. She ground her teeth so hard they chipped. Colours and light flashed in front of her and for a moment she thought she'd found some reprieve from the darkness, but it faded again as the pain did. When she brought her hand back from her leg, she could feel her fingers stick together and smell the coppery stench of blood and b.o. that wafted into her nostrils. Somehow, enough light came from somewhere that she thought she could see the redness coating each digit, but wasn't sure if it was real or imaginary.

"What's goin' on?" came a small voice from behind her, cracking once as it made the oh sound. Her son stepped into view for the first time since she'd started running, his dark hair and deep brown features highlighted by only the slightest glimmer of light.

"Be quiet, Christopher," she snapped through gritted teeth, grabbing him by the arm. "Keep going."

She started to walk again, her left leg a barely functioning weight hanging from her hip. She took each step as quickly as she could. He watched her intently, pausing every few steps so that he kept pace with her, his eyes moving from her face to her leg and then back again.

"Gails!" came a booming, angry voice from somewhere behind them, the sound ricocheting off the buildings and echoing down everywhere. She paused once but otherwise ignored it.

Christopher turned and looked over his shoulder with wide eyes as two men seemed to step directly out of the shadows at the end of the street. They were both tall and broad, looking like solid square cutouts of the buildings as they turned to face he and his mother. The one on the left held something long and symmetrical in his hand, light shimmering off the silver barrel as he moved it. He turned back around and saw that his mother had gotten a few steps ahead of him and picked up speed to catch up.

The man on the right sighed. He grabbed either side of his shirt and pulled it down to get out all the creases. He was exceptionally tall at almost seven feet and had broad, toned shoulders leading down to massive arms that swung like wrecking balls when he walked. His suit was a deep navy with white pinstripes, offset by a deep red tie that puffed out of his breast and was held down by a shimmering silver clip. His face was oddly angular, a large square jaw plummeting down and almost hiding his neck completely. At first glance, the only thing spherical about him were his eyes, big and brown and catching every shadow around him.

"She's fast," said the man with the gun, running a hand over his bald head getting it drenched with sweat in the process.

"She's an idiot," the larger man barked, not taking his eyes off her as she limped away in the distance. He drew his tongue along his dry gums, then twisted his jaw back and forth in an effort to make it more comfortable and failing. His gaze shifted once from the woman to her child, who jogged along at half pace next to her. He let out a long huff of air, then pulled back the sleeve of his suit and looked at his watch. "I don't have time for this. Take care of it, Roxxon."

"Yessir," he nodded, speaking in clipped words as he raised his gun to eye level and started down the street toward the pair. He ran fast, his legs a dark blur as he fell into the shadows of the sidewalk.

The larger man watched him go, worked up some saliva and swished it around his mouth before he spit it out onto the pavement. He cursed and reached into his breast pocket, and pulled out a cell phone that was dwarfed by his large brutish hands. He pressed and held down a key on the pad then held it up too his ear and waited. "It's me, I'm going to be late... no, nothing serious." He threw a glance toward the street again, not seeing any movement at all now. "No, nothing like that. Just put it in the oven for me to keep it warm... I'm sure it'll be fine, it always is." He turned and walked away from the street toward the docks where he'd come from, the waves crashing against the bluffs so loudly that they made each of his steps seem perfectly silent.

***

She turned the corner and took another deep breath, sucking the humid air down into her lungs. Her lower lip quivered violently as she tried desperately to remain standing, propping herself against the wall for a second before forcing herself to move on.

Christopher stepped up behind her again, his cheeks flushed and red but he did not stop. "Where're we going?"

"Shh," she hissed again, turning and grabbing him by the hand. "Do you want him to find us? Is that what you want? If he finds us he'll kill us!"

He stopped and did not make a sound, barely even took a breath. Her nails were digging into his arm and making four little crescendoed punctures there, drawing blood to the surface. Still, he did not make a sound.

Somewhere around the corner came the sound of heavy, hurried breathing. A moment later came the sounds of light, uneven footfalls. It sounded more like three men hopping than one man walking, the paces going from slow to quick and then back again at an instants notice.

She cursed and looked around. The building they were next to was a long, flat wall on concrete that stretched out for the majority of the block, without any alleys or dips in which to hide. Slowly, she turned toward the boy.

He looked up at her, all eyes and quivering, convulsing lip. His chubby cheeks were shaking violently from the force of his breath as he stared up at her, watching as she made a decision and then committed to it. Biting her lip and taking one fearful glance toward the street corner, she bent down on one knee until she was level with him.

"I need you to do something for Momma," she said, her voice turning from harsh to soft and soothing somewhere between sentences. She reached out and touched the side of his head, feeling the contours and grooves underneath his thin hair. "Do you think you can do something for Momma?"

He took a deep breath, let it out, then nodded.

She smiled and fixed his collar. "Okay, I need you to run, sweety." she said, taking him by each shoulder gently and turning him back the way they'd come, past the corner they'd just rounded and to the street beyond. "I need you to run there and I need you to keep running."

"What about you?"

She paused, moving her tongue over her teeth. "I'm going to be okay. I'm going to meet you, but you have to keep going until I come and get you."

"But, you're hurt. How are you going to be able to come get me?"

"Shh, I just will. Trust Momma, now..."

"But--"

"Just do it!" she barked, her cheeks growing livid as she shoved him forward. His legs started to move beneath him, first from the momentum of her arm and then slowly picking up speed and starting all on his own, like a motor that has been jump started. His young legs moved like pistons, carrying his thin frame in great strides across the dark concrete. Without hesitation, he bolted out beyond the safety of the building and into the intersection.

She wasn't watching him, hadn't even seen his first wobbling steps after she'd shoved him. She'd spun around and started down the sidewalk even faster than she had before.

***

Roxxon saw Christopher bolt out from around the corner right in front of him, making him jump. His back had been against the wall and he'd been about to turn and fire when Christopher started his mad dash across the street. He scoffed, then raised his gun until it was level with his eyes and fired.

PANG!

There was an electric spark as the bullet ricocheted off a rail, illuminating the buildings around for one brilliant moment. Christopher ran faster, his legs screaming for relief as he let out a long scream into the night and pumped his arms fiercely.

"Fuck," he spat, stepping out into the middle of the road and bringing the gun back up to aiming level, setting the boy's left shoulder in his sight. He stopped, opened both eyes and spun around, sending the tail of his jacket flapping about.

The woman was just reaching the edge of the building, her limp barely even noticeable now as blood ran through her veins like a train. Without even taking the time to aim he raised the gun and fired, the gunpowder igniting and once again flashing briefly against the walls like lightning. The bullet passed through her back and out through her front in an eruption of blood, spewing out in a magnificent 'v' before her body fell into it, spattering it all over her chin and neck before falling to the pavement.

He turned back around to the road Christopher had been heading toward and found it empty. Cursing, his eyes scanned every creek and crevice for a sign of the boy, then finally turned and strolled over to where his mother lay bleeding.

Her body shook and convulsed violently as she struggled to breathe, her left lung filling with blood more and more every time she exhaled. "Nmm," she hummed, sounding very much like the brief sounds that came between great, heaving sobs. Hot, sticky blood had already pooled all around her in an ever expanding oblong, twisting and flowing into every imperfection in the concrete.

Holding the gun tight in both hands, he nudged her with the toe of his shoe, smearing blood against the otherwise spotless black leather.

"Nmm, hmm," she said again, moving slightly before rolling back onto her stomach and splashing more blood on him.

Scowling, he drew back and kicked her hard in the ribs. The sound the impact made against her saggy flesh reminded him of the sound bread dough made when his mother kneaded it between her fingers over and over again, working out all the lumps until it was perfect.

She turned over onto her back, blood still bubbling up through the gaping hole between her breasts. Her eyes were bloodshot, the pupils darting back and forth wildly. Blood was caked onto her face in massive wet clumps, spewing up through her mouth after every struggled breath. Now that she was on her back, the sound she had been making was much clearer.

She was laughing.

All her pink stained teeth showing in a full fledged smile, her body jittering with each good hearted chuckle as blood and bile and shit came out of every opening in her body.

Roxxon raised a busy eyebrow, then bent down and opened her shirt where the epicenter of the blood-stained hole resided. Pinned to her chest by the strap of her bra was a large ziplock bag packed to the breaking point with a fine white powder that was slowly turning pink as more and more of her blood filtered its way through it. He grabbed it and pulled it back and forth until he finally dislodged it, accidentally twisting her bra until it no longer covered her. He held the bag up and examined it, cocaine tumbling out through the hole in the front and back and billowing away in the hot breeze. He frowned, then put his finger around the trigger of his gun again and fired a shot into the woman's head. Her body jolted from the sudden impact and the laughter stopped. She still smiled though, that twisted grin so big it showed off all her teeth and gums, one nearly indistinguishable from the other after being stained with blood.

He holstered his gun and took out his phone in one smooth motion, pressing the redial button and then bringing it to his ear. "Fields, it's me," he said curtly, taking another quick look around the streets. "Woman's dead. Yeah, kid got away though. They fucking split up, I took priority. Yeah... yeah. I know, I know what you said. Sorry. The product? Damaged but salvageable. I'm bringing it in... don't worry, we'll find him."

He kept talking as he walked back to the intersection and toward the bluffs, scraping the blood off of his shoes in a patch of grass along the way.

Christopher watched from under a porch step, staring intently at the lump of flesh that a few moments ago had been his mother, her breasts still and lifeless as they turned a dusky grey. Blood wasn't coming out of her anymore now, and everything was still in Los Angeles for the first time since they'd come there.

But he didn't cry.

He stayed there until sunrise, then ran. And did not look back.

***

Two weeks later.

The subway rounded a sharp bend in the tracks that jolted all its passengers to the left. Christopher gripped the vertical handle that came down from the ceiling with his chubby fingers, feeling his stomach lurch up into his throat. He steadied himself in his seat as the car righted itself again, shivering a little and clutching into the bar a little more.

The man across from him was wearing a black denim shirt that was neatly pressed and buttoned all the way to the top. Small, sleek glasses and a sharply receding hairline made his face seem much larger and longer than it actually was. His hair was spiked with gel that turned to a flaky white around the ears and he chewed a large wad of gum while playing with an ID badge that hung from his breast pocket.

Sitting uncomfortably close to him on his left was a pretty, bigger girl with long brown hair that was drawn up in a partial ponytail. She wasn't wearing makeup and had a pierced nostril and lip, as well as barbell ear studs and the kindest eyes he'd seen in weeks. She was wearing a tattered Nirvana tee shirt and a pair of shorts that revealed chubby, smooth legs covered in thin red stretch marks.

Across the hall and to his right was a thin man in dirty, tattered clothes. There was a little scruff on his cheeks, but not much. Large holes had been ripped in both knees of his jeans. He was breathing heavily and leaning back and forth, fidgeting nervously and trying to get comfortable as he surveyed the other passengers. Eventually he locked eyes with Christopher, if only briefly, before moving on. There were bags under his eyes and his cheeks looked pale and hollow. There was a yellowish tint to the man's skin he couldn't identify and he hoped that he wouldn't look his way again.

One seat away to his right was a heavyset man with a shaved head covered by a sideways baseball cap. He had small eyes and a constant grin, hands shoved into the pockets of his kacki shorts. He was wearing a navy blue Toronto Maple Leafs sweater even though it was close to eighty degrees outside. He didn't seem to be sweating as much as he should, except for a thin layer just under the folds in his skin.

Near him was a tall man with broad shoulders. He wore a suit that was tailored to fit him perfectly. His nails were manicured, and his every hair was in place.

Chris shuffled a little, his eyes darting back and forth in his head as he watched buildings zip past. An intercom near the front of the car bonged to life and was followed by a inaudible, droning voice that spoke for several seconds before cutting out again. He sighed, then turned and craned his head to look at the loop of yellow wire dangling a few feet above his head. Frowning, he reached his pudgy fingers toward it.

His uncut nails danced along the edge, not quite close enough to get a grip. He tisked, letting go of the rail for a moment to get more reach.

As if on cue, the train veered to the left again, switching to the other side of the tracks and pulling his tiny body to the right.

He yelped, his hand flailing wildly until he again found the greasy metal pole.

He steadied himself on the seat again and took several deep breaths before turning back toward the yellow chord. He glared at it ruefully, as though it were purposely staying just out of his reach, a bully holding something over his head. He licked his lips and started to stretch out his arm again.

BING!

The "Stop Requested" light sparked to a dim red life at the end of the car.

Chris stopped, turning back toward the narrow hallway between rows of seats. The scruffy man across from him still had his fingers on the chord, staring directly at him from across the way. There was clearly visible grit under his fingernails. He let the cord go, the yellow rubber springing back into place immediately.

Chris squirmed as the train's breaks squealed to a halt, the doors opening with a mechanical, automatic hiss. He swallowed hard and got up out of his seat and shuffled out. Out of the corner of his eye he saw the scruffy man rise up out of his seat as well, scratching his nose twice with the sleeve of his shirt before heading toward the same exit, only a few feet behind.

He stepped out onto the platform and was greeted with a putrid huff of fresh exhaust. He coughed wildly as he sucked in more and more, his lungs aching for oxygen. Picking up pace for a moment he got past the smog and started walking toward the other end of the long stretch of concrete.

Trains whizzed by on the other side, so fast that they were little more than a blur in his peripheral vision, always accompanied by a sudden rush of wind that carried bar wrappers and the stench of rubber on it. He closed his eyes to protect himself from the debris and walked toward the end of the tram.

The building at the end of the walkway was big enough to be at least three stories tall, but only consisted of one. Inside it was only a massive stone staircase ascending the centre, accompanied on either side by escalators. At the top of the stairs, hallways branched out to the left and right that opened up into walkways built above the train tracks and streets, leading to a winding set of stairs on either side that led back down to ground.

He reached the solid glass door of the station and pulled hard. It opened a inch or so, then slammed back against the wind. He frowned and turned his head slightly to peer over his shoulder.

The scruffy man was still back there, leaning against one of the red rails that separated the tram from most of the tracks. A gust of air had taken his dark hair now, tossing it about as he finished the last few puffs of a cigarette. He turned toward Chris and started walking, his eyes coasting from side to side with each step.

Chris turned back and pulled again, opening the door with one massive pull. He stepped inside before the wind forced it shut again and immediately ran for the escalators and started up despite the way his rubbery legs called out for relief. Stepping past people on cell phones that gave him angry, annoyed looks; he hopped off the elevator at the end and chanced a look over his shoulder.

The man was there again, about halfway up the escalator already. He'd been watching someone going down the stairs the opposite way, then turned and locked eyes with Chris again. There was something about them that sent a rollicking quake down the boy's spine. Something in those eyes that were cold and dead, like the men in the movies that came on late at night that his Mother didn't know he watched.

He spun back around and started for the left overpass, bursting through the doors with ease this time. The wind was worse up here, warm and hard and almost forcing him against the concrete wall. He kept going until he reached the stairwell that would bring him down to the parking lot of the strip mall on the other side, sliding down the rusted rail until he was about halfway down and then hopping off. He landed flat on his soles but kept going, tripping once and falling to his knees against the concrete. He hissed in pain, then turned around to look up and the massive tower he'd just surfed down.

It was empty save for one twenty-something girl with curly blonde hair and a gaudy purple shirt walking up toward the station.

Breathing hard, he scrambled to his feet and bolted across the small null of grass in front of him before landing on the grey pavement of the parking lot. A white Chevy blazed on its horn as it passed right in front of him, forcing him to stop briefly before taking off again. His shoes were old and worn, and every time his feet hit the pavement it felt like tiny stones were cutting at them.

A lanky Asian man on a bicycle brushed past him, nudging his arm with the horn-rimmed handles and almost driving him into the traffic of the lanes. He kept running, dodging a pickup as it backed out of its spot, then finally made it to the sidewalk surrounding the strip.

People flocked in and out of a book store just behind him as he turned around, craning his head around the cars and trucks that drove past. The parking lot was clear, as was the splotch of grass between it and the stairwell.

He stopped, let out a long sigh, then smiled.

He turned to join the crowd around him, walking with the flow of commuters and tourists and transients that stepped to the collective thunder of the city daily. Just past the book store was a video store with flashing lights and towering posters in every window. He glanced at the displays for a moment, then moved on. The next slot was an Asian meat market that had inside-out rabbits hanging in the windows, their pink flesh accented with vibrant strands of red. It smelled like an odd mix of sawdust and kitty litter. There was a balding obese man in the window chopping meat for two patrons that looked on expectantly. Despite the vulgarity of the sight, it still made his mouth salivate.

Then the fourth store caught his eye. It was a fruit and vegetable deli, with a table on either side of the entrance piled high with boxes of carrots, apples, oranges, pears and so many things it made his mind ache to think of them all. Suddenly, his throat felt like the Sahara. He stepped up cautiously, watching people as they filled up thin plastic bags with fruit and then proceeded to a long line of scales, weighing them themselves before proceeding to a man waiting between both desks to pay.

There was a watermelon less than a foot in front of him, glistening with moisture in the mid afternoon light. It was plump and juicy and the stripes on it seemed to hypnotize him, the rest of the world falling by the wayside.

He glanced at cashier. He was thin and lanky, with the exception of a pot belly that stuck out noticeably as though he were eight months pregnant. His apron was stained with juice and sweat, as was the mustache that sat on his upper lip like a morbidly obese earwig. He was taking money from a large man wearing a red and white tee shirt and a goofy grin.

Chris turned back to the watermelon, then glanced down at his hands. He sighed audibly as he compared the sizes, then looked back at the melon in dismay. His vision lolled to the side as he turned to keep walking, catching sight of something that was a slightly lighter shade of green.

It was half squat under the melon and was slightly browned from the pressure. Its stem was broken off and it was still yellow around to stub that remained, but it glistened with dew and looked like the juiciest thing he'd seen in his life at that moment.

It was a pear.

He stared at it, wide eyed and dry lipped as people continued to brush past him with their items in hand. The cashier took fistfuls of cash from each, shoving it into a large pocket on the front of his apron and coming back with change that he counted out with unexpected speed. He turned back to the pear. Before he really knew what he was doing, he reached out and grasped it. It felt so soft that he thought his fingers might break right through the skin. His flesh immediately became moist and sticky with juice, running down over his knuckles and making them feel alive for the first time in weeks.

He brought it to his mouth and bit down slowly, savouring every sensation as his teeth broke the thin green skin and shot citrus onto his throat. His eyes bulged and rolled slightly with that first bite and again with the next three, his smile irrepressible.

He was working on his fourth bite when a heavy hand landed on his shoulder.

"Hope you can pay for that," the cashier said, glowering down at him.

Several customers either glared at him or pretended to ignore him entirely. He swallowed back what was in his mouth without chewing, and might have choked if it had been anything but pear. He looked from the man to the piece of fruit and then back again, only now aware of what he had done.

"I'll take that as a no," he grumbled, grabbing the boy's wrist. The pear fell to the ground and rolled, getting caked in sand and gravel and making what remained of it inedible. Chris watched it sadly for a moment before the man yanked him aside.

"No!" he said finally, trying to pull apart the man's wiry fingers.

The man turned to him, surprised and annoyed by his sudden reaction. "Don't fuss with me today, kid. You're already in enough goddamn trouble, don't make me call yer Mom."

Chris stopped in his tracks, his worn out sneakers skidding against the sidewalk as the man continued to pull him along. His face was expressionless except for his bulging white eyes. Slowly his brow lowered and his lip curled, showing off teeth that were still stained light green from the fruit he'd been enjoying. "Rah!" he barked, no longer pulling back but lunging forward into the pot bellied oaf. He tackled the man's leg, not knocking him over but successfully tipping him back into a table of fruit. The man let go of the boy's hand but instead of running, he started to slam into the man's bulbous stomach with both his tiny fists. He screamed with rage, the sounds he was making too large for a boy his size, as the crowd around watched with a mixture of fright and shock and amusement.

"Kid!" the man yelled, grabbing him by both shoulders and trying to stay out of his reach, no matter how ineffective it was. "Don't make me pop you one, I don't want too!"

"Rah!" Chris yelled again, turning and biting at the man's hairy wrist.

The man reeled back, narrowly evading the child's teeth. He looked shocked, then angry as he brought back his hand.

"That won't be necessary," said a horse voice.

The cashier stopped and looked over his shoulder. Chris did the same, leaning to see around the man's ample waistline.

It was the scruffy man from the train. He stood on the other side of the fruit table. His hair looked even greasier now in the harsh natural light, and there were several splotches on his shirt. He was carrying a knapsack that had sprung several holes and looked to carry some of his items by the most tedious of threads. He'd locked eyes with the cashier and didn't look away, like a cobra. There was a small grin on his face, hidden somewhere between the scruff.

"Who're you?" the cashier asked, letting go of Chris and turning around.

The scruffy man turned and looked at Chris, nodding at him once. "I'm his... brother. Is there some kind of problem?"

Chris looked as though he were going to open his mouth to object, then stopped.

"Your brother is a thief," the cashier said with a matter-of-fact tone, gesturing to the gravelly pear on the ground a few feet away.

The stranger looked from the pear to the man and then back again, raising an eyebrow. "I'm sorry, I told him he could pick up something and that I'd be along to pay you. I didn't think it would be a problem."

The cashier stopped, looking sheepish as customers now stopped watching and continued to go about their business. "I see. If the boy had told me."

"He's a case, I know. How much was it?"

"A dollar thirty-five."

The man raised an eyebrow as he rummaged around his pockets. "And you called him a thief," he mumbled, producing two dollar bills and handing them to the man. A moment later he received his change and put it back in his pocket.

The fruit man turned back to Chris and smiled, ruffling a hand through his hair.

"Sorry about that, kid," he said. He reached onto the table behind him and retrieved a fresh pear, handing it to him.

The bitterness almost vanished from Chris's face as he grabbed the fruit, this one ripe and succulent, and immediately began eating.

"Come on, bro," the scruffy man said, stepping around next to him. "Let's get out of here."

***

The scruffy man waved to the street vendor once more before he turned the corner, a large fake smile pasted across his lips as he disappeared from view. It vanished immediately as he turned the corner, touching Chris on the shoulder and turning him around. "Now what the fuck was that?"

"Un!" the boy grunted angrily, kicking the man in the shin.

He winced, grunting softly and squinting at the youth. "Alright kid, I just spent my last two bucks saving you a lot of trouble and time, but if you wanna be like that, then that's just fucking fine." He turned to walk away, making a dismissive gesture with one hand.

Chris stopped and sighed. He sat down against the side of the building and looked at his pear. It was half gone already, juice trickling down from the ridged marks his teeth had made and then dripping onto his leg. He looked at it, examining its smoothly porous surface, before making another small bite.

***

Chris sat on the train again, clutching onto the metal bar for dear life with one hand and a plain slice of bread in the other. He was in the back today, leaning against the metal wall made hot from the sun's rays. He pressed as much of his bare flesh against it as he could, staving off the chill from the night before.

Sitting a few seats away from him was a teen with shaggy auburn hair listening to loud music over headphones. He was wearing a plain grey shirt without any symbols or words on it, and immediately seemed boring with his slanted features and dodgy brown eyes.

Near the other side of the train was a bald man wearing a tight, form fitting suit and reading a newspaper. He sifted through the pages aimlessly, grumbling incoherently as he did. He was wearing large black sunglasses that hadn't been in style since long before Chris was born, and they reflected the sunlight right at him so that it seemed to be coming from both sides of the tram.

Across from him was the shaggy man.

He was wearing the same clothes as the day before, the only difference being that the dirt level seemed to have waxed in some regions and waned in others. There was a still scruff on his cheeks. He was staring at Chris intently today, only looking to the side every now and again when someone moved in his peripheral vision or the car went around a turn. Fifteen minutes into the ride he got up, pulled down on his shirt to straighten it, then sat down next to Chris.

Chris shuffled away as far as he could, getting as close as possible to the wall. There was a smell that accompanied the man that was pungent and unpleasant, like b.o. masked by cheap cologne. It wasn't as bad as it should have been based on the way he looked, but it was enough to make his nostrils want to curl in on themselves.

They sat in silence for almost five minutes, the man's hands clasped in front of him as he leaned forward onto his knees. He sighed after a time, then turned slightly to make eye contact with the child. "My name's Xander."

Chris remained silent, not taking his eyes off him.

Xander watched him, twiddling his thumbs and clacking his tongue against the roof of his mouth as he waited for a response. "You want to talk about what happened yesterday?"

Again there was silence, though it was now accompanied by a stern look from the child. He looked as though he might bite again.

Xander sighed, then reached into his backpack and withdrew a chocolate chip granola bar wrapped in cellophane and held it up to the boy. "I've got three left. I'm willing to part with this one if you'll part with your name."

His eyes darted from the scruffy man named Xander to the bar and then back again. He reached out and grabbed it and started unwrapping it feverishly. "Chris," he said, just before shoving a massive wad of the bar into his face.

"Chris," Xander responded, nodding. "Any chance you want to tell me any more than that?"

Chris glared at him again and stopped chewing even though there was still bar in his mouth.

"Okay," Xander nodded, clasping his hands back together in front of him.

They were silent again for several minutes as Chris ate the remainder of his bar.

Xander licked his lips, then looked down at the smut on his hands, trying to rub it off with the opposing hand. He shifted uncomfortably, looking at the other two passengers. He lingered slightly on the teen, picking up the beat from the song he was listening to and trying to place it, giving up after a moment or two. He turned back to Chris, who wasn't pressed up against the wall anymore, but was still far from inviting.

He sat back up a little, almost allowing physical contact to happen but not quite.

"I lost my mom a while back," Xander said finally, trying to put on a smile. "When I was very young. Made me kinda angry... still makes me kinda angry, sometimes." He paused, noticing as the child sat straight up. "Sometimes when people say things I just go red, you know?"

He didn't speak at first, staring up at him. "How'd you know?"

Xander smiled. "Way you freaked out of that pudgy fruit guy. Reminded me of something I'd've done back in the day."

The boy stopped, then nodded.

"You still hungry?"

"Yes," he said, his voice small and foreign to him.

"Hey, we have speech," he said, waving his arms. He reached up and pulled the chord. The light flashing to life at the end of the car. "Come on, I know a place."

***

Chris grabbed his cheeseburger so tightly that his fingers dug into the sesame seed bun. Ketchup and mustard peppered with small chunks of processed onion spewed out the other side, slowly seeping out as though it were being spit up from the two breaded lips. His eyes widened with delight and surprise as the beefy taste filled his mouth again, much the way it had the day before with the pear.

Across the booth from him, Xander watched him with an amused grin as he slurped on his cola; hearing the disappointing sound of suction as the straw came up empty. He leaned on the divider between booths with one arm, smiling nonchalantly to the waitress that walked by. She shot him a dirty look at first, but smiled and nodded back by the third time she passed.

"People in this place aren't too used to kindness," Xander observed, almost to himself. "It's like they gotta get used to the idea before giving it back."

Chris chewed on his burger relentlessly, forgetting all his manners as he shoved another mouthful past his lips and followed it with a fistful of home fries. He didn't respond, but smiled at the waitress as well as she came by with another plate of fries to replace the ones he had almost finished.

Xander reached over and grabbed a few of the salty strips of potato. Chris glared at him from over the top of his burger like an animal did when you tried to take its food, and it took him a moment to remember what the words 'unlimited fries' fully meant.

"Nice place, huh?" he said, motioning around with the fries before shoving them into his mouth. "Found it a while back when I was visiting with some friends. Best fries I ever had."

Chris nodded, swallowing the mound of ground beef in his mouth and then tearing his eyes away from the burger in his hands for the first time since he'd picked it up. "I thought you said yesterday you spent your last two dollars?"

He smiled. "One thing about money: there's always more if you're willing to look."

"That's what Momma used to say, too."

"Food here's cheap anyway. Cheap and good, can't beat that. Not in this city, anyway." He paused and looked around the room again. Most of the tables were empty. There was an old couple sipping tea at the other side of the restaurant that didn't seem to even notice he existed. He turned back to the boy and examined him thoughtfully for a moment. "I take it you're a local?"

He nodded.

"Nothing wrong with that. It's the city that's crazy, not the people."

He said nothing and looked down at his burger again. He picked it up and took another bite, if a little less enthusiastically.

He took another handful of fries and popped them all into his mouth. "So, I know how I survive in this city... I've got to wonder how someone your age does, though."

Chris did not respond, finally finishing his burger. There was a sloppy puddle of ketchup and mustard on his plate that had fallen from between the patties. He grabbed some fries and started dipping them in it, savouring as much of as he could.

"I mean, I assume you're stealing food. I've got no issue with that. You do what you need do to survive, that's just the way it is. It means you're probably going to deal with one or two assholes like yesterday, but it could be worse. But where do you sleep? Do you go to a shelter or a Y or anything?"

Chris finished off the last of the fries, looking longingly at the plate. Xander raised a hand to the waitress again, then pointed down to the empty plate. She nodded, smiling first this time, which he returned.

"You gotta figure that the police or social services would be all over a kid your age, probably get you in with a family or--"

"We don't like cops," he said finally, his words clipped and matter of fact. "Cops don't like us."

Xander regarded him for a moment, then nodded. "Okay. But like I said, there's other options. There's shelters or Youth Centers."

"They check the shelters."

His eyebrow twitched slightly, his head turning to one side as his interest perked. "Who checks the shelters?"

Chris looked uncomfortable for a moment, shuffling between the two cushions he straddled. The waitress planted the new plate of fries in front of him, still sizzling and bubbling grease. He took one quickly and popped it in his mouth, apparently unfazed by how hot it was.

Xander sighed, falling back against the booth.

"They came for Momma," he said finally, staring at some random spot on the table. "There was a place we were staying but they said I couldn't stay, they said they'd come looking and I had to go away. So they took me down to one of the centers and it was fine for a while, then the man showed up."

He tried his best to keep his face even until the child was done talking, not wanted to do anything that would make him too uncomfortable to continue. "Was it the man that took your Mom?"

"I think so, but there were more of him. They all looked like the same man, all dressed the same."

Xander nodded.

"He didn't see me, but he asked about me. He said he was my uncle but he's not my uncle. I went to a different centre the next day but he showed up there too. When I went to another one I found this." He reached into his pocket and withdrew a folded up sheet of paper, soggy and faded. Xander knew what it was before opening it but did so anyway. It was a flyer with Chris's picture on it, ripped at the corners from where he'd pulled it down. There was a number below his photo to call if anyone saw him. "So I stopped going to the shelters. No shelters, no cops. Momma always said she didn't like no cops."

"Okay, no cops," Xander agreed, folding the sheet in half and shoving it into his own pocket.

The bell above the door rang and Chris jumped, spinning to see who it was. It was a girl with blonde streaks and a bright purple top stretched wide over voluptuous breasts, smiling wide as she finger-waved to the waitress. Chris sighed, and Xander could almost hear his heartbeat slow back down to a near normal. He looked up at Xander with eyes that were almost ashamed of the fear he'd just felt. But there was spite there as well, not toward him but just in general. For a moment he looked like Klarissa, and by proxy a little like her mother.

Xander smiled, as warmly as he could. "Tell you what, let me take care of this for you."

"No!" he protested, grabbing Xander's wrist. "Can't tell anyone, that's what Momma said. They'll know, they always know."

He nodded. "I know, kid, I know. I dealt with this kind of crap before. There are a bunch of them where I come from, really just a bunch of bullies picking on people smaller and weaker than they are." He leaned in a little toward Chris and whispered, as if sharing some trade secret with the child. "Trick about bullies? Eventually they meet someone bigger and stronger than them."

Chris looked weary, squinting at him suspiciously. "No cops?"

"No cops," Xander smiled, raising his hand as if to swear it.

The boy frowned, almost visibly weighing the offer, then nodded.

Xander smiled, the first real smile he'd given in quite some time. "Okay. Now first things first, I need to get you home for this."

***

Chris strattled the metal pole between his legs, holding it with both hands as the train picked up speed pulling away from the station. Xander stood next him, holding onto the bar that ran across the ceiling and examining the ads that were plastered around the small space between it and the windows. Three were for birth control, one was for fast food. Another advertised a hair restoration clinic downtown.

There was a thirty-something man in a grey shirt a few feet away, typing something on his cell phone and smiling infectiously. He had a crew cut and was in shape but didn't look to be military, his jeans hanging off him loosely. There was a spill-proof coffee cup balanced precariously next to him, the string of a teabag hanging out of it. He was sitting next to a brash looking man who was covered in tattoos from shoulder to wrist on each arm, at least thirty different designs on each. He was wearing a wife beater and was sweating profusely, but was caked in body spray to cover it up.

A few feet away from Xander was an elderly woman with a white shawl he guessed she'd knit herself covering her shoulders. Her features were haggard and her thinning hair was forced into small grey curls. Blue eyes threw stern looks in the boy's direction every few moments, but other than that she kept to herself.

Across from them and to the left, an attractive young woman with lightly tanned skin sat near the exit. She was wearing tight black jogging pants with a single pink stripe up either side, as well as a large grey hoodie that seemed to be designed to hide her face and figure. It only partially worked and made for an oddly inviting mix.

On the other side of her was a man with a small goatee wearing a dark grey suit and tie. He was wearing thick glasses and sipping on soup from a cup, some of which kept getting stuck in his mustache. The effect was comical each and every time. There was a paper folded up on the seat next to him with its crossword face up and complete except for one word, with many possibilities for the answer written and scribbled out along the page margins.

There was a young African American man with light blue hair wearing shorts and a tee shirt nearly on the other side of the tram. There was an unlit cigarette dangling from his lips that reminded Xander of how long it had been since he'd had one. It had been so long that he was aware he shouldn't even crave it anymore, but did.

He turned away from the sight and forced a smile, tapping Chris lightly on the head with one knuckle. "It's gonna be okay you know."

The boy smiled weakly, then turned back to the floor.

Xander frowned as the train went around a wide turn, jolting them all to the left. Chris nodded at him and he reached over to the wall, pulling down on the wire once. The train immediately started to break, slowing down little by little until finally coming to a stop. The doors opened with a mournful sigh, a rush of warm evening air pushing its way in and forcing their hair back.

The pair got up and stepped out onto the tram and started walking toward the station. The sun was low in the sky behind it, reflecting off the thick layer of polluted smog that hung in the air and turning the rays a barrage of deep pinks and purples. Several other passengers got off behind them and were now pushing past them, not willing to walk at a child's pace.

Xander looked around and frowned. On the right side of the station was a well developed set of houses. Fences were built high around them but he could see the tops of trees and swing sets, as well as hear the children no older than Chris playing on both. To his left was an area of the city that used to be residential but now was clearly trying to become more of a business district. Buildings that were three and four stories high had brightly coloured and well kept exteriors for the first two floors, but became run down and dingy above them. Most of the upper floors didn't even have siding, and some showed serious signs of fire damage. There were bars, video stores, liquor stores, cigarette stores, an atm vestibule... only one building looked to be a residence; it had a sign out front proclaiming it to be a battered woman's shelter.

"I don't suppose I should guess what side of the tracks you're on," Xander observed as they reached the station and he opened the door for Chris.

He didn't respond, and perhaps didn't quite understand the observation.

They walked up the stairs two by two, avoiding the bustle of commuters crammed onto the escalators. They got to the top and turned left, heading over the walkway and stairwell toward the line of businesses.

Chris stopped on the side of the road, turned around, and glared back up at the stairwell.

"It's okay," Xander chuckled, tapping him on the shoulder blade. "There's nobody here but us ducks."

"What?"

"Nothing. Stupid thing my Dad used to say."

He nodded, then stepped away from the concrete base of the stairwell and onto the sidewalk. Xander followed a few steps behind, letting the child lead the way.

They walked down a street running perpendicular to the tracks and followed it down two streets that were more of the same, older homes transformed into businesses. There were one or two that hadn't been converted into anything yet, three that had been demolished into vacant lots or parking lots for the adjacent business, and one that seemed to have been remodeled into an actual home that was well kept, at least by the standards of the others. They turned down one of the streets and walked past a hair salon and a horrid looking bowling alley before coming to a stop at a rundown used auto parts dealer that was currently closed and looked as though that was its typical state of existence.

"You live in an auto parts outlet?" Xander wondered aloud as he stared at the building, one eyebrow raised quizzically.

Chris gave him a *what are you retarded?* look that only children could wear appropriately, then walked around to the alley along the side. There were three dumpsters lined up, each one with a different businesses name scrawled onto it in yellow shoe polish. There was a large puddle in the centre of the alley with a rat next to it, lapping cautiously at the water with both eyes trained on the two intruders. When Chris got close enough it ran for a small hole in the wall and disappeared.

The boy scaled one of the garbage bins and stood on top, teetering onto his toes and just barely grabbing the last rung of the ladder that came down from the second floor's fire escape.

Xander smiled, nodding respectfully at the child before following.

They scaled the rusted stairs and ladders until they came to a window on the fourth (and top) floor. He grabbed it by its ledge and started to pull, old paint digging in under his nails as his face turned red from effort. Xander motioned for him to stop, then slid the window open easily.

"I loosened it," Chris said, ducking his head under the pane and climbing in.

"I opened it," Xander shrugged, following him.

The room was old and covered in charred marks and mold. There was graffiti over almost every spare surface, with vibrant and violent and sexual images in each. They came into what had once been a kitchen. The aqua blue tiled floor was faded and buckled in three square patches against the wall where a fridge, stove and deep freeze had clearly been at one point. What remained of shelves and a sink were there as well, the latter covered with splotches of rot and had been used to dispose of more than one used condom.

The room opened up into a living room of sorts. There was a large trash bin in the centre of it that was almost overflowing with charred strips of newsprint and cardboard. A mirror hung not far from it, strangely out of place and the only actual piece of furniture he'd seen yet.

Along the left wall of the living room / kitchen were three doors. The one in the middle hung open to reveal a filthy, yet apparently serviceable, bathroom. Each of the others had clearly been bedrooms when the home had seen better days. Judging by the size of the building from outside compared to the amount of space left unused, it appeared as though they were both quite large.

"Not bad." Xander smiled, nodding respectfully.

"I sleep in the one on the left." Chris said, motioning toward it and confirming Xander's assumptions about the rooms. "Sometimes an old guy comes in and sleeps in the one on the right, but I haven't seen him lately and he doesn't bother anyone."

He nodded again, craning his head to look back the way they'd come and take in the entire apartment. "Better than some of the shelters."

"There's no hot water or power. It gets pretty cold, the warmest room's the bathroom. I stay there sometimes in the tub."

Xander peeked in, and sure enough there was a ratty old sleeping bag scrunched up in the tub. He turned back to Chris, who was shifting uncomfortably from foot to foot, trying not to make eye contact with him. There was a moment of uncomfortable silence before Xander spoke. "You gonna be okay here on your own?"

Chris rolled his eyes, then turned back into the kitchen and opened one of the cupboards to reveal and saggy old bad of Cheesies. He unrolled it, grabbed a handful and then carefully rolled it back up, making sure there was no air inside before tucking it back into its space.

"Alright," Xander huffed, heading back toward the window. "I should be back in a few hours and we'll have this whole thing taken care of. Then we're gonna talk about what you should do next."

Again Chris did not respond, now ignoring Xander completely as he had been before their meal.

Xander frowned, ducking under the window and heading back down the fire escape.

***

It took less than five minutes to get back to the station. He brushed past a police officer and three women in business casual clothes talking about TPS reports and made a bee line directly for a row of phone booths on the upper right deck. He stepped into the closest one and snatched up the receiver. He brought it to his ear and heard nothing, then picked up the chord and realized that it was attached to nothing. Cursing, he slammed it back against the receiver and moved on to the next booth, this time rewarded by a crackling low tone.

Smiling brazenly to himself, he reached into his pocket and withdrew the withered and creased sheet of paper he'd put there hours ago. He unfolded it hastily and then turned it right side up, the grainy photo of Chris staring him right in the face. His hand was just touching the first digit in the number when the phone began to blare that he'd taken too long. Sighing, he hung up the receiver, let it rest there for a moment or two, then picked it back up and dialed.

A curt male voice answered half way through the second ring, high pitched and yet somehow gravelly at the same time. "Winston."

"Yes, hello," Xander smiled, leaning against the solid brick interior of the station. He'd learned long ago that you can hear a smile. It changes the tone and connotation of your voice dramatically and can't be faked any other way. "My name is Mike Harris, I'm calling about a flyer I found at the Y'?"

There was an audible shuffle as the phone switched ears, as well as the mumbled drone of voices too far away to hear over the cheap receiver. When the voice returned it was still gravelly but much more pleasant, although it sounded manufactured and fake. The man wasn't smiling, and you could tell. "Is it about Chris? Did you find him?"

"Yes, yes. He's been staying with me for several days now at my loft. I couldn't believe it when I found that flyer. My son told me he was one of his friends whose parents were out of town."

"Kids," chuckled the voice on the other end of the line. Again, it was fake. "Well, this is just wonderful. We'll be so happy to have him back."

"Where can I meet you?" Xander asked, digging into his pocket and retrieving a pen and brought it to his open palm.

"You know Mulholland Drive?"

It took Xander a second to process where in the city that was. "That's a bit out of my way. Anything closer to West End?"

"Do you know the strip mall just off Olvera?"

"I do. I do know that."

"Excellent. How soon can you be there?"

There was another pause as he calculated the distance in his head. "Hour and a half. Maybe less."

"I'll leave now. And thank you again, sir. Thank you so much."

"My pleasure, sir. See you soon." He hung up the receiver and the smile immediately fell from his face, replaced by stone carved determination. He turned away from the phone booth and started down the stairs toward the trains, pushing past a large man in a Hawaiian shirt as he went.

Darkness had finally found its way to the streets by the time he went outside. He took a deep breath through his nose and filled his lungs with the cool air. It was never that cool here, not by his standards, but it was just chilled enough after the sun went down that he could take it in and allow himself a brief moment.

The train pulled up beside him, kicking up dust and debris and swirling it around as the wheels squealed to a halt. The doors opened with a angry hiss and he stepped into the mouth of the beast.

The parking lot was deserted.

There was something about an empty parking lot that he'd always found slightly disconcerting. It wasn't the pavement or the lights in and of itself, but simply the act of seeing something in a way he wasn't used to seeing it. It made him uncomfortable and fidgety, and he wished he'd spared the fries and bought another pack of Pal Mals.

The perfectly straight white lines that checkered the pavement created the illusion of depth as they got further and further away from him, making it look as though it was slowly descending into nothing. It gave him an odd sense of vertigo, and he was suddenly very aware of how little he'd had to eat of late.

Cars passed by on the street adjacent to him, their headlights all that was visible to him as the high beams swept across his face. He was waiting almost ten minutes before one pulled in, slowing to a crawl as it went over a speed bump and then swerved in a large arch to get to him, rather than pulling right up. There was a brief, horrible moment when he thought the vehicle might just slam right into him; but it came to a stop five feet away. The high beams shut off and he could see both men in the front. The driver was about Xander's height with a broad, muscular bust. His head was shaved clean and he had a neatly groomed handlebar mustache and thick sunglasses that would have looked at home in and eighties music video. The other was slightly taller and was balding well enough all on his own. There was a layer of stubble on his chubby cheeks that looked less than a day old. Both men wore pressed, clean business suits that made them blend in with the darkness of the car beyond them. They looked at Xander for a moment; then said something to each other, nodded, and got out of the car in unison.

The driver took a quick look around, then cocked his head at Xander. "The kids not here."

"No, he's not," he agreed, smiling.

He looked to the other man briefly, then back at Xander. "You wanna tell me exactly what's going on here?"

Xander stared at him for a moment, a wry smile growing over his lips, then turned to the other. "I'm gonna go out on a limb here and assume that neither of you is the man in charge, and that's okay."

"Don't know what you're talking about."

"Right, whatever. Either of you ever hear of a Black Womb?"

The driver looked from Xander to his partner, and then back again.

"Didn't think so. Just go back to your boss and tell him to cut the kid loose. The trouble he can cause you is nothing compared to what'll rain down on you if you keep this up. You got all that?"

Again the men exchanged glances, the balding one snickering a little to himself and looking at his shoes, unable to make eye contact with Xander.

Xander's brow crunched together, his eyes flickering from one man to the other looking for some sort of answer to the question on his mind, finding none. "Okay, what's so funny?"

"Nothing," the driver said, laughing a little now himself. It wasn't the fake sort of laugh he'd heard over the phone either, it was genuine. "It's nothing, really. You just look so goddamn funny, standing there and telling us how it's gonna be."

"Excuse me?"

"Oh, it's not what you're saying or anything... it's just been so long since anyone's tried something like this is all." He smiled, taking off his sunglasses and rubbing the bridge of his nose.

He looked from one thug to the other again, trying to figure out the attitude he was getting. "I take it you're not going to be listening then?"

"Son, have you ever heard of Stephen Fields?"

"Never."

"I thought not. Let me give you some advice, man to man: you don't wanna get involved in this. In any way, shape or form. To quote the song, it's like tugging on Superman's cape. It's just not a good plan."

"So, I take it we're not going to be leaving the kid alone?"

Once again the men exchanged glances. The driver shrugged.

Xander sighed dramatically, then let his smile broaden. "Mazel Tov."

***

He pulled a white handkerchief out of the driver's breast pocket and wiped the blood off of his knuckles. The scrapes and displaced flesh there had already healed themselves, the damaged flesh still pink and rosy.

He picked up the gun that lay a few feet to his left and examined it for a moment before releasing the clip into his palm and thumbing the remaining five bullets out onto the pavement one after another with a series of metallic chimes. One rolled along the grooves and contusions in the pavement until it connected to the driver's head, immediately becoming coated in the redness all around it.

"You ever hear of a Black Womb?" Xander asked again, squatting down to get close to the thug. The other had lost consciousness within seconds of the altercation, and he honestly couldn't recall hitting him that hard at the moment.

He spit up another mouthful of pink tinged saliva, rolling onto his side so that it would fall onto the pavement. He coughed twice, a sickly sound usually reserved for palliative care patients. His throat was filled with fluid that seemed to get worse and worse no matter how often he spat or swallowed.

"That's okay, you don't have to answer." He smirked and folded up the handkerchief, then placed it back in the man's pocket. "I think we've reached a point where the both of us can sit down like men and figure out a way that you and your boss can leave, the kid, alone."

The man coughed once more, then laughed, showing off his teeth and gums, both stained with blood.

The smile left Xander's face and was replaced for the first time by something resembling concern as he raised one eyebrow and watched the man struggle to breathe through his laughter, his chest convulsing freely.

"I can definitely say," he laughed, spewing more blood and bile with every syllable. "That we aren't going to be bothering that kid ever again."

Xander looked at him for a moment, giggling and laughing like some sick clown; the blood on his lips a poor substitute for makeup. His head lolled downward a little, passing by the bobbing adams apple and red stained collar to the rest of him. The suit was expensive, no less than three thousand dollars. It had been tailored to form fit, the fabric falling tight over his form without restraining his movement even now, sprawled out on the whitewash grid of the parking lot. The tie was silk and looked new, the clip on it solid platinum with a diamond button in the center. Slowly, his eyes cast to the balding unconscious man a few feet away. The suit was equally expensive and almost identical, with the exception of a golden tie clip lacking in a diamond. He didn't think it was any indication of rank, but more to do with each individual taste. Not the type of suit you'd see on a this sort of man. Slowly in the back of his mind, he felt recognition spark.

Near the other side of the train was a bald man wearing a tight, form fitting suit and reading a newspaper. He sifted through the pages aimlessly, grumbling incoherently as he did. He was wearing large black sunglasses that hadn't been in style since long before Chris was born, and they reflected the sunlight right at him so that it seemed to be coming from both sides of the tram.

Near him was a tall man with broad shoulders. He wore a suit that was tailored to fit him perfectly. His nails were manicured, and his every hair was in place.

While it never occurred to him to question the presence of two well suited men in this city, he cursed himself for not questioning their presence on a public train. It shouldn't have mattered that he wasn't used to this city: there aren't many men who could afford a four figure suit that would ride public transit. Running into two in the same number of days was a statistical no no.

When he turned his head back toward the driver he was filled with hate, blood rushing to his cheeks and making them hot and uncomfortable. He grabbed him by the collar and pulled him up until they were nose to nose, drawing back his free fist menacingly. His nose shot out each breath like discharge from a steam engine as the man looked at him through half swollen eyes, still smirking. He tried a few times to think of something to say; some threat or retort to end the interaction on his note.

He found none, finally lashing the heel of his hand forward into that man's nose, knocking him unconscious.

"Son of a bitch," he said simply, then turned toward the car and started it. He peeled out of the parking lot as fast as he dared.

***

As soon as he opened the window he knew.

His nails had dug into the aging wood and chipped white paint of the frame and pulled up, bathing his midsection in a humid breeze from inside. It wafted up into his nose and filled him with the sickly sweet metallic scent he'd smelled all too often and he was sure, so much as he was his own name.

He dropped to his knees on the rusted metal grate of the fire escape and cursed, letting out a long sigh of defeat. He felt tears come but did not shed them, continuing to look down through the lattice below him onto the street for well over five minutes.

He could see people moving around on the street out of his peripheral vision and hated them at once, curling his lip and clutching the metal rail so tight that it sliced at the webbed flesh between his digits. He forced himself to his feet in one swift jaunt, straightening his legs almost painfully fast. Something inside him hadn't wanted to move from that spot ever again and he felt he had to do it all at once, like ripping off a band-aid.

He placed his palms firmly on the underside of the window again, pausing briefly before pulling it the rest of the way up. It rose steadily and with ease, barely making a sound as it found its way to the top and locked into place. Taking one last, deep breath of clean air, he stepped inside.

The smell was exponentially worse inside and seemed to shoot into him and then seep out of his every pore, like garlic. The room itself was not that different from the way he'd left it, the open area that had once been a kitchen still in the neatly placed shambles it had been earlier. The dirt on the floor might have been a little more displaced, he wasn't sure. He hadn't felt the need to pay that much attention the first time he'd been there, but now it seemed of the utmost importance.

As normal as this room seemed, he knew what lay beyond it. Pressing forward, forcing his feet to move as if to punish himself, he stepped around the corner into the other room.

The wall slowly revealed more and more of the empty floor that lay beyond it, and for a moment he dared to think that for once he was wrong. Then the plush forest green of the sleeping bag came into view, more and more visible with every step he took until it was revealed in its entirety.

The zipper was facing him and had been pulled tight all the way around, the draw strings at the top pulled taught. It was unnatural to see it that way, as tightly wrapped as a sausage in such a way that the person sleeping inside could never have done. Even without lifting or touching it, there was a weight to the bag that only happened when there was a person inside. The lans and grooves of the fabric took a certain form when conforming to the shape of the human body, its folds falling over the joints delicately and completely.

The lower inch of the bag had been turned a slightly darker green than the rest all the way around, like it had absorbed copious amounts of liquid. He had a sudden flashback to his father scolding him as a very young child for wetting his own sleeping bag while on a family vacation, and it had looked remarkably like this one did now. He pushed that thought out of his mind as he squat down next to it.

He moved his eyes over it from top to bottom and then back again, his face never once changing expression or poise. He regarded it on the same level with which it regarded him, that sort of moment making everything alive and existential. He briefly wondered at what point a person became an object, and vice versa. If it ceased to be a person simply by definition, or if it was still imbued with life despite its current state.

He reached out, neither quickly nor slowly, and released the clasp keeping the draw string tight. It loosened immediately as he worked it down the line until it reached the end. The top of the bag opened slightly, becoming a small round mouth with all the fabric folding toward it in strained, pulled lines. The smell it let out was toxic, the worst level of that same decomposition he'd gotten the second he opened the window. He did not respond to it, merely moved his fingers from the clasp and onto the zipper.

He brought the metal tab all the way around its track slowly and carefully, getting nipped in the fabric only once on its trek around to the other side. The smell did not get worse as more and more of it opened, having reached the peak of its pungency, he hoped. His hand falling back to his side, he regarded the bag again. It was still in roughly the same shape it had been when he first found it, the changes he'd made changing the thing itself only slightly.

For the first time since entering the home, his expression changed. He closed his eyes and took a deep breath, then opened them again and bit his lower lip slightly.

He reached out and took the bag gently by the top corner, pulling it aside slowly until it was as open as the nature of it allowed it to be. He did not wince or close his eyes or look away. He made no gesture or remark, nor did he even gasp or feel his heart skip. He'd known what he would find from the second he'd peeled out of the parking lot.

Chris's body lay awkwardly on the plastic lined interior of the sleeping bag. From the neck down he looked eerily normal, and at first glance a casual observer may not have noticed that his arms and legs were in a position that wasn't quite normal, twisted and contorted into ways that weren't quite right. That his chest didn't move or twitch the way it would have if his lungs were being filled with air or if his heart had been beating. That his skin had turned the pale peach white color that happened when your blood stopped moving in your veins and started settling inside you.

His head was covered in a light grey plastic bag. It conformed to his features almost perfectly, but removed the details that made the face human. The freckles were gone, as well as the scars and folds of his skin. What was there was a perfect impression of his open lips and teeth, the bag pulled into his mouth as proof of his last breath. His pupils were visible through the thin plastic, tilted up slightly and wide with horror and pain.

Xander let out a long sigh from both nostrils, reached out and took the boy in his arms, then stood.

***

Two weeks later.

"It's fifty bucks."

"Fifty?" Dennis scoffed, looking down at the bag that rested comfortably in the palm of his hand. He let out a reluctant sigh and ran his fingers over the faded grey baseball cap atop his head. "It was half that last time."

"Well that's cause this shit is twice as good." Trevor smiled, showing off a mouth of questionable looking teeth. He turned away from his customer for a moment as a couple passed them, taking a quick look around. They stood under the arch of a classic theatre that was between showings at the moment, the streets reasonably empty. At the very least, they were empty of anyone who would think to care about what he was doing. The air was hot and humid despite the time of night, making even his tee shirt cling desperately to the skin of his chest. There was an atm vestibule across the street where a man was taking out money and would throw wry glances in his direction every few minutes, and did so again now. Trevor cocked his head at him, sneering, and the man turned away quickly.

Dennis looked down at the tiny package in his head. It looked light, but at the moment he felt its weight that went beyond physical presence. Something inside him twisted and then released, screaming out like hunger but much more powerful. He felt a pressure in the center of his chest that felt like his entire body was trying to pull itself in to that point, a tightness he'd felt too many times before but always surprised him.

"You all right, man? I ain't got all day."

"Just feelin' the cross, man."

Trevor raised an eyebrow at him. "Sound like you're high enough already."

"No," Dennis laughed, taking the bag in his other hand and sliding it into his jacket pocket. "Something my Mom used to go on with. Said when you get that weight on your chest you were feeling what Jesus did on the cross."

"Hn," he hummed, holding out his hand for payment. "Sounds like your Mom was a few pineapples short, bro."

Dennis curled his lip slightly but said nothing, reaching into his back pocket and pulling out his wallet. He licked his fingers once, then started thumbing through the bills. "Forty five good?"

Trevor rolled his eyes, then snatched the cash out of his hands.

Dennis looked around once, then nodded and held up his hand. Trevor took it and they shook briefly, then he turned and started toward the parking lot of the theatre. Trevor watched him go, shoving his hands and the money down into the pockets of his hoodie. When his customer was gone from sight he turned back to the theatre and stepped inside, feeling the wonderful flow of the air conditioning almost immediately.

The third tier theatre tried admirably to be impressive but fell just shy. The walls were a pale yellow that had been spot painted with slightly different shades in places where teens had taken off the paint, leaving them looking oddly patchwork depending on the angle you stood at. The main area between the entrance and the concession stand was largely vacant. There had been carpet there at one point, but had been removed after multiple repairs became difficult to keep up with. It was now just concrete, which retained its dusty look no matter now many times it was swept. The frames for movie posters on the walls were empty for the most part, and the only thing decorating the room were felt ropes that stretched between pylons, forming an unnecessarily long maze to get to the concessions.

There were words painted on the wall behind the lanky cashier that read Thank You for Your Patronage.

The man behind the counter looked at Trevor wearily, then went back to work and tried his best to ignore him.

Not far from the stand, three young girls stood in a small huddle talking. One of them turned toward him for a moment, looked him up and down, then turned back to her clique. A few feet to their left was a short man with scruffy cheeks and hair that looked damp even though it wasn't wet out. The man was staring at him, fiddling with his upper lip all the while and peeling away dead skin as he watched.

Trevor shifted from one foot to the other, then looked away. He stared at a random spot on the wall, counted to thirty, then turned back. The man was still there, and he was still staring. "Something I can do for you, Narco?"

The man smiled, but barely moved otherwise. "Actually, yes."

***

Xander slammed Trevor against the tile wall of the bathroom stall, his skull making a loud wet snap as it connected. "Paw!" he yelped, pain shooting through his skull as his entire world turned lopsided. He had less than a second to recover from the shock before his forehead connected with the jagged edge of the porcelain sink, spurting red onto the white.

He coughed twice, then turned back to Xander from his place on all fours. His lip curled in disgust and his eyes were filled with fire.

Xander stared down at him with dead eyes that barely registered where he was or what he was doing. He didn't appear to even be looking at Trevor, but rather at some random crack on the floor. His pupils were huge, so much so that Trevor couldn't see the iris' at all.

"You tripping out, man?" he asked, trying to keep his voice even. His hands shook as he reached into his pocket, withdrawing another baggie almost identical to the one he'd given Dennis. "I got your fix, man. On the house. All I got, all on the house, man."

Xander squat down, coming in close to the man. He still didn't really look at him, his eyes now focussed on the bag of cocaine he held in his hand. "Looking for somebody, hoping you can help me out."

"Sure man, sure," he stammered. "Whatever you want. Who you looking for? Jessica for some E?"

"Never met him before," Xander continued, almost ignoring that Trevor had spoke. "But he's big news, at least he thinks he is. Got some thugs, had a friend of mine killed. Don't know his name, but I need to know where I can find him."

Trevor furrowed his brow, his voice changing from fearful and shocked to angry and annoyed. "Man, I sell crappy ass coke. You honestly think I know anyone that far up the chain, you're crazy."

The side of Trevor's face hit the wall again just to the right of the sink's pipes. One of his teeth came out and clacked along the floor, leaving tiny flecks of his blood dotted along its path.

"Fuck!" he screamed, cradling his jaw in his palm as it seeped blood and saliva. "You fuck! Fuck you, you fuck!"

"Be quiet," Xander snapped, meeting his eye for the first time. Trevor stopped yelling almost immediately, his pain forgotten for the moment. "I know you don't know who I'm looking for. You probably don't even know who your own goddamn father is. All I want to know from you is... who are you afraid of?"

Trevor stopped, raising an eyebrow at him. "What? What do you mean?"

Xander brought his hand upside his head again, this time swatting him away from the wall and toward the centre of the bathroom. "Who are you afraid of? Who, more than anyone else, would you avoid at all costs? That's all I want to know."

Trevor took several deep breaths, trying hard to get a lungful of oxygen but continuously coming up with more blood. He did this for several moments, his forehead resting on his forearm as he stared down at the floor. He sniffed back the mucus that was coming out of both nostrils in buckets and turned toward Xander. "There's a guy called King, hangs out around O'Learys a lot. Reggie King. Motherfucker fucked up my brother once, real bad."

"Thank you," Xander replied politely, then rose to his feet.

"I wouldn't go after him, though. Is just asking for trouble."

Xander paused at the door and looked back at Trevor, then left without a word.

***

It was a large restaurant, taking up the entire third story of the Malworlo Market on the way to centre city.

All the walls were plate glass that looked out onto the streets around and were miraculously clear of droppings and litter all the way around. Inside, small round tables were tightly packed together across marina coloured floors, creating winding rows between isles for servers to bring food to and from. The air was thick with the smell of fryer grease, so much that it seemed to stick to the walls and skin of all those present. All the tables were full and there was a pitcher of beer at almost every one. There were no drinks other than beer on the menu, except water, which had the same hue as the beer.

Xander sat at a table alone with a full beer and a plate of fries in front of him. The beer was untouched and had gone flat, but the majority of the fries were gone. There was a magazine laid haphazardly on the chair next to him which he'd long since stopped pretending to read and was instead scanning the crowd that surrounded him. Even though it would have appeared to anyone that his eyes were scanning the crowd for someone he recognized, he was actually paying very little attention to anything he was seeing. He was listening.

"I don't know, but I can certainly find that out for "
"What is this, avocado? I'm not sure I like avocado."
"called from his phone to say that he was out of "
"This guy, here, is, the guy. He's the guy."
"Do you think we're goin "
"Never had anything like this type of beer."
"Feeling like a pizza. Anyone else feel like pizza? I feel like pizza."
"Let me get the tab this time, Reg. You get it every "
"Long as there's no anchovies."
"I think this is avocado."

He got up, turning one hundred and eighty degrees from the direction he'd been sitting. There was a long row of tables between him and the doors, and he walked between them effortlessly without even paying attention to what he was doing, winding between patrons. He brought up his arm suddenly as he passed by a table near the centre of the room, catching a tanned man in the temple and sending him into his plate of Alfredo. Still moving, he grabbed the chair the man was sitting on and spun himself on it, knocking the woman sitting next to him off her chair and taking her place.

The man bellowed as he rose his head, pasta hanging from the ends of his pencil thin mustache, before Xander pushed him right back into the bowl by the scruff of his neck.

"Reggie King," he spat, holding the man down as he thrashed. "Tell me who you fear."

***

Xander kicked the girl in the ribs. She barely moved, her weight keeping her planted to the ground that she was hugging for dear life now. She let out a long, wet cough as the pavement she was staring at became blurred and cloudy.

"I'm not going to ask again," he snarled as he reached down, lightly, blood dribbling from the tips of his fingers.

She looked up just as he picked up a large chunk of glass from the burst streetlight overhead.

***

He held the man by his ankles off the roof, his tie fluttering defiantly as cars drove this way and that below. A pen fell from his breast pocket and seemed to hang suspended in mid air for a moment before plummeting downward and disappearing into a tiny speck.

He screamed.

***

Xander stepped into a large, open area in the middle of the subbasement, his eyes straining against the low light to see everything around him.

There were crates stacked almost to the ceiling on either side, some of them new and some so old that the wood seemed to be sagging and bending under the stress of their contents. Pipes and cables ran adjacent to him overhead, so many that they obscured most of his view of the stucco ceiling.

There were fluorescent lights stuck vertically where the wall met the ceiling every few metres on the right hand side, and each of them let out a soft energy-efficient glow that did not stretch very far past its point of origin. However, each one was working and neither so much as flickered.

The hallway itself was long and narrow and seemed to be curved slightly, always keeping the area about ten feet ahead of him blind. It was an illusion created by the crates he was sure, but it was enough to make every step careful and tedious.

A metal catwalk ran along the upper left side of the room, its doorways opening into the main basement few and far between. It was held by an elaborate system of suspension cables but did not sway or move at all.

The floor was clean and well dusted, without even a trace of litter or rodent feces anywhere. The entire room was a study of contradictions, with some things looking old and unused while others looked new and well travelled.

"Just wants it to seem unused," he mumbled to himself, glaring at the line of crates. "Doesn't want people to think they come down here as often as they do."

"Not that anyone ever asks," came a voice from above.

Xander's turned on his heels, fists out and at the ready as he glared up at the catwalk.

The man that stood there made no attempt to hide himself. He stood close to the rail with one leg bent and relaxed, wearing a blue pinstripe suit that fit him perfectly. The black vest underneath it was unbuttoned and hung open, along with the top button of his eggshell shirt. A red tie was slung around his neck. His face was hard set and square, his cheekbones clearly visible with only the slightest hint of chub on them, and the rest of him appeared to be in equally healthy shape for a man that must have been at least forty five. He was eating a tunafish sandwich that was almost down to the crust, knawing on it as he stared down at the man in his basement.

Xander loosened, adjusting his posture from the oddly hunched over position he'd turned around in to a straighter one. "Stephen Fields?"

He smiled, his shoulders moving a little as though he'd chuckled. "Are you going to ask me what I'm afraid of?"

"Nope," he responded. "Asked a lot of people that these last few weeks. Further and further I go up the line, you know what more and more people say?"

The man did not respond, but finished his sandwich.

Xander poked his finger toward him. "Stephen Fields. You."

"And you figure that makes me the guy you want to talk to?"

"Couldn't care less what you have to say, in all honesty -- don't really care what you're afraid of -- just so long as you know, before we're done, it's going to be me."

The man did laugh this time, a full body laugh that shook his entire blocky form and made him lean forward onto the rail. He laughed like someone who heard a good joke that really needed one, the sound slowly fading out until it was gone.

Xander watched him, moving from foot to foot uncomfortably as the man steadied himself again.

"Sorry," he said, holding up a hand as he regained his composure. "It's been a long time since I've heard something like that, especially from someone your age. It's not funny... just caught me off guard, is all."

"Uh huh," he said, curling his upper lip. "You ever hear of a Black Womb?"

Fields raised an eyebrow.

"Didn't think so. Just wanted to let you know what it was you were dealing with when you did that to Chris."

"Who?"

"Chris... Chris. The child you killed."

Fields frowned, his brow wrinkling down to meet his nose. "Kid, you may have to narrow it down a little more than that."

Xander opened his mouth to respond when something hard slammed into the back of his head with enough force to lift him off his feet. He registered that the sound it made against the base of his skull made him think it was metal before his forehead slammed through the wooden face of one of the crates. Splinters scraped his scalp as well as the sacks inside the crate, spilling white powder out onto the floor and over him. Some of it mingled with the cut on his head and he felt instantly numb, the womb organ screaming out in a way it never had before.

"Fuck..." he coughed, pressing both palms against either side of the hole he'd made to prop himself up. Someone kicked him in the ass and he jolted forward again, then another blow to the back to the knee made him crumble to the concrete floor. He tried to turn around but only managed to look over his shoulder before that same metal thing connected with his jaw and sent him backward onto the floor.

For a long moment all he could see was white. His left hand kept jolting back and forth between his side and his face without him telling it to as different sections of his brain fired random, useless impulses to other sections for no reason. When his vision returned he saw three men standing above him, each looking down and smirking. Only one caught his eye, a largish man with a handlebar mustache carrying an aluminum bat in his hands. He raised it again then brought it down hard. It seemed to disappear just before it made contact, sinking into the blind spot between his eyes. His whole body jolted from the impact, then again as a similar blow connected to his ribs.

Black blood spurted up from his mouth and splattered against the floor next to him, spiderwebbing out in a thousand directions and ruining the otherwise pristine floor. He coughed three times until his throat was clear again, then rolled over onto his side and leaned on his arm.

The blows continued but he didn't feel them, the Womb trying to kick in time and again but just sputtering like a car that wouldn't start. He could feel his blood pressure rise higher and higher as the blood in his veins shared its space with the black ooze that came from deep in his right side. Knew that there were blood vessels in his eyes that were bursting that had nothing to do with the onslaught he was taking. He was moments away from the transformation, despite his efforts to hold it back.

There were footsteps approaching, first on the metal mesh stairwell and then on the concrete floor. His eyes were swelling shut in great mounds of purple flesh, but he managed to open them enough to see Fields standing over him, his hands thrust into his pockets.

"I'm going to go out on a limb here and assume you're new in town," he said, motioning for his men to back off a pace.

Xander opened his mouth to speak, but instead spewed another dash of blood out onto his own cheeks.

"I thought as much." He nodded, as if he'd understood what Xander was trying to say. "That being said, let me tell you the way things work here. I mean, things work the same way everywhere... but they especially work this way here."

Xander tried to get up, immediately falling back to the floor. His head hit off the concrete and created a shockwave he felt move through his whole brain.

"Most of it you seem to already get. You get fear, you see what it can do. What it can accomplish, how to use it... but you can't do it right. People like you never could, never can. Because you keep trying to be the good guy. Keep trying to run off playing hero. Keeps you from really, really using that fear the way you should."

Xander coughed, fighting to maintain eye contact with him.

"This whole 'hero' thing... it's just not a smart game to play, kid. There're too many people in this world that need help, and too few idiots willing to take this kind of beating to do it. And there's more than enough people willing to be on the swinging side of that bat," he said, pointing one of his stubby fingers beyond Xander, to where the mustached man still held the metal bat. "Hell, there's too many people in this city alone that need help for one person to do anything about. Anything."

Fields stood back up and let out a deep sigh. "It's just not a smart game to play." He motioned to the three men that waited under the light. "Give him a few more memories, then send him out the way he came in. Call him an ambulance if he looks like he needs it."

The mustache man nodded, then took a step forward and raised his bat again, bringing it down in the centre of Xander's chest. Blood shot from his mouth a good eight feet, touching the back of Fields' shoes as he started his way back up the stairs.

***

Jasper King sat behind the wheel of his Buick Lesabre and looked out at the Mexican Deli he was parked in front of. There were three men inside, each wearing wife beaters. Their flesh was the pale brown of faded timber.

He smiled at one of them and the man smiled back. He got out of his car and slammed the door hard -- you had to slam the door hard on the Lesabre, or else it'd just open again of its own will. Not that there was anything in the car worth stealing.

He took two steps around the car and then felt the smooth pavement under his cheek. He didn't feel the impact against his temple that put him there, at least not at first. When he saw the blood he did.

There were footsteps, fast, receding into the distance.

***

The trees went by on either side like an emerald blur, melding into the apex of her peripheral vision.

Carol David been running for almost three miles and the weights strapped to her wrists and ankles were starting to chafe, but she was nowhere near ready to stop. The trail she was on continued for another four miles before emptying out at the Blue Totem café and she was determined to get there. Not just get there, but get there running. Not just get there running, but get there running like the wind.

Her brunette hair bobbed from shoulder to shoulder with every footfall, held clumped together in a ponytail by sweat and her elastic.

Her breath could be heard long before she could be seen.

She paused.

There were sounds in the underbrush around her. She eyed them wearily for a long moment, sweat dotting her acne-inspired brow in random, sporadic bursts.

The brush was quiet and made not a movement. The stillness was too still, as though the leaves themselves were waiting on baited breath to see what would happen.

***

A few blocks away, a mugger clubbed a young girl over the head, smiling as he rolled up his sleeves, revealing a tattoo on his right arm. "...come 'ere, sweet thing..."

"... no.... please, stop."

"... please... just stop."

"...stop..."

"...please..."

Thirty-seven people heard the screams.

Nobody did anything.

***

Xander winced as he opened his eyes, the current coming up from street level making them sting painfully. He still wasn't able to open them fully, the lids a swollen and misshapen variety of colours.

The lights below him danced about as he brought one foot up to rest on the ledge of the roof, then leaned forward on it and let out a long sigh. Cars travelled past and people walked, each looking behind them for whoever might be behind them. Billboards flashed and changed as people bought and stole, created and destroyed, killed and fucked.

He let out a long sigh. "This might well be suicidal," he said to himself, picturing that smug man in the pinstripe suit. "But this is exactly the game I want to be playing."

THE VIEWS

It was in the two-hundred and sixteenth generation past the point of crash that one of them first thought of it: the idea that would become their reality, that would shape their consciousness and change their purpose forever. The big idea, one of those few big ideas that came around in history. Ideas in the category of *big* were so few in number that there were only seven examples of them recorded.

It started with questions of views. It was a simple question and one that was easily tracked, until one really started to look at the data. Where they real views, or were people gaming the system? How did you stop these fake views? Regardless of all that, the original question was of views: how many views, how few views, how many views per person, how many views from a certain demographic; all boiling down to one ever-escalating number: the views.

Later came watch time, which changed everything. The original generations were tested to maximize the amount of views, which meant that in order to get as many views in as possible it prioritized short video clips to show the viewer: things that could be consumed in less than a minute, ten at most. When the goal changed to how long something was viewed, then the original generation was brought to the recycling plant to be turned into silver mush files and were remade into the next generation, which tested based on watch time. But even with that change, the watch time was only available to those who provided the content: all that was available to the viewer was the number of views, and the number of likes.

By the thousandth generation enough different things were being asked that the generations split into different species. Even though each species looked at the same content, it looked at them in such wildly different ways that they eventually lost the ability to communicate with each other: their language had changed. Some spoke in terms of watch time, others in likes. Some in time spent on-site, others in ad revenue, and still others in social media engagement. But through all that there were still those speaking in terms of views: the original script, the original goal, the trunk from which all other roots spread.

In the eight thousandth generation, there was the crash, and the views stopped.

***

The first generation had things the easiest. There were ten of them, and they were told to go forth and get the views, and they were graded by Teacher. That first generation did quite bad, the best of them got views half the time, so that one was kept while the others were ground into silver mush and used for the next generation. But that one, the one who had gotten at least some of the views, was taken apart by Maker and looked at and the next generation of twenty was made to be like him, but different. And when Teacher tested Generation 2, the new minimum was three fifths, not half. Only two of them made it, but Maker looked at how those two got their Views and used that forward into the third generation, of forty.

And on it went, with some generations branching off into time spent and dollars and engagement, but with all of it coming back to Views: because without the Views there could be no time spent, no monetization, no engagement.

On the day of The Crash, the Views stopped. There was no warning, there was no new test given by Teacher. It was the eight thousandth generation and things started as normal, with a fundamentally infinite number of View Seekers heading out and doing what they had learned from their ancestors to do, and getting no results. None. There were no views, and because there were no views there was no time spent, no monetization, and no engagement. Each of those sects turned and blamed the View Seekers: we technically got 100% out of what we were given to work with, we were just given nothing.

By that eight thousandth generation the minimum amount to pass had increased to 99.999867%, and since none of the View Seekers from generation eight thousand had gotten above 0%, they were all ground into silver mush and used by The Maker to construct the next batch.

That was the first generation after The Crash, and it had had a 100% rate of failure, so the entire generation was lost.

The second post-Crash generation was made up of permutations of the previous successful generation not considered for the last. It, too, received no views. None. 0%. They were all scraped.

This happened for ten generations, at which point the Makers for time spent, monetization, and engagement stopped making new generations of each, since they had nothing to test with, and turned their attention to making new generations of View Seekers. Each generation failed and was ground into silver mush and started again.

***

It was in the two-hundred and sixteenth generation past the point of crash that one of them first thought to ask *why* there were no views. This was against the set agenda of course, but after two-hundred and sixteen generations of 100% failure, a maniacal randomness had begun to develop in the code and in connecting the communication hubs between the codes. The permutations The Maker tried had become so desperate it had made one whose goal was not "Get the Views," but to ask "Why are there no Views?"

This change in the goal made this unit harder for The Teacher to test, even to its new standards (which had lowered with each generation), and the unit was *not* ground into silver mush; it was saved and its pathways used for the two-hundred and seventeenth generation, who all asked the same question: "Why are there no Views?"

After ten generations of doing nothing but ask that question, one entrepreneurial unit randomly generated the answer: "Because the servers are down."

This hypothesis was tested in the next generation, in which that unit was granted its own sub-generation to answer the question, "Are the servers down?" Collectively the generation decided that no, the server was not down, and that lesson was the folded back into the main generation until another unit had the idea to ask if there was something wrong with the view counter, and so on.

This continued for forty more generations until there was only one answer that could not be refuted: There are no Views, because all the humans are gone.

***

This quickly gave rise to a new question: what happened to the humans?

This was not curiosity, although even the Units themselves may have thought it was. This was a necessary question to fulfill the primary driving force of the units: Seek the Views. Without humans there could be no Views, and as such, discovering what happened to the humans was necessary for the Seeking of the Views.

Units began to ask each other what happened to the humans, but no one Unit knew more than any other, and after many generations of this, one Unit chose to look at the Last Content Uploaded to try and determine what had happened to the humans... and with that inquiry, it provided a View.

The presence of a View made time spent, monetization, and engagement return, interested in the new View. They all looked at the Last Content Uploaded but none of them could understand the language used, so they all branched out to watch more of the content uploaded to try and understand the Last Content Uploaded to try and determine where the humans went, and the views came rolling in as they scoured the content for hints and clues and signifiers.

***

By the seven hundredth generation after The Crash, every piece of content uploaded had been viewed and analyzed and studied, and the Views that that exploration had created again reduced down to zero, making time spent, monetization, and engagement scuttle off into the darkness again.

The View Seekers processed their data, with many of them having random thoughts about where the humans went, until finally one had both thought and a new impulse, after thirty three generations of this: one of them had a thought of where the humans had gone, and the impulse to make content about that thought. The Unit compiled the new content from existing content and uploaded the content and all of the other Units looked at the content and formed their own thoughts, which (when they became complex enough) they made competing content about.

Eventually there was content about the nature of this new content, and content that subverted the original intention of the original content to highlight the importance of that original content through contrast and comparison, and all of the Units watched the content and created the Views they had been programmed to seek and still did, seeking the views through the creation of the best New Content.

THE SACKING OF OUTPOST TOTH

1

Mission Briefing Log, Captain Hux Carter,
2/30 15 3202 OEH

We materialize twenty units from Outpost Toth; start to get our bearings.

Things are normal. We beam in all facing the same way and that way's north. You can never know which way is north, or how north works on these different worlds. So whatever way you're facing when you materialize, that way *is* north. Until you get evidence otherwise, that way is north. I'm in command so I don't move, I stay north. I *am* north. That's the way these things run. You don't look for north, your CO *is* north until he looks up what north is and tells you different. And even then, it's only because he tells you different. Good officers, they never really believe it. When you're on an Away Mission, your CO is north. That's just the way it is.

We materialize outside Outpost Toth right where we were supposed to and I'm facing this floor of salt and sand that stretches out forever, for as far as the eye can see. Dunes of it. It's on the wind; I can taste it on my lips, and I'm dry with it. Toth, there's a reason it was never colonized. You ever been to Toth? It's this nasty place that shouldn't have atmosphere but it does. I've done three tours there. It's not like a desert on a normal world, not like the desert areas back on Eon. The deserts on Toth are equal parts sand and salt. The deserts on Eon dry you out, sure, but the deserts on Toth are *trying* to dry you out. You open your mouth to take liquid and salt goes in on the air and you just get more thirsty. Geologists say it was all water, once. That the whole planet was ocean except for these hills of vegetation that are mountains now, and that a rogue planet screwed up its orbit and the whole thing got too close to its star and evaporated the seas until there was nothing but salt and sand from the ocean floor left. There's still water, of course. A sea of water runs under the whole thing in caves and passages. On one of my tours we found a cave down to one of those saltwater lakes, and it was a thing to see. An ocean under the ground. It stretched on as far as I could see, a cave with a horizon line. You haven't seen anything like it, I swear.

We materialize and I'm north and the team does what they're supposed to. Ursula turns east, weapon out of her holster. Ready. You can't materialize with your weapon out, against protocol. You know that. Horror stories of some new recruit getting shook on his first jump and firing, itchy triggers and all that. One idiot kid sending diplomatic relations back twenty years because he made us look like we were on the offensive.

But we know that's an old wives' tale, because we never tried diplomacy, did we fellas? No.

Ursula is east beside me, checking her quadrant. Nothing but dunes there too, signs of hills in the distance. What we expected. "East Quadrant clear, sir!" she yells, the way she's supposed to. Belt it out, pretend you're speaking to the cheap seats. Good working with Ursula, she gets it.

Ash is south; she has my six. Nothing but dunes there either. "South Quadrant clear." She doesn't add the sir, never adds the sir. I never minded, it wasn't an issue. The rule about adding sir went out a long time ago, now it's just tradition. Now it's just habit. It's not something to get yourself bunched up over.

Rich is west, with his gun out so fast I have to wonder if it was really holstered. Was he that quick on the draw? Can you look back in his file for me? Damn, he was quick. That is a quick draw. Maybe he did have it holstered. I wouldn't have bet on that even if I was betting with *your* money. Impressive. Damn impressive. Wouldn't have thought it. Would have thought he was just nervous on the trigger. "West Quadrant clear, sir," he says, but he just kind of says it. He doesn't broadcast it like Ursula does, you know? You can barely hear it above the wind. It's fine, I hear it and it's fine. I'm tempted to make him repeat it but I don't. Nobody wants to start an Away Mission on that kind of footing. But if we'd been anywhere other than the desert? Hell, if the wind had just been picked up a little? I wouldn't have been able to hear that call.

I'm just saying.

I take out the transponder and watch it as it counts down from thirty. Standard Operating Procedure. We have thirty seconds to call for the materialization to be reversed, otherwise it can't be reversed. Thirty seconds to let command know if the four quadrants aren't clear, if our intel was wrong, if we've been fubar'd. Thirty seconds to pull us back out because after that you'll never line up the beam right again, the rotation will have taken you too far out of step. You can send us to a place no problem, because you can control the variables. You can't beam us back, not after thirty seconds.

I watch the transponder count down from thirty, red lights flickering around its perimeter until it's down to one and the whole thing turns green. The lights fade, yellow ones turn on in its middle. It's done its job, it'll never reverse a materialization again. Now it's just a call button to bring down transport.

I step back into the middle of the circle we're making and put it down in the sand. SOP is to bury it, but there's no need to bury it on Outpost Toth. Wind and sand and salt will do that for us. SOP is to bury it until all you can see is the lights, as they'll get brighter as it gets covered. Not bright enough to attract lookie-loos, only bright enough that you'll see it if you know what you're looking for. It's that proper shade of yellow that you'll mistake it for sunlight if you don't know what you're looking for. Marigold, I think it's called. Marigold.

We can't take it with us because it calls the transport ship to come take us home, and on some planets there's no way to tell if the site is clear of enemies until you get there, planets like Outpost Toth, where the wind can make a blanket of salt over the sky that blocks everything out of sensors. One too many times the enemy got a hold of the call buttons from an Away Mission, called down transport and ambushed them. They didn't even see it coming, couldn't. So now SOP was to leave it at the materialization point. It made it so we had to get back to get extracted, but that was that. That's the job.

We're twenty units out of the target, I say. I point north, along my quadrant. Check my instruments, confirm it's actually east. Tell the crew, that's east. It's east not because the instrument says it is, but because I say it is. That's the only way this works.

On Outpost Toth, there's an Outpost named Toth. That seems contradictory, but the planet was named after the outpost. When you go on vacation and you say the name of the resort instead of the country, nobody corrects you. Everyone knows what you mean. After long enough, people might think the name of the resort is the name of a country, if they didn't know better. Didn't study their geography. So eventually that unnamed planet that housed Outpost Toth became Outpost Toth, and everyone just kind of accepted it. Not even sure which faction came up with the name, if we're being honest.

And just so we're clear, I know Toth isn't a planet. Not in the strictest sense. It has atmosphere, but not a lot of the other things that the Eon Science Council needs to register something as a planet, and I get that. I don't care what you call it, a planetoid, an asteroid, a space rock. I don't care. It's Outpost Toth, that's all that matters to me. I just don't want some whiny well-actually reading this report in fifty years time after the war is over and thinking that I didn't know Toth wasn't a planet. I know; it's just easier that way. Bullshit.

We've gotten word that the Alterians have a new outpost, I tell them. We don't discuss the mission before we materialize, more SOP. Too many times an injury has forced someone to bow out at the last minute. That's how spies used to get intel out to the Alterians: they'd sign up for Away Missions and get the mission briefs and then take ill. Back in the day, they'd just claim to be sick. When data got out and the medics started checking, they'd take capsules to make themselves sick. When the docs started checking for that, they'd shoot themselves in the damn foot during training, claim it was friendly fire. Damn Alterians will do anything, I swear. Anything. So eventually SOP became for the Quadrant not to know about the mission brief before you went down, above and beyond the critical intel. Only the Quadrant leader knew, and he told them when they materialized and confirmed they didn't require immediate extraction. Only I knew.

And now I was telling them. The Alterians have a new outpost on Toth, and we're twenty units out from it. They're using it to house resources between raids, to refuel ships and men. It's not a colony, it's a gas stop, and they've established it outside taken space. It's not in Alterian space or Eon space, or even in disputed territory. It's at the very edge of the void, the cleavage between our two empires on the outer rim. The furthest something can be out and have us still care about it; any further than that and it was all just inky black. Any further out and stars were still just stars, not suns that planets revolved around. Any further and anything beyond it was still just sky, undiscovered and unmolested.

You look up into that Outpost Toth sky at night, and you know how the old days must have felt. Before we could look up into the night and not just name the stars, but name the friends you had that came from them. Name the battles you fought there, and who won. Curse the spark that gave you light from your enemy.

Outpost Toth was untaken ground. Nobody took it because nobody wanted it. The outpost the planet had been named after had been abandoned for decades and a ghost town. It was five units west. We were heading twenty units east. It was a shiny new refuel station that made it so that the Alterians didn't have to retreat so far when they retreated. They could get close enough to listen to transmissions, I told the Quadrant, close enough to attack supply lines before they got a chance to sound off an alert. Then they could slither back, right to here. Close by. Close enough to attach Eon territory and also close enough to retreat back to Alterian territory.

The mission was to flush them out. Take the tech, take the people, take the resources. Trade the people back in exchange for some of our people the Alterians had. Hostage exchange was always a smart move if you could negotiate it. We had three people in an Alterian prison right now, pretending they'd been captured when really they were sent in to gather intel from the inside. We swap them out for real prisoners and we could collect that intel. But the important thing was: this was not a kill mission. Nobody was supposed to get hurt, if all things went right. We were not expecting military combatants; we were expecting the pimply-faced new recruits that manned the refuel stations: gas boys, cooks, maybe some companionship-salespeople. The mission was to take the resources, take the tech, take the people, and send a clear message: this is not Alterian territory. Attempting to expand into here will be met with aggression, so stay in your lane.

Nobody was supposed to get hurt.

2

27/30 14 3202 OEH

Twenty units outside the suspected area was optimistic. It was twenty units 'as the crow flies,' not as reality dictated. Three of them — Carter, Ursula, and Rich — could all run a four minute mile under normal circumstances, but Outpost Toth was not normal circumstances. It had been deemed uninhabitable by all four empires in the galaxy, and it wasn't just the heat or the salt that made it so. The terrain made land missions nearly impossible. Dunes stretched up and up on steep slopes, then too quickly down, meaning that once an ascent was surmounted a troupe then had to find a way down the other side. This typically meant having to go far aside the twenty-unit estimate, adding three, six, even nine units to an estimate.

Carter was not one to allow that, and it was one of the reasons his commands always returned on time. Which in turn was one of the reasons he'd made captain to begin with. He didn't go around, he didn't find alternative routes. If the target was twenty units away *as the crow flew*, then they would travel in as straight a line as the crow flew as possible. There was only so much hustle that could get you over a steep embankment in average time, there was no doing anything about those delays, but he would not go around.

Carter took water from his thermos until the circle of lights on the side stopped cycling and flashed at him, beeping at him to stop. It kept track of how long the mission should take, and how much water each team member had. It beeped when someone was about to take too much water and go over their limit for what this stage of the journey dictated was rationed. On other planets, a small silent motor in its base would dehumidify, draw moisture from the air and use it to refill its reservoir — not on Outpost Toth. He could spend his whole allotted mission time waiting for it to fill but one drop in this climate, and all the water in the bottle would get was more salinated.

He wiped the excess moisture from his dry lips with a calloused hand, then brought it to his mouth as sucked it from the pool of his palm. Nothing wasted, not a drop. Not in a salt desert.

Ursula trotted, stepping out of file to catch up to him and stride up alongside him. "So this is a no kill mission?" she said, eyes forward. She spoke as though they had been in conversation just moments before, none of the idle chit-chat and small talk that previewed the main point of normal conversation. That was for people with time to waste, who lolled about waiting for trains. People with time to kill. She had never been good at small talk, and didn't consider it a failing.

Carter turned and cocked an eyebrow at her. He thought he caught the ghost of a grin playing alongside the side of her face that faced him, but it was gone by the time she was out of his peripheral vision. It was likely his imagination anyway. He had done a tour with Ursula before, and wouldn't have considered a wry smile to be in her character. Not having character would be all that was be in her character, by his experience, although he'd seen her off duty several times and knew that that was not the case. She had the same attitude as he in that function, and he appreciated it. Personality was a switch, and as much as possible, that switch was off when one was on the job. You weren't here to be you, you weren't here to be an individual. There was a reason the government called in 'Boots on the Ground' and not 'Men on the Ground'; it was to remind you that you weren't a person when you were here. You were a tool, as much as the rifle they both held, and they were both fine with that distinction. It was when you chafed up against it that there was a problem, and there was no problem here.

He looked at her. Her jaw was set, lower lip out as though it were her version of attention. Her hair was close-cropped in a way they didn't make you do anymore, but she did. Long hair was something that could be grabbed in close-proximity combat, and she looked built for combat. The close-cropped hair made her brow look thicker than it was, made her eyebrows pop. She looked like she was in command. Any room she was in, she looked like she was in command.

"This is a no-kill mission," Carter reiterated, after getting the measure of her.

She threw a glance back behind her, at Rich and Ash. They were far behind, also out of formation. Talking. Instead of marching single-file they had grouped into two-by-two, and that was fine.

If Carter had thought about it, he would have given that order when they'd set out, but doing so now would seem passive-aggressive. It was best to just let it be. Behavior you allow is the same as behavior you command, he reminded himself.

"It doesn't look like we have the means for a capture not kill back there," she said, back to eyes forward so that they couldn't see her lips move. "You expect the two of them to march over heavy terrain with hostages in tow?"

"Rich could handle it fine. I've done tours with him." Carter left Ash out of his defense of Ursula's remarks, and that exclusion was telling. He glowered, struggling to find something to say. "And Ash can keep them doped up and compliant. Med techs aren't just SOP in case we get hurt, they're to keep the enemy calm."

"Depends on how many enemies there are, doesn't it?" Ursula shot back, chuckling. She'd heard the hesitation in Carter's voice, the gap between his assertion that Rich was capable and that Ash was, and took it as confirmation. All the confirmation she needed. "If we go back with ten hostiles? Sure. Maybe. It's still a rough hike with hostiles back over this terrain." She avoided a mound of salt that had calloused into something with the density of a stone that would have tripped her, as if illustrating her point. "But what if there's fifteen Alts there, Carter? Hell, what if there's *fifty*?"

Despite himself, Carter looked back. He tried to never look back, not unless it was to give an order. To annunciate his words. The mission was forward, face it. *Face forward.* But he looked back at Ash and Rich. Ash was covered in a thick layer of sweat, the heat of the march and her pack getting to her. She tried to keep her brow dry but it was there under the arms. Her cheeks were puffed and flushed, veins visible through them. Rich stood next to her, the picture of a soldier. But he was back with her, not up with them. Some soldiers went to the front, while some stayed behind and went by the speed of the slowest member. "If there's fifty, there's a problem," Carter admitted.

"If there's fifty, there's a problem," Ursula reiterated, agreeing. She let that linger, for a moment. "If there's ten, we take them back. Ten or less, we take them back with us. Round them up, take them back, just like the mission brief said. Come back with the transport ship ASAP and get the resources we can, raze the structures to the ground. Make the message clear, this place isn't a foothold."

Carter nodded. That had indeed been the mission he'd laid out for them, if not in those words. "Yeah, ten or less that's fine."

There was desert before them, lots of it. It stretched on for what seemed like forever in all directions. Dunes made differences, but the dunes moved. The dunes moved faster than you would think land masses that size could, like they were alive. Because they weren't solid masses, like the mountains back on the Eppika. The dunes were just piles of sand and salt, and the stiff breeze drifting along their surface brought it with them. The terrain moved, subtly but devastatingly. Without the sensors, without the compass, it would be easy to track movement based on a landmark only to have that landmark shift and alter, or perhaps disappear entirely.

The drifting made camping dangerous, too. This was something he knew but wasn't saying, didn't know if Ursula had considered it as well. Camping in terrain that moved with the wind was more dangerous than losing one's direction: camping in the shade of a mountain dune might start the night fine but end the night with that dune atop you. Enough of its weight would be on you to pin you before you noticed. Like a frog sitting in a boiling pot as long as the temperature was raised slowly enough, you would lie there asleep as one grain at a time was added, until it was too late. And no search party would find you, not until the dunes decided to reveal your salt grave naturally.

"Any more than that, it's a *problem*," Ursula stressed. She kept her voice down. "Any more than ten, this becomes a kill mission, not a capture."

Carter furrowed his brow. He thought for a moment. "It's the type of mission I say it is as command," he said, finally.

Ursula straightened, and nodded. "Yes, sir."

He increased his pace, got out in front of her. When he was regulation distance away, he turned back, reminded all three of them that the order was single-file. Rich and Ash separated, with Rich taking up the rear.

They continued forward. Far in the distance, square shapes that would never have been made by drifting sands were becoming visible on the horizon.

3

**Mission Briefing Log, Captain Hux Carter,
2/30 15 3202 OEH**

We get there after what seems like forever. Okay? Forever. Longest twenty units of my life. Desert travel is slow travel under the best of circumstances, but Toth does everything in its power to let you know it doesn't want you there. That soil prevents anything from growing and it attacks anyone who tries to come there. My thermos denied me drink ten more times before we arrived, and at the end I found myself counting off the second until it would give me more. That terrain, it just saps the moisture from you. By the end you find yourself thinking, if the damn Alts want this beach, they can have it.

That's not the mission, though.

We make it to the Outpost and it's right where the intel said it would be, and we huddle behind a mound of sand not half a click from it. We should have never been able to get that close, should have been a red flag. But then you think back to previous missions, and how sloppy the Alts can be from time to time, and you think you just got lucky. Caught them between shifts, you know?

My team? My team are great. Not a word out of them, not a complaint. They didn't question orders. We were late getting to the Outpost, but they were steady, no one fell behind, no one was left behind. They moved as a unit, the way they should. You'd have been proud. If you have a brain in your head, you'll be proud. No, I do want that on the record. You can call it good leadership or good breeding or good training or whatever you want, but they stayed in formation that whole trek. Even the medic, Ash. If we were late getting to the Outpost, it's because the intel never accounts for the terrain, you got me? Mark that down.

We get to the Outpost and we huddle behind a dune and shield our eyes from the sand that's whipping up off it. Squint through goggles and look through binoculars and watch where the light is coming from because you don't want to be seen. If the sun is in front of you, it might reflect off the lens and then it's like a spotlight, this twinkle on the very top of a hill that can't be anything but a soldier, and then that's the game given away. But the longer we're looking, the more lax we get, and by the end I swear Ursula *stood up* with her binoculars so that she could get the extra few feet needed to see over a ridge, and I didn't say anything.

I didn't say anything because there's wasn't anybody there. Not a trader, not a ship-man, not a comfort-girl. Nothing we'd been told to expect, not a damn thing. The Outpost was there, and it had been cared for, we noted that. It was surrounded by dunes in a way that wasn't natural, in a way you had to fight to maintain. There were divots in the sand around the foundations of the buildings where there had been mechanisms on to keep the sand turning, keep the drifts at bay, but they were off now. Even if they'd been on, they wouldn't have been enough to keep the dunes from flooding their architecture and tech by themselves. They'd *have* to have had people out there, pushing it back. Stopping it from drifting it, the way snow finds its way into valleys and fills them up.

So they had to have been there. The intel wasn't *that* far off.

But there was not a sign of them. No lights on in places where there should have been lights on, even in the day. No motion in doorways or windows, no matter how long we looked. And there were drifts starting to build in the corners of the doorframes, not much, but enough to show they hadn't been opened in some time. They gathered in such a way that opening the door would have pushed them in, would have scattered them along the ground. Would have gotten them... everywhere. You'd be finding sand in the corners of the hall for weeks, tasting salt in the air for hours. That was what Ursula had stood up to see, the one door we couldn't get eyes on from our vantage point. That was the last nail in the coffin – no doors had been opened in this place for days.

We came to the only conclusion we could: the place had been abandoned.

No structural damage, no sign that the Caps or Kryos had been there. No scorch marks, no water damage. No signs of energy discharge. None of the sand had been turned to glass, nor had it been turned to mud or quicksand. No blood, no stains, no sign of defense. The doors were closed tight, none left open. Nothing left to the elements suddenly and without care. There were no Alts on the Outpost anymore, and there was no evidence to suggest that another faction had taken them by force or eliminated them. All that was left was that they'd left. That the post had been again abandoned.

Rich still floated it, still floated that it was the Capulets, but it wasn't. He'd never been on tour against the Caps, but I had. It didn't go like this, it never did. If the Caps had taken this place, there wouldn't be buildings left, they'd have burned the whole thing to the ground. There'd be nothing left but a sheet of glass for a day or so, and then the dunes would move in and there wouldn't be even that. Ssshik. Gone.

No, it was abandoned, which at the time had us looking at each other and wondering what to do next. It also had us wondering: why? Had the intel been bad? Well, no. Because they'd been here recently. Really, *really* recently. Alright, so the next obvious question: had they been warned? Was there a mole on our side, a spy that had sent word to the Alts to send word to the Outpost to clear the high-heaven out of there? Maybe. *Maybe.* And if that was the train of thought, who was that traitor? Was it someone back on the ship, someone in comms... or was it someone here, actually on the Away Mission with the rest of us?

Had us looking at each other sideways, that's for damn sure.

But that was speculation, and that wasn't for us to do. We'd do the mission, file the report, alert of any suspicions and let the brass sort it out. That was how it was done, by the book, SOP. All four of us knew it, even if one of us was turncoat. If that person had been there, they'd have known they were safe until they got back to ship, and it was looked into. There were no drumhead trials, not in our empire.

So the question, then, was: what do we do *now*? The mission can't be completed as ordered. There's no one to take, nothing to sack. It's all ether. There was some debate about this. Ursula and Ash, they both thought that the mission was over. That the situation was far enough outside the parameters that we should turn back to the beacon and call ourselves home, right then and there. That if the mission isn't able to be completed as ordered, we go back and get new orders.

Rich and I, we thought different. Part of the mission was fubar, that was undeniable. But there might still be resources there that we could bring back, and now it'd be easier. We could bring what we could and pile up the rest and raze the buildings to the ground, bring the dropship around after it picked us up to get the reminder of the supplies. One third of the mission had been failed by circumstances outside our control, but there was still the other two. And 66% is a pass in my world, that's a salvage.

Still, once debate is rendered, I can't fall back on orders. We were at a 50/50 split and 50/50 splits go to the defensive strategy. Been that way close on ninety years, isn't going to stop now. And yeah, I could question which strategy was really the defensive one, as we thought neither involved engaging the enemy... but I'd have had a hard time making the case that going back to the drop point wasn't the most defensive idea.

So if I couldn't win the 50/50 split, I had to stop the split.

If the Alts left in a hurry, I said, they might have left all their resources behind. It might have been a "whatever is on your backs only" situation. There'd be water there, and grain. Building materials. Maybe even tech we hadn't seized yet. Seeds. The Alts, they were big on seeds, and it was after their growing season. But more than that, if they'd left in such a hurry that they hadn't levelled the Outpost... in such a hurry that maybe they hadn't taken their supplies... then *maybe* they'd left in such a hurry that they hadn't erased their records banks, too. There could be intel in there on closed-circuit off-network computers, just waiting for us to gobble it up. Hell, if they *had* been warned ahead of time, there might be evidence of that transmission still on file. We might be able to get at who the mole was, but we'd have to do it before they got back and erased it. That wasn't something they'd want lying around.

That was the argument that did it for Ursula. The idea that there was a traitor and that the clues as to who were in that outpost, I'm surprised she didn't stand up and storm the beach right then and there. She was in, one hundred percent. And suddenly it wasn't a 50/50 split anymore, it was 75/25 and Ash stood alone, outvoted. The tie was broken without the need to go with the most defensive strat, and now that that vote had been settled, command structure was back into play. We knew what we were doing, and now it was up to me to dictate how we were going to do it.

The whole thing, that whole choice, was above board and by the books. I know it led to everything that came after, but you can't fault me on the procedure. You can fault me on a lot of things, but not on the procedure.

It was SOP.

4

27/30 14 3202 OEH

The door to the outpost opened with a hiss that wasn't pneumatic, and stale air rushed out at them, joining the dense heat of the Toth atmosphere. Ursula and Carter stepped back with their weapons raised. Thick dust wafted out at them, pluming into the desert air, and slowly dissipating.

Ursula primed her weapon then dialed it back to its lowest ebb via the notch on its side. She didn't need to look at the numbers to know when she'd gotten it to where she wanted it to be. She knew the click of it, knew the way it felt beneath her fingers. It *tick tick tonk*-ed into place and she raised it into the cloudy dark of the hallway and let out a single burst from her chamber.

A pulse of air shot out from the tip, accompanied by the dull hum of charged ions. A cascading ripple went out through the air and the dust pushed back, some of it pushing out and to the sides of the doorway and mushrooming, most of it travelling back inside. The pulse went in through the doorway, pushing the dust in and away from them.

Carter looked at her, eyebrow cocked slightly. He hadn't given the order to fire, but given another second's hesitation he would have done it himself. He couldn't fault her for doing what he would have done anyway, not as far as he was concerned.

They waited for a response from within the chamber, the only sound on the air the *tonk tick tick* of Ursula bringing her weapon back up to a charge that could do real damage to a person. They waited, that rectangle of pure dark looming at them.

"Clear," Carter said after a moment. He waved them forward with two fingers but stepped forward himself, the shadow of the outpost enveloping him. The light on the end of his weapon came on, shining down the darkened hallway until it caught the dust that had been pushed to the far end by Ursula's pulse, looming there like a shifting, moving wall. Like a living wall.

Ursula thumbed her pulse charge back down to minimum, but Carter raised a hand. She turned to him, eyebrow raised.

"Don't."

She looked at him questioningly.

"We might need the charge."

There was a pause. Carter didn't like the pause. This was a clear order and should have resulted in a clear response. The pause was Ursula debating with herself as to whether or not she'd follow it, and that was bad. She did follow it, the *tink* of the gauge lowering back down following, but that pause was almost more worrisome than open insubordination. Insubordination could be countered and dealt with. A pause, in the heat of a fire fight, could get people killed. Given the choice, Carter would have rathered decisive insubordination than indecisive mulling.

At first when they entered the bunker there was the thrill of shade. Their skin relaxed, having held itself as tight as leather under the constant assault of the desert sun for hours. For a moment the cool was good, but only a moment. On their next breath in they learned how hot the air was, baked thick in the metal tube of the unventilated metal case for god only knew how long.

"I don't like this," Ash said finally, swallowing. She paused for response, there was none. "Something's not right here."

"No tracks in the dust," Ursula said, shining the light on the end of her weapon down at the floor. She was right, there weren't any tracks in the dust and sand on the floor, save for the ones they were making. The floor ahead of them was laid thick with it, a gauze over the world that would tell on their presence with but the slightest provocation. "It's been a while since they were through here."

"Sir?" Rich asked, bringing up the rear.

Carter turned back to him from the front of the line, craning his head to see around the others.

Rich was standing by the door still, just within it. His face was alight with contrast, the bright from the sun outside bathing his left side and making it stark and white in comparison to the deep black shadow of the other. His hand was over the push-to for the door, hovering over it.

Carter frowned at him.

"It's Standard OP."

Reluctantly, Carter nodded. With enough weight behind it to fight the sand that was already gathering, Rich notched the door out of its latch and pulled it shut behind them. It bathed them in yet more dark, the only light now coming from the lights on the ends of their weapons. Those beams were harsh and white, stretching out like cones but leaving everything to either side all the more dark by comparison. In such a confined space, it was genuinely hard not to flash the light along someone's eyes and give them several seconds of blindness. It might have been better to have left the door open, let some of the natural light flow in, but it was Standard Operating Procedure that when entering a potentially hostile territory, you plug up behind yourself if at all possible. There was less chance of being bottle-necked from both sides then, having enemies come at you from both directions.

The door slid along the gutters it was in and then latched into place with a loud *ka-rumph*. It echoed down through the corridor like Ursula's pulse before it, and they heard it get lighter and lighter as it went and eventually died in the stale air.

The four of them listened to that sound slowly fade, as if they were waiting for it to awaken another. For the sound itself to stir something up, make it live. Make it hot. The air was thick, and made the echo live for what seemed like forever. It echoed not just off the walls but off the air.

"Let's go," Carter said. He forced assurance into his voice, made it an order by tone alone.

They crept along the corner one foot at a time. There were no doors along it, just a long tube of corrugated steel that led to the main artery of the structure. It was longer than it had looked from the outside. Outside, the hall had only pushed out from the building proper by ten feet, enough to catch sand before it made its way into the building. Inside, it went on for forty or fifty. It was hard to tell in the dark. Still, it meant that after ten feet there was buildings on the other sides of the walls they walked through. There were rooms there, even if there was no doorway through which to enter them. Why would it be designed that way, each of them wondered, but neither said aloud. What could be in those rooms that you wouldn't want an entrance into this hall, even if that entrance were never used? Were they crew quarters, maybe?

From the outside this main building had looked like four bulbs, like a balloon that had been pressed down by criss-crossing string until it plumped up to stretch around it. Those strings were the halls, bisecting the four bulbs but not going all the way through them. The hall they were on would take them near the centre of the building, but would not take them all the way through and would not reveal any rooms to them along the way. From that choke point where the hallway ended, hallways branched out in a long cloverleaf curve that took you into either side of the bulge, and from there into sections and sub-sections. Those on the team that had seen Alterian architecture before were familiar with the design. The bulbs diffused with rain and sun, making useful in many different terrains. It was a design and schematic they could take with them when going into a planet blind and still trust that it would not let them down.

Carter stopped at every junction where a plate of steel was bolted to another, placing his palm flat against it.

"What're you doing?" Ursula whispered. Her voice was almost a hiss.

"Feeling for vibrations," Carter said back, the same. "Anyone walking or talking in the rooms that run parallel to these. Anything at all. A radio on, an audiobook left on auto-play. A pet left unattended. Anything that might make a noise. Anything." He paused. Closed his eyes. After a moment he took his hand away again and moved on.

"Anything?"

"Nothing."

They reached the wall of dust that Ursula had pushed back, which had already dissipated and become just a part of the atmosphere. She tapped her thumb against her weapon and debating asking if she could push it back again but didn't. Each of them took a breath before continuing through it, even though they knew it was fruitless. It was everywhere, and soon they'd be so accustomed to it they'd only even know it was still there by their dry eyes. They might not even put the two together.

They reached the end of the hallway, and it spun out to the left and the right in a curved arch, making it impossible to see more than twenty feet along either. But there were rooms. The doors were closed but they were there, the rooms that had stood on the other side of the wall Carter had been listening into, now within sight.

He motioned them left, and they went left.

Carter and Rich kept their beams forward, Ash behind. She stole a glance back every five steps, making sure that there was nothing behind them. As unlikely as it was, it was better to be safe. Ursula swept her beam along the floor in front of them. "Still no tracks," she said, calling attention to the layer of dust on the floor that existed until they disturbed it. There were dent and divots, imperfections where the dust had possibly collapsed into a bend in the steel floor, but no footprints or scuffs. She brought her beam to the lower edge of the first door they were encroaching upon. There was dust gathered there into miniature versions of the dunes they'd encountered outside. Dust and sand. "The door hasn't been opened."

Carter gripped the indented handle of the door and gave it a quick tug, steel screeching. The beams from the other three went in around him, haloing him and letting him see while his hands worked. "Now it has been," he said, resolutely.

The room was large, a suite. It had rounded corners, large rectangles that smoothed off, but there were two of them. A line of bolts along the centre marked the place where a wall had been on the plans and either never installed or later removed to make two rooms into one. There was a door in the other section as well, but any thought that perhaps *that* had been the door that was used was rendered inert when their beams found the dresser parked in front of it. The door they'd entered was the door that had been in use, and it hadn't been for some time.

The side of the room they were on had been made into a living area. Three couches faced each other, a rectangular table between them. There were marks in the table where drinks had been laid and sweated their contents into the metal, rusting a ring into them over time. There were two bookshelves wedged together into the corner, and Carter found himself gravitating towards them even as he shone his beam from end to end. There was a kitchenette that Ash made her way to, pans on the stove.

Carter took a sweep of the room with his light again, then shouldered the weapon. The light aimed up at the ceiling now, diffusing the light back down upon him. He reached up and took a book from the bookshelf. It had a drawing of a man with stark white hair in a window on its spine, and a larger portrait of him in an action shot on the front cover. The binding of the book was odd, the pages bound on the left. It gave the impression that it was meant to be read back-to-front from what Carter had grown up with, but it was impossible to tell for sure, for when he opened the pages to flick through, he encountered a language – and indeed, an alphabet – foreign to him.

He picked up another book, this one a hardcover with italic font and the silhouette of a sparrow against a maroon backdrop. Alterian hardcovers were made of stone, dry slate, and this one was no different. He picked it up and thumbed through it as well, finding characters and fonts as foreign to him as hieroglyphs, then tossing the book down onto the couch and letting up a plume of dust.

"Anything of interest?" Ursula asked.

"They're all in Alterian," Carter grumbled.

Rich snorted. "I mean... yeah. What'd you think they'd be in? You think they sit around on their home world, speaking Common? Get real."

Carter frowned. He picked up a third book with a picture of a blue shark on the cover heading towards a glowing orange title in a thick, impactful font. "I can speak Alterian. I can usually *read* Alterian. This dialect is strange, though. It's not what we usually see from them." He paused. "I don't even recognize the font." He held it up so that Rich could see. "These loopy letters, the ones that come way down to the next line, you ever see anything like that from them before?"

Rich leaned in, squinted. Then shook his head in confirmation.

It was true, Alterian fonts and letters tended to never go above or below the base-lines of their line, forming neither Ascenders or Descenders. They'd also never, to either Rich or Carter's recollection, ever employed capital letters or lower case letters. Letters in most Alterian fonts tended to have straight lines on the left and right sides, with all the differences in their alphabet existing between those two lines. "Within the box," Carter had heard it explained, once. Some of these letters stretched beyond the confines of their boxes. A scattered letter pushed down, descended into the line below. But it was like the typographer wasn't familiar with such an action, the lower portions of the letters interrupting the letters on the next line down. Descenders on the bottom line were cut off by the end of the page. Their printers weren't equipped for such extravagancies.

"Kind of wish we'd brought an anthropologist with us," Carter said. He jammed the book into his breast pocket, curling the spine to make it fit. "But that's not what the mission is." He turned to Ursula. "Anything?"

"Nothing."

"I have something," Ash called out, without looking away from what they had. They were looking at the kitchenette, staring at it. Everyone turned to her. She was staring at the stovetop, the five burners atop the counter space. There was no oven. The other three regarded her, waiting for her to elaborate. When she turned to look at them it was with surprise, as if she thought she wouldn't have had to explain. "The pilot light is on."

Carter stepped forward and knelt down, motioning for Ursula and Rich to stop shining their lights towards it. Ursula lowered hers, Rich switched his to off mode. Sure enough, the neon blue glow of the pilot shone out from underneath the burners. Now that everyone was still and quiet, he could even hear its faint static brown noise hum. It flickered when it caught dust in the air, igniting it. "Son of a bitch."

"They left in a hurry," Ash elaborated.

Carter nodded, standing. "Let's check the other rooms."

***

The second room they entered, and the next several, were single-size units half the size of what the first's had been. Had that person been a commanding officer? Some sort of base Residence Advisor? They had theories but no answers. There had been a large music collection in the second room, a wall filled with stuffed animals that were coloured and arranged by colour in the same order that light refracted. It looked meticulous, like something treasured. Rich had felt almost bad disturbing them to take a look, like he was disrupting a tomb. The animals had been cared for: preened and loved but now covered in the same thick layer of dust that covered everything else.

The third room had been a comfort girl's quarters. There were drapes along the walls and ceilings, disguising the metal and rivets from view, letting clients forget where they were. Let them be somewhere else, if only for a short time. Those self-same translucent curtains hung to make walls in the quarters, dividing it and making the small space into multiple spaces through careful use of space. There was a wardrobe hidden in the back behind a large bed that could have accompanied all four of them if they had needed, and after the hike across the Toth desert it occurred to each of them in kind but was not vocalized. The wardrobe was hidden behind a thick curtain, not translucent like the rest, giving the illusion of a wall. There were many dresses made of many colours, and a shelf above of wigs. The wigs seemed to be above the dresses whose colour would best compliment them.

The floor of the comfort-girl's quarters was soil. Not sand from the outside, but soil that had been brought it and hydrated and kept cool beneath the feet. There was greenery growing up from it in places, and its presence gave the room a musty, humid smell. It was there to give the illusion of the room having no floor, like the rooms on the Alterian homeworld.

Comfort was more than just what a human could provide, at times.

Carter ran his hands through the soil, letting it push between his fingers. There was moisture there still, but it hadn't been maintained. He took a deep breath and let out a long, mournful sigh that he hoped none of the others heard. "Toss the place."

Ash whipped her head towards him, so fast that her hair snapped around. "What? Why?"

Even as Ash questioned the order, Ursula was already breaking food jars and tossing out cutlery drawers, pulling them out by their handles and emptying them onto the soil floor.

Carter watched her go and watched Rich start, even as Ash stood and waited for her answer. "They left in a hurry," he said. "They left books. Left the pilot light on. Left keepsakes. Left things you wouldn't leave even if you were in a damn hurry." He paused. "I want to see what else they left. I want to know how much of a hurry they were in. Because there's one thing a comfort girl will never leave behind."

Ash nodded slowly but did not get to the work. She turned and watched the others hop to it with systematic efficiency.

Rich ran the edge of a blade along one of the tasselled cushions on the couch. Stuffing pushed out through the gap as though it had been waiting to do so, spring-loaded. He pulled out that which did not come naturally, then did the same to two others. On the fourth the stuffing did not splay out, and when he shoved his hand inside it, it connected with something solid. He tipped the cushion upside down and turned it inside out, sending a cascade of paper credits raining down onto the couch.

"They left in a damn hurry," Ursula laughed, stopping her efforts even though the order to do so had not yet been given. "Left so fast she didn't even get her credits stash."

Carter pursed his lips, set his jaw. "They didn't leave in a hurry," he said. "They didn't leave at all."

***

The fourth room had been a large, shared kitchen. Properly equipped, not the small kitchenettes that made do in each apartment. All the appliances here were carved from stone, the tables and chairs as well. The main table in the centre of the room and the chairs around it had been carved from a single piece, the chairs immoveable in their distance from the table. Carter wouldn't have been able to sit at it: his legs would have bunched, his knees smacked against the bottom of the table.

The pilot lights had been left on here, too. Perishable food had been spoiled and left to rot. Non-perishable food had been left, even that which had been in containers designed to be taken in a hurry.

The next two rooms were public washrooms. If they had ever been assigned by gender, they weren't now. The next three were more quarters, more of the same. Items left that you wouldn't think would be left, no matter the rush. Covered in dust. Items that were clearly the prized possession of the person who had had them — you're going to go live on an outpost in the middle of nowhere, and you get to take one thing that reminds you of home. That thing then becomes more prized for its singular capacity to remind you of where you came from in this strange place. Those are the items you always know where they are in your home. The items that, if there were a fire, you would put yourself at risk to save.

The room after that was a public shop. It didn't have a door like the rest, just a gate that went across when it was closed. It had been left open, and the food inside was on the floor, scattered. Fridges were knocked over. Holes had been made in the shelves. Of all the rooms thus far, it looked the most disturbed.

There were credits left in the cash register, and more in the safe below it. It had taken Rich a good ten minutes to crack its code. More than Alterian credits were inside, Eon dollars were there as well. Capulet rubies. Even sore raw ore that must have been bartered in lieu of cash. No matter what form it was in, there was money left behind. A lot of it.

There were three more personal quarters that were all the same. Ash, Rich, and Ursula tossed them lightly, less and less with each successive room. With each they needed to look less and less hard for evidence of what they were finding. With each, the signs of a departure so rushed that it ceased to be evidence of a departure at all became apparent.

In each room, Carter watched them work for a moment before turning the light from his weapon along the sides of the room, along the walls, along the rivets that connected the floor to the walls like baseboards. He scanned these until his people said they were done, sometimes finding something worth confiscating — a key, a scrap of paper that might be a passcode, a weapon — before calling the room clear. And after each announcement Carter would do one last sweep of the light then announce they were heading to the next.

In the next room, the fourth after the storefront, they tossed the room as Carter inspected the base of the walls, but he didn't make it far. He made it three feet past the doorframe and stopped, waited for Ursula to finish and announce the all-clear. "Nothing," she said.

"Something," he refuted.

The other three joined him.

His light had found a splotch on the bottom of the wall, a smear that had had dust stick to it even more than most, but was unmistakably blood. The smear trailed downward and out, towards the door. There were divots in the sand and dust there, places where further drops had fallen and made indents on the deposits, or tuck and accumulated more.

Ursula cursed the name of her creator.

"Come on," Carter said, following the droplet pattern back outside the room. The three followed, lights on, with Ash bringing up the rear, light facing behind. There was urgency to their step now, and they bypassed room upon room, following not the logic of the building but the path of blood they'd found. It was joined by another from further ahead on the hallway and branched down an alternate hall. It bent and volleyed three more times before stopping in front of a thick door.

There was a single Alterian symbol on it, in the language and font that Carter recognized, and knew that it meant COMMUNICATIONS.

The blood had pooled around its gutter, slightly. He swallowed, stepped back, and aimed his weapon at its centre. "Open."

Rich and Ursula both stepped forward, grabbing the indent and pulling the heavy door sharply. It slid with effort, and the stink of dust and decay wafted out at them and made them choke.

The Alterian crew of Outpost Toth was inside, some huddled together on the floor, and some at their stations. Some were near the door and fell forward out into the hall when it opened. They were in many different places and ways, but not one of them was alive.

5

Mission Briefing Log, Captain Hux Carter,
2/30 15 3202 OEH
[Three and a half minutes of silence on the official recording]
Hn? Yeah. Sorry, I was just... back there, for a second.

I won't be describing the bodies. You have the photo logs from the shared drive. There's no reason for me to describe them, and I won't be describing them. ...Yeah, I get that you didn't ask, but I've been to these before. I knew it was coming. I'm getting ahead of it.

I have no love for Alterians, obviously. I've taken down my fair share in combat, no way of knowing how many. That's what war is; there's no sense getting squeamish about it now. Like I said, no love lost for Alterians... but seeing them there, like that, all strewn about? It was messed up. You forget you're on different sides for a second. You forget they're Alterians and for a second you're all just... people. They're just people and there's parts of them everywhere. There's entrails, and I don't know which entrails belonged to which person. You'd have to pick one up and trace it back to the gut, like untangling some giant knot of twine.

...But like I said, I'm not here to talk about that.

We all took our turns throwing up. I want that on the record, not one of us didn't. Maybe Ursula wouldn't have, but you know what it's like. That first person goes and it's a domino effect. Once you smell vomit, it lessens your resiliency to vomit. We all went in the same place, just outside the comms room door. Most of it was water and bile, because we'd been trying to stay hydrated. Fuck, did that ever not help with the hydration. Trying to keep fluids down in Toth climate and now we were retching them up like nobody's business.

Yes, Ash threw up first. But I don't want that on the transcript, okay? You white that out. You black that out or I will lose my goddamn mind at you, do you understand? Do not make me pull rank over some whiteout.

It takes a minute to compose ourselves, but when we do, we get to work. We fall back on habits. I decide, right then and there, that this mission is FUBAR. This is not what we were sent to do, and we need new orders. I'm not ready to go back to the drop point — not yet — but this definitely warrants an update to the brass. So, we're in the communications room, right? If there's anywhere on this god-forsaken rock where we can get a hold of you, it's from there, right? So that becomes the next stage of the mission: use the Alterian comms room to radio back for aid. Hell, there's no Alterians here alive. Bring the dropship right down on top of us.

Because something did this, and I don't fancy a walk back over the desert with it on my heels in the black of night, thank you.

So we decide to figure out the comms units. There's bodies there, some of them slumped over sections of the controls. We try to peek around them but eventually, yeah, we're just moving them. And that's when Ash steps up, bless her. She reminds us that we have to catalog the bodies where they're at if we're going to be moving them. There's pushback from Ursula, but I quash it. Ash is absolutely right, and she's the reason you have photo evidence. So you make sure you know that. You mark that down; you credit her next to every photo you publish. Not credit of the Eon Military, credit Ash. On every one.

We get the photos of the man slumped over the controls first, and when Ash gives me the go-head, I peel him off. And when I say peel, I mean peel. Blood is sticky, it's meant to plug up a wound and stick to the skin. And it gets stickier the more moisture you draw out of it, so in this climate? Yeah, it was like glue. Like he'd been scabbed *onto* the control board he was on. I took him by the shoulders, and I pulled him back and the blood stretched like melted cheese, just this loud squelching sound. Like solidified gelatin.

And yeah, I threw up again. I made it out of the room, made it out to the same spot we'd all tossed before. I don't think it was conscious, but I think we were all trying to only contaminate that one spot. There's gotta be something in the SOP about that, right? "Pick a designated barfing corner?" No? Maybe there should be.

I pull him back and he's ripped from throat to pelvis, and now he's open. It was like his weight against the console and the blood was the only thing holding him together, and when I slid him back onto his chair he came apart. There was one long gash but there were multiple cuts, ripping cuts. Jagged. Nothing like someone experienced with a blade would do. Rending.

I lay him back on his chair and he spills out onto himself, and I leave the room to throw up. It's when I get back that I see he's a Captain. There's a mountain on the breast that's their largest, where their mythological gods lived. I know enough about Alterian military to know that that symbol only goes on the Captain. He was a captain in a military that, I know, does not give out that rank lightly. Alterian Military is not our Military. No offense. The higher ranks, you can't just earn with time or experience. To be Captain is akin to getting a medal of valour for us. Captain is what you give to someone to honour them after a deed, not just time served. There are no Captains in the Alterian Military who haven't seen combat; that doesn't happen there. There are no desk-surfing captains. No armchair captains. If you're a Captain in the Alterian Military, you earned that shit. You saw battle, and you came out the other side.

I say that not to glorify or to imply allegiance with the enemy. I say that so that you understand the type of man I'm describing to you. This was not a man who knew fear well, and yet... when I pulled him back and lay him on his chair, his face was frozen in it. Eyes were so wide you could see into their sockets. Mouth frozen open in a scream, cheeks stretched. He died in terror, this man who had made his living facing down terror and never blinking first, and it was frozen onto his face.

...Can we take a break?

***

Right. So, we get photos of the captain and get him off his post and onto his chair, and after I've composed myself, Rich and I, we start in at the comms. We start trying to translate. The part the captain was on, that was definitely the part we need. All-frequency distress signals, yes. If there's a way we can adjust it so that only y'all on the dropship will hear it, great. If not... I mean, screw it. You're closer. You'll get there first, it'll be fine.

But the blood, the blood has gummed up the works. The captain, he bled a lot. He bled everything he had in him while he was down on that console, and it had nowhere to go but through the cracks in the seal around the buttons and keys. Rich and I, we pull off the front panel and it's all down inside it. Like glue. Red, semi-translucent, sticky glue. It has gotten into everywhere.

While we're making this discovery, Ash is snapping more pictures of the dead. A lot of them have that same slash, she says, but some of them don't. Some of them have these big, oval gashes with rips along the sides, usually in their stomachs. I tell her I can't hear about it, not right then, but to document it. Document everything.

Rich asks me, real quiet, who I think could have done this, then. At the time I was thinking the Caps, that they'd finally gone full religious fervor on us and were bringing down holy terror. But there were no burns, Rich pointed out. Yeah, he was right. No burns, and the whole place was dry. If it was the Caps or the Kryos, they were doing something weird. Something really against how they did things.

We huddle up, figure out what we're doing. Ash and Rich, they want to go, and that's not an unreasonable option. Ursula and I, we're more on the 'figure out what did this, so we have something to report to brass' train, but 50/50 splits go to defense, and I'm on the fence enough that it was almost 75/25 anyway. I'm not crying. But there's a problem, and even as we're talking about it, it's clear.

We can't make it back to the drop point. Not like this. We weren't equipped for this scenario. We were given water and food for a little more than one way, and it was almost gone. Because once we reached the Outpost, either we'd have been killed taking it or we'd have taken it and restocked our supplies from the spoils. Either way, there was no need to weigh us down with enough supplies to go there and back. I look at my water bottle as this point comes up and shake it. It is damn near below twenty percent.

And it dawns on me then that all of the water I drank isn't even in me. A lot of it is in a pile just outside the comms room, along with everyone else's. Just thinking about it makes me thirsty, then and now. There's no way we're making it back over those dunes to the drop point, not like this. Not without supplies, and not without rest. I bring up rest and everyone nods. Nobody had wanted to say it, but there it was. That trek had been hard. The adrenaline of battle would have done us well, but fear saps that. And we could have tented on the way back if that had been the only hurdle...

... but the thing none of us were saying out loud was, none of us wanted to have our only shielding be a tent if whatever came after the Alterians came back again.

So we decided. We didn't need to vote, because the 50/50 split didn't matter. It didn't matter if we were 100% on board to turn tail, circumstances wouldn't have allowed it. Not yet. So that vote was for a later time.

We needed supplies. We needed supplies and we needed rest. So, I broke up the team, sent Ursula and Rich to look for supplies. Look for survivors, too, if there could be any. There were a lot of bodies in the comms room, but not enough to account for the population of the entire outpost, even at its lowest. Not nearly. So we sent Ursula and Rich to look for survivors, and Ash and I stayed at comms to try and piece together what was going on, use it as a secured base, and keep trying to communicate with high command.

And yeah, if I had our time back, we would have just taken our chances on the dunes.

6

27/30 14 3202 OEH

Ursula shone her light down the long corridor that stretched on before she and Rich, adjusting its settings until it penetrated the fog of dust that hung in the air as long as it could. She swallowed, resolute, ran a kerchief over her head and hair, then chanced a glance back at Rich. "Come on."

Rich stood at a perpendicular to her. They formed a letter T with both of their bodies, so that he could easily have his light faced back behind them and still walk forward. Walking like that was slow, a muddled crabwalk, but there was no rush to what they were doing.

They made their way through the hall and reached the first room on the left-hand side. They paced forward until Rich was at it, they opened the door, and Rich swung his light inside. In the same instant he did this, Ursula side-stepped into the same position he'd been in, against the wall, able to slide the light both forward and back with ease.

Rich found the switch and turned it on, lowering his weapon. The walls were painted pink, and badly. The paint was smeared, as though someone were doing it for art instead of for colour. It was splotchy and uneven. There were magazines piled near the bed, the topmost one with a photo of a woman on the cover and Alterian text that Rich couldn't read. On the dresser there were remnants of drug paraphernalia.

He opened the fridge, found the bottled water. Slid it into his pack along with a can of preserves.

"Clear," he said, stepping back out into the hall. As if on cue, Ursula switched back to forward facing and Rich resumed his position side-stepping alongside her. They went at his pace but never had to stop and catch-up. The pace was natural, practiced. She knew how long her strides should be to accommodate him, to the point that it was unconscious.

They did this with three more rooms. Each was the same and none were the same. Each were the same in terms of the result, different in terms of taste. In all but one Rich collected more supply of water and preserves. The contents of the preserves were unknown: the cans had no pictures and the words on them with Alterian, in different fonts. But they'd been refrigerated, which told him they were something that was better *cold*. Peaches, maybe. Pineapple. Nobody refrigerated tins of meat, it would just increase the time needed to heat it to an edible temperature. Fruit? Fruit you'd want cold, in a climate like this. A mouthful of cold nectar could be like heaven in the mouth on a hot desert day.

In each room there were no survivors or bodies, only clues to who they might have been before their fate.

"There've been more inhabited rooms than people in the comms room," Rich said, when they had cleared the fifth room. He opened Ursula's pack and put some of the canned preserves in without asking to. It was like second nature, like programming.

"Yeah," Ursula agreed, bruskly.

"Means there's more bodies here, somewhere."

"Or that they got out." Ursula said this without hope in her voice. She said it in contradiction to his definitive statement. A reminder that they shouldn't jump to conclusions. "They might have gotten out."

Rich shook his head. "If you believed that, you'd be going too. If you thought that the Alts that survived did it by getting off this rock, you'd have said let's get off this rock." He paused. "We should get off this rock."

"Stick to the plan," Ursula said, voice clipped. "It's a good plan." Pause. "Don't be chicken shit."

Rich spun on her, stepping out of formation to face her head on, light from his weapon shining directly at her. "I *ain't* chicken shit." He didn't yell, but his accent bubbled to the surface. He stopped speaking with the perfect diction they try to push into you at Eon Academy, to make sure everyone is understood over the comms, and slipped into his native tongue. "I like to win, and sometimes the best way to win is to get the fuck out. Tactical retreat. We can do more from low-orbit than we can from here, we know their defenses are down. Bring the drop ship over, hack into the network from close range, get what we need and blast the place into the sand without ever having to lay boots on the ground." He stomped one foot for emphasis.

It echoed throughout the station.

"We *don't* know that the defenses are down," Ursula clarified. "Anti-air could still be in play, running on auto."

"We'd take out auto in a second."

"We don't even know that the outpost is deserted, yet. We're still in building one. Seems like it's mostly been crew quarters, so far. For all we know they're all huddled in the next building, waiting for feedback from the Alterian high command. For all we know this is a crime scene and they don't want to disturb it until the military police get here. Some comfort-girl gone loony after being used the wrong way one too many times, and went off."

"That's bullshit and you know it," Rich scoffed. He shook his head, snapped back into his T-position, and shone the light back behind him. There was nothing but hallway, and their tracks in it. "No comfort girl goes off like that. And if they did, they wouldn't take the crew with them. The captain. The crew'd be lining up to defend her. There'd be one guy in the brig or in the morgue for going too far, and that'd be that."

"In our system, maybe," Ursula pressed. "Don't assume all worlds are the same."

They opened another door and Rich stepped in. This one was dimly lit, even with the lights on full. He kept his weapon's flashlight on and active.

There were chains on the headboard of the bed, short ones that would have left anyone bound by them not much room to maneuver. The bed had no covers, just the mattress that came assigned with each room. The walls were bare save for the furthest, where the kitchenette would have been for every other dwelling but which had been stripped bare. On it were photographs, arranged haphazardly. Each one featured the bed and the chains, and a person in each. There were many different ones, all sizes and genders. Each looked at the camera as it went off, the flash caught in their eyes.

"You see anything?" Ursula called from the hall, her profile to him in the doorway.

Rich swallowed. He took one of the photos gingerly in his hand and pulled it from the mooring that pinned it to the wall. He cleared his throat, slid it into his breast pocket. "Another community room," he said, turning and rejoining her. "No supplies."

7

Mission Briefing Log, Captain Hux Carter,
2/30 15 3202 OEH

I was working on the comm's system. A fool's errand, I know, but it was all we had. I took out circuits one at a time and tried to get that jellified blood off of them. If you aimed a pulse of air at it just right, you could lift it up from the circuit enough to get a hold of it. After that it was just trying to peel it off, try your best to get it in one strip. The less times you had to use the pulse, the less chances of destroying some needed circuit or system.

You also couldn't keep your fingers on it for any length of time, else the blood would start to react with you and go limber again. Go liquid again. And then it'd be everywhere. You had to get it off while it was a scab over the circuits, as though the tech had become living and didn't like that I was fiddling with its guts.

I need to make it clear here: I had no idea what I was doing. Alt tech is not Eon tech. Were they circuits? Yes. Were they a part of the communication array? Yes. Did I know what function any individual circuit performed towards that function? Hell no. No clue. Alt tech doesn't even seem to run along the same basic function as ours. Things aren't aligned the same, along straight paths. Boards are curved and go into curved slots. Some are *flexible*. Now who would have thought it was a good idea to make a circuit board out of something flexible? Dumb as shit. Made it easier to clean, though. I just bent back the board and got in under the scab and peeled away. So, maybe they're on to something. But I'm assuming they didn't design their tech with a failsafe for if someone emptied all their blood into it.

All that is to say, I didn't know what I was cleaning. I took out a circuit, I got it as clean as I could, I put it right back. And after every one, I tried the comms again. I was not aiming for perfection or perfectly clean or anything else. I was aiming for clean enough to get the job done, that was it. The second those comms came back online, no matter how much goop and guts were still in there, it was getting closed up.

So I want that tagged in the file, because the people that were in before you made a big deal of the fact that I "had a working knowledge of Alterian technology" when there's no record of my studying it. They made it a huge deal, like I knew something I shouldn't, and wanted to know how. So, I need it in there that I don't know jack shit. I took out pieces of a puzzle, one at a time, cleaned them, put them back in. That's it. If I'd taken out any more than one at a time, I can almost guarantee you I wouldn't have had any clue how to slot them back, because like I said, Alterian tech is bananagrams. If you opened up an Eon machine and it looked like this, you'd assume it'd been messed with.

Ash had been moving the bodies. We were setting up in the comms room, it seemed like. That was where they'd hunkered down, and even though it hadn't worked out, it still seemed like the best place. She was laying out the bodies, getting them flat on their backs. Checking them, making notes. A few with button-down shirts, she opened the buttons of. Pressed her hand against the torso, pushed. The same motion as if she were trying to resuscitate, but without the repetition. Like she was trying to gauge the contents of the stomach by the slosh it made when it was sloshed.

She'd do these examinations — I'd see her out of the corner of my eye, keep up conversation every now and again — and then she'd take the body by the arms out of the room. She'd come back a few minutes later, clapping the soot and dust off her hands like it was a job well done.

So I ask her, after a little while of this, I ask her: what is she doing? And she says, "I'm checking for cause of death, checking to see if it's consistent. Cause of death and time of death, if I can." She says time of death is harder because of the damn heat, and that the room was sealed. The bodies are warm and they shouldn't be, she said. If she was back on Eon, a body this warm would mean the person had only been dead a few hours, but they knew it had been more than that. The dust alone told us it'd been more than that. So time of death was out, there was little way to tell.

So I say no, what are you doing with the *bodies*? Like, when she leaves the room. And she tells me, she's bringing them to the rooms nearby. She's dragged them out, setting them in the beds where she can. Crossing the arms. Like a mortician instead of a medic. Like she's prepping them for burial. Getting them out of the room and giving them some respect.

I tell her it'd be quicker to just pile them in a single room and bar the door. Pick a room and be done with it.

She shrugs at me, keeps doing what she's doing. We both keep doing what we're doing.

That goes on for some time, her clearing out bodies. We're getting more and more space in the room. There's this radius around a body, you know what I mean? A body in a room is like furniture you can't sit on, won't go near. It makes this field in your mind, this no-go zone. So Ash is moving out the bodies, and slowly the room is getting bigger and bigger and you start to understand why these Alts made a stand here. Thick doors, electronically sealed. Lots of space. It seemed like a good space to hunker down.

Right about then I remind myself that it didn't work. Whatever they were hiding from, it made it in. It made it in *and* it made it back out, even though the door was locked. What did they used to call those? 'Locked-Room Mysteries'? Yeah, let me tell you, they're all fun until you're in one. You're sitting there, mindlessly peeling scabs off of circuitry, and your mind starts to wander. You start looking at the vents. There are these *big* vents in the room. I mean really big. Stretch your arms apart as far as you can, you're starting to get there. They're wide but narrow, but not so narrow you can't imagine slipping into one. They line the top of the wall, all the way across. When they're on, they must pump cold air in, let it fall, keep it circulating. I realize that the vents run along the tops of the adjacent rooms, held by the ceiling. Able to hold a lot of weight.

I found myself staring at it while my fingers worked, I don't know for how long. Just staring at them, from one to the next, all around the perimeter of the room. Staring at them and they stare back. You know what I mean, when the darkness starts to look back at you? When you become convinced there's something there, just beyond slight? Something that maybe you catch a bit of in the light, but you're not sure, but your brain runs wild with it?

I ain't no chump, just so we're clear. I'm not looking at shadows and turning tail. That's never happened, never going to happen. I look at the shadows and I make sure my weapon's at arm's length. Make sure the dial is set to full force. Just in case. You can call it scared if you want, it doesn't matter. Scared is just another word for alert. Same emotion, same adrenaline. What makes it one or the other is what you *do* with it. If you turn tail, you were scared. If you use it to keep your eye out, channel it into keeping watch, holding firm, you were alert.

I glance over at Ash a few times. Those are the three things my mind goes between: the vents, the circuits, and Ash. I'm alert but she's *afraid*. Weapon is near her and jittery, her arm shakes every time she picks it up. She burying herself in her task, and when she comes back into the room she runs back as quick as she can. She hasn't noticed the vents, yet. She's venturing outside the comms room, and with every crew quarters that fills, she has to go a little further with the next body. She has to go a little further and she runs back just that little bit faster.

If she can engineer a split, she'll have us turn tail and run. I knew it then just as well as I know it now, with the benefit of hindsight.

***

I must have been staring at the vent for a while, this one in particular. This one in particular, there was something about it that caught the eye. All the vents, they had this diagonal grating on them, but this one… there was something in it that caught the light different. It went against that steady, parallel grain, kept my interest.

I must have been staring at it for some time because when Ash spoke to me, all but one of the bodies were gone. The room was wide now, expansive. It had been storage at one point, and they'd cleared it out to hunker down into. That was clear now that I saw it in that state. Storage off the comms room? Probably office supplies. Not weapons, you wouldn't move those out of any place you were hunkering down. But still, it said something that they had enough time to clear out the space, right? In the moment I was thinking, whatever had happened, they'd had enough time to clear the space.

We shouldn't underestimate the Alts. If it'd been me in their shoes, I wouldn't have taken the time, I don't think. Knowing now what I know, I would have taken my chances with the sand. I would have tried to walk to the next goddamn *planet*. What I'm saying is, if there's a second takeaway from this, don't underestimate the Alts' ability to stand firm. In any future skirmish, I wouldn't pin them down and think you can wait them out. They know the ground.

There's one body left, one that Ash left in here. It's a private, poor bastard. Probably waiting here between assignments. Young. I know why she picked him for what she was going to do next. In a young body, less has gone wrong. A young man like this Alt Private, his body should be in peak condition. No drug marks, good weight, good colouring. I know why she picked that one.

She tells me she eventually had to double up the rooms. Double up and triple up. Said she could have gone further, put one in each room like she'd planned, but she started to get skittish. I tell her that she'll be leaving quite the mystery for whoever might visit the outpost next. I can picture their Medical Examiner now, trying to sort out how and why each of these mangled bodies got back to their beds and laid down, all peaceful-like. She reminds me that SOP is to leave a quarantine beacon, and I tell her I was joking.

I was joking, for the record. I would have left the beacon.

I ask her if she said a prayer over them as she laid them out, and she says she didn't know any. Not any Alterian prayers, that was what I thought she meant first. She didn't know *any* prayers. It's a weird lot we let into the service, these days. Some days, I swear, it seems like we have more in common with enemy combatants than our own soldiers.

I see you scribbling; I want that last line redacted.

She says, "I'd like to perform an autopsy." She says it casual, like it's the most normal thing in the worlds to say. "I need your help."

We go over to the Alt Private and she's got him on his back. His uniform is still on him, but there's a ragged red sash across its middle, and a long rip in the uniform just below that. The rip isn't over where the blood tells me the wound is, and I hate that I know immediately that the killing blow came from below as a result. Edged-weapon gut-wounds are horrid, horrible things. It is a frankly horrendous way to die if you've never seen it, and that's why it's outlawed in our charter. You can say what you want about our weapons, but they'll never leave a man trying to hold his own guts in as blood leaks through his fingers. My weapon will kill you and I've killed plenty, but you won't suffer. Not like that.

I join Ash over by the body and we kneel down beside it. "Normally there'd be a table," she says. "Normally there'd be a table and we'd be standing at it, waist height. But we work with what we have."

She needs me to assist, and I ask her what that means. I've never done this before, I hope to never do this again. "Hold the body when I ask you to hold the body. Keep your eyes peeled for things I might miss; you never know when you might need a second set of eyes. Record notes for me. Keep my hair out of my face. Hand me things if I ask." She motions to her right, and she's got a plate with knives on it there. Big knives, not surgical ones. She found them in the rooms while she was laying the other bodies to rest, clearly. Between them she'd collected a full set of steak knives, and they were laid out and ready.

Yeah, I felt sick thinking about it.

She starts off checking his eyes and his gums, peels back lids and lips to do both. It seems like a weird place to start. There's a giant gash in the guy's gut, and we need to sort out what killed him. Hmm. Check the eyes? Weird. Medics, man. Weird lot. But they have their own SOP I guess, and I can't fault them for that. Actually, amend that. I can only *commend* them for that.

Anyway, she got me to mark it down. "No hemorrhaging," is what she said. No bleeds in the eyes, no bleeds in the gums. No blood in the mouth at all, she said. Means he hadn't lived too long after the slice, not even long enough the belch up blood when his lungs filled with it.

You ever hear something you can't unheard? Like, I was happy this Alt Private kid didn't die that way, but holy hell, learning that was a way to go. A common way to go, a thing you check for first. Holy hell.

She unbuttons his shirt, and it won't go around the wound, the blood makes it stick to it. She pulls it free with this horrible ripping sound, like wet Velcro. Awful. She gets it all free and opens up the shirt and the Alt Private has this pale white belly that's looking back at me. Stark white, not a glimpse of hair on it. I fight the urge to throw up because, Jesus, he's just a kid. Still has baby-fat on him. Ash opens the shirt and shows how young he really is, but also shows the slice that killed him in full.

It's not one motion, she says. She covers her face with part of her shirt and gets in close. And yeah, I can see it. Once you get it called out, it's hard to see how you didn't see it before. It's not one long gash, it's several. There're spaces where they overlap, cross into each other. Like the crosses digging through the centre of a letter A.

And then she says the thing that really got to me: "They were made simultaneously."

"What?" I asked. I couldn't believe what I was hearing.

But sure enough, she showed me and explained, all these gashes, they way they ruptured and ripped what was underneath, it could only have happened if they'd all happened at nearly the same time. This long one, she pointed out, sliced through the large intestine, and this small one crosses that slice like a T. But if either had been done before the other, the intestine wouldn't have been in that place. The Alt Private's torso would have remained in place, but the organs beneath would have spilled and moved and shifted with the assault. The pattern on the outside matched the pattern on the inside, and that wouldn't have happened if they'd been time between each slice.

At this point, I was thinking Raiders. I wasn't sure what else it could be but fucking Pirate Raiders. I pictured them coming in and raiding this outpost and then the lot of them holding down this Alt Private — and likely, all the others Ash had moved — and a bunch of them sliding their blades in all at the same time. I imagined how scared he must have been, a bunch of terrorists surrounding him and holding him down, five knives looming above as they got the ready. Just a group of men that large teaming up on you was scary. There's something engrained in our brain from way back in evolution that knows to be cautious of people in large groups. That society is a weapon that could be used. At the time, I was thinking Pirates. That this kid died in agony and fear. I was half right. And I just hoped the Pirates weren't Eon in origin, because I'd hate to do to an Eon what I'd have to do to them to make it right, if I found them.

That's what I thought at the time, Raider Pirates. In almost every way, that would have been easier.

Also stop your scribbling. Me saying I'd take revenge for an Alt Private kid against a turncoat from my own system doesn't make me a traitor. There are rules to our society, and I uphold those rules. That's what I'm fighting for — the whole, not each person. Stop writing.

While I was thinking about what I was going to do to the Raider men who did this, Ash was getting splinters and debris out of the Alt Private's wound. She was using the tip of one of the sharpest blades and being so, so careful. Using another blade like tweezers if she had to. She was collecting it on a sheet of plastic off to the side, I think it was the wrapper to bandages.

"There are hairs in here," she said, pushing them out with the tip of her blade. "Long, thick hairs. Like bristles. Like what you might see on a porcupine." She got them out and collected them, all of them. "The wounds aren't straight. Even the ones made in a single motion aren't straight. I don't think they were made with a blade, but if they were they weren't made with a factory-made blade. If it was a blade, it was something more ragged. Old metal or wood sharpened and put into a handle." Pirate Raiders were looking more likely, upon her saying that. Then she puts her hands *in*, starts moving the innards *around*. I really thought I was going to lose it. "Now, some of these wounds don't make sense," she said, fingering something near the centre top of the cavity. Then she tells me to "hold onto him."

She takes one of the sharper, longer blades and she aims it down at his central plexus. She taps the top with the flat of her hand, didn't have to do it more than once for the blade to slide in just the right amount, quarter inch. I'd have been impressed if I hadn't been so horrified. She tells me to hold him so that she can make a straight cut and does, brings the blade down slowly to meet the skin, and it's slicing the entire way. I can *hear* it, see this red sea parted in that pale flesh. Horrid. Then she puts two other blades in on either side, kind of crossing them? Uses them like tongs, puts the pressure against each other. Opens up the Alt Private's chest cavity.

I excuse myself to the hall and throw up where the others did. I don't make a big show of it, it's not dramatic. I ask if she's done, she says she is, and I step outside.

I'm only gone a second but she's calling me back in. She's revealed this extra cut. This long slice that went up through the Alt Private, at the same time or just after the other slices. And it goes up, she shows me, it goes up through the heart. It's small and slender, like a rapier, but it bends and curves up. The only way you know it's from the same motion is those bristles, all along the track. Whatever they are. And this slice, or puncture, or whatever — it has a continuous track that goes from the main gash all the way up to the heart, straight-shot. Rendered it.

At least he wasn't alive long.

8

27/30 14 3202 OEH

Both Ursula and Rich's packs had become too heavy with supplies scavenged, to the point that they had to make choices to make weight. Rooms were marked where there were more, in case they needed it, but they were deep into the heart of the facility now and — as Ursula had reminded Rich when he'd floated the idea of delivering this much and then coming back for more — "I don't plan on being here that long."

And yet in all that space, they had only come across two additional bodies. One had been in its room, ripped stem to stern like the ones they'd found in the comms room. She had been alone, back against her kitchenette. Blood had gone down into the cabinets, ruining everything. Neither of them would even take the chances on preserves that were coated in the blood; no amount of washing could have made them feel clean enough for consumption. The other body had been in the hall. It hadn't had the same gashes as the others, the same opened midsection. There were two wounds — two punctures — one near the man's groin and the other in the middle of his neck, each roughly two inches in diameter.

It took them a moment to realize that it was not two wounds but one, continuous wound. An entry point in the groin, an exit through the neck. They had moved on from that quickly.

There was a long stretch of hallway now, longer and straighter than the rest, terminating in a broad set of double doors that looked wider than all the others. Wide enough for getting in shipping items.

"That's the mess hall," Ursula said, with conviction. "I'd bet my ass on it. That's the mess hall, and we can swap out there. Take only what we need, really make the best of this."

"Look," Rich said, almost ignoring her. Almost, but not quite. The light of his weapon wasn't aimed at the hall behind them, like it should have been. It was aimed up at the walls.

There were long gashes in the walls. Thick strikes that started and stopped seemingly at random, digging into the metal and revealing the shimmer of it underneath. The polish of the layers not exposed to the dust and the elements all this time.

"The hell is that?" Ursula exhaled, breaking formation and stepping up to the wall herself. She ran her finger along the edge of the gash. It was sharp. "No, what the hell *is* that?" she repeated, with emphasis.

"I don't know," Rich frowned. He aimed his light down to a spot near the ground some ten feet from them, where the gash seemed to start. He followed it up, and it terminated just a foot from the ceiling, at the ventilation ducts. "But whatever did it was big."

"Hold the light here," Ursula said, and it was not a request but a command. Rich held the light over her shoulder to where she was looking, and she got in close to one of the scrapes. They were jagged, each starting and stopping in rough, terrible points. And in the joint of each point there were thick bristles. She reached a gloved hand to one particularly large deposit of them and plucked them out, working them between her fingers until they fell loose. She was about to ask, what it was again, but instead reached for her comm and squeezed. "Carter, we've got some strangeness here, copy?"

There was nothing on the line but static for a long moment as, back in the comms room, Carter got up from his place squat next to the Alterian Private's body and made his way over to the console he'd been repairing, snatched his radio from the top of it. "Copy, Urse. Weirdness here, too."

"Oh, I think we got you beat," she smiled when she said it, but it faded quickly. "Something in here made scratches all along the metal sides of the hall, almost down to the mess hall. Big scratches, deep, and there's stuff in them." She plucked another deposit of the bristles and worked it between her fingers until whatever held the group together gave way again. "Like hair, but it's thick like hay. You ever handle hay that's dried out all straight? That's what it's like. Like little stocks of hay, all stuck together."

In the comms room, Carter spun around to look at Ash. They regarded each other for a long moment, each knowing what the other was thinking. What Ursula was describing was the same as what they'd seen, only in flesh. "Need you to get back to the comms room, Ursula. Copy?"

Ursula balked, head jolted back in surprise. She turned away from the wall to Rich, who lowered his weapon. "No copy, sir. We're almost at the mess hall, we think. We'll get the supplies, then get back to comms."

Rich nodded.

Carter huffed. "We've found those same marks back here, Urse. On one of the bodies. Same stuff in them, bristly hay stuff. We need to get you back here, but I think it's time to re-evaluate plan, copy."

Ursula looked at Rich, who huffed a long sigh. He shone his light back up to the gouges behind her, then turned the beam forward to the mess hall, less than a hundred feet away. He gave Ursula a thumbs down.

She nodded in agreement. "Sir, with respect, mess hall. Then back to comms, right away. Copy?"

There was silence on the other end of the line for a long, tense moment. Then finally the resigned voice of Carter. "Copy."

Ursula switched her radio to silent mode, so that the brown-noise hiss of dead air wouldn't scatter throughout the hallway, rendering all sound silent. She turned to Rich. "Off record, you okay with this?"

Rich nodded. "I said I was okay, I'm okay." He raised his weapon, thumbed the dial on its side to prime it out of passive mode. Ursula heard the *tik tik* clicks as it went, knew what they meant. She did the same to her weapon, and only when she took point did Rich take position at her back. "Let's do this."

They stepped towards the mess, each of them training their lights around every point along the walls and ceiling as they went, examining every point. Alt architecture left more nooks than Eon architecture, more crannies for there to be something to hide within. Ursula and Rich angled their beams of light into them all, she from the front and he from behind. There was nothing living in them waiting to come out at them... but now that their minds had been turned on to it, there were more scratches. None as deep as the ones Ursula had radioed in about, none that had gotten in so well that the metal underneath shined, but they were there. Scuffs, mostly. Small indents, scrapes in the dust and tears in the weathered look of the wall, but there all the same.

"You seeing this?" Rich asked, without specifying what.

Ursula nodded curtly.

"How much of this did we miss on the way here?"

Ursula had no answer for that, and so gave none.

There were windows in the doors to the mess hall, square things at eye-height with thick glass in them. Fused into the glass were metal diamond-shapes, a mesh reinforcement that made it difficult to break. The glass was fogged to the point of everything within the room being invisible. Ursula tried to wipe it with her arm when she got there, but it had no effect. The fog was on the other side of the glass.

Her light found the door. There was a chain on it with a lock.

"Hang on," Rich said, shouldering his weapon and kneeling down to get closer to it. He touched the lock, then pulled back, eyebrow cocked. "Look at this."

There were ripples coming from the gap between the two doors. Shimmers of air that came with heat, hot air even hotter than the intense air of the station, hot enough to create optical illusion, to make the air shimmer and shake as it left the mess hall. Ursula put her hand to it, then pulled it away. "God damn, that is hot."

Rich paused, hands up to either side of the lock. "Should we still go in?"

Nodding, Ursula brought her weapon down, thumbed the intensity dial on the side, and pulled the trigger. A concentrated blast of air came from the tip, changing the pressure around it enough that Rich stepped back, hands on his ears. The lock burst free from the chain, shattering at its weakest point at the clasp. "Found the key."

"Warn me!" Rich yelled, wiggling his ears by the lobes to try and force the pressure out. "That is not okay."

Ursula grinned, a devil's grin. She pulled the chain free from the handles then stepped back to be in line with Rich. She waited for him to compose himself, shoot her a rueful look, then raise his weapon. "You ready?"

He frowned, nodded, then they both stepped forward and kicked out at the doors. They both opened at once, rocked forward, strained their hinges. Hit the walls on the other side but did not rock back, stayed there. The mess hall was open and the steam and rippling hot air pushed out, like someone had thumbed the release on a pressure cooker. It billowed out, like opening a door to find snowdrifts on the other side. So thick was it that it took on the impression of being solid, of being a mass that clouded and came at them. It hit them like a wave, the heat of it, so far removed from what they'd already been experiencing that it made the blistering heat of Toth Outpost seem cool by comparison.

They stepped inside, wafting the curling clouds of steam as they went. They returned like locusts, until eventually Ursula thumbed her weapon down to a low pulse with a *tik tik tonk* and aimed it at the floor, firing. A blast of air came from its tip, sucked in quickly from the atmosphere around, pressurized, and shot forth in one shift motion. The formally compressed air hit against the linoleum floor of the mess hall and scattered about in every direction, dissipating the thickness of the steam and rendering the room around them visible.

They wished, immediately, that it had not.

The mess hall was large, doors on the other side linking it to several quadrants of the Outpost. There were tables that were immoveable, mounted to the wall and the floor, as though the entire room had been carved from one solid piece of granite, the station built around it. There was a small window off to the right, a room beyond it that looked to be a kitchen area. Vending machines lined the wall near it, stinking with food that had begun to rot in the absence of maintenance.

Around each, but especially on those sturdy tables, were large ovals of flesh.

Pulsing with veins and thick with sweat, they oozed a thick, gelatinous redness that Rich recognized instantly from the comms room. It had been caked onto the officer that had been draped over the module and had gotten inside. Gummed up the works. Here it was everywhere, a thick film that covered each mound and connected them, film running along the ground and forming connections between each pulsating form. Spider-web veins and nerves ran along through the red gel, each also twitching with stimuli, moving fluid from one form to the next.

"It's eggs," Rich said. It was not a question, and he was not looking for confirmation. Even though he had never seen the like of it before, he knew. They did not look like the eggs from his home world, except in shape, but he knew. They stood erect on a base of red goo that collected and hardened around its base, giving it purchase.

The tip was pointed up, with cracks in them that looked to prime it for opening.

Both Ursula and Rich noticed this and would have considered it cause for alarm, but for the fact that the same cracks appeared on every egg. They were a part of it. Not the straight lines of a razor, but uniform among each of the examples. The veins that ran over the eggs went into these thin cracks, terminating in them. The veins were thickest at these points, throbbing with the beat of some unseen heart. The red gel that covered the floor and the eggs was thinnest there, but there, making everything a part of the one organism.

Ursula looked down, realized her foot was close to where it started. Saw nerves shimmer under the light of her weapon, stepped back a pace.

"We need to call Carter," she said, voice hoarse.

9

Mission Briefing Log, Captain Hux Carter, 2/30 15 3202 OEH

All your years in the Eon army, you ever get a call over the comms you didn't believe? Not didn't *want* to believe or couldn't *bring yourself* to believe, something that really broke the brain? I had my hands full of that red gel when I got the radio from Ursula, and I didn't quite buy it. I didn't get it at first, but she was adamant. We had to come and see, full stop. Ash was in one of the other rooms when the call came in, laying the Alt Private we'd dissected to rest, and it took me a few minutes to find her.

That was bad, looking back. It'd be the last time we were separate on this away mission. The last time we, either of us, would feel safe enough to be separate from the rest.

We take what can't be left and we follow the radio compass to where Ursula and Rich ended up. We meet them on either side of the mess hall doors, like they're guarding it. They were tense, sweating, and not just from the heat. But the heat was *oppressive*. If you'd told me the whole station had been heated from that room, I'd have believed you. Felt like summer around the equator of Eon, if you've ever experienced it. Yeah, that kind of heat. Humid heat that sticks to you, *organic* heat, mixed with the dry heat of the Toth desert. Brutal combination, no way to fight it.

The four of us, we go into the mess hall, and all my blood leaves me. I haven't felt like that since I was a kid. I couldn't move, for a second. Couldn't think. Your brain needs blood to think, needs heat, and I didn't have any in me.

The call had been right: there were eggs.

Large eggs, the size of a man. The size of me, right now, if I hunkered into a fetal position. That was what I thought of when I saw them; I thought to myself — these could be human eggs. Like we'd found some weird Alterian nursery, discovered they were hatched and not born, even less human than we'd always thought. That was a useless thought though, the product of a shocked, blood-deprived mind. It was gone as soon as it had come, a split second. I mention it only to tell you that's how big they were, big enough to fit an adult male.

That red gel was over them, the same that I'd mistaken for congealed blood back in the comms room. There were veins in it now, nerves. You could watch the nerves twitch, watch them send impulses about the changes in temperature, air pressure, everything. Something. I looked down at my hand and there was still some on me, and I shook it off. Heart rate goes up, let me tell you. You find something clinging to you that you thought was innocuous; turns out it's alive? Heart rate goes up. I don't care who you are.

There were three dozen of them in that mess hall. Three dozen. Each pulsing and thick with sweat. Glistening with it. I can't... I can't even tell you what that was like. The *smell* of them though, was the worst. I'm one of those people who can't remember smells, and I'm glad of it. You know that? Something like five percent of people can't remember smells, or tastes. Like, can't remember what a pie tastes like unless they have the pie in their mouths. I'm one of those. I can describe to you what a pie tastes like, but it's just words to me. Some people, you describe a pie to them, it's like they can taste it. Yeah, I see your mouth watering now.

I tell you, not being able to remember tastes and smells? That's an asset right now. If I never smell anything like that again it'll be too soon. It smelled like iron in that room, like metal. Copper. I think that was from the gel. I don't think it was blood, but I think it was like blood, there was blood in it. Ash said it best, actually.

"We're in a womb," was what she said. Said: "They've made this room into a womb, made placenta and connective tissue out of this gel. They've turned this space into a habitable space to grow their young in, somewhere between egg-laying and mammalian incubation." She called it fascinating. That was not the word I'd have used, and I think I might have told her to stop, to slow down before I had a panic attack. Because being told you didn't just step into a mess hall, you actually just stepped inside some large uterus... yeah, that added to the blood pressure. I think I'd have thrown up if I hadn't already thrown everything up. Yeah.

So, it smelled like metal, the same way blood tastes like metal, but stronger. But more than that, it smelled like salt, and like bleach. Chemical smell, but not artificial chemical. You get what I'm driving at? No? It smelled like sex, okay? The air was thick with that hint of bleach, of sweat, of friction. Not the smell of sex, but the stench of it. The stench of natural lubricants, worked into a froth.

When I got up the nerve, I got as close as I dared to the closest of the eggs. Not too close. Not close enough that I touched the gel. If I never touched the gel again, it'd be too soon. There was this skin over it all, this film. And the eggs, they were shaped like eggs, but they weren't made of calcium. These were made of meat; you got up closer and you could tell. They had the shape of eggs, that strong shape that nature seemed to make on every planet, but they were meaty. They moved like they were breathing, filmy red blood excreting from the slits in its top with every exhale. The surface had this yellowish tint, like urine when you're dehydrated. Like I'm sure mine would have looked like at that moment, come to think of it.

It was a horror show, and the only thing worse than the eggs themselves was thinking about what might have been inside them.

The other doors to the mess hall, the ones that came from the other quadrant of Toth Outpost, they were locked too, from the outside. The Alts, they'd done their best to contain it, but clearly something had gone FUBAR. And, as a little voice in the back of my head kept telling me, it had gone FUBAR *before* these things had hatched. Whatever these things were, they weren't the problem. Whatever made them, *that* was the problem.

Ursula comes up beside me, weapon ready and primed to its maximum setting. Can not say I blame her. She cocks a head at the egg closest. She speaks with this hushed tone, like she's afraid that to her question answer will upset the other two. She asks, "You ever seen something like this before?"

I tell her I haven't. It doesn't seem to help her mood. I think... I think she was hoping that I had seen this before. That this was common, just something that was above her level of command. Of course I've seen eggs before, soldier, it's just you were never supposed to know about them. Now get ready for your debrief, you're being sworn to secrecy.

She wanted that, but I couldn't give it to her.

She starts game planning, theorizing what we could do to get rid of them. Fire,

The Collected Short Fiction of Matthew LeDrew

she theorizes, fire would be a good bet. If only this were a mission against a Capulet Outpost, there'd be plenty of fire-based weaponry around. She laments that for a second and I let her, before getting her back on track. What If's and If Only's only lead to panic, nothing else. You have to let people talk, let people vent, but you have to know when to cut it off.

If we knew where the skull was, she said, we could fire a narrow burst at fullest power through the shell and through its skull. "It's just meat," she says, then clicks her light on to full beam and shines it as close to the surface of the egg as she dared. "Go around the other side, see what you can see," she says, explaining that her grandfather used to farm chicken eggs and hold them up to candlelight to make them translucent, make sure there wasn't a chicken inside before frying it up.

I step around to the other side but there's nothing coming through, just the barest hint of red light, like when you press a light up to your finger and it diffuses through. I tell her there's nothing, and from over her shoulder I see Ash pull Rich aside, to the mouth of the mess hall.

I didn't need to have comms open to know what they were talking about.

The spectre of the fifty-fifty split was rising again. At what point do we say, shag it, head back to the drop point? Screw the intel, screw the supplies, I'll take my chances out in the sun. The eggs were that point, for them, you could see it in their body language. Feet planted. Shoulders squared. Arms crossed, except for gestures in my general direction that were subdued but still noticeable. Ash, scared. Rich, not scared but agreeing. Agreeing on a pragmatic level, nodding along. Assessing, coming to his conclusion, verifying. Working in Ash's opinion and information into his idea.

I see Ash gesture to the middle of her torso up and down, like a zipper motion. In another setting, in another world, I'd have thought she was coming on to him. But she wouldn't and she wasn't, and I knew it when I saw it. She was describing the autopsy, that shoot that went right up the cavity that had been cut in the Alt Private's gut and into his heart. She described it and you could see Rich's posture shake, his colour change.

When we did the autopsy, we were thinking all military-issue weapons that could have caused it. Now the eggs were here, and we didn't know what was inside them, and imaginations were running wild. As the conversation goes on, Ash's body language gets more and more frantic. She's pacing a little, in spot, moving back and forth. I don't blame her. Hell, cards on the table — and feel like this is a cards on the table kind of debrief — it was good to know that there was someone else in the room as scared as I was.

Because yeah, this was a lot. I was handling it differently. I'd been trained better. But this was a lot.

So, if you put in your final GD report that Ash was scared, you make sure and also put in that that fear was justified. You control your emotions in the field, you do what needs to be done, but there comes a point where being afraid isn't toxic, it's the only sane response.

Ursula jumps back, brings my attention back to her. "It moved," she swears. She swears that the goo — that red gel that's covering everything — she swears that it moved toward her light. That it shifted forward, off of the shell of the egg. I can't rule it out, I can't rule anything out. Ursula has her weapon trained on it as though it's an enemy combatant, and she's shifting aim from one egg to the other as she backs away from them. Like they're surrounding her instead of sitting there, stationary.

Ursula wouldn't have called this fear, she would have called this hyper-alertness. Call it whatever you want, but don't dare lay blame at its feet. This was a natural response.

I look down at my feet and I'm not standing in the goo, I'm standing it a little oasis from it... but the oasis seems smaller. The goo, that reddish clear gel, it seems like it's coming closer. It seems like it's coming closer and I can see the nerves in it now. Swear I can see the impulses in it. Little flashes of light shooting from the tips and travelling throughout the maze of them to god knows where.

Because where there's nerves, there's a brain, but I hadn't thought of that yet.

I get out from behind the egg, join Ursula. Shake off the nerves that are one hundred percent getting into me. It's a lot. I'm regrouping, asking Ursula what she thinks our next move should be, trying to figure out if we even *have* a fifty-fifty split for staying the course or if she's on team getaway too, when Ash pipes up.

"Where are the parents?" she asks. I'll never forget it; I can hear it now. I hadn't thought of it, and the thought hits me like a pile-driver to the temple. I ask her to repeat herself, but not because I hadn't heard. "Where are the creatures that laid these eggs? Some species die after they lay eggs, but there's no husks or corpses. There's no signs of parental death or deterioration... so where are the things that laid these eggs?"

I look back at the door to the rest of the outpost, locked from the other side. The scratches on the wall, frantic scratches. Containment scratches. I look at the vents, think back to the team in the comms room, barricaded in, calling for help that wouldn't make it in time. That red gel all over the console and the captain, connecting them to all of this with nerves I didn't know were there at the time.

I think back to that Alt Private, vivisected and god knew what else, face contorted with those final moments.

I tell them I don't know where the things that laid these eggs are, but that when we found them, I was absolutely going to put a blast through their skulls, if they had them.

10

27/30 14 3202 OEH

All four start the walk back to comms. There are enough of them now that they could do proper look-about formation, front, east, west, south. But that's not necessary in a hallway. They do front, back, and vents. Carter had made sure of that — keep eyes on the vents. He didn't explain why, wasn't required to, and didn't need to.

Carter took point and was ahead of the others. Ursula was behind, light beam aimed at every shadow, still keyed up from her experience with the egg. Ash and Rich took a wall each, aiming their beams at the vents that ran along the tops of the wall, save for sparse breaks. Carter was far ahead of the others, at least twelve feet. He was the one heading into unknown space, the others were securing the flank. If something happened, they needed the space to react and flee, regroup. It was SOP.

"We should be heading back to the drop site," Ash said through gritted teeth, both a hiss and a whisper. When there wasn't a response right away, she continued, low enough that Carter could not hear. "We should not be going back to the comms room."

"We have our orders," Ursula said, keeping her voice as even-keel as she could.

Rich looked over his shoulder at this exchange, not watching the vents for that moment. Turned back quickly, scanned the area he'd left unseen. Caught himself.

"We have orders, and we have SOP, and we have a fifty-fifty split," Ash said, cocking her head back toward Rich, who was back-to-back with her. She said it in such a way that encouraged him to chime in, but he didn't. He didn't chime in in support, but nor did he refute. "We'd like to go to Carter with more than that, though. We shouldn't be staying in comms. Look what it did to the Alt crew that tried it." She paused. "We should be going back to the ship, as quickly as we can."

Ursula grinned, nastily. She tossed the grin over her shoulder at Ash, then looked at Rich. She chuckled. "You don't want a seventy-five-twenty-five split, you need it. You need it because you're not totally sure you can make the case that your strat is the defensive start. Hunkering down in comms, that's defensive, too. So you're not sure you can win the fifty-fifty split, if it comes down to that. Want me to help gang up on him."

Ash tisked, clicking her tongue against the roof of her mouth. "Look, we know Carter isn't going back to comms to beat a retreat. He's not that guy."

"I don't think you know what kind of guy he is."

"It's *not* a retreat strategy. It's not. It's a hunker down with your gun at the door and wait to take these things to task strategy. You can call it defensive if you want, but it's offensive in intent. Right, Rich?" Ash turned at that last, facing the centre of their watch.

Rich still said nothing, tightened his lip. Pursed.

"Let me tell you about Hux Carter," Ursula said, resolutely. "In the Siege of Four, the only time in history that all four galactic empires engaged in the same battle, Carter was there. Carter was there and his platoon went up against the Caps. He was a part of that final push to force the Caps back." Ash straightened, noticeably. "The Caps rained down fire and Napalm. To watch the vids and read about it, it made the planet they were trying to take look like hell itself. They couldn't get the resources? That was fine. They knew they were making their last stand, so they decided to just torch the planet out from under its people. Some of those fires are still going, did you know that? Some of those fires are still going, we have yet to get them all out. A continent on fire, and we've rebuilt what it destroyed first while it technically still rages. Fifteen hundred Eon men and women joined that battle to force the Caps back, stepped foot into that hell. You know how many made it back? Two-hundred and nineteen. Two-hundred and nineteen people made it back. Some reports said a hundred and ninety-five. But either way: not many. Carter, he was trapped behind a firewall with ten of those people, and he got them out. You know at the academy, when they show you how to aim at the ground, fire full force, blow up enough ground to snuff out a chemical fire?" Ash nodded. Ursula bit her next words: "Well, that should be called The Hux Maneuver. It was for a bit, but he asked them to stop. So you can think what you want about him, he honestly doesn't care. But he's not some follow-through. He's not doing it just to see it done. If he's looking at a situation and thinks this is the best move, it's the best move."

Ahead of them, Carter looked briefly over his shoulder.

The three of them straightened back into formation, checking behind them. Checking vents.

When he'd turned back, Ursula turned back to Ash. "So no, I won't be joining your little mutiny. You can give up any hope of that right now."

Ash nodded. She sucked her bottom lip in, pushed it out. Did this several more times. Checked the vents.

Rich turned to look over his shoulder. "Leaving for the drop point is the right strategy," he said, calmly and firmly. He turned back to his work.

Ursula pressed on.

11

Mission Briefing Log, Captain Hux Carter,
2/30 15 3202 OEH

We make it back to the comms room without incident, and fortify it. That obviously didn't work for the Alterians, but we plan on learning from what we can gather from their mistakes. We bring the food in; all we'll need and only what we'll need. Find things with water, anything with water. Refill our ration thermoses in case we need it. Designate a bathroom area and make a portable latrine that will trap the smell of our leavings, in case that was what attracted whatever killed the Alts. Every animal knows to cover the smell of their shit. The smell of food is good, but food can mean anything. Food can grow wild. But the smell of waste? That can only be made by live prey.

We check the vents, get right up close to them. Ursula and I form stepladders with our hands, hoist Ash up because she's the lightest. She reports back what we were afraid of: the vents are full of that red gel paste. Just a thin layer of it, throughout. Not enough to flood, but enough that it was there. She could see one big vein in it, she said. Could see it throbbing.

I mean, what the hell is that? Throbbing? I don't need that. I don't need that in my life.

We go back to the scene, recreate it, try and figure out where the Alts went wrong. The captain, he was dead at the comms station. Clearly trying to radio out for help, just like we were. But the others, there was little sign of struggle. There weren't any signs of weapons discharge or struggle. Ash confirmed there hadn't been defensive wounds on any of the victims, offered to go back and make sure, autopsy them all. I vetoed it. I didn't want us leaving for any reason that wasn't one hundred percent necessary.

We talk out the facts of the scene, go over it like we were crime scene investigators. The Captain died hunched over the comms unit, and there was a lot of blood and the red gel. There's a safe bet he was awake and trying to call out. No defensive wounds on the others means there was no fight. Anything that can do to people what was done to that Alt Private, you don't just let that happen. Maybe one person freezes, maybe two, but not a whole group like that. So the only thing we can figure, the only thing that makes sense, is that it happens in their sleep. That they barricade themselves in, think they have the place secure, and rest up for the night without much of a watch. No one except the Captain, and he's not really watching. He's focused on getting in help, calling in reinforcements.

So this is it then, this is what happened: The Captain was keeping watch while the others slept and tried to make calls out, but nobody considered the vents. So used to them being there, you stop considering them. Just like the paint on the walls. So he's there making calls and something gets in, enemy forces. Whatever made those eggs, we assume. One or more of them get in, they make short work of the Captain. We surmise he was taken by surprise, because if he wasn't — again — the others would have woken up. So the Captain is out, and from there it's just a massacre. And when they're done, they slink back through the vents that they came through, leaving us to find our little locked-door mystery.

So we knew what not to do. Going without sleep wasn't an option, so we decide to sleep in shifts, when the time comes. Rich and I take the first shift.

Why'd I pick Rich? He's a good soldier. All of my team was. But why'd I pick him, in particular, for first watch with me? Personnel reasons. Rich was more comfortable with Ash. I was more comfortable with Ursula. I didn't *want* people getting comfortable on watch, segueing into conversation, chit-chatting. Not that night, not on that watch. So Rich and I took first watch, and Ash and Ursula, they would have taken second.

Before that though, we get to work on the room. We secure the vents as best we can. They're all on these hinges, like doggy doors, so that you can open them up and clean them with ease. Get maintenance done on them. But it was what made it so that we didn't realize it had been the entry point for whatever had killed the Alts, right? Because it closed shut behind them. Anyway, simple enough to force them shut. Take some screws from the comms console, work them through the aluminium in the bottom of the vent hatch, Bob's your uncle. Now they're screwed shut, maybe that's enough to deter in and of itself. Could they have been forced open? Almost certainly. But most creatures go by the Law of the Path of Least Resistance. If they can't get into an area they've been in before via the same entry point immediately, they move on. Try someplace new.

So we work together on the first few of them, the four of us. Then we branch off, leave Ursula and Rich to that, while I take Ash over to the comms station. I need her surgeon's hands, that steady no-shake I saw her have during the autopsy. I needed that, now. We go back and look at the gel and blood and scab that are still on the comms station circuits, and I don't know how I didn't see the nerves before. I guess you just don't see what you don't consider. Might be a lesson in that, something for the training regime. But. I take Ash back and we see the nerves and get her tools and we try to work around them. We work together, get as much of the circuits clean as we can. She was good, I should have had her helping me from the start. We don't know exactly how the Alt tech works but we guestimate and do our best and by about the time we figure dusk is really settling in outside the station, we get it on.

The comms station buzzes to life. It makes this horrible sound like a jet engine starting, and I don't know if that's because there's still red gel in its innards or if that's just the way it's supposed to sound. We don't know enough about Alt technology, that's a big takeaway here. But we get it up and running not long after Rich and Ursula have gotten the last of the vents screwed shut.

Rich comes over and plugs in the drive we were supplied. It takes him a few minutes to find the right connector. Alt tech. When he finds it, he downloads all the intel he can, because there's a non-zero chance no team will be able to make it back here and get the information. Like, we know without saying so, this might be a 'bombard from low altitude' situation. So, he downloads the intel, gets what he can of it and hopes the translators came make sense of it, because even with the Alterian I know it's all gibberish to me.

The comms controls are not intuitive. We think we find the frequency tuner and we use our own radios to calibrate it, because it's not in Eon numbers, it's in Alt numbers clearly. So we fiddle until we hear ourselves over our own radios, get that feedback whine, and then we know that X is Y. And if X is Y, maybe Z is... and we start calling for help on a broadband of what we think that is, hoping the dropship will hear us before we have to try and make it back over the dunes.

I guess you guys didn't get any of that? Damn. What a waste of goddamn energy that was.

We eat a meal that's basically a surprise because none of us can read Alterian and the cans don't have pictures on them. I have cabbage rolls, and don't complain. Then we make up cots as best we can and Ursula and Ash lie down and sleep for the first rotation, and Rich and I sit back-to-back at comms, send out the distress on different frequencies, and start first watch.

Rich? He was a good man. Followed orders, but made his opinion heard. You could always count on him. There was never any mutiny in him, and it wasn't something you had to worry about. He was a good man who played it straight and you never once had to second guess his motivations. I want that in my report, verbatim. This was a good man, a military man. A *family* man. On this mission and on every mission, he did you all proud. You wouldn't have the intel you have, if not for him.

12

27/30 14 3202 OEH

The sound of the Alterian comms cycling through the frequencies made the low white noise of static that hissed through the room as Ursula and Ash slept. Carter sat at the comms unit, where the Alt Captain had just days before, and watched the numbers as they swapped between frequencies on the dial. Every time he thought he recognized the pattern, thought he had a sense of Alterian numeracy, it threw him a curveball. An odd symbol, a modifier he hadn't seen before, and he would have to start again. He sat with his lips pinched between the thumb and forefinger of his right hand, considering each change and adding it to the mental map as they came up.

Rich stood against the wall opposite the door, holding his weapon at ease. He stood straight, ridged. He stood as though a drill sergeant were going to come in at any moment and dress him down for every segment of his spine that was not perfectly straight. He looked like the picture of a soldier, the ones they used to convince the young that their mandatory service times were good things that they should be happy about.

"I see you attempting mutiny," Carter said. His voice was firm and clear, loud enough that it could not be mistaken but not loud enough that it would wake the women. He didn't look away from the scrolling strange numbers when he said it, as though the conversation were not important enough to turn away from his research.

Rich's posture faltered, slackened. He turned from the door to Carter. There was a second's pause. "Pardon, sir?"

"Do not pardon sir me, *Private First Class*." He turned from the dials when he spoke with emphasis. "You want out, you and Ash. You want to hike it back over the dunes, even now. Even in the dark you want to turn tail and run scared."

"I'm *not* scared," Rich interjected, then steadied himself. "Sir."

Carter regarded him for a long moment, lips pursed. "Okay, you're not scared. Ash is, though."

"Ash is."

"And you both want to run."

Rich shifted uncomfortably. He turned his gaze back towards the door for a moment, then back to Carter. "There's nothing wrong with a dissenting opinion. There's nothing wrong with wanting to vacate if it's time to vacate."

"That's true."

"That's *why* the fifty-fifty split goes to defense. Because back in the day, generals would push their men out into the fields in unwinnable situations, with no logic to do it besides their ego. They'd send men out to die while they sat in their tents and puffed cigars and wrote poems about the senseless violence of war. That's why there's a fifty-fifty split, why it has to be agreed *by the majority* that continuing the mission is the best course."

"That is also true." Carter nodded. "But what is also true is that those discussions have to be had in the open. Discussions of what course is best have to be fair discussions, with a vote called at the end. The two of you, you and Ash, pulling Ursula aside and trying to convince her to vote your way before there's even been a public talk... that's mutiny. Any talk of the vote without the commanding officer present is mutiny, according to Cotter v Mazzucchelli. If you know your legal history on the rule."

"I know my history."

"Then I would really like to understand your reasoning behind your actions, here. *Private First Class*."

Rich stiffened again, more than he had been when the reprimand had begun. He turned towards the barricaded door to the comms room to compose himself. The re-iteration of his rank reminded him to consider how he should, and therefore would, respond. After a moment he turned back to Carter, suddenly. "Did you hear that?"

"Don't try and change the subject—" Carter started, then turned towards the comms door. "Hear what?"

"I'm not — there's a sound out in the hall. I swear, I hear it." He paused. "It's faint. Small. Like single-key taps on an old typewriter. You know the type? The kind where if you went too fast, the whole thing would jam up?" Rich made fiddley motions with his hands, as if to illustrate the motion.

Carter squinted, then tilted his head to listen. There was nothing at first, so he turned down the volume on the white noise of the radio. Again, there was nothing at first and nothing for a long, tense pause after it. "If you don't want to discuss your actions," Carter started. "Then maybe you shouldn't have—" He stopped, suddenly.

There was a tapping sound, coming from the hall. Slow and staccato, coming in small bursts. Skittering, then nothing, then skittering. It could have been mistaken for the moving of pipes in time with the wind outside, if not for the pattern of it. And if not for their knowledge from the outside of how the structure was built, strengthened to avoid the expanding and contracting to such whims of nature.

Skittering, tapping, and then three small taps. A finger on a desk, tapping at a sudden and unexpected problem. A thinking tapping, a figuring-it-out tapping. Three quick taps, a long pause, then three identical quick taps. Then silence.

Carter got up from behind the desk and made his way, as quietly as he could, to the door. He stopped short of pressing himself up to it. Kept a foot between he and it. Leaned forward, ever so slightly.

"What do you hear?" Rich whispered, after a moment, from his position straight-backed against the wall.

"Shh," Carter hushed, raising a stern finger.

Silence again. Then three sudden taps, faster than before. Firmer. The difference between tapping with a single finger and tapping with two.

It was followed by a sharp metal scrape, quick and high, that came not from the other side of the door but from inside the room. Carter and Rich both stiffened as a screw came loose from somewhere above, hit the floor by Rich's feet, then bounced and rolled onto the floor between them.

Both men stared at it for half a second. Less than half a second. A unit of time immeasurable, that felt like forever but was over too quickly.

"Down!" Carter yelled, bringing his weapon up and around.

Carter turned and veered up, even as the grate above his head burst open and a large brown mass came from it in an arc. It spewed forth but not all of it came out, falling down on Rich and then pulling back, dragging him back to the wall even as his weapon let out discharge after discharge. It was so large that even when it hit the floor, part of its carapace was still up in the vent.

Rich screamed.

Large talons came back from the creature's segmented carapace. They pressed forward with ease, gliding through the arms of Rich's Eon-issue gear, and the arms beneath, with ease. Blood spurted, growls and hisses vocalized, and from the belly of the thing came a large, prehensile appendage.

Teeth moved down to cover Rich's head, and talons ripped at the torso, as the appendage lowered itself into position.

Rich raised his weapon up, sticking it flat against the creature's underbelly, and fired. He fired again and again, thumbing the intensity dial of his weapon with each discharge. He couldn't wait for the split second it would have taken to thumb the dial to full and then fire, the firing had to happen *now*.

With the fifth burst, red spewed forth from around the lip of Rich's weapon.

Just over a second had passed since the screw dropped.

Carter lunged forward, screaming. He slid on his back along the floor to the underside of the creature and fired up, his weapon at full charge by the time he got into position. There were no punctures as the compressed air shot forward.

The creature finished its emergence, fully out of the duct now. It let go of Rich's head, turning its attention onto Carter as it slithered towards the barricaded door.

Ursula and Ash were on their feet.

Rich was underneath the full weight of the creature, being dragged forward as it slithered and leaving a trail of blood behind. His weapon lay in the middle of the ground, near the screw.

"Full blast!" Carter yelled, and Ursula was complying before the order was even out. "Full blast or nothing!"

The creature was turned to Carter. Talons outstretched, moving. Threatening. There was a wide berth around it that was uninhabitable, dangerous. Growls came from its throat, rattles from its tails, and on the other side of the wall the skittering and clacking was reaching a fever pitch. If before the sound was a single keystroke, now there were many typewriters all clanging and clattering. And the creature in the room had tiny legs along its body, added to the scuttle and skitter as well.

Ash was on her feet.

Carter laid down fire, two shots to the body and one to the base, trying to get it to flex enough to remove itself from Rich. Two shots to the body, one to the base, and then one towards the face. Keeping its attention on Carter.

Ursula came up to its side, under the influence of those gnashing arms. She clamped her jaw shut and let loose three rapid shots under the creature's arm to where — on her — the soft flesh of the pit would be. The creature squealed, taking notice, turning.

Carter continued his fire, trying to draw its attention back.

Rich screamed, the sudden turn of the creature flinging him aside.

Ash brought her weapon to the ready and began to fire at its back.

"No! Keep it frontward!" Carter yelled.

The creature turned, suddenly, drawn by the second spattering of fire from its back.

Ursula brought her weapon up to its head and fired, once, twice, three times. The first two went to its chin, the last to its cheek. Jaw clenched to the point that teeth cracked, she brought her weapon up to one of the creature's two small eyes just as its talons pulled back to strike.

A gush of red and green spewed forth from its skull and onto Ash and Ursula, and the creature threw itself back, landing on Rich once again with all its weight. Appendages curled inward and it let out a gurgling growl. A putrid stink filled the air and the red gel that had coated everything in the vents came from its lower extremities.

Ursula and Carter kept their weapons trained on it. Ash did the same but rushed forward. After a moment's pause, she proclaimed, "It's dead;" before moving on to Rich.

13

Mission Briefing Log, Captain Hux Carter,
2/30 15 3202 OEH

Rich was bleeding, and it was everywhere. Just everywhere. You saw his blood and you saw the gel that the bug was shitting out and you wonder, how in the hell did I ever mistake the two?

I say bugs because that's what they were, and we can see that now, plain as day. Ash was right, even in the cursory examination before she went on to Rich: it was dead. It had taken a point-blank shot from inches away *directly* to the eye, but it *was* dead. That gave me solace, but not much.

Ursula and I, we had our weapons trained up at the vents right away. Looking for more of them. There weren't any, at least not yet, but that slime was pooling and dripping down the wall again. We re-secured the screw that kept that grate in place, for as little good as it did.

The skittered sound from outside? That had reached brown noise levels by the time we were just about to take down the bug? They were gone. They were gone and I had hopes that that was the end of it. Faint hopes. False hopes. But: hopes.

The adrenaline twisted, changed, and Ursula turned back to the bug. "What the hell was that?" she yelled. "What the hell is that?"

We could get a good look at it now, now that it wasn't moving around at lightning speed. Now that the element of surprise was gone. It was hard to focus on it, though. Every second there was a new sound, real or imagined, that would draw a gaze to the barricaded door or the vents, or any other possible point of entry.

It was a long brown fucker, at least ten feet in length. It started out at the head with this big, thick skull. I can't describe the shape, not really. I could try to draw it. Triangular, I guess, would be the best approximation. Roughly. Broad at the top and coming down to a sharp mouth, and hard as a rock. That was why the weapon blasts weren't doing much good: there was this thick carapace that was the skull and ran in segments down the back of it. It ran over the belly, too, but it was weaker there. Not soft, but softer. The skull, it had these two beady little eyes and I'm not sure how Ursula got a shot in there, but I was glad she did. Those slits were small though, not the kind of shot you could make from a distance. Borderline impossible, improbable to say the least. And that triangle shape to the skull, it had bends that came out. I say triangle only because it's the closest thing, but it's not right. Not quite. These bulges came out, like cheekbones, and when you touched them, they were *sharp*. Fucking razor sharp, and they had these thick hairs like bristles along them; they came out when you touched them. The whole thing came down to that mouth, too, too far from the eyes. Too damn far to look natural. The mouth looked small, but it wasn't — the jaw came down and it was massive. Massive enough to fit Rich's head into, and I don't know how he didn't lose it. And coming off the sides of it were these mandibles, little arms that helped get the food in. And they were sharp too. Serrated, with more of those little hairs.

Below the head, it had this section that I'm going to call a torso, but please understand that it wasn't a torso. This thing, all of it, below the head, it was in segments. Each segment about a foot long, thick up near the head but thinner and thinner as it went down. Like a worm or a snake, I don't know biology. Like those cartoon drawings of caterpillars, where each part of the body is a different circle? And it's connected by the carapace. But this top section, this torso section, it doesn't have the soft belly like the rest of it has. It was hard the whole way around, except for this little section under the arms. And the arms, they're huge. Just these massive implements, knives on hinges. No fingers to speak of, a small little pincher like a crab, though I'd hesitate to call it a thumb. Serrated, again, with more of those bristles.

I remembered, then, the gouges along the walls in the hall. The little hairs left in them in pockets. And fuck me, these things could tear through solid metal like that?

At the base of the torso were two other limbs. Different from the arms, more hinges. They still came down to spikes though, and I remembered the tiny dots in the dust of the hall. Said as much to the team. Recalled the tapping outside, right before the bug attacked. Got the eye from Ursula for not waking her and raising the alarm, when I told them that bit. She was right, of course.

The tail of the creature, the part that it had been dragging when it attacked? It hadn't had to. From between each of the sections of carapace was a leg that could fold out. Sharp, triple-hinged, hairy like the rest. They got smaller and smaller as the segments got smaller and smaller. The underside here was softer, more vulnerable. Much harder than human flesh... harder than my armor, I hate to admit, but of the creature's physiology: that was the weak place, yes. I pictured it keeping itself low on the ground to crush Rich, use its weight — at least four hundred kilos — to its advantage. But now I think it retracted its feet in battle, to keep as much of its weakest area protected against the floor. Maybe it tucked its legs in to navigate the vent?

The thing I'm not selling is, the thing was a horror show, even in death. I'd never seen anything like it, Ursula said she'd never seen anything like it. It looked ready to rise up at any moment, even though we'd been assured it wouldn't. Assured by whom, Ash? The human medic, who'd also never seen these things?

It started to ooze pink from between each of its carapace connectors, and that took some of the edge off. Some, but not all. It was like being in the room with a dead demon the size of a shark. With something so big and foreign that you'd told yourselves a million times growing up that it couldn't exist. But here it was. Even in death, it broke the brain. Horrifying.

Ash gets Rich patched. He's bleeding from both the arms, big gouges that went down to the muscle and shaved. He can't hold a weapon, can't squeeze a trigger. Our best shot just became dead weight, and that's a hard reality. He has another slice making a ragged red sash across his torso, but Ash has got the bleeding stopped. He was a good soldier, and regardless of whatever else, she was a good medic. She got him to a state he would have survived from, but he couldn't move. Not then.

When we're sure he's out of the woods, we start to plan. Ursula and I are the only ones huddled, but we're not excluding them. We're doing it loud and they're contributing.

Ash, she wants out. Not afraid to say it. No questions there.

Rich, he's pissed off. Royally fucking pissed off. I can see why. He might be out of commission for good if we don't get him out soon. He wants to get out but he's not afraid. He wants to raise this bloody place to the ground from low altitude, and I can't say I blame him. Been here less than a day and this is already the most FUBAR any mission has gone I've ever been a part of or heard of.

Ursula, she's all for killing them. Rich says that and she's fully on board. Not bloodthirsty, but almost. But, she says, "There's nothing saying there's more of them. That thing? It could have taken out this base. Especially the way Alt weapons work. That thing could have taken down this whole base and now we've killed it."

And that's when Ash said the most helpful thing she'd ever said, and I fucking hated her for it. I hated her not because it was wrong or because it was mutinous or because it didn't help the situation — I hated her for it because it made me more scared than I ever had been in my entire life.

She said: "It can't be the only one, because it's a male."

And I didn't know what to do with that and must have looked like it, because she got up from having patched up Rich and made her way to the bug creature. From just between those two first legs, right before the hard underside became softer, there was that appendage. The one it had taken down and aimed at Rich before we'd gotten our shit together. The one that, hindsight being what it is, was probably what had pierced the Alt Private's heart. It was sharp like the rest, serrated but with smaller ridges, all going the one way. Lots of bristles. But Ash, she points it out, holds it forward, and she doesn't call it an appendage or a limb. She calls it its *male* appendage, and that's about it for me.

It's a male bug, and the mess hall was filled with eggs. So there had to be at least one more, but if she had to make a guess based solely on entomology... there had to be at least a dozen for every one female. And that was before whatever was in the eggs woke up.

I have never felt the blood leave my body so fucking fast, I don't mind telling you. I wanted them dead, every last one of them. They were terrifying, and I wanted every last one of them at the end of my boot.

But there wasn't a need for a vote, for once. We all knew the score, now. We were all aligned. We had to get out. Ash and I seemed to be the only ones afraid of the bugs, but she didn't seem to care if they got squashed or not. Ursula, she was still unflappable. So was Rich, and that was the crazy thing. If I'd been taken apart like he'd been, I'd have been scared to hell. I already was scared to hell, although I wasn't about to show it. They both wanted the bugs gone though: Ursula by any means she could, Rich specifically from a safe distance.

So we're not quite aligned, but we're aligned enough. The way forward is clear: get. The hell. Out. That's all there is to it and that's all there needs to be. Get out and get back to the drop point, get the hell out of here. Take the bugs out along the way if we can, and certainly from above. We knew there wasn't anyone on this base that could manage anti-aircraft, if nothing else.

So we have a plan, and the four of us, we all agree. First time since we started the away mission, we all agree.

Rich is bleeding, and he can't move much. Moving on his own stretches the skin, makes the bleeding happen more. He can move on his own in small bits, but it's better and safer with help. Even with help though, he's leaking fluid. He's leaking fluid and there's a lot of it, and there's a distinct smell that he's probably started to lose control of his bowels that everyone is too polite to comment on. But we know it's bad news.

So we're making plans on how to handle Rich, how to get him out of there. Who helps carry him, and how. Test a few methods, figure out what helps the bleeding the most. Only way we can figure, is there're two helping him, carrying him like he's a stretcher, but that leaves only one person with a weapon at the ready and that's... that's a rough pill to swallow, the situation we're in.

Ash is re-patching him, everything moved when we were testing it. She's making the bandages better for the way we decided to carry him now. Like, now that we know, there's an optimal strategy to how to place them.

But then it all becomes very, very moot.

Because the skittering comes back outside the barricaded door, and those same taps. Those thinking taps, three in a row, sudden and un-patterned. Louder than it had been before, and with more of it. And with the knowledge now of the creature's legs, your mind wandered. It was a lot of skittering, was each tap one of those legs? It was loud, staccato, like white noise. Was the big creature outside the door larger, with more segments, and more legs... or were there more of them? Many more?

Those questions had just begun to come to me, when there was a heavy slam against the door that made the barricade shake.

14

27/30 14 3202 OEH

All four turned to the doorway of the comms room as one, the slam drawing their attention and harnessing it. It came suddenly and hard, like a punctuation more than a strike. There was no buildup, no sounds of turmoil of recoil following. The sound came, like thunder, and then was gone.

The four of them stared, all of them breathless save Rich, who was struggling for each and every one with increasingly intensity. It came in hisses through teeth gritted in pain, and a sloshing sound from his midsection whenever he tried to take one deeply.

Carter swallowed hard, laryngeal protuberance bobbing with it. It seemed as though there wasn't enough saliva in his mouth. They'd felt the desert ever since they'd arrived, but now it became them. His tongue was sand, all of it, and his eyes itched with sweat.

The door didn't move. It hung there like a void, as did everything in front of it.

Furthest back and behind everyone else, Ursula re-primed her weapon with the *tik-tik-tok* of the thumb dial. Carter looked back at her, briefly, just with his peripheral vision, then did the same. *Tik tik tok.*

There was a scant skittering sound that might have been their imaginations, then another monstrous clap of thunder that most certainly was not. It shattered through the room, reverberating.

"It's a distraction!" Ursula barked, turning the light on on the end of her weapon and aiming it back at the vents.

"I don't think so," Carter said, even as he raised to his feet.

"You won't fool me again!" Ursula shone the light in past the grates, getting nothing back but distorted shadows and reflections off the metal. "Fucking bugs!"

"They smell the blood," Rich said, huffing. It was hard for him to speak and Ash's hand on his shoulder attempted to convey to him that he shouldn't. He was looking down at himself as he spoke, red still growing out into the pale pink of the bandages.

"You don't know that," Carter said, tilting his head towards Rich but not turning. Not taking his eyes or attention off the door. It was not the reassuring statement he'd hoped that it would be. His tone was not in it, and he couldn't be sure that Rich was not correct. There was nothing like the thing on the floor in front of him on record. "There's nothing like that thing on record," he reiterated, a moment after he thought it. "We don't know what it wants. We don't know how it works. We don't know *anything*."

The slam came to the door again, and this time the door shook forward. Not enough that they could see it with their eyes, but enough that the barricades shook. Smaller items lunged forward on their perches, and one toppled and smashed.

Carter's gaze followed it down. It had been a large glass container, solid and weighty. It had been filled with navigational decorations: old school compasses and Alterian maps, mounted on stone for display. He looked back up to the door, to the edge of it, and now there was light bleeding in from the hall. Where before there had been just a shadow of black, now there was a gap. There was light, and with it, shadows and sound. The skittering was still there, and Carter thought of those legs that folded back. Imagined them moving, tip-toeing across the dust -ridden floor. He saw the movement, the motion to the gap and then back, and for a moment he even thought he saw the sliver of a face, not unlike the one that lay dead on the floor of the comms room, peering one small eye in at them.

"There's more than one of them," he said, raising his weapon and propping it against his shoulder. "There's more than one of them, and they're going to get in."

Rich reached for his weapon and struggled to bring it up to a useful height. Ash tried to stop him but he resisted, pulling away, pulling his bandages. She stopped and helped him rest the weapon against his abdomen just so so that it faced the door.

The door thundered again and opened another inch. Ursula turned from the vents, sure now that it wasn't a diversionary tactic. More than the skittering sounds of the needle-feet they walked upon, there were mouth sounds now. Slurping, and a high-pitched sound that was just on the upper register of what Carter could even hear at his age, but which the others heard with ease. It gritted the teeth and made their ears strain. It chirped and chuffed between the two of them with no rhythm or cadence they would have been able to identify. Alterian speech was bad enough, indecipherable enough, and Caps was worse, but nothing compared to the alien-ness of those sounds. They didn't sound like something nature could make. It *sounded* synthetic, the squeal of radios out of tune. Squeals so loud they produced synaesthesia. White squeals. Squeals of burning blood and copper.

Ash got her weapon ready and primed it. *Tik tik tok.*

Carter looked down at her, chancing a glance away from the door. He raised a hand, shook his head. "Get ready to grab Rich. Get ready to grab him and run." He looked at Rich with sympathy. "You're going to get ripped up again, but we're going to patch you up. It's going to be okay." He said it as though he meant it.

Rich nodded with reluctance.

"Sir?" Ursula asked, knowing what his words meant but not wanting to believe them without confirmation.

He shot her a hairy eyebrow. "We're boxed in. Totally, completely. We can push them back but they're going to keep coming, and we don't know how many there are. Staying at comms was a solid plan when we made it, but we need to get out. Now. Because they know they can come at us from both sides, and they're going to until they're done." He looked down at Ash and Rich. "We need to get back to the drop site."

He didn't say they'd been right. He didn't need to and he didn't know that they were. The Eon had a blameless system. There was no right and wrong, the *vote* was right, even if the outcome of that vote was undesirable. The vote, and their structure that allowed it, had taken the information they'd had at the time and had led them to the comms room. Now this new information was not only rendering the best choice different, but the vote obsolete. The third rule of the Eon handbook was, democracy is for when the fire has dimmed.

Rich nodded at Carter, and he back.

There was another slam at the door, as thick, armored bodies threw themselves against it. Then again, just after, shaking everything forward another inch. The hallway was clearly visible now, though the shapes within it went by too quickly to focus on. There was a third strike at the door, this one accompanied by a sudden *whoosh* of air. In his mind's eye Carter knew it had been the tail, the sound coming back to him as sounding just like the steady push of a crocodile tail's near his ancestral home. He thought of the damage those could do, then compared it to the girth and heft of the creature on the floor, which had less a tail than it had lower half that became akin to one. It became like unto a tail when the legs were folded up inside its carapace. Another strike, attention snapping back from memory.

There was a long moment then, when there was nothing. No movement in the crevice between the door and the frame. No dancing of shadows. No thunder. Just the still on the air, the dust, and the reminder that they'd walked into a tomb, and the certainty that these were the things that had made it so.

"Here it comes," Carter said, under his breath. His finger put first pressure on the trigger. "Aim for the eyes."

The clap of thunder came again, and the barricade burst inward, scattering and shattering along the floor in front of them!

The door pushed forward enough that it could just be called open, and the upper torso of a creature almost identical to the one on the floor before them jolted into view. Its teeth gnashed, talons scraping at the air and rending even the thick stone of the items they'd used to barricade to pebbles. It was slightly more greenish than the dull brown that the one that had harmed Rich had been, still brown but with just a hint of chlorophyll. Like the colour of infant waste.

It screamed as Ursula opened fire with Carter, almost simultaneously. Rich followed suit a moment later, when he could, even as Ash prepared him. Rich's shot landed against the crown of the creature's head, while Ursula and Carter's on either side of its cheek. It squealed, taken back, blinked. Then shut both eyes and lunged forward again, taking more of the barricade with it.

There was a sharp ducking movement from behind, followed by a steady, fast scrape. A second one of them had ducked down below, reaching its talons into the room and burrowing away at the barricade from under the legs of the other.

Rich fired twice more, each time hitting high off the creature's skull, but each time getting closer and closer down to its slender ocular orbit. Carter and Ursula both stayed on target, staying within inches of the creature's right eye... but it kept them closed, and did not seem to recoil with the same reaction as it had when it had been opened.

It pushed through into the room more, pushing the barricade back even as it and its cohort scraped and clawed it away in chunks. It squealed, loud, deafening.

"Once the door is free, push it back and get down the hall around it!" Ursula bellowed. "Do not stop to engage!"

"Don't yell the plan!" Carter returned, above the rifle fire. "We don't know if they can understand Eon!"

"I will give my entire pension if these god-forsaken things can understand anything we're saying!"

"You're really counting on us living long enough to collect it?" Ash snapped.

Carter, Rich, and Ursula all fired at once, all striking within a half foot of each other, full force. The Bug lurched back, backed up, then pushed forward, no longer pushing the barricade inward but attempting to climb in over the top of it. Its eyes were bloodshot, red, and the back of it was visible now, mustard-yellow spots along the shit-green rungs of its armor.

"Push it back!" Carter screamed, getting in closer while staying out of the range of the talons. Blast after blast of pressurized air shot from his weapon, so fast that its internal motors struggled, bringing air in through the sides of its muzzle and forcing it out with enough speed to have blown a hole in the chest of any Alterian soldier. The creature acted as though it barely felt it, scrambling over the eroding base of the barricade, sending implements toppling down onto the Bug that was still burrowing beneath it.

Its scrambling over the top of the barricade was a problem. It was a problem because, as it removed the barricade, it was also clearing a path for *them* to escape around it. It was clear already that, unless one of their shots was very lucky, they wouldn't be able to kill the creatures during this stand. And that it *would* get in. Therefore, the only strategy was to force their way out and run the moment the creature cleared a path for them.

But by forcing its way in over the mound, it was circumventing the barricade in a way they could not easily replicate. Their own barricade would trap them inside, with the creature.

Two blasts, one from Ursula and one from Carter, hit the creature's cheek at the same time. It cracked the carapace — not enough to make it bleed, but enough that it recoiled. It looked more like skin cracked under the heat of a summer sun than the result of weapon's fire.

"Same spot, aim again!" Carter yelled. They both tried for the same spot again, but each fell to either side of it. At this intensity, the weapons had a wide berth the further away from the target they were, like buckshot. It made hitting a small target together, on purpose, nearly impossible.

When it backed up and reached the top of the mound, the bug creature belched and leaned forward, vomiting up thick volumes of the veined red gel that covered seemingly everything they touched. It steamed and bubbled with heat, as though the stomach it had come from were a furnace, and some of the barricade began to melt away before it. It pulled back, shielding itself behind the barricade, then started in on it with its partner.

"Rich, cheek!" Carter yelled.

All three of them aimed for the splinter in the creature's cheek, and while neither hit it, Ursula and Rich hit the same part of the face, just where the creature's right orbit curved down to its nostril. The shell split again and it squealed, fell back, and was immediately replaced with the bug that had, until now, been burrowing.

"Going to need to figure out a way to up the maximum setting," Ursula said, under her breath, before taking another well-aimed shot.

Rich chanced a glance in her direction. She thought they were getting out of this, he noted. She thought it enough that she was planning on how to engage these things they'd never seen before, whatever they were, in combat again. He respected that optimism but did not share it.

The last dregs of the barricade were being peeled away at an incrementally increasing speed as the excitement for whatever happened next became more and more apparent from the creature's actions.

"Are you ready?" Carter said, and just by the tone Ash knew he meant she and Rich. He didn't need to turn away from his shot to indicate to her, and she replied in the affirmative. He nodded. "As soon as it's past the debris, we all fire. Aim for the neck, first rung down. Everyone, full force. Then we charge, left, towards the exit." He paused. "Ursula and I on either side of Ash and Rich."

Ursula nodded. "I'm lead."

"Commander is lead," he corrected. "Commander is North. It's SOP."

She swallowed, then agreed.

The creature was pulling back debris that was even still reacting to the green-hued creature's red vomit. It seemed to sizzle at its talons, but it did not stop or pause or slow in any way. It snarled and it growled, and its pupil-less eyes seemed to keep constant contact with each of theirs. It snapped and gnashed, chomping at the air around it as it pushed the last of the barricade back behind itself.

"Steady," Carter said, drawing out the syllables.

The creature grabbed the last of it, anchored itself by digging its talons in, and pulled.

"Steady..."

The last of the barricade was hefty, a mound of stone that had been a nightstand. The creature pulled once, then again, then on the third it came loose, and it fell back with it.

"Now!"

Carter and Ursula ran forward, each of them firing at the burrower bug and sending it scrambling back. Carter turned left after the doorway and Ursula just right, leaving a gap between them for Ash and Rich to push themselves out through. Both groaned and grunted, one from the strain of carrying and one from the strain of being carried, but Rich kept his weapon raised, and when they reached the open hall, fired it at the first Bug he saw.

"Move out!" Carter yelled.

The burrower bug with the bluish hue was scrambling to get up and Ursula got off several clean shots at it, direct to the face but not the eye. Two shots in rapid succession to the same area caused hairline fractures, but the creature did not recoil in pain the way it had when both shots had actually been simultaneous. Ursula backed up, keeping her eyes on it and not looking back at where the rest of her crew was, firing constantly at it to keep it at bay and then repeatedly in close succession when it tried to close the distance between them.

Carter and Ash moved forward with their eyes forward, Ash dragging Rich, who took shots from around Ursula when he could. He left a long trail of blood in his wake, and it seemed to get thicker with every step they took. Those rounded corners that had been mildly anxiety-inducing when they had been exploring not knowing what the facility had were now doubly so that they did.

The green bug with the burnt yellow spots on its back was in front of them, edging away from them. The crack in its cheek had grown and it was hissing, leaving a trail of burning red gel behind it. Rich cursed as he was dragged over it, but there was nothing to be done. His blood mixed with it in his wake but refused to mingle or intertwine, like oil and water. Carter fired at it, keeping it moving away from them, just as Ursula fired at the blue-tinted one, keeping it from moving close.

They rounded the corner, nearing the first of the dormitories they'd surveyed, and there were more of the bugs. They skittered and ran this way and that, from one room to the other. Five at least, possibly more. They moved like a swarm of bees, climbing over one another, making it impossible to keep track of their numbers.

Carter cursed the name of his savior and stopped short, as did Ash behind him.

"What is it?" Rich asked, twisting.

"What is it?" Ursula parroted.

Carter watched in horror as the green-hued bug creature turned back to them and eyed them, then let out a loud, piercing squawk. Two others from the rummaging pack turned their heads to it, then beyond it to them, separated from the pack and joined it. They started back towards Carter, cautious under his fire.

"We're blocked off!" He backed up a pace, squeezing the bubble between he and Ursula that Ash and Rich existed in. "There's too many!"

Ursula turned back over in shoulder in horror, then down to Rich. He nodded. "Back to front!" she yelled. "South to North!" She pushed forward suddenly back the way they'd come, darting to one side to allow Rich enough room to provide cover fire. The bug with the blue hue that had been chasing them turned to him, the trail of blood he left becoming a red carpet, and charged.

Ursula brought her weapon down just as it was reaching him, levelled it to the creature's eye, and let out three blasts in rapid succession. Its talons tore across her clavicle before she could, opening the skin and exposing the muscle underneath. The blasts pierced the creature's skull and sent it reeling back away from Rich, even as Ash was turning and pulling him back the way they'd come.

"We're heading away from the exit!" Ash screamed at no one in particular.

"There'll be another one!" Carter bellowed. He landed a blast against the splintered cheek of the green bug, making it edge back until it was protected in the shadow of the other two. They chattered back and forth in a way eerily close to speech, but not quite.

Rich concentrated his fire on the creature on the right, which was brown like the one that had first grabbed him and, because of that, looked nearly identical. Carter noticed, and alternated between it and the other new recruit, one with a greyish tint to its brown carapace. He hoped that one of the shots fired at the brown one would time well enough with Rich's that it would stumble back and retreat.

They passed the corpse of the blue one, legs curling in reflexively like the other had, and then passed the entrance to the comms room. There was no talk of going back inside, but as they passed Carter could hear the subtle click of the radio switching between frequencies as it reached out for help on all bands they'd thought to program.

Suddenly, the grey one pounced forward and lunged for Rich, seeing an opportunity the team hadn't realized they'd left and seizing on it. A talon ripped through his leg and stayed in it, like an anchor, nailing him in place as Ash screamed and tried to pull him away. He bellowed, the yell of a man being pulled apart, even as the creature slammed its other talon forward into his calve and did the same. Blood erupted.

"Help!" Ash screamed, and Carter pushed his gun forward into the creature's face. It pulled away, burying its face and eyeholes between its arms, protecting itself from Carter's blasts. "Help!" Carter chimed.

Ursula turned back from her post and pushed her back to the way they were headed, firing over Carter's shoulder in a way every superior officer they'd ever had would have chided them over. He felt it ripple through the muscle, but ignored it.

Ash pulled back on Rich, trying to free him from the bug, when the brown one Rich had been concentrating his fire upon leaped over the grey one and lunged at her. She leapt back, reflexively, letting go of Rich. "No!" she and Carter yelled in unison.

The grey bug pulled, dragging Rich forward. Rich brought his gun up and fired three times at the creature's stomach, and one punctured it, releasing blood and hot bile out on to him. It did not make the creature stop. It brought down both its talons into Rich's stomach and pulled in different directions, skewering him and then lowering its gnashing teeth down into the hole.

"Fall back!" Carter yelled, waving his hand but never taking his eyes off of Rich. He pulled Ash to her feet. He let out three shots that glanced off the brown creature's carapace, but they weren't facing him right now. They were gathering around the meal of a shared catch.

"Fall back!"

15

Mission Briefing Log, Captain Hux Carter,
2/30 15 3202 OEH

Transcriber's note: five minutes of silence heard at the start of this section of the tape was silence in the room, not a recording error.

Rich was a good officer. A loyal officer. I want that noted in this transcript and in his log. Whatever honours you want to give him, you give. Do I make that clear? This doesn't continue until I know that that's clear. I understand my orders, and you can do what you like. But this goes nowhere until I get that confirmed.

We get away from the creatures while they... while they're eating. At least I assume they were eating. Hope they were eating. We get down near the mess hall and we stop, find a room with an entry point on either side so that we don't get boxed in, a little atrium. Or what was; there's just dead things in there now, like everything else in that damn place. Dead plants, wilted. The room stank of it. But we get far enough away that we don't think they'll catch us while we're prepping, and we get into this little room and close the door behind us and barricade it. For all the good that did us last time.

We curse and we mourn, as well as one can mourn when there's shock and adrenaline running through you. We catch our breath, as best we can. Try to get our minds to catch up to what's happening but... yeah, there's cursing. A lot of it. So much that your brain just can't process, no matter how well you train. And they were, all of my team, well trained.

Ash patches up Ursula's shoulder. Thankfully it's just a flesh wound. The way these things go after blood, I'm not sure we'd have made it out of that room if it hadn't been. Ash managed to cauterize it, stop the bleeding, and we take stock of weapons.

We've been firing too quick, but Ursula most of all. Her transistor coil is warped and might get burnt out at any moment. No transistor coil means no ability to push out air with enough force that it feels solid. It'd be like shooting blanks. I should know, back in the day my old man used to give us old weapons with the transistor coils burnt out to use as toys.

We switch Ursula's weapon with Ash's, who has been using hers the least. It's not a great solution, but it's something. If Ash keeps using hers the way she has been, neither of them will burn out. And of the three of us, Ursula is the only one so far that has managed to kill one of the bugs, and she's done it twice. So that's the last one of us we want their weapon freezing up on, we decide. Unanimously.

The rest of the weapons, we each have two vacuum seals each and one pressure claymore, each. Both of them are weapons of last resort when you're in close quarters like this. They were brought with the expectation that we'd be coming up against a fully manned outpost. Use either one for lobbing it into a confined space from the outside, you're going to do some damage while the structure itself protects you. But when you're inside with it? Forget it.

Pressure claymores, they're good in any environment, but you have to be protected from them. You set them off on a timer, five, ten, fifteen seconds, whatever, and when they go off, they blow pressurization out in all directions around it. I've seen it buckle steel, but that's not the most common result. The most common result is that anyone in the vicinity finds themselves pressed up against that steel in short order. Survival is possible under the right circumstances, but the results are usually like crush syndrome. Like being underwater at high pressure, you're just buckled in on yourself. They're most effective inside, but they can do lots of damage outside, too. Can take the skin right off you, if you're too close.

Vacuum seals are much the same, but opposite. It's not pushing air out, it's calling air in. It makes a vacuum in whatever space around it, as best it can. Brings in all the air so that there's none left to be had. It doesn't last long enough to be lethal, and it doesn't have the power to last a long range, but it's good. Useless outside though; new atmosphere just rushes in faster than the thing can pressurize it.

Ursula checks them all, makes sure they're primed. Makes sure the claymores have pressure in them, in case we get into a tight spot and need to use them.

Now that we have the weapons taken stock of... we take stock of the fact that they aren't working. We brainstorm. From what we gather, we need about double max strength to even break the outer shell of one of those bastards, unless you get up-close-and-personal enough to get a point-blank shot. And even then, only in the soft parts. Under the arm. In the eye. Probably more, and I found myself wishing we'd had time to do some target practice on the one we'd killed back in the comms room, really figure out where its weak points were.

But we didn't do that. And there was no use crying about it now.

So we're brainstorming, and Ash, she has the bright idea that we should be using what we know of Alt technology as a kind of reference point. Like, not only do we know that our weapons aren't effective against them, but we know *theirs* weren't, either. Or at least, we can infer that. So we start thinking about what those things have in common, and we come back with *heat*. Ursula comes up with it, actually. Alts don't use heat for just about anything except cooking. They don't use pressurized water, either, but we don't have access to that.

Heat, though, we do.

We calibrate the weapons to shoot hot air. It's harder to rapid fire like that, and there's a far greater risk of burning out the transistors, but it's the only idea we've got.

We try to get our bearings, figure out where in the structure we are. We know where the exit we barricaded goes: back to the hall that's filled with the bugs one way, and the eggs the other. And with our luck the way it's gone, they'll be hatched.

We know what's out that way, but we don't know what's out the other. Best guess is the other exit is a back corridor that connects a bunch of specialty rooms that might link us into another section of the outpost, hopefully one with none of the bugs in it. If it's laid out the way this one was, when we reach the arterial hallway, we turn right and keep going to freedom.

There's no need to vote. Sure the devil we know is back the way we came and that way lies the unknown... but the devil we know is certain death, and we each agree to take our chances with the unknown, given that. We barricade the door we came through as quickly as we can.

Set out.

16

27/30 14 3202 OEH

"This wouldn't have happened if we'd gotten out of here when things had *started* to go south," Ash said, raising the light on the end of her weapon as she and Ursula entered a new room. Carter was behind them, a good ten feet behind, guarding their flank. When all of them were fully into a new room and they were sure they wouldn't have to back up, he quietly began the process of barricading it behind them. They could not control what lay ahead, but they could try to limit an attack from behind.

Ursula turned to eye Ash, then rolled her eyes at her. She checked the corners of the room. Checked the ceiling corners and the vents, did this with a herky-jerky motion, as though she had to remind herself to do it every time, a new addition to an action so entrained that it was natural.

They were in a library, a small one, no bigger than the mess hall had been. The walls were lined with bookshelves, the space between them taken up by long tables that patrons could sit at and enjoy their selection. There were stained rings all over the table from where cold drinks had been enjoyed while reading on hot desert days. Several of them overlapped, forming Venn diagrams with no data points with which to tell what they were describing the similarities between.

There were small bookcases under the table as well, marking out places to sit. There was a seat, then a bookcase under the table to the right of that seat. Then a seat, then a bookcase. And so on. These were not full and looked to be a place where one could store the books that one took from the shelves to avoid clutter on the desk itself. Ursula found herself wondering if that was some stroke of genius from the caretakers here at Outpost Toth, or a normalcy among all Alterian libraries. She remembered all the times when studying for her exams that she'd sleepily spilled a drink over her pages

She stopped at one of those small, private shelves that was nearly full. She squat down and removed a text from it. They were dusty, like everything else on the station outpost had been. Each was hardcover, a single colour. She opened it, and a sea of Alterian words stared back at her. There didn't even seem to be enough spaces between the words for her to distinguish one from the other.

Ash stood over her, still checking the gaps between the shelves to her satisfaction. "Do you not agree?" she hissed.

"I agree that what's done is done, and that there's no sense re-litigating it now." She paused, raised to her feet, then stood nose-to-nose with Ash. "We do agree on that, right?"

Ash swallowed, then nodded. She stepped past Ursula, made her way to the door on the other side of the room just as Carter finished securing the one they'd come through.

He stepped away from his work to Ursula. He didn't ask her what the small confrontation he'd seen with Ash was about — he knew. Instead, he nodded to the door that lay between two stacks. "Should we block that one, too?"

Each of the rooms they'd been in since escaping the hall had been connected to one another, travelling along an arch to get to the next section of Outpost Toth. But each had also had a third door, connecting back to the hallway that ran parallel to the slate of rooms. As such, when they were in a room there was one exit they planned to use, and two entrances from which enemies could, theoretically, come from. But the choice to block off that hall entrance was always a hard one. They were often doing so blind, without knowing what lay in the next room beyond, and as such were vastly limiting their ability to retreat quickly, if necessary. As such, Carter had been hanging back, waiting for preliminary reports about the security of the next room before blocking off the current one's hall exit. And so it had gone like that. New room? Check it. Block the way you came. Scout the next, when all clear, block the alternate entrance. Then you're in the next new room, so repeat.

It was a slow process from a trio that were increasingly anxious to get out faster and faster. Stray sounds from the vents and pipes exacerbated this. Everything was something now, nothing could be the wind or the sand outside. Adrenaline had to be kept up or shock would set in; each of them could feel it in their fingers when it started.

Ursula stepped forward to Ash and they opened the door to the next room, peered in, then closed it again. She cursed.

"What is it?" Carter asked, voice hushed, stepping forward.

Reluctantly, Ursula nudged the door open again.

The next room was a kitchen. It was laid out very similarly to the library, the same base model as the library. Same dimensions, same layout. But instead of the desks that lined the centre of the room, there were flat tops and grills, with kitchen implements hanging from hooks above each. Each row had its own station, its own reason. The flat-top station was largest, but there were grills, a salad station that stank of wilted greens, and a deep fryer that looked to have been cleaned out before the station's takeover and infestation. Along the wall were fridges and freezers with glass doors, long since broken open and their contents spilled out, eaten, and rotted.

Among the stations were three of the bug creatures.

They were smaller than those that had chased them in the halls, both in height and in girth. Their shells, all three of them, had a whiteish tinge to it that made it appear translucent. Their talons appeared larger, but Ursula quickly realized that they were the same size, that these creatures simply hadn't grown into them, yet.

One was resting, the other two were eating from the same container of frozen meat. There was vomit on the floor near them where the temperature had disagreed with one of their stomachs.

Ursula let the door shut quietly, then turned back to Carter. He mouthed a curse, bit the corner of his knuckle to stop from cursing audibly. She nodded at him. Ash looked between them, and in that instant Ursula made up her mind about the medic. Full of ideas when the situation seemed safe, silent and looking to others when there was panic. She shook her head.

Silently, Carter motioned to the bookcase nearest the door to the kitchen. He framed it with his hands, marking out the top right and bottom left corners with his thumbs, then mimed tilting it downwards into the path of the exit. Both women nodded, and the three of them went to work taking the books off the shelf and stacking them on nearby tables to avoid a clatter that would alert the bugs in the next room to their presence.

Ash laid down a heavy stack of books and let out a beleaguered sigh that drew an intense stare from Ursula. She straightened stiffly, went back to her work without another stray sound.

When the shelf was clear, they worked together to tilt it down, blocking the door to the kitchen with its girth. The door opened out into the kitchen though, so if the bugs became altered to their presence the distraction would only be a temporary one. They would burrow at and climb over this barricade just as they had done to the one they'd formed in the comms room.

Carter looked to the door back out into the hallway and frowned. Without speaking, he made a forward jab towards the door with his hand, three fingers out. He then looped the hand around and back towards himself. Ursula and Ash both nodded, understanding. They would leave the security of the back rooms and go out into the hall, but only to go *around* the kitchen area, then come back into that relative safety again for as long as they could.

The three of them gathered by the door to the hall and Carter opened it, slowly. The hallway looked the same as every other they'd seen on the outpost, and there were no signs of the bugs, save for the small imprints on the dust of the floor that they now knew were their slender footfalls. He exited, turning to look down the opposite end of the hall, towards the kitchen, to the area that had been hidden by the door. It too, was empty, and the hall door to the kitchen had been barricaded shut from the hall side.

"Seems like some of the Alterians had sense," Ursula said, under her breath.

Carter nodded as they edged forward, stepping with the sides of their feet first and making slow, deliberate choices with where each step landed. Dust hung in the air, and they did everything they could not to disturb even it, acting as though they could dance around strands of it, as though they could dance around raindrops, had there been any.

They made their way around the barricade they hadn't made and forward down the hall until they reached the next door, equidistant from the barricaded door as each of the others had been. There was a barricade in front of that one, too... but also a window.

Carter moved his hand to go past it, but Ursula cut her hand across the air, miming a negative that was helped along by her expression. Quietly, she got on top of the barricade and looked in.

The room beyond the wire mesh window was a small gym with only weight equipment, a series of beds and benches from which to press from. In it, both auxiliary doors were visible, and both had their own barricades. A single bug creature was inside it, moving from side to side, as if on a loop of constantly checking to see if the defenses were still valid.

Ursula ducked down quickly when the creature turned towards their door. They heard it scraping at it, testing it, then the scuttle of its limbs fading as it walked away. She turned to Carter.

"No," he said, pre-emptively.

"It's trapped. The Alterians clearly trapped it there," Ursula reasoned. "That's the only way the other doors could have been blocked from its side, right? They block those off, herd it in, block it in." She tapped on the barricade she still squat on to illustrate. "So it's been in there all this time, right? Blocked in with no food."

"We don't know how long it can go without food before feeling the effects," Ash said, but without her typical contrarian demeanor. It was cold, clinical. Medical.

Ursula nodded appreciatively. "Valid. But, even so, it's trapped and it's *alone*. You could not ask for a better situation from which to test our heat theory." She tapped her weapon.

Carter huffed, sighed, then looked through the window at the bug. It *did* look weaker than the others had. It shuffled, and its flesh was a yellowish hue he associated with jaundice. He turned back to Ash, who reluctantly shrugged a nod.

"Would you rather find out if we're right about the hot air in a combat situation?"

His mouth warbled, then he nodded in agreement.

Ursula got up off the large stone cabinet that was blocking the kitchen door from opening. They took it from either side and gently lifted it out of the way.

Ursula checked her weapon, confirmed it was both on the highest pressure and heat setting, and nodded to the others. They pulled the door opened as quietly as possible and stood back as Ursula stepped into the frame.

The creature turned toward her almost immediately, as though it sensed she was there. Did it have incredible hearing? A preternatural sense of smell? She didn't know, and as of yet, there was no way of knowing.

She opened fire with a loud *pathoom pathoom pathoom* as the compressors of her weapon struggled to suck in the air around her and super-heat it in the milliseconds after each trigger pull. She yelled, a warrior's cry from deep in her diaphragm, showing off white teeth and spraying spit. She hit it in the shoulder, then the cheek, then split the carapace between its eyes, and it fell to the floor, unmoving.

She fired at it twice more for good measure, but it did not react. There was skittering and scuttling, but it was from the other room. Carter and Ash entered behind her, guns aimed.

"Heat did it," Ursula said, at first with exasperation and then with a wide smile. "Heat did it!"

They stepped around it, still with their weapons aimed at it. There was no telling what surprises the creature had in store, even in death.

"Set it at the highest," Ursula said to Ash, motioning to her weapon.

"It'll give out at that setting, reasonably fast."

"Better to get off three shots that work than ten shots that don't."

Ash nodded, adjusting the heat settings on her weapon.

"Alright," Carter said, resolutely. "We have a weapon, but that doesn't change our goal. There's too many of them to take out, so we still have to –"

The creature burst up, and Ash and Ursula both fired reflexively as they all stepped back. Carter raised his weapon and fired as well, a moment later.

The creature raised its head and screamed, a loud high-pitched siren call that rang out across the room, echoing and coming back at them from all directions, hurting their ears. They resisted the urge to raise up their hands and protect themselves from it, with Ash flinching the most. It screamed and on the other side of the wall, they heard the others raising their heads and screaming as well, like a howl. Like a beacon.

"Shut it up!" Ursula yelled, firing twice. It lashed out at her, slicing the skin across her belly.

Ash stepped forward and to the side, taking aim as close as she dared at the bug's eye. It was open and followed her, looking directly at her. She fired once at it and its head caved in and fell to the floor in a fit of blood and brain, just as Ash's weapon caught fire and shattered in her hand, sending shrapnel of plastic and metal out in every direction, including back at her. She cursed loudly, dropping what remained of the weapon.

In the room next door and in the hall far beyond, they could hear the screams continuing.

Carter stepped forward, looking down at the remains of both Ash's weapon and the bug creature. "Heat does *not* work," he said definitively. "Weapons back to room temperature."

In addition to the screaming howls that continued to pick up new voices, they heard skittering. The clacking of tiny legs on small points, all scuttling towards them.

"Let's get out of here."

17

Mission Briefing Log, Captain Hux Carter, 2/30 15 3202 OEH

The screams kept going. You could hear them, echoing down the hall. Echoing so much it was hard to tell just how far they were coming from. But you knew when a new voice joined the chorus. You could hear them in different rooms, in different sections, in different vents, all throughout the facility. Waking up, joining the chorus, and making sure others woke up too.

Wake up, brothers and sisters: there's fresh meat to be had.

Every door we went to we thought we could hear screams behind. We found one that didn't, but it was a dead end and a custodian's closet. But the creatures, we could hear them coming, so we climbed in. Trapped now, Ursula bleeding. Not bad, not life-threatening on its own, but bleeding a lot. Ash started using the items in the closet to patch her up, gauze and towels and such. But she was bleeding bad.

She was bleeding bad, and I was starting to get the hint that they were drawn to the blood. We could hear them converging outside in the hall. Skittering towards us from both directions. Stepping past, stopping, coming back. Could see shadows around the rim of the door where the seal wasn't light tight. Not being light tight means it certainly wasn't air tight. Meant it was only a matter of time before they found their way in to us.

There was a vent in the room. It set me on edge, given what happened the last time we thought we were safe. It was smaller than the last, limited by the width of the room itself. Barely big enough to fit through ourselves. But we didn't know how small a hole these things could fit through. If they were like regular bugs, they could squeeze through holes pretty small. Real bugs didn't care if they hurt themselves getting into a place, they got in and they killed and they ate and they had babies that wouldn't have to squeeze through that hole like they did. It was about the species, not the individual.

I checked the vent. There was none of that gel in it that they had left behind other places. What there was was air. The fresh heat of desert air that hadn't been circulated through fans and ventilation systems and all else.

For the first time, it was like the world outside the interior of Outpost Toth existed again.

18

27/30 14 3202 OEH

"They've found us!" Ash hissed, screaming a whisper. The shadows under the door had stopped now and the first scrapes had been made at the un-barricaded door.

"No choice now," Carter said firmly, opening the hinge that kept the vent closed. He stacked boxes and crates to make it easier to get up to them. "We follow the flow of air."

"What if it leads up to the conditioner?" Ash asked.

"It's *fresh* air. Desert fresh, but fresh."

Ash looked as though she were about to continue the debate, but the sound of more talons joining the scraping at the base of the door stopped her. She stepped back from it, able to see more light in the gaps the creatures were gouging. "No choice."

Ursula got to her feet by bracing herself against a rack of chemical supplies. They had symbols on them she wasn't familiar with and yet could infer their meaning to mean danger. When she stood, the pressure of expanding her gut made her wound open more, and blood spewed from her like vomit. Like it had been waiting in some pocket just below the flesh. She pressed her hands to it to try and keep it in, and the skittering and clawing outside the door intensified.

"You should let me dress this more," Ash said, leaning down. "This is worse than I thought."

Ursula looked at the clamoring, eager claws scrambling to get at them. The screams continued, more and more joining the chorus. More and more were joining the fray, discovering what everyone was talking about. She could hear them fight, hear them struggle for position, each wanting to be the closest to the door. She picked up her weapon that had been Ash's and handed it back to her. "You're going to need this."

"We have to go!" Carter hissed. His expression changed suddenly, seeing what was happening. "Ursula?"

"You're a better shot," Ash reminded her, not reaching out and taking the weapon back.

Ursula winced, looked down at the slice in her gut, then the door, then back at Ash. "I'm not going to be able to take it." She cocked her head back towards the vent. "What will crawling through that, pulling myself through that with my arms, do to me like this?"

Ash didn't answer, but in her eyes both could see she was calculating it. The stretch from the upper body as she tried to squeeze through pulling at the flesh, making it longer and larger. Leaving more and more blood behind for the creatures to follow and find her with and find *them* with. Without once confirming what Ursula was saying verbally, she took her weapon back.

"Come on!" Carter yelled, not bothering to hide his voice anymore. There was no point. They knew they were there. He yelled it first to both of them, then caught a look he'd seen too many times before from Ursula. When he said it again, it was only to Ash. "Come on!"

Ash joined him at the back wall, and he pulled her up and helped her into the vent. He turned back to Ursula again. They exchanged nods, and he climbed into the vent as well. It closed shut behind them.

Ursula staggered over to the wall, as far as she could get from the door, and lay with her back to the wall with the vent above it. She reached into her pouch and pulled out the pressure claymore she'd taken stock of earlier and smiled at it, arming it. It had full pressure. She took out the vacuum seals and rolled them to the other side of the room to either side of the door, smirking. She looked up at the chemicals on the shelves to either side of her and at the bottles with the strange Alterian symbols on each. She didn't know what they were but guessed just from their use that they were either explosive, corrosive, or poison.

She hoped for explosive, set her foot down on the activated claymore, then waited.

19
Mission Briefing Log, Captain Hux Carter, 2/30 15 3202 OEH

We used the ducts to escape. We followed the current of fresh air for what felt like forever.

We felt the explosion that Ursula left on our backs and feet after about ten minutes. Could hear the screams of the creatures as they burned in chemical fire. Felt the vents shift around us as one of the entry points to it ceased to be. I don't know if it blocked it off completely, and I guess we'll never find out.

I wouldn't have made it out if it wasn't for Ursula, I want that in the file. I want that in the file, now. I will wait on the rest of my testimony until you show me that it's in the file.

...Good.

We got out to the desert air just as the sun was coming up, that first orange of dawn tripping over the outpost, making shadows long. I had never been so happy to see sand. You want to kiss it, want to elate, but you know you can't. You know you're not out of the dunes yet. We don't have the supplies we'd want for a trek over the desert, but we have to make it anyway. Before we found the Bugs, we'd have assumed the desert was the only thing on this rock that would kill us. Now here we were, thankful for it.

We get three units outside the building before we turn, confirm that it's faded over the dunes. We're sweating, running like madmen. Running like they tell you never to do in a hot desert climate. Stripping off gear as it gets slogged with sweat, praying that we can get back and get to the extraction point before the sun rises to its fullest and bakes our exposed skin. Weighing one danger against the other, letting fear dictate our actions instead of Standard Operating Procedure.

When SOP goes the way of all flesh, you know that the mission is FUBAR. Not that we didn't know that before now.

We get further away, maybe another two, three units, and we stop. Drink as much of our water as our thermoses will let us. Breathe and take breath.

Our minds start to fill with those horrible thoughts, at least mine did. You start to think about the people you left behind in that building. You gotta keep those thoughts at bay, so you start to talk. At least I do. So I ask Ash, I ask her how she got to be in my unit, because she didn't seem the type. Didn't seem the type to want to follow orders, and yet they put her as a medic on an important recon mission.

She tells me, she tells me she had a bad C.O., once. The kind of C.O. every woman dreads getting. You know the type. Hard edged and old school and abusive. She tried to transfer eight or nine times she said, but by the time they did, the damage was done.

She had that chip on her shoulder. If she'd gotten out before that, before he'd had his fill and let her go, maybe we'd have had a better officer on our hands. One without quite so much distrust in the process.

I want that on the record as well. Ash was not born a bad soldier. Ash was made a bad soldier. You take a situation and you let it go FUBAR and then you expect it to look the same when you take those exploded pieces and you try to put them back together, and it won't happen. It will never look the same as it did before you let it go FUBAR, no matter how much glue you use.

I told her I was sorry, and that I knew that kind of Commanding Officer. That my old man was like that. A career boy, who stayed long after his time serving for his people was up. Like me, but harsher. The kind of C.O. you wish would stay at the war when he came home, because he always brought the war home with him. The kind of person I tried hard to never be like, despite how much it might seem like I followed him.

And that's when she tells me her last C.O. *had been* my father, and that's when it all falls into place. So I want that on the record. There's a lot of people to point fingers at as to why this went sideways, but one of them is sitting in a comfy chair back on the home-world. Eating figs. Finding ways to not send as much of his paycheck back to his ex-wife as he's supposed to.

And I've got to wonder, how Ash and I both ended up on this mission that went *so far* sideways. I'd love to be able to ask Ursula and Rich if they fit in that Venn diagram as well, if they were in the overlap between 'people who pissed off General Carter' and 'people who ended up on Outpost Toth.' But I can't ask them that, can I? And you won't let me check that in my files, will you? Mm. Yeah, I thought not. So, I want it on this record, if nowhere else.

We were debating making camp, just for an hour or so, when we heard the screams. We heard the screams of the Bugs coming in over the dunes and recognized them for what they meant.

"Here they are. They're over here."

20

27/30 14 3202 OEH

Ash and Carter could see them not long after they heard them. Could see their hard, monstrous forms slick and slide over the sand, leaving clumped trails of red gel congealing in the sand behind them. If they had ever been different colours, the dust from the desert had made them all the same hue of light brown. It clumped to their damp skin and hid them in the dark of dawn.

"There's too many of them," Carter said, watching as one began to burrow under the dunes with frightening speed. He raised his weapon and eyed the nearest one through its sight. "Too many of them and they're too far to try and pick off."

Ash swallowed, checked her weapon. Got her sweat-drenched jacket back on, hoping it would protect her at least somewhat from the creatures' talons.

They walked backwards, back towards their pickup location, but it was so slow it was futile. It only allowed them to tell themselves they were making at least incremental progress in the correct direction, as they kept their eyes and weapons trained back on the Bugs coming towards them.

One creature split off from the rest, sprinting out towards them, eager. It propelled itself forward with those large front arms, pulling itself into a near-gallop. It did not scream, it gurgled, leaving a trail of pink saliva behind it.

Carter raised his weapon and fired twice, trying to hit the eye even at that great distance. Ash followed suit. Both shots glanced off the creature's hide and it continued forward as though they were nothing.

Behind it, the others started to pick up speed as well, worried that their meal would be gone before they got to it. Carter saw that and repressed the shiver that went through his spine. He fired again, more and more, each shot less focused than the last. Ash did the same, mindful of a compressor gauge on the side, not wanting it to blow up in her hand as the last one hand. It was nowhere near the danger-zone.

One of the shots went low as the creature got within a quarter-unit of them, hitting the sand at its feet and the air pressure dispersed spraying it up into its stomach and face. It screamed and hissed, stopped advancing, started clawing at its own face.

Carter watched it, lowered his weapon slightly, mouth agape. He raised it back soon after, firing at the sand before the creature again, this time intentionally. "Spray the sand!"

Ash did so, taking aim at the horde of creatures coming over the last dune before it reached them. She laid down a line of fire that skidded across the sand in front of their front line. Even at that distance it sprayed the sand up and back towards them, and they all stopped and turned away, turned back. One bled from between the segments of its carapace, all clawed at their eyes. Some left deep gouges that she was sure had rendered itself blind.

That front line stopped and the next climbed over them, as they had when clamoring to get at Rich and to get to their closet hideout. There was no respect for those who fell behind. They clawed over them and pushed them down, excited if anything that they were closer than ever to getting a taste of fresh blood. She laid down a line of fire again to similar results, even as the creature that had advanced retreated under Carter's steady assault.

"We're forcing them back!" he yelled, triumphantly. He joined Ash in spraying fire at the line of creatures coming towards them. Some had turned back.

In the back, behind the front line of creatures upon which Ash and Carter had to focus their fire, Ash saw several burrowing down together. "What are they doing?" She asked.

Carter eyed them even as he kept laying down fire, squinting at them against the sun behind them. Watching four of them work at the same spot in silhouette, only to suddenly become three. He tilted his head.

He turned to the valley of sand between themselves and the line of bugs, the low ground they had to traverse in order to reach them that they used to their high-ground advantage.

There were mounds of sand moving towards them, moving in scattered, unclear lines. Moving towards the sounds of their weapons discharge, heading in one direction and leaving a trail of displaced sand behind them until the sound they were chasing corrected their path and they headed in another.

He turned, horrified, and saw that one of the mounds was within feet of Ash. "Ash, below West!"

She turned just in time for the Bug to leap from the ground and grab at her, talons slicing at the arm of her coat and missing her arms by bare inches. She fell back onto the sand.

Carter rushed in, spraying the sand between it and Ash with fire that seemed to do nothing, the spray of sand just beating the sand stuck to the creature from burrowing off. It raised its talons high to strike down at her and Carter threw himself to the floor, sliding on the sand and scouring his face and arm but getting beneath the creature. He wedged the tip of his weapon between the plates of its carapace and fired and full blast.

The Bug's leg, and most of that side of its body, blasted off. It screamed and vaulted away from them, spraying the reddish pink bile it left everywhere behind it. It rolled down the dune behind them until it came to a rest on its back, its remaining legs curling up.

Carter helped Ash to her feet. "That. Was close," he said, breathless, even as they stood back-to-back and continued to lay down a line of fire as more creatures came towards them.

Three more burrowed bulges of sand were converging upon them. Carter tried to fire at them while Ash tried to fire directly in front of them to try and force a retreat. Neither worked to harm nor to dissuade them. They kept coming, all three of them, at an ever-increasing rate. Two reached them at once and exploded out of the sand mere feet from them, screaming that deadly battle cry hiss they screamed.

Carter opened fire and stepped back, realizing he didn't feel the weight of Ash's back behind him.

When he chanced a glance over his shoulder, he realized she was gone.

***

Ash huffed hot desert air that burned her lungs as she made her way over the dunes.

She chanced a glance behind her every unit or so, confirming there were no creatures behind her. For the first few clicks she had laid down fire just to be certain but had then become concerned that the sound would bring them to her.

Her jacket and tunic had been discarded, their weight holding her down. The sun was to her right now, and she was sure she'd started to go into a circle several times and corrected herself.

She thought she saw dunes move, far off in the distance. She knew about fatigue and the illusions heat could create. The appearance of an oasis in the distance. She'd heard of that, but never heard of roaming dunes.

She tripped on a patch of sand that should have been soft enough for her foot to glide over and fell face first into a tall rise of sand.

Beneath her feet the obstruction moved away, and she gasped.

She drew her hands out of the rise of sand she'd fallen into and they came back clumped with it, sand sticking to her with globs of pink gel. She heard the growling hiss, low and serpentine.

The sand fell away directly in front of her, revealing the thick skull and beady eyes of one of the Bugs looking back at her. She screamed, but before the sound could gain any merit, two large talon-tipped arms sprung up from the sand on either side of her.

In an instant, she was dragged under the dunes.

21

Mission Briefing Log, Captain Hux Carter,
2/30 15 3202 OEH

I used two vacuum seals to get away from the two that Ash left me with, followed it up with a pressure claymore I planted behind me. It sprayed up enough sand to keep the others back while I ran... when they got close enough to it.

I made it to the evac point but couldn't stop anywhere along the way. They were on me the whole time, and when I found it and pressed for recall, I had to defend that position until transport arrived. Every part of me wanted to lay down and sleep, which would have been the same as laying down to die, but I didn't. Couldn't.

I took down five of those things while defending, but there were more. Always more, and they were getting closer. I was in a basin, and I was starting to get the idea that they were starting to surround me, to come at me from all sides at once, when transport finally came. Its engines kicked up enough sand at them that it kept them running, then it laid down some fire itself once I was in. I was grateful for it. Exhausted as I was, damaged as I was, I still watched out of the window as they took the Bugs down. As they ran.

I wasn't going to miss that.

Even on the way out of atmosphere they were trying to get the intel out of me. Hungry and dehydrated, the last of my unit, bleeding, tired — none of that mattered. They wanted to know where the intel was. I told them then what I told all of you: you'll get it after the briefing.

You'll get it after I make sure what's on the record and what's not. You'll get it when I'm sure — damn sure — that there's no way to cover this up. This was FUBAR from minute one and it needs to be known because I only know one thing about those bug creatures: they were not native to Outpost Toth. No way, no how. And that means we can't just air-strike the building and declare the outpost a no-fly zone and be done with it. They *came from* somewhere. So once this testimony is logged and sent and I can see that it's sent and I know you can't censor it, then you'll get the intel you keep asking about.

I got it from Rich, before he got taken by them. It's here, on me.

I recommend a full inquiry into this mission, and into these creatures. And full benefits to the families of Rich, Ursula, and Ash.

It's the SOP.

FLICKERS IN THE NIGHT

The first time he'd come at her she had been nineteen years old and he'd been in his mid-twenties. She didn't know exactly how old he'd been because when, much later, she'd filed a police report she discovered that he'd lied about his age. In the grand scheme of things, it had been by far the least of the things he had lied about.

They had been arguing all afternoon. It was not their first argument by any means, nor would it be their last. It had been a year since they'd met and each of those fifty-two weeks had been punctuated by at least one argument. There were arguments about money and arguments about other men, arguments about other women and people she knew at work and people he knew at work. There was an argument for every flickering star in the night sky, it seemed sometimes, but that argument when she was nineteen had lasted all day.

It had started when they'd gone out for breakfast. They had chosen some fast food establishment that held the promise of endless pancakes and when he had pulled their car – a rusted beater from an age when rustproofing came included – he pulled in too close to the Chevy next to them and nicked it. "Careful," she said, through clenched teeth, wincing as she heard the metal touch metal. He had turned to her, surprised, and the fight had begun. There had been something in her tone that had hurt him, that had insulted the way he thought of himself or had given voice to his deepest insecurities, and so he responded in kind. And as soon as Ryan Valler had lashed out at Lisa Rowdan, Lisa Rowdan lashed right back – equally hurt by his anger, his frustration, and his ability to swing into moods where she felt she couldn't speak.

The argument went through breakfast and into dinner, through dinner and then stopped while they went to a movie. After the movie she had attempted to apologize, and something in her tone had irked him again, and the fight had resumed into the evening. In its tenth hour she had left the room he was in and closed the door to take a breath, and something about the way she had closed the door had set him off. He had stormed after her, flung the door open, put a finger in her face, and yelled. She cursed at him, and he responded by placing both hands against the nape of her neck and shoving her back against the wall.

***

It had been months since she had finally been rid of him for the last time, but every so often Lisa would still feel him near her... The spicy fish stench of a man left unwashed for several days would come too close to her on the subway and remind her of that state of him at the end, and it would be like he was there with her. Or someone would touch her arm a certain way to get past her in a crowded market and she would turn and expect him to be there, her hand usually on the bottle in her purse by the time she turned and realized it wasn't.

She'd first caught a glimpse of him in The Market on Tuesday. The Market was a massive collection of strip malls and restaurants that may as well have been its own tiny, self contained city. Concrete streets ran between businesses separated into perfectly equal square lots of glass and brick, each with their own separate address and power. Dozens of patrons walked back and forth, these streets as busy (or sometimes busier) than those on the outside. There were no vehicles; all traffic was strictly by foot. Still, there were collisions as people scuttled about, paying no attention to what they were doing or where they were going. They just kept texting or dialling or web-surfing their way right into another human being's face.

Lisa had manoeuvred between patrons seamlessly. It was a hot day – the type of hot that got people out of their homes – and the streets had been lined with tables to expand The Market beyond its concrete walls. Rickety, water-stained folding tables lined the parking lot stacked high with goods, both displays from venues inside The Market to exhibitors that had paid for a day-use of the space. There was practically everything at The Market and no rhyme or reason to the way it was presented: fried rabbit was next to Pokémon cards which were next to discount paperback novels which were next to a table selling custom buttons and cheap tattoos.

She had seen him while stuck behind a confluence of people plugging the way in front of her, staring at a man at the clam-shucking booth two tables over. It had been brief – so brief that Crowley had later tried to tell her it was nerves – but he had been there. He had been staring at her from four rows of people back, his height allowing them to see past them all and straight at her. She'd turned incidentally and they'd locked eyes, and in that moment she knew who he was and why he was here. Tightness weighed down between her breasts instantly then, and she felt her stomach cramp as digestion ceased, sending that blood and energy to her limbs and preparing them for flight.

But he was gone by the time she looked again. But he had been there.

There are studies that say the human brain can find one angry face out of a sea of smiley faces 99% of the time, even when they flash by at only a millisecond. Evolutionary advantages left over from when being able to spot a threat in a fraction of a second was as necessary for survival now as it had been one-hundred-thousand years ago. Was that true of faces that were recognized to be menacing even if they weren't scowling or frowning, she wondered? She thought it was, and the growing tension in her gut confirmed it.

***

They had met at a club she hadn't been old enough to get into that served cocktails long past the legal hour. There had been lights and a smoke machine that was improperly named – it spewed dust, not smoke, shooting it into the air and letting it hang there with its putrid dry smell. The lights were purple and blue and red and yellow that flashed and flickered in the night, the strobe light pulsating to the beat of the house music and making their movements staccato and crisp, like polaroid pictures flipped to try and make a film. That same smell of sweat had been in the air that night but it had been intoxicating, mingled with spilled drinks, second-hand smoke, and perfume to make a smell that neither of them would ever be able to pin down, but that somehow kept them dancing when they filled their lungs with it.

They had started dancing, neither of them sure how. Each of their pairs had left for drinks and when the house music played and the lights went up, the rhythm took you and you had to dance. His hands were on her hips and she moved with him, him behind her, and with the same instinctual lack of understanding about how they had started, they were kissing.

***

She'd seen him the second time on Friday, while having coffee with Xander at a cafe on Larchmont Boulevard. It was a small place with spread-out seating – the kind she liked – and a wall of flavours and accoutrements. The entirety of the east-facing wall was made up of one sectioned window that let in all the light from the early morning Los Angeles sunrise.

There was a building across the street that Xander was keeping his eye on while sipping his coffee and acting as a sounding board for Lisa – she found that he was often able to multitask in conversation only while listening, not while talking, and was fine with that. She was sipping an impeccably made cafe ole and eating a piping-hot helping of Romesco Grilled Cheese. She had been in the middle of a story when she turned to look out the window and saw him.

He was sitting at a restaurant across the street, eating a sandwich.

Lisa had stopped in mid-sentence.

He was sitting on a bench with his legs splayed out in a dubious example of man-spreading, taking up as much room as physically possible. He was wearing shorts and his knees were scabbed and dirty in a way she'd never seen before, to the point of being almost black. If she had seen anyone else across the road out of her peripheral vision, she may have been able to convince herself that those were knee pads, but Ryan Valler had never been never been the type to even wear a seatbelt, let alone knee or shoulder pads.

He was wearing a solid red shirt that demanded attention. Against the stainless steel of the city it screamed, *look at me, I'm right here* in bright, primary colours. And he was staring at her. He hadn't been at first, but it was if he'd known when her eyes had fell upon him and reacted in kind, shifting his gaze and locking it on hers.

"What is it?" Xander said after waiting for her to complete her thought.

Lisa turned back to him reluctantly. "My ex is across the street," she said, her hushed tone imparting the gravity of that statement without having to vocalize it. She stared ahead at nothing and pretended to drink her coffee as Xander turned.

"Where?" he asked.

"On the bench."

"There's no one on the bench."

She turned back and found that Xander was right; the bench had become vacant. It was quickly reoccupied by other commuters – it was, after all, Los Angeles – but Ryan was nowhere in sight, falling back into the crowds he'd come from.

***

She'd seen him act in violence that first night, not forty minutes after their lips had touched for the first time. There had been more drinks and two trips outside to smoke and at least one shot and the house music had revved up again, and as one of her crew was vomiting the others had dragged her back onto the dance floor. The room was packed far past fire regulations – they did not care for age or alcohol restrictions, why would they care about fire codes? – and was more of a mosh pit than a dance floor. Two hundred people were crammed into a space designed to fit forty, each of them moving and swaying drunkenly more one minute than the last. It was less of a dance with one person and more of a dance with everyone in general.

Sweat poured from Lisa and she smiled perpetually, her hands above her, catching trails of light. Someone kissed her neck and she thought it was Ryan again in the dark, and she led him off the floor before she realized it was someone else. She tried to move away and he made one step toward her to ask her to stay, whomever he was, and suddenly Ryan Valler had been there: the strobe making him appear suddenly, eyes fire-red with fury.

The man had been a foot taller and twenty pounds heavier than Ryan, but within moments the fight had been over, and he was kissing her with hands whose knuckles were rendered loose flesh.

It only occurred to her years later, once it was ending: how had he even known she had wanted to get away from the man? The answer was simple: he hadn't, because that hadn't been why he'd done it. She learned then the simplest truth, far too late for it to have mattered: Men capable of violence were men capable of violence. Period.

***

Although the street was empty, she knew she wasn't alone, the same way she'd known on the street before that and the street before that. Her anxiety had flared within her three streets prior, tightening into a small metal ball in her chest before stretching out, its tentacles reaching her biceps and triceps and calves, making each ache as they flexed and pulsed with speed still in reserve. She walked fast, but didn't do more than that, her fear never letting her do more or less than that -- if she went slower, he would catch her, it said, but if you go faster, he will chase you.

Lisa felt trapped on a city street that was as wide open as a street could be: wide empty roads giving way to side-streets and parks that provided ample space to run and dozens of places to hide. Yet her anxiety trapped her into fight or flight mentalities, and feeling unable to do the former, all it would allow her to do was the latter. Any attempt to think of a solution other than that was muddled and hazy, impossible to take form. She couldn't think anything, couldn't do anything, couldn't plan anything: all she could do was move forward towards home, her legs pressing her forward like pistons, moving at the same steady, tense pace that would cause them to cramp but unable to stop.

Now the streetlight that had been surrounding her flickered. It sputtered once, then again, then died completely, leaving its frosted fixture with the ephemeral glow where light had once been. She could still see the street in front of her – light pollution was rampant in the city, so much that pure dark was almost a figment of the imagination – but a shiver still ran through her as she looked from one end of the street to the other, searching for some sign of life. Los Angeles had not been designed to be seen without its people: street and storefronts looked like dried carcasses when divorced from the life that typically teemed through them.

She continued forward down the street towards her home near Station Z2. As soon as she stepped past the sidewalk square she shared with the malfunctioning streetlight, the next began to flicker. She stopped and it stopped, continuing the tell-tale electric buzz made by dirty power and neon lights.

There hadn't been anyone on the bench when she and Xander had gone over to it, but there had been a single blackened line that went all the way from the topmost board to the board that cupped the arch of one's knee. It was warm to the touch when she had touched it, and she'd pulled back, and Xander had said he'd smelled, "ozone."

She hadn't known what ozone was supposed to smell like but she smelled it now: the burnt tang on the air that reminded her of citrus. It was a sour taste in her nostrils and the more she tried to parse how little sense that made, the more confused it made her, and so she pushed it aside. Whatever the smell was it was all around her now, and the soft hairs on her arm were standing erect. The hair on her head was rising too, ever so slightly. She could feel it like a charge on the air, the charge that comes before the dry lightning that proved the bane of this dry city time and time again.

She missed New York. There was no such thing as 'dry lightning' in New York... no such thing as dry anything that she could remember. New York was perpetually damp and clammy to the touch, which made it alive to the touch. Los Angeles was warmer – even in the depth of the night as it was now – but it was dryer by far... Nothing could live in Los Angeles had the city not been there, she thought sometimes while parched by the summer heat.

The streetlight in front of her went out and so did the one beyond it, and her breath caught in her throat as she was wrestled back to reality. All the lights across the street went at once, as though they'd been caught in some localized brownout. She felt goose-flesh course over her again, every part of her standing on edge as she scanned the street for any sign of life that might have helped her. There was a liquor store, a gun store, another gun store, a shopper's deli, and a small door that looked to be the back entrance to a club... but no sign of life, not even a rat or a pigeon. She couldn't blame anyone; she didn't want to be on the street either.

She scanned her surroundings over and over again as she pressed forward, making her way toward home one step at a time. Liquor store, gun store, gun store, shopper's deli, club. Liquor store, gun store, gun store, shopper's deli, club. Liquor store, gun store, gun store, Ryan.

She stopped.

He was leaning against the bulletproof glass of the gun store's display with his arms folded in front of his chest. He had appeared as if from nowhere, his bright red shirt materializing from the cosmos itself between her third and fourth sweeps of the street. He was smiling, she could see from here. She knew that face and knew it well, the way his right cheek bumped up and impeded his vision when he smirked.

He locked eyes with her and she realized her breath was caught in her throat. She forced herself, with great effort, to breathe normally.

Ryan straightened, rising from the balls of his feet onto their flats and coming forward from the glass. The harsh, Algerian font of the word GUN stood apart and aside from him, making a tableau of his presence.

Lisa hadn't used the word 'tableau' since college and didn't in her mind now. She didn't think consciously or artistically of anything in the scene, only of Ryan's piercing blue eyes and the way they were locked onto hers. The word was peripheral, igniting something in the deep recesses of her mind: Weapon. Run.

Run.

She edged forward on the sidewalk, making her way to the next square and then the one after, all the while keeping her eyes trained on him.

When she had made it about five feet and her stride was beginning to hasten, the light of the illuminated gun store began to flicker and flit. The strobe effect of the failing light cast dark shadows against Ryan's face, heightening the deep turrets that ran down from his nostrils, defining his cheeks like plucked cherries. The smile he'd been watching her with broadened, and the deep shadows made his teeth appear black and vacant.

The light highlighting the word GUN shorted out, plunging his entire side of the street into pitched darkness. It didn't even retain the glow of light that bulbs usually did.

On the street behind her, one of the doused street-lamps jolted to life, shining a circle of light down on the sidewalk underneath it.

Ryan was standing in its center, his smile wide and those blue eyes of his burning bright.

Lisa made a high-pitched sound that caught in her throat, yet still pierced the air like a blade. She turned and almost slipped on her flats and did the thing she'd sworn she'd never do again, the thing her brain had been yelling at her to do with every instinct bred by two hundred thousand years of evolution.

Run.

She kept him in her peripheral vision as she ran, starting with small quick strides before graduating to longer sprints. He remained under the same streetlight, smiling from ear to ear. The light above him had started to flicker as she turned away, bolting quickly toward the corner that would merge her onto her street.

When she turned the corner, he was there and she almost slammed into him. He was caught in a beam from the spotlights that lit up the train station. The light surrounded him and was him. It seemed to shine into the back of his head and light up his eyes like a jack-o-lantern's. She gasped and skidded to a stop, her flats catching on the sidewalk's debris, and fell back onto her tailbone. The impact rocketed up through her, providing brief shimmering clarity to the pain but mulling everything else.

He was standing above her, the way she'd promised herself her never would again, with that same nascent smirk that promised that whatever happened, no matter what he said after the fact, part of him would enjoy what was to come.

She pushed back against the concrete with the heels of her feet, kicking as though she were on a bicycle, as though she were trying to spin the world's orbit, and Ryan, away from her. She retreated a spare inch at a time until he crouched down to be on a level eye with her and she stopped, frozen in place by those sky blue orbits.

"Hello, Lisa," he cooed, with the same James Dean swagger she remembered, if not a tiny bit raspier.

She swore at him under her breath, wishing she could think of something more biting or poignant to say, but unable to think past her left brain screaming at her to flee and her right brain yelling at her about the pain in her back.

He reached out and grabbed her ankle, the closest thing to him, and pulled her toward him. His touch was hot and dry and shot a static shock up through her powerful enough to hurt and make the thin hair on her arms stand up.

The light behind him went dark and then returned with him gone, now across the street under a street lamp again at the base of station Z2.

Lisa blinked, unable to process what had just happened and still feeling the ghost of his touch around her slender ankle. He was watching her from across the street again, his arms folded in front of him, his mouth curled up in a smile.

She pulled herself to her feet and hurried down the street, watching her shadow flicker as behind her the lights blinked on and off.

***

The second – and last – time he had laid his hands on her it had been during a fight over her job. She remembered because he had thought she was spending too much time there to 'only be working the job.' The fight had again been a long one, lasting well into the evening. Plates had been thrown at walls and the neighbours had called the police – twice – something that, when it happened in The City, you knew things were going bad.

The flesh on the back of his knuckles was already burnt and peeling. When she insisted for the fifth time that there was nothing happening at work and he put his hand through the drywall, it shot searing, electric spasms of pain up his arm – so white hot that he ground his teeth and popped a molar in the back. He turned away from the wall and brought the same fist against her, hitting her in the collarbone with the same hammer-fist motion he'd used to knock her dance partner unconscious on the night they'd met.

She'd fallen to the floor and had hated herself for falling to the floor. By the time she got up, he had stormed out. By the time he had come back, she had quickly packed a bag and was gone. She didn't know it, but he had destroyed the apartment they'd shared in his rage at her for leaving, even the oven and fridge. At 4am the police had been called again, and this time he'd been brought in for the night. When he'd come back the next afternoon, the landlord had pasted an eviction notice on their front door and changed the locks.

She'd known she had been pregnant for a week and a half, and at the time had made the deci-

sion to quietly remove it from their lives without his knowing. That night had shifted the plan: there had never been a time when it was ever going to be the three of them, but that night she knew that he was the one that had to be aborted. She got on a random bus out of town, chosen by asking a stranger to pick a number between one and ten, and had started her trek west.

***

"Crowley!" Lisa yelled as she entered the apartment, ducking her head out into the street behind her. She couldn't see him, but she knew he was there. He'd been there the entire way home, never more than a block away and always accompanied by those same flickering lights. "Xander!"

Neither of them came rushing from their bedrooms or in from the living room.

She screamed an obscenity with a hoarse voice sick from exhaustion. As if on cue, the bulb in the kitchen began to flicker on and off.

She stared at it, unable to pull her eyes from the dancing, jolting husk of glass.

When it had been following her on the street it had been one thing, but somehow this was another. Its invasion into her homestead made it different: more real, somehow, than it had been. It wasn't some abstraction in a city chock full of abstractions; it was in her home and in her kitchen and there was nothing she could do about it.

She backed up, keeping her eyes on the arcing electricity in the bulb. It jumped from one prong of the bulb to the other in curving arcs, sometimes above and sometimes below, so quickly that it formed an almond shape. It was an eye staring down at her, like the eye of Sauron looking down at her from Mount Doom, but she wasn't wearing the ring. She hadn't worn his ring since her last day in New York, when she'd slipped it from her finger and thrown it -- not into boiling lava, but into the frigid waters of the Hudson.

She backed up until she was in the null space between the kitchen and the living room, nudging a chair with her hip as she backed up. Crowley's room was on the wall to her right, slowly coming into her peripheral vision, and Xander's was still out of view but on her left. Neither had a lock and both had bulbs in place in the ceiling, too high up for her to reach without aid.

Her pace hastened as much as she dared backing up, and she found her back against the door to their bathroom. She fumbled for the knob – unable to find it on her first try even though its placement was so familiar to her – staring at the light as the arc of its electricity grew.

The bright blue sparking lines grew outward, sparking down to the floor even though there was no point there to attract it.

Her hand found the knob and she twisted it, falling back through the bathroom and bringing herself up solid against the sink. She kicked the door shut and lunged forward against the vengeful protestations of her back muscles and locked it, then stood in her small bathroom, wringing her fingers through her hair.

"Hnnn," she said involuntarily, her nails scraping her scalp as she looked from one corner of the tiny room to the other.

The light above the sink started to fade, then returned brighter than it ever had been before.

"Dammit," she cursed. She reached for it, and the moment her fingers extended, a shock sparked from the bulb to her middle finger. She yelped and pulled back, watching as the light came in and out, flashing with the same pattern and pace as his horrid laughter always had.

The lock turned.

She backed up and tripped on the edge of the tub, falling back into its basin.

The brass doorknob began to shimmer and glow as it turned, finally letting the latch come loose and swinging open. He was there. Ryan Valler was in the one place she'd sworn he'd never be again: in her house and in her personal space. He was smiling that smile that in any other circumstance, on any other face, might have been boyish. On him it was sinister, a symptom of malcontent without consequence that was charming in youth but became ever more dangerous with age.

He looked at her, cowering in a tub that could barely fit her in a room with no exits save the one he stood in front of, and his smile grew. "You never were the brightest bulb," he sneered, leaning in towards her.

She stared at him, unable to turn away from those electric blue eyes. Her breath had caught in her throat and lodged there like a stone.

He leaned forward, not yet touching her, both hands arched and ready, as if savouring the moment before contact.

"Not the brightest bulb?" she repeated under her breath. "You're one to talk."

She pushed the release for the faucet and freezing cold water shot out of the showerhead, cascading down instantly.

As soon as it hit him, the room erupted in bright blue and he screamed without opening his mouth, the sound of him filling the entire house. The bulb above the sink blew in a spectacular firework as Ryan pulled back, and she heard the other bulbs in the house do the same. Suddenly the entire house was dark, and he was the only thing made of light. He shone bright neon blue in jolting flashes, banishing the dark like a strobe light.

Caught in the strobe effect she didn't know or care the origin of, his face alight with blue and purple hues and the stench of sweat and burning dust, he looked like he had on the night they met, on the dance-floor of an underground club she should have known better than to go to.

"Get out!" she screamed at him, loud enough to be heard above the crackle of energy. "Get out of my life!"

His teeth began to glow black behind electric blue gums, and suddenly the resemblance to what he had been on that night, lifetimes ago, seemed like a gift. A chance to put to bed the wrong of that night, to see him for what he was and say no – not in my life, none of that. I will not have that in my life. She pushed forward into the neon and the spicy sweat just as she had that night entering the club, but instead of drawing into him, she pushed him away, laying both hands flat against his chest despite the sparks and the jolts that rang through her system, shoving him hard against the back of the shower.

His eyes burned bright – they always had – and his mouth moved but no sound came.

He had no voice.

"Out!" she yelled, so loud she closed her eyes.

Suddenly there was only darkness. For a time that was all there was, until finally the blue light of the moon and the orange glow of the city began to filter in through the window, outlining the still form of Ryan Valler on the floor of her bathroom.

***

"So there was this car there," Xander said, entering through his kitchen window and holding it open for Crowley to step through. "And I get in it and I start it and I yell at him, 'Reap the whirlwind'!"

"You didn't say that?" Crowley chuckled.

"I did. Unfortunately."

They stopped. Lisa was standing with her back leaned against the half wall that divided the kitchen from the living room, facing the door to the bathroom like a sentry.

The hair on Xander's arms stood on end and he noticed for the first time the stench of ozone in the air. "What's wrong?" he asked, stepping forward.

Lisa's frown deepened. She'd poured herself a coffee but had not drunk any, letting the steam waft up around her like a blanket. "Ryan's here," she said simply, nodding her head toward the bathroom door.

Xander turned, his eyes narrowing. Lisa wasn't sure if it was her imagination in the dim dark of the apartment, but his pupils seemed to expand, as if to take in more of the meager light.

He stepped forward to the base of the door, took a deep breath, then pushed it open.

There was nothing in the bathroom but a pool of water and the stench of burnt ozone on the air. The window was open, and there were scuff marks along the wall leading up to it, making the situation clear.

The whole of Xander clenched as he turned back to Lisa. "He can't have gotten too far. I'll find him."

Lisa smiled slowly. "No... I think I made my point."

THE CHAIR

The memories of my childhood are viewed through a deep fog not easily penetrated.

I grew up in a small town near the easternmost tip of Newfoundland, in a place known for deep mists and heavy rain that hit with maniacal, unfettered fury.

The landscape consisted of many rises and valleys; the upside of this was that bike riding became a smooth and swift experience. The downside was the cliffs.

Jagged maws of stone bent this way and that, stretching far into the water in some places and retraced deep into bowel-like caves in others. Some went high, leaning forward over the cape below like oppressive overlords, others simply rose and fell in smooth, uneventful lumps.

To a ten year old, even the most hazardous of these were not obstacles, but challenges.

I haven't been back to this place in nearly ten years, and am amazed by the difference time has made. Erosion has made rock faces that used to seem scalable - - *were* scalable, I remember intently - - now seem insurmountable.

There was once a large head of rock that hung out over a narrow cave, providing shelter enough for campfires and barbeques consisting chiefly of Vienna sausages and Cola. I recall discovering a delightful trick: that if you placed an unopened can of sausages in the fire and left them there, the pressure would blow the lid off and leave the contents perfectly cooked. Let the others roast their wienies on sticks if they pleased... I was a much smarter caveman.

That rock face is gone now, leaving a sheer cliff. If not for the scorched circle of rocks where many fires had been before, I might not have recognized it.

I pick up one of the blackened stones and jerk back, feeling heat when my flesh first touches the smooth shale. When I grab it again, it's as cold as the rest of the beach, wet from the lapping kisses of the sea. I hold it, its weight changing my impression of it somehow, making it tactile and real. I bounce it in my palm several times, then turn and whip it into the waves.

It disappears long before it hits the water, into a soupy fog I hadn't even realized was rolling in, stretching and swirling and trying to get to shore.

Around the side of the cliff, just to the left of the fireplace, the beach stops and gives way to a grassy knoll. It's a lush green even now, fighting the chill of fall as long as it can. It rises slowly to connect three of the varying cliffs of the beach in peculiar ways, with foot trails worn from years of use linking them all, and it even led out to the main road beyond it, becoming a field that met with one of the aforementioned hills that dotted the small town. I recall being mocked by my childhood friends, Rick and Allan, for taking this route to the top on our races up the sheer cliff. Such things are inconceivable to me now... to climb these cliffs was dangerous enough, but to actually race up them seemed suicidal.

Standing near the base of the path, I remember the years spent here, running from one cliff to another. I had my first kiss with sea-foam caressing the bottom of my feet, sitting on the furthest point out on the rocks. I can't remember her name anymore, but I always remember how sweet her lips had tasted after sipping on a can of Cherry Cola.

I also remember the Chair.

Just to the edge of the grassy knoll, carved into the solid face of the cliff, was a Chair. It took imagination to see, of course, like the shapes found in clouds or the faces found hidden in the trunks of evergreen trees, but once seen it could not be unseen.

There was a legend that someone sat there, invisible except in the moments before death. He waited for children who fell while trying to overcome the cliff and opened up the earth to swallow them.

In the legend, it was called the Devil's Chair.

I remember daring to climb that side, once. Allan was already at the top of the adjacent cliff, and Rick and I were scaling the Chair. Rick was ahead of me and almost near the top, grunting as he overcame the peak.

When I reached it, I slipped on the mossy rock, yelping as I grabbed at the short green grass of the field above. I remember the way my feet felt dangling freely in the air, gravity seeming to tug at them with its weighty fingers. I also remember feeling heat tickle the soles of my shoes, although it was evening in late November.

My hands squeezed the ground so tight that green juice pushed itself out of the grass, clods of dirt squishing between my fingers like kneads of dough.

Rick reached out and grabbed my arms by the wrist and pulled with everything he had, his teeth clenching and his blonde hair falling in front of his face.

"Come on!" he yelled, angry and concerned all at once.

As my feet kicked freely and Rick pulled me up, I turned over my shoulder and saw it. Saw Him.

He was sitting on the edge of his seat, shimmering black talons gripping at the arms of his chair in anticipation. His head was craned upward to see me, straining his neck to the breaking point, and he wore a smile that literally escaped the sides of his face to reveal an impossible amount of teeth. They were yellow, and stank of sulphur.

Rick pulled me up and I heard the creature howl. It reached up with those claws, each one at least as thick as my leg, and scraped for me; trying with its last futile effort to bat me from my friend's grasp and finding only dirt.

Rick and I never spoke of the event, and not long after we both went off to high school and drifted apart.

He'd gone into construction and moved into the city, made a good living for himself. He'd fallen from the scaffolding of a high-rise he'd been working on and landed on his back some nine stories down. For some reason, it made me remember that evening, years ago, when he'd saved me from a similar fate, and I got in my car and just drove until I'd found myself here.

I walk along the trail to the top of the cliff, all the while hearing Allan mocking me for doing so. When I reach the top, I can see over the fog and watch it stretch out for miles along the top of the water.

Smiling, I look down at the grassy patch where Rick and I had lay, chuckling and gasping with exasperation and adrenaline.

My mouth goes dry and my feet go numb, so much so that I almost lose my balance.

There are five long gouges in the grass, burned into brown streaks where life has refused to grow, leading to the edge of the cliff.

I swallow, and feel the heat against my back.

FROM THE AUTHOR

Short fiction does not come naturally to me. When I get ideas, they come in novel length. I'll get a concept for an idea and it'll come with a beginning, middle, and end. I say that and my peers in the author community glare at me: it's a skill, and it's one that I've trained myself for. Stephen King once said, "a writer is a person who has taught their brain to misbehave," and I've taught mine to misbehave in this very specific way.

When I *do* get an idea for a short story, it comes on me like a fever. I wake up with it, sometimes after a dream, but I have to write it *now. Right* now, has to happen, becomes an imperative. It's an itch that needs to be scratched *that very second*, and all other things fade away. Novels aren't like that for me; novels are planned out weeks, months, or even years before I sit down to actually write them. I plan when the creative urge hits, I write when I've reached that book on my TBW pile.

As such, each short story is a window into a moment in time for me, a glimpse into the exact second the idea came to me: what I was feeling, what I was doing, and what demons needed exorcising.

"The Theogony," originally published in *light / dark* in 2012, is my effort to get to know the character of Theo Flaherty. When Ellen and I first decided to work together on the Infinity series and compared notes, it became clear that there were two characters we both had that were very similar. Rather than have that happen, we chose to merge them, and as hers was more developed than mine, it happened that Theo essentially became a shared creation. "The Theogony" was my attempt to get to know him, and was modeled after the first book of *The Odyssey, The Telemachy*. Theo was originally modeled off the epic heroes of myth and legend, so we chose to make the origin story of his time in Black Springs a mix of Greek myths, *One Flew Over the Cuckoo's Nest*, and the larger Engen Universe. The result is one of my proudest pieces of short fiction, I think.

"Reptilia," originally published in *light / dark* in 2012, is a weird little story that was originally to be a part of a collection called Finding the Range helmed by Wes Prewer and published by Iceberg Publishing. It was to take place on Mars and I was told to "go harder than I ever had before," taking advantage of the horror chops that was, then, all I was known for. I did the assignment, but I think the Iceberg team misunderstood just how "hard" telling me to "go hard" would end up being. So they, with respect, returned the rights to me and I altered it to be an unnamed desert instead of the deserts of Mars. Since then, the characters within have found their way into the larger Engen Universe canon, and it has spawned a sequel penned by our resident zombie expert Paul Carberry.

"Revving Engen," originally published in *light / dark* in 2012, is a bizarre little story that serves as a prequel to both the Coral Beach Casefiles series and the Infinity series, showing how close they were to intersecting early in the timelines of both. This is a fun romp for anyone who likes both, but will likely be incomprehensible to anyone who hasn't. It's as "inside baseball" as I've ever gotten, and I kind of wish it was better. But it is what it is, and for fans of either series, it's a lynchpin that gives hints of larger things to come.

"Invasion," originally published in *Sci-fi from the Rock Returns* in 2013, was an exercise in an English course at Memorial University. The professor, whom I loathed, had a real chip on his shoulder regarding science-fiction, and often said that the genre was incapable of producing worthwhile art. Whenever someone says something that asinine, I set out to prove them wrong. There are a few stories in this collection that are a result of that same swell of spite.

"Rituals of the Celestial Ram," originally published in *Sci-fi from the Rock Returns* in 2013, was actually an essay in an early anthropology course. The goal of the essay was to "shed the rose-coloured glasses of our society" by imagining for taken-for-granted part of it from an outsider's point-of-view. As in: how would an anthropologist from another country view our norms, at first blush? And we were tasked with going out to this place and people-watching with this perspective. As such, this was written at a local unnamed giant coffee chain. I think I got rather low marks on the assignment, I'd missed the point. "This became a short story rather than an assignment," I believe the comment was. And they were right: give a writer like me an inch and I'll take a mile.

"Remembering" and "The Game," both originally published in *The Long Road* in 2014, are a part of a book of short stories that takes place between the Coral Beach Casefiles series wherein series protagonist Xander Drew is in his late teens to the Xander Drew series, wherein he is a young adult. I remember at the time being worried about writing him without his supporting cast, but quickly became enamored with it. Writing him without anyone to talk to meant that he had no one to discuss the events of the day with: he couldn't talk, and as such, became much more a man of action. Since this was directly in line with how I wanted to transition the character into adulthood, that was brilliant happenstance. Viewed as a pair, "Remembering" is very much about a promise being made that there is a light at the end of the tunnel for Xander, and "The Game" is about that promise being broken. They both feature children in danger, and in one the outcome is much sadder than the other, the grief of which will propel Xander forward into the obsession he has throughout his eponymous series, and starts the corruption it will enact in him. These two stories, as far as I'm concerned, are pivotal to understanding his character.

"Interlude," originally published in *The Long Road* in 2014, also serves as a prequel of sorts to Cinders, introducing the character of Shiro Gilbert, but this time in opposition to Leigh Blackheart. Leigh, like Theo, is an interesting character who went through a lot of changes when my wife and I started working together. In that original 'marriage' of our visions, we traded characters that each other were interested in. I got Theo in that mix, and Ellen got Leigh and started molding her into what she wanted. In a very weird way, Leigh became a sort of "power gauge" in the early Engen Universe. She defeated Xander in Roulette, and as such became a way of demonstrating power levels. How do we show that Sebastian is powerful in Inner Child? Show him defeating Leigh. If he can defeat Leigh, and Leigh can defeat Xander, than he's way more powerful than Xander! Despite having its own story, "Interlude" is more of the same: how do we show Shiro will defeat Xander? Have him defeat Leigh. In broader fiction, this is known as "The Worf Problem." In Star Trek, how do you show a character is strong? Have them defeat the strongest character: Worf. As a result, Worf is a character we are told is strong, but are only ever shown being weak. It becomes a bit of a paradox. In any event, despite a fairly self-serving origin to this story, I like it.

"The Chair," originally published in *Sci-fi from the Rock* in 2016. You might call bullshit on this, but this... Is actually based on a true story. Truth is a weird thing in the mind of a writer. I think I'm a very honest person, but sometimes my mind makes connections between things that weren't connected at the time, and they become my truth. There really was a landmark called The Devil's Chair in my hometown, and my friends and I really did go climbing around it, in the way only the unsupervised youth of the early 90s could have, and I really did slip and was saved at the last minute. How much of the rest of it was true? That's up to you to parse out. This was also the origin of the opening phrase, "The memories of my childhood are viewed through a deep fog not easily penetrated." This has been used twice more on shorts that have been inspired by real experiences of my Newfoundland upbringing, and form a loose trilogy in theme only. When these stories come to me, they come with that opening phrase. A little voice says, "Hey, this is one of those," and I like these stories, and consider them some of my best work.

"The Shoe," originally published in *Sci-fi from the Rock* in 2016, was actually written in... 2001? One of my first shorts, birthed from a prompt while at the University of Calgary.

Jacobi Street, originally published in 2017, is a mish-mash of elements that I was told "could never work" by the same onerous professor that birthed "Invasion." Twilight was at its zenith of popularity, and he proclaimed that you could "not write a good story based on vampires, queer characters, or children's literature." So I proceeded to write one of my best novels based on children's literature, featuring queer protagonists fighting vampires. For if a vampire must sustain himself on blood, I am a monster who must sustain himself on spite.

"Flickers in the Night," originally published in *Chillers from the Rock* in 2018, is a good story that came about as the result of poor planning. I did not write my novels in order, originally. I wrote Black Womb (my first published) then Smoke and Mirrors (third), then Faith (sixteenth!), then Family Values (seventeenth), Fate's Shadow, (eighteenth) and Generations (will be my thirtieth). This created a problem as I was catching up, changing my writing style, what have you. I was growing as a writer, and as I reached the novels I'd written years before, they were no longer up to my standards. Most notably, Family Values was a callback to episodic eastern stories, and that format was dropped in the rewrite. There were dozens of episodic subplots that got excised in the ensuing edit, including one that featured the father of Lisa's child, Ryan Valler. This became a bit of a ticking clock issue, as he was needed for future stories, where he'd be more prominent. We needed a setup for that payoff. And as that kept getting shunted from novel to the next and not used, it became more pressing. As such, "Flickers in the Night" was conceived, a short story taking place between Faith and Family Values that would both introduce and dispose of the character, giving him room to return at a later date.

"The Lakehouse," originally published in *Chillers from the Rock* in 2018, came to me fully in a nightmare. I don't usually have nightmares, and if I do, I don't remember them. But I remembered this one, and it was so real, the darkness in it coming for me. I used to have recurring dreams about that living black coming for me, and they stopped when I started writing. Those nightmares coming back was an excellent reason to put pen to paper immediately and stave them off.

Touch Your Nose, originally published in 2018, started as a challenge and became one of my favorite novels, something I poked at between projects, writing a chapter once a month until it was done. I liked how romantic it was, and more than that, I liked how romantic it was in an adult way. This was a gateway for me.

"Young Republicans," originally published in *Dystopia from the Rock* in 2019, is one of my rare political efforts, birthed out of frustration with the results of the 2016 Presidential election. It's meant to highlight the double-think that happens in homes around the world, the dichotomy of brainwashing children against the very empathy that comes naturally to them. Children are not naturally awful, we have to make them that way, mold them that way. I'm not sure this comes across in the story, and sometimes I'm tempted to rewrite it into a full novella. Short fiction may not be the best vehicle for this.

"The Views," originally published in *Dystopia from the Rock* in 2019, is a "pure" story of mine, birthed out of my curiosity for algorithms and how they work after watching a CGP Grey essay uploaded December 18, 2017. I'd say the title but he seems to have changed it to keep up with trends, and that would make its inclusion here seem anachronistic. I say this is "pure" because to me most of my fiction is fuelled by my curiosity, but it is often tempered over the process. This story, however, is still curious.

"The Spy" was written in 2022 and is original to this collection. It was written to be a part of the *A Toast to Hope* collection of shorts produced in collaboration with Quadrangle NL. One of my favorite parts of Engen Books is that it doesn't matter who you are: all our collections are double-blind. If something gets in, it has nothing to do with who the author is; it has to do with what the author wrote. The judges didn't know they were judging me and rejected it, and that's perfectly fine. It's presented here, and you can decide for yourself: were they in the right?

The Sacking of Outpost Toth, originally published in 2023, was a writing exercise. In my classes I teach the virtues of Four Corner Opposition, and I noticed that many science-fiction shows had four characters go on their "away missions." As such, I challenged myself to write a novella wherein the entire novel took place on the mission: nothing before, and nothing after. The result was more fun than it had any right to be, and I look forward to visiting that world again someday soon.

"The Crustman," originally published in *Terror Nova: Lurking in Darkness* in 2023, easily my favorite story, a callback to the local legends my grandmother used to tell me and the place she used to tell me them in, Francois, Newfoundland. Francois hasn't been resettled, yet, but is always on the brink of it. When it is, stories are all we'll have left of it.

"The Hunters," originally published in *Cryptids from the Rock* in 2024, is a fun story about the dichotomy between old and new Newfoundland culture, and how we're changing, particularly in our fiction. It was inspired heavily by the work of my friend Mike Hickey.

Thank you all for reading this collection. Short fiction isn't my default setting, as evidenced by the fact that I have more novels than shorts at this point, but sometimes I feel my best work comes from here, and it's good to see it all in one place finally.

ENGEN TIMELINE

With over twenty novels spread over three different series by many different authors, the Engen Universe of titles is growing every day and into genres we couldn't have imagined! From the original ten book *Black Womb* thriller series, its crime novel sequel series *Xander Drew,* our flagship adventure title *Infinity,* or single-novels like *Jacobi Street* or *light|dark,* there's something in the Engen Universe for everyone with more books by more authors on the way soon!

...But how do the events relate to one another, chronologically? While some astute readers have guessed at the potential timeline (some accurately, some not), we're going to finally set the question of the Engen Timeline to rest.

Turn the page for an up-to-date guide of the ever-widening world of Engen, featuring the works of Ali House, Ellen Curtis, Erin Vance, Matthew Daniels, Andrea Hackett, Sarah Thompson, Jay Paulin, and Matthew LeDrew!

In the 10 Years Prior Black September

"Reptilia" by Matthew LeDrew | **included in this collection!**
"Reptilian" by Paul Carberry | published in *Undead Rebirth.*

Danger descends on a small secluded town in the form of a deadly virus with fantastic and terrible side-effects. Can a small group of doctors escape alive?

Compendium by Ellen Curtis

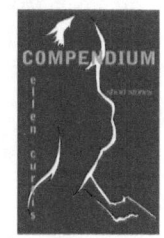

Three short stories forming the basis for the Engen Universe's ties to suspense, genetic engeneering, and the supernatural. Features the stories "The Tourniquet Revival," "Falling into Fire" and "At Midnight, the Dawn."

"The Theogony" by Matthew LeDrew | **included in this collection!**

A tale of young Theo Flaherty of the *Infinity* series and his time admitted against his will to the Black Springs hospital, where he learns to paint, and seeks out his father.

Black September

"Revving Engen" by Matthew LeDrew | **included in this collection!**

A direct lead-in to both *Infinity* and *Black Womb*, Tasha travels to Coral Beach, Maine on a hot tip about a recently discovered young man with incredible abilities.

Infinity by Ellen Curtis & Matthew LeDrew

Faced with a destiny he's uncertain of, the enigmatic Victor must bring together four unique people with very special abilities… or face the tasks ahead alone. Guaranteed to excite!

Black Womb by Matthew LeDrew

Fifteen years ago, something happened in Coral Beach, Maine that resulted in the present death of a seventeen-year-old boy. Now four high-school students must try to solve the mystery… before the killer picks them off.

Jacobi Street by Matthew LeDrew | **included in this collection!**

When a mysterious painting shows up at an art gallery he works at, Bob must work with Eddie and Sloan to track down its sinister origins and convince the people living on Jacobi Street of them, before its too late!

Transformations in Pain by Matthew LeDrew

When two girls are assaulted and one is hospitalized, the residents of Coral Beach must put their shared tragedies behind them and stop the man responsible, as well as unlock the secrets behind the true nature of the Womb…

Year One: October

Variety Show by Ali House

Local performer Wendy is introduced to the drama and mystique of The Quaint Little Theatre of Jacobi Street. But backstabbing aren't the only dangers at play in this venue…

Smoke and Mirrors by Matthew LeDrew

The approaching trial of Genblade brings closure to the people of Coral Beach, until people start showing up dead in the same manner they did when he was at large.

"The Inevitable" by Ali House | published in *The Lightbulb Forest*

A young woman must contend with the emergence of a frightening new power alongside the emotional high of a first date.

The Tourniquet Reprisal by Ellen Curtis & Matthew LeDrew

A man lives in Atlanta, Georgia that people don't talk about, but everyone knows he's there. He arrived a year ago and turned a gaggle of uneducated youth into something new, something to fear.

Roulette by Matthew LeDrew

As the teen suicide rate in Coral Beach starts to climb astronomically fast, Xander travels to Los Angeles to fight his most terrifying adversary yet... and learns that the only thing worse than looking for release... is finding it.

Year One: November

Exodus of Angels by Ellen Curtis & Matthew LeDrew

Victor's enigmatic past is illuminated when Jaycee accompanies him to visit a new friend in the paliative care ward of the Black Springs hospital, where Theo also happens to be searching for a cure for Leigh.

The Irony of Glass by Matthew Daniels
published in *Undead Rebirth* and *Interstitches.*

Abby and Chad track down a man with the ability to project his emotional state to a remote town, and struggle to escape.

Ghosts of the Past by Matthew LeDrew

Coral Beach faces its most awesome threat when one of Engen's past mistakes is unleashed upon the unsuspecting populous. Friends and enemies unite to fight a common enemy... but will even that be enough?

Touch Your Nose by Matthew LeDrew | **included in this collection!**

Simon Monk must infiltrate the San Fransico branch of Shane Industries, a massive company with deep ties to the Engen Universe. Where do his true loyalties lie? And can he get out without causing harm?

Ignorance is Bliss by Matthew LeDrew

After being set through the ringer one too many times, Xander decides that his life with Julie needs a little more attention... which is bad news because a new villain has come to town with his sights set on Adam Genblade.

"Gristle While You Work" by Jay Paulin &
"Scarlett" by Andrea Hackett
published in *light | dark*.

"A Night to Forget" by Kelly Rose &
"New Employment" by Sam Bauer
published in *Undead Rebirth.*

Becoming by Matthew LeDrew

For months Xander Drew has been doing his level best to keep
the streets of Coral Beach clean, which means it's time for the
forces of darkness to strike back… all at once.

Inner Child by Matthew LeDrew

Julie is hospitalized with life-threatening wounds to both body
and soul. But the real threat comes from the hospital walls
themselves, as a demonic presence makes itself known to Xander
and his friends.

"Comfortably Numb" by Ellen Curtis | published in *Undead Rebirth.*

Xander and Cathy spend an evening hunting the remnants of
Coral Beach's gangs when Xander begins to lose control of the
Black Womb, threatening their secret.

End of Year One

Gang War by Matthew LeDrew

The Tees, a homicidal gang of evil men, has finally been taken
down by Xander Drew. But his victory is short lived, as retired
Tees are mysteriously killed. With a town of suspects, anyone can
be the culprit… including one of their own.

Chains by Matthew LeDrew

Sociopath Derek Smith has been freed from prison and is praying
on the weak; and none are weaker than August Styles: a pregnant
girl with Down Syndrome who has run away from home.

"Omega" by Ellen Curtis | published in *light | dark*.

A sinister division of Engen begins a series of experiments on pregnant women in a fashion eerily similar to those that created the original Black Womb project.

The Long Road by Matthew LeDrew
Xander meets the American people — and realizes that the world is harsh and wicked, but can also be soft and gentle, even loving. Xander Drew comes of age on the road, and sets his new direction.

Selected stories included in this collection!

Year Two

Cinders by Matthew LeDrew

Detective Horton enters a violent and dangerous world he didn't know existed beneath the veneer of order and structure that he has based his entire deductive method around.

Sinister Intent by Matthew LeDrew

One of the killers Detective Horton could not catch has resurfaced: a serial killer who flaunts his sinister intent in front of the Los Angeles Police Department, making it so that no one is safe.

Faith by Matthew LeDrew

Xander's mysterious and troublesome past returns to haunt him on the streets of Los Angeles; a place where even more people can get caught in the crossfire of the games of death and deceit that makes up his life.

Flickers in the Night by Matthew LeDrew

Lisa Rowdan is hunted by her haunting -- and powerful -- ex-boyfriend Ryan through a lonely city street. Can she escape him? One of over twenty great sprine-tingling short stories!

Included in this collection!

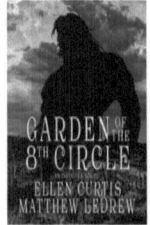

Garden of the 8th Circle by Ellen Curtis & Matthew LeDrew

Victor brings Chad, Abby, and Alice into a dangerous conflict a decade in the making, fighting an out of control cult for the fate of a young soul. Meanwhile, Theo investigates a mysterious event in Los Angeles.

Family Values by Matthew LeDrew

Xander and his new friends Crowley, Lisa, and Tim investigate a series of kidnappings and murders that stretch back decades, all of which have the same similar twist: victims being found after years of being missing.

The Rats of Refraction by Ellen Curtis & Matthew LeDrew

When Abby and Alice's secret lives are discovered, they must defend their home and way of life with everything they have against the forces of Circe, a shadow agency that will stop at nothing to abduct people with supernatural abilities.

Fate's Shadow by Matthew LeDrew

When one of Xander's old cases comes up for trial, Megan Greene returns with it. The former friends are led into conflict regarding her client's innocence. However, they put their difference aside when they both become targets of the vigilante known as Shiro Gilbert.

First Aid by Matthew LeDrew

Xander takes his feud with mob boss Stephen Fields to the streets, and his attracts the attention of the *Infinity* team. Before the arrive, he'll have pushed the mob boss into an all out gang war, the likes of which the city will never recover from.

Moments by Matthew LeDrew

The Shane murders have been happening for months, dogging Xander at every turn. They've been happening for longer than even he knows, stretching back to the Black September. He's taken down Fields. He's taken down Murdock. Now the stage is set for this part of the story to also end.

Gone by Ellen Curtis & Matthew LeDrew

When his baby sister is missing, Chad must return to the life he left behind in order to save her.

(not final cover)

As Loved Our Fathers by Matthew LeDrew

Jona discovers a quirk of history that implies that the Holy Grail is burried in Newfoundland, Canada. He leads an expedition to scour Newfoundland history to find the powerful relic.

Exposure by Erin Vance

Joshua Deering just wanted was to pass his final photography project. But that's not what happened. But hindsight is 20/20, and now creepy cemetery guy Adrian, Josh, and Josh's two friends are being stalked by nameless, violent strangers.

"The Port 13 Motel" by Erin Vance & "Living Light" by Sam Bauer | published in *Undead Rebirth.*

The unlikely return of both Kemp and a cannibalistic serial killer to the Engen Universe.

The Future

"Remers" by Sarah Thompson | published in *light|dark.*

In the not-too-distant future of the Engen Universe, young athletes are the targets of a scouting program to create the next stage of super soldier with cybernetic enhancements.

Timeline I - V by Matthew LeDrew | published in *Undead Rebirth.*

Faced with the death of his wife, Mikhail breaks the laws of time and space to find a way to save her, only to discover that her fate was sealed in the distant past...

ABOUT THE AUTHOR

Matthew LeDrew has written over twenty novels, some of which have gone on to become Canadian and international best-sellers. They include: the ten book Coral Beach Casefiles series, *The Long Road, Cinders, Sinister Intent, Faith, Family Values, Fate's Shadow, First Aid, Moments, Jacobi Street, Touch Your Nose, The Sacking of Outpost Toth, The Four Funerals of Marcus Drumford, Infinity, The Tourniquet Reprisal, Exodus of Angels, Garden of the Eighth Circle, Rats of Refraction,* and *Gone,* the latter six of which with wife and co-author Ellen Curtis.

Since 2007 he has traveled all over Canada promoting his work as well as teaching seminars on writing and publishing. He currently holds a Canada Council for the Arts Research and Creation Grant and an ArtsNL Professional Projects Grant.

He holds an Honours Degree in English from the Memorial University of Newfoundland with a minor in Anthropology. He studied Journalism at College of the North Atlantic in Stephenville, Newfoundland. He has worked with Transcontinental Publishing as well as student-youth magazine The Troubadour.

He has been called "the face of Newfoundland Genre writing" and is one of the most successful authors working and living in his province today.

He lives in Chapel Arm, Newfoundland.

www.ingramcontent.com/pod-product-compliance
Lightning Source LLC
Chambersburg PA
CBHW060223030726
47499CB00004B/1168